EVERYMAN,
I WILL GO WITH THEE,
AND BE THY GUIDE,
IN THY MOST NEED
TO GO BY THY SIDE

W. SOMERSET MAUGHAM

COLLECTED STORIES

WITH AN INTRODUCTION BY
NICHOLAS SHAKESPEARE

EVERYMAN'S LIBRARY
Alfred A. Knopf New York London Toronto
276

THIS IS A BORZOI BOOK

PUBLISHED BY ALFRED A. KNOPF

First included in Everyman's Library, 2004
This selection Copyright © 2004 by Everyman's Library

Copyright information (UK):
Copyright © The Royal Literary Fund
The Complete Short Stories first published in Great Britain in 1951 by
William Heinemann
First published in four volumes as *Collected Short Stories* in 1975 by
Pan Books Ltd.
Published in four volumes as *Collected Short Stories* in 2002 by Vintage

Copyright information (US):
Copyright © The Estate of W. Somerset Maugham

Introduction Copyright © 2004 by Nicholas Shakespeare
Bibliography and Chronology Copyright © 2004 by Everyman's Library
Typography by Peter B. Willberg
Second printing (US)

All rights reserved under International and Pan-American Copyright
Conventions. Published in the United States by Alfred A. Knopf,
a division of Random House, Inc., New York, and simultaneously in
Canada by Random House of Canada Limited, Toronto. Distributed
by Random House, Inc., New York. Published in the United Kingdom
by Everyman's Library, Northburgh House, 10 Northburgh Street,
London EC1V 0AT, and distributed by Random House (UK) Ltd.

US website: www.randomhouse.com/everymans

ISBN: 1-4000-4253-4 (US)
1-85715-276-X (UK)

A CIP catalogue reference for this book is available from the British Library

Library of Congress Cataloging-in-Publication Data
Maugham, W. Somerset (William Somerset), 1874–1965.
[Short stories. Selections]
Collected stories / W. Somerset Maugham; with an introduction by
Nicholas Shakespeare.
p.   cm.—(Everyman's library)
Includes bibliographical references.
ISBN 1-4000-4253-4
1. British—Foreign countries—Fiction. I. Title.
PR6025.A86A6 2004
823'.912—dc22   2004046931

Book design by Barbara de Wilde and Carol Devine Carson

Printed and bound in Germany by GGP Media GmbH, Pössneck

W. SOMERSET MAUGHAM

———

CONTENTS

_____

INTRODUCTION

When you come down to brass tacks the value of a work of art depends on the artist's personality.

W. Somerset Maugham

Towards the end of his life, the most widely read English writer since Dickens, and the highest paid in history, was observed by an old woman on Vevey railway station trying to play hide-and-seek with his male secretary. 'Yoo-hoo,' he called from behind a pillar. When the secretary began to reprimand him, the woman moved to intercede: 'You should be gentle with that nice old man. He thinks he's Somerset Maugham.'

Hide-and-seek was a game that Maugham had made his profession, a game of concealment and catching other people out. At the height of his powers he would have savoured the excruciating irony: the writer in decline accused of impersonating himself. This was the type of story closest to his heart. Perhaps like the old lady, and perhaps because he was so adept at constructing a monolithic persona, we all feel we know who Somerset Maugham is. But his large audience, swollen by screen and television adaptations, has tended to undermine his critical reputation. There hangs over his name a suspicion of something middle-brow that his personality has failed to dispel. Among the words he attracted were: misogynist, cynic, mysterious, sensitive, malicious, vulnerable, racist, suspicious, sophisticated, inscrutable. His authorial gaze has the expression of a tribal mask nailed to the wall, surmising you. A friend commented: 'Not once in all the years that I've known him have I seen the mask drop. He's on guard all the time, alert as a hawk, watching everything he does and says.' Only at one remove, in remarks he made about others – El Greco, Arnold Bennett, Maupassant – does there appear the occasional suggestive crack. Otherwise he maintains the pose in Graham Sutherland's portrait of him. The defiant, unblinking, arms-crossed pose of a mandarin in a smoking-jacket.

Maugham was more than happy to probe into the lives of

other writers, especially those he admired, but he was a litigious curmudgeon when it came to anyone investigating his biography. He behaved as if he could control its shape and content like one of his stories, but life has a tremendous resistance to being twisted and squeezed. It is not – as Maugham knew to his cost – a mask. In his essay *The Art of Fiction*, he observed with habitual common sense: 'Sometimes people carry to such perfection the mask they have assumed that in due course they actually become the person they seem. But in his book or picture the real man delivers himself defenceless.' Maugham proved no exception to his own rule. He understood that what a writer writes is 'the expression of his personality and the manifestation of his instincts, his emotions, his intuitions and his experience'. In a body of seventy-three works nowhere does Maugham's truest self call out louder to be recognized than in two or three of his novels and in his twelve volumes of short stories.

*

Interviewed in 1933, Maugham remarked: 'It has always seemed to me that literature can only find its fullest and freest expression in the essay or short story.' He wrote more than one hundred stories, at least fourteen of which he burned on one of his 'bonfire nights', after Winston Churchill warned that they contravened the Official Secrets Act. Of the stories that do survive, he estimated that maybe a dozen would find their way into anthologies, 'if only because some of them deal with circumstances and places to which the passage of time and the growth of civilization will give a romantic glamour'. When assessing his worth, Maugham had not too many illusions.

In a writing career spanning sixty-five years, he produced much that is well forgotten. At his worst, as David Garnett said of him, he reads like 'a choppy sea'. He has a fatal fondness for the surprise twist which can, on occasions, rip the head right off a story. There are moments when he stirs in the reader the uneasy sense that he shares the prejudices of those he dissects with such pitilessness. ('I think of those thin black arms of hers around you and it fills me with a physical nausea.') As for his women! When a woman in Maugham says: 'One must behave like a gentleman', you suspect that that is what originally she was. It comes hardly as a surprise, for instance, to learn that the model for the parlourmaid in 'The Treasure' was a valet. Then there is the accusation that for all his genius at narrative, he has no depth. You wait for him to go to another level, but something always pulls him back, as in his own description of the fever bird. 'It has three notes and it just misses the fourth which would make the chord and the ear waits for it maddeningly.' He lacks, in other words, that extra note which might rank him with the greatest.

Maugham demanded, quite rightly, that a writer should be judged by his best work. He believed that this, rather like his talent at the bridge table, placed him 'in the very first row of the second-raters' – a judgement with which the intelligentsia whom he loathed concurred. 'Division II, Class 1,' reckoned Lytton Strachey, after reading one of Maugham's books during a bout of flu. His harshest critics, such as Edmund Wilson, positioned him still further back, on the level of 'one of the less brilliant contributions to a prep-school magazine'. Perhaps his talent was, in the final analysis, a Gentleman's Relish that he spread too thin, but his finest stories leave a taste that is not in doubt. At his best, his clear, painterly prose seems written by the light of the Mediterranean sun that fell across his page at the Villa Mauresque, streaming into his study through the Gauguin glass window of a Tahitian woman and a rabbit. To Desmond MacCarthy, he was 'the English Maupassant'; to Cyril Connolly, who rated him the best short-story writer of the twentieth century, 'the Kipling of the Pacific'. His admirers number Evelyn Waugh ('the only living studio-master under whom one can study with profit'), Gabriel García Márquez ('one of my favourite writers') and George Orwell ('I believe the modern writer who has influenced me most is Somerset Maugham, whom I admire immensely for his power of telling a story straightforwardly and without frills.'). James Michener went further. Any time he hankered to set a story in Maugham's world, he took down 'Rain' and reread the first three paragraphs. 'I hold those passages to be about the best beginning of a mood story extant.'

W. SOMERSET MAUGHAM

In an essay on the short story, Maugham set out his credo for the genre. 'It is natural for men to tell tales and I suppose the short story was created in the night of time when the hunter, to beguile the leisure of his fellows when they had eaten and drunk their fill, narrated by the cavern fire some fantastic incident he had heard of.' Maugham tells his tales after the same fashion, within the radius of an acetylene lamp, over a cigar and a whisky and soda, at the card table, in a liner, a railway carriage, an outstation. A cramped and circumscribed stage, in other words, where all concentration is on him.

About the form, he had definite ideas. No Alice Monro ambiguities for Maugham. He liked a story that fitted. As his narrator says in 'The Human Element': 'I like a story to have a beginning, a middle, and an end. I have a weakness for a point.' Best of all he liked the sort of story he could write himself. 'This is the sort of story that many people have written well, but no one more brilliantly than Guy de Maupassant.' When a medical student in London, Maugham often revisited Paris, where he had passed his first ten years, and combed the book-stores for editions of Maupassant, reading them sometimes standing up and 'peering between the uncut pages'. He singled out 'La Parure' as a model: 'You can tell it over the dinner-table or in a ship's smoking-room and hold the attention of your listeners. It relates a curious, but not improbable incident. The scene is set before you with brevity, as the medium requires, but with clearness; and the persons concerned, the kind of life they lead and their deterioration, are shown to you with just the amount of detail that is needed to make the circumstances of the case plain.' Another model was Chekhov, who taught him to rid his story of anything superfluous, to keep his description of nature brief, and to narrate the facts, leaving it to the reader to decide what should be done about them. Lucidity, euphony, simplicity – these were his lodestars.

The stories Maugham most liked to tell were sparked by incidents that he had heard about, or, preferably, witnessed himself. Those that made up *Ashenden* (1928) were, he wrote, 'on the whole a very truthful account of my experiences during the war when I was in the Secret Service'. In his other collections, too, he depended on that confirmative grain of truth before he could let his imagination run. 'To know a thing actually happened gives it a poignancy, touches a chord, which a piece of acknowledged fiction misses.' Like many writers, he was not good at pure invention.

In his most famous story, 'Rain', Maugham did not even bother to change the name of the plump, pretty prostitute, Miss Thompson, whom he had met on the deck of a cruise ship from Honolulu. About 'The Vessel of Wrath', he maintained: 'All the people I have described in this story I met at one time or another.' An entry in his notebook, describing a Resident in an outstation who took a bottle of whisky to bed every night, was the source of 'Before the Party'. A story he particularly liked, 'The Alien Corn', was based on a young man he knew who had made 'a hash of his life' – while 'The Colonel's Lady' incubated for many years on the back of an envelope, Maugham dashing off the anecdote that he had heard when staying at the New York Ritz.

Three of his best stories – 'The Letter', 'Footprints in the Jungle', 'The Book-bag' – were told to him straight. He came upon the incidents described in 'The Letter' while on a visit to the Far East where he learned how Mrs Ethel Proudlock, wife of the acting head of the Victoria Institution in Kuala Lumpur, had shot dead on her veranda the manager of a tin-mine, not once but six times, after he tried to kiss her. 'I had nothing to do but make them probable, coherent and dramatic.' Likewise, the story behind 'Footprints in the Jungle', involving another murder, was given to him 'word for word' one evening in a club in a town in Malaya. 'I was shown two of the people concerned in it and, believe me, when I looked at them, knowing their story, I could hardly believe my eyes.' The rest, he maintained, were invented 'by the accident of my happening upon persons here and there, who in themselves or from something I heard about them, suggested a theme that seemed suitable for a short story'.

His themes elaborate a sceptical world view derived from Schopenhauer and La Rochefoucauld. Many of his stories read like dramatized maxims. Only a trembling leaf separates hope from despair. Suffering doesn't ennoble. The murderer doesn't get caught. The wages of sin aren't always death. Men hate those they have injured. Beneath the mousiest woman lurks the most vicious Valkyrie.

If he had few illusions about himself, he had none whatsoever about his characters. 'As a rule my characters are suggested by someone I have known,' he told *The Bookman* in 1926, in answer to a questionnaire. He was drawn to those men and women who were destroyed by a code of honour, an appetite, a passion. By the time he had finished with them, however, little remained of the original. Asked about his favourite characters, he singled out two for the reason that they were 'gay, amusing and unscrupulous'. Rather like Maugham himself.

*

'The *I* who writes is just as much a character in the story as the other persons with whom it is concerned.'

By common consent, Maugham's most satisfying character is the 'I' who sets the scene, the Marlow-like narrator who beckons you closer into the lamplight, the cigar-smoke, and over a gin pahit guides you by the elbow through several discussions until the conversation, so to speak, gets into its shirtsleeves and the guts of the story are laid out bare. To start with, though, we meet him in evening dress or white ducks. In the majority of stories, he is a middle-aged English author, married, although appearing to travel alone, which he does first-class, with infinite time on his hands, gliding at leisure through the South Seas, the Far East, the French penal colonies, the Riviera, Capri, Mayfair. He is at ease equally with prisoners, parlourmaids and Foreign Secretaries. By the same token, he cares precious little for those people whose tragedies he is swift to tap, his deeper emotions being reserved for a fine Havana or a cold grouse. 'My sympathies were not deeply engaged in the matter,' is his typical response. For Anthony Burgess, who lived in Malaya, this narrator was 'something that English fiction needed – the dispassionate commentator, the "raisonneur", the man at home in Paris and Vienna but also in Seoul and Djakarta, convivial and clubbable, as ready for a game of poker as for a discussion on the Racine alexandrine, the antithesis of the slippered bookman'. Burgess was not alone in considering this poker-faced persona the character of Maugham's most likely to endure. To V. S. Pritchett, Maugham's uninvolved and cosmopolitan narrator was 'the Great Dry Martini in person' and gratified the reader's wish 'to see oneself as worldly-wise and sagacious, to have impenetrable savoir-faire, to call for that dry Martini and light a sceptical cigar at the end of the day'. He reminds you of none other than the character he helped to inspire, save that unlike James Bond he would not have wished to be disturbed in bed. Whatever hidden steps Maugham's narrator takes elsewhere in the territory of sex, almost the only lapse in the entire short-story canon is Ashenden's flirtation with Baroness von Higgins – a flirtation he considers, then rejects.

Maugham, of course, took pains to point out that the first-person narrator is a convention as old as the caves, the object being to create credibility. It had also the virtue of compactness, of limiting time and space. 'When you are shut up with a man for ten days in a railway carriage you can hardly fail to learn most of what there is to know about him.' But the narrator in Maugham's confined setting is much more than a technical device. He is also a thin disguise for the author. In few places is he so thinly disguised as in the character he named Willie Ashenden, a figure cited by Goebbels in a 1941 radio speech as an example of the repellent cynicism of the British Secret Service to which Maugham once belonged.

Like Willie Maugham, Ashenden was a student at Heidelberg; had an affair – long past – with a Russian lady who ate only scrambled eggs; lived in Chesterfield Street, Mayfair; used the codename Somerville, and once saw Ibsen in the flesh drink a glass of beer at the Maximilianhof. He bears the same relation to Maugham as, say, the Ambassador in 'His Excellency' bears to the character in the story that the Ambassador offloads to Ashenden, about 'a fellow I knew when I was a very junior clerk at the FO' – who is, of course, the Ambassador.

Maugham's formula changes little, causing him to title one of his collections *The Mixture as Before*. An ordinary-looking man, thin, elderly, bald, at first sight with nothing to attract his attention – or it could be a prim, demure wife, 'the sort of woman you simply didn't notice' – sinks into a cane chair, glares at the narrator with pregnant eyes and says: 'I'm afraid you'll think it awfully strange of me to talk to you like this. I'm at the end of my tether. If I don't talk to somebody I shall go off my head' – whereupon out tumbles a melodrama of incest, jealousy and parricide. It was a discovery of terrific consequence to Maugham that people at the end of their tether at the end of the world 'find it a relief to tell someone whom in all probability they will never meet again the story that had burdened perhaps for years their waking thoughts and their dreams at night'. And, of course, the more cold, distinguished and snobbish the British official whom Ashenden/ Maugham encounters, the more consuming and degrading the passion to which inevitably they confess. The nectar sucked, the narrator is free to flutter on. 'I like meeting people whom I shall never meet again. No one is boring whom you will never see but once in your life.'

*

Maugham rooted his stories in direct observations that beg certain questions of the unrooted author. He defined a work of fiction as 'an arrangement which the author makes of the facts of his experience with the idiosyncrasies of his own personality'. In the end, the point of Henry James – for Maugham – was his personality, not his artistry. What, after all, has a writer to give you but himself? A writer has to write as he can 'and as he must because he is a certain sort of man'. But what sort of man was Maugham? He exploited the 'I' more so than most authors, and yet about himself he was astonishingly reticent.

It was well observed by one of his biographers, Anthony Curtis, that 'everything there is to say about Maugham has (so it seems) already been said by Maugham himself'. The facts of his life are well known, but as Maugham observed, 'fact is a poor story-teller'. They deserve retelling.

*

INTRODUCTION

The author of the stories selected here was a stateless atheist born in an Embassy and raised from the age of ten to seventeen in a vicarage. His birthplace in 1874 was a parcel of English territory abroad, the second floor of the British Embassy in Faubourg St Honoré that had been turned into a maternity ward in order to exempt him from French military service. His russet-haired mother was known to British diplomats as 'Beauty'; his father, a diminutive, sallow-faced solicitor who worked for the Embassy, as 'the Beast'. Willie, their fourth son, resembled his father. He looked in point of fact like a 'sick monkey', wrote Evelyn May Wiehe. As for his short height, this no doubt contributed to the fierce, Napoleonic angle of his gaze. 'The world is an entirely different place to the man of five foot seven from what it is to the man of six foot two.' His smallness gave him the perspective and the disadvantages of a child. Travelling with his lover, Gerald Haxton in Sarawak in 1921, his boat capsized in circumstances that he describes in 'The Yellow Streak'. 'Gerald cried out that he could touch bottom. I put down my legs, but could feel nothing.' Feeling nothing was an emotion with which Maugham was familiar. While he had few scales in front of his eyes, plenty encased his heart.

He spent his first ten years in France and until he was twelve spoke better French than English. It was a Proustian childhood, of salons and servants and excursions to the coast. The first author he read was La Fontaine, whose fables he recited to his mother at teatime; the first sand that he played on was the beach at Deauville where he once spotted Lillie Langtry. 'It was France that educated me, France that taught me to value beauty, distinction, wit and good sense, France that taught me to write.' Right up until the Second World War, his stories were more popular in France than in Britain. His French upbringing instilled in him two codes of life, two liberties, two points of view. But this duality, he believed, had a dislocating effect – and 'prevented me from ever identifying myself completely with the instincts and prejudices of one people or another'.

From his ravishing mother he inherited an impossible, idealized notion of love as well as a susceptibility to tuberculosis. Mrs Maugham's doctor believed that having another child would cure her. Actually, it killed both the child, who died on Maugham's eighth birthday, and six days later the mother. Her death at the age of forty-one was the tragedy of his life, concluded another of Maugham's biographers, Ted Morgan. 'If in some lives there is an original sin, in Maugham's there was an original wound, from which, by his own admission, he never recovered.' Nearly sixty years later he broke down and wept as he talked of it. 'I shall never get over her death. I shall never get over it,' he railed to his nephew. In his most persistent dream he would wake to find himself at home with his mother. When he died, her picture was on his bedside table. Her sudden disappearance, so early on, coloured his subsequent dealings with women. He never trusted any woman enough to replace her in his affections. At the same time, he clenched himself against the likelihood of being abruptly deserted. One of his favourite aphorisms was by Logan Pearsall Smith: 'If we shake hands with icy fingers, it is because we have burnt them so horribly before.' There smoulders in the name of his alter ego the aroma of someone irredeemably scalded. 'The first syllable had to me a particular connotation which I found suggestive.' Where Graham Greene had a splinter of ice in his heart, Maugham had a small mound of ash.

Two years later, in 1884, his father died and he was properly alone. His French nurse took him to Whitstable, to stay with his uncle Henry, a deep-eyed, snobbish parson married to a German aristocrat. Almost Henry's first act was to sack the nurse. Maugham took eventual revenge on his uncle by drawing on him for the missionary figure in the story 'Rain' – prompting Greene to observe that Maugham had done more than anyone 'to stamp the idea of the repressed strait-laced clergyman on the popular imagination'.

The effect of being orphaned and uprooted had a further alienating impact. 'Tell him I stammer, Uncle,' said the ten-year old Willie as they prepared to meet the headmaster of King's School, Canterbury, where he would board for the next seven years. It was the stammer, wrote Morgan, of someone getting stuck on one word 'like a typewriter key', and it started more or less upon Maugham's arrival at the ivy-covered vicarage, when overnight he had to exchange his primary language. Whatever the cause of his speech impediment, it indicated the separateness that already he felt from others, the sense that he did not fit in. As often is pointed out, his handicap was no less attention-drawing than the clubfoot that he gives to his autobiographical hero in *Of Human Bondage*. In Maugham's case, it encouraged his natural shyness which he later described as a 'mixture of diffidence and conceit'. He admitted: 'My life and my production has been greatly influenced by my stammer.' Without it, he probably would have become a lawyer like his father and his brother Freddy, who rose to be Lord Chancellor. Instead, it hastened his retreat into the aloof, unobtrusive observer of the sort that he detected in Arnold Bennett, who suffered from the same thing: 'It may be that except for the stammer which forced him to introspection, Arnold would never have become a writer.'

On top of everything, there was his homosexuality. The first glimmerings appear in an attachment he formed at King's School, Canterbury. Possibly the other boy was Leonard Ashenden, with whom he shared a prize. At any rate, his sexual make-up – three-quarters 'queer', one quarter 'normal' in Maugham's arithmetic – was made conspicuous to him during a year he spent in Heidelberg, arranged by his German aunt. His seduction by a twenty-six-year-old Cambridge graduate, John Ellingham Brooks, who later fled to Capri, launched Maugham into a life of unavoidable pretence and façade that must have been especially galling for a man who in most respects could not look at a façade without wishing to blow-torch it.

In Heidelberg, he discovered also the European writers and philosophers who would shape his literary tastes. La Rochefoucauld, Maupassant, Racine, Ibsen, whose influence saturates his earliest stories like 'A Bad Example' and 'Daisy'; and Schopenhauer, who believed, as Maugham came to believe, that religion was an illusion to help us endure the accident of existence. Their outlook chimed with Maugham's association of love with suffering and his pessimistic view of human nature following his mother's death. An entry in his notebook reads: 'Everything in life is meaningless, the pain and the suffering are fruitless and futile. There is no object in life.' He returned to England equipped to see the worst in anything. To recreate Whitstable as Blackstable.

Turning down a chance to go to Cambridge – a decision he later regretted – he worked for a firm of accountants, a situation that he could only tolerate for a few weeks. He had started writing in a dedicated way from the age of fifteen, but could not explain to his uncle that this was the profession on which he had set his heart. 'Why not try medicine?' suggested his uncle's doctor in Whitstable, and so he enrolled at St Thomas's. If he could not yet be a writer, at least he could study medicine like some of the writers he admired: Chekhov, Conan Doyle, Keats.

He was grateful for his five years' training at the London hospital. 'There I saw human nature in the raw.' As it had granted Chekhov, his profession gave him access to places where his stammer and his reticence denied him. In the slums of Lambeth, in kerosene-smoked rooms, he opened his doctor's black bag, as later he opened the notebooks that he bought from the Papeterie Brocchi, 30 Faubourg St Honoré – and experienced the privilege and thrill of having utter strangers trust him with their lives. In one period of three weeks, he calculated that he delivered sixty-three babies.

He had no intention of practising. He had a mind, as Edward Garnett said, like a pair of scissors, but he would not have made a good surgeon. 'One of our failures, I'm afraid,' recalled a doctor who had worked alongside him as a dresser. Fumbling to dissect a body in anatomy class, he could not for the life of him find an obvious nerve. His professor helped him to locate it, with a remark that Maugham took as his motto: 'You see, the normal is the rarest thing in the world.' Once the pen had replaced the scalpel, as shortly it did, he never lost the vital habit of regarding all he met as patients to be dispassionately listened to and diagnosed. He behaved like Willie Ashenden, unmoved by the grief of Giulia Lazzari: 'He felt his relation to her as impersonal as a doctor's in the presence of a pain that he cannot alleviate. He saw now why

R. had given him this peculiar task; it needed a cool head and an emotion well under control.'

Doctor, writer, spy: each operates from the assumption that the people around him nurse secrets, and his business is to chivvy them out. R.'s true identity was Sir John Wallinger, a former India policeman, who during the First World War was in charge of deploying British Intelligence agents in France and Switzerland. Wallinger was also the lover of a friend of Syrie Wellcome, whom Maugham was squiring at the time, and later disastrously married. She arranged a meeting. Maugham turned up at a red-brick house where there was a 'For Sale' sign. The upshot was that Maugham, already a successful playwright, agreed to go to Lucerne in neutral Switzerland where he would take a room in the Hotel Beau Rivage and there, while pretending to write a play, investigate an Englishman, married to a German wife, whom R. suspected of being a traitor. On assignments like these, he gathered the stories that he collected, ten years later, in *Ashenden*.

Maugham's Swiss winter affected his lungs. It was partly to recover his health that in 1916 he travelled to the South Seas with his lover Gerald Haxton, a San Franciscan whom he had met two years earlier, in Flanders. Both were serving in the same ambulance unit. Maugham was forty at the time; Haxton twenty-two, with a pock-marked face that sometimes he disguised with make-up, and an appetite for gambling and alcohol. 'He stank,' wrote Beverly Nichols, who considered Haxton a liar, a forger and a cheat. 'If he thought it would be of the faintest advantage he'd jump into bed with a hyena.' Maugham in his stories makes extraordinarily few glances to his personal life, but the rare nod speaks volumes. 'I know nothing more shattering than to love with all your heart ... someone who is worthless.' That Haxton led Maugham on a dance as merry as it must have been painful is suggested by an uncharacteristic flight into verse (*In weariness, and not in death or parting, is / The bitterness of love. Spent is my passion / Like a river dried up by the sun's fierce rays*) and further supported by his confession to Godfrey Winn: 'You do not know what it is like, Godfrey, and I hope you never will, to be married to someone who is married to drink.' But Maugham loved Haxton, and his best stories were collected and written in his company. As he revealed in *Ashenden*: 'In these stories no more than the barest suggestion has been made that Ashenden was capable on occasions of the passion ironically called tender ... but even when suffering most acutely from the pangs of unrequited love he had been able to say to himself, albeit with a wry face, after all, it's grist to the mill.'

In 1915, Haxton was arrested in a Covent Garden hotel and indicted on six counts of gross indecency. A cloud hung over him – 'a cloud no bigger than a boy's hand,' sighed a friend of Maugham's on Capri, exiled for a similar reason. Not long afterwards Haxton was deported as an undesirable alien. The refusal of the authorities ever to let his lover enter England was the principal reason that Maugham left England, to live in France, but there were other factors, as he mentioned in *The Summing Up*: 'I am attached to England but I have never felt myself very much at home there. I have always been shy with English people. To me England has been a country where I had obligations that I did not want to fulfil and responsibilities that irked me. I have never felt entirely myself till I had put at least the Channel between my native country and me. Some fortunate persons find freedom in their own minds; I, with less spiritual power than they, find it in travel.'

By the end of his life, Maugham could claim with reason: 'I have sojourned in most parts of the world.' Among the widest travelled of English authors, he even endowed a prize in his name that stipulated the money should be spent purely on travel. In travel, he could yield to the illusion that he might, just possibly, arrive at an answer to the riddle of life. 'My whole soul aches for the East, for Egypt, and India and Japan,' says the doctor in Maugham's 1904 novel, *The Merry-Go-Round*, a man who wants nothing more than to follow the example of his author and abandon medicine. 'I want to know the corrupt eager life of the Malays and the violent adventures of the South Sea Islands.'

In 1916, Maugham sailed from San Francisco with Haxton to do just that.

*

INTRODUCTION

Patagonia, Morocco, South Africa, Australia, India, Canada – wherever there is a restless Englishman abroad within reach of a bridge table, a cocktail cabinet and a soda syphon.

There is plenty to say against Maugham, and yet when all is said and done, I side with the Waughs and the Micheners, and not with the Edmund Wilsons. For sheer narrative cunning Maugham is as good as it gets in the twentieth century. There is a quality to his writing, in these days easy to ignore, which looks like champagne to everyone else's lager. He did not write beautifully. He wrote ordinarily, like a speaker in prose. But for the authentic old-world pleasure he gave to the reader – pleasure in the words, pleasure in the atmosphere, pleasure in the brilliance of the artifice – he has few rivals. What might seem now anachronistic – i.e. escape into old-fashioned story-telling – is also the key to his endurance. When people look back and ask who could offer this escape, they will have to say Saki, they will have to say William Maxwell, Raymond Carver and Frank O'Connor. And they will have to say Maugham too. Connolly was quite right. 'If all else perish, there will remain a story-teller's world from Singapore to the Marquesas that is exclusively and forever Maugham, a world of veranda and prahu which we enter, as we do that of Conan Doyle's Baker Street, with a sense of happy and eternal homecoming.'

Nicholas Shakespeare

SELECT BIBLIOGRAPHY

———

WORKS BY SOMERSET MAUGHAM
A Writer's Notebook, William Heinemann, 1949.
Ten Novels and their Authors, William Heinemann, 1954.
The Vagrant Mood, William Heinemann, 1952.
A Traveller in Romance, Anthony Blond, 1984.
Selected Prefaces and Introductions, William Heinemann, 1963.

BIOGRAPHY AND CRITICISM
L. BRANDER, *Somerset Maugham: A Guide*, Oliver & Boyd, 1963.
ROBERT CALDER, *W. Somerset Maugham and the Quest for Freedom*, William Heinemann, 1972.
RICHARD CORDELL, *Somerset Maugham: A biographical and critical study*, Indiana University Press, 1961.
ANTHONY CURTIS, *The Pattern of Maugham*, Hamish Hamilton, 1974.
ANTHONY CURTIS, *Somerset Maugham*, Weidenfeld and Nicolson, 1977.
KLAUS W. JONAS (ed.), *The Maugham Enigma*, Peter Owen, 1954.
ROBIN MAUGHAM, *Somerset and all the Maughams*, William Heinemann, 1966.
TED MORGAN, *Somerset Maugham*, Jonathan Cape, 1980.

CHRONOLOGY

DATE	AUTHOR'S LIFE	LITERARY CONTEXT
1874	William Somerset Maugham is born in Paris, the youngest of four brothers. His father is a lawyer attached to the British Embassy.	Hardy: *Far From the Madding Crowd*. Rimbaud: *Les Illuminations*. Verlaine: *Romances sans paroles*.
1875		Boucicault: *The Shaughraun*. Gilbert and Sullivan: *Trial by Jury*.
1880		Maupassant: 'Boule de suif'.
1882	Maugham's mother dies.	Ibsen: *The Master Builder*. Stevenson: *New Arabian Nights*.
1884	The author is orphaned when his father dies. He is sent to England to live with his uncle, the vicar of Whitstable.	Twain: *Huckleberry Finn*. Ibsen: *The Wild Duck*. Maupassant: 'La Parure'.
1885	Maugham is educated at King's School, Canterbury (to 1889).	Zola: *Germinal*. Maupassant: *Bel-Ami*. Pinero: *The Magistrate*.
1886		Stevenson: *Dr Jekyll and Mr Hyde*; *Kidnapped*.
1890	Educated at Heidelberg (to 1892).	Ibsen: *Hedda Gabler*. Maupassant: *L'Inutile beauté*.
1892	The author turns down a chance to attend Cambridge University and trains as a doctor at St Thomas's Teaching Hospital, London.	Guy de Maupassant is admitted to an asylum after attempting to cut his throat. He dies there the following year.
1894	Maugham works as an intern and obstetric clerk.	Conan Doyle: *The Memoirs of Sherlock Holmes*. Kipling: *The Jungle Book*.
1895		Wilde: *The Importance of Being Earnest*; *An Ideal Husband*.
1897	Publication of *Liza of Lambeth*, Maugham's first novel, influenced by his experience as an obstetric clerk in the slums.	Conrad: *The Nigger of the 'Narcissus'*. Shaw: *Candida*. Wells: *The Invisible Man*. James: *What Maisie Knew*. Rostand: *Cyrano de Bergerac*.
1898	*The Making of a Saint* (novel).	Wells: *The War of the Worlds*. Pinero: *Trelawny of the 'Wells'*.
1899	*Orientations* (short stories).	Chekhov: 'Lady with a Lapdog'.

Disraeli Prime Minister (to 1880). Impressionist exhibition in Paris.

New Republican Constitution in France. Britain buys Suez Canal shares.

Gladstone Prime Minister (to 1885).
Phoenix Park murders in Dublin.

Death of General Gordon at Khartoum. Pasteur's anti-rabies vaccine.
Karl Benz's engine for motor-car.

Kaiser Wilhelm II forces Bismarck to resign.

Gladstone Prime Minister (to 1894). Panama scandal in France.

Gladsone resigns over Home Rule for Ireland. Dreyfus case begins in
France. Nicholas II becomes Tsar of Russia.

Trial of Oscar Wilde. Freud's *Studien über Hysterie* inaugurates psychoanalysis.
Jameson Raid on Transvaal.
Queen Victoria's Diamond Jubilee. Marconi's wireless telegraph company
founded. First monotype typesetting machine. Klondike Gold Rush begins.

Gladstone dies. The Curies discover radium. Britain granted 99-year lease
on Hong Kong by Chinese government.
Boer War begins (to 1902).

DATE	AUTHOR'S LIFE	LITERARY CONTEXT
1900		Death of Wilde.
		Conrad: *Lord Jim*.
		Freud: *The Interpretation of Dreams*.
1901	*The Hero* (novel).	Kipling: *Kim*.
		Chekhov: *The Seagull*.
1902	*Mrs Craddock* (novel).	Barrie: *The Admirable Crichton*.
		Bennett: *Anna of the Five Towns*.
		Conan Doyle: *The Hound of the Baskervilles*.
		Gide: *L'Immoraliste*.
1903	*A Man of Honour* (play).	Birth of Waugh.
		James: *The Ambassadors*.
		Shaw: *Man and Superman*.
		Butler: *The Way of All Flesh*.
		Childers: *The Riddle of the Sands*.
1904	*The Merry-Go-Round* (novel).	James: *The Golden Bowl*.
		Conrad: *Nostromo*.
		Barrie: *Peter Pan*.
		Kipling: *Traffics and Discoveries*.
1905	*The Land of the Blessed Virgin: Sketches and Impressions of Andalusia* (travel writing).	Granville-Barker: *The Voysey Inheritance*. Shaw: *Major Barbara*.
1906	*The Bishop's Apron* (novel).	Galsworthy: *A Man of Property* (vol. 1 of *The Forsyte Saga*).
1907	Maugham's acclaimed comedy of manners, *Lady Frederick*, is published.	Conrad: *The Secret Agent*. Granville-Barker: *Waste*.
1908	*The Explorer, The Magician* (novels). *The Noble Spaniard* (play) is written but not published. The author has four plays running in London.	Forster: *A Room with a View*. Bennett: *The Old Wives' Tale*.
1909		Galsworthy: *Strife*.
		Gide: *La Porte étroite*.
1910		Forster: *Howard's End*.
1911	Maugham meets Syrie Wellcome, daughter of Dr Thomas Barnardo. This meeting marks the beginning of an unconventional relationship.	Lawrence: *The White Peacock*. Bennett: *Clayhanger*. Wells: *The Country of the Blind*. Saki: *The Chronicles of Clovis*.
1912	*Jack Straw, Mrs Dot, Penelope, The Explorer* (plays).	Mann: *Death in Venice*. Bennett: *Milestones*.

CHRONOLOGY

HISTORICAL EVENTS

Annexation of Transvaal and Orange Free State. Labour Party is founded in Britain. Planck's quantum theory. First Zeppelin built.

Queen Victoria dies. Accession of Edward VII. Roosevelt President of USA. Marconi transmits messages across the Atlantic.
Balfour Prime Minister (to 1905). *Times Literary Supplement* started. Education Act in England and Wales makes provision for secondary education.

Emmeline Pankhurst founds the Women's Social and Political Union. Begininning of *Entente Cordiale* between Britain and France. Wright brothers make first powered flight.

Russo-Japanese War (to 1905).

First Russian revolution. Einstein's special theory of relativity.

Liberals win landslide victory in General Election. Launch of HMS *Dreadnought,* first modern battleship.
Triple Entente between Britain, France and Russia. The world's first purpose-built cinema opens at Colne, Lancashire.

Asquith becomes Prime Minister (to 1916) with Lloyd George as Chancellor of the Exchequer. Austria annexes Bosnia and Herzegovina. Old-age pensions introduced in Britain.

House of Lords rejects Lloyd George's Budget: constitutional crisis.
Ford's Model T car. Blériot crosses the Channel by monoplane.
Death of Edward VII. First Post-Impressionist exhibition held in London.
Coronation of George V. Agadir Crisis. Industrial unrest in Britain.
Suffragette riots. First British Official Secrets Act. Amundsen reaches South Pole.

The *Titanic* sinks.

DATE	AUTHOR'S LIFE	LITERARY CONTEXT
1913	*The Tenth Man, Landed Gentry, Smith, The Land of Promise* (plays).	Lawrence: *Sons and Lovers.* Shaw: *Pygmalion.* Proust: *A la Recherche du temps perdu.* Alain-Fournier: *Le Grand Meaulnes.*
1914	Maugham enlists in a British Red Cross Ambulance unit working alongside the French army, joining other literary ambulance drivers including Ernest Hemingway, John Masefield and e e cummings. One of his co-drivers is Desmond MacCarthy, who later becomes a critic for the *Sunday Times*, describing Maugham as 'the English Maupassant'. During this time, he meets Gerald Haxton, who becomes his lover for the next 30 years.	Conrad: *Chance.* Joyce: *Dubliners.* Lawrence: *The Prussian Officer.* Saki: *Beasts and Super-Beasts.*
1915	Maugham and Syrie's daughter Liza is born. *Of Human Bondage* (novel): the lonely boyhood and later training of Philip Carey mirrors Maugham's own experience. The author is sent as a secret agent to Geneva.	Madox Ford: *The Good Soldier.* Conrad: *Victory.* Lawrence: *The Rainbow.* Buchan: *The Thirty-nine Steps.* Woolf: *The Voyage Out.*
1916	Maugham and Haxton set off for the South Seas on the first of their many journeys together. Syrie Wellcome makes a permanent split from her husband Henry, who cites the author as a co-respondent in the subsequent divorce case.	Joyce: *A Portrait of the Artist as a Young Man.* Constance Garnett's translation of the complete stories of Chekhov (to 1922). Brighouse: *Hobson's Choice.*
1917	Maugham and Wellcome marry. Syrie is to be celebrated as an interior decorator in the 1920s, famous for creating the white room. The British government sends Maugham to Petrograd, where he is charged with the task of preventing the Russian Revolution from taking place.	Eliot: *Prufrock and Other Observations.* Yeats: *The Wild Swans at Coole.* Barrie: *Dear Brutus.* Kipling: *A Diversity of Creatures.*

CHRONOLOGY

HISTORICAL EVENTS

Crisis in Ireland: Ulster opposes Home Rule.

Outbreak of World War I following the assassination of Archduke Franz Ferdinand at Sarajevo on 28 June. Trench warfare on Western Front.

Asquith forms coalition government with Balfour. Zeppelin raids. Heavy fighting at Gallipoli. *Lusitania* sunk by German submarine. Einstein's general theory of relativity.

First battle of the Somme commences at 7.30 am on 1 July. By the end of the day, there are 58,000 casualties, a third of them fatal. Battles of Verdun and Jutland. Lloyd George becomes Prime Minister (to 1922). Easter Rising in Dublin.

February and October (Bolshevik) Revolutions in Russia. Abdication of Nicholas II. Russia makes separate peace with Germany. US joins war. Battle of Passchendaele. Balfour Declaration on Palestine.

DATE	AUTHOR'S LIFE	LITERARY CONTEXT
1918		Strachey: *Eminent Victorians*. Brooke: *Collected Poems*. Apollinaire: *Calligrammes*.
1919	*The Moon and Sixpence* (novel) chronicles the life of Charles Strickland, an artist who abandons Europe for Tahiti like the Post-Impressionist Gauguin, neglecting duty in favour of art.	Shaw: *Heartbreak House*. Wodehouse: *My Man Jeeves*. Gide: *La Symphonie pastorale*. Colette: *Chérie*.
1920	*The Unknown* (play).	Mansfield: *Bliss*. Lawrence: *Women in Love*. Wharton: *The Age of Innocence*. Pound: *Hugh Selwyn Mauberly*.
1921	*The Circle* is published, a play based on the life of a young married woman who elopes with a Malayan rubber planter. *The Trembling of a Leaf* (short stories: includes 'Rain'). Maugham travels in Sarawak with Haxton.	Huxley: *Crome Yellow*. Christie: *The Mysterious Affair at Styles*. Dos Passos: *Three Soldiers*. Pirandello: *Six Characters in Search of an Author*.
1922	*East of Suez, Caesar's Wife* (plays). *On a Chinese Screen* (travel writing).	Joyce: *Ulysses*. Eliot: *The Waste Land*. Mansfield: *The Garden Party*. Lawrence: *England, My England*.
1923	*Home and Beauty, The Unattainable, Our Betters* (plays).	Huxley: *Antic Hay*. Cummings: *The Enormous Room*.
1924	*Loaves and Fishes* (play).	Forster: *A Passage to India*. Ford: *Parade's End* (to 1928). Shaw: *Saint Joan*. O'Casey: *Juno and the Paycock*. O'Neill: *Desire Under the Elms*.
1925	*The Painted Veil* (novel). Further travels in South-east Asia.	Scott Fitzgerald: *The Great Gatsby*. Woolf: *Mrs Dalloway*. Kafka: *The Trial*.
1926	Maugham purchases a house at St Jean Cap Ferrat on the French Riviera. The Villa Mauresque is to be frequented by writers and politicians for the rest of the author's life, and an invitation to spend time there becomes a cherished commodity amongst the social set and literati. *The Constant Wife* (play). *The Casuarina Tree* (short stories).	O'Casey: *The Plough and the Stars*. Kipling: *Debits and Credits*. Henry Green: *Blindness*. Hemingway: *The Sun Also Rises*. Faulkner: *Soldier's Pay*. Nabokov: *Mary*. Kafka: *The Castle*.

CHRONOLOGY

HISTORICAL EVENTS

Execution of Nicholas II and his family. Second battle of the Marne: tanks help final Allied advance. Armistice (11 November). Women over 30 gain the vote in Britain.
Versailles Peace Conference. Weimar Republic formed. The Third International. Alcock and Brown fly the Atlantic.

League of Nations formed. Prohibition in the US. First public broadcasting station in Britain.

Civil war in Ireland. Mussolini marches on Rome. Stalin becomes General Secretary of the Communist Party Central Committee. Coalition falls and Bonar Law forms Conservative ministry.

Baldwin becomes Prime Minister. Women gain legal equality in divorce suits. Hitler's coup in Munich fails.
First Labour government formed by Ramsay MacDonald. Death of Lenin. Baldwin becomes Prime Minister again after a Conservative election victory.

An agreement is signed by the Germans after the Locarno Conference in October, recognizing the western border established during the Treaty of Versailles. Hitler: *Mein Kampf.*
British general strike. First television demonstrated.

DATE	AUTHOR'S LIFE	LITERARY CONTEXT
1927	*The Letter* (play).	Woolf: *To the Lighthouse.* Wodehouse: *Meet Mr Mulliner.* Dunne: *An Experiment with Time.*
1928	*The Sacred Flame* (play). *Ashenden* (short stories) is published, based on Maugham's wartime experiences in the Secret Service.	Death of Hardy. Lawrence: *Lady Chatterley's Lover.* Waugh: *Decline and Fall.*
1929		Faulkner: *The Sound and the Fury.* Hemingway: *A Farewell to Arms.* Priestley: *The Good Companions.* Remarque: *All Quiet on the Western Front.* Cocteau: *Les Enfants terribles.*
1930	Maugham publishes *Cakes and Ale,* a satirical novel. *The Bread-Winner* (play). *The Gentleman in the Parlour* (travel writing).	Eliot: *Ash Wednesday.* Waugh: *Vile Bodies.* Pritchett: *The Spanish Virgin.* Coward: *Private Lives.* Faulkner: *As I Lay Dying.*
1931	*Six Stories Written in the Fist Person Singular* (short stories).	Woolf: *The Waves.* Waugh: *Remote People.* O'Neill: *Mourning Becomes Electra.*
1932	*For Services Rendered* (anti-war drama). *The Narrow Corner* (novel).	Waugh: *Black Mischief.* Huxley: *Brave New World.* Céline: *Voyage au bout de la nuit.*
1933	*Ah King* (short stories). *Sheppey* (play).	Coward: *Design for Living.* Malraux: *La Condition humaine.* Giraudoux: *Intermezzo.*
1934		Bowen: *The Cat Jumps.* Waugh: *A Handful of Dust; Ninety-two Days.*
1935	*Don Fernando: or Variations on Some Spanish Themes* (travel writing).	Isherwood: *Mr Norris Changes Trains.* Eliot: *Murder in the Cathedral.* Greene: *England Made Me.*
1936	*Cosmopolitans* (short stories).	Orwell: *Keep the Aspidistra Flying.* Wodehouse: *Laughing Gas.* Céline: *Mort à crédit.*
1937	*Theatre* (novel).	Priestley: *Time and the Conways.* Christie: *Death on the Nile.*

CHRONOLOGY

HISTORICAL EVENTS

Stalin expels Trotsky from Communist Party. German economy collapses. BBC founded. Fleming discovers Penicillin.

Hoover becomes US President. Women over 21 enfranchised in Britain. Stalin launches Soviet collectivization.

Wall Street crash. Beginning of worldwide economic depression. Second Labour government under MacDonald (to 1931).

Gandhi begins civil disobedience campaign in India. Nazis win seats from the moderates in German election. Airship disaster (*R101*) in France.

Britain abandons the Gold Standard. Macdonald forms National Government (to 1935).

Hunger marches in Britain. Mosley's British Union of Fascists formed. F. D. Roosevelt's landslide victory in the US. Geneva Disarmament Conference.

Hitler becomes Chancellor of Germany. Nazi persecution of Jews begins.

Stavisky scandal in France. Riots in Paris: Doumerge forms National Union ministry to avert civil war. Hitler becomes Führer.

Italy invades Abyssinia. Baldwin Prime Minister (to 1937).

Abdication of Edward VIII. Spanish Civil War (to 1939). German troops enter Rhineland. Churchill calls for re-armament. Blum forms Popular Front government in France.

Guernica, Spain, bombed by German planes. Rome–Berlin Axis formed.

DATE	AUTHOR'S LIFE	LITERARY CONTEXT
1938	*The Summing Up* (autobiography). Maugham writes: 'An occasional glance at the obituary column of *The Times* has suggested to me that the sixties are very unhealthy; I have long thought it would exasperate me to die before I had written this book.' He lives for another 27 years.	Waugh: *Scoop.* Greene: *Brighton Rock.* Pritchett: *You Make Your Own Life.* Priestley: *When We Are Married.* Sartre: *La Nausée.* Cocteau: *La Voix humaine.*
1939	*Christmas Holiday* (novel).	Joyce: *Finnegans Wake.* Eliot: *The Family Reunion.* Greene: *The Confidential Agent.* Steinbeck: *The Grapes of Wrath.*
1940	In June Maugham flees France with a single suitcase, joining other refugees on a coal-steamer to Gibraltar. Later in the year he sails to New York where he gives a series of lectures on behalf of the Ministry of Information. He spends the rest of the war in the US. *The Mixture as Before* (short stories). *France at War. Books and You.*	Hemingway: *For Whom the Bell Tolls.* Greene: *The Power and the Glory.* Dylan Thomas: *Portrait of the Artist as a Young Dog.* Auden: *Another Time.*
1941	*Up at the Villa* (novel). *Strictly Personal.*	Coward: *Blithe Spirit.* Fitzgerald: *The Last Tycoon.*
1942	*The Hour Before the Dawn* (novel).	Camus: *L'Etranger.*
1943		Colette: *Gigi.*
1944	*The Razor's Edge* (novel).	Eliot: *Four Quartets.* Anouilh: *Antigone.* Sartre: *Huis clos.* Frank O'Connor: *Crab Apple Jelly.*
1945		Orwell: *Animal Farm.* Waugh: *Brideshead Revisited.* Betjeman: *New Bats in Old Belfries.* Pritchett: *It May Never Happen.*
1946	*Then and Now* (novel).	Dylan Thomas: *Deaths and Entrances.* Rattigan: *The Winslow Boy.*
1947	*Creatures of Circumstance* (short stories).	Priestley: *An Inspector Calls.* Rattigan: *The Browning Version.* Williams: *A Streetcar Named Desire.* Anouilh: *L'Invitation au château.*

CHRONOLOGY

HISTORICAL EVENTS

Fall of Blum and collapse of the Popular Front in France. Daladier forms right-wing government. Germany annexes Austria. Munich crisis. Germany occupies disputed areas of Czechoslovakia.

Molotov–Ribbentrop pact between Germany and the USSR. Germany invades Poland; Britain and France declare war on 3 September.

Churchill becomes Prime Minister. Fall of France. Evacuation of Dunkirk. Battle of Britain. The Blitz. Italy joins the war in alliance with Germany.

USSR is invaded. Japanese attack Pearl Harbor. US joins war.

Fall of Singapore. Germans reach Stalingrad. Battle of El-Alamein. Germans retreat in Russia, Africa and Italy.
Normandy landings. Red Army reaches Belgrade and Budapest. Butler's Education Act.

Hitler commits suicide. Germany surrenders. World War II ends after nuclear bombs are dropped on Hiroshima and Nagasaki. United Nations founded. Attlee forms Labour government.

Nuremberg trials. Churchill's 'Iron Curtain' speech. Beginning of Cold War. National Health Service founded in Britain.

Independence of India and Pakistan. Marshall Plan: US gives aid for European postwar recovery.

DATE	AUTHOR'S LIFE	LITERARY CONTEXT
1948	*Catalina* (novel). *Quartet* (short stories). *Great Novelists and their Novels*.	Waugh: *The Loved One*. Camus: *La Peste*. Brecht: *The Caucasian Chalk Circle*.
1949	*A Writer's Notebook*.	Orwell: *Nineteen Eighty-four*. Greene: *The Third Man*. Fry: *The Lady's not for Burning*. Miller: *Death of a Salesman*.
1950	*Trio* (short stories).	Lawrence Durrell: *Sappho*. Salinger: *The Catcher in the Rye*. Powell: *A Question of Upbringing* (vol. 1 of *A Dance to the Music of Time*).
1951	*The Writer's Point of View*.	Frank O'Connor: *Traveller's Samples*. Beckett: *Molloy*; *Malone meurt*.
1952	*Encore* (short stories). *The Vagrant Mood*.	Waugh: *Men at Arms* (vol. 1 of *The Sword of Honour* trilogy). Beckett: *Waiting for Godot*. Rattigan: *The Deep Blue Sea*. Miller: *The Crucible*.
1953	*The Noble Spaniard* (play) is finally published.	Hartley: *The Go-Between*. Fleming: *Casino Royale*. Anouilh: *L'Alouette*.
1954	*Ten Novels and their Authors*. Maugham is created a Companion of Honour.	Amis: *Lucky Jim*. Rattigan: *Separate Tables*.
1955		Nabokov: *Lolita*. Miller: *A View from the Bridge*. Williams: *Cat on a Hot Tin Roof*.
1956		Burgess: *Time for a Tiger* (vol. 1 of *The Malayan Trilogy*). Camus: *La Chute*.
1957		Waugh: *The Ordeal of Gilbert Pinfold*. Pasternak: *Doctor Zhivago*. Nabokov: *Pnin*.
1958	*Points of View*.	Greene: *Our Man in Havana*. Murdoch: *The Bell*. Pinter: *The Birthday Party*.
1959	Maugham visits Japan, where he is mobbed by thousands of fans.	Spark: *Memento Mori*. Beckett: *Endgame*.
1961	Maugham is made a Companion of Literature by the Royal Literary Society, and is also created Honorary Senator of Heidelberg.	Albee: *The American Dream*. Spark: *The Prime of Miss Jean Brodie*. Pritchett: *When My Girl Comes Home*.

CHRONOLOGY

DATE	AUTHOR'S LIFE	LITERARY CONTEXT
1962	Maugham's memoirs (*Looking Back*) are serialized in the *Sunday Express*.	Albee: *Who's Afraid of Virginia Woolf?* Burgess: *A Clockwork Orange.*
1963	*Selected Prefaces and Introductions.*	Spark: *The Girls of Slender Means.* Le Carré: *The Spy Who Came in from the Cold.* Pinter: *The Lover.*
1964		Isherwood: *A Single Man.* Snow: *The Corridors of Power.* Bellow: *Herzog.*
1965	Maugham dies in Nice at the age of 91.	Pinter: *The Homecoming.* Osborne: *A Patriot for Me.* Le Carré: *The Looking Glass War.*

CHRONOLOGY

Cuban missile crisis. Anglo-French agreement on the construction of Concorde.

Assassination of President Kennedy. Profumo affair. Douglas-Home becomes Prime Minister.

Wilson forms a Labour Government. Martin Luther King is awarded the Nobel Peace Prize. Fall of Khrushchev.

W. SOMERSET MAUGHAM

COLLECTED STORIES

IN A STRANGE LAND

I AM OF a roving disposition; but I travel not to see imposing monuments, which indeed somewhat bore me, nor beautiful scenery, of which I soon tire; I travel to see men. I avoid the great. I would not cross the road to meet a president or a king; I am content to know the writer in the pages of his book and the painter in his picture; but I have journeyed a hundred leagues to see a missionary of whom I had heard a strange story and I have spent a fortnight in a vile hotel in order to improve my acquaintance with a billiard-marker. I should be inclined to say that I am not surprised to meet any sort of person were it not that there is one sort that I am constantly running against and that never fails to give me a little shock of amused astonishment. This is the elderly Englishwoman, generally of adequate means, who is to be found living alone, up and down the world, in unexpected places. You do not wonder when you hear of her living in a villa on a hill outside a small Italian town, the only Englishwoman in the neighbourhood, and you are almost prepared for it when a lonely *hacienda* is pointed out to you in Andalusia and you are told that there has dwelt for many years an English lady. But it is more surprising when you hear that the only white person in a Chinese city is an Englishwoman, not a missionary, who lives there none knows why; and there is another who inhabits an island in the South Seas, and a third who has a bungalow on the outskirts of a large village in the centre of Java. They live solitary lives, these women, without friends, and they do not welcome the stranger. Though they may not have seen one of their own race for months they will pass you on the road as though they did not see you, and if, presuming on your nationality, you should call, as likely as not they will decline to see you; but if they do, they will give you a cup of tea from a silver teapot and on a plate of Old Worcester you will find Scotch scones. They will talk to you politely, as though they were entertaining you in a Kentish vicarage, but when you take your leave will show no particular desire to continue the acquaintance. One wonders in vain what strange instinct it is that has driven them

3

to separate themselves from their kith and kin and thus to live apart from all their natural interests in an alien land. Is it romance they have sought, or freedom?

But of all these Englishwomen whom I have met or perhaps only heard of (for as I have said they are difficult to access) the one who remains most vividly in my memory is an elderly person who lived in Asia Minor. I had arrived after a tedious journey at a little town from which I proposed to make the ascent of a celebrated mountain and I was taken to a rambling hotel that stood at its foot. I arrived late at night and signed my name in the book. I went up to my room. It was cold and I shivered as I undressed, but in a moment there was a knock at the door and the dragoman came in.

"Signora Niccolini's compliments," he said.

To my astonishment he handed me a hot-water bottle. I took it with grateful hands.

"Who is Signora Niccolini?" I asked.

"She is the proprietor of this hotel," he answered.

I sent her my thanks and he withdrew. The last thing I expected in a scrubby hotel in Asia Minor kept by an old Italian woman was a beautiful hot-water bottle. There is nothing I like more (if we were not all sick to death of the war I would tell you the story of how six men risked their lives to fetch a hot-water bottle from a château in Flanders that was being bombarded); and next morning, so that I might thank her in person, I asked if I might see the Signora Niccolini. While I waited for her I racked my brains to think what hot-water bottle could possibly be in Italian. In a moment she came in. She was a little stout woman, not without dignity, and she wore a black apron trimmed with lace and a small black lace cap. She stood with her hands crossed. I was astonished at her appearance for she looked exactly like a housekeeper in a great English house.

"Did you wish to speak to me, sir?"

She was an Englishwoman and in those few words I surely recognized the trace of a cockney accent.

"I wanted to thank you for the hot-water bottle," I replied in some confusion.

"I saw by the visitors' book that you were English, sir, and I always send up a 'ot-water bottle to English gentlemen."

"Believe me, it was very welcome."

"I was for many years in the service of the late Lord Ormskirk, sir. He always used to travel with a 'ot-water bottle. Is there anything else, sir?"

"Not at the moment, thank you."

She gave me a polite little nod and withdrew. I wondered how on earth it came about that a funny old Englishwoman like that should be the landlady of a hotel in Asia Minor. It was not easy to make her acquaintance, for she knew her place, as she would herself have put it, and she kept me at a distance. It was not for nothing that she had been in service in a noble English family. But I was persistent and I induced her at last to ask me to have a cup of tea in her own little parlour. I learnt that she had been lady's-maid to a certain Lady Ormskirk, and Signor Niccolini (for she never alluded to her deceased husband in any other way) had been his lordship's chef. Signor Niccolini was a very handsome man and for some years there had been an "understanding" between them. When they had both saved a certain amount of money they were married, retired from service, and looked about for a hotel. They had bought this one on an advertisement because Signor Niccolini thought he would like to see something of the world. That was nearly thirty years ago and Signor Niccolini had been dead for fifteen. His widow had not once been back to England. I asked her if she was never homesick.

"I don't say as I wouldn't like to go back on a visit, though I expect I'd find many changes. But my family didn't like the idea of me marrying a foreigner and I 'aven't spoken to them since. Of course there are many things here that are not the same as what they 'ave at 'ome, but it's surprising what you get used to. I see a lot of life. I don't know as I should care to live the 'umdrum life they do in a place like London."

I smiled. For what she said was strangely incongruous with her manner. She was a pattern of decorum. It was extraordinary that she could have lived for thirty years in this wild and almost barbaric country without its having touched her. Though I knew no Turkish and she spoke it with ease I was convinced that she spoke it most incorrectly and with a cockney accent. I suppose she had remained the precise, prim English lady's-maid, knowing her place, through all these vicissitudes, because she had no faculty of surprise. She took everything that came as a matter of course.

5

She looked upon everyone who wasn't English as a foreigner and therefore as someone, almost imbecile, for whom allowances must be made. She ruled her staff despotically – for did she not know how an upper servant in a great house should exercise his authority over the under servants? – and everything about the hotel was clean and neat.

"I do my best," she said, when I congratulated her on this, standing, as always when she spoke to me, with her hands respectfully crossed. "Of course one can't expect foreigners to 'ave the same ideas what we 'ave, but as his lordship used to say to me, what we've got to do, Parker, he said to me, what we've got to do in this life is to make the best of our raw material."

But she kept her greatest surprise for the eve of my departure.

"I'm glad you're not going before you've seen my two sons, sir."

"I didn't know you had any."

"They've been away on business, but they've just come back. You'll be surprised when you've seen them. I've trained them with me own 'ands so to speak, and when I'm gone they'll carry on the 'otel between them."

In a moment two tall, swarthy, strapping young fellows entered the hall. Her eyes lit up with pleasure. They went up to her and took her in their arms and gave her resounding kisses.

"They don't speak English, sir, but they understand a little, and of course they speak Turkish like natives, and Greek and Italian." I shook hands with the pair and then Signora Niccolini said something to them and they went away.

"They're handsome fellows, Signora," I said. "You must be very proud of them."

"I am, sir, and they're good boys, both of them. They've never give me a moment's trouble from the day they was born and they're the very image of Signor Niccolini."

"I must say no one would think they had an English mother."

"I'm not exactly their mother, sir. I've just sent them along to say 'ow do you do to 'er."

I dare say I looked a little confused.

"They're the sons that Signor Niccolini 'ad by a Greek girl that used to work in the 'otel, and 'aving no children of me own I adopted them."

6

I sought for some remark to make.

"I 'ope you don't think that there's any blame attaches to Signor Niccolini," she said, drawing herself up a little. "I shouldn't like you to think that, sir." She folded her hands again and with a mixture of pride, primness, and satisfaction added the final word: "Signor Niccolini was a very full-blooded man."

RAIN

IT WAS NEARLY bed-time and when they awoke next morning land would be in sight. Dr Macphail lit his pipe and, leaning over the rail, searched the heavens for the Southern Cross. After two years at the front and a wound that had taken longer to heal than it should, he was glad to settle down quietly at Apia for twelve months at least, and he felt already better for the journey. Since some of the passengers were leaving the ship next day at Pago-Pago they had had a little dance that evening and in his ears hammered still the harsh notes of the mechanical piano. But the deck was quiet at last. A little way off he saw his wife in a long chair talking with the Davidsons, and he strolled over to her. When he sat down under the light and took off his hat you saw that he had very red hair, with a bald patch on the crown, and the red, freckled skin which accompanies red hair; he was a man of forty, thin, with a pinched face, precise and rather pedantic; and he spoke with a Scots accent in a very low, quiet voice.

Between the Macphails and the Davidsons, who were missionaries, there had arisen the intimacy of shipboard, which is due to propinquity rather than to any community of taste. Their chief tie was the disapproval they shared of the men who spent their days and nights in the smoking-room playing poker or bridge and drinking. Mrs Macphail was not a little flattered to think that she and her husband were the only people on board with whom the Davidsons were willing to associate, and even the doctor, shy but no fool, half unconsciously acknowledged the compliment. It was only because he was of an argumentative mind that in their cabin at night he permitted himself to carp.

"Mrs Davidson was saying she didn't know how they'd have got through the journey if it hadn't been for us," said Mrs Macphail, as she neatly brushed out her transformation. "She said we were really the only people on the ship they cared to know."

"I shouldn't have thought a missionary was such a big bug that he could afford to put on frills."

"It's not frills. I quite understand what she means. It wouldn't have been very nice for the Davidsons to have to mix with all that rough lot in the smoking-room."

"The founder of their religion wasn't so exclusive," said Dr Macphail with a chuckle.

"I've asked you over and over again not to joke about religion," answered his wife. "I shouldn't like to have a nature like yours, Alec. You never look for the best in people."

He gave her a sidelong glance with his pale, blue eyes, but did not reply. After many years of married life he had learned that it was more conducive to peace to leave his wife with the last word. He was undressed before she was, and climbing into the upper bunk he settled down to read himself to sleep.

When he came on deck next morning they were close to land. He looked at it with greedy eyes. There was a thin strip of silver beach rising quickly to hills covered to the top with luxuriant vegetation. The coconut trees, thick and green, came nearly to the water's edge, and among them you saw the grass houses of the Samoans; and here and there, gleaming white, a little church. Mrs Davidson came and stood beside him. She was dressed in black and wore round her neck a gold chain, from which dangled a small cross. She was a little woman, with brown, dull hair very elaborately arranged, and she had prominent blue eyes behind invisible pince-nez. Her face was long, like a sheep's, but she gave no impression of foolishness, rather of extreme alertness; she had the quick movements of a bird. The most remarkable thing about her was her voice, high, metallic, and without inflexion; it fell on the ear with a hard monotony, irritating to the nerves like the pitiless clamour of the pneumatic drill.

"This must seem like home to you," said Dr Macphail, with his thin, difficult smile.

"Ours are low islands, you know, not like these. Coral. These are volcanic. We've got another ten days' journey to reach them."

"In these parts that's almost like being in the next street at home," said Dr Macphail facetiously.

"Well, that's rather an exaggerated way of putting it, but one does look at distances differently in the South Seas. So far you're right."

Dr Macphail sighed faintly.

"I'm glad we're not stationed here," she went on. "They say this is a terribly difficult place to work in. The steamers' touching makes the people unsettled; and then there's the naval station; that's bad for the natives. In our district we don't have difficulties like that to contend with. There are one or two traders, of course, but we take care to make them behave, and if they don't we make the place so hot for them they're glad to go."

Fixing the glasses on her nose she looked at the green island with a ruthless stare.

"It's almost a hopeless task for the missionaries here. I can never be sufficiently thankful to God that we are at least spared that."

Davidson's district consisted of a group of islands to the North of Samoa; they were widely separated and he had frequently to go long distances by canoe. At these times his wife remained at their head-quarters and managed the mission. Dr Macphail felt his heart sink when he considered the efficiency with which she certainly managed it. She spoke of the depravity of the natives in a voice which nothing could hush, but with a vehemently unctuous horror. Her sense of delicacy was singular. Early in their acquaintance she had said to him:

"You know, their marriage customs when we first settled in the islands were so shocking that I couldn't possibly describe them to you. But I'll tell Mrs Macphail and she'll tell you."

Then he had seen his wife and Mrs Davidson, their deck-chairs close together, in earnest conversation for about two hours. As he walked past them backwards and forwards for the sake of exercise, he had heard Mrs Davidson's agitated whisper, like the distant flow of a mountain torrent, and he saw by his wife's open mouth and pale face that she was enjoying an alarming experience. At night in their cabin she repeated to him with bated breath all she had heard.

"Well, what did I say to you?" cried Mrs Davidson, exultant next morning. "Did you ever hear anything more dreadful? You don't wonder that I couldn't tell you myself, do you? Even though you are a doctor."

Mrs Davidson scanned his face. She had a dramatic eagerness to see that she had achieved the desired effect.

"Can you wonder that when we first went there our hearts sank? You'll hardly believe me when I tell you it was impossible to find a single good girl in any of the villages."

She used the word *good* in a severely technical manner.

"Mr Davidson and I talked it over, and we made up our minds the first thing to do was to put down the dancing. The natives were crazy about dancing."

"I was not averse to it myself when I was a young man," said Dr Macphail.

"I guessed as much when I heard you ask Mrs Macphail to have a turn with you last night. I don't think there's any real harm if a man dances with his wife, but I was relieved that she wouldn't. Under the circumstances I thought it better that we should keep ourselves to ourselves."

"Under what circumstances?"

Mrs Davidson gave him a quick look through her pince-nez, but did not answer his question.

"But among white people it's not quite the same," she went on, "though I must say I agree with Mr Davidson, who says he can't understand how a husband can stand by and see his wife in another man's arms, and as far as I'm concerned I've never danced a step since I married. But the native dancing is quite another matter. It's not only immoral in itself, but it distinctly leads to immorality. However, I'm thankful to God that we stamped it out, and I don't think I'm wrong in saying that no one has danced in our district for eight years."

But now they came to the mouth of the harbour and Mrs Macphail joined them. The ship turned sharply and steamed slowly in. It was a great land-locked harbour big enough to hold a fleet of battleships; and all around it rose, high and steep, the green hills. Near the entrance, getting such breeze as blew from the sea, stood the governor's house in a garden. The Stars and Stripes dangled languidly from a flagstaff. They passed two or three trim bungalows, and a tennis court, and then they came to the quay with its warehouses. Mrs Davidson pointed out the schooner, moored two or three hundred yards from the side, which was to take them to Apia. There was a crowd of eager, noisy, and good-humoured natives come from all parts of the island, some from curiosity, others to barter with the travellers on their way to Sydney; and they brought pineapples and huge bunches of bananas, tapa cloths, necklaces of shells or sharks' teeth, *kava*-bowls, and models of war canoes. American sailors, neat and trim, clean-shaven and frank of face, sauntered among them, and there was a little group of officials. While their luggage was being landed the Macphails and Mrs Davidson watched the crowd. Dr Macphail looked at the yaws from which most of the children and the young boys seemed to suffer, disfiguring sores like torpid ulcers, and his professional eyes glistened when he saw for the first time in his experience cases of elephantiasis, men going about with a huge, heavy arm or dragging along a grossly disfigured leg. Men and women wore the lava-lava.

"It's a very indecent costume," said Mrs Davidson. "Mr Davidson thinks it should be prohibited by law. How can you expect people to be moral when they wear nothing but a strip of red cotton round their loins?"

"It's suitable enough to the climate," said the doctor, wiping the sweat off his head.

Now that they were on land the heat, though it was so early in the morning, was already oppressive. Closed in by its hills, not a breath of air came in to Pago-Pago.

"In our islands," Mrs Davidson went on in her high-pitched tones, "we've practically eradicated the lava-lava. A few old men still continue to wear it, but that's all. The women have all taken to the Mother Hubbard, and the men wear trousers and singlets. At the beginning of our stay Mr Davidson said in one of his reports: the inhabitants of these islands will never be thoroughly Christianized till every boy of more than ten years is made to wear a pair of trousers."

But Mrs Davidson had given two or three of her birdlike glances at heavy grey clouds that came floating over the mouth of the harbour. A few drops began to fall.

"We'd better take shelter," she said.

They made their way with all the crowd to a great shed of corrugated iron, and the rain began to fall in torrents. They stood there for some time and then were joined by Mr Davidson. He had been polite enough to the Macphails during the journey, but he had not his wife's sociability, and had spent much of his time reading. He was a silent, rather sullen man, and you felt that his affability was a duty that he imposed upon himself Christianly; he was by nature reserved and even morose. His appearance was singular. He was very tall and thin, with long limbs loosely jointed; hollow cheeks, and curiously high cheek-bones; he had so cadaverous an air that it surprised you to notice how full and sensual were his lips. He wore his hair very long. His dark eyes, set deep in their sockets, were large and tragic; and his hands with their big, long fingers, were finely shaped; they gave him a look of great strength. But the most striking thing about him was the feeling he gave you of suppressed fire. It was impressive and vaguely troubling. He was not a man with whom any intimacy was possible.

He brought now unwelcome news. There was an epidemic of measles, a serious and often fatal disease among the Kanakas, on the island, and a case had developed among the crew of the schooner which was to take them on their journey. The sick man had been brought ashore and put in hospital on the quarantine station, but telegraphic instructions had been sent from Apia to say that the schooner would not be allowed to enter the harbour till it was certain no other member of the crew was affected.

"It means we shall have to stay here for ten days at least."

"But I'm urgently needed at Apia," said Dr Macphail.

"That can't be helped. If no more cases develop on board, the schooner will be allowed to sail with white passengers, but all native traffic is prohibited for three months."

"Is there a hotel here?" asked Mrs Macphail.

Davidson gave a low chuckle.

"There's not."

"What shall we do then?"

"I've been talking to the governor. There's a trader along the front who has rooms that he rents, and my proposition is that as soon as the rain lets up we should go along there and see what we can do. Don't expect comfort. You've just got to be thankful if we get a bed to sleep on and a roof over our heads."

But the rain showed no signs of stopping, and at length with umbrellas and waterproofs they set out. There was no town, but merely a group of official buildings, a store or two, and at the back, among the coconut trees and plantains, a few native dwellings. The house they sought was about five minutes' walk from the wharf. It was a frame house of two storeys, with broad verandas on both floors and a roof of corrugated iron. The owner was a half-caste named Horn, with a native wife surrounded by little brown children, and on the ground-floor he had a store where he sold canned goods and cottons. The rooms he showed them were almost bare of furniture. In the Macphails' there was nothing but a poor, worn bed with a ragged mosquito net, a rickety chair, and a washstand. They looked round with dismay. The rain poured down without ceasing.

"I'm not going to unpack more than we actually need," said Mrs Macphail.

Mrs Davidson came into the room as she was unlocking a portmanteau. She was very brisk and alert. The cheerless surroundings had no effect on her.

"If you'll take my advice you'll get a needle and cotton and start right in to mend the mosquito net," she said, "or you'll not be able to get a wink of sleep tonight."

"Will they be very bad?" asked Dr Macphail.

"This is the season for them. When you're asked to a party at Government House at Apia you'll notice that all the ladies are given a pillowslip to put their – their lower extremities in."

"I wish the rain would stop for a moment," said Mrs Macphail. "I could try to make the place comfortable with more heart if the sun were shining."

"Oh, if you wait for that, you'll wait a long time. Pago-Pago is about the rainiest place in the Pacific. You see, the hills, and that bay, they attract the water, and one expects rain at this time of year anyway."

She looked from Macphail to his wife, standing helplessly in different parts of the room, like lost souls, and she pursed her lips. She saw that she must take them in hand. Feckless people like that made her impatient, but her hands itched to put everything in the order which came so naturally to her.

"Here, you give me a needle and cotton and I'll mend that net of yours, while you go on with your unpacking. Dinner's at one. Dr Macphail, you'd better go down to the wharf and see that your heavy luggage has been put in a dry place. You know what these natives are, they're quite capable of storing it where the rain will beat in on it all the time."

The doctor put on his waterproof again and went downstairs. At the door Mr Horn was standing in conversation with the quartermaster of the ship they had just arrived in and a second-class passenger whom Dr Macphail had seen several times on board. The quartermaster, a little, shrivelled man, extremely dirty, nodded to him as he passed.

"This is a bad job about the measles, doc," he said. "I see you've fixed yourself up already."

Dr Macphail thought he was rather familiar, but he was a timid man and he did not take offence easily.

"Yes, we've got a room upstairs."

"Miss Thompson was sailing with you to Apia, so I've brought her along here."

The quartermaster pointed with his thumb to the woman standing by his side. She was twenty-seven perhaps, plump, and in a coarse fashion pretty. She wore a white dress and a large white hat. Her fat calves in white cotton stockings bulged over the tops of long white boots in glacé kid. She gave Macphail an ingratiating smile.

"The feller's tryin' to soak me a dollar and a half a day for the meanest-sized room," she said in a hoarse voice.

"I tell you she's a friend of mine, Jo," said the quartermaster. "She can't pay more than a dollar, and you've sure got to take her for that."

The trader was fat and smooth and quietly smiling.

"Well, if you put it like that, Mr Swan, I'll see what I can do about it. I'll talk to Mrs Horn and if we think we can make a reduction we will."

"Don't try to pull that stuff with me," said Miss Thompson. "We'll settle this right now. You get a dollar a day for the room and not one bean more."

Dr Macphail smiled. He admired the effrontery with which she bargained. He was the sort of man who always paid what he was asked. He preferred to be over-charged than to haggle. The trader sighed.

"Well, to oblige Mr Swan I'll take it."

"That's the goods," said Miss Thompson. "Come right in and have a shot of hooch. I've got some real good rye in that grip if you'll bring it along, Mr Swan. You come along too, doctor."

"Oh, I don't think I will, thank you," he answered. "I'm just going down to see that our luggage is all right."

He stepped out into the rain. It swept in from the opening of the harbour in sheets and the opposite shore was all blurred. He passed two or three natives clad in nothing but the lava-lava, with huge umbrellas over them. They walked finely, with leisurely movements, very upright; and they smiled and greeted him in a strange tongue as they went by.

It was nearly dinner-time when he got back, and their meal was laid in the trader's parlour. It was a room designed not to live in but for purposes of prestige, and it had a musty, melancholy air. A suite of stamped plush was arranged neatly round the walls, and from the middle of the ceiling, protected from the flies by yellow tissue-paper, hung a gilt chandelier. Davidson did not come.

"I know he went to call on the governor," said Mrs Davidson, "and I guess he's kept him to dinner."

A little native girl brought them a dish of Hamburger steak, and after a while the trader came up to see that they had everything they wanted.

"I see we have a fellow lodger, Mr Horn," said Dr Macphail.

"She's taken a room, that's all," answered the trader. "She's getting her own board."

He looked at the two ladies with an obsequious air.

"I put her downstairs so she shouldn't be in the way. She won't be any trouble to you."

"Is it someone who was on the boat?" asked Mrs Macphail.

"Yes, ma'am, she was in the second cabin. She was going to Apia. She has a position as cashier waiting for her."

"Oh!"

When the trader was gone Macphail said:

"I shouldn't think she'd find it exactly cheerful having her meals in her room."

"If she was in the second cabin I guess she'd rather," answered Mrs Davidson. "I don't exactly know who it can be."

"I happened to be there when the quartermaster brought her along. Her name's Thompson."

"It's not the woman who was dancing with the quartermaster last night?" asked Mrs Davidson.

"That's who it must be," said Mrs Macphail. "I wondered at the time what she was. She looked rather fast to me."

"Not good style at all," said Mrs Davidson.

They began to talk of other things, and after dinner, tired with their early rise, they separated and slept. When they awoke, though the sky was still grey and the clouds hung low, it was not raining and they went for a walk on the high road which the Americans had built along the bay.

On their return they found that Davidson had just come in.

"We may be here for a fortnight," he said irritably. "I've argued it out with the governor, but he says there is nothing to be done."

"Mr Davidson's just longing to get back to his work," said his wife, with an anxious glance at him.

"We've been away for a year," he said, walking up and down the veranda. "The mission has been in charge of native missionaries and I'm terribly nervous that they've let things slide. They're good men, I'm not saying a word against them, God-fearing, devout, and truly Christian men – their Christianity would put many so-called Christians at home to the blush – but they're pitifully lacking in energy. They can make a stand once, they can make a stand twice, but they can't make a stand all the time. If you leave a mission in charge of a native missionary, no matter how trustworthy he seems, in course of time you'll find he's let abuses creep in."

Mr Davidson stood still. With his tall, spare form, and his great eyes flashing out of his pale face, he was an impressive figure. His sincerity was obvious in the fire of his gestures and in his deep, ringing voice.

"I expect to have my work cut out for me. I shall act and I shall act promptly. If the tree is rotten it shall be cut down and cast into the flames."

And in the evening after the high tea which was their last meal, while they sat in the stiff parlour, the ladies working and

16

Dr Macphail smoking his pipe, the missionary told them of his work in the islands.

"When we went there they had no sense of sin at all," he said. "They broke the commandments one after the other and never knew they were doing wrong. And I think that was the most difficult part of my work, to instil into the natives the sense of sin."

The Macphails knew already that Davidson had worked in the Solomons for five years before he met his wife. She had been a missionary in China, and they had become acquainted in Boston, where they were both spending part of their leave to attend a missionary congress. On their marriage they had been appointed to the islands in which they had laboured ever since.

In the course of all the conversations they had had with Mr Davidson one thing had shone out clearly and that was the man's unflinching courage. He was a medical missionary, and he was liable to be called at any time to one or other of the islands in the group. Even the whaleboat is not so very safe a conveyance in the stormy Pacific of the wet season, but often he would be sent for in a canoe, and then the danger was great. In cases of illness or accident he never hesitated. A dozen times he had spent the whole night baling for his life, and more than once Mrs Davidson had given him up for lost.

"I'd beg him not to go sometimes," she said, "or at least to wait till the weather was more settled, but he'd never listen. He's obstinate, and when he's once made up his mind, nothing can move him."

"How can I ask the natives to put their trust in the Lord if I am afraid to do so myself?" cried Davidson. "And I'm not, I'm not. They know that if they send for me in their trouble I'll come if it's humanly possible. And do you think the Lord is going to abandon me when I am on his business? The wind blows at his bidding and the waves toss and rage at his word."

Dr Macphail was a timid man. He had never been able to get used to the hurtling of the shells over the trenches, and when he was operating in an advanced dressing-station the sweat poured from his brow and dimmed his spectacles in the effort he made to control his unsteady hand. He shuddered a little as he looked at the missionary.

"I wish I could say that I've never been afraid," he said.

"I wish you could say that you believed in God," retorted the other.

But for some reason, that evening the missionary's thoughts travelled back to the early days he and his wife had spent on the islands.

"Sometimes Mrs Davidson and I would look at one another and the tears would stream down our cheeks. We worked without ceasing, day and night, and we seemed to make no progress. I don't know what I should have done without her then. When I felt my heart sink, when I was very near despair, she gave me courage and hope."

Mrs Davidson looked down at her work, and a slight colour rose to her thin cheeks. Her hands trembled a little. She did not trust herself to speak.

"We had no one to help us. We were alone, thousands of miles from any of our own people, surrounded by darkness. When I was broken and weary she would put her work aside and take the Bible and read to me till peace came and settled upon me like sleep upon the eyelids of a child, and when at last she closed the book she'd say: 'We'll save them in spite of themselves.' And I felt strong again in the Lord, and I answered: 'Yes, with God's help I'll save them. I must save them.'"

He came over to the table and stood in front of it as though it were a lectern.

"You see, they were so naturally depraved that they couldn't be brought to see their wickedness. We had to make sins out of what they thought were natural actions. We had to make it a sin, not only to commit adultery and to lie and thieve, but to expose their bodies, and to dance and not to come to church. I made it a sin for a girl to show her bosom and a sin for a man not to wear trousers."

"How?" asked Dr Macphail, not without surprise.

"I instituted fines. Obviously the only way to make people realize that an action is sinful is to punish them if they commit it. I fined them if they didn't come to church, and I fined them if they danced. I fined them if they were improperly dressed. I had a tariff, and every sin had to be paid for either in money or work. And at last I made them understand."

"But did they never refuse to pay?"

"How could they?" asked the missionary.

"It would be a brave man who tried to stand up against Mr Davidson," said his wife, tightening her lips.

Dr Macphail looked at Davidson with troubled eyes. What he heard shocked him, but he hesitated to express his disapproval.

"You must remember that in the last resort I could expel them from their church membership."

"Did they mind that?"

Davidson smiled a little and gently rubbed his hands.

"They couldn't sell their copra. When the men fished they got no share of the catch. It meant something very like starvation. Yes, they minded quite a lot."

"Tell him about Fred Ohlson," said Mrs Davidson.

The missionary fixed his fiery eyes on Dr Macphail.

"Fred Ohlson was a Danish trader who had been in the islands a good many years. He was a pretty rich man as traders go and he wasn't very pleased when we came. You see, he'd had things very much his own way. He paid the natives what he liked for their copra, and he paid in goods and whisky. He had a native wife, but he was flagrantly unfaithful to her. He was a drunkard. I gave him a chance to mend his ways, but he wouldn't take it. He laughed at me."

Davidson's voice fell to a deep bass as he said the last words, and he was silent for a minute or two. The silence was heavy with menace.

"In two years he was a ruined man. He'd lost everything he'd saved in a quarter of a century. I broke him, and at last he was forced to come to me like a beggar and beseech me to give him a passage back to Sydney."

"I wish you could have seen him when he came to see Mr Davidson," said the missionary's wife. "He had been a fine, powerful man, with a lot of fat on him, and he had a great big voice, but now he was half the size, and he was shaking all over. He'd suddenly become an old man."

With abstracted gaze Davidson looked out into the night. The rain was falling again.

Suddenly from below came a sound, and Davidson turned and looked questioningly at his wife. It was the sound of a gramophone, harsh and loud, wheezing out a syncopated tune.

"What's that?" he asked.

Mrs Davidson fixed her pince-nez more firmly on her nose.

"One of the second-class passengers has a room in the house. I guess it comes from there."

They listened in silence, and presently they heard the sound of dancing. Then the music stopped, and they heard the popping of corks and voices raised in animated conversation.

"I daresay she's giving a farewell party to her friends on board," said Dr Macphail. "The ship sails at twelve, doesn't it?"

Davidson made no remark, but he looked at his watch.

"Are you ready?" he asked his wife.

She got up and folded her work.

"Yes, I guess I am," she answered.

"It's early to go to bed yet, isn't it?" said the doctor.

"We have a good deal of reading to do," explained Mrs Davidson. "Wherever we are, we read a chapter of the Bible before retiring for the night and we study it with the commentaries, you know, and discuss it thoroughly. It's a wonderful training for the mind."

The two couples bade one another good night. Dr and Mrs Macphail were left alone. For two or three minutes they did not speak.

"I think I'll go and fetch the cards," the doctor said at last.

Mrs Macphail looked at him doubtfully. Her conversation with the Davidsons had left her a little uneasy, but she did not like to say that she thought they had better not play cards when the Davidsons might come in at any moment. Dr Macphail brought them and she watched him, though with a vague sense of guilt, while he laid out his patience. Below the sound of revelry continued.

It was fine enough next day, and the Macphails, condemned to spend a fortnight of idleness at Pago-Pago, set about making the best of things. They went down to the quay and got out of their boxes a number of books. The doctor called on the chief surgeon of the naval hospital and went round the beds with him. They left cards on the governor. They passed Miss Thompson on the road. The doctor took off his hat, and she gave him a "Good morning doc," in a loud, cheerful voice. She was dressed as on the day before, in a white frock, and her shiny white boots with their high heels, her fat legs bulging over the tops of them, were strange things on that exotic scene.

"I don't think she's very suitably dressed, I must say," said Mrs Macphail. "She looks extremely common to me."

When they got back to their house, she was on the veranda playing with one of the trader's dark children.

"Say a word to her," Dr Macphail whispered to his wife. "She's all alone here, and it seems rather unkind to ignore her."

Mrs Macphail was shy, but she was in the habit of doing what her husband bade her.

"I think we're fellow lodgers here," she said, rather foolishly.

"Terrible, ain't it, bein' cooped up in a one-horse burg like this?" answered Miss Thompson. "And they tell me I'm lucky to have gotten a room. I don't see myself livin' in a native house, and that's what some have to do. I don't know why they don't have a hotel."

They exchanged a few more words. Miss Thompson, loud-voiced and garrulous, was evidently quite willing to gossip, but Mrs Macphail had a poor stock of small talk and presently she said:

"Well, I think we must go upstairs."

In the evening when they sat down to their high tea, Davidson on coming in said:

"I see that woman downstairs has a couple of sailors sitting there. I wonder how she's gotten acquainted with them."

"She can't be very particular," said Mrs Davidson.

They were all rather tired after the idle, aimless day.

"If there's going to be a fortnight of this I don't know what we shall feel like at the end of it," said Dr Macphail.

"The only thing to do is to portion out the day to different activities," answered the missionary. "I shall set aside a certain number of hours to study and a certain number to exercise, rain or fine – in the wet season you can't afford to pay any attention to the rain – and a certain number to recreation."

Dr Macphail looked at his companion with misgiving. Davidson's programme oppressed him. They were eating Hamburger steak again. It seemed the only dish the cook knew how to make. Then below the gramophone began. Davidson started nervously when he heard it, but said nothing. Men's voices floated up. Miss Thompson's guests were joining in a well-known song and presently they heard her voice too, hoarse and loud. There was a good deal of shouting and laughing. The four people upstairs, trying to make conversation, listened despite themselves to the clink of glasses and the scrape of chairs. More people had evidently come. Miss Thompson was giving a party.

"I wonder how she gets them all in," said Mrs Macphail suddenly breaking into a medical conversation between the missionary and her husband.

It showed whither her thoughts were wandering. The twitch of Davidson's face proved that, though he spoke of scientific things, his mind was busy in the same direction. Suddenly, while the doctor was giving some experience of practice on the Flanders front, rather prosily, he sprang to his feet with a cry.

"What's the matter, Alfred?" asked Mrs Davidson.

"Of course! It never occurred to me. She's out of Iwelei."

"She can't be."

"She came on board at Honolulu. It's obvious. And she's carrying on her trade here. Here."

He uttered the last word with a passion of indignation.

"What's Iwelei?" asked Mrs Macphail.

He turned his gloomy eyes on her and his voice trembled with horror.

"The plague spot of Honolulu. The Red Light district. It was a blot on our civilization."

Iwelei was on the edge of the city. You went down side streets by the harbour, in the darkness, across a rickety bridge, till you came to a deserted road, all ruts and holes, and then suddenly you came out into the light. There was parking room for motors on each side of the road, and there were saloons, tawdry and bright, each one noisy with its mechanical piano, and there were barbers' shops and tobacconists. There was a stir in the air and a sense of expectant gaiety. You turned down a narrow alley, either to the right or to the left, for the road divided Iwelei into two parts, and you found yourself in the district. There were rows of little bungalows, trim and neatly painted in green, and the pathway between them was broad and straight. It was laid out like a garden-city. In its respectable regularity, its order and spruceness, it gave an impression of sardonic horror; for never can the search for love have been so systematized and ordered. The pathways were lit by a rare lamp, but they would have been dark except for the lights that came from the open windows of the bungalows. Men wandered about, looking at the women who sat at their windows, reading or sewing, for the most part taking no notice of the passers-by; and like the women they were of all nationalities. There were Americans, sailors from the ships in port, enlisted men off the gunboats, sombrely drunk, and soldiers from the regiments, white and black, quartered on the island; there were Japanese, walking in twos and threes; Hawaiians, Chinese in long robes, and Filipinos in preposterous hats. They were silent and as it were oppressed. Desire is sad.

"It was the most crying scandal of the Pacific," exclaimed Davidson vehemently. "The missionaries had been agitating against it for years, and at last the local press took it up. The police refused to stir. You know their argument. They say that vice is inevitable and consequently the best thing is to localize and control it. The truth is, they were paid. Paid. They were paid by the saloon-keepers, paid by the bullies, paid by the women themselves. At last they were forced to move."

"I read about it in the papers that came on board in Honolulu," said Dr Macphail.

"Iwelei, with its sin and shame, ceased to exist on the very day we arrived. The whole population was brought before the justices. I don't know why I didn't understand at once what that woman was."

"Now you come to speak of it," said Mrs Macphail, "I remember seeing her come on board only a few minutes before the boat sailed. I remember thinking at the time she was cutting it rather fine."

"How dare she come here!" cried Davidson indignantly. "I'm not going to allow it."

He strode towards the door.

"What are you going to do?" asked Macphail.

"What do you expect me to? I'm going to stop it. I'm not going to have this house turned into – into . . . "

He sought for a word that should not offend the ladies' ears. His eyes were flashing and his pale face was paler still in his emotion.

"It sounds as though there were three or four men down there," said the doctor. "Don't you think it's rather rash to go in just now?"

The missionary gave him a contemptuous look and without a word flung out of the room.

"You know Mr Davidson very little if you think the fear of personal danger can stop him in the performance of his duty," said his wife.

She sat with her hands nervously clasped, a spot of colour on her high cheek-bones, listening to what was about to happen below. They all listened. They heard him clatter down the wooden stairs and throw open the door. The singing stopped suddenly, but the gramophone continued to bray out its vulgar tune. They heard Davidson's voice and then the noise of something heavy falling. The music stopped. He had hurled the gramophone on the floor. Then again they heard Davidson's voice, they could not make out the words, then Miss Thompson's, loud and shrill, then a confused clamour as though several people were shouting together at the top of their lungs. Mrs Davidson gave a little gasp, and she clenched her hands more tightly. Dr Macphail looked uncertainly from her to his wife. He did not want to go down, but he wondered if they expected him to. Then there was something that sounded like a scuffle. The noise now was more distinct. It might be that Davidson was being thrown out of the room. The door was slammed. There was a moment's silence and they heard Davidson come up the stairs again. He went to his room.

"I think I'll go to him," said Mrs Davidson.

She got up and went out.

"If you want me, just call," said Mrs Macphail, and then when the other was gone: "I hope he isn't hurt."

"Why couldn't he mind his own business?" said Dr Macphail.

They sat in silence for a minute or two and then they both started, for the gramophone began to play once more, defiantly, and mocking voices shouted hoarsely the words of an obscene song.

Next day Mrs Davidson was pale and tired. She complained of headache, and she looked old and wizened. She told Mrs Macphail that the missionary had not slept at all; he had passed the night in a state of frightful agitation and at five had got up and gone out. A glass of beer had been thrown over him and his clothes were stained and stinking. But a sombre fire glowed in Mrs Davidson's eyes when she spoke of Miss Thompson.

"She'll bitterly rue the day when she flouted Mr Davidson," she said. "Mr Davidson has a wonderful heart and no one who is in trouble has ever gone to him without being comforted, but he has no mercy for sin, and when his righteous wrath is excited he's terrible."

"Why, what will he do?" asked Mrs Macphail.

"I don't know, but I wouldn't stand in that creature's shoes for anything in the world."

Mrs Macphail shuddered. There was something positively alarming in the triumphant assurance of the little woman's manner. They were going out together that morning, and they went down the stairs side by side. Miss Thompson's door was open, and they saw her in a bedraggled dressing-gown, cooking something in a chafing-dish.

"Good morning," she called. "Is Mr Davidson better this morning?"

They passed her in silence, with their noses in the air, as if she did not exist. They flushed, however, when she burst into a shout of derisive laughter. Mrs Davidson turned on her suddenly.

"Don't you dare to speak to me," she screamed. "If you insult me I shall have you turned out of here."

"Say, did I ask Mr Davidson to visit with me?"

"Don't answer her," whispered Mrs Macphail hurriedly.

They walked on till they were out of earshot.

"She's brazen, brazen," burst from Mrs Davidson.

Her anger almost suffocated her.

And on their way home they met her strolling towards the quay. She had all her finery on. Her great white hat with its vulgar, showy flowers was an affront. She called out cheerily to them as she went by, and a couple of American sailors who were standing there grinned as the ladies set their faces to an icy stare. They got in just before the rain began to fall again.

"I guess she'll get her fine clothes spoilt," said Mrs Davidson with a bitter sneer.

Davidson did not come in till they were half-way through dinner. He was wet through, but he would not change. He sat, morose and silent, refusing to eat more than a mouthful, and he stared at the slanting rain. When Mrs Davidson told him of their two encounters with Miss Thompson he did not answer. His deepening frown alone showed that he had heard.

"Don't you think we ought to make Mr Horn turn her out of here?" asked Mrs Davidson. "We can't allow her to insult us."

"There doesn't seem to be any other place for her to go," said Macphail.

"She can live with one of the natives."

"In weather like this a native hut must be a rather uncomfortable place to live in."

"I lived in one for years," said the missionary.

When the little native girl brought in the fried bananas which formed the sweet they had every day, Davidson turned to her.

"Ask Miss Thompson when it would be convenient for me to see her," he said.

The girl nodded shyly and went out.

"What do you want to see her for, Alfred?" asked his wife.

"It's my duty to see her. I won't act till I've given her every chance."

"You don't know what she is. She'll insult you."

"Let her insult me. Let her spit on me. She has an immortal soul, and I must do all that is in my power to save it."

Mrs Davidson's ears rang still with the harlot's mocking laughter.

"She's gone too far."

"Too far for the mercy of God?" His eyes lit up suddenly and his voice grew mellow and soft. "Never. The sinner may be deeper in sin than the depth of hell itself, but the love of the Lord Jesus can reach him still."

The girl came back with the message.

"Miss Thompson's compliments and as long as Rev. Davidson don't come in business hours she'll be glad to see him any time."

The party received it in stony silence, and Dr Macphail quickly effaced from his lips the smile which had come upon them. He knew his wife would be vexed with him if he found Miss Thompson's effrontery amusing.

They finished the meal in silence. When it was over the two ladies got up and took their work. Mrs Macphail was making another of the innumerable comforters which she had turned out since the beginning of the war, and the doctor lit his pipe. But Davidson remained in his chair and with abstracted eyes stared at the table. At last he got up and without a word went out of the room. They heard him go down and they heard Miss Thompson's defiant "Come in" when he knocked at the door. He remained with her for an hour. And Dr Macphail watched the rain. It was beginning to get on his nerves. It was not like our soft English rain that drops gently on the earth; it was unmerciful and somehow terrible; you felt in it the malignancy of the primitive powers of nature. It did not pour, it flowed. It was like a deluge from heaven, and it rattled on the roof of corrugated iron with a steady persistence that was maddening. It seemed to have a fury of its own. And sometimes you felt that you must scream if it did not stop, and then suddenly you felt powerless, as though your bones had suddenly become soft; and you were miserable and hopeless.

Macphail turned his head when the missionary came back. The two women looked up.

"I've given her every chance. I have exhorted her to repent. She is an evil woman."

He paused, and Dr Macphail saw his eyes darken and his pale face grow hard and stern.

"Now I shall take the whips with which the Lord Jesus drove the usurers and the money changers out of the Temple of the Most High."

He walked up and down the room. His mouth was close set, and his black brows were frowning.

"If she fled to the uttermost parts of the earth I should pursue her."

With a sudden movement he turned round and strode out of the room. They heard him go downstairs again.

"What is he going to do?" asked Mrs Macphail.

"I don't know." Mrs Davidson took off her pince-nez and wiped them. "When he is on the Lord's work I never ask him questions."

She sighed a little.

"What is the matter?"

"He'll wear himself out. He doesn't know what it is to spare himself."

Dr Macphail learnt the first results of the missionary's activity from the half-caste trader in whose house they lodged. He stopped the doctor when he passed the store and came out to speak to him on the stoop. His fat face was worried.

"The Rev. Davidson has been at me for letting Miss Thompson have a room here," he said, "but I didn't know what she was when I rented it to her. When people come and ask if I can rent them a room all I want to know is if they've the money to pay for it. And she paid me for hers a week in advance."

Dr Macphail did not want to commit himself.

"When all's said and done it's your house. We're very much obliged to you for taking us in at all."

Horn looked at him doubtfully. He was not certain yet how definitely Macphail stood on the missionary's side.

"The missionaries are in with one another," he said, hesitatingly. "If they get it in for a trader he may just as well shut up his store and quit."

"Did he want you to turn her out?"

"No, he said so long as she behaved herself he couldn't ask me to do that. He said he wanted to be just to me. I promised she shouldn't have no more visitors. I've just been and told her."

"How did she take it?"

"She gave me Hell."

The trader squirmed in his old ducks. He had found Miss Thompson a rough customer.

"Oh, well, I daresay she'll get out. I don't suppose she wants to stay here if she can't have anyone in."

"There's nowhere she can go, only a native house, and no native'll take her now, not now that the missionaries have got their knife in her."

Dr Macphail looked at the falling rain.

"Well, I don't suppose it's any good waiting for it to clear up."

In the evening when they sat in the parlour Davidson talked to them of his early days at college. He had had no means and had worked his way through by doing odd jobs during the vacations. There was silence downstairs. Miss Thompson was sitting in her little room alone. But suddenly the gramophone began to play. She had set it on in defiance, to cheat her loneliness, but there was no one to sing, and it had a melancholy note. It was like a cry for help. Davidson took no notice. He was in the middle of a long anecdote and without change of expression went on. The gramophone continued. Miss Thompson put on one reel after another. It looked as though the silence of the night were getting on her nerves. It was breathless and sultry. When the Macphails went to bed they could not sleep. They lay side by side with their eyes wide open, listening to the cruel singing of the mosquitoes outside their curtain.

"What's that?" whispered Mrs Macphail at last.

They heard a voice, Davidson's voice, through the wooden partition. It went on with a monotonous, earnest insistence. He was praying aloud. He was praying for the soul of Miss Thompson.

Two or three days went by. Now when they passed Miss Thompson on the road she did not greet them with ironic cordiality or smile; she passed with her nose in the air, a sulky look on her painted face, frowning, as though she did not see them. The trader told Macphail that she had tried to get lodging elsewhere, but had failed. In the evening she played through the various reels of her gramophone, but the pretence of mirth was obvious now. The ragtime had a cracked, heart-broken rhythm as though it were a one-step of despair. When she began to play on Sunday Davidson sent Horn to beg her to stop at once since it was the Lord's day. The reel was taken off and the house was silent except for the steady pattering of the rain on the iron roof.

"I think she's getting a bit worked up," said the trader next day to Macphail. "She don't know what Mr Davidson's up to and it makes her scared."

Macphail had caught a glimpse of her that morning and it struck him that her arrogant expression had changed. There was in her face a hunted look. The half-caste gave him a sidelong glance.

"I suppose you don't know what Mr Davidson is doing about it?" he hazarded.

"No, I don't."

It was singular that Horn should ask him that question, for he also had the idea that the missionary was mysteriously at work.

He had an impression that he was weaving a net around the woman, carefully, systematically, and suddenly, when everything was ready, would pull the strings tight.

"He told me to tell her," said the trader, "that if at any time she wanted him she only had to send and he'd come."

"What did she say when you told her that?"

"She didn't say nothing. I didn't stop. I just said what he said I was to and then I beat it. I thought she might be going to start weepin'."

"I have no doubt the loneliness is getting on her nerves," said the doctor. "And the rain – that's enough to make anyone jumpy," he continued irritably. "Doesn't it ever stop in this confounded place?"

"It goes on pretty steady in the rainy season. We have three hundred inches in the year. You see, it's the shape of the bay. It seems to attract the rain from all over the Pacific."

"Damn the shape of the bay," said the doctor.

He scratched his mosquito bites. He felt very short-tempered. When the rain stopped and the sun shone, it was like a hot-house, seething, humid, sultry, breathless, and you had a strange feeling that everything was growing with a savage violence. The natives, blithe and childlike by reputation, seemed then, with their tattooing and their dyed hair, to have something sinister in their appearance; and when they pattered along at your heels with their naked feet you looked back instinctively. You felt they might at any moment come behind you swiftly and thrust a long knife between your shoulder-blades. You could not tell what dark thoughts lurked behind their wide-set eyes. They had a little the look of ancient Egyptians painted on a temple wall, and there was about them the terror of what is immeasurably old.

The missionary came and went. He was busy, but the Macphails did not know what he was doing. Horn told the doctor that he saw the governor every day, and once Davidson mentioned him.

"He looks as if he had plenty of determination," he said, "but when you come down to brass tacks he has no backbone."

"I suppose that means he won't do exactly what you want," suggested the doctor facetiously.

The missionary did not smile.

"I want him to do what's right. It shouldn't be necessary to persuade a man to do that."

"But there may be differences of opinion about what is right."

"If a man had a gangrenous foot would you have patience with anyone who hesitated to amputate it?"

"Gangrene is a matter of fact."

"And Evil?"

What Davidson had done soon appeared. The four of them had just finished their midday meal, and they had not yet separated for the siesta which the heat imposed on the ladies and on the doctor. Davidson had little patience with the slothful habit. The door was suddenly flung open and Miss Thompson came in. She looked round the room and then went up to Davidson.

"You low-down skunk, what have you been saying about me to the governor?"

She was spluttering with rage. There was a moment's pause. Then the missionary drew forward a chair.

"Won't you be seated, Miss Thompson? I've been hoping to have another talk with you."

"You poor low-life bastard."

She burst into a torrent of insult, foul and insolent. Davidson kept his grave eyes on her.

"I'm indifferent to the abuse you think fit to heap on me, Miss Thompson," he said, "but I must beg you to remember that ladies are present."

Tears by now were struggling with her anger. Her face was red and swollen as though she were choking.

"What has happened?" asked Dr Macphail.

"A feller's just been in here and he says I gotter beat it on the next boat."

Was there a gleam in the missionary's eyes? His face remained impassive.

"You could hardly expect the governor to let you stay here under the circumstances."

"You done it," she shrieked. "You can't kid me. You done it."

"I don't want to deceive you. I urged the governor to take the only possible step consistent with his obligations."

"Why couldn't you leave me be? I wasn't doin' you no harm."

"You may be sure that if you had I should be the last man to resent it."

"Do you think I want to stay on in this poor imitation of a burg? I don't look no busher, do I?"

"In that case I don't see what cause of complaint you have," he answered.

She gave an inarticulate cry of rage and flung out of the room. There was a short silence.

"It's a relief to know that the governor has acted at last," said Davidson finally. "He's a weak man and he shilly-shallied. He said she was only here for a fortnight anyway, and if she went on to Apia, that was under British jurisdiction and had nothing to do with him."

The missionary sprang to his feet and strode across the room.

"It's terrible the way the men who are in authority seek to evade their responsibility. They speak as though evil that was out of sight ceased to be evil. The very existence of that woman is a scandal and it does not help matters to shift it to another of the islands. In the end I had to speak straight from the shoulder."

Davidson's brow lowered, and he protruded his firm chin. He looked fierce and determined.

"What do you mean by that?"

"Our mission is not entirely without influence at Washington. I pointed out to the governor that it wouldn't do him any good if there was a complaint about the way he managed things here."

"When has she got to go?" asked the doctor, after a pause.

"The San Francisco boat is due here from Sydney next Tuesday. She's to sail on that."

That was in five days' time. It was next day, when he was coming back from the hospital where for want of something better to do Macphail spent most of his mornings, that the half-caste stopped him as he was going upstairs.

"Excuse me, Dr Macphail, Miss Thompson's sick. Will you have a look at her?"

"Certainly."

Horn led him to her room. She was sitting in a chair idly, neither reading nor sewing, staring in front of her. She wore her white dress and the large hat with the flowers on it. Macphail noticed that her skin was yellow and muddy under her powder, and her eyes were heavy.

"I'm sorry to hear you're not well," he said.

"Oh, I ain't sick really. I just said that, because I just had to see you. I've got to clear on a boat that's going to 'Frisco."

She looked at him and he saw that her eyes were suddenly startled. She opened and clenched her hands spasmodically. The trader stood at the door, listening.

"So I understand," said the doctor.

She gave a little gulp.

"I guess it ain't very convenient for me to go to 'Frisco just now. I went to see the governor yesterday afternoon, but I couldn't get to him. I saw the secretary, and he told me I'd got to take that boat and that was all there was to it. I just had to see the governor, so I waited outside his house this morning, and when he come out I spoke to him. He didn't want to speak to me, I'll say, but I wouldn't let him shake me off, and at last he said he hadn't no objection to my staying here till the next boat to Sydney if the Rev. Davidson will stand for it."

She stopped and looked at Dr Macphail anxiously.

"I don't know exactly what I can do," he said.

"Well, I thought maybe you wouldn't mind asking him. I swear to God I won't start anything here if he'll just only let me stay. I won't go out of the house if that'll suit him. It's no more'n a fortnight."

"I'll ask him."

"He won't stand for it," said Horn. "He'll have you out on Tuesday, so you may as well make up your mind to it."

"Tell him I can get work in Sydney, straight stuff, I mean. 'Tain't asking very much."

"I'll do what I can."

"And come and tell me right away, will you? I can't set down to a thing till I get the dope one way or the other."

It was not an errand that much pleased the doctor, and, characteristically perhaps, he went about it indirectly. He told his wife what Miss Thompson had said to him and asked her to speak to Mrs Davidson. The missionary's attitude seemed rather arbitrary and it could do no harm if the girl were allowed to stay in Pago-Pago another fortnight. But he was not prepared for the result of his diplomacy. The missionary came to him straightaway.

"Mrs Davidson tells me that Thompson has been speaking to you."

Dr Macphail, thus directly tackled, had the shy man's resentment at being forced out into the open. He felt his temper rising and he flushed.

"I don't see that it can make any difference if she goes to Sydney rather than to San Francisco, and so long as she promises to behave while she's here it's dashed hard to persecute her."

The missionary fixed him with his stern eyes.

"Why is she unwilling to go back to San Francisco?"

"I didn't inquire," answered the doctor with some asperity. "And I think one does better to mind one's own business."

Perhaps it was not a very tactful answer.

"The governor has ordered her to be deported by the first boat that leaves the island. He's only done his duty and I will not interfere. Her presence is a peril here."

"I think you're very harsh and tyrannical."

The two ladies looked up at the doctor with some alarm, but they need not have feared a quarrel, for the missionary smiled gently.

"I'm terribly sorry you should think that of me, Dr Macphail. Believe me, my heart bleeds for that unfortunate woman, but I'm only trying to do my duty."

The doctor made no answer. He looked out of the window sullenly. For once it was not raining and across the bay you saw nestling among the trees the huts of a native village.

"I think I'll take advantage of the rain stopping to go out," he said.

"Please don't bear me malice because I can't accede to your wish," said Davidson, with a melancholy smile. "I respect you very much, doctor, and I should be sorry if you thought ill of me."

"I have no doubt you have a sufficiently good opinion of yourself to bear mine with equanimity," he retorted.

"That's one on me," chuckled Davidson.

When Dr Macphail, vexed with himself because he had been uncivil to no purpose, went downstairs, Miss Thompson was waiting for him with her door ajar.

"Well," she said, "have you spoken to him?"

"Yes, I'm sorry, he won't do anything," he answered, not looking at her in his embarrassment.

But then he gave her a quick glance, for a sob broke from her. He saw that her face was white with fear. It gave him a shock of dismay. And suddenly he had an idea.

"But don't give up hope yet. I think it's a shame the way they're treating you and I'm going to see the governor myself."

"Now?"

He nodded. Her face brightened.

"Say, that's real good of you. I'm sure he'll let me stay if you speak for me. I just won't do a thing I didn't ought all the time I'm here."

Dr Macphail hardly knew why he had made up his mind to appeal to the governor. He was perfectly indifferent to Miss Thompson's affairs, but the missionary had irritated him, and with him temper was a smouldering thing. He found the governor at home. He was a large, handsome man, a sailor, with a grey toothbrush moustache; and he wore a spotless uniform of white drill.

"I've come to see you about a woman who's lodging in the same house as we are," he said. "Her name's Thompson."

"I guess I've heard nearly enough about her, Dr Macphail," said the governor, smiling. "I've given her the order to get out next Tuesday and that's all I can do."

"I wanted to ask you if you couldn't stretch a point and let her stay here till the boat comes in from San Francisco so that she can go to Sydney. I will guarantee her good behaviour."

The governor continued to smile, but his eyes grew small and serious.

"I'd be very glad to oblige you, Dr Macphail, but I've given the order and it must stand."

The doctor put the case as reasonably as he could, but now the governor ceased to smile at all. He listened sullenly, with averted gaze. Macphail saw that he was making no impression.

"I'm sorry to cause any lady inconvenience, but she'll have to sail on Tuesday and that's all there is to it."

"But what difference can it make?"

"Pardon me, doctor, but I don't feel called upon to explain my official actions except to the proper authorities."

Macphail looked at him shrewdly. He remembered Davidson's hint that he had used threats, and in the governor's attitude he read a singular embarrassment.

"Davidson's a damned busybody," he said hotly.

"Between ourselves, Dr Macphail, I don't say that I have formed a very favourable opinion of Mr Davidson, but I am bound to confess that he was within his rights in pointing out to me the danger that the presence of a woman of Miss Thompson's character was to a place like this where a number of enlisted men are stationed among a native population."

He got up and Dr Macphail was obliged to do so too.

"I must ask you to excuse me. I have an engagement. Please give my respects to Mrs Macphail."

The doctor left him crestfallen. He knew that Miss Thompson would be waiting for him, and, unwilling to tell her himself that he had failed, he went into the house by the back door and sneaked up the stairs as though he had something to hide.

At supper he was silent and ill-at-ease, but the missionary was jovial and animated. Dr Macphail thought his eyes rested on him now and then with triumphant good-humour. It struck him suddenly that Davidson knew of his visit to the governor and of its ill success. But how on earth could he have heard of it? There was something sinister about the power of that man. After supper he saw Horn on the veranda and, as though to have a casual word with him, went out.

"She wants to know if you've seen the governor," the trader whispered.

"Yes. He wouldn't do anything. I'm awfully sorry, I can't do anything more."

"I knew he wouldn't. They daren't go against the missionaries."

"What are you talking about?" said Davidson affably, coming out to join them.

"I was just saying there was no chance of your getting over to Apia for at least another week," said the trader glibly.

He left them, and the two men returned into the parlour. Mr Davidson devoted one hour after each meal to recreation. Presently a timid knock was heard at the door.

"Come in," said Mrs Davidson, in her sharp voice.

The door was not opened. She got up and opened it. They saw Miss Thompson standing at the threshold. But the change in her appearance was extraordinary. This was no longer the flaunting hussy who had jeered at them in the road, but a broken, frightened woman. Her hair, as a rule so elaborately arranged, was tumbling untidily over her neck. She wore bedroom slippers and a skirt and blouse. They were unfresh and bedraggled. She stood at the door with the tears streaming down her face and did not dare to enter.

"What do you want?" said Mrs Davidson harshly.

"May I speak to Mr Davidson?" she said in a choking voice.

The missionary rose and went towards her.

"Come right in, Miss Thompson," he said in cordial tones. "What can I do for you?"

She entered the room.

"Say, I'm sorry for what I said to you the other day an' for – for everythin' else. I guess I was a bit lit up. I beg pardon."

"Oh, it was nothing. I guess my back's broad enough to bear a few hard words."

She stepped towards him with a movement that was horribly cringing.

"You've got me beat. I'm all in. You won't make me go back to 'Frisco?"

His genial manner vanished and his voice grew on a sudden hard and stern.

"Why don't you want to go back there?"

She cowered before him.

"I guess my people live there. I don't want them to see me like this. I'll go anywhere else you say."

"Why don't you want to go back to San Francisco?"

"I've told you."

He leaned forward, staring at her, and his great, shining eyes seemed to try to bore into her soul. He gave a sudden gasp.

"The penitentiary."

She screamed, and then she fell at his feet, clasping his legs.

"Don't send me back there. I swear to you before God I'll be a good woman. I'll give all this up."

She burst into a torrent of confused supplication and the tears coursed down her painted cheeks. He leaned over her and, lifting her face, forced her to look at him.

"Is that it, the penitentiary?"

"I beat it before they could get me," she gasped. "If the bulls grab me it's three years for mine."

He let go his hold of her and she fell in a heap on the floor, sobbing bitterly. Dr Macphail stood up.

"This alters the whole thing," he said. "You can't make her go back when you know this. Give her another chance. She wants to turn over a new leaf."

"I'm going to give her the finest chance she's ever had. If she repents let her accept her punishment."

She misunderstood the words and looked up. There was a gleam of hope in her heavy eyes.

"You'll let me go?"

"No. You shall sail for San Francisco on Tuesday."

She gave a groan of horror and then burst into low, hoarse shrieks which sounded hardly human, and she beat her head passionately on the ground. Dr Macphail sprang to her and lifted her up.

"Come on, you mustn't do that. You'd better go to your room and lie down. I'll get you something."

He raised her to her feet and partly dragging her, partly carrying her, got her downstairs. He was furious with Mrs Davidson and with his wife because they made no effort to help. The half-caste was standing on the landing and with his assistance he managed to get her on the bed. She was moaning and crying. She was almost insensible. He gave her a hypodermic injection. He was hot and exhausted when he went upstairs again.

"I've got her to lie down."

The two women and Davidson were in the same positions as when he had left them. They could not have moved or spoken since he went.

"I was waiting for you," said Davidson, in a strange, distant voice. "I want you all to pray with me for the soul of our erring sister."

He took the Bible off a shelf, and sat down at the table at which they had supped. It had not been cleared, and he pushed the tea-pot out of the way. In a powerful voice, resonant and deep, he read to them the chapter in which is narrated the meeting of Jesus Christ with the woman taken in adultery.

"Now kneel with me and let us pray for the soul of our dear sister, Sadie Thompson."

He burst into a long, passionate prayer in which he implored God to have mercy on the sinful woman. Mrs Macphail and Mrs Davidson knelt with covered eyes. The doctor, taken by surprise, awkward and sheepish, knelt too. The missionary's prayer had a savage eloquence. He was extraordinarily moved, and as he spoke the tears ran down his cheeks. Outside, the pitiless rain fell, fell steadily, with a fierce malignity that was all too human.

At last he stopped. He paused for a moment and said:

"We will now repeat the Lord's prayer."

They said it and then, following him, they rose from their knees. Mrs Davidson's face was pale and restful. She was comforted and at peace, but the Macphails felt suddenly bashful. They did not know which way to look.

"I'll just go down and see how she is now," said Dr Macphail.

When he knocked at her door it was opened for him by Horn. Miss Thompson was in a rocking-chair, sobbing quietly.

"What are you doing there?" exclaimed Macphail. "I told you to lie down."

"I can't lie down. I want to see Mr Davidson."

"My poor child, what do you think is the good of it? You'll never move him."

"He said he'd come if I sent for him."

Macphail motioned to the trader.

"Go and fetch him."

He waited with her in silence while the trader went upstairs. Davidson came in.

"Excuse me for asking you to come here," she said, looking at him sombrely.

"I was expecting you to send for me. I knew the Lord would answer my prayer."

They stared at one another for a moment and then she looked away. She kept her eyes averted when she spoke.

"I've been a bad woman. I want to repent."

"Thank God! thank God! He has heard our prayers."

He turned to the two men.

"Leave me alone with her. Tell Mrs Davidson that our prayers have been answered."

They went out and closed the door behind them.

"Gee whizz," said the trader.

That night Dr Macphail could not get to sleep till late, and when he heard the missionary come upstairs he looked at his watch. It was two o'clock. But even then he did not go to bed at once, for through the wooden partition that separated their rooms he heard him praying aloud, till he himself, exhausted, fell asleep.

When he saw him next morning he was surprised at his appearance. He was paler than ever, tired, but his eyes shone with inhuman fire. It looked as though he were filled with an overwhelming joy.

"I want you to go down presently and see Sadie," he said. "I can't hope that her body is better, but her soul – her soul is transformed."

The doctor was feeling wan and nervous.

"You were with her very late last night," he said.

"Yes, she couldn't bear to have me leave her."

"You look as pleased as Punch," the doctor said irritably.

Davidson's eyes shone with ecstasy.

"A great mercy has been vouchsafed me. Last night I was privileged to bring a lost soul to the loving arms of Jesus."

Miss Thompson was again in the rocking-chair. The bed had not been made. The room was in disorder. She had not troubled to dress herself, but wore a dirty dressing-gown, and her hair was tied in a sluttish knot. She had given her face a dab with a wet towel, but it was all swollen and creased with crying. She looked a drab.

She raised her eyes dully when the doctor came in. She was cowed and broken.

"Where's Mr Davidson?" she asked.

"He'll come presently if you want him," answered Macphail acidly. "I came here to see how you were."

"Oh, I guess I'm OK. You needn't worry about that."

"Have you had anything to eat?"

"Horn brought me some coffee."

She looked anxiously at the door.

"D'you think he'll come down soon? I feel as if it wasn't so terrible when he's with me."

"Are you still going on Tuesday?"

"Yes, he says I've got to go. Please tell him to come right along. You can't do me any good. He's the only one as can help me now."

"Very well," said Dr Macphail.

During the next three days the missionary spent almost all his time with Sadie Thompson. He joined the others only to have his meals. Dr Macphail noticed that he hardly ate.

"He's wearing himself out," said Mrs Davidson pitifully. "He'll have a breakdown if he doesn't take care, but he won't spare himself."

She herself was white and pale. She told Mrs Macphail that she had no sleep. When the missionary came upstairs from Miss Thompson he prayed till he was exhausted, but even then he did not sleep for long. After an hour or two he got up and dressed himself, and went for a tramp along the bay. He had strange dreams.

"This morning he told me that he'd been dreaming about the mountains of Nebraska," said Mrs Davidson.

"That's curious," said Dr Macphail.

He remembered seeing them from the windows of the train when he crossed America. They were like huge mole-hills, rounded and smooth, and they rose from the plain abruptly. Dr Macphail remembered how it struck him that they were like a woman's breasts.

Davidson's restlessness was intolerable even to himself. But he was buoyed up by a wonderful exhilaration. He was tearing out by the roots the last vestiges of sin that lurked in the hidden corners of that poor woman's heart. He read with her and prayed with her.

"It's wonderful," he said to them one day at supper. "It's a true rebirth. Her soul, which was black as night, is now pure and white like the new-fallen snow. I am humble and afraid. Her remorse for all her sins is beautiful. I am not worthy to touch the hem of her garment."

"Have you the heart to send her back to San Francisco?" said the doctor. "Three years in an American prison. I should have thought you might have saved her from that."

"Ah, but don't you see? It's necessary. Do you think my heart doesn't bleed for her? I love her as I love my wife and my sister. All the time that she is in prison I shall suffer all the pain that she suffers."

"Bunkum," cried the doctor impatiently.

"You don't understand because you're blind. She's sinned, and she must suffer. I know what she'll endure. She'll be starved and tortured and humiliated. I want her to accept the punishment of man as a sacrifice to God. I want her to accept it joyfully. She has an opportunity which is offered to very few of us. God is very good and very merciful."

Davidson's voice trembled with excitement. He could hardly articulate the words that tumbled passionately from his lips.

"All day I pray with her and when I leave her I pray again, I pray with all my might and main, so that Jesus may grant her this great mercy. I want to put in her heart the passionate desire to be punished so that at the end, even if I offered to let her go, she would refuse. I want her to feel that the bitter punishment of prison is the thank-offering that she places at the feet of our Blessed Lord, who gave his life for her."

The days passed slowly. The whole household, intent on the wretched, tortured woman downstairs, lived in a state of unnatural excitement. She was like a victim that was being prepared for the savage rites of a bloody idolatry. Her terror numbed her. She could not bear to let Davidson out of her sight; it was only when he was with her that she had courage, and she hung upon him with a slavish dependence. She cried a great deal, and she read the Bible, and prayed. Sometimes she was exhausted and apathetic. Then she did indeed look forward to her ordeal, for it seemed to offer an escape, direct and concrete, from the anguish she was enduring. She could not bear much longer the vague terrors which now assailed her. With her sins she had put aside all personal vanity, and she slopped about her room, unkempt and dishevelled, in her tawdry dressing-gown. She had not taken off her night-dress for four days, nor put on stockings. Her room was littered and untidy. Meanwhile the rain fell with a cruel persistence. You felt that the heavens must at last be empty of water, but still it poured down, straight and heavy, with a maddening iteration, on the iron roof. Everything was damp and clammy. There was mildew on the walls and on the boots that stood on the floor. Through the sleepless nights the mosquitoes droned their angry chant.

"If it would only stop raining for a single day it wouldn't be so bad," said Dr Macphail.

They all looked forward to the Tuesday when the boat for San Francisco was to arrive from Sydney. The strain was intolerable. So far as Dr Macphail was concerned, his pity and his resentment were alike extinguished by his desire to be rid of the unfortunate woman. The inevitable must be accepted. He felt he would breathe more freely when the ship had sailed. Sadie Thompson was to be escorted on board by a clerk in the governor's office. This person called on the Monday evening and told Miss Thompson to be prepared at eleven in the morning. Davidson was with her.

"I'll see that everything is ready. I mean to come on board with her myself."

Miss Thompson did not speak.

When Dr Macphail blew out his candle and crawled cautiously under his mosquito curtains, he gave a sigh of relief.

"Well, thank God that's over. By this time tomorrow she'll be gone."

"Mrs Davidson will be glad too. She says he's wearing himself to a shadow," said Mrs Macphail. "She's a different woman."

"Who?"

"Sadie. I should never have thought it possible. It makes one humble."

Dr Macphail did not answer, and presently he fell asleep. He was tired out, and he slept more soundly than usual.

He was awakened in the morning by a hand placed on his arm, and, starting up, saw Horn by the side of his bed. The trader put his finger on his mouth to prevent any exclamation from Dr Macphail and beckoned to him to come. As a rule he wore shabby ducks, but now he was barefoot and wore only the lava-lava of the natives. He looked suddenly savage, and Dr Macphail, getting out of bed, saw that he was heavily tattooed. Horn made him a sign to come on to the veranda. Dr Macphail got out of bed and followed the trader out.

"Don't make a noise," he whispered. "You're wanted. Put on a coat and some shoes. Quick."

Dr Macphail's first thought was that something had happened to Miss Thompson.

"What is it? Shall I bring my instruments?"

"Hurry, please, hurry."

Dr Macphail crept back into the bedroom, put on a waterproof over his pyjamas, and a pair of rubber-soled shoes. He rejoined the trader, and together they tiptoed down the stairs. The door leading out to the road was open and at it were standing half a dozen natives.

"What is it?" repeated the doctor.

"Come along with me," said Horn.

He walked out and the doctor followed him. The natives came after them in a little bunch. They crossed the road and came on to the beach. The doctor saw a group of natives standing round some object at the water's edge. They hurried along, a couple of dozen yards perhaps, and the natives opened out as the doctor came up. The trader pushed him forwards. Then he saw, lying half in the water and half out, a dreadful object, the body of Davidson. Dr Macphail bent down – he was not a man to lose his head in an emergency – and turned the body over. The throat was cut from ear to ear, and in the right hand was still the razor with which the deed was done.

"He's quite cold," said the doctor. "He must have been dead some time."

"One of the boys saw him lying there on his way to work just now and came and told me. Do you think he did it himself?"

"Yes. Someone ought to go for the police."

Horn said something in the native tongue, and two youths started off.

"We must leave him here till they come," said the doctor.

"They mustn't take him into my house. I won't have him in my house."

"You'll do what the authorities say," replied the doctor sharply. "In point of fact I expect they'll take him to the mortuary."

They stood waiting where they were. The trader took a cigarette from a fold in his lava-lava and gave one to Dr Macphail. They smoked while they stared at the corpse. Dr Macphail could not understand.

"Why do you think he did it?" asked Horn.

The doctor shrugged his shoulders. In a little while native police came along, under the charge of a marine, with a stretcher, and immediately afterwards a couple of naval officers and a naval doctor. They managed everything in a businesslike manner.

"What about the wife?" said one of the officers.

"Now that you've come I'll go back to the house and get some things on. I'll see that it's broken to her. She'd better not see him till he's been fixed up a little."

"I guess that's right," said the naval doctor.

When Dr Macphail went back he found his wife nearly dressed.

"Mrs Davidson's in a dreadful state about her husband," she said to him as soon as he appeared. "He hasn't been to bed all night. She heard him leave Miss Thompson's room at two, but he went out. If he's been walking about since then he'll be absolutely dead."

Dr Macphail told her what had happened and asked her to break the news to Mrs Davidson.

"But why did he do it?" she asked, horror-stricken.

"I don't know."

"But I can't. I can't."

"You must."

She gave him a frightened look and went out. He heard her go into Mrs Davidson's room. He waited a minute to gather himself together and then began to shave and wash. When he was dressed he sat down on the bed and waited for his wife. At last she came.

"She wants to see him," she said.

"They've taken him to the mortuary. We'd better go down with her. How did she take it?"

"I think she's stunned. She didn't cry. But she's trembling like a leaf."

"We'd better go at once."

When they knocked at her door Mrs Davidson came out. She was very pale, but dry-eyed. To the doctor she seemed unnaturally composed. No word was exchanged, and they set out in silence down the road. When they arrived at the mortuary Mrs Davidson spoke.

"Let me go in and see him alone."

They stood aside. A native opened a door for her and closed it behind her. They sat down and waited. One or two white men came and talked to them in undertones. Dr Macphail told them again what he knew of the tragedy. At last the door was quietly opened and Mrs Davidson came out. Silence fell upon them.

"I'm ready to go back now," she said.

Her voice was hard and steady. Dr Macphail could not understand the look in her eyes. Her pale face was very stern. They walked back slowly, never saying a word, and at last they came round the bend on the other side of which stood their house. Mrs Davidson gave a gasp, and for a moment they stopped still. An incredible sound assaulted their ears. The gramophone which had been silent for so long was playing, playing ragtime loud and harsh.

"What's that?" cried Mrs Macphail with horror.

"Let's go on," said Mrs Davidson.

They walked up the steps and entered the hall. Miss Thompson was standing at her door, chatting with a sailor. A sudden change had taken place in her. She was no longer the cowed drudge of the last days. She was dressed in all her finery, in her white dress, with the high shiny boots over which her fat legs bulged in their cotton stockings; her hair was elaborately arranged; and she wore that enormous hat covered with gaudy flowers. Her face was painted, her eyebrows were boldly black, and her lips were scarlet. She held herself erect. She was the flaunting queen that they had known at first. As they came in she broke into a loud, jeering laugh; and then, when Mrs Davidson involuntarily stopped, she collected the spittle in her mouth and spat. Mrs Davidson cowered back, and two red spots rose suddenly to her cheeks. Then, covering her face with her hands, she broke away and ran quickly up the stairs. Dr Macphail was outraged. He pushed past the woman into her room.

"What the devil are you doing?" he cried. "Stop that damned machine."

He went up to it and tore the record off. She turned on him.

"Say, doc, you can that stuff with me. What the hell are you doin' in my room?"

"What do you mean?" he cried. "What d'you mean?"

She gathered herself together. No one could describe the scorn of her expression or the contemptuous hatred she put into her answer.

"You men! You filthy, dirty pigs! You're all the same, all of you. Pigs! Pigs!"

Dr Macphail gasped. He understood.

THE FALL OF EDWARD BARNARD

BATEMAN HUNTER SLEPT badly. For a fortnight on the boat that brought him from Tahiti to San Francisco he had been thinking of the story he had to tell, and for three days on the train he had repeated to himself the words in which he meant to tell it. But in a few hours now he would be in Chicago, and doubts assailed him. His conscience, always very sensitive, was not at ease. He was uncertain that he had done all that was possible, it was on his honour to do much more than the possible, and the thought was disturbing that, in a matter which so nearly touched his own interest, he had allowed his interest to prevail over his quixotry. Self-sacrifice appealed so keenly to his imagination that the inability to exercise it gave him a sense of disillusion. He was like the philanthropist who with altruistic motives builds model dwellings for the poor and finds that he has made a lucrative investment. He cannot prevent the satisfaction he feels in the ten per cent which rewards the bread he had cast upon the waters, but he has an awkward feeling that it detracts somewhat from the savour of his virtue. Bateman Hunter knew that his heart was pure, but he was not quite sure how steadfastly, when he told her his story, he would endure the scrutiny of Isabel Longstaffe's cool grey eyes. They were far-seeing and wise. She measured the standards of others by her own meticulous uprightness and there could be no greater censure than the cold silence with which she expressed her disapproval of a conduct that did not satisfy her exacting code. There was no appeal from her judgement, for, having made up her mind, she never changed it. But Bateman would not have had her different. He loved not only the beauty of her person, slim and straight, with the proud carriage of her head, but still more the beauty of her soul. With her truthfulness, her rigid sense of honour, her fearless outlook, she seemed to him to collect in herself all that was most admirable in his countrywomen. But he saw in her something more than the perfect type of the American girl, he felt that her exquisiteness was peculiar in a way to her environment, and he was assured that no city in the world could have produced her but Chicago. A pang seized him when he remembered that he must deal so bitter a blow to her pride, and anger flamed up in his heart when he thought of Edward Barnard.

But at last the train steamed in to Chicago and he exulted when he saw the long streets of grey houses. He could hardly bear his impatience at the thought of State and Wabash with their crowded pavements, their hustling traffic, and their noise. He was at home. And he was glad that he had been born in the most important city in the United States. San Francisco was provincial, New York was effete; the future of America lay in the development of its economic possibilities, and Chicago, by its position and by the energy of its citizens, was destined to become the real capital of the country.

"I guess I shall live long enough to see it the biggest city in the world," Bateman said to himself as he stepped down to the platform.

His father had come to meet him, and after a hearty handshake, the pair of them, tall, slender, and well-made, with the same fine, ascetic features and thin lips, walked out of the station. Mr Hunter's automobile was waiting for them and they got in. Mr Hunter caught his son's proud and happy glance as he looked at the street.

"Glad to be back, son?" he asked.

"I should just think I was," said Bateman.

His eyes devoured the restless scene.

"I guess there's a bit more traffic here than in your South Sea island," laughed Mr Hunter. "Did you like it there?"

"Give me Chicago, dad," answered Bateman.

"You haven't brought Edward Barnard back with you."

"No."

"How was he?"

Bateman was silent for a moment, and his handsome, sensitive face darkened.

"I'd sooner not speak about him, dad," he said at last.

"That's all right, my son. I guess your mother will be a happy woman today."

They passed out of the crowded streets in the Loop and drove along the lake till they came to the imposing house, an exact copy of a château on the Loire, which Mr Hunter had built himself some years before. As soon as Bateman was alone in his room he asked for a number on the telephone. His heart leaped when he heard the voice that answered him.

"Good morning, Isabel," he said gaily.

"Good morning, Bateman."

"How did you recognize my voice?"

"It is not so long since I heard it last. Besides, I was expecting you."

"When may I see you?"

"Unless you have anything better to do perhaps you'll dine with us tonight."

"You know very well that I couldn't possibly have anything better to do."

"I suppose that you're full of news?"

He thought he detected in her voice a note of apprehension.

"Yes," he answered.

"Well, you must tell me tonight. Good-bye."

She rang off. It was characteristic of her that she should be able to wait so many unnecessary hours to know what so immensely concerned her. To Bateman there was an admirable fortitude in her restraint.

At dinner, at which beside himself and Isabel no one was present but her father and mother, he watched her guide the conversation into the channels of an urbane small-talk, and it occurred to him that in just such a manner would a marquise under the shadow of the guillotine toy with the affairs of a day that would know no morrow. Her delicate features, the aristocratic shortness of her upper lip, and her wealth of fair hair suggested the marquise again, and it must have been obvious, even if it were not notorious, that in her veins flowed the best blood in Chicago. The dining-room was a fitting frame to her fragile beauty, for Isabel had caused the house, a replica of a palace on the Grand Canal at Venice, to be furnished by an English expert in the style of Louis XV; and the graceful decoration linked with the name of that amorous monarch enhanced her loveliness and at the same time acquired from it a more profound significance. For Isabel's mind was richly stored, and her conversation, however light, was never flippant. She spoke now of the Musicale to which she and her mother had been in the afternoon, of the lectures which an English poet was giving at the Auditorium, of the political situation, and of the Old Master which her father had recently bought for fifty thousand dollars in New York. It comforted Bateman to hear her. He felt that he was once more in the civilized world, at the centre of culture and distinction; and certain voices, troubling and yet against his will refusing to still their clamour, were at last silent in his heart.

"Gee, but it's good to be back in Chicago," he said.

At last dinner was over, and when they went out of the dining-room Isabel said to her mother:

"I'm going to take Bateman along to my den. We have various things to talk about."

"Very well, my dear," said Mrs Longstaffe. "You'll find your father and me in the Madame du Barry room when you're through."

Isabel led the young man upstairs and showed him into the room of which he had so many charming memories. Though he knew it so well he could not repress the exclamation of delight which it always wrung from him. She looked round with a smile.

"I think it's a success," she said. "The main thing is that it's right. There's not even an ash-tray that isn't of the period."

"I suppose that's what makes it so wonderful. Like all you do it's so superlatively right."

They sat down in front of a log fire and Isabel looked at him with calm grave eyes.

"Now what have you to say to me?" she asked.

"I hardly know how to begin."

"Is Edward Barnard coming back?"

"No."

There was a long silence before Bateman spoke again, and with each of them it was filled with many thoughts. It was a difficult story he had to tell, for there were things in it which were so offensive to her sensitive ears that he could not bear to tell them, and yet in justice to her, no less than in justice to himself, he must tell her the whole truth.

It had all begun long ago when he and Edward Barnard, still at college, had met Isabel Longstaffe at the tea-party given to introduce her to society. They had both known her when she was a child and they long-legged boys, but for two years she had been in Europe to finish her education and it was with a surprised delight that they renewed acquaintance with the lovely girl who returned. Both of them fell desperately in love with her, but Bateman saw quickly that she had eyes only for Edward, and, devoted to his friend, he resigned himself to the role of confidant. He passed bitter moments, but he could not deny that Edward was worthy of his good fortune, and, anxious that nothing should impair the friendship he so greatly valued, he took care never by a hint to disclose his own feelings. In six months the young couple were engaged. But they were very young and Isabel's father decided that they should not marry at least till Edward graduated. They had to wait a year. Bateman remembered the winter at the end of which Isabel and Edward were to be married, a winter of dances and theatre-parties and of informal gaieties at which he, the constant third, was always present. He loved her no less because she would shortly be his friend's wife; her smile, a gay word she flung him, the confidence of her affection, never ceased to delight him; and he congratulated himself, somewhat complacently, because he did not envy them their happiness. Then an accident happened. A great bank failed, there was a panic on the exchange, and Edward Barnard's father found himself a ruined man. He came home one night, told his wife he was penniless, and after dinner, going into his study, shot himself.

A week later, Edward Barnard, with a tired, white face, went to Isabel and asked her to release him. Her only answer was to throw her arms round his neck and burst into tears.

"Don't make it harder for me, sweet," he said.

"Do you think I can let you go now? I love you."

"How can I ask you to marry me? The whole thing's hopeless. Your father would never let you. I haven't a cent."

"What do I care? I love you."

He told her his plans. He had to earn money at once, and George Braunschmidt, an old friend of his family, had offered to take him into his own business. He was a South Sea merchant, and he had agencies in many of the islands of the Pacific. He had suggested that Edward should go to Tahiti for a year or two, where under the best of his managers he could learn the details of that varied trade, and at the end of that time he promised the young man a position in Chicago. It was a wonderful opportunity, and when he had finished his explanations Isabel was once more all smiles.

"You foolish boy, why have you been trying to make me miserable?"

His face lit up at her words and his eyes flashed.

"Isabel, you don't mean to say you'll wait for me?"

"Don't you think you're worth it?" she smiled.

"Ah, don't laugh at me now. I beseech you to be serious. It may be for two years."

"Have no fear. I love you, Edward. When you come back I will marry you."

Edward's employer was a man who did not like delay and he had told him that if he took the post he offered he must sail that day week from San Francisco. Edward spent his last evening with Isabel. It was after dinner that Mr Longstaffe, saying he wanted a word with Edward, took him into the smoking-room. Mr Longstaffe had accepted good-naturedly the arrangement which his daughter had told him of and Edward could not imagine what mysterious communication he had now to make. He was not a little perplexed to see that his host was embarrassed. He faltered. He talked of trivial things. At last he blurted it out.

"I guess you've heard of Arnold Jackson," he said, looking at Edward with a frown.

Edward hesitated. His natural truthfulness obliged him to admit a knowledge he would gladly have been able to deny.

"Yes, I have. But it's a long time ago. I guess I didn't pay very much attention."

"There are not many people in Chicago who haven't heard of Arnold Jackson," said Mr Longstaffe bitterly, "and if there are they'll have no difficulty in finding someone who'll be glad to tell them. Did you know he was Mrs Longstaffe's brother?"

"Yes, I knew that."

"Of course we've had no communication with him for many years. He left the country as soon as he was able to, and I guess the country wasn't sorry to see the last of him. We understand he lives in Tahiti. My advice to you is to give him a wide berth, but if you do hear anything about him Mrs Longstaffe and I would be very glad if you'd let us know."

"Sure."

"That was all I wanted to say to you. Now I daresay you'd like to join the ladies."

There are few families that have not among their members one whom, if their neighbours permitted, they would willingly forget, and they are fortunate when the lapse of a generation or two has invested his vagaries with a romantic glamour. But when he is actually alive, if his peculiarities are not of the kind that can be condoned by the phrase, "he is nobody's enemy but his own", a safe one when the culprit has no worse to answer for than alcoholism or wandering affections, the only possible course is silence. And it was this which the Longstaffes had adopted towards Arnold Jackson. They never talked of him. They would not even pass through the street in which he had lived. Too kind to make his wife and children suffer for his misdeeds, they had supported them for years, but on the understanding that they should live in Europe. They did everything they could to blot out all recollection of Arnold Jackson and yet were conscious that the story was as fresh in the public mind as when first the scandal burst upon a gaping world. Arnold Jackson was as black a sheep as any family could suffer from. A wealthy banker, prominent in his church, a philanthropist, a man respected by all, not only for his connexions (in his veins ran the blue blood of Chicago), but also for his upright character, he was arrested one day on a charge of fraud; and the dishonesty which the trial brought to light was not the sort which could be explained by a sudden temptation; it was deliberate and systematic. Arnold Jackson was a rogue. When he was sent to the penitentiary for seven years there were few who did not think he had escaped lightly.

When at the end of this last evening the lovers separated it was with many protestations of devotion. Isabel, all tears, was consoled a little by her certainty of Edward's passionate love. It was a strange feeling that she had. It made her wretched to part from him and yet she was happy because he adored her.

This was more than two years ago.

He had written to her by every mail since then, twenty-four letters in all, for the mail went but once a month, and his letters had been all that a lover's letters should be. They were intimate and charming, humorous sometimes, especially of late, and tender. At first they suggested that he was homesick, they were full of his desire to get back to Chicago and Isabel; and, a little anxiously, she wrote begging him to persevere. She was afraid that he might throw up his opportunity and come racing back. She did not want her lover to lack endurance and she quoted to him the lines:

> I could not love thee, dear, so much,
> Loved I not honour more.

But presently he seemed to settle down and it made Isabel very happy to observe his growing enthusiasm to introduce American methods into that forgotten corner of the world. But she knew him, and at the end of the year, which was the shortest time he could possibly stay in Tahiti, she expected to have to use all her influence to dissuade him from coming home. It was much better that he should learn the business thoroughly, and if they had been able to wait a year there seemed no reason why they should not wait another. She talked it over with Bateman Hunter, always the most generous of friends (during those first few days after Edward went she did not know what she would have done without him), and they decided that Edward's future must stand before everything. It was with relief that she found as the time passed that he made no suggestion of returning.

"He's splendid, isn't he?" she exclaimed to Bateman.

"He's white, through and through."

"Reading between the lines of his letter I know he hates it over there, but he's sticking it out because . . . "

She blushed a little and Bateman, with the grave smile which was so attractive in him, finished the sentence for her.

"Because he loves you."

"It makes me feel so humble," she said.

"You're wonderful, Isabel, you're perfectly wonderful."

But the second year passed and every month Isabel continued to receive a letter from Edward, and presently it began to seem a little strange that he did not speak of coming back. He wrote as though he were settled definitely in Tahiti, and what was more, comfortably settled. She was surprised. Then she read his letters again, all of them, several times; and now, reading between the lines indeed, she was puzzled to notice a change which had escaped her. The later letters were as tender and as delightful as the first, but the tone was different. She was vaguely suspicious of their humour, she had the instinctive mistrust of her sex for that unaccountable quality, and she discerned in them now a flippancy which perplexed her. She was not quite certain that the Edward who wrote to her now was the same Edward that she had known. One afternoon, the day after a mail had arrived from Tahiti, when she was driving with Bateman he said to her:

"Did Edward tell you when he was sailing?"

"No, he didn't mention it. I thought he might have said something to you about it."

"Not a word."

"You know what Edward is," she laughed in reply, "he has no sense of time. If it occurs to you next time you write you might ask him when he's thinking of coming."

Her manner was so unconcerned that only Bateman's acute sensitiveness could have discerned in her request a very urgent desire. He laughed lightly.

"Yes. I'll ask him. I can't imagine what he's thinking about."

A few days later, meeting him again, she noticed that something troubled him. They had been much together since Edward left Chicago; they were both devoted to him and each in his desire to talk of the absent one found a willing listener; the consequence was that Isabel knew every expression of Bateman's face, and his denials now were useless against her keen instinct. Something told her that his harassed look had to do with Edward and she did not rest till she had made him confess.

"The fact is," he said at last, "I heard in a roundabout way that Edward was no longer working for Braunschmidt and Co., and yesterday I took the opportunity to ask Mr Braunschmidt himself."

"Well?"

"Edward left his employment with them nearly a year ago."

"How strange he should have said nothing about it!"

Bateman hesitated, but he had gone so far now that he was obliged to tell the rest. It made him feel dreadfully embarrassed.

"He was fired."

"In heaven's name what for?"

"It appears they warned him once or twice, and at last they told him to get out. They say he was lazy and incompetent."

"Edward?"

They were silent for a while, and then he saw that Isabel was crying. Instinctively he seized her hand.

"Oh, my dear, don't, don't," he said. "I can't bear to see it."

She was so unstrung that she let her hand rest in his. He tried to console her.

"It's incomprehensible, isn't it? It's so unlike Edward. I can't help feeling there must be some mistake."

She did not say anything for a while, and when she spoke it was hesitatingly.

"Has it struck you that there was anything queer in his letters lately?" she asked, looking away, her eyes all bright with tears.

He did not quite know how to answer.

"I have noticed a change in them," he admitted. "He seems to have lost that high seriousness which I admired so much in him. One would almost think that the things that matter – well, don't matter."

Isabel did not reply. She was vaguely uneasy.

"Perhaps in his answer to your letter he'll say when he's coming home. All we can do is to wait for that."

Another letter came from Edward for each of them, and still he made no mention of his return; but when he wrote he could not have received Bateman's inquiry. The next mail would bring them an answer to that. The next mail came, and Bateman brought Isabel the letter he had just received; but the first glance of his face was enough to tell her that he was disconcerted. She read it through carefully and then, with slightly tightened lips, read it again.

"It's a very strange letter," she said. "I don't quite understand it."

"One might almost think that he was joshing me," said Bateman, flushing.

"It reads like that, but it must be unintentional. That's so unlike Edward."

"He says nothing about coming back."

"If I weren't so confident of his love I should think . . . I hardly know what I should think."

It was then that Bateman had broached the scheme which during the afternoon had formed itself in his brain. The firm, founded by his father, in which he was now a partner, a firm which manufactured all manner of motor vehicles, was about to establish agencies in Honolulu, Sydney, and Wellington; and Bateman proposed that himself should go instead of the manager, who had been suggested. He could return by Tahiti; in fact, travelling from Wellington, it was inevitable to do so; and he could see Edward.

"There's some mystery and I'm going to clear it up. That's the only way to do it."

"Oh, Bateman, how can you be so good and kind?" she exclaimed.

"You know there's nothing in the world I want more than your happiness, Isabel."

She looked at him and she gave him her hands.

"You're wonderful, Bateman. I didn't know there was anyone in the world like you. How can I ever thank you?"

"I don't want your thanks. I only want to be allowed to help you."

She dropped her eyes and flushed a little. She was so used to him that she had forgotten how handsome he was. He was as tall as Edward and as well made, but he was dark and pale of face, while Edward was ruddy. Of course she knew he loved her. It touched her. She felt very tenderly towards him.

It was from this journey that Bateman Hunter was now returned.

The business part of it took him somewhat longer than he expected and he had much time to think of his two friends. He had come to the conclusion that it could be nothing serious that prevented Edward from coming home, a pride, perhaps, which made him determined to make good before he claimed the bride he adored; but it was a pride that must be reasoned with. Isabel was unhappy. Edward must come back to Chicago with him and marry her at once. A position could be found for him in the works of the Hunter Motor Traction and Automobile Company. Bateman, with a bleeding heart, exulted at the prospect of giving happiness to the two persons he loved best in the world at the cost of his own. He would never marry. He would be godfather to the children of Edward and Isabel, and many years later when they were both dead he would tell Isabel's daughter how long, long ago he had loved her mother. Bateman's eyes were veiled with tears when he pictured this scene to himself.

Meaning to take Edward by surprise he had not cabled to announce his arrival, and when at last he landed at Tahiti he allowed a youth, who said he was the son of the house, to lead him to the

Hôtel de la Fleur. He chuckled when he thought of his friend's amazement on seeing him, the most unexpected of visitors, walk into his office.

"By the way," he asked, as they went along, "can you tell me where I shall find Mr Edward Barnard?"

"Barnard?" said the youth. "I seem to know the name."

"He's an American. A tall fellow with light brown hair and blue eyes. He's been here over two years."

"Of course. Now I know who you mean. You mean Mr Jackson's nephew."

"Whose nephew?"

"Mr Arnold Jackson."

"I don't think we're speaking of the same person," answered Bateman, frigidly.

He was startled. It was queer that Arnold Jackson, known apparently to all and sundry, should live here under the disgraceful name in which he had been convicted. But Bateman could not imagine whom it was that he passed off as his nephew. Mrs Longstaffe was his only sister and he had never had a brother. The young man by his side talked volubly in an English that had something in it of the intonation of a foreign tongue, and Bateman, with a sidelong glance, saw, what he had not noticed before, that there was in him a good deal of native blood. A touch of hauteur involuntarily entered into his manner. They reached the hotel. When he had arranged about his room Bateman asked to be directed to the premises of Braunschmidt and Co. They were on the front, facing the lagoon, and, glad to feel the solid earth under his feet after eight days at sea, he sauntered down the sunny road to the water's edge. Having found the place he sought, Bateman sent in his card to the manager and was led through a lofty barn-like room, half store and half warehouse, to an office in which sat a stout, spectacled, bald-headed man.

"Can you tell me where I shall find Mr Edward Barnard? I understand he was in this office for some time."

"That is so. I don't know just where he is."

"But I thought he came here with a particular recommendation from Mr Braunschmidt. I know Mr Braunschmidt very well."

The fat man looked at Bateman with shrewd, suspicious eyes. He called to one of the boys in the warehouse.

"Say, Henry, where's Barnard now, d'you know?"

"He's working at Cameron's, I think," came the answer from someone who did not trouble to move.

The fat man nodded.

"If you turn to your left when you get out of here you'll come to Cameron's in about three minutes."

Bateman hesitated.

"I think I should tell you that Edward Barnard is my greatest friend. I was very much surprised when I heard he'd left Braunschmidt and Co."

The fat man's eyes contracted till they seemed like pin-points, and their scrutiny made Bateman so uncomfortable that he felt himself blushing.

"I guess Braunschmidt and Co. and Edward Barnard didn't see eye to eye on certain matters," he replied.

Bateman did not quite like the fellow's manner, so he got up, not without dignity, and with an apology for troubling him bade him good day. He left the place with a singular feeling that the man he had just interviewed had much to tell him, but no intention of telling it. He walked in the direction indicated and soon found himself at Cameron's. It was a trader's store, such as he had passed half a dozen of on his way, and when he entered the first person he saw, in his shirt-sleeves, measuring out a length of trade cotton, was Edward. It gave him a start to see him engaged in so humble an occupation. But he had scarcely appeared when Edward, looking up, caught sight of him, and gave a joyful cry of surprise.

"Bateman! Who ever thought of seeing you here?"

He stretched his arm across the counter and wrung Bateman's hand. There was no self-consciousness in his manner and the embarrassment was all on Bateman's side.

"Just wait till I've wrapped this package."

With perfect assurance he ran his scissors across the stuff, folded it, made it into a parcel, and handed it to the dark-skinned customer.

"Pay at the desk, please."

Then, smiling, with bright eyes, he turned to Bateman.

"How did you show up here? Gee, I am delighted to see you. Sit down, old man. Make yourself at home."

"We can't talk here. Come along to my hotel. I suppose you can get away?"

This he added with some apprehension.

"Of course I can get away. We're not so business-like as all that in Tahiti." He called out to a Chinese who was standing behind the opposite counter. "Ah-Ling, when the boss comes tell him a friend of mine's just arrived from America and I've gone out to have a drain with him."

"All-light," said the Chinese, with a grin.

Edward slipped on a coat and, putting on his hat, accompanied Bateman out of the store. Bateman attempted to put the matter facetiously.

"I didn't expect to find you selling three and a half yards of rotten cotton to a greasy nigger," he laughed.

"Braunschmidt fired me, you know, and I thought that would do as well as anything else."

Edward's candour seemed to Bateman very surprising, but he thought it indiscreet to pursue the subject.

"I guess you won't make a fortune where you are," he answered, somewhat dryly.

"I guess not. But I earn enough to keep body and soul together, and I'm quite satisfied with that."

"You wouldn't have been two years ago."

"We grow wiser as we grow older," retorted Edward, gaily.

Bateman took a glance at him. Edward was dressed in a suit of shabby white ducks, none too clean, and a large straw hat of native make. He was thinner than he had been, deeply burned by the sun, and he was certainly better-looking than ever. But there was something in his appearance that disconcerted Bateman. He walked with a new jauntiness; there was a carelessness in his demeanour, a gaiety about nothing in particular, which Bateman could not precisely blame, but which exceedingly puzzled him.

"I'm blest if I can see what he's got to be so darned cheerful about," he said to himself.

They arrived at the hotel and sat on the terrace. A Chinese boy brought them cocktails. Edward was most anxious to hear all the news of Chicago and bombarded his friend with eager questions. His interest was natural and sincere. But the odd thing was that it seemed equally divided among a multitude of subjects. He was as eager to know how Bateman's father was as what Isabel was doing. He talked of her without a shade of embarrassment, but she might just as well have been his sister as his promised wife; and before Bateman had done analysing the exact meaning of Edward's remarks he found that the conversation had drifted to his own work and the buildings his father had lately erected. He was determined to bring the conversation back to Isabel and was looking for the occasion when he saw Edward wave his hand cordially. A man was advancing towards them on the terrace, but Bateman's back was turned to him and he could not see him.

"Come and sit down," said Edward gaily.

The new-comer approached. He was a very tall, thin man, in white ducks, with a fine head of curly white hair. His face was thin too, long, with a large, hooked nose and a beautiful, expressive mouth.

"This is my old friend Bateman Hunter. I've told you about him," said Edward, his constant smile breaking on his lips.

"I'm pleased to meet you, Mr Hunter. I used to know your father."

The stranger held out his hand and took the young man's in a strong, friendly grasp. It was not till then that Edward mentioned the other's name.

"Mr Arnold Jackson."

Bateman turned white and he felt his hands grow cold. This was the forger, the convict, this was Isabel's uncle. He did not know what to say. He tried to conceal his confusion. Arnold Jackson looked at him with twinkling eyes.

"I daresay my name is familiar to you."

Bateman did not know whether to say yes or no, and what made it more awkward was that both Jackson and Edward seemed to be amused. It was bad enough to have forced on him the acquaintance of the one man on the island he would rather have avoided, but worse to discern that he was being made a fool of. Perhaps, however, he had reached this conclusion too quickly, for Jackson, without a pause, added:

"I understand you're very friendly with the Longstaffes. Mary Longstaffe is my sister."

Now Bateman asked himself if Arnold Jackson could think him ignorant of the most terrible scandal that Chicago had ever known. But Jackson put his hand on Edward's shoulder.

"I can't sit down, Teddie," he said. "I'm busy. But you two boys had better come up and dine tonight."

"That'll be fine," said Edward.

"It's very kind of you, Mr Jackson," said Bateman, frigidly, "but I'm here for so short a time; my boat sails tomorrow, you know; I think if you'll forgive me, I won't come."

"Oh, nonsense. I'll give you a native dinner. My wife's a wonderful cook. Teddie will show you the way. Come early so as to see the sunset. I can give you both a shakedown if you like."

"Of course we'll come," said Edward. "There's always the devil of a row in the hotel on the night a boat arrives and we can have a good yarn up at the bungalow."

"I can't let you off, Mr Hunter," Jackson continued with the utmost cordiality. "I want to hear all about Chicago and Mary."

He nodded and walked away before Bateman could say another word.

"We don't take refusals in Tahiti," laughed Edward. "Besides, you'll get the best dinner on the island."

"What did he mean by saying his wife was a good cook? I happen to know his wife's in Geneva."

"That's a long way off for a wife, isn't it?" said Edward. "And it's a long time since he saw her. I guess it's another wife he's talking about."

For some time Bateman was silent. His face was set in grave lines. But looking up he caught the amused look in Edward's eyes, and he flushed darkly.

"Arnold Jackson is a despicable rogue," he said.

"I greatly fear he is," answered Edward, smiling.

"I don't see how any decent man can have anything to do with him."

"Perhaps I'm not a decent man."

"Do you see much of him, Edward?"

"Yes, quite a lot. He's adopted me as his nephew."

Bateman leaned forward and fixed Edward with his searching eyes.

"Do you like him?"

"Very much."

"But don't you know, doesn't everyone here know, that he's a forger and that he's been a convict? He ought to be hounded out of civilized society."

Edward watched a ring of smoke that floated from his cigar into the still, scented air.

"I suppose he is a pretty unmitigated rascal," he said at last. "And I can't flatter myself that any repentance for his misdeeds offers one an excuse for condoning them. He was a swindler and a hypocrite. You can't get away from it. I never met a more agreeable companion. He's taught me everything I know."

"What has he taught you?" cried Bateman in amazement.

"How to live."

Bateman broke into ironical laughter.

"A fine master. Is it owing to his lessons that you lost the chance of making a fortune and earn your living now by serving behind a counter in a ten-cent store?"

"He has a wonderful personality," said Edward, smiling good-naturedly. "Perhaps you'll see what I mean tonight."

"I'm not going to dine with him if that's what you mean. Nothing would induce me to set foot within that man's house."

"Come to oblige me, Bateman. We've been friends for so many years, you won't refuse me a favour when I ask it."

Edward's tone had in it a quality new to Bateman. Its gentleness was singularly persuasive.

"If you put it like that, Edward, I'm bound to come," he smiled.

Bateman reflected, moreover, that it would be as well to learn what he could about Arnold Jackson. It was plain that he had a great ascendancy over Edward, and if it was to be combated it was necessary to discover in what exactly it consisted. The more he talked with Edward the more conscious he became that a change had taken place in him. He had an instinct that it behoved him to walk warily, and he made up his mind not to broach the real purport of his visit till he saw his way more clearly. He began to talk of one thing and another, of his journey and what he had achieved by it, of politics in Chicago, of this common friend and that, of their days together at college.

At last Edward said he must get back to his work and proposed that he should fetch Bateman at five so that they could drive out together to Arnold Jackson's house.

"By the way, I rather thought you'd be living at this hotel," said Bateman, as he strolled out of the garden with Edward. "I understand it's the only decent one here."

"Not I," laughed Edward. "It's a deal too grand for me. I rent a room just outside the town. It's cheap and clean."

"If I remember right those weren't the points that seemed most important to you when you lived in Chicago."

"Chicago!"

"I don't know what you mean by that, Edward. It's the greatest city in the world."

"I know," said Edward.

Bateman glanced at him quickly, but his face was inscrutable.

"When are you coming back to it?"

"I often wonder," smiled Edward.

This answer, and the manner of it, staggered Bateman, but before he could ask for an explanation Edward waved to a half-caste who was driving a passing motor.

"Give us a ride down, Charlie," he said.

He nodded to Bateman, and ran after the machine that had pulled up a few yards in front. Bateman was left to piece together a mass of perplexing impressions.

Edward called for him in a rickety trap drawn by an old mare, and they drove along a road that ran by the sea. On each side of it were plantations, coconut and vanilla; and now and then they saw a great mango, its fruit yellow and red and purple among the massy green of the leaves, now and then they had a glimpse of the lagoon, smooth and blue, with here and there a tiny islet graceful with tall palms. Arnold Jackson's house stood on a little hill and only a path led to it, so they unharnessed the mare and tied her to a tree, leaving the trap by the side of the road. To Bateman it seemed a happy-go-lucky way of doing things. But when they went up to the house they were met by a tall, handsome native woman, no longer young, with whom Edward cordially shook hands. He introduced Bateman to her.

"This is my friend Mr Hunter. We're going to dine with you, Lavina."

"All right," she said, with a quick smile. "Arnold ain't back yet."

"We'll go down and bathe. Let us have a couple of pareos."

The woman nodded and went into the house.

"Who is that?" asked Bateman.

"Oh, that's Lavina. She's Arnold's wife."

Bateman tightened his lips, but said nothing. In a moment the woman returned with a bundle, which she gave to Edward; and the two men, scrambling down a steep path, made their way to a grove of coconut trees on the beach. They undressed and Edward showed his friend how to make the strip of red trade cotton which is called a pareo into a very neat pair of bathing-drawers. Soon they were splashing in the warm, shallow water. Edward was in great spirits. He laughed and shouted and sang. He might have been fifteen. Bateman had never seen him so gay, and afterwards when they lay on the beach, smoking cigarettes, in the limpid air, there was such an irresistible light-heartedness in him that Bateman was taken aback.

"You seem to find life mighty pleasant," said he.

"I do."

They heard a soft movement and looking round saw that Arnold Jackson was coming towards them.

"I thought I'd come down and fetch you two boys back," he said. "Did you enjoy your bath, Mr Hunter?"

"Very much," said Bateman.

Arnold Jackson, no longer in spruce ducks, wore nothing but a pareo round his loins and walked barefoot. His body was deeply browned by the sun. With his long, curling white hair and his ascetic face he made a fantastic figure in the native dress, but he bore himself without a trace of self-consciousness.

"If you're ready we'll go right up," said Jackson.

"I'll just put on my clothes," said Bateman.

"Why, Teddie, didn't you bring a pareo for your friend?"

"I guess he'd rather wear clothes," smiled Edward.

"I certainly would," answered Bateman, grimly, as he saw Edward gird himself in the loincloth and stand ready to start before he himself had got his shirt on.

"Won't you find it rough walking without your shoes?" he asked Edward. "It struck me the path was a trifle rocky."

"Oh, I'm used to it."

"It's a comfort to get into a pareo when one gets back from town," said Jackson. "If you were going to stay here I should strongly recommend you to adopt it. It's one of the most sensible costumes I have ever come across. It's cool, convenient, and inexpensive."

They walked up to the house, and Jackson took them into a large room with white-washed walls and an open ceiling in which a table was laid for dinner. Bateman noticed that it was set for five.

"Eva, come and show yourself to Teddie's friend, and then shake us a cocktail," called Jackson.

Then he led Bateman to a long low window.

"Look at that," he said, with a dramatic gesture. "Look well."

Below them coconut trees tumbled down steeply to the lagoon, and the lagoon in the evening light had the colour, tender and varied, of a dove's breast. On a creek, at a little distance, were the clustered huts of a native village, and towards the reef was a canoe, sharply silhouetted, in which were a couple of natives fishing. Then, beyond, you saw the vast calmness of the Pacific and twenty miles away, airy and unsubstantial like the fabric of a poet's fancy, the unimaginable beauty of the island which is called Murea. It was all so lovely that Bateman stood abashed.

"I've never seen anything like it," he said at last.

Arnold Jackson stood staring in front of him, and in his eyes was a dreamy softness. His thin, thoughtful face was very grave. Bateman, glancing at it, was once more conscious of its intense spirituality.

"Beauty," murmured Arnold Jackson. "You seldom see beauty face to face. Look at it well, Mr Hunter, for what you see now you will never see again, since the moment is transitory, but it will be an imperishable memory in your heart. You touch eternity."

His voice was deep and resonant. He seemed to breathe forth the purest idealism, and Bateman had to urge himself to remember that the man who spoke was a criminal and a cruel cheat. But Edward, as though he heard a sound, turned round quickly.

"Here is my daughter, Mr Hunter."

Bateman shook hands with her. She had dark, splendid eyes and a red mouth tremulous with laughter; but her skin was brown, and her curling hair, rippling down her shoulders, was coal-black. She wore but one garment, a Mother Hubbard of pink cotton, her feet were bare, and she was crowned with a wreath of white scented flowers. She was a lovely creature. She was like a goddess of the Polynesian spring.

She was a little shy, but not more shy than Bateman, to whom the whole situation was highly embarrassing, and it did not put him at his ease to see this sylph-like thing take a shaker and with a practised hand mix three cocktails.

"Let us have a kick in them, child," said Jackson.

She poured them out and smiling delightfully handed one to each of the men. Bateman flattered himself on his skill in the subtle art of shaking cocktails and he was not a little astonished, on tasting this one, to find that it was excellent. Jackson laughed proudly when he saw his guest's involuntary look of appreciation.

"Not bad, is it? I taught the child myself, and in the old days in Chicago I considered that there wasn't a bar-tender in the city that could hold a candle to me. When I had nothing better to do in the penitentiary I used to amuse myself by thinking out new cocktails, but when you come down to brass tacks there's nothing to beat a dry Martini."

Bateman felt as though someone had given him a violent blow on the funny-bone and he was conscious that he turned red and then white. But before he could think of anything to say a native boy brought in a great bowl of soup and the whole party sat down to dinner. Arnold Jackson's remark seemed to have aroused in him a train of recollections, for he began to talk of his prison days. He talked quite naturally, without malice, as though he were relating his experiences at a foreign university. He addressed himself to Bateman and Bateman was confused and then confounded. He saw Edward's eyes fixed on him and there was in them a flicker of amusement. He blushed scarlet, for it struck him that Jackson was making a fool of him, and then because he felt absurd – and knew there was no reason why he should – he grew angry. Arnold Jackson was impudent – there was no other word for it – and his callousness, whether assumed or not, was outrageous. The dinner proceeded. Bateman was asked to eat sundry messes, raw fish and he knew not what, which only his civility induced him to swallow, but which he was amazed to find very good eating. Then an incident happened which to Bateman was the most mortifying experience of the evening. There was a little circlet of flowers in front of him, and for the sake of conversation he hazarded a remark about it.

"It's a wreath that Eva made for you," said Jackson, "but I guess she was too shy to give it to you."

Bateman took it up in his hand and made a polite little speech of thanks to the girl.

"You must put it on," she said, with a smile and a blush.

"I? I don't think I'll do that."

"It's the charming custom of the country," said Arnold Jackson. There was one in front of him and he placed it on his hair. Edward did the same.

"I guess I'm not dressed for the part," said Bateman, uneasily.

"Would you like a pareo?" said Eva quickly. "I'll get you one in a minute."

"No, thank you. I'm quite comfortable as I am."

"Show him how to put it on, Eva," said Edward.

At that moment Bateman hated his greatest friend. Eva got up from the table and with much laughter placed the wreath on his black hair.

"It suits you very well," said Mrs Jackson. "Don't it suit him, Arnold?"

"Of course it does."

Bateman sweated at every pore.

"Isn't it a pity it's dark?" said Eva. "We could photograph you all three together."

Bateman thanked his stars it was. He felt that he must look prodigiously foolish in his blue serge suit and high collar – very neat and gentlemanly – with that ridiculous wreath of flowers on his head. He was seething with indignation, and he had never in his life exercised more self-control than now when he presented an affable exterior. He was furious with that old man, sitting at the head of the table, half-naked, with his saintly face and the flowers on his handsome white locks. The whole position was monstrous.

Then dinner came to an end, and Eva and her mother remained to clear away while the three men sat on the veranda. It was very warm and the air was scented with the white flowers of the night. The full moon, sailing across an unclouded sky, made a pathway on the broad sea that led to the boundless realms of Forever. Arnold Jackson began to talk. His voice was rich and musical. He talked now of the natives and of the old legends of the country. He told strange stories of the past, stories of hazardous expeditions into the unknown, of love and death, of hatred and revenge. He told of the adventurers who had discovered those distant islands, of the sailors who, settling in them, had married the daughters of great chieftains, and of the beach-combers who had led their varied lives on those silvery shores. Bateman, mortified and exasperated, at first listened sullenly, but presently some magic in the words possessed him and he sat entranced. The mirage of romance obscured the light of common day. Had he forgotten that Arnold Jackson had a tongue of silver, a tongue by which he had charmed vast sums out of the credulous public, a tongue which very nearly enabled him to escape the penalty of his crimes? No one had a sweeter eloquence, and no one had a more acute sense of climax. Suddenly he rose.

"Well, you two boys haven't seen one another for a long time. I shall leave you to have a yarn. Teddie will show you your quarters when you want to go to bed."

"Oh, but I wasn't thinking of spending the night, Mr Jackson," said Bateman.

"You'll find it more comfortable. We'll see that you're called in good time."

Then with a courteous shake of the hand, stately as though he were a bishop in canonicals, Arnold Jackson took leave of his guest.

"Of course I'll drive you back to Papeete if you like," said Edward, "but I advise you to stay. It's bully driving in the early morning."

For a few minutes neither of them spoke. Bateman wondered how he should begin on the conversation which all the events of the day made him think more urgent.

"When are you coming back to Chicago?" he asked, suddenly.

For a moment Edward did not answer. Then he turned rather lazily to look at his friend and smiled.

"I don't know. Perhaps never."

"What in heaven's name do you mean?" cried Bateman.

"I'm very happy here. Wouldn't it be folly to make a change?"

"Man alive, you can't live here all your life. This is no life for a man. It's a living death. Oh, Edward, come away at once, before it's too late. I've felt that something was wrong. You're infatuated with the place, you've succumbed to evil influences, but it only requires a wrench, and when you're free from these surroundings you'll thank all the gods there be. You'll be like a dope-fiend when he's broken from his drug. You'll see then that for two years you've been breathing poisoned air. You can't imagine what a relief it will be when you fill your lungs once more with the fresh pure air of your native country."

He spoke quickly, the words tumbling over one another in his excitement, and there was in his voice sincere and affectionate emotion. Edward was touched.

"It is good of you to care so much, old friend."

"Come with me tomorrow, Edward. It was a mistake that you ever came to this place. This is no life for you."

"You talk of this sort of life and that. How do you think a man gets the best out of life?"

"Why, I should have thought there could be no two answers to that. By doing his duty, by hard work, by meeting all the obligations of his state and station."

"And what is his reward?"

"His reward is the consciousness of having achieved what he set out to do."

"It all sounds a little portentous to me," said Edward, and in the lightness of the night Bateman could see that he was smiling. "I'm afraid you'll think I've degenerated sadly. There are several things I think now which I daresay would have seemed outrageous to me three years ago."

"Have you learnt them from Arnold Jackson?" asked Bateman, scornfully.

"You don't like him? Perhaps you couldn't be expected to. I didn't when I first came. I had just the same prejudice as you. He's a very extraordinary man. You saw for yourself that he makes no secret of the fact that he was in a penitentiary. I do not know that he regrets it or the crimes that led him there. The only complaint he ever made in my hearing was that when he came out his health was impaired. I think he does not know what remorse is. He is completely unmoral. He accepts everything and he accepts himself as well. He's generous and kind."

"He always was," interrupted Bateman, "on other people's money."

"I've found him a very good friend. Is it unnatural that I should take a man as I find him?"

"The result is that you lose the distinction between right and wrong."

"No, they remain just as clearly divided in my mind as before, but what has become a little confused in me is the distinction between the bad man and the good one. Is Arnold Jackson a bad man who does good things or a good man who does bad things? It's a difficult question to answer. Perhaps we make too much of the difference between one man and another. Perhaps even the best of us are sinners and the worst of us are saints. Who knows?"

"You will never persuade me that white is black and that black is white," said Bateman.

"I'm sure I shan't, Bateman."

Bateman could not understand why the flicker of a smile crossed Edward's lips when he thus agreed with him. Edward was silent for a minute.

"When I saw you this morning, Bateman," he said then, "I seemed to see myself as I was two years ago. The same collar, and the same shoes, the same blue suit, the same energy. The same determination. By God, I was energetic. The sleepy methods of this place made my blood tingle. I went about and everywhere I saw possibilities for development and enterprise. There were fortunes to be made here. It seemed to me absurd that the copra should be taken away from here in sacks and the oil extracted in America. It would be far more economical to do all that on the spot, with cheap labour, and save freight, and I saw already the vast factories springing up on the island. Then the way they extracted it from the coconut seemed to me hopelessly inadequate and I invented a machine which divided the nut and scooped out the meat at the rate of two hundred and forty an hour. The harbour was not large enough. I made plans to enlarge it, then to form a syndicate to buy land, put up two or three large hotels, and bungalows for occasional residents;

I had a scheme for improving the steamer service in order to attract visitors from California. In twenty years, instead of this half-French, lazy little town of Papeete I saw a great American city with ten-storey buildings and street-cars, a theatre and an opera house, a stock exchange and a mayor."

"But go ahead, Edward," cried Bateman, springing up from the chair in excitement. "You've got the ideas and the capacity. Why, you'll become the richest man between Australia and the States."

Edward chuckled softly.

"But I don't want to," he said.

"Do you mean to say you don't want money, big money, money running into millions? Do you know what you can do with it? Do you know the power it brings? And if you don't care about it for yourself think what you can do, opening new channels for human enterprise, giving occupation to thousands. My brain reels at the visions your words have conjured up."

"Sit down, then, my dear Bateman," laughed Edward. "My machine for cutting the coconuts will always remain unused, and so far as I'm concerned street-cars shall never run in the idle streets of Papeete."

Bateman sank heavily into his chair.

"I don't understand you," he said.

"It came upon me little by little. I came to like the life here, with its ease and its leisure, and the people, with their good-nature and their happy smiling faces. I began to think. I'd never had time to do that before. I began to read."

"You always read."

"I read for examinations. I read in order to be able to hold my own in conversation. I read for instruction. Here I learned to read for pleasure. I learned to talk. Do you know that conversation is one of the greatest pleasures in life? But it wants leisure. I'd always been too busy before. And gradually all the life that had seemed so important to me began to seem rather trivial and vulgar. What is the use of all this hustle and this constant striving? I think of Chicago now and I see a dark, grey city, all stone – it is like a prison – and a ceaseless turmoil. And what does all that activity amount to? Does one get there the best out of life? Is that what we come into the world for, to hurry to an office, and work hour after hour till night, then hurry home and dine and go to a theatre? Is that how I must spend my youth? Youth lasts so short a time, Bateman. And when I am old, what have I to look forward to? To hurry from my home in the morning to my office and work hour after hour till night, and then hurry home again, and dine and go to a theatre? That may be worth while if you make a fortune; I don't know, it depends on your nature; but if you don't, is it worth while then? I want to make more out of my life than that, Bateman."

"What do you value in life then?"

"I'm afraid you'll laugh at me. Beauty, truth, and goodness."

"Don't you think you can have those in Chicago?"

"Some men can, perhaps, but not I." Edward sprang up now. "I tell you when I think of the life I led in the old days I am filled with horror," he cried violently. "I tremble with fear when I think of the danger I have escaped. I never knew I had a soul till I found it here. If I had remained a rich man I might have lost it for good and all."

"I don't know how you can say that," cried Bateman indignantly. "We often used to have discussions about it."

"Yes, I know. They were about as effectual as the discussions of deaf mutes about harmony. I shall never come back to Chicago, Bateman."

"And what about Isabel?"

Edward walked to the edge of the veranda and leaning over looked intently at the blue magic of the night. There was a slight smile on his face when he turned back to Bateman.

"Isabel is infinitely too good for me. I admire her more than any woman I have ever known. She has a wonderful brain and she's as good as she's beautiful. I respect her energy and her ambition. She was born to make a success of life. I am entirely unworthy of her."

"She doesn't think so."

"But you must tell her so, Bateman."

"I?" cried Bateman. "I'm the last person who could ever do that."

Edward had his back to the vivid light of the moon and his face could not be seen. Is it possible that he smiled again?

"It's no good your trying to conceal anything from her, Bateman. With her quick intelligence she'll turn you inside out in five minutes. You'd better make a clean breast of it right away."

"I don't know what you mean. Of course I shall tell her I've seen you." Bateman spoke in some agitation. "Honestly I don't know what to say to her."

"Tell her that I haven't made good. Tell her that I'm not only poor, but that I'm content to be poor. Tell her I was fired from my job because I was idle and inattentive. Tell her all you've seen tonight and all I've told you."

The idea which on a sudden flashed through Bateman's brain brought him to his feet and in uncontrollable perturbation he faced Edward.

"Man alive, don't you want to marry her?"

Edward looked at him gravely.

"I can never ask her to release me. If she wishes to hold me to my word I will do my best to make her a good and loving husband."

"Do you wish me to give her that message, Edward? Oh, I can't. It's terrible. It's never dawned on her for a moment that you don't want to marry her. She loves you. How can I inflict such a mortification on her?"

Edward smiled again.

"Why don't you marry her yourself, Bateman? You've been in love with her for ages. You're perfectly suited to one another. You'll make her very happy."

"Don't talk to me like that. I can't bear it."

"I resign in your favour, Bateman. You are the better man."

There was something in Edward's tone that made Bateman look up quickly, but Edward's eyes were grave and unsmiling. Bateman did not know what to say. He was disconcerted. He wondered whether Edward could possibly suspect that he had come to Tahiti on a special errand. And though he knew it was horrible he could not prevent the exultation in his heart.

"What will you do if Isabel writes and puts an end to her engagement with you?" he said, slowly.

"Survive," said Edward.

Bateman was so agitated that he did not hear the answer.

"I wish you had ordinary clothes on," he said, somewhat irritably. "It's such a tremendously serious decision you're taking. That fantastic costume of yours makes it seem terribly casual."

"I assure you, I can be just as solemn in a pareo and a wreath of roses, as in a high hat and a cut-away coat."

Then another thought struck Bateman.

"Edward, it's not for my sake you're doing this? I don't know, but perhaps this is going to make a tremendous difference to my future. You're not sacrificing yourself for me? I couldn't stand for that, you know."

"No, Bateman, I have learnt not to be silly and sentimental here. I should like you and Isabel to be happy, but I have not the least wish to be unhappy myself."

The answer somewhat chilled Bateman. It seemed to him a little cynical. He would not have been sorry to act a noble part.

"Do you mean to say you're content to waste your life here? It's nothing less than suicide. When I think of the great hopes you had when we left college it seems terrible that you should be content to be no more than a salesman in a cheap-John store."

"Oh, I'm only doing that for the present, and I'm gaining a great deal of valuable experience. I have another plan in my head. Arnold Jackson has a small island in the Paumotas, about a thousand miles from here, a ring of land round a lagoon. He's planted coconut there. He's offered to give it me."

"Why should he do that?" asked Bateman.

"Because if Isabel releases me I shall marry his daughter."

"You?" Bateman was thunderstruck. "You can't marry a half-caste. You wouldn't be so crazy as that."

"She's a good girl, and she has a sweet and gentle nature. I think she would make me very happy."

"Are you in love with her?"

"I don't know," answered Edward reflectively. "I'm not in love with her as I was in love with Isabel. I worshipped Isabel. I thought she was the most wonderful creature I had ever seen. I was not half good enough for her. I don't feel like that with Eva. She's like a beautiful exotic flower that must be sheltered from bitter winds. I want to protect her. No one ever thought of protecting Isabel. I think she loves me for myself and not for what I may become. Whatever happens to me I shall never disappoint her. She suits me."

Bateman was silent.

"We must turn out early in the morning," said Edward at last. "It's really about time we went to bed."

Then Bateman spoke and his voice had in it a genuine distress.

"I'm so bewildered, I don't know what to say. I came here because I thought something was wrong. I thought you hadn't succeeded in what you set out to do and were ashamed to come back when you'd failed. I never guessed I should be faced with this. I'm so desperately sorry, Edward. I'm so disappointed. I hoped you would do great things. It's almost more than I can bear to think of you wasting your talents and your youth and your chance in this lamentable way."

"Don't be grieved, old friend," said Edward. "I haven't failed. I've succeeded. You can't think with what zest I look forward to life, how full it seems to me and how significant. Sometimes, when you are married to Isabel, you will think of me. I shall build myself a house on my coral island and I shall live there, looking after my trees – getting the fruit out of the nuts in the same old way that they have done for unnumbered years – I shall grow all sorts of things in my garden, and I shall fish. There will be enough work to keep me busy and not enough to make me dull. I shall have my books and Eva, children, I hope, and above all, the infinite variety of the sea and the sky, the freshness of the dawn and the beauty of the sunset, and the rich magnificence of the night. I shall make a garden out of what so short a while ago was a wilderness. I shall have created something. The years will pass insensibly, and when I am an old man I hope I shall be able to look back on a happy, simple, peaceful life. In my small way I too shall have lived in beauty. Do you think it is so little to have enjoyed contentment? We know that it will profit a man little if he gain the whole world and lose his soul. I think I have won mine."

Edward led him to a room in which there were two beds and he threw himself on one of them. In ten minutes Bateman knew by his regular breathing, peaceful as a child's, that Edward was asleep. But for his part he had no rest, he was disturbed in mind, and it was not till the dawn crept into the room, ghostlike and silent, that he fell asleep.

Bateman finished telling Isabel his long story. He had hidden nothing from her except what he thought would wound her or what made himself ridiculous. He did not tell her that he had been forced to sit at dinner with a wreath of flowers round his head and he did not tell her that Edward was prepared to marry her uncle's half-caste daughter the moment she set him free. But perhaps Isabel had keener intuitions than he knew, for as he went on with his tale her eyes grew colder and her lips closed upon one another more tightly. Now and then she looked at him closely, and if he had been less intent on his narrative he might have wondered at her expression.

"What was this girl like?" she asked when he finished. "Uncle Arnold's daughter. Would you say there was any resemblance between her and me?"

Bateman was surprised at the question.

"It never struck me. You know I've never had eyes for anyone but you and I could never think that anyone was like you. Who could resemble you?"

"Was she pretty?" said Isabel, smiling slightly at his words.

"I suppose so. I daresay some men would say she was very beautiful."

"Well, it's of no consequence. I don't think we need give her any more of our attention."

"What are you going to do, Isabel?" he asked then.

Isabel looked down at the hand which still bore the ring Edward had given her on their betrothal.

"I wouldn't let Edward break our engagement because I thought it would be an incentive to him. I wanted to be an inspiration to him. I thought if anything could enable him to achieve success it was the thought that I loved him. I have done all I could. It's hopeless. It would only be weakness on my part not to recognize the facts. Poor Edward, he's nobody's enemy but his own. He was a dear, nice fellow, but there was something lacking in him, I suppose it was backbone. I hope he'll be happy."

She slipped the ring off her finger and placed it on the table. Bateman watched her with a heart beating so rapidly that he could hardly breathe.

"You're wonderful, Isabel, you're simply wonderful."

She smiled, and, standing up, held out her hand to him.

"How can I ever thank you for what you've done for me?" she said. "You have done me a great service. I knew I could trust you."

He took her hand and held it. She had never looked more beautiful.

"Oh, Isabel, I would do so much more for you than that. You know that I only ask to be allowed to love and serve you."

"You're so strong, Bateman," she sighed. "It gives me such a delicious feeling of confidence."

"Isabel, I adore you."

He hardly knew how the inspiration had come to him, but suddenly he clasped her in his arms; she, all unresisting, smiled into his eyes.

"Isabel, you know I wanted to marry you the very first day I saw you," he cried passionately.

"Then why on earth didn't you ask me?" she replied.

She loved him. He could hardly believe it was true. She gave him her lovely lips to kiss. And as he held her in his arms he had a vision of the works of the Hunter Motor Traction and Automobile Company growing in size and importance till they covered a hundred acres, and of the millions of motors they would turn out, and of the great collection of pictures he would form which should beat anything they had in New York. He would wear horn spectacles. And she, with the delicious pressure of his arms about her, sighed with happiness, for she thought of the exquisite house she would have, full of antique furniture, and of the concerts she would give, and of the *thés dansants*, and the dinners to which only the most cultured people would come.

"Poor Edward," she sighed.

THE POOL

WHEN I WAS introduced to Lawson by Chaplin, the owner of the Hotel Metropole at Apia, I paid no particular attention to him. We were sitting in the lounge over an early cocktail and I was listening with amusement to the gossip of the island.

Chaplin entertained me. He was by profession a mining engineer and perhaps it was characteristic of him that he had settled in a place where his professional attainments were of no possible value.

It was, however, generally reported that he was an extremely clever mining engineer. He was a small man, neither fat nor thin, with black hair, scanty on the crown, turning grey, and a small, untidy moustache; his face, partly from the sun and partly from liquor, was very red. He was but a figurehead, for the hotel, though so grandly named but a frame building of two storeys, was managed by his wife, a tall, gaunt Australian of five-and-forty, with an imposing presence and a determined air. The little man, excitable and often tipsy, was terrified of her, and the stranger soon heard of domestic quarrels in which she used her fist and her foot in order to keep him in subjection. She had been known after a night of drunkenness to confine him for twenty-four hours to his own room, and then he could be seen, afraid to leave his prison, talking somewhat pathetically from his veranda to people in the street below.

He was a character, and his reminiscences of a varied life, whether true or not, made him worth listening to, so that when Lawson strolled in I was inclined to resent the interruption. Although not midday, it was clear that he had had enough to drink, and it was without enthusiasm that I yielded to his persistence and accepted his offer of another cocktail. I knew already that Chaplin's head was weak. The next round which in common politeness I should be forced to order would be enough to make him lively, and then Mrs Chaplin would give me black looks.

Nor was there anything attractive in Lawson's appearance. He was a little thin man, with a long, sallow face and a narrow, weak chin, a prominent nose, large and bony, and great shaggy black eyebrows. They gave him a peculiar look. His eyes, very large and very dark, were magnificent. He was jolly, but his jollity did not seem to me sincere; it was on the surface, a mask which he wore to deceive the world, and I suspected that it concealed a mean nature. He was plainly anxious to be thought a "good sport" and he was hail-fellow-well-met; but, I do not know why, I felt that he was cunning and shifty. He talked a great deal in a raucous voice, and he and Chaplin capped one another's stories of beanos which had become legendary, stories of "wet" nights at the English Club, of shooting expeditions where an incredible amount of whisky had been consumed, and of jaunts to Sydney of which their pride was that they could remember nothing from the time they landed till the time they sailed. A pair of drunken swine. But even in their intoxication, for by now, after four cocktails each, neither was sober, there was a great difference between Chaplin, rough and vulgar, and Lawson: Lawson might be drunk, but he was certainly a gentleman.

At last he got out of his chair, a little unsteadily.

"Well, I'll be getting along home," he said. "See you before dinner."

"Missus all right?" said Chaplin.

"Yes."

He went out. There was a peculiar note in the monosyllable of his answer which made me look up.

"Good chap," said Chaplin flatly, as Lawson went out of the door into the sunshine. "One of the best. Pity he drinks."

This from Chaplin was an observation not without humour.

"And when he's drunk he wants to fight people."

"Is he often drunk?"

"Dead drunk, three or four days a week. It's the island done it, and Ethel."

"Who's Ethel?"

"Ethel's his wife. Married a half-caste. Old Brevald's daughter. Took her away from here. Only thing to do. But she couldn't stand it, and now they're back again. He'll hang himself one of these days, if he don't drink himself to death. Good chap. Nasty when he's drunk."

Chaplin belched loudly.

"I'll go and put my head under the shower. I oughtn't to have had that last cocktail. It's always the last one that does you in."

He looked uncertainly at the staircase as he made up his mind to go to the cubby hole in which was the shower, and then with unnatural seriousness got up.

"Pay you to cultivate Lawson," he said. "A well-read chap. You'd be surprised when he's sober. Clever too. Worth talking to."

Chaplin had told me the whole story in these few speeches.

When I came in towards evening from a ride along the seashore Lawson was again in the hotel. He was heavily sunk in one of the cane chairs in the lounge and he looked at me with glassy eyes. It was plain that he had been drinking all the afternoon. He was torpid, and the look on his face was sullen and vindictive. His glance rested on me for a moment, but I could see that he did not recognize me. Two or three other men were sitting there, shaking dice, and they took no notice of him. His condition was evidently too usual to attract attention. I sat down and began to play.

"You're a damned sociable lot," said Lawson suddenly.

He got out of his chair and waddled with bent knees towards the door. I do not know whether the spectacle was more ridiculous than revolting. When he had gone one of the men sniggered.

"Lawson's fairly soused today," he said.

"If I couldn't carry my liquor better than that," said another, "I'd climb on the waggon and stay there."

Who would have thought that this wretched object was in his way a romantic figure or that his life had in it those elements of pity and terror which the theorist tells us are necessary to achieve the effect of tragedy?

I did not see him again for two or three days.

I was sitting one evening on the first floor of the hotel on a veranda that overlooked the street when Lawson came up and sank into a chair beside me. He was quite sober. He made a casual remark and then, when I had replied somewhat indifferently, added with a laugh which had in it an apologetic tone:

"I was devilish soused the other day."

I did not answer. There was really nothing to say. I pulled away at my pipe in the vain hope of keeping the mosquitoes away, and looked at the natives going home from their work. They walked with long steps, slowly, with care and dignity, and the soft patter of their naked feet was strange to hear. Their dark hair, curling or straight, was often white with lime, and then they had a look of extraordinary distinction. They were tall and finely built. Then a gang of Solomon Islanders, indentured labourers, passed by, singing; they were shorter and slighter than the Samoans, coal-black, with great heads of fuzzy hair dyed red. Now and then a white man drove past in his buggy or rode into the hotel yard. In the lagoon two or three schooners reflected their grace in the tranquil water.

"I don't know what there is to do in a place like this except to get soused," said Lawson at last.

"Don't you like Samoa?" I asked casually, for something to say.

"It's pretty, isn't it?"

The word he chose seemed so inadequate to describe the unimaginable beauty of the island that I smiled, and smiling I turned to look at him. I was startled by the expression in those fine sombre eyes of his, an expression of intolerable anguish; they betrayed a tragic depth of emotion of which I should never have thought him capable. But the expression passed away and he smiled. His smile was simple and a little naïve. It changed his face so that I wavered in my first feeling of aversion from him.

"I was all over the place when I first came out," he said.

He was silent for a moment.

"I went away for good about three years ago, but I came back." He hesitated. "My wife wanted to come back. She was born here, you know."

"Oh yes."

He was silent again, and then hazarded a remark about Robert Louis Stevenson. He asked me if I had been up to Vailima. For some reason he was making an effort to be agreeable to me. He began to talk of Stevenson's books, and presently the conversation drifted to London.

"I suppose Covent Garden's still going strong," he said. "I think I miss the opera as much as anything here. Have you seen *Tristan and Isolde*?"

He asked me the question as though the answer was really important to him, and when I said, a little casually I daresay, that I had, he seemed pleased. He began to speak of Wagner, not as a musician, but as the plain man who received from him an emotional satisfaction that he could not analyse.

"I suppose Bayreuth was the place to go really," he said. "I never had the money, worse luck. But of course one might do worse than Covent Garden, all the lights and the women dressed up to the nines, and the music. The first act of the *Walküre*'s all right, isn't it? And the end of *Tristan*. Golly!"

His eyes were flashing now and his face was lit up so that he hardly seemed the same man. There was a flush on his sallow, thin cheeks, and I forgot that his voice was harsh and unpleasant. There was even a certain charm about him.

"By George, I'd like to be in London tonight. Do you know the Pall Mall restaurant? I used to go there a lot. Piccadilly Circus with the shops all lit up, and the crowd. I think it's stunning to stand there and watch the buses and taxis streaming along as though they'd never stop. And I like the Strand too. What are those lines about God and Charing Cross?"

I was taken aback.

"Thompson's, d'you mean?" I asked.

I quoted them:

> "And when so sad, thou canst not sadder,
> Cry, and upon thy so sore loss
> Shall shine the traffic of Jacob's ladder
> Pitched between Heaven and Charing Cross."

He gave a faint sigh.

"I've read *The Hound of Heaven*. It's a bit of all right."

"It's generally thought so," I murmured.

"You don't meet anybody here who's read anything. They think it's swank."

There was a wistful look on his face, and I thought I divined the feeling that made him come to me. I was a link with the world he regretted and a life that he would know no more. Because not so very long before I had been in the London which he loved, he looked upon me with awe and envy. He had not spoken for five minutes perhaps when he broke out with words that startled me by their intensity.

"I'm fed up," he said. "I'm fed up."

"Then why don't you clear out?" I asked.

His face grew sullen.

"My lungs are a bit dicky. I couldn't stand an English winter now."

At that moment another man joined us on the veranda and Lawson sank into a moody silence.

"It's about time for a drain," said the newcomer. "Who'll have a drop of Scotch with me? Lawson?"

Lawson seemed to arise from a distant world. He got up.

"Let's go down to the bar," he said.

When he left me I remained with a more kindly feeling towards him than I should have expected. He puzzled and interested me. And a few days later I met his wife. I knew they had been married for five or six years, and I was surprised to see that she was still extremely young. When he married her she could not have been more than sixteen. She was adorably pretty. She was no darker than a Spaniard, small and very beautifully made, with tiny hands and feet, and a slight, lithe figure. Her features were lovely; but I think what struck me most was the delicacy of her appearance; the half-castes as a rule have a certain coarseness, they seem a little roughly formed, but she had an exquisite daintiness which took your breath away. There was something extremely civilized about her, so that it surprised you to see her in those surroundings, and you thought of those famous beauties who had set all the world talking at the Court of the Emperor Napoleon III. Though she wore but a muslin frock and a straw hat she wore them with an elegance that suggested the woman of fashion. She must have been ravishing when Lawson first saw her.

He had but lately come out from England to manage the local branch of an English bank, and, reaching Samoa at the beginning of the dry season, he had taken a room at the hotel. He quickly made the acquaintance of all and sundry. The life of the island is pleasant and easy. He enjoyed the long idle talks in the lounge of the hotel and the gay evenings at the English Club when a group of fellows would play pool. He liked Apia straggling along the edge of the lagoon, with its stores and bungalows, and its native village. Then there were week-ends when he would ride over to the house of one planter or another and spend a couple of nights on the hills. He had never before known freedom or leisure. And he was intoxicated by the sunshine. When he rode through the bush his head reeled a little at the beauty that surrounded him. The country was indescribably fertile. In parts the forest was still virgin, a tangle of strange trees, luxuriant undergrowth, and vine; it gave an impression that was mysterious and troubling.

But the spot that entranced him was a pool a mile or two away from Apia to which in the evenings he often went to bathe. There was a little river that bubbled over the rocks in a swift stream, and then, after forming the deep pool, ran on, shallow and crystalline, past a ford made by great stones where the natives came sometimes to bathe or to wash their clothes. The coconut trees, with their frivolous elegance, grew thickly on the banks, all clad with trailing plants, and they were reflected in the green water. It was just such a scene as you might see in Devonshire among the hills and yet with a difference, for it had a tropical richness, a passion, a scented languor which seemed to melt the heart. The water was fresh, but not cold; and it was delicious after the heat of the day. To bathe there refreshed not only the body but the soul.

At the hour when Lawson went, there was not a soul and he lingered for a long time, now floating idly in the water, now drying himself in the evening sun, enjoying the solitude and the friendly silence. He did not regret London then, nor the life that he had abandoned, for life as it was seemed complete and exquisite.

It was here that he first saw Ethel.

Occupied till late by letters which had to be finished for the monthly sailing of the boat next day, he rode down one evening to the pool when the light was almost failing. He tied up his horse and sauntered to the bank. A girl was sitting there. She glanced round as he came and noiselessly slid into the water. She vanished like a naiad startled by the approach of a mortal. He was surprised and amused. He wondered where she had hidden herself. He swam downstream and presently saw her sitting on a rock. She looked at him with uncurious eyes. He called out a greeting in Samoan.

"*Talofa.*"

She answered him, suddenly smiling, and then let herself into the water again. She swam easily and her hair spread out behind her. He watched her cross the pool and climb out on the bank. Like all the natives she bathed in a Mother Hubbard, and the water had made it cling to her slight body. She wrung out her hair, and as she stood there, unconcerned, she looked more than ever like a wild creature of the water or the woods. He saw now that she was half-caste. He swam towards her and, getting out, addressed her in English.

"You're having a late swim."

She shook back her hair and then let it spread over her shoulders in luxuriant curls.

"I like it when I'm alone," she said.

"So do I."

She laughed with the childlike frankness of the native. She slipped a dry Mother Hubbard over her head and, letting down the wet one, stepped out of it. She wrung it out and was ready to go. She paused a moment irresolutely and then sauntered off. The night fell suddenly.

Lawson went back to the hotel and, describing her to the men who were in the lounge shaking dice for drinks, soon discovered who she was. Her father was a Norwegian called Brevald who was often to be seen in the bar of the Hotel Metropole drinking rum and water. He was a little old man, knotted and gnarled like an ancient tree, who had come out to the islands forty years before as mate of a sailing vessel. He had been a blacksmith, a trader, a planter, and at one time fairly well-to-do; but, ruined by the great hurricane of the nineties, he had now nothing to live on but a small plantation of coconut trees. He had had four native wives and, as he told you with a cracked chuckle, more children than he could count. But some had died and some had gone out into the world, so that now the only one left at home was Ethel.

"She's a peach," said Nelson, the super-cargo of the *Moana*. "I've given her the glad eye once or twice, but I guess there's nothing doing."

"Old Brevald's not that sort of a fool, sonny," put in another, a man called Miller. "He wants a son-in-law who's prepared to keep him in comfort for the rest of his life."

It was distasteful to Lawson that they should speak of the girl in that fashion. He made a remark about the departing mail and so distracted their attention. But next evening he went again to the pool. Ethel was there; and the mystery of the sunset, the deep silence of the water, the lithe grace of the coconut trees, added to her beauty, giving it a profundity, a magic, which stirred the heart to unknown emotions. For some reason that time he had the whim not to speak to her. She took no notice of him. She did not even glance in his direction. She swam about the green pool. She dived, she rested on the bank, as though she were quite alone: he had a queer feeling that he was invisible. Scraps of poetry, half forgotten, floated across his memory, and vague recollections of the Greece he had negligently studied in his school days. When she had changed her wet clothes for dry ones and sauntered away he found a scarlet hibiscus where she had been. It was a flower that she had worn in her hair when she came to bathe and, having taken it out on getting into the water, had forgotten or not cared to put in again. He took it in his hands and looked at it with a singular emotion. He had an instinct to keep it, but his sentimentality irritated him, and he flung it away. It gave him quite a little pang to see it float down the stream.

He wondered what strangeness it was in her nature that urged her to go down to this hidden pool when there was no likelihood that anyone should be there. The natives of the islands are devoted to the water. They bathe, somewhere or other, every day, once always, and often twice; but they bathe in bands, laughing and joyous, a whole family together; and you often saw a group of girls, dappled by the sun shining through the trees, with the half-castes among them, splashing about the shallows of the stream. It looked as though there were in this pool some secret which attracted Ethel against her will.

Now the night had fallen, mysterious and silent, and he let himself down in the water softly, in order to make no sound, and swam lazily in the warm darkness. The water seemed fragrant still from her slender body. He rode back to the town under the starry sky. He felt at peace with the world.

Now he went every evening to the pool and every evening he saw Ethel. Presently he overcame her timidity. She became playful and friendly. They sat together on the rocks above the pool, where the water ran fast, and they lay side by side on the ledge that overlooked it, watching the gathering dusk envelop it with mystery. It was inevitable that their meetings should become known – in the South Seas everyone seems to know everyone's business – and he was subjected to much rude chaff by the men at the hotel. He smiled and let them talk. It was not even worth while to deny their coarse suggestions. His feelings were absolutely pure. He loved Ethel as a poet might love the moon. He thought of her not as a woman but as something not of this earth. She was the spirit of the pool.

One day at the hotel, passing through the bar, he saw that old Brevald, as ever in his shabby blue overalls, was standing there. Because he was Ethel's father he had a desire to speak to him, so he went in, nodded and, ordering his own drink, casually turned and invited the old man to have one with him. They chatted for a few minutes of local affairs, and Lawson was uneasily conscious that the Norwegian was scrutinizing him with sly blue eyes. His manner was not agreeable. It was sycophantic, and yet behind the cringing air of an old man who had been worsted in his struggle with fate was a shadow of old truculence. Lawson remembered that he had once been captain of a schooner engaged in the slave trade, a blackbirder they call it in the Pacific, and he had a large hernia in the chest which was the result of a wound received in a scrap with Solomon Islanders. The bell rang for luncheon.

"Well, I must be off," said Lawson.

"Why don't you come along to my place one time?" said Brevald, in his wheezy voice. "It's not very grand, but you'll be welcome. You know Ethel."

"I'll come with pleasure."

"Sunday afternoon's the best time."

Brevald's bungalow, shabby and bedraggled, stood among the coconut trees of the plantation, a little away from the main road that ran up to Vailima. Immediately around it grew huge plantains. With their tattered leaves they had the tragic beauty of a lovely woman in rags. Everything was slovenly and neglected. Little black pigs, thin and high-backed, rooted about, and chickens clucked noisily as they picked at the refuse scattered here and there. Three or four natives were lounging about the veranda. When Lawson asked for Brevald the old man's cracked voice called out to him, and he found him in the sitting-room smoking an old briar pipe.

"Sit down and make yerself at home," he said. "Ethel's just titivating."

She came in. She wore a blouse and skirt and her hair was done in the European fashion. Although she had not the wild, timid grace of the girl who came down every evening to the pool, she seemed now more usual and consequently more approachable. She shook hands with Lawson. It was the first time he had touched her hand.

"I hope you'll have a cup of tea with us," she said.

He knew she had been at a mission school, and he was amused, and at the same time touched, by the company manners she was putting on for his benefit. Tea was already set out on the table and in a minute old Brevald's fourth wife brought in the tea-pot. She was a handsome native, no longer very young, and she spoke but a few words of English. She smiled and smiled. Tea was rather a solemn meal, with a great deal of bread and butter and a variety of very sweet cakes, and the conversation was formal. Then a wrinkled old woman came in softly.

"That's Ethel's granny," said old Brevald, noisily spitting on the floor.

She sat on the edge of a chair, uncomfortably, so that you saw it was unusual for her and she would have been more at ease on the ground, and remained silently staring at Lawson with fixed, shining eyes. In the kitchen behind the bungalow someone began to play the concertina and two or three voices were raised in a hymn. But they sang for the pleasure of the sounds rather than from piety.

When Lawson walked back to the hotel he was strangely happy. He was touched by the higgledy-piggledy way in which those people lived; and in the smiling good-nature of Mrs Brevald, in the little Norwegian's fantastic career, and in the shining mysterious eyes of the old grandmother he found something unusual and fascinating. It was a more natural life than any he had known, it was nearer to the friendly, fertile earth; civilization repelled him at that moment, and by mere contact with these creatures of a more primitive nature he felt a greater freedom.

He saw himself rid of the hotel which already was beginning to irk him, settled in a little bungalow of his own, trim and white, in front of the sea so that he had before his eyes always the multi-coloured variety of the lagoon. He loved the beautiful island. London and England meant nothing to him any more, he was content to spend the rest of his days in that forgotten spot, rich in the best of the world's goods, love and happiness. He made up his mind that whatever the obstacles nothing should prevent him from marrying Ethel.

But there were no obstacles. He was always welcome at the Brevalds' house. The old man was ingratiating and Mrs Brevald smiled without ceasing. He had brief glimpses of natives who seemed somehow to belong to the establishment, and once he found a tall youth in a lava-lava, his body tattooed, his hair white with lime, sitting with Brevald, and was told he was Mrs Brevald's brother's son; but for the most part they kept out of his way. Ethel was delightful with him. The light in her eyes when she saw him filled him with ecstasy. She was charming and naïve. He listened enraptured when she told him of the mission school at which she was educated, and of the sisters. He went with her to the cinema which was given once a fortnight and danced with her at the dance which followed it. They came from all parts of the island for this, since gaieties are few in Upolu; and you saw there all the society of the place, the white ladies keeping a good deal to themselves, the half-castes very elegant in American clothes, the natives, strings of dark girls in white Mother Hubbards and young men in unaccustomed ducks and white shoes. It was all very smart and gay. Ethel was pleased to show her friends the white admirer who did not leave her side. The rumour was soon spread that he meant to marry her and her friends looked at her with envy. It was a great thing for a half-caste to get a white man to marry her, even the less regular relation was better than nothing, but one could never tell what it would lead to; and Lawson's position as manager of the bank made him one of the catches of the island. If he had not been so absorbed in Ethel he would have noticed that many eyes were fixed on him curiously, and he would have seen the glances of the white ladies and noticed how they put their heads together and gossiped.

Afterwards, when the men who lived at the hotel were having a whisky before turning in, Nelson burst out with:

"Say, they say Lawson's going to marry that girl."

"He's a damned fool then," said Miller.

Miller was a German–American who had changed his name from Müller, a big man, fat and bald-headed, with a round, clean-shaven face. He wore large gold-rimmed spectacles, which gave him a benign look, and his ducks were always clean and white. He was a heavy drinker, invariably ready to stay up all night with the "boys", but he never got drunk; he was jolly and affable, but very shrewd. Nothing interfered with his business; he represented a firm in San Francisco, jobbers of the goods sold in the islands, calico, machinery and what not; and his good-fellowship was part of his stock-in-trade.

"He don't know what he's up against," said Nelson. "Someone ought to put him wise."

"If you'll take my advice you won't interfere in what don't concern you," said Miller. "When a man's made up his mind to make a fool of himself, there's nothing like letting him."

"I'm all for having a good time with the girls out here, but when it comes to marrying them – this child ain't taking any, I'll tell the world."

Chaplin was there, and now he had his say.

"I've seen a lot of fellows do it, and it's no good."

"You ought to have a talk with him, Chaplin," said Nelson. "You know him better than anyone else does."

"My advice to Chaplin is to leave it alone," said Miller.

Even in those days Lawson was not popular and really no one took enough interest in him to bother. Mrs Chaplin talked it over with two or three of the white ladies, but they contented themselves with saying that it was a pity; and when he told her definitely that he was going to be married it seemed too late to do anything.

For a year Lawson was happy. He took a bungalow at the point of the bay round which Apia is built, on the borders of a native village. It nestled charmingly among the coconut trees and faced the passionate blue of the Pacific. Ethel was lovely as she went about the little house, lithe and graceful like some young animal of the woods, and she was gay. They laughed a great deal. They talked nonsense. Sometimes one or two of the men at the hotel would come over and spend the evening, and often on a Sunday they would go for a day to some planter who had married a native; now and then one or other of the half-caste traders who had a store in Apia would give a party and they went to it. The half-castes treated Lawson quite differently now. His marriage had made him one of themselves and they called him Bertie. They put their arms through his and smacked him on the back. He liked to see Ethel at these gatherings. Her eyes shone and she laughed. It did him good to see her radiant happiness. Sometimes Ethel's relations would come to the bungalow, old Brevald of course, and her mother, but cousins too, vague native women in Mother Hubbards and men and boys in lava-lavas, with their hair dyed red and their bodies elaborately tattooed. He would find them sitting there when he got back from the bank. He laughed indulgently.

"Don't let them eat us out of hearth and home," he said.

"They're my own family. I can't help doing something for them when they ask me."

He knew that when a white man marries a native or a half-caste he must expect her relations to look upon him as a gold mine. He took Ethel's face in his hands and kissed her red lips. Perhaps he could not expect her to understand that the salary which had amply sufficed for a bachelor must be managed with some care when it had to support a wife and a house. Then Ethel was delivered of a son.

It was when Lawson first held the child in his arms that a sudden pang shot through his heart. He had not expected it to be so dark. After all it had but a fourth part of native blood, and there was no reason really why it should not look just like an English baby; but, huddled together in his arms, sallow, its head covered already with black hair, with huge black eyes, it might have been a native child. Since his marriage he had been ignored by the white ladies of the colony. When he came across men in whose houses he had been accustomed to dine as a bachelor, they were a little self-conscious with him; and they sought to cover their embarrassment by an exaggerated cordiality.

"Mrs Lawson well?" they would say. "You're a lucky fellow. Damned pretty girl."

But if they were with their wives and met him and Ethel they would feel it awkward when their wives gave Ethel a patronizing nod. Lawson had laughed.

"They're as dull as ditchwater, the whole gang of them," he said. "It's not going to disturb my night's rest if they don't ask me to their dirty parties."

But now it irked him a little.

The little dark baby screwed up its face. That was his son. He thought of the half-caste children in Apia. They had an unhealthy look, sallow and pale, and they were odiously precocious. He had seen them on the boat going to school in New Zealand, and a school had to be chosen which took children with native blood in them; they were huddled together, brazen and yet timid, with traits which set them apart strangely from white people. They spoke the native language among themselves. And when they grew up the men accepted smaller salaries because of their native blood; girls might marry a white man, but boys had no chance; they must marry a half-caste like themselves, or a native. Lawson made up his mind passionately that he would take his son away from the humiliation of such a life. At whatever cost he must get back to Europe. And when he went in to see Ethel, frail and lovely in her bed, surrounded by native women, his determination was strengthened. If he took her away among his own people she would belong more completely to him. He loved her so passionately he wanted her to be one soul and one body with him; and he was conscious that here, with those deep roots attaching her to the native life, she would always keep something from him.

He went to work quietly, urged by an obscure instinct of secrecy, and wrote to a cousin who was a partner in a shipping firm in Aberdeen, saying that his health (on account of which like so many more he had come out to the islands) was so much better, there seemed no reason why he should not return to Europe. He asked him to use what influence he could to get him a job, no matter how poorly paid, on Deeside, where the climate was particularly suitable to such as suffered from diseases of the lungs. It takes five or six weeks for letters to get from Aberdeen to Samoa, and several had to be exchanged. He had plenty of time to prepare Ethel. She was as delighted as a child. He was amused to see how she boasted to her friends that she was going to England; it was a step up for her; she would be quite English there; and she was excited at the interest the approaching departure gave her. When at length a cable came offering him a post in a bank in Kincardineshire she was beside herself with joy.

When, their long journey over, they were settled in the little Scots town with its granite houses Lawson realized how much it meant to him to live once more among his own people. He looked back on the three years he had spent in Apia as exile, and returned to the life that seemed the only normal one with a sigh of relief. It was good to play golf once more, and to fish – to fish properly, that was poor fun in the Pacific when you just threw in your line and pulled out one big sluggish fish after another from the crowded sea – and it was good to see a paper every day with that day's news, and to meet men and women of your own sort, people you could talk to; and it was good to eat meat that was not frozen and to drink milk that was not canned. They were thrown upon their own resources much more than in the Pacific, and he was glad to have Ethel exclusively to himself. After two years of marriage he loved her more devotedly than ever, he could hardly bear her out of his sight, and the need in him grew urgent for a more intimate communion between them. But it was strange that after the first excitement of arrival she seemed to take less interest in the new life than he had expected. She did not accustom herself to her surroundings. She was a little lethargic. As the fine autumn darkened into winter she complained of the cold. She lay half the morning in bed and the rest of the day on a sofa, reading novels sometimes, but more often doing nothing. She looked pinched.

"Never mind, darling," he said. "You'll get used to it very soon. And wait till the summer comes. It can be almost as hot as in Apia."

He felt better and stronger than he had done for years.

The carelessness with which she managed her house had not mattered in Samoa, but here it was out of place. When anyone came he did not want the place to look untidy; and, laughing, chaffing Ethel a little, he set about putting things in order. Ethel watched him indolently. She spent long hours playing with her son. She talked to him in the baby language of her own country. To distract her, Lawson bestirred himself to make friends among the neighbours, and now and then they went to little parties where the ladies sang drawing-room ballads and the men beamed in silent good nature. Ethel was shy. She seemed to sit apart. Sometimes Lawson, seized with a sudden anxiety, would ask her if she was happy.

"Yes, I'm quite happy," she answered.

But her eyes were veiled by some thought he could not guess. She seemed to withdraw into herself so that he was conscious that he knew no more of her than when he had first seen her bathing in the pool. He had an uneasy feeling that she was concealing something from him, and because he adored her it tortured him.

"You don't regret Apia, do you?" he asked her once.

"Oh, no – I think it's very nice here."

An obscure misgiving drove him to make disparaging remarks about the island and the people there. She smiled and did not answer. Very rarely she received a bundle of letters from Samoa and then she went about for a day or two with a set, pale face.

"Nothing would induce me ever to go back there," he said once. "It's no place for a white man."

But he grew conscious that sometimes, when he was away, Ethel cried. In Apia she had been talkative, chatting volubly about all the little details of their common life, the gossip of the place; but now she gradually became silent, and, though he increased his efforts to amuse her, she remained listless. It seemed to him that her recollections of the old life were drawing her away from him, and he was madly jealous of the island and of the sea, of Brevald, and all the dark-skinned people whom he remembered now with horror. When she spoke of Samoa he was bitter and satirical. One evening late in the spring when the birch trees were bursting into leaf, coming home from a round of golf, he found her not as usual lying on the sofa, but at the window, standing. She had evidently been waiting for his return. She addressed him the moment he came into the room. To his amazement she spoke in Samoan.

"I can't stand it. I can't live here any more. I hate it. I hate it."

"For God's sake speak in a civilized language," he said irritably. She went up to him and clasped her arms around his body awkwardly, with a gesture that had in it something barbaric. "Let's go away from here. Let's go back to Samoa. If you make me stay here I shall die. I want to go home."

Her passion broke suddenly and she burst into tears. His anger vanished and he drew her down on his knees. He explained to her that it was impossible for him to throw up his job, which after all meant his bread and butter. His place in Apia was long since filled. He had nothing to go back to there. He tried to put it to her reasonably, the inconveniences of life there, the humiliation to which they must be exposed, and the bitterness it must cause their son.

"Scotland's wonderful for education and that sort of thing. Schools are good and cheap, and he can go to the University at Aberdeen. I'll make a real Scot of him."

They had called him Andrew. Lawson wanted him to become a doctor. He would marry a white woman.

"I'm not ashamed of being half native," Ethel said sullenly.

"Of course not, darling. There's nothing to be ashamed of."

With her soft cheek against his he felt incredibly weak.

"You don't know how much I love you," he said. "I'd give anything in the world to be able to tell you what I've got in my heart."

He sought her lips.

The summer came. The highland valley was green and fragrant and the hills were gay with the heather. One sunny day followed another in that sheltered spot, and the shade of the birch trees was grateful after the glare of the high road. Ethel spoke no more of Samoa and Lawson grew less nervous. He thought that she was resigned to her surroundings, and he felt that his love for her was so passionate that it could leave no room in her heart for any longing. One day the local doctor stopped him in the street.

"I say, Lawson, your missus ought to be careful how she bathes in our highland streams. It's not like the Pacific, you know."

Lawson was surprised, and had not the presence of mind to conceal the fact.

"I didn't know she was bathing."

The doctor laughed.

"A good many people have seen her. It makes them talk a bit, you know, because it seems a rum place to choose, the pool up above the bridge, and bathing isn't allowed there, but there's no harm in that. I don't know how she can stand the water."

Lawson knew the pool the doctor spoke of, and suddenly it occurred to him that in a way it was just like that pool at Upolu where Ethel had been in the habit of bathing every evening. A clear highland stream ran down a sinuous course, rocky, splashing gaily, and then formed a deep, smooth pool, with a little sandy beach. Trees overshadowed it thickly, not coconut trees, but beeches, and the sun played fitfully through the leaves on the sparkling water. It gave him a shock. With his imagination he saw Ethel go there every day and undress on the bank and slip into the water, cold, colder than that of the pool she loved at home, and for a moment regain the feeling of the past. He saw her once more as the strange, wild spirit of the stream, and it seemed to him fantastically that the running water called her. That afternoon he went along to the river. He made his way cautiously among the trees and the grassy path deadened the sound of his steps. Presently he came to a spot from which he could see the pool. Ethel was sitting on the bank, looking down at the water. She sat quite still. It seemed as though the water drew her irresistibly. He wondered what strange thoughts wandered through her head. At last she got up, and for a minute or two she was hidden from his gaze; then he saw her again, wearing a Mother Hubbard, and with her little bare feet she stepped delicately over the mossy bank. She came to the water's edge, and softly, without a splash, let herself down. She swam about quietly, and there was something not quite of a human being in the way she swam. He did not know why it affected him so queerly. He waited till she clambered out. She stood for a moment with the wet folds of her dress clinging to her body, so that its shape was outlined, and then, passing her hands slowly over her breasts, gave a little sigh of delight. Then she disappeared. Lawson turned away and walked back to the village. He had a bitter pain in his heart, for he knew that she was still a stranger to him and his hungry love was destined ever to remain unsatisfied.

He did not make any mention of what he had seen. He ignored the incident completely, but he looked at her curiously, trying to divine what was in her mind. He redoubled the tenderness with which he used her. He sought to make her forget the deep longing of her soul by the passion of his love.

Then one day, when he came home, he was astonished to find her not in the house.

"Where's Mrs Lawson?" he asked the maid.

"She went into Aberdeen, Sir, with the baby," the maid answered, a little surprised at the question. "She said she would not be back till the last train."

"Oh, all right."

He was vexed that Ethel had said nothing to him about the excursion, but he was not disturbed, since of late she had been in now and again to Aberdeen, and he was glad that she should look at the shops and perhaps visit a cinema. He went to meet the last train, but when she did not come he grew suddenly frightened. He went up to the bedroom and saw at once that her toilet things were no longer in their place. He opened the wardrobe and the drawers. They were half empty. She had bolted.

He was seized with a passion of anger. It was too late that night to telephone to Aberdeen and make inquiries, but he knew already all that his inquiries might have taught him. With fiendish cunning she had chosen a time when they were making up their periodical accounts at the bank and there was no chance that he could follow her. He was imprisoned by his work. He took up a paper and saw that there was a boat sailing for Australia next morning. She must be now well on the way to London. He could not prevent the sobs that were wrung painfully from him.

"I've done everything in the world for her," he cried, "and she had the heart to treat me like this. How cruel, how monstrously cruel!"

After two days of misery he received a letter from her. It was written in her school-girl hand. She had always written with difficulty:

Dear Bertie –
  I couldn't stand it any more. I'm going home.
Good-bye.
Ethel

She did not say a single word of regret. She did not even ask him to come too. Lawson was prostrated. He found out where the ship made its first stop, and, though he knew very well she would not come, sent a cable beseeching her to return. He waited with pitiful anxiety. He wanted her to send him just one word of love; she did not even answer. He passed through one violent phase after another. At one moment he told himself that he was well rid of her, and at the next that he would force her to return by withholding money. He was lonely and wretched. He wanted his boy and he wanted her. He knew that, whatever he pretended to himself, there was only one thing to do and that was to follow her. He could never live without her now. All his plans for the future were like a house of cards and he scattered them with angry impatience. He did not care whether he threw away his chances for the future, for nothing in the world mattered but that he should get Ethel back again. As soon as he could he went into Aberdeen and told the manager of his bank that he meant to leave at once. The manager remonstrated. The short notice was inconvenient. Lawson would not listen to reason. He was determined to be free before the next boat sailed; and it was not until he was on board of her, having sold everything he possessed, that in some measure he regained his calm. Till then to those who had come in contact with him he seemed hardly sane. His last action in England was to cable to Ethel at Apia that he was joining her.

He sent another cable from Sydney, and when at last with the dawn his boat crossed the bar at Apia and he saw once more the white houses straggling along the bay he felt an immense relief.

The doctor came on board, and the agent. They were both old acquaintances and he felt kindly towards their familiar faces. He had a drink or two with them for old times' sake, and also because he was desperately nervous. He was not sure if Ethel would be glad to see him. When he got into the launch and approached the wharf he scanned anxiously the little crowd that waited. She was not there and his heart sank, but then he saw Brevald, in his old blue clothes, and his heart warmed towards him.

"Where's Ethel?" he said, as he jumped on shore.

"She's down at the bungalow. She's living with us."

Lawson was dismayed, but he put on a jovial air.

"Well, have you got room for me? I daresay it'll take a week or two to fix ourselves up."

"Oh, yes, I guess we can make room for you."

After passing through the custom-house they went to the hotel and there Lawson was greeted by several of his old friends. There were a good many rounds of drinks before it seemed possible to get away and when they did go at last to Brevald's house they were both rather gay. He clasped Ethel in his arms. He had forgotten all his bitter thoughts in the joy of beholding her once more. His mother-in-law was pleased to see him, and so was the old, wrinkled beldame, her mother; natives and half-castes came in, and they all sat round, beaming on him. Brevald had a bottle of whisky and everyone who came was given a nip. Lawson sat with his little dark-skinned boy on his knees, they had taken his English clothes off him and he was stark, with Ethel by his side in a Mother Hubbard. He felt like a returning prodigal. In the afternoon he went down to the hotel again and when he got back he was more than gay, he was drunk. Ethel and her mother knew that white men got drunk now and then, it was what you expected of them, and they laughed good-naturedly as they helped him to bed.

But in a day or two he set about looking for a job. He knew that he could not hope for such a position as that which he had thrown away to go to England; but with his training he could not fail to be useful to one of the trading firms, and perhaps in the end he would not lose by the change.

"After all, you can't make money in a bank," he said. "Trade's the thing."

He had hopes that he would soon make himself so indispensable that he would get someone to take him into partnership, and there was no reason why in a few years he should not be a rich man.

"As soon as I'm fixed up we'll find ourselves a shack," he told Ethel. "We can't go on living here."

Brevald's bungalow was so small that they were all piled on one another, and there was no chance of ever being alone. There was neither peace nor privacy.

"Well, there's no hurry. We shall be all right here till we find just what we want."

It took him a week to get settled and then he entered the firm of a man called Bain. But when he talked to Ethel about moving she said she wanted to stay where she was till her baby was born, for she was expecting another child. Lawson tried to argue with her.

"If you don't like it," she said, "go and live at the hotel."

He grew suddenly pale.

"Ethel, how can you suggest that!"

She shrugged her shoulders.

"What's the good of having a house of our own when we can live here."

He yielded.

When Lawson, after his work, went back to the bungalow he found it crowded with natives. They lay about smoking, sleeping, drinking *kava*; and they talked incessantly. The place was grubby and untidy. His child crawled about, playing with native children, and it heard nothing spoken but Samoan. He fell into the habit of dropping into the hotel on his way home to have a few cocktails, for he could only face the evening and the crowd of friendly natives when he was fortified with liquor. And all the time, though he loved her more passionately than ever, he felt that Ethel was slipping away from him. When the baby was born he suggested that they should get into a house of their own, but Ethel refused. Her stay in Scotland seemed to have thrown her back on her own people, now that she was once more among them, with a passionate zest, and she turned to her native ways with abandon. Lawson began to drink more. Every Saturday night he went to the English Club and got blind drunk.

He had the peculiarity that as he grew drunk he grew quarrelsome and once he had a violent dispute with Bain, his employer. Bain dismissed him, and he had to look out for another job. He was idle for two or three weeks and during these, sooner than sit in the bungalow, he lounged about in the hotel or at the English Club, and drank. It was more out of pity than anything else that Miller, the German-American, took him into his office; but he was a business-man, and though Lawson's financial skill made him valuable, the circumstances were such that he could hardly refuse a smaller salary than he had had before, and Miller did not hesitate to offer it to him. Ethel and Brevald blamed him for taking it, since Pedersen, the half-caste, offered him more. But he resented bitterly the thought of being under the orders of a half-caste. When Ethel nagged him he burst out furiously:

"I'll see myself dead before I work for a nigger."

"You may have to," she said.

And in six months he found himself forced to this final humili-ation. The passion for liquor had been gaining on him, he was often heavy with drink, and he did his work badly. Miller warned him once or twice and Lawson was not the man to accept remonstrance easily. One day in the midst of an altercation he put on his hat and walked out. But by now his reputation was well known and he could find no one to engage him. For a while he idled, and then he had an attack of delirium tremens. When he recovered, shameful and weak, he could no longer resist the constant pressure and he went to Pedersen and asked him for a job. Pedersen was glad to have a white man in his store and Lawson's skill at figures made him useful.

From that time his degeneration was rapid. The white people gave him the cold shoulder. They were only prevented from cutting him completely by disdainful pity and by a certain dread of his angry violence when he was drunk. He became extremely susceptible and was always on the lookout for affront.

He lived entirely among the natives and half-castes, but he had no longer the prestige of the white man. They felt his loathing for them and they resented his attitude of superiority. He was one of themselves now and they did not see why he should put on airs. Brevald, who had been ingratiating and obsequious, now treated him with contempt. Ethel had made a bad bargain. There were disgrace-ful scenes and once or twice the two men came to blows. When there was a quarrel Ethel took the part of her family. They found he was better drunk than sober, for when he was drunk he would lie on the bed or on the floor, sleeping heavily.

Then he became aware that something was being hidden from him.

When he got back to the bungalow for the wretched, half-native supper which was his evening meal, often Ethel was not in. If he asked where she was Brevald told him she had gone to spend the evening with one or other of her friends. Once he followed her to the house Brevald had mentioned and found she was not there. On her return he asked her where she had been and she told him her father had made a mistake; she had been to so-and-so's. But he knew that she was lying. She was in her best clothes; her eyes were shining, and she looked lovely.

"Don't try any monkey tricks on me, my girl," he said, "or I'll break every bone in your body."

"You drunken beast," she said, scornfully.

He fancied that Mrs Brevald and the old grandmother looked at him maliciously and he ascribed Brevald's good humour with him, so unusual those days, to his satisfaction at having something up his sleeve against his son-in-law. And then, his suspicions aroused, he imagined that the white men gave him curious glances. When he came into the lounge of the hotel the sudden silence which fell upon the company convinced him that he had been the subject of the conversation. Something was going on and everyone knew it but himself. He was seized with furious jealousy. He believed that Ethel was carrying on with one of the white men, and he looked at one after the other with scrutinizing eyes; but there was nothing to give him even a hint. He was helpless. Because he could find no one on whom definitely to fix his suspicions, he went about like a raving maniac, looking for someone on whom to vent his wrath. Chance caused him in the end to hit upon the man who of all others least deserved to suffer from his violence. One afternoon, when he was sitting in the hotel by himself, moodily, Chaplin came in and sat down beside him. Perhaps Chaplin was the only man on the island who had any sympathy for him. They ordered drinks and chatted a few minutes about the races that were shortly to be run. Then Chaplin said: "I guess we shall all have to fork out money for new dresses." Lawson sniggered. Since Mrs Chaplin held the purse-strings, if she wanted a new frock for the occasion she would certainly not ask her husband for the money.

"How is your missus?" asked Chaplin, desiring to be friendly.

"What the hell's that got to do with you?" said Lawson, knitting his dark brows.

"I was only asking a civil question."

"Well, keep your civil questions to yourself."

Chaplin was not a patient man; his long residence in the tropics, the whisky bottle, and his domestic affairs had given him a temper hardly more under control than Lawson's.

"Look here, my boy, when you're in my hotel you behave like a gentleman or you'll find yourself in the street before you can say knife."

Lawson's lowering face grew dark and red.

"Let me just tell you once for all and you can pass it on to the others," he said, panting with rage. "If any of you fellows come messing round with my wife he'd better look out."

"Who do you think wants to mess around with your wife?"

"I'm not such a fool as you think. I can see a stone wall in front of me as well as most men, and I warn you straight, that's all. I'm not going to put up with any hanky-panky, not on your life."

"Look here, you'd better clear out of here, and come back when you're sober."

"I shall clear out when I choose and not a minute before," said Lawson.

It was an unfortunate boast, for Chaplin in the course of his experience as a hotel-keeper had acquired a peculiar skill in dealing with gentlemen whose room he preferred to their company, and the words were hardly out of Lawson's mouth before he found himself caught by the collar and arm and hustled not without force into the street. He stumbled down the steps into the blinding glare of the sun.

It was in consequence of this that he had his first violent scene with Ethel. Smarting with humiliation and unwilling to go back to the hotel, he went home that afternoon earlier than usual. He found Ethel dressing to go out. As a rule she lay about in a Mother Hubbard, barefoot, with a flower in her dark hair; but now, in white silk stockings and high-heeled shoes, she was doing up a pink muslin dress which was the newest she had.

"You're making yourself very smart," he said. "Where are you going?"

"I'm going to the Crossleys."

"I'll come with you."

"Why?" she asked coolly.

"I don't want you to gad about by yourself all the time."

"You're not asked."

"I don't care a damn about that. You're not going without me."

"You'd better lie down till I'm ready."

She thought he was drunk and if he once settled himself on the bed would quickly drop off to sleep. He sat down on a chair and began to smoke a cigarette. She watched him with increasing irritation. When she was ready he got up. It happened by an unusual chance that there was no one in the bungalow. Brevald was working on the plantation and his wife had gone into Apia. Ethel faced him.

"I'm not going with you. You're drunk."

"That's a lie. You're not going without me."

She shrugged her shoulders and tried to pass him, but he caught her by the arm and held her.

"Let me go, you devil," she said, breaking into Samoan.

"Why do you want to go without me? Haven't I told you I'm not going to put up with any monkey tricks?"

She clenched her fist and hit him in the face. He lost all control of himself. All his love, all his hatred, welled up in him and he was beside himself.

"I'll teach you," he shouted. "I'll teach you."

He seized a riding-whip which happened to be under his hand, and struck her with it. She screamed, and the scream maddened him so that he went on striking her, again and again. Her shrieks rang through the bungalow and he cursed her as he hit. Then he flung her on the bed. She lay there sobbing with pain and terror. He threw the whip away from him and rushed out of the room. Ethel heard him go and she stopped crying. She looked round cautiously, then she raised herself. She was sore, but she had not been badly hurt, and she looked at her dress to see if it was damaged. The native women are not unused to blows. What he had done did not outrage her. When she looked at herself in the glass and arranged her hair, her eyes were shining. There was a strange look in them.

Perhaps then she was nearer loving him than she had ever been before.

But Lawson, driven forth blindly, stumbled through the plantation and, suddenly exhausted, weak as a child, flung himself on the ground at the foot of a tree. He was miserable and ashamed. He thought of Ethel, and in the yielding tenderness of his love all his bones seemed to grow soft within him. He thought of the past, and of his hopes, and he was aghast at what he had done. He wanted her more than ever. He wanted to take her in his arms. He must go to her at once. He got up. He was so weak that he staggered as he walked. He went into the house and she was sitting in their cramped bedroom in front of her looking-glass.

"Oh, Ethel, forgive me. I'm so awfully ashamed of myself. I didn't know what I was doing."

He fell on his knees before her and timidly stroked the skirt of her dress.

"I can't bear to think of what I did. It's awful. I think I was mad. There's no one in the world I love as I love you. I'd do anything to save you from pain and I've hurt you. I can never forgive myself, but for God's sake say you forgive me."

He heard her shrieks still. It was unendurable. She looked at him silently. He tried to take her hands and the tears streamed from his eyes. In his humiliation he hid his face in her lap and his frail body shook with sobs. An expression of utter contempt came over her face. She had the native woman's disdain of a man who abased himself before a woman. A weak creature! And for a moment she had been on the point of thinking there was something in him. He grovelled at her feet like a cur. She gave him a little scornful kick.

"Get out," she said. "I hate you."

He tried to hold her, but she pushed him aside. She stood up. She began to take off her dress. She kicked off her shoes and slid the stockings off her feet, then she slipped on her old Mother Hubbard.

"Where are you going?"

"What's that got to do with you? I'm going down to the pool."

"Let me come too," he said.

He asked as though he were a child.

"Can't you even leave me that?"

He hid his face in his hands, crying miserably, while she, her eyes hard and cold, stepped past him and went out.

From that time she entirely despised him; and though, herded together in the small bungalow, Lawson and Ethel with her two children, Brevald, his wife and her mother, and the vague relations and hangers-on who were always in and about, they had to live cheek by jowl, Lawson, ceasing to be of any account, was hardly noticed. He left in the morning after breakfast, and came back only to have supper. He gave up the struggle, and when for want of money he could not go to the English Club he spent the evening playing hearts with old Brevald and the natives. Except when he was drunk he was cowed and listless. Ethel treated him like a dog. She submitted at times to his fits of wild passion, and she was frightened by the gusts of hatred with which they were followed; but when, afterwards, he was cringing and lachrymose she had such a contempt for him that she could have spat in his face. Sometimes he was violent, but now she was prepared for him, and when he hit her she kicked and scratched and bit. They had horrible battles in which he had not always the best of it. Very soon it was known all over Apia that they got on badly. There was little sympathy for Lawson, and at the hotel the general surprise was that old Brevald did not kick him out of the place.

"Brevald's a pretty ugly customer," said one of the men. "I shouldn't be surprised if he put a bullet into Lawson's carcass one of these days."

Ethel still went in the evenings to bathe in the silent pool. It seemed to have an attraction for her that was not quite human, just that attraction you might imagine that a mermaid who had won a soul would have for the cool salt waves of the sea; and sometimes Lawson went also. I do not know what urged him to go, for Ethel was obviously irritated by his presence; perhaps it was because in that spot he hoped to regain the clean rapture which had filled his heart when first he saw her; perhaps only, with the madness of those who love them that love them not, from the feeling that his obstinacy could force love. One day he strolled down there with a feeling that was rare with him now. He felt suddenly at peace with the world. The evening was drawing in and the dusk seemed to cling to the leaves of the coconut trees like a little thin cloud. A faint breeze stirred them noiselessly. A crescent moon hung just over their tops. He made his way to the bank. He saw Ethel in the water floating on her back. Her hair streamed out all round her, and she was holding in her hand a large hibiscus. He stopped a moment to admire her; she was like Ophelia.

"Hullo, Ethel," he cried joyfully.

She made a sudden movement and dropped the red flower. It floated idly away. She swam a stroke or two till she knew there was ground within her depth and then stood up.

"Go away," she said. "Go away."

He laughed.

"Don't be selfish. There's plenty of room for both of us."

"Why can't you leave me alone? I want to be by myself."

"Hang it all, I want to bathe," he answered, good-humouredly.

"Go down to the bridge. I don't want you here."

"I'm sorry for that," he said, smiling still.

He was not in the least angry, and he hardly noticed that she was in a passion. He began to take off his coat.

"Go away," she shrieked. "I won't have you here. Can't you even leave me this? Go away."

"Don't be silly, darling."

She bent down and picked up a sharp stone and flung it quickly at him. He had no time to duck. It hit him on the temple. With a cry he put his hand to his head and when he took it away it was wet with blood. Ethel stood still, panting with rage. He turned very pale, and without a word, taking up his coat, went away. Ethel let herself fall back into the water and the stream carried her slowly down to the ford.

The stone had made a jagged wound and for some days Lawson went about with a bandaged head. He had invented a likely story to account for the accident when the fellows at the club asked him about it, but he had no occasion to use it. No one referred to the matter. He saw them cast surreptitious glances at his head, but not a word was said. The silence could only mean that they knew how he came by his wound. He was certain now that Ethel had a lover, and they all knew who it was. But there was not the smallest indication to guide him. He never saw Ethel with anyone; no one showed a wish to be with her, or treated him in a manner that seemed strange. Wild rage seized him, and having no one to vent it on he drank more and more heavily. A little while before I came to the island he had had another attack of delirium tremens.

I met Ethel at the house of a man called Caster, who lived two or three miles from Apia with a native wife. I had been playing tennis with him and when we were tired he suggested a cup of tea. We went into the house and in the untidy living-room found Ethel chatting with Mrs Caster.

"Hullo, Ethel," he said, "I didn't know you were here."

I could not help looking at her with curiosity. I tried to see what there was in her to have excited in Lawson such a devastating passion. But who can explain these things? It was true that she was lovely; she reminded one of the red hibiscus, the common flower of the hedge-row in Samoa, with its grace and its languor and its passion; but what surprised me most, taking into consideration the story I knew even then a good deal of, was her freshness and simplicity. She was quiet and a little shy. There was nothing coarse or loud about her; she had not the exuberance common to the half-caste; and it was almost impossible to believe that she could be the virago that the horrible scenes between husband and wife, which were now common knowledge, indicated. In her pretty pink frock and high-heeled shoes she looked quite European. You could hardly have guessed at that dark background of native life in which she felt herself so much more at home. I did not imagine that she was at all intelligent, and I should not have been surprised if a man, after living with her for some time, had found the passion which had drawn him to her sink into boredom. It suggested itself to me that in her elusiveness, like a thought that presents itself to consciousness and vanishes before it can be captured by words, lay her peculiar charm; but perhaps that was merely fancy, and if I had known nothing about her I should have seen in her only a pretty little half-caste like another.

She talked to me of the various things which they talk of to the stranger in Samoa, of the journey, and whether I had slid down the water rock at Papaseea, and if I meant to stay in a native village. She talked to me of Scotland, and perhaps I noticed in her a tendency to enlarge on the sumptuousness of her establishment there. She asked me naïvely if I knew Mrs This and Mrs That, with whom she had been acquainted when she lived in the north.

Then Miller, the fat German-American, came in. He shook hands all round very cordially and sat down, asking in his loud, cheerful voice for a whisky and soda. He was very fat and he sweated profusely. He took off his gold-rimmed spectacles and wiped them; you saw then that his little eyes, benevolent behind the large round glasses, were shrewd and cunning; the party had been somewhat dull till he came, but he was a good story-teller and a jovial fellow. Soon he had the two women, Ethel and my friend's wife, laughing delightedly at his sallies. He had a reputation on the island of a lady's man, and you could see how this fat, gross fellow, old and ugly, had yet the possibility of fascination. His humour was on a level with the understanding of his company, an affair of vitality and assurance, and his Western accent gave a peculiar point to what he said. At last he turned to me:

"Well, if we want to get back for dinner we'd better be getting. I'll take you along in my machine if you like."

I thanked him and got up. He shook hands with the others, went out of the room, massive and strong in his walk, and climbed into his car.

"Pretty little thing, Lawson's wife," I said, as we drove along. "Too bad the way he treats her. Knocks her about. Gets my dander up when I hear of a man hitting a woman."

We went on a little. Then he said:

"He was a darned fool to marry her. I said so at the time. If he hadn't, he'd have had the whip hand over her. He's yaller, that's what he is, yaller."

The year was drawing to its end and the time approached when I was to leave Samoa. My boat was scheduled to sail for Sydney on the fourth of January. Christmas Day had been celebrated at the hotel with suitable ceremonies, but it was looked upon as no more than a rehearsal for New Year, and the men who were accustomed to foregather in the lounge determined on New Year's Eve to make a night of it. There was an uproarious dinner, after which the party sauntered down to the English Club, a simple little frame house, to play pool. There was a great deal of talking, laughing, and betting, but some very poor play, except on the part of Miller, who had drunk as much as any of them, all far younger than he, but had kept unimpaired the keenness of his eye and the sureness of his hand.

He pocketed the young men's money with humour and urbanity. After an hour of this I grew tired and went out. I crossed the road and came to the beach. Three coconut trees grew there, like three moon maidens waiting for their lovers to ride out of the sea, and I sat at the foot of one of them, watching the lagoon and the nightly assemblage of the stars.

I do not know where Lawson had been during the evening, but between ten and eleven he came along to the club. He shambled down the dusty, empty road, feeling dull and bored, and when he reached the club, before going into the billiard-room, went into the bar to have a drink by himself. He had a shyness now about joining the company of white men when there were a lot of them together and needed a stiff dose of whisky to give him confidence. He was standing with the glass in his hand when Miller came in to him. He was in his shirt-sleeves and still held his cue. He gave the bar-tender a glance.

"Get out, Jack," he said.

The bar-tender, a native in a white jacket and a red lava-lava, without a word slid out of the small room.

"Look here, I've been wanting to have a few words with you, Lawson," said the big American.

"Well, that's one of the few things you can have free, gratis, and for nothing on this damned island."

Miller fixed his gold spectacles more firmly on his nose and held Lawson with his cold determined eyes.

"See here, young fellow, I understand you've been knocking Mrs Lawson about again. I'm not going to stand for that. If you don't stop it right now I'll break every bone of your dirty little body."

Then Lawson knew what he had been trying to find out so long. It was Miller. The appearance of the man, fat, bald-headed, with his round bare face and double chin and the gold spectacles, his age, his benign, shrewd look, like that of a renegade priest, and the thought of Ethel, so slim and virginal, filled him with a sudden horror. Whatever his faults Lawson was no coward, and without a word he hit out violently at Miller. Miller quickly warded the blow with the hand that held the cue, and then with a great swing of his right arm brought his fist down on Lawson's ear. Lawson was four inches shorter than the American and he was slightly built, frail and weakened not only by illness and the enervating tropics, but by drink. He fell like a log and lay half dazed at the foot of the bar. Miller took off his spectacles and wiped them with his handkerchief.

"I guess you know what to expect now. You've had your warning and you'd better take it."

He took up his cue and went back into the billiard-room. There was so much noise there that no one knew what had happened. Lawson picked himself up. He put his hand to his ear, which was singing still. Then he slunk out of the club.

I saw a man cross the road, a patch of white against the darkness of the night, but did not know who it was. He came down to the beach, passed me sitting at the foot of the tree, and looked down. I saw then that it was Lawson, but since he was doubtless drunk, did not speak. He went on, walked irresolutely two or three steps, and turned back. He came up to me and bending down stared in my face.

"I thought it was you," he said.

He sat down and took out his pipe.

"It was hot and noisy in the club," I volunteered.

"Why are you sitting here?"

"I was waiting about for the midnight mass at the Cathedral."

"If you like I'll come with you."

Lawson was quite sober. We sat for a while smoking in silence. Now and then in the lagoon was the splash of some big fish, and a little way out towards the opening in the reef was the light of a schooner.

"You're sailing next week, aren't you?" he said.

"Yes."

"It would be jolly to go home once more. But I could never stand it now. The cold, you know."

"It's odd to think that in England now they're shivering round the fire," I said.

There was not even a breath of wind. The balminess of the night was like a spell. I wore nothing but a thin shirt and a suit of ducks. I enjoyed the exquisite languor of the night, and stretched my limbs voluptuously.

"This isn't the sort of New Year's Eve that persuades one to make good resolutions for the future," I smiled.

He made no answer, but I do not know what train of thought my casual remark had suggested in him, for presently he began to speak. He spoke in a low voice, without any expression, but his accents were educated, and it was a relief to hear him after the twang and the vulgar intonations which for some time had wounded my ears.

"I've made an awful hash of things. That's obvious, isn't it? I'm right down at the bottom of the pit and there's no getting out for me. '*Black as the pit from pole to pole.*'" I felt him smile as he made the quotation. "And the strange thing is that I don't see how I went wrong."

I held my breath, for to me there is nothing more awe-inspiring than when a man discovers to you the nakedness of his soul. Then you see that no one is so trivial or debased but that in him is a spark of something to excite compassion.

"It wouldn't be so rotten if I could see that it was all my own fault. It's true I drink, but I shouldn't have taken to that if things had gone differently. I wasn't really fond of liquor. I suppose I ought not to have married Ethel. If I'd kept her it would be all right. But I did love her so."

His voice faltered.

"She's not a bad lot, you know, not really. It's just rotten luck. We might have been as happy as lords. When she bolted I suppose I ought to have let her go, but I couldn't do that – I was dead stuck on her then; and there was the kid."

"Are you fond of the kid?" I asked.

"I was. There are two, you know. But they don't mean so much to me now. You'd take them for natives anywhere. I have to talk to them in Samoan."

"Is it too late for you to start fresh? Couldn't you make a dash for it and leave the place?"

"I haven't the strength. I'm done for."

"Are you still in love with your wife?"

"Not now. Not now." He repeated the two words with a kind of horror in his voice. "I haven't even got that now. I'm down and out."

The bells of the Cathedral were ringing.

"If you really want to come to the midnight mass we'd better go along," I said.

"Come on."

We got up and walked along the road. The Cathedral, all white, stood facing the sea not without impressiveness, and beside it the Protestant chapels had the look of meeting-houses. In the road were two or three cars, and a great number of traps, and traps were put up against the walls at the side. People had come from all parts of the island for the service, and through the great open doors we saw that the place was crowded. The high altar was all ablaze with light. There were a few whites and a good many half-castes, but the great majority were natives. All the men wore trousers, for the Church had decided that the lava-lava is indecent. We found chairs at the back, near the open door, and sat down. Presently, following Lawson's eyes, I saw Ethel come in with a party of half-castes. They were all very much dressed up, the men in high, stiff collars and shiny boots, the women in large, gay hats. Ethel nodded and smiled to her friends as she passed up the aisle. The service began.

When it was over Lawson and I stood on one side for a while to watch the crowd stream out, then he held out his hand.

"Good night," he said. "I hope you'll have a pleasant journey home."

"Oh, but I shall see you before I go."

He sniggered.

"The question is if you'll see me drunk or sober."

He turned and left me. I had a recollection of those very large black eyes, shining wildly under the shaggy brows. I paused irresolutely. I did not feel sleepy and I thought I would at all events go along to the club for an hour before turning in. When I got there I found the billiard-room empty, but half-a-dozen men were sitting round a table in the lounge, playing poker. Miller looked up as I came in.

"Sit down and take a hand," he said.

"All right."

I bought some chips and began to play. Of course it is the most fascinating game in the world and my hour lengthened out to two, and then to three. The native bar-tender, cheery and wide-awake notwithstanding the time, was at our elbow to supply us with drinks and from somewhere or other he produced a ham and a loaf of bread. We played on. Most of the party had drunk more than was good for them and the play was high and reckless. I played modestly, neither wishing to win nor anxious to lose, but I watched Miller with a fascinated interest. He drank glass for glass with the rest of the company, but remained cool and level-headed. His pile of chips increased in size and he had a neat little paper in front of him on which he had marked various sums lent to players in distress. He beamed amiably at the young men whose money he was taking. He kept up interminably his stream of jest and anecdote, but he never missed a draw, he never let an expression of the face pass him. At last the dawn crept into the windows, gently, with a sort of deprecating shyness, as though it had no business there, and then it was day.

"Well," said Miller. "I reckon we've seen the old year out in style. Now let's have a round of jackpots and me for my mosquito net. I'm fifty, remember, I can't keep these late hours."

The morning was beautiful and fresh when we stood on the veranda, and the lagoon was like a sheet of multi-coloured glass. Someone suggested a dip before going to bed, but none cared to bathe in the lagoon, sticky and treacherous to the feet. Miller had his car at the door and he offered to take us down to the pool. We jumped in and drove along the deserted road. When we reached the pool it seemed as though the day had hardly risen there yet. Under the trees the water was all in shadow and the night had the effects of lurking still. We were in great spirits. We had no towels or any costume and in my prudence I wondered how we were going to dry ourselves. None of us had much on and it did not take us long to snatch off our clothes. Nelson, the little super-cargo, was stripped first.

"I'm going down to the bottom," he said.

He dived and in a moment another man dived too, but shallow, and was out of the water before him. Then Nelson came up and scrambled to the side.

"I say, get me out," he said.

"What's up?"

Something was evidently the matter. His face was terrified. Two fellows gave him their hands and he slithered up.

"I say, there's a man down there."

"Don't be a fool. You're drunk."

"Well, if there isn't I'm in for DTs. But I tell you there's a man down there. It just scared me out of my wits."

Miller looked at him for a moment. The little man was all white. He was actually trembling.

"Come on, Caster," said Miller to the big Australian, "we'd better go down and see."

"He was standing up," said Nelson, "all dressed. I saw him. He tried to catch hold of me."

"Hold your row," said Miller. "Are you ready?"

They dived in. We waited on the bank, silent. It really seemed as though they were underwater longer than any men could breathe. Then Caster came up, and immediately after him, red in the face as though he were going to have a fit, Miller. They were pulling something behind them. Another man jumped in to help them, and the three together dragged their burden to the side. They shoved it up. Then we saw that it was Lawson, with a great stone tied up in his coat and bound to his feet.

"He was set on making a good job of it," said Miller, as he wiped the water from his short-sighted eyes.

MACKINTOSH

HE SPLASHED ABOUT for a few minutes in the sea; it was too shallow to swim in and for fear of sharks he could not go out of his depth; then he got out and went into the bath-house for a shower. The coldness of the fresh water was grateful after the heavy stickiness of the salt Pacific, so warm, though it was only just after seven, that to bathe in it did not brace you but rather increased your languor; and when he had dried himself, slipping into a bath-gown, he called out to the Chinese cook that he would be ready for breakfast in five minutes. He walked barefoot across the patch of coarse grass which Walker, the administrator, proudly thought was a lawn, to his own quarters and dressed. This did not take long, for he put on nothing but a shirt and a pair of duck trousers and then went over to his chief's house on the other side of the compound. The two men had their meals together, but the Chinese cook told him that

Walker had set out on horseback at five and would not be back for another hour.

Mackintosh had slept badly and he looked with distaste at the paw-paw and the eggs and bacon which were set before him. The mosquitoes had been maddening that night; they flew about the net under which he slept in such numbers that their humming, pitiless and menacing, had the effect of a note, infinitely drawn out, played on a distant organ, and whenever he dozed off he awoke with a start in the belief that one had found its way inside his curtains. It was so hot that he lay naked. He turned from side to side. And gradually the dull roar of the breakers on the reef, so unceasing and so regular that generally you did not hear it, grew distinct on his consciousness, its rhythm hammered on his tired nerves and he held himself with clenched hands in the effort to bear it. The thought that nothing could stop that sound, for it would continue to all eternity, was almost impossible to bear, and, as though his strength were a match for the ruthless forces of nature, he had an insane impulse to do some violent thing. He felt he must cling to his self-control or he would go mad. And now, looking out of the window at the lagoon and the strip of foam which marked the reef, he shuddered with hatred of the brilliant scene. The cloudless sky was like an inverted bowl that hemmed it in. He lit his pipe and turned over the pile of Auckland papers that had come over from Apia a few days before. The newest of them was three weeks old. They gave an impression of incredible dullness.

Then he went into the office. It was a large, bare room with two desks in it and a bench along one side. A number of natives were seated on this, and a couple of women. They gossiped while they waited for the administrator, and when Mackintosh came in they greeted him.

"*Talofa-li.*"

He returned their greeting and sat down at his desk. He began to write, working on a report which the governor of Samoa had been clamouring for and which Walker, with his usual dilatoriness, had neglected to prepare. Mackintosh as he made his notes reflected vindictively that Walker was late with his report because he was so illiterate that he had an invincible distaste for anything to do with pens and paper; and now when it was at last ready, concise and neatly official, he would accept his subordinate's work without a word of appreciation, with a sneer rather or a gibe, and send it on to his own superior as though it were his own composition. He could not have written a word of it. Mackintosh thought with rage that if his chief pencilled in some insertion it would be childish in expression and faulty in language. If he remonstrated or sought to put his meaning into an intelligible phrase, Walker would fly into a passion and cry:

"What the hell do I care about grammar? That's what I want to say and that's how I want to say it."

At last Walker came in. The natives surrounded him as he entered, trying to get his immediate attention, but he turned on them roughly and told them to sit down and hold their tongues. He threatened that if they were not quiet he would have them all turned out and see none of them that day. He nodded to Mackintosh.

"Hullo, Mac; up at last? I don't know how you can waste the best part of the day in bed. You ought to have been up before dawn like me. Lazy beggar."

He threw himself heavily into his chair and wiped his face with a large bandana.

"By heaven, I've got a thirst."

He turned to the policeman who stood at the door, a picturesque figure in his white jacket and lava-lava, the loincloth of the Samoan, and told him to bring *kava*. The *kava* bowl stood on the floor in the corner of the room, and the policeman filled a half coconut shell and brought it to Walker. He poured a few drops on the ground, murmured the customary words to the company, and drank with relish. Then he told the policeman to serve the waiting natives, and the shell was handed to each one in order of birth or importance and emptied with the same ceremonies.

Then he set about the day's work. He was a little man, considerably less than of middle height, and enormously stout; he had a large, fleshy face, clean-shaven, with the cheeks hanging on each side in great dew-laps, and three vast chins; his small features were all dissolved in fat; and, but for a crescent of white hair at the back of his head, he was completely bald. He reminded you of Mr Pickwick. He was grotesque, a figure of fun, and yet, strangely enough, not without dignity. His blue eyes, behind large gold-rimmed spectacles, were shrewd and vivacious, and there was a great deal of determination in his face. He was sixty, but his native vitality triumphed over advancing years. Notwithstanding his corpulence his movements were quick, and he walked with a heavy, resolute tread as though he sought to impress his weight upon the earth. He spoke in a loud, gruff voice.

It was two years now since Mackintosh had been appointed Walker's assistant. Walker, who had been for a quarter of a century administrator of Talua, one of the larger islands in the Samoan group, was a man known in person or by report through the length and breadth of the South Seas; and it was with lively curiosity that Mackintosh looked forward to his first meeting with him. For one reason or another he stayed a couple of weeks at Apia before he took up his post and both at Chaplin's hotel and at the English Club he heard innumerable stories about the administrator. He thought now with irony of his interest in them. Since then he had heard them a hundred times from Walker himself. Walker knew that he was a character and, proud of his reputation, deliberately acted up to it. He was jealous of his "legend" and anxious that you should know the exact details of any of the celebrated stories that were told of him. He was ludicrously angry with anyone who had told them to the stranger incorrectly.

There was a rough cordiality about Walker which Mackintosh at first found not unattractive, and Walker, glad to have a listener to whom all he said was fresh, gave of his best. He was good-humoured, hearty, and considerate. To Mackintosh, who had lived the sheltered life of a government official in London till at the age of thirty-four an attack of pneumonia, leaving him with the threat of tuberculosis, had forced him to seek a post in the Pacific, Walker's existence seemed extraordinarily romantic. The adventure with which he started on his conquest of circumstance was typical of the man. He ran away to sea when he was fifteen and for over a year was employed in shovelling coal on a collier. He was an undersized boy and both men and mates were kind to him, but the captain for some reason conceived a savage dislike of him. He used the lad cruelly so that, beaten and kicked, he often could not sleep for the pain that racked his limbs. He loathed the captain with all his soul. Then he was given a tip for some race and managed to borrow twenty-five pounds from a friend he had picked up in Belfast. He put it on the horse, an outsider, at long odds. He had no means of repaying the money if he lost, but it never occurred to him that he could lose. He felt himself in luck. The horse won and he found himself with something over a thousand pounds in hard cash. Now his chance had come. He found out who was the best solicitor in the town – the collier lay then somewhere on the Irish coast – went to him, and, telling him that he heard the ship was for sale, asked him to arrange the purchase for him. The solicitor was amused at his small client, he was only sixteen and did not look so old, and, moved perhaps by sympathy, promised not only to arrange the matter for him but to see that he made a good bargain. After a little while Walker found himself the owner of the ship. He went back to her and had what he described as the most glorious moment of his life when he gave the skipper notice and told him that he must get off *his* ship in half an hour. He made the mate captain and sailed on the collier for another nine months, at the end of which he sold her at a profit.

He came out to the islands at the age of twenty-six as a planter. He was one of the few white men settled in Talua at the time of the German occupation and had then already some influence with the natives. The Germans made him administrator, a position which he occupied for twenty years, and when the island was seized by the British he was confirmed in his post. He ruled the island despotically, but with complete success. The prestige of this success was another reason for the interest that Mackintosh took in him.

But the two men were not made to get on. Mackintosh was an ugly man, with ungainly gestures, a tall thin fellow, with a narrow chest and bowed shoulders. He had sallow, sunken cheeks, and his eyes were large and sombre. He was a great reader, and when his books arrived and were unpacked Walker came over to his quarters and looked at them. Then he turned to Mackintosh with a coarse laugh.

"What in Hell have you brought all this muck for?" he asked. Mackintosh flushed darkly.

"I'm sorry you think it muck. I brought my books because I want to read them."

"When you said you'd got a lot of books coming I thought there'd be something for me to read. Haven't you got any detective stories?"

"Detective stories don't interest me."

"You're a damned fool then."

"I'm content that you should think so."

Every mail brought Walker a mass of periodical literature, papers from New Zealand and magazines from America, and it exasperated him that Mackintosh showed his contempt for these ephemeral publications. He had no patience with the books that absorbed Mackintosh's leisure and thought it only a pose that he read Gibbon's *Decline and Fall* or Burton's *Anatomy of Melancholy*. And since he had never learned to put any restraint on his tongue, he expressed his opinion of his assistant freely. Mackintosh began to see the real man, and under the boisterous good-humour he discerned a vulgar cunning which was hateful; he was vain and domineering, and it was strange that he had notwithstanding a shyness which made him dislike people who were not quite of his kidney. He judged others, naïvely, by their language, and if it was free from the oaths and the obscenity which made up the greater part of his own conversation, he looked upon them with suspicion. In the evening the two men played piquet. He played badly but vaingloriously, crowing over his opponent when he won and losing his temper when he lost. On rare occasions a couple of planters or traders would drive over to play bridge, and then Walker showed himself in what Mackintosh considered a characteristic light. He played regardless of his partner, calling up in his desire to play the hand, and argued interminably, beating down opposition by the loudness of his voice. He constantly revoked, and when he did so said with an ingratiating whine: "Oh, you wouldn't count it against an old man who can hardly see." Did he know that his opponents thought it as well to keep on the right side of him and hesitated to insist on the rigour of the game? Mackintosh watched him with an icy contempt. When the game was over, while they smoked their pipes and drank whisky, they would begin telling stories. Walker told with gusto the story of his marriage. He had got so drunk at the wedding feast that the bride had fled and he had never seen her since. He had had numberless adventures, commonplace and sordid, with the women of the island and he described them with a pride in his own prowess which was an offence to Mackintosh's fastidious ears. He was a gross, sensual old man. He thought Mackintosh a poor fellow because he would not share his promiscuous amours and remained sober when the company was drunk.

He despised him also for the orderliness with which he did his official work. Mackintosh liked to do everything just so. His desk was always tidy, his papers were always neatly docketed, he could put his hand on any document that was needed, and he had at his fingers' ends all the regulations that were required for the business of their administration.

"Fudge, fudge," said Walker. "I've run this island for twenty years without red tape, and I don't want it now."

"Does it make it any easier for you that when you want a letter you have to hunt half an hour for it?" answered Mackintosh.

"You're nothing but a damned official. But you're not a bad fellow; when you've been out here a year or two you'll be all right. What's wrong about you is that you won't drink. You wouldn't be a bad sort if you got soused once a week."

The curious thing was that Walker remained perfectly unconscious of the dislike for him which every month increased in the breast of his subordinate. Although he laughed at him, as he grew accustomed to him, he began almost to like him. He had a certain tolerance for the peculiarities of others, and he accepted Mackintosh as a queer fish. Perhaps he liked him, unconsciously, because he could chaff him. His humour consisted of coarse banter and he wanted a butt. Mackintosh's exactness, his morality, his sobriety, were all fruitful subjects; his Scots name gave an opportunity for the usual jokes about Scotland; he enjoyed himself thoroughly when two or three men were there and he could make them all laugh at the expense of Mackintosh. He would say ridiculous things about him to the natives, and Mackintosh, his knowledge of Samoan still imperfect, would see their unrestrained mirth when Walker had made an obscene reference to him. He smiled good-humouredly.

"I'll say this for you, Mac," Walker would say in his gruff loud voice, "you can take a joke."

"Was it a joke?" smiled Mackintosh. "I didn't know."

"Scots wha hae!" shouted Walker, with a bellow of laughter. "There's only one way to make a Scotchman see a joke and that's by a surgical operation."

Walker little knew that there was nothing Mackintosh could stand less than chaff. He would wake in the night, the breathless night of the rainy season, and brood sullenly over the gibe that Walker had uttered carelessly days before. It rankled. His heart swelled with rage, and he pictured to himself ways in which he might get even with the bully. He had tried answering him, but Walker had a gift of repartee, coarse and obvious, which gave him an advantage. The dullness of his intellect made him impervious to a delicate shaft. His self-satisfaction made it impossible to wound him. His loud voice, his bellow of laughter, were weapons against which Mackintosh had nothing to counter, and he learned that the wisest thing was never to betray his irritation. He learned to control himself. But his hatred grew till it was a monomania. He watched Walker with an insane vigilance. He fed his own self-esteem by every instance of meanness on Walker's part, by every exhibition of childish vanity, of cunning, and of vulgarity. Walker ate greedily, noisily, filthily, and Mackintosh watched him with satisfaction. He took note of the foolish things he said and of his mistakes in grammar. He knew that Walker held him in small esteem, and he found a bitter satisfaction in his chief's opinion of him; it increased his own contempt for the narrow, complacent old man. And it gave him a singular pleasure to know that Walker was entirely unconscious of the hatred he felt for him. He was a fool who liked popularity, and he blandly fancied that everyone admired him. Once Mackintosh had overheard Walker speaking of him.

"He'll be all right when I've licked him into shape," he said. "He's a good dog and he loves his master."

Mackintosh silently, without a movement of his long, sallow face, laughed long and heartily.

But his hatred was not blind; on the contrary, it was peculiarly clear-sighted, and he judged Walker's capabilities with precision. He ruled his small kingdom with efficiency. He was just and honest. With opportunities to make money he was a poorer man than when he was first appointed to his post, and his only support for his old age was the pension which he expected when at last he retired from official life. His pride was that with an assistant and a half-caste clerk he was able to administer the island more competently than Upolu, the island of which Apia is the chief town, was administered with its army of functionaries. He had a few native policemen to sustain his authority, but he made no use of them. He governed by bluff and his Irish humour.

"They insisted on building a jail for me," he said. "What the devil do I want a jail for? I'm not going to put the natives in prison. If they do wrong I know how to deal with them."

One of his quarrels with the higher authorities at Apia was that he claimed entire jurisdiction over the natives of his island. Whatever their crimes he would not give them up to courts competent to deal with them, and several times an angry correspondence had passed between him and the governor at Upolu. For he looked upon the natives as his children. And that was the amazing thing about this coarse, vulgar, selfish man; he loved the island on which he had lived so long with passion, and he had for the natives a strange rough tenderness which was quite wonderful.

He loved to ride about the island on his old grey mare and he was never tired of its beauty. Sauntering along the grassy roads among the coconut trees he would stop every now and then to admire the loveliness of the scene. Now and then he would come upon a native village and stop while the headman brought him a bowl of *kava*. He would look at the little group of bell-shape huts with their high thatched roofs, like beehives, and a smile would spread over his fat face. His eyes rested happily on the spreading green of the bread-fruit trees.

"By George, it's like the garden of Eden."

Sometimes his rides took him along the coast and through the trees he had a glimpse of the wide sea, empty, with never a sail to disturb the loneliness; sometimes he climbed a hill so that a great stretch of country, with little villages nestling among the tall trees, was spread out before him like the kingdom of the world, and he would sit there for an hour in an ecstasy of delight. But he had no words to express his feelings and to relieve them would utter an obscene jest; it was as though his emotion was so violent that he needed vulgarity to break the tension.

Mackintosh observed this sentiment with an icy disdain. Walker had always been a heavy drinker, he was proud of his capacity to see men half his age under the table when he spent a night in Apia, and he had the sentimentality of the toper. He could cry over the stories he read in his magazines and yet would refuse a loan to some trader in difficulties whom he had known for twenty years. He was close with his money. Once Mackintosh said to him:

"No one could accuse you of giving money away."

He took it as a compliment. His enthusiasm for nature was but the drivelling sensibility of the drunkard. Nor had Mackintosh any sympathy for his chief's feelings towards the natives. He loved them because they were in his power, as a selfish man loves his dog, and his mentality was on a level with theirs. Their humour was obscene and he was never at a loss for the lewd remark. He understood them and they understood him. He was proud of his influence over them. He looked upon them as his children and he mixed himself in all their affairs. But he was very jealous of his authority; if he ruled them with a rod of iron, brooking no contradiction, he would not suffer any of the white men on the island to take advantage of them. He watched the missionaries suspiciously and, if they did anything of which he disapproved, was able to make life so unendurable to them that if he could not get them removed they were glad to go of their own accord. His power over the natives was so great that on his word they would refuse labour and food to their pastor. On the other hand he showed the traders no favour. He took care that they should not cheat the natives; he saw that they got a fair reward for their work and their copra and that the traders made no extravagant profit on the wares they sold them. He was merciless to a bargain that he thought unfair. Sometimes the traders would complain at Apia that they did not get fair opportunities. They suffered for it. Walker then hesitated at no calumny, at no outrageous lie, to get even with them, and they found that if they wanted not only to live at peace, but to exist at all, they had to accept the situation on his own terms. More than once the store of a trader obnoxious to him had been burned down, and there was only the appositeness of the event to show that the administrator had instigated it. Once a Swedish half-caste, ruined by the burning, had gone to him and roundly accused him of arson. Walker laughed in his face.

"You dirty dog. Your mother was a native and you try to cheat the natives. If your rotten old store is burned down it's a judgement of Providence; that's what it is, a judgement of Providence. Get out."

And as the man was hustled out by two native policemen the administrator laughed fatly.

"A judgement of Providence."

And now Mackintosh watched him enter upon the day's work. He began with the sick, for Walker added doctoring to his other activities, and he had a small room behind the office full of drugs. An elderly man came forward, a man with a crop of curly grey hair, in a blue lava-lava, elaborately tattooed, with the skin of his body wrinkled like a wine-skin.

"What have you come for?" Walker asked him abruptly.

In a whining voice the man said that he could not eat without vomiting and that he had pains here and pains there.

"Go to the missionaries," said Walker. "You know that I only cure children."

"I have been to the missionaries and they do me no good."

"Then go home and prepare yourself to die. Have you lived so long and still want to go on living? You're a fool."

The man broke into querulous expostulation, but Walker, pointing to a woman with a sick child in her arms, told her to bring it to his desk. He asked her questions and looked at the child.

"I will give you medicine," he said. He turned to the half-caste clerk. "Go into the dispensary and bring me some calomel pills."

He made the child swallow one there and then and gave another to the mother.

"Take the child away and keep it warm. Tomorrow it will be dead or better."

He leaned back in his chair and lit his pipe.

"Wonderful stuff, calomel. I've saved more lives with it than all the hospital doctors at Apia put together."

Walker was very proud of his skill, and with the dogmatism of ignorance had no patience with the members of the medical profession.

"The sort of case I like," he said, "is the one that all the doctors have given up as hopeless. When the doctors have said they can't cure you, I say to them, 'Come to me.' Did I ever tell you about the fellow who had a cancer?"

"Frequently," said Mackintosh.

"I got him right in three months."

"You've never told me about the people you haven't cured."

He finished this part of the work and went on to the rest. It was a queer medley. There was a woman who could not get on with her husband and a man who complained that his wife had run away from him.

"Lucky dog," said Walker. "Most men wish their wives would too."

There was a long complicated quarrel about the ownership of a few yards of land. There was a dispute about the sharing out of a catch of fish. There was a complaint against a white trader because he had given short measure. Walker listened attentively to every case, made up his mind quickly, and gave his decision. Then he would listen to nothing more; if the complainant went on he was hustled out of the office by a policeman. Mackintosh listened to it all with sullen irritation. On the whole, perhaps, it might be admitted that rough justice was done, but it exasperated the assistant that his chief trusted his instinct rather than the evidence. He would not listen to reason. He browbeat the witnesses and when they did not see what he wished them to called them thieves and liars.

He left to the last a group of men who were sitting in the corner of the room. He had deliberately ignored them. The party consisted of an old chief, a tall, dignified man with short, white hair, in a new lava-lava, bearing a huge fly wisp as a badge of office, his son, and half a dozen of the important men of the village. Walker had had a feud with them and had beaten them. As was characteristic of him he meant now to rub in his victory, and because he had them down to profit by their helplessness. The facts were peculiar. Walker had a passion for building roads. When he had come to Talua there were but a few tracks here and there, but in course of time he had cut roads through the country, joining the villages together, and it was to this that a great part of the island's prosperity was due. Whereas in the old days it had been impossible to get the produce of the land, copra chiefly, down to the coast where it could be put on schooners or motor launches and so taken to Apia, now transport was easy and simple. His ambition was to make a road right round the island and a great part of it was already built.

"In two years I shall have done it, and then I can die or they can fire me, I don't care."

His roads were the joy of his heart and he made excursions constantly to see that they were kept in order. They were simple enough, wide tracks, grass-covered, cut through the scrub or through the plantations; but trees had to be rooted out, rocks dug up or blasted, and here and there levelling had been necessary. He was proud that he had surmounted by his own skill such difficulties as they presented. He rejoiced in his disposition of them so that they were not only convenient, but showed off the beauties of the island which his soul loved. When he spoke of his roads he was almost a poet. They meandered through those lovely scenes, and Walker had taken care that here and there they should run in a straight line, giving you a green vista through the tall trees, and here and there should turn and curve so that the heart was rested by the diversity. It was amazing that this coarse and sensual man should exercise so subtle an ingenuity to get the effects which his fancy suggested to him. He had used in making his roads all the fantastic skill of a Japanese gardener. He received a grant from headquarters for the work but took a curious pride in using but a small part of it, and the year before had spent only a hundred pounds of the thousand assigned to him.

"What do they want money for?" he boomed. "They'll only spend it on all kinds of muck they don't want; what the missionaries leave them, that is to say."

For no particular reason, except perhaps pride in the economy of his administration and the desire to contrast his efficiency with the wasteful methods of the authorities at Apia, he got the natives to do the work he wanted for wages that were almost nominal. It was owing to this that he had lately had difficulty with the village whose chief men now were come to see him. The chief's son had been in Upolu for a year and on coming back had told his people of the large sums that were paid at Apia for the public works. In long, idle talks he had inflamed their hearts with the desire for gain. He held out to them visions of vast wealth and they thought of the whisky they could buy – it was dear, since there was a law that it must not be sold to natives, and so it cost them double what the white man had to pay for it – they thought of the great sandalwood boxes in which they kept their treasures, and the scented soap and potted salmon, the luxuries for which the Kanaka will sell his soul; so that when the administrator sent for them and told them he wanted a road made from their village to a certain point along the coast and offered them twenty pounds, they asked him a hundred. The chief's son was called Manuma. He was a tall, handsome fellow, copper-coloured, with his fuzzy hair dyed red with lime, a wreath of red berries round his neck, and behind his ear a flower like a scarlet flame against his brown face. The upper part of his body was naked, but to show that he was no longer a savage, since he had lived in Apia, he wore a pair of dungarees instead of a lava-lava. He told them that if they held together the administrator would be obliged to accept their terms. His heart was set on building the road and when he found they would not work for less he would give them what they asked. But they must not move; whatever he said they must not abate their claim; they had asked a hundred and that they must keep to. When they mentioned the figure, Walker burst into a shout of his long, deep-voiced laughter. He told them not to make fools of themselves, but to set about the work at once. Because he was in a good humour that day he promised to give them a feast when the road was finished. But when he found that no attempt was made to start work, he went to the village and asked the men what silly game they were playing. Manuma had coached them well. They were quite calm, they did not attempt to argue – and argument is a passion with the Kanaka – they merely shrugged their shoulders: they would do it for a hundred pounds, and if he would not give them that they would do no work. He could please himself. They did not care. Then Walker flew into a passion. He was ugly then. His short fat neck swelled ominously, his red face grew purple, he foamed at the mouth. He set upon the natives with invective. He knew well how to wound and how to humiliate. He was terrifying. The older men grew pale and uneasy. They hesitated. If it had not been for Manuma, with his knowledge of the great world, and their dread of his ridicule, they would have yielded. It was Manuma who answered Walker.

"Pay us a hundred pounds and we will work."

Walker, shaking his fist at him, called him every name he could think of. He riddled him with scorn. Manuma sat still and smiled. There may have been more bravado than confidence in his smile, but he had to make a good show before the others. He repeated his words.

"Pay us a hundred pounds and we will work."

They thought that Walker would spring on him. It would not have been the first time that he had thrashed a native with his own hands; they knew his strength, and though Walker was three times the age of the young man and six inches shorter they did not doubt that he was more than a match for Manuma. No one had ever thought of resisting the savage onslaught of the administrator. But Walker said nothing. He chuckled.

"I am not going to waste my time with a pack of fools," he said. "Talk it over again. You know what I have offered. If you do not start in a week, take care."

He turned round and walked out of the chief's hut. He untied his old mare and it was typical of the relations between him and the natives that one of the elder men hung on to the off stirrup while Walker from a convenient boulder hoisted himself heavily into the saddle.

That same night when Walker according to his habit was strolling along the road that ran past his house, he heard something whizz past him and with a thud strike a tree. Something had been thrown at him. He ducked instinctively. With a shout, "Who's that?" he ran towards the place from which the missile had come and he heard the sound of a man escaping through the bush. He knew it was hopeless to pursue in the darkness, and besides he was soon out of breath, so he stopped and made his way back to the road. He looked about for what had been thrown, but could find nothing. It was quite dark. He went quickly back to the house and called Mackintosh and the Chinese boy.

"One of those devils has thrown something at me. Come along and let's find out what it was."

He told the boy to bring a lantern and the three of them made their way back to the place. They hunted about the ground, but could not find what they sought. Suddenly the boy gave a guttural cry. They turned to look. He held up the lantern, and there, sinister in the light that cut the surrounding darkness, was a long knife sticking into the trunk of a coconut tree. It had been thrown with such force that it required quite an effort to pull it out.

"By George, if he hadn't missed me I'd have been in a nice state."

Walker handled the knife. It was one of those knives, made in imitation of the sailor knives brought to the islands a hundred years before by the first white men, used to divide the coconuts in two so that the copra might be dried. It was a murderous weapon, and the blade, twelve inches long, was very sharp. Walker chuckled softly.

"The devil, the impudent devil."

He had no doubt it was Manuma who had flung the knife. He had escaped death by three inches. He was not angry. On the contrary, he was in high spirits; the adventure exhilarated him, and when they got back to the house, calling for drinks, he rubbed his hands gleefully.

"I'll make them pay for this!"

His little eyes twinkled. He blew himself out like a turkey-cock, and for the second time within half an hour insisted on telling Mackintosh every detail of the affair. Then he asked him to play piquet, and while they played he boasted of his intentions. Mackintosh listened with tightened lips.

"But why should you grind them down like this?" he asked. "Twenty pounds is precious little for the work you want them to do."

"They ought to be precious thankful I give them anything."

"Hang it all, it's not your own money. The government allots you a reasonable sum. They won't complain if you spend it."

"They're a bunch of fools at Apia."

Mackintosh saw that Walker's motive was merely vanity. He shrugged his shoulders.

"It won't do you much good to score off the fellows at Apia at the cost of your life."

"Bless you, they wouldn't hurt me, these people. They couldn't do without me. They worship me. Manuma is a fool. He only threw that knife to frighten me."

The next day Walker rode over again to the village. It was called Matautu. He did not get off his horse. When he reached the chief's house he saw that the men were sitting round the floor in a circle, talking, and he guessed they were discussing again the question of the road. The Samoan huts are formed in this way: trunks of slender trees are placed in a circle at intervals of perhaps five or six feet; a tall tree is set in the middle and from this downwards slopes the thatched roof. Venetian blinds of coconut leaves can be pulled down at night or when it is raining. Ordinarily the hut is open all round so that the breeze can blow through freely. Walker rode to the edge of the hut and called out to the chief.

"Oh, there, Tangatu, your son left his knife in a tree last night. I have brought it back to you."

He flung it down on the ground in the midst of the circle, and with a low burst of laughter ambled off.

On Monday he went out to see if they had started work. There was no sign of it. He rode through the village. The inhabitants were about their ordinary avocations. Some were weaving mats of the pandanus leaf, one old man was busy with a *kava* bowl, the children were playing, the women went about their household chores. Walker, a smile on his lips, came to the chief's house.

"*Talofa-li*," said the chief.

"*Talofa*," answered Walker.

Manuma was making a net. He sat with a cigarette between his lips and looked up at Walker with a smile of triumph.

"You have decided that you will not make the road?"

The chief answered.

"Not unless you pay us one hundred pounds."

"You will regret it." He turned to Manuma. "And you, my lad, I shouldn't wonder if your back was very sore before you're much older."

He rode away chuckling. He left the natives vaguely uneasy. They feared the fat sinful old man, and neither the missionaries' abuse of him nor the scorn which Manuma had learnt in Apia made them forget that he had a devilish cunning and that no man had ever braved him without in the long run suffering for it. They found out within twenty-four hours what scheme he had devised. It was characteristic. For next morning a great band of men, women, and children came into the village and the chief men said that they had made a bargain with Walker to build the road. He had offered them twenty pounds and they had accepted. Now the cunning lay in this, that the Polynesians have rules of hospitality which have all the force of laws; an etiquette of absolute rigidity made it necessary for the people of the village not only to give lodging to the strangers, but to provide them with food and drink as long as they wished to stay. The inhabitants of Matautu were outwitted. Every morning the workers went out in a joyous band, cut down trees, blasted rocks, levelled here and there and then in the evening tramped back again, and ate and drank, ate heartily, danced, sang hymns, and enjoyed life. For them it was a picnic. But soon their hosts began to wear long faces; the strangers had enormous appetites, and the plantains and the bread-fruit vanished before their rapacity; the alligator-pear trees, whose fruit sent to Apia might sell for good money, were stripped bare. Ruin stared them in the face. And then they found that the strangers were working very slowly. Had they received a hint from Walker that they might take their time? At this rate by the time the road was finished there would not be a scrap of food in the village. And worse than this, they were a laughing-stock; when one or other of them went to some distant hamlet on an errand he found that the story had got there before him, and he was met with derisive laughter. There is nothing the Kanaka can endure less than ridicule. It was not long before much angry talk passed among the sufferers. Manuma was no longer a hero; he had to put up with a good deal of plain speaking, and one day what Walker had suggested came to pass: a heated argument turned into a quarrel and half a dozen of the young men set upon the chief's son and gave him such a beating that for a week he lay bruised and sore on the pandanus mats. He turned from side to side and could find no ease. Every day or two the administrator rode over on his old mare and watched the progress of the road. He was not a man to resist the temptation of taunting the fallen foe, and he missed no opportunity to rub into the shamed inhabitants of Matautu the bitterness of their humiliation. He broke their spirit. And one morning, putting their pride in their pockets — a figure of speech, since pockets they had not — they all set out with the strangers and started working on the road. It was urgent to get it done quickly if they wanted to save any food at all, and the whole village joined in. But they worked silently, with rage and mortification in their hearts, and even the children toiled in silence. The women wept as they carried away bundles of brushwood. When Walker saw them he laughed so much that he almost rolled out of his saddle. The news spread quickly and tickled the people of the island to death. This was the greatest joke of all, the crowning triumph of that cunning old white man whom no Kanaka had ever been able to circumvent; and they came from distant villages, with their wives and children, to look at the foolish folk who had refused twenty pounds to make the road and now were forced to work for nothing. But the harder they worked the more easily went the guests. Why should they hurry, when they were getting good food for nothing and the longer they took about the job the better the joke became? At last the wretched villagers could stand it no longer, and they were come this morning to beg the administrator to send the strangers back to their own homes. If he would do this they promised to finish the road themselves for nothing. For him it was a victory complete and unqualified. They were humbled. A look of arrogant complacence spread over his large, naked face, and he seemed to swell in his chair like a great bullfrog. There was something sinister in his appearance, so that Mackintosh shivered with disgust. Then in his booming tones he began to speak.

"Is it for my good that I make the road? What benefit do you think I get out of it? It is for you, so that you can walk in comfort and carry your copra in comfort. I offered to pay you for your work, though it was for your own sake the work was done. I offered to pay you generously. Now *you* must pay. I will send the people of Manua back to their homes if you will finish the road and pay the twenty pounds that I have to pay them."

There was an outcry. They sought to reason with him. They told him they had not the money. But to everything they said he replied with brutal gibes. Then the clock struck.

"Dinner time," he said. "Turn them all out."

He raised himself heavily from his chair and walked out of the room. When Mackintosh followed him, he found him already seated at table, a napkin tied round his neck, holding his knife and fork in readiness for the meal the Chinese cook was about to bring. He was in high spirits.

"I did 'em down fine," he said, as Mackintosh sat down. "I shan't have much trouble with the roads after this."

"I suppose you were joking," said Mackintosh icily.

"What do you mean by that?"

"You're not really going to make them pay twenty pounds?"

"You bet your life I am."

"I'm not sure you've got any right to."

"Ain't you? I guess I've got the right to do any damned thing I like on this island."

"I think you've bullied them quite enough."

Walker laughed fatly. He did not care what Mackintosh thought.

"When I want your opinion I'll ask for it."

Mackintosh grew very white. He knew by bitter experience that he could do nothing but keep silence, and the violent effort at self-control made him sick and faint. He could not eat the food that was before him and with disgust he watched Walker shovel meat into his vast mouth. He was a dirty feeder, and to sit at table with him needed a strong stomach. Mackintosh shuddered. A tremendous desire seized him to humiliate that gross and cruel man; he would give anything in the world to see him in the dust, suffering as much as he had made others suffer. He had never loathed the bully with such loathing as now.

The day wore on. Mackintosh tried to sleep after dinner, but the passion in his heart prevented him; he tried to read, but the letters swam before his eyes. The sun beat down pitilessly, and he longed for rain; but he knew that rain would bring no coolness; it would only make it hotter and more steamy. He was a native of Aberdeen and his heart yearned suddenly for the icy winds that whistled through the granite streets of that city. Here he was a prisoner, imprisoned not only by that placid sea, but by his hatred for that horrible old man. He pressed his hands to his aching head. He would like to kill him. But he pulled himself together. He must do something to distract his mind, and since he could not read he thought he would set his private papers in order. It was a job which he had long meant to do and which he had constantly put off. He unlocked the drawer of his desk and took out a handful of letters. He caught sight of his revolver. An impulse, no sooner realized than set aside, to put a bullet through his head and so escape from the intolerable bondage of life flashed through his mind. He noticed that in the damp air the revolver was slightly rusted, and he got an oil-rag and began to clean it. It was while he was thus occupied that he grew aware of someone slinking round the door. He looked up and called:

"Who is there?"

There was a moment's pause, then Manuma showed himself.

"What do you want?"

The chief's son stood for a moment, sullen and silent, and when he spoke it was with a strangled voice.

"We can't pay twenty pounds. We haven't the money."

"What am I to do?" said Mackintosh. "You heard what Mr Walker said."

Manuma began to plead, half in Samoan and half in English. It was a sing-song whine, with the quavering intonations of a beggar, and it filled Mackintosh with disgust. It outraged him that the man should let himself be so crushed. He was a pitiful object.

"I can do nothing," said Mackintosh irritably. "You know that Mr Walker is master here."

Manuma was silent again. He still stood in the doorway.

"I am sick," he said at last. "Give me some medicine."

"What is the matter with you?"

"I do not know. I am sick. I have pains in my body."

"Don't stand there," said Mackintosh sharply. "Come in and let me look at you."

Manuma entered the little room and stood before the desk.

"I have pains here and here."

He put his hands to his loins and his face assumed an expression of pain. Suddenly Mackintosh grew conscious that the boy's eyes were resting on the revolver which he had laid on the desk when Manuma appeared in the doorway. There was a silence between the two which to Mackintosh was endless. He seemed to read the thoughts which were in the Kanaka's mind. His heart beat violently. And then he felt as though something possessed him so that he acted under the compulsion of a foreign will. Himself did not make the movements of his body, but a power that was strange to him. His throat was suddenly dry, and he put his hand to it mechanically in order to help his speech. He was impelled to avoid Manuma's eyes.

"Just wait here," he said, his voice sounding as though someone had seized him by the windpipe, "and I'll fetch you something from the dispensary."

He got up. Was it his fancy that he staggered a little? Manuma stood silently, and though he kept his eyes averted, Mackintosh knew that he was looking dully out of the door. It was this other person that possessed him that drove him out of the room, but it was himself that took a handful of muddled papers and threw them on the revolver in order to hide it from view. He went to the dispensary. He got a pill and poured out some blue draught into a small bottle, and then came out into the compound. He did not want to go back into his own bungalow, so he called to Manuma.

"Come here."

He gave him the drugs and instructions how to take them. He did not know what it was that made it impossible for him to look at the Kanaka. While he was speaking to him he kept his eyes on his shoulder. Manuma took the medicine and slunk out of the gate.

Mackintosh went into the dining-room and turned over once more the old newspapers. But he could not read them. The house was very still. Walker was upstairs in his room asleep, the Chinese cook was busy in the kitchen, the two policemen were out fishing. The silence that seemed to brood over the house was unearthly, and there hammered in Mackintosh's head the question whether the revolver still lay where he had placed it. He could not bring himself to look. The uncertainty was horrible, but the certainty would be more horrible still. He sweated. At last he could stand the silence no longer, and he made up his mind to go down the road to the trader's, a man named Jervis, who had a store about a mile away. He was a half-caste, but even that amount of white blood made him possible to talk to. He wanted to get away from his bungalow, with the desk littered with untidy papers, and underneath them something, or nothing. He walked along the road. As he passed the fine hut of a chief a greeting was called out to him. Then he came to the store. Behind the counter sat the trader's daughter, a swarthy broad-featured girl in a pink blouse and a white drill skirt. Jervis hoped he would marry her. He had money, and he had told Mackintosh that his daughter's husband would be well-to-do. She flushed a little when she saw Mackintosh.

"Father's just unpacking some cases that have come in this morning. I'll tell him you're here."

He sat down and the girl went out behind the shop. In a moment her mother waddled in, a huge old woman, a chiefess, who owned much land in her own right; and gave him her hand. Her monstrous obesity was an offence, but she managed to convey an impression of dignity. She was cordial without obsequiousness; affable, but conscious of her station.

"You're quite a stranger, Mr Mackintosh. Teresa was saying only this morning: 'Why, we never see Mr Mackintosh now.'"

He shuddered a little as he thought of himself as that old native's son-in-law. It was notorious that she ruled her husband, notwithstanding his white blood, with a firm hand. Hers was the authority and hers the business head. She might be no more than Mrs Jervis to the white people, but her father had been a chief of the blood royal, and his father and his father's father had ruled as kings. The trader came in, small beside his imposing wife, a dark man with a black beard going grey, in ducks, with handsome eyes and flashing teeth. He was very British, and his conversation was slangy, but you felt he spoke English as a foreign tongue; with his family he used the language of his native mother. He was a servile man, cringing and obsequious.

"Ah, Mr Mackintosh, this is a joyful surprise. Get the whisky, Teresa; Mr Mackintosh will have a gargle with us."

He gave all the latest news of Apia, watching his guest's eyes the while, so that he might know the welcome thing to say.

"And how is Walker? We've not seen him just lately. Mrs Jervis is going to send him a sucking-pig one day this week."

"I saw him riding home this morning," said Teresa.

"Here's how," said Jervis, holding up his whisky.

Mackintosh drank. The two women sat and looked at him, Mrs Jervis in her black Mother Hubbard, placid and haughty, and Teresa anxious to smile whenever she caught his eye, while the trader gossiped insufferably.

"They were saying in Apia it was about time Walker retired. He ain't so young as he was. Things have changed since he first come to the islands and he ain't changed with them."

"He'll go too far," said the old chiefess. "The natives aren't satisfied."

"That was a good joke about the road," laughed the trader. "When I told them about it in Apia they fair split their sides with laughing. Good old Walker."

Mackintosh looked at him savagely. What did he mean by talking of him in that fashion? To a half-caste trader he was Mr Walker. It was on his tongue to utter a harsh rebuke for the impertinence. He did not know what held him back.

"When he goes I hope you'll take his place, Mr Mackintosh," said Jervis. "We all like you on the island. You understand the natives. They're educated now, they must be treated differently to the old days. It wants an educated man to be administrator now. Walker was only a trader same as I am."

Teresa's eyes glistened.

"When the time comes if there's anything anyone can do here, you bet your bottom dollar we'll do it. I'd get all the chiefs to go over to Apia and make a petition."

Mackintosh felt horribly sick. It had not struck him that if anything happened to Walker it might be he who would succeed him. It was true that no one in his official position knew the island so well. He got up suddenly and scarcely taking his leave walked back to the compound. And now he went straight to his room. He took a quick look at his desk. He rummaged among the papers.

The revolver was not there.

His heart thumped violently against his ribs. He looked for the revolver everywhere. He hunted in the chairs and in the drawers. He looked desperately, and all the time he knew he would not find it. Suddenly he heard Walker's gruff, hearty voice.

"What the devil are you up to, Mac?"

He started. Walker was standing in the doorway and instinctively he turned round to hide what lay upon his desk.

"Tidying up?" quizzed Walker. "I've told 'em to put the grey in the trap. I'm going down to Tafoni to bathe. You'd better come along."

"All right," said Mackintosh.

So long as he was with Walker nothing could happen. The place they were bound for was about three miles away, and there was a fresh-water pool, separated by a thin barrier of rock from the sea, which the administrator had blasted out for the natives to bathe in. He had done this at spots round the island, wherever there was a spring; and the fresh water, compared with the sticky warmth of the sea, was cool and invigorating. They drove along the silent grassy road, splashing now and then through fords, where the sea had forced its way in, past a couple of native villages, the bell-shaped huts spaced out roomily and the white chapel in the middle, and at the third village they got out of the trap, tied up the horse, and walked down to the pool. They were accompanied by four or five girls and a dozen children. Soon they were all splashing about, shouting and laughing, while Walker, in a lava-lava, swam to and fro like an unwieldy porpoise. He made lewd jokes with the girls, and they amused themselves by diving under him and wriggling away when he tried to catch them. When he was tired he lay down on a rock, while the girls and the children surrounded him; it was a happy family; and the old man, huge, with his crescent of white hair and his shining bald crown, looked like some old sea god. Once Mackintosh caught a queer soft look in his eyes.

"They're dear children," he said. "They look upon me as their father."

And then without a pause he turned to one of the girls and made an obscene remark which sent them all into fits of laughter. Mackintosh started to dress. With his thin legs and thin arms he made a grotesque figure, a sinister Don Quixote, and Walker began to make coarse jokes about him. They were acknowledged with little smothered laughs. Mackintosh struggled with his shirt. He knew he looked absurd, but he hated being laughed at. He stood silent and glowering.

"If you want to get back in time for dinner you ought to come soon."

"You're not a bad fellow, Mac. Only you're a fool. When you're doing one thing you always want to do another. That's not the way we live."

But all the same he raised himself slowly to his feet and began to put on his clothes. They sauntered back to the village, drank a bowl of *kava* with the chief, and then, after a joyful farewell from all the lazy villagers, drove home.

After dinner, according to his habit, Walker, lighting his cigar, prepared to go for a stroll. Mackintosh was suddenly seized with fear.

"Don't you think it's rather unwise to go out at night by yourself just now?"

Walker stared at him with his round blue eyes.

"What the devil do you mean?"

"Remember the knife the other night. You've got those fellows' backs up."

"Pooh! They wouldn't dare."

"Someone dared before."

"That was only a bluff. They wouldn't hurt me. They look upon me as a father. They know that whatever I do is for their own good."

Mackintosh watched him with contempt in his heart. The man's self-complacency outraged him, and yet something, he knew not what, made him insist.

"Remember what happened this morning. It wouldn't hurt you to stay at home just tonight. I'll play piquet with you."

"I'll play piquet with you when I come back. The Kanaka isn't born yet who can make me alter my plans."

"You'd better let me come with you."

"You stay where you are."

Mackintosh shrugged his shoulders. He had given the man full warning. If he did not heed it that was his own lookout. Walker put on his hat and went out. Mackintosh began to read; but then he thought of something; perhaps it would be as well to have his own whereabouts quite clear. He crossed over to the kitchen and, inventing some pretext, talked for a few minutes with the cook. Then he got out the gramophone and put a record on it, but while it ground out its melancholy tune, some comic song of a London music-hall, his ear was strained for a sound away there in the night. At his elbow the record reeled out its loudness, the words were raucous, but notwithstanding he seemed to be surrounded by an unearthly silence. He heard the dull roar of the breakers against the reef. He heard the breeze sigh, far up, in the leaves of the coconut trees. How long would it be? It was awful.

He heard a hoarse laugh.

"Wonders will never cease. It's not often you play yourself a tune, Mac."

Walker stood at the window, red-faced, bluff and jovial.

"Well, you see I'm alive and kicking. What were you playing for?"

Walker came in.

"Nerves a bit dicky, eh? Playing a tune to keep your pecker up?"

"I was playing your requiem."

"What the devil's that?"

"'Alf o' bitter an' a pint of stout."

"A rattling good song too. I don't mind how often I hear it. Now I'm ready to take your money off you at piquet."

They played and Walker bullied his way to victory, bluffing his opponent, chaffing him, jeering at his mistakes, up to every dodge, browbeating him, exulting. Presently Mackintosh recovered his coolness, and standing outside himself, as it were, he was able to take a detached pleasure in watching the overbearing old man and in his own cold reserve. Somewhere Manuma sat quietly and awaited his opportunity.

Walker won game after game and pocketed his winnings at the end of the evening in high good-humour.

"You'll have to grow a little bit older before you stand much chance against me, Mac. The fact is I have a natural gift for cards."

"I don't know that there's much gift about it when I happen to deal you fourteen aces."

"Good cards come to good players," retorted Walker. "I'd have won if I'd had your hands."

He went on to tell long stories of the various occasions on which he had played cards with notorious sharpers and to their consternation had taken all their money from them. He boasted. He praised himself. And Mackintosh listened with absorption. He wanted now to feed his hatred; and everything Walker said, every gesture, made him more detestable. At last Walker got up.

"Well, I'm going to turn in," he said with a loud yawn. "I've got a long day tomorrow."

"What are you going to do?"

"I'm driving over to the other side of the island. I'll start at five, but I don't expect I shall get back to dinner till late."

They generally dined at seven.

"We'd better make it half past seven then."

"I guess it would be as well."

Mackintosh watched him knock the ashes out of his pipe. His vitality was rude and exuberant. It was strange to think that death hung over him. A faint smile flickered in Mackintosh's cold, gloomy eyes.

"Would you like me to come with you?"

"What in God's name should I want that for? I'm using the mare and she'll have enough to do to carry me; she don't want to drag you over thirty miles of road."

"Perhaps you don't quite realize what the feeling is at Matautu. I think it would be safer if I came with you."

Walker burst out into contemptuous laughter.

"You'd be a fine lot of use in a scrap. I'm not a great hand at getting the wind up."

Now the smile passed from Mackintosh's eyes to his lips. It distorted them painfully.

"*Quem deus vult perdere prius dementat.*"

"What the hell is that?" said Walker.

"Latin," answered Mackintosh as he went out.

And now he chuckled. His mood had changed. He had done all he could and the matter was in the hands of fate. He slept more soundly than he had done for weeks. When he awoke next morning he went out. After a good night he found a pleasant exhilaration in the freshness of the early air. The sea was a more vivid blue, the sky more brilliant, than on most days, the trade wind was fresh, and there was a ripple on the lagoon as the breeze brushed over it like velvet brushed the wrong way. He felt himself stronger and younger. He entered upon the day's work with zest. After luncheon he slept again, and as evening drew on he had the bay saddled and sauntered through the bush. He seemed to see it all with new eyes. He felt more normal. The extraordinary thing was that he was able to put Walker out of his mind altogether. So far as he was concerned he might never have existed.

He returned late, hot after his ride, and bathed again. Then he sat on the veranda, smoking his pipe, and looked at the day declining over the lagoon. In the sunset the lagoon, rosy and purple and green, was very beautiful. He felt at peace with the world and with himself. When the cook came out to say that dinner was ready and to ask whether he should wait, Mackintosh smiled at him with friendly eyes. He looked at his watch.

"It's half past seven. Better not wait. One can't tell when the boss'll be back."

The boy nodded, and in a moment Mackintosh saw him carry across the yard a bowl of steaming soup. He got up lazily, went into the dining-room, and ate his dinner. Had it happened? The uncertainty was amusing and Mackintosh chuckled in the silence. The food did not seem so monotonous as usual, and even though there was Hamburger steak, the cook's invariable dish when his poor invention failed him, it tasted by some miracle succulent and spiced. After dinner he strolled over lazily to his bungalow to get a book. He liked the intense stillness, and now that the night had fallen the stars were blazing in the sky. He shouted for a lamp and in a moment the Chink pattered over on his bare feet, piercing the darkness with a ray of light. He put the lamp on the desk and noiselessly slipped out of the room. Mackintosh stood rooted to the floor, for there, half hidden by untidy papers, was his revolver. His heart throbbed painfully, and he broke into a sweat. It was done then.

He took up the revolver with a shaking hand. Four of the chambers were empty. He paused a moment and looked suspiciously out into the night, but there was no one there. He quickly slipped four cartridges into the empty chambers and locked the revolver in his drawer.

He sat down to wait.

An hour passed, a second hour passed. There was nothing. He sat at his desk as though he were writing, but he neither wrote nor read. He merely listened. He strained his ears for a sound travelling from a far distance. At last he heard hesitating footsteps and knew it was the Chinese cook.

"Ah-Sung," he called.

The boy came to the door.

"Boss velly late," he said. "Dinner no good."

Mackintosh stared at him, wondering whether he knew what had happened, and whether, when he knew, he would realize on what terms he and Walker had been. He went about his work, sleek, silent, and smiling, and who could tell his thoughts?

"I expect he's had dinner on the way, but you must keep the soup hot at all events."

The words were hardly out of his mouth when the silence was suddenly broken into by a confusion, cries, and a rapid patter of naked feet. A number of natives ran into the compound, men and women and children; they crowded round Mackintosh and they all talked at once. They were unintelligible. They were excited and frightened and some of them were crying. Mackintosh pushed his way through them and went to the gateway. Though he had scarcely understood what they said he knew quite well what had happened. And as he reached the gate the dog-cart arrived. The old mare was being led by a tall Kanaka, and in the dog-cart crouched two men, trying to hold Walker up. A little crowd of natives surrounded it.

The mare was led into the yard and the natives surged in after it. Mackintosh shouted to them to stand back and the two policemen, appearing suddenly from God knows where, pushed them violently aside. By now he had managed to understand that some lads, who had been fishing, on their way back to their village had come across the cart on the home side of the ford. The mare was nuzzling about the herbage and in the darkness they could just see the great white bulk of the old man sunk between the seat and the dashboard. At first they thought he was drunk and they peered in, grinning, but then they heard him groan, and guessed that something was amiss. They ran to the village and called for help. It was when they returned, accompanied by half a hundred people, that they discovered Walker had been shot.

With a sudden thrill of horror Mackintosh asked himself whether he was already dead. The first thing at all events was to get him out of the cart, and that, owing to Walker's corpulence, was a difficult job. It took four strong men to lift him. They jolted him and he uttered a dull groan. He was still alive. At last they carried him into the house, up the stairs, and placed him on his bed. Then Mackintosh was able to see him, for in the yard, lit only by half a dozen hurricane lamps, everything had been obscured. Walker's white ducks were stained with blood, and the men who had carried him wiped their hands, red and sticky, on their lava-lavas. Mackintosh held up the lamp. He had not expected the old man to be so pale. His eyes were closed. He was breathing still, his pulse could be just felt but it was obvious that he was dying. Mackintosh had not bargained for the shock of horror that convulsed him. He saw that the native clerk was there, and in a voice hoarse with fear told him to go into the dispensary and get what was necessary for a hypodermic injection. One of the policemen had brought up the whisky, and Mackintosh forced a little into the old man's mouth. The room was crowded with natives. They sat about the floor, speechless now and terrified, and every now and then one wailed aloud. It was very hot, but Mackintosh felt cold, his hands and his feet were like ice, and he had to make a violent effort not to tremble in all his limbs. He did not know what to do. He did not know if Walker was bleeding still, and if he was, how he could stop the bleeding.

The clerk brought the hypodermic needle.

"You give it to him," said Mackintosh. "You're more used to that sort of thing than I am."

His head ached horribly. It felt as though all sorts of little savage things were beating inside it, trying to get out. They watched for the effect of the injection. Presently Walker opened his eyes slowly. He did not seem to know where he was.

"Keep quiet," said Mackintosh. "You're at home. You're quite safe."

Walker's lips outlined a shadowy smile.

"They've got me," he whispered.

"I'll get Jervis to send his motor-boat to Apia at once. We'll get a doctor out by tomorrow afternoon."

There was a long pause before the old man answered.

"I shall be dead by then."

A ghastly expression passed over Mackintosh's pale face. He forced himself to laugh.

"What rot! You keep quiet and you'll be as right as rain."

"Give me a drink," said Walker. "A stiff one."

With shaking hand Mackintosh poured out whisky and water, half and half, and held the glass while Walker drank greedily. It seemed to restore him. He gave a long sigh and a little colour came into his great fleshy face. Mackintosh felt extraordinarily helpless. He stood and stared at the old man.

"If you'll tell me what to do I'll do it," he said.

"There's nothing to do. Just leave me alone. I'm done for."

He looked dreadfully pitiful as he lay on the great bed, a huge, bloated, old man; but so wan, so weak, it was heart-rending. As he rested, his mind seemed to grow clearer.

"You were right, Mac," he said presently. "You warned me."

"I wish to God I'd come with you."

"You're a good chap, Mac, only you don't drink."

There was another long silence, and it was clear that Walker was sinking. There was an internal haemorrhage and even Mackintosh in his ignorance could not fail to see that his chief had but an hour or two to live. He stood by the side of the bed stock-still. For half an hour perhaps Walker lay with his eyes closed, then he opened them.

"They'll give you my job," he said, slowly. "Last time I was in Apia I told them you were all right. Finish my road. I want to think that'll be done. All round the island."

"I don't want your job. You'll get all right."

Walker shook his head wearily.

"I've had my day. Treat them fairly, that's the great thing. They're children. You must always remember that. You must be firm with them, but you must be kind. And you must be just. I've never made a bob out of them. I haven't saved a hundred pounds in twenty years. The road's the great thing. Get the road finished."

Something very like a sob was wrung from Mackintosh.

"You're a good fellow, Mac. I always liked you."

He closed his eyes, and Mackintosh thought that he would never open them again. His mouth was so dry that he had to get himself something to drink. The Chinese cook silently put a chair for him. He sat down by the side of the bed and waited. He did not know how long a time passed. The night was endless. Suddenly one of the men sitting there broke into uncontrollable sobbing, loudly, like a child, and Mackintosh grew aware that the room was crowded by this time with natives. They sat all over the floor on their haunches, men and women, staring at the bed.

"What are all these people doing here?" said Mackintosh. "They've got no right. Turn them out, turn them out, all of them."

His words seemed to rouse Walker, for he opened his eyes once more, and now they were all misty. He wanted to speak, but he was so weak that Mackintosh had to strain his ears to catch what he said.

"Let them stay. They're my children. They ought to be here."

Mackintosh turned to the natives.

"Stay where you are. He wants you. But be silent."

A faint smile came over the old man's white face.

"Come nearer," he said.

Mackintosh bent over him. His eyes were closed and the words he said were like a wind sighing through the fronds of the coconut trees.

"Give me another drink. I've got something to say."

This time Mackintosh gave him his whisky neat. Walker collected his strength in a final effort of will.

"Don't make a fuss about this. In 'ninety-five when there were troubles white men were killed, and the fleet came and shelled the villages. A lot of people were killed who'd had nothing to do with it. They're damned fools at Apia. If they make a fuss they'll only punish the wrong people. I don't want anyone punished."

He paused for a while to rest.

"You must say it was an accident. No one's to blame. Promise me that."

"I'll do anything you like," whispered Mackintosh.

"Good chap. One of the best. They're children. I'm their father. A father don't let his children get into trouble if he can help it."

A ghost of a chuckle came out of his throat. It was astonishingly weird and ghastly.

"You're a religious chap, Mac. What's that about forgiving them? You know."

For a while Mackintosh did not answer. His lips trembled.

"Forgive them, for they know not what they do?"

"That's right. Forgive them. I've loved them, you know, always loved them."

He sighed. His lips faintly moved, and now Mackintosh had to put his ears quite close to them in order to hear.

"Hold my hand," he said.

Mackintosh gave a gasp. His heart seemed wrenched. He took the old man's hand, so cold and weak, a coarse, rough hand, and held it in his own. And thus he sat until he nearly started out of his seat, for the silence was suddenly broken by a long rattle. It was terrible and unearthly. Walker was dead. Then the natives broke out with loud cries. The tears ran down their faces, and they beat their breasts.

Mackintosh disengaged his hand from the dead man's and staggering like one drunk with sleep he went out of the room. He went to the locked drawer in his writing-desk and took out the revolver. He walked down to the sea and walked into the lagoon; he waded out cautiously, so that he should not trip against a coral rock, till the water came to his arm-pits. Then he put a bullet through his head.

An hour later half a dozen slim brown sharks were splashing and struggling at the spot where he fell.

I DON'T KNOW that I very much liked Landon. He was a member of a club I belonged to, and I had often sat next to him at lunch. He was a judge at the Old Bailey, and it was through him I was able to get a privileged seat in court when there was an interesting trial that I wanted to attend. He was an imposing figure on the bench in his great full-bottomed wig, his red robes, and his ermine tippet: and with his long, white face, thin lips, and pale blue eyes, a somewhat terrifying one. He was just, but harsh; and sometimes it made me uncomfortable to hear the bitter scolding he gave a convicted prisoner whom he was about to sentence to a long term of imprisonment. But his acid humour at the lunch-table and his willingness to discuss the cases he had tried made him sufficiently good company for me to disregard the slight malaise I felt in his presence. I asked him once whether he did not feel a certain uneasiness of mind after he had sent a man to the gallows. He smiled as he sipped his glass of port.

"Not at all. The man's had a fair trial; I've summed up as fairly as I could, and the jury has found him guilty. When I condemn him to death, I sentence him to a punishment he richly deserves; and when the court rises, I put the case out of my head. Nobody but a sentimental fool would do anything else."

I knew he liked to talk to me, but I never thought he looked upon me as anything but a club acquaintance, so I was not a little surprised when one day I received a telegram from him saying that he was spending his vacation on the Riviera, and would like to stay with me for two or three days on his way to Italy. I wired that I should be glad to see him. But it was with a certain trepidation that I met him at the station.

On the day of his arrival, to help me out, I asked Miss Gray, a neighbour and an old friend of mine, to dinner. She was of mature age, but charming, and she had a flow of lively conversation which I knew nothing could discourage. I gave them a very good dinner, and though I had no port to offer the judge, I was able to provide him with a good bottle of Montrachet and an even better bottle of Mouton Rothschild. He enjoyed them both; and I was glad of that, because when I had offered him a cocktail, he had refused with indignation.

"I have never understood," he said, "how people presumably civilized can indulge in a habit that is not only barbarous but disgusting."

I may state that this did not deter Miss Gray and me from having a couple of dry Martinis, though it was with impatience and distaste that he watched us drink them.

But the dinner was a success. The good wine and Miss Gray's sprightly chatter combined to give Landon a geniality I had never before seen in him. It was plain to me that notwithstanding his austere appearance he liked feminine society; and Miss Gray in a becoming dress, with her neat head only just touched with grey and her delicate features, her sparkling eyes, was still alluring. After dinner the judge, with some old brandy still further to mellow him, let himself go, and for a couple of hours held us entranced while he told us of celebrated trials in which he had been concerned. I was not surprised therefore that when Miss Gray asked us to lunch with her next day, Landon, even before I could answer, accepted with alacrity.

"A very nice woman," he said when she had left us. "And a head on her shoulders. She must have been very pretty as a girl. She's not bad now. Why isn't she married?"

"She always says nobody asked her."

"Stuff and nonsense! Women ought to marry. Too many of these women about who want their independence. I have no patience with them."

Miss Gray lived in a little house facing the sea at St Jean, which is a couple of miles from my own house at Cap Ferrat. We drove down next day at one and were shown into her sitting-room.

"I have a surprise for you," she said to me, as we shook hands. "The Craigs are coming."

"You've got to know them at last."

"Well, I thought it was too absurd that we should live next door to one another, and bathe from the same beach every day and not speak. So I forced myself on them, and they've promised to come to lunch today. I wanted you to meet them, to see what you make of them." She turned to Landon. "I hope you don't mind."

But he was on his best behaviour.

"I'm sure I shall be delighted to meet any friends of yours, Miss Gray," he said.

"But they're not friends of mine. I've seen a lot of them, but I never spoke to them till yesterday. It'll be a treat for them to meet an author and a celebrated judge."

I had heard a good deal of the Craigs from Miss Gray during the previous three weeks. They had taken the cottage next to hers, and at first she feared they would be a nuisance. She liked her own company and did not want to be bothered with the trivialities of social intercourse. But she very quickly discovered that the Craigs were as plainly disinclined to strike up an acquaintance with her as she with them. Though in that little place they could not but meet two or three times a day, the Craigs never by so much as a glance gave an indication that they had ever seen her before. Miss Gray told me she thought it very tactful of them to make no attempt to intrude upon her privacy, but I had an idea that she was not affronted, a little puzzled rather, that they apparently wanted to know her as little as she wanted to know them. I had guessed some time before that she would not be able to resist making the first advance. On one occasion, while we were walking we passed them, and I was able to have a good look at them. Craig was a handsome man, with a red, honest face, a grey moustache, and thick strong grey hair. He held himself well, and there was a bluff heartiness of manner about him that suggested a broker who had retired on a handsome fortune. His wife was a woman hard of visage, tall, and of masculine appearance, with dull, fair hair too elaborately dressed, a large nose, a large mouth, and a weather-beaten skin. She was not only plain but grim. Her clothes, pretty, flimsy and graceful, sat oddly upon her, for they would better have suited a girl of eighteen, and Mrs Craig was certainly forty. Miss Gray told me they were well cut and expensive. I thought he looked commonplace and she looked disagreeable, and I told Miss Gray she was lucky that they were obviously disposed to keep themselves to themselves.

"There's something rather sweet about them," she answered.

"What?"

"They love one another. And they adore the baby."

For they had a child that was not more than a year old; and from this Miss Gray had concluded that they had not long been married. She liked to watch them with their baby. A nurse took it out every morning in a pram, but before this, father and mother spent an ecstatic quarter of an hour teaching it to walk. They stood a few yards apart and urged the child to flounder from one to the other; and each time it tumbled into the parental arms it was lifted up and rapturously embraced. And when finally it was tucked up in the smart pram, they hung over it with charming baby talk and watched it out of sight as though they couldn't bear to let it go.

Miss Gray used often to see them walking up and down the lawn of their garden arm in arm; they did not talk, as though they were so happy to be together that conversation was unnecessary; and it warmed her heart to observe the affection which that dour, unsympathetic woman so obviously felt for her tall, handsome husband. It was a pretty sight to see Mrs Craig brush an invisible speck of dust off his coat, and Miss Gray was convinced that she purposely made holes in his socks in order to have the pleasure of darning them. And it looked as though he loved her as much as she loved him. Every now and then he would give her a glance, and she would look up at him and smile, and he gave her cheek a little pat. Because they were no longer young, their mutual devotion was peculiarly touching.

I never knew why Miss Gray had never married; I felt as certain as the judge that she had had plenty of chances; and I asked myself, when she talked to me about the Craigs, whether the sight of this matrimonial felicity didn't give her a slight pang. I suppose complete happiness is very rare in this world, but these two people seemed to enjoy it, and it may be that Miss Gray was so strangely interested in them only because she could not quite suppress the feeling in her heart that by remaining single she had missed something.

Because she didn't know what their first names were, she called them Edwin and Angelina. She made up a story about them. She told it to me one day; and when I ridiculed it, she was quite short with me. This, as far as I can remember, is how it went: They had fallen in love with one another years before – perhaps twenty years – when Angelina, a young girl then, had the fresh grace of her teens and Edwin was a brave youth setting out joyously on the journey of life. And since the gods, who are said to look upon young love with kindliness, nevertheless do not bother their heads with practical matters, neither Edwin nor Angelina had a penny. It was impossible for them to marry, but they had courage, hope, and confidence. Edwin made up his mind to go out to South America or Malaya or where you like, make his fortune and return to marry the girl who had patiently waited for him. It couldn't take more than two or three years, five at the utmost; and what is that, when you're twenty and the whole of life is before you? Meanwhile of course Angelina would live with her widowed mother.

But things didn't pan out according to schedule. Edwin found it more difficult than he had expected to make a fortune; in fact, he found it hard to earn enough money to keep body and soul together, and only Angelina's love and her tender letters gave him the heart to continue the struggle. At the end of five years he was not much better off than when he started. Angelina would willingly have joined him and shared his poverty, but it was impossible for her to leave her mother, bed-ridden as she was, poor thing, and there was nothing for them to do but have patience. And so the years passed slowly, and Edwin's hair grew grey, and Angelina became grim and haggard. Hers was the harder lot, for she could do nothing but wait. The cruel glass showed such charms as she had possessed slipping away from her one by one; and at last she discovered that youth, with a mocking laugh and a pirouette, had left her for good. Her sweetness turned sour from long tending of a querulous invalid; her mind was narrowed by the society of the small town in which she lived. Her friends married and had children, but she remained a prisoner to duty.

She wondered if Edwin still loved her. She wondered if he would ever come back. She often despaired. Ten years went by, and fifteen, and twenty. Then Edwin wrote to say that his affairs were settled, and he had made enough money for them to live upon in comfort, and if she were still willing to marry him, he would return at once. By a merciful interposition of providence, Angelina's mother chose that very moment to abandon a world in which she had made herself a thorough nuisance. But when after so long a separation they met, Angelina saw with dismay that Edwin was as young as ever. It's true his hair was grey, but it infinitely became him. He had always been good-looking, but now he was a very handsome man in the flower of his age. She felt as old as the hills. She was conscious of her narrowness, her terrible provincialism, compared with the breadth he had acquired by his long sojourn in foreign countries. He was gay and breezy as of old, but her spirit was crushed. The bitterness of life had warped her soul. It seemed monstrous to bind that alert and active man to her by a promise twenty years old, and she offered him his release. He went deathly pale.

"Don't you care for me any more?" he cried brokenly.

And she realized on a sudden – oh, the rapture, oh, the relief! – that to him she was just the same as she had ever been. He had thought of her always as she was; her portrait had been, as it were, stamped on his heart, so that now, when the real woman stood before him, she was, to him, still eighteen.

So they were married.

"I don't believe a word of it," I said when Miss Gray had brought her story to its happy ending.

"I insist on your believing it," she said. "I'm convinced it's true, and I haven't the smallest doubt that they'll live happily together to a ripe old age." Then she made a remark that I thought rather shrewd. "Their love is founded on an illusion, perhaps; but since it has to them all the appearance of reality, what does it matter?"

While I have told you this idyllic story of Miss Gray's invention, the three of us, our hostess, Landon, and myself, waited for the Craigs to come.

"Have you ever noticed that if people live next door to you, they're invariably late?" Miss Gray asked the judge.

"No, I haven't," he answered acidly. "I'm always punctual myself, and I expect other people to be punctual."

"I suppose it's no good offering you a cocktail?"

"None whatever, madam."

"But I have some sherry that they tell me isn't bad."

The judge took the bottle out of her hands and looked at the label. A faint smile broke on his thin lips.

"This is a civilized drink, Miss Gray. With your permission I will help myself. I never knew a woman yet who knew how to pour out a glass of wine. One should hold a woman by the waist, but a bottle by the neck."

While he was sipping the old sherry with every sign of satisfaction, Miss Gray glanced out of the window.

"Oh, that's why the Craigs are late. They were waiting for the baby to come back."

I followed her eyes and saw that the nurse had just pushed the pram past Miss Gray's house on her way home. Craig took the baby out of the pram and lifted it high in the air. The baby, trying to tug at his moustache, crowed gleefully. Mrs Craig stood by, watching, and the smile on her face made her harsh features almost pleasant. The window was open, and we heard her speak.

"Come along, darling," she said, "we're late."

He put the baby back in the pram, and they came up to the door of Miss Gray's house and rang the bell. The maid showed them in. They shook hands with Miss Gray, and because I was standing near, she introduced me to them. Then she turned to the judge.

"And this is Sir Edward Landon – Mr and Mrs Craig."

One would have expected the judge to move forward with an outstretched hand, but he remained stock-still. He put his eyeglass up to his eye, that eyeglass that I had on more than one occasion seen him use with devastating effect in court, and stared at the newcomers.

"Gosh, what a dirty customer," I said to myself.

He let the glass drop from his eye.

"How do you do," he said. "Am I mistaken in thinking that we've met before?"

The question turned my eyes to the Craigs. They stood side by side close to one another, as though they had drawn together for mutual protection. They did not speak. Mrs Craig looked terrified. Craig's red face was darkened by a purple flush, and his eyes appeared almost to start out of his head. But that only lasted a second.

"I don't think so," he said in a rich, deep voice. "Of course I've heard of you, Sir Edward."

"More people know Tom Fool than Tom Fool knows," said he.

Miss Gray meanwhile had been giving the cocktail-shaker a shake, and now she handed cocktails to her two guests. She had noticed nothing. I didn't know what it all meant; in fact, I wasn't sure it meant anything. The incident, if incident there was, passed so quickly that I was half inclined to think that I had read into the strangers' momentary embarrassment on being introduced to a celebrated man something for which there was no foundation. I set about making myself pleasant. I asked them how they liked the Riviera and if they were comfortable in their house. Miss Gray joined in, and we chatted, as one does with strangers, of commonplace things. They talked easily and pleasantly. Mrs Craig said how much they enjoyed the bathing and complained of the difficulty of getting fish at the seaside. I was aware that the judge did not join in the conversation, but looked down at his feet as though he were unconscious of the company.

Lunch was announced. We went into the dining-room. We were only five, and it was a small round table, so the conversation could not be anything but general. I must confess that it was carried on chiefly by Miss Gray and myself. The judge was silent, but he often was, for he was a moody creature, and I paid no attention. I noticed that he ate the omelette with good appetite, and when it was passed round again took a second helping. The Craigs struck me as a little shy, but that didn't surprise me, and as the second course was produced they began to talk more freely. It didn't strike me that they were very amusing people; they didn't seem interested in very much besides their baby, the vagaries of the two Italian maids they had, and an occasional flutter at Monte Carlo; and I couldn't help thinking that Miss Gray had erred in making their acquaintance. Then suddenly something happened: Craig rose abruptly from his chair and fell headlong to the floor. We jumped up. Mrs Craig threw herself down, over her husband, and took his head in her hands.

"It's all right, George," she cried in an agonized tone. "It's all right!"

"Put his head down," I said. "He's only fainted."

I felt his pulse and could feel nothing. I said he had fainted, but I wasn't sure it wasn't a stroke. He was the sort of heavy, plethoric man who might easily have one. Miss Gray dipped her napkin into water and dabbed his forehead. Mrs Craig seemed distraught. Then I noticed that Landon had remained quietly sitting in his chair.

"If he's fainted, you're not helping him to recover by crowding round him," he said acidly.

Mrs Craig turned her head and gave him a look of bitter hatred.

"I'll ring up the doctor," said Miss Gray.

"No, I don't think that's necessary," I said. "He's coming to."

I could feel his pulse growing stronger, and in a minute or two he opened his eyes. He gasped when he realized what had happened, and tried to struggle to his feet.

"Don't move," I said. "Lie still a little longer."

I got him to drink a glass of brandy, and the colour came back to his face.

"I feel all right now," he said.

"We'll get you into the next room, and you can lie on the sofa for a bit."

"No, I'd sooner go home. It's only a step."

He got up from the floor.

"Yes, let's go back," said Mrs Craig. She turned to Miss Gray. "I'm so sorry; he's never done anything like this before."

They were determined to go, and I thought myself it was the best thing for them to do.

"Put him to bed and keep him there, and he'll be as right as rain tomorrow."

Mrs Craig took one of his arms and I took the other; Miss Gray opened the door, and though still a bit shaky, he was able to walk. When we arrived at the Craigs' home, I offered to go in and help undress him; but they would neither of them hear of it. I went back to Miss Gray's and found them at dessert.

"I wonder why he fainted," Miss Gray was saying. "All the windows are open, and it's not particularly hot today."

"I wonder," said the judge.

I noticed that his thin pale face bore an expression of some complacency. We had our coffee; and then, since the judge and I were going to play golf, we got into the car and drove up the hill to my house.

"How did Miss Gray get to know those people?" Landon asked me. "They struck me as rather second-rate. I shouldn't have thought they were very much her mark."

"You know women. She likes her privacy, and when they settled in next door, she was quite decided that she wouldn't have anything to do with them; but when she discovered that they didn't want to have anything to do with her, she couldn't rest till she'd made their acquaintance."

I told him the story she had invented about her neighbours. He listened with an expressionless face.

"I'm afraid your friend Miss Gray is a sentimental donkey, my dear fellow," he said when I had come to an end. "I tell you, women ought to marry. She'd soon have had all that nonsense knocked out of her if she'd had half a dozen brats."

"What do you know about the Craigs?" I asked.

He gave me a frigid glance.

"I? Why should I know anything about them? I thought they were very ordinary people."

I wish I knew how to describe the strong impression he gave me, both by the glacial austerity of his look and by the rasping finality of his tone, that he was not prepared to say anything more. We finished the drive in silence.

Landon was well on in his sixties, and he was the kind of golfer who never hits a long ball but is never off the straight, and he was a deadly putter, so, though he gave me strokes, he beat me handsomely. After dinner I took him in to Monte Carlo, where he finished the evening by winning a couple of thousand francs at the roulette table. These successive events put him into a remarkably good humour.

"A very pleasant day," he said when we parted for the night. "I've thoroughly enjoyed it."

I spent the next morning at work, and we did not meet till lunch. We were just finishing when I was called to the telephone.

When I came back, my guest was drinking a second cup of coffee.

"That was Miss Gray," I said.

"Oh? What had she to say?"

"The Craigs have done a bolt. They disappeared last night. The maids live in the village; and when they came this morning, they found the house empty. They'd skipped – the Craigs, the nurse, and the baby – and taken their luggage with them. They left money on the table for the maids' wages, the rent to the end of their tenancy, and the tradesmen's bills."

The judge said nothing. He took a cigar from the box, examined it carefully and then lit it with deliberation.

"What have you got to say about that?" I asked.

"My dear fellow, are you obliged to use these American phrases? Isn't English good enough for you?"

"Is that an American phrase? It expresses exactly what I mean. You can't imagine I'm such a fool as not to have noticed that you and the Craigs had met before; and if they've vanished into thin air like figments of the imagination, it's a fairly reasonable conclusion that the circumstances under which you met were not altogether pleasant."

The judge gave a little chuckle, and there was a twinkle in his cold blue eyes.

"That was a very good brandy you gave me last night," he said. "It's against my principles to drink liqueurs after lunch, but it's a very dull man who allows his principles to enslave him, and for once I think I should enjoy one."

I sent for the brandy and watched the judge while he poured himself out a generous measure. He took a sip with obvious satisfaction.

"Do you remember the Wingford murder?" he asked me.

"No."

"Perhaps you weren't in England at the time. Pity – you might have come to the trial. You'd have enjoyed it. It caused a lot of excitement; the papers were full of it.

"Miss Wingford was a rich spinster of mature age who lived in the country with a companion. She was a healthy woman for her age; and when she died rather suddenly, her friends were surprised. Her physician, a fellow called Brandon, signed the certificate and she was duly buried. The will was read, and it appeared that she had left everything she had, something between sixty and seventy thousand pounds, to her companion. The relations were very sore, but there was nothing they could do about it. The will had been drawn up by her lawyer and witnessed by his clerk and Dr Brandon.

"But Miss Wingford had a maid who had been with her for thirty years and had always understood that she would be remembered in the will; she claimed that Miss Wingford had promised to leave her well provided for, and when she found that she wasn't even mentioned she flew into a passion. She told the nephew and the two nieces who had come down for the funeral that she was sure Miss Wingford had been poisoned, and she said that if they didn't go to the police, she'd go herself. Well, they didn't do that, but they went to see Dr Brandon. He laughed. He said that Miss Wingford had had a weak heart and he'd been treating her for years. She died just as he had always expected her to die, peacefully in her sleep; and he advised them not to pay any attention to what the maid said. She had always hated the companion, a Miss Starling, and had been jealous of her. Dr Brandon was highly respected; he had been Miss Wingford's doctor for a long time, and the two nieces, who'd stayed with her often, knew him well. He was not profiting by the will, and there seemed no reason to doubt his word, so the family thought there was nothing to do but make the best of a bad job and went back to London.

"But the maid went on talking; she talked so much that at last the police, much against their will, I must admit, were obliged to take notice, and an order to exhume the body was made. There was an inquest, and it was found that Miss Wingford had died from an overdose of veronal. The coroner's jury found that it had been administered by Miss Starling, and she was arrested. A detective was sent down from Scotland Yard, and he got together some unexpected evidence. It appeared that there'd been a good deal of gossip about Miss Starling and Dr Brandon. They'd been seen a lot together in places in which there was no reason for them to be except that they wanted to be together, and the general impression in the village was that they were only waiting for Miss Wingford to die to get married. That put a very different complexion on the case. To make a long story short, the police got enough evidence in their opinion to justify them in arresting the doctor and charging him and Miss Starling with the murder of the old lady."

The judge took another sip of brandy.

"The case came up for trial before me. The case for the prosecution was that the accused were madly in love with one another and had done the poor old lady to death so that they could marry on the fortune Miss Starling had wheedled her employer into leaving her. Miss Wingford always had a cup of cocoa when she went to bed, which Miss Starling prepared for her; and the counsel for the prosecution claimed that it was in this that Miss Starling had dissolved the tablets that caused Miss Wingford's death. The accused elected to give evidence on their own behalf, and they made a miserable showing in the witness-box. They lied their heads off. Though witnesses testified they had seen them walking together at night with their arms round one another's waists, though Brandon's maid testified she had seen them kissing one another in the doctor's house, they swore they were no more than friends. And oddly enough medical evidence proved that Miss Starling was *virgo intacta*.

"Brandon admitted that he had given Miss Wingford a bottle of veronal tablets because she complained of sleeplessness, but declared he had warned her never to take more than one, and then only when absolutely necessary. The defence sought to prove that she had taken the tablets either by accident or because she wanted to commit suicide. That didn't hold water for a moment. Miss Wingford was a jolly, normal old lady who thoroughly enjoyed life; and her death occurred two days before the expected arrival of an old friend for a week's visit. She hadn't complained to the maid of sleeping badly – in fact, her maid had always thought her a very good sleeper. It was impossible to believe that she had accidentally taken a sufficient number of tablets to kill herself. Personally, I had no doubt that it was a put-up job between the doctor and the companion. The motive was obvious and sufficient. I summed up and I hope summed up fairly; but it was my duty to put the facts before the jury, and to my mind the facts were damning. The jury filed out. I don't suppose you know that when you are sitting on the bench, you somehow get the feeling of the court. You have to be on your guard against it, to be sure it doesn't influence you. I never had it more strongly than on that day that there wasn't a soul in court who wasn't convinced that those two people had committed the crime with which they were charged. I hadn't the shadow of a doubt that the jury would bring in a verdict of guilty. Juries are incalculable. They were out for three hours, and when they came back I knew at once that I was mistaken. In a murder case, when a jury is going to bring in a verdict of guilty they won't look at the prisoner; they look away. I noticed that three or four of the jurymen glanced at the two prisoners in the dock. They brought in a verdict of not guilty. The real names of Mr and Mrs Craig are Dr and Mrs Brandon. I'm just as certain as I am that I'm sitting here that they committed between them a cruel and heartless murder and richly deserved to be hanged."

"What do you think made the jury find them not guilty?"

"I've asked myself that; and do you know the only explanation I can give? The fact that it was conclusively proved that they had never been lovers. And if you come to think of it, that's one of the most curious features of the whole case. That woman was prepared to commit murder to get the man she loved, but she wasn't prepared to have an illicit love-affair with him."

"Human nature is very odd, isn't it?"

"Very," said Landon, helping himself to another glass of brandy.

THE UNCONQUERED

HE CAME BACK into the kitchen. The man was still on the floor, lying where he had hit him, and his face was bloody. He was moaning. The woman had backed against the wall and was staring with terrified eyes at Willi, his friend, and when he came in she gave a gasp and broke into loud sobbing. Willi was sitting at the table, his revolver in his hand, with a half empty glass of wine beside him. Hans went up to the table, filled his glass and emptied it at a gulp.

"You look as though you'd had trouble, young fellow," said Willi with a grin.

Hans's face was blood-stained and you could see the gashes of five sharp finger-nails. He put his hand gingerly to his cheek.

"She'd have scratched my eyes out if she could, the bitch. I shall have to put some iodine on. But she's all right now. You go along."

"I don't know. Shall I? It's getting late."

"Don't be a fool. You're a man, aren't you? What if it is getting late? We lost our way."

It was still light and the westering sun streamed into the kitchen windows of the farm-house. Willi hesitated a moment. He was a little fellow, dark and thin-faced, a dress designer in civil life, and he didn't want Hans to think him a cissy. He got up and went towards the door through which Hans had come. When the woman saw what he was going to do she gave a shriek and sprang forwards.

"*Non, non,*" she cried.

With one step Hans was in front of her. He seized her by the shoulders and flung her violently back. She tottered and fell. He took Willi's revolver.

"Stop still, both of you," he rasped in French, but with his guttural German accent. He nodded his head towards the door. "Go on. I'll look after them."

161

Willi went out, but in a moment was back again.

"She's unconscious."

"Well, what of it?"

"I can't. It's no good."

"Stupid, that's what you are. *Ein Weibchen*. A woman."
Willi flushed.

"We'd better be getting on our way."

Hans shrugged a scornful shoulder.

"I'll just finish the bottle of wine and then we'll go."

He was feeling at ease and it would have been pleasant to linger.
He had been on the job since morning and after so many hours on his
motor-cycle his limbs ached. Luckily they hadn't far to go, only
to Soissons – ten or fifteen kilometres. He wondered if he'd have
the luck to get a bed to sleep in. Of course all this wouldn't
have happened if the girl hadn't been a fool. They had lost their
way, he and Willi, they had stopped a peasant working in a field and
he had deliberately misled them, and they found themselves on a side
road. When they came to the farm they stopped to ask for a direction. They'd asked very politely, for orders were to treat the French
population well as long as they behaved themselves. The door was
opened for them by the girl and she said she didn't know the way to
Soissons, so they pushed in; then the woman, her mother, Hans
guessed, told them. The three of them, the farmer, his wife and
daughter, had just finished supper and there was a bottle of wine on
the table. It reminded Hans that he was as thirsty as the devil. The day
had been sweltering and he hadn't had a drink since noon. He asked
them for a bottle of wine and Willi had added that they would pay
them well for it. Willi was a good little chap, but soft. After all, they
were the victors. Where was the French army? In headlong flight.
And the English, leaving everything behind, had scuttled like rabbits
back to their island. The conquerors took what they wanted, didn't
they? But Willi had worked at a Paris dressmaker's for two years. It's
true he spoke French well, that's why he had his present job, but it
had done something to him. A decadent people. It did a German no
good to live among them.

The farmer's wife put a couple of bottles of wine on the table and
Willi took twenty francs out of his pocket and gave it to her. She
didn't even say thank you. Hans's French wasn't as good as Willi's,

but he could make himself understood, and he and Willi spoke it together all the time. Willi corrected his mistakes. It was because Willi was so useful to him in this way that he had made him his friend, and he knew that Willi admired him. He admired him because he was so tall, slim, and broad-shouldered, because his curly hair was so fair and his eyes so blue. He never lost an opportunity to practise his French, and he tried to talk now, but those three French people wouldn't meet him half-way. He told them that he was a farmer's son himself and when the war was over was going back to the farm. He had been sent to school in Munich because his mother wanted him to go into business, but his heart wasn't in it, and so after matriculating he had gone to an agricultural college.

"You came here to ask your way and now you know it," said the girl. "Drink up your wine and go."

He had hardly looked at her before. She wasn't pretty, but she had fine dark eyes and a straight nose. Her face was very pale. She was plainly dressed, but somehow she didn't look quite like what she evidently was. There was a sort of distinction about her. Ever since the war started he'd heard fellows talk about the French girls. They had something the German girls hadn't. Chic, Willi said it was, but when he asked him just what he meant by that Willi could only say that you had to see it to understand. Of course he'd heard others say that they were mercenary and hard as nails. Well, they'd be in Paris in a week and he'd find out for himself. They said the High Command had already arranged for houses for the men to go to.

"Finish your wine and let's go," said Willi.

But Hans was feeling comfortable and didn't want to be hurried.

"You don't look like a farmer's daughter," he said to the girl.

"And so what?" she answered.

"She's a teacher," said her mother.

"Then you've had a good education." She shrugged her shoulders, but he went on good-humouredly in his bad French. "You ought to understand that this is the best thing that has ever happened to the French people. We didn't declare war. You declared war. And now we're going to make France a decent country. We're going to put order into it. We're going to teach you to work. You'll learn obedience and discipline."

She clenched her fists and looked at him, her eyes black with hatred. But she did not speak.

"You're drunk, Hans," said Willi.

"I'm as sober as a judge. I'm only telling them the truth and they may just as well know it at once."

"He's right," she cried out, unable any longer to contain herself. "You're drunk. Now go. Go."

"Oh, you understand German, do you? All right, I'll go. But you must give me a kiss first."

She took a step back to avoid him, but he seized her wrist.

"Father," she cried. "Father."

The farmer flung himself on the German. Hans let go of her and with all his might hit him in the face. He crumpled up on the floor. Then, before she could escape him, he caught the girl in his arms. She gave him a swinging blow on the cheek...He chuckled grimly.

"Is that how you take it when a German soldier wants to kiss you? You'll pay for this."

With his great strength he pinioned her arms and was dragging her out of the door, but her mother rushed at him and catching him by the clothes tried to pull him away. With one arm holding the girl close to him, with the flat of his other hand he gave the woman a great push and she staggered back to the wall.

"Hans, Hans," cried Willi.

"Shut up, damn you."

He put his hands over the girl's mouth to stop her shrieking and carried her out of the room. That was how it had happened and you had to admit that she'd brought it on herself. She shouldn't have slapped him. If she'd given him the kiss he'd asked for he'd have gone away. He gave a glance at the farmer still lying where he had fallen and he could hardly help laughing at his funny face. There was a smile in his eyes when he looked at the woman cowering against the wall. Was she afraid it was her turn next? Not likely. He remembered a French proverb.

"*C'est le premier pas qui coûte.* There's nothing to cry about, old woman. It had to come sooner or later." He put his hand to his hip pocket and pulled out a wallet. "Look, here's a hundred francs so that mademoiselle can buy herself a new dress. There's not much left of that one." He placed the note on the table and put his helmet back on his head. "Let's go."

They slammed the door behind them and got on their motor-cycles. The woman went into the parlour. Her daughter was lying on the divan. She was lying as he had left her and she was weeping bitterly.

Three months later Hans found himself in Soissons again. He had been in Paris with the conquering army and had ridden through the Arc de Triomphe on his motor-cycle. He had advanced with the army first to Tours and then to Bordeaux. He'd seen very little fighting. The only French soldiers he'd seen were prisoners. The campaign had been the greatest spree he could ever have imagined. After the armistice he had spent a month in Paris. He'd sent picture postcards to his family in Bavaria and bought them all presents. Willi, because he knew the city like the palm of his hand, had stayed on, but he and the rest of his unit were sent to Soissons to join the force that was holding it. It was a nice little town and he was comfortably billeted. Plenty to eat and champagne for less than a mark a bottle in German money. When he was ordered to proceed there it had occurred to him that it would be fun to go and have a look at the girl he'd had. He'd take her a pair of silk stockings to show there was no ill-feeling. He had a good bump of locality and he thought he would be able to find the farm without difficulty. So one afternoon, when he had nothing to do, he put the silk stockings in his pocket and got on his machine. It was a lovely autumn day, with hardly a cloud in the sky, and it was pretty, undulating country that he rode through. It had been fine and dry for so long that, though it was September, not even the restless poplars gave sign that the summer was drawing to an end. He took one wrong turning, which delayed him, but for all that he got to the place he sought in less than half an hour. A mongrel dog barked at him as he walked up to the door. He did not knock, but turned the handle and stepped in. The girl was sitting at the table peeling potatoes. She sprang to her feet when she saw the uniformed man.

"What d'you want?" Then she recognized him. She backed to the wall, clutching the knife in her hands. "It's you. *Cochon.*"

"Don't get excited. I'm not going to hurt you. Look. I've brought you some silk stockings."

"Take them away and take yourself off with them."

"Don't be silly. Drop that knife. You'll only get hurt if you try to be nasty. You needn't be afraid of me."

"I'm not afraid of you," she said.

She let the knife fall to the floor. He took off his helmet and sat down. He reached out with his foot and drew the knife towards him.

"Shall I peel some of your potatoes for you?" She did not answer. He bent down for the knife and then took a potato out of the bowl and went to work on it. Her face hard, her eyes hostile, she stood against the wall and watched him. He smiled at her disarmingly. "Why do you look so cross? I didn't do you much harm, you know. I was excited, we all were, they'd talked of the invincible French army and the Maginot line..." he finished the sentence with a chuckle. "And the wine went to my head. You might have fared worse. Women have told me that I'm not a bad-looking fellow."

She looked him up and down scornfully.

"Get out of here."

"Not until I choose."

"If you don't go my father will go to Soissons and complain to the general."

"Much he'll care. Our orders are to make friends with the population. What's your name?"

"That's not your business."

There was a flush in her cheeks now and her angry eyes were blazing. She was prettier than he remembered her. He hadn't done so badly. She had a refinement that suggested the city-dweller rather than the peasant. He remembered her mother saying she was a teacher. Because she was almost a lady it amused him to torment her. He felt strong and healthy. He passed his hand through his curly blond hair, and giggled when he thought that many girls would have jumped at the chance she had had. His face was so deeply tanned by the summer that his eyes were startlingly blue.

"Where are your father and mother?"

"Working in the fields."

"I'm hungry. Give me a bit of bread and cheese and a glass of wine. I'll pay."

She gave a harsh laugh.

"We haven't seen cheese for three months. We haven't enough bread to stay our hunger. The French took our horses a year ago and now the Boches have taken our cows, our pigs, our chickens, everything."

"Well, they paid you for them."

"Can we eat the worthless paper they gave us?"

She began to cry.

"Are you hungry?"

"Oh, no," she answered bitterly, "we can eat like kings on potatoes and bread and turnips and lettuce. Tomorrow my father's going to Soissons to see if he can buy some horse meat."

"Listen, Miss. I'm not a bad fellow. I'll bring you a cheese, and I think I can get hold of a bit of ham."

"I don't want your presents. I'll starve before I touch the food you swine have stolen from us."

"We'll see," he said good-humouredly.

He put on his hat, got up, and with an *Au revoir, mademoiselle*, walked out.

He wasn't supposed to go joy-riding round the country and he had to wait to be sent on an errand before he was able to get to the farm again. It was ten days later. He walked in as unceremoniously as before and this time he found the farmer and his wife in the kitchen. It was round about noon and the woman was stirring a pot on the stove. The man was seated at table. They gave him a glance when he came in, but there was no surprise in it. Their daughter had evidently told them of his visit. They did not speak. The woman went on with her cooking, and the man, a surly look on his face, stared at the oil-cloth on the table. But it required more than this to disconcert the good-humoured Hans.

"*Bonjour, la compagnie,*" he said cheerfully. "I've brought you a present."

He undid the package he had with him and set out a sizable piece of Gruyère cheese, a piece of pork, and a couple of tins of sardines. The woman turned round and he smiled when he saw the light of greed in her eyes. The man looked at the foodstuff sullenly. Hans gave him his sunny grin.

"I'm sorry we had a misunderstanding the first time I came here. But you shouldn't have interfered."

At that moment the girl came in.

"What are you doing here?" she cried harshly. Then her eyes fell on the things he had brought. She swept them together and flung them at him. "Take them away. Take them."

But her mother sprang forward.

"Annette, you're crazy."

"I won't take his presents."

"It's our own food that they've stolen from us. Look at the sardines. They're Bordeaux sardines."

She picked the things up. Hans looked at the girl with a mocking smile in his light blue eyes.

"Annette's your name, is it? A pretty name. Do you grudge your parents a little food? You said you hadn't had cheese for three months. I couldn't get any ham; I did the best I could."

The farmer's wife took the lump of meat in her hands and pressed it to her bosom. You felt that she could have kissed it. Tears ran down Annette's cheeks.

"The shame of it," she groaned.

"Oh, come now, there's no shame in a bit of Gruyère and a piece of pork."

Hans sat down and lit a cigarette. Then he passed the packet over to the old man. The farmer hesitated for a moment, but the temptation was too strong for him; he took one and handed back the packet.

"Keep it," said Hans. "I can get plenty more." He inhaled the smoke and blew a cloud of it from his nostrils. "Why can't we be friends? What's done can't be undone. War is war, and, well, you know what I mean. I know Annette's an educated girl and I want her to think well of me. I expect we shall be in Soissons for quite a while and I can bring you something now and then to help out. You know, we do all we can to make friends with the townspeople, but they won't let us. They won't even look at us when we pass them in the street. After all, it was an accident, what happened that time I came here with Willi. You needn't be afraid of me. I'll respect Annette as if she was my own sister."

"Why do you want to come here? Why can't you leave us alone?" asked Annette.

He really didn't know. He didn't like to say that he wanted a little human friendship. The silent hostility that surrounded them all at Soissons got on his nerves so that sometimes he wanted to go up to a Frenchman who looked at him as if he wasn't there and knock him down, and sometimes it affected him so that he was almost inclined to cry. It would be nice if he had some place to go where he was welcome. He spoke the truth when he said he had no desire for Annette. She wasn't the sort of woman he fancied. He liked women to be tall and full-breasted, blue-eyed, and fair-haired like himself; he liked them to be strong and hefty and well-covered. That refinement which he couldn't account for, that thin fine nose and those dark eyes, the long pale face – there was something intimidating about the girl, so that if he hadn't been excited by the great victories of the German armies, if he hadn't been so tired and yet so elated, if he hadn't drunk all that wine on an empty stomach, it would never have crossed his mind that he could have anything to do with her.

For a fortnight after that Hans couldn't get away. He'd left the food at the farm and he had no doubt that the old people had wolfed it. He wondered if Annette had eaten it too; he wouldn't have been surprised to discover that the moment his back was turned she had set to with the others. These French people, they couldn't resist getting something for nothing. They were weak and decadent. She hated him, yes, God, how she hated him, but pork was pork, and cheese was cheese. He thought of her quite a lot. It tantalized him that she should have such a loathing for him. He was used to being liked by women. It would be funny if one of these days she fell in love with him. He'd been her first lover and he'd heard the students in Munich over their beer saying that it was her first lover a woman loved, after that it was love. When he'd set his mind on getting a girl he'd never failed yet. Hans laughed to himself and a sly look came into his eyes.

At last he got his chance to go to the farm. He got hold of cheese and butter, sugar, a tin of sausages, and some coffee, and set off on his motor-cycle. But that time he didn't see Annette. She and her father were at work in the fields. The old woman was in the yard and her face lit up when she saw the parcel he was bringing. She led him into the kitchen. Her hands trembled a little as she untied the string and when she saw what he had brought her eyes filled with tears.

"You're very good," she said.

"May I sit down?" he asked politely.

"Of course." She looked out of the window and Hans guessed that she wanted to make sure that Annette was not coming. "Can I offer you a glass of wine."

"I'd be glad of it."

He was sharp enough to see that her greed for food had made her, if not friendly to him, at least willing to come to terms with him. That look out of the window made them almost fellow conspirators.

"Did you like the pork?" he asked.

"It was a treat."

"I'll try to bring you some more next time I come. Did Annette like it?"

"She wouldn't touch a thing you'd left. She said she'd rather starve."

"Silly."

"That's what I said to her. As long as the food is there, I said, there's nothing to be gained by not eating it."

They chatted quite amicably while Hans sipped his wine. He discovered that she was called Madame Périer. He asked her whether there were any other members of the family. She sighed. No, they'd had a son, but he'd been mobilized at the beginning of the war and he'd died. He hadn't been killed, he'd got pneumonia and died in the hospital at Nancy.

"I'm sorry," said Hans.

"Perhaps he's better off than if he'd lived. He was like Annette in many ways. He could never have borne the shame of defeat." She sighed again. "Oh, my poor friend, we've been betrayed."

"Why did you want to fight for the Poles? What were they to you?"

"You're right. If we had let your Hitler take Poland he would have left us alone."

When Hans got up to go he said he would come again soon.

"I shan't forget the pork."

Then Hans had a lucky break; he was given a job that took him twice a week to a town in the vicinity so that he was able to get to the farm much oftener. He took care never to come without bringing something. But he made no headway with Annette. Seeking to ingratiate himself with her, he used the simple wiles that he had discovered went down with women; but they only excited her derision. Thin-lipped and hard, she looked at him as though he were dirt. On more than one occasion she made him so angry that he would have liked to take her by the shoulders and shake the life out of her. Once he found her alone, and when she got up to go he barred her passage.

"Stop where you are. I want to talk to you."

"Talk. I am a woman and defenceless."

"What I want to say is this: for all I know I may be here for a long time. Things aren't going to get easier for you French, they're going to get harder. I can be useful to you. Why don't you be reasonable like your father and mother?"

It was true that old Périer had come round. You couldn't say that he was cordial, he was indeed cold and gruff, but he was civil. He had even asked Hans to bring him some tobacco, and when he wouldn't accept payment for it had thanked him. He was pleased to hear the news of Soissons and grabbed the paper that Hans brought him. Hans, a farmer's son, could talk about the farm as one who knew. It was a good farm, not too big and not too small, well watered, for a sizable brook ran through it, and well wooded, with arable land and pasture. Hans listened with understanding sympathy when the old man bewailed himself because without labour, without fertilizers, his stock taken from him, it was all going to rack and ruin.

"You ask me why I can't be reasonable like my father and mother," said Annette.

She pulled her dress tight and showed herself to him. He couldn't believe his eyes. What he saw caused such a convulsion in his soul as he had never known. The blood rushed to his cheeks.

"You're pregnant."

She sank back on her chair and leaning her head on her hands began to weep as though her heart would break.

"The shame of it. The shame."

He sprang towards her to take her in his arms.

"My sweet," he cried.

But she sprang to her feet and pushed him away.

"Don't touch me. Go away. Go away. Haven't you done me enough harm already?"

She flung out of the room. He waited by himself for a few minutes. He was bewildered. His thoughts in a whirl, he rode slowly back to Soissons, and when he went to bed he couldn't get to sleep for hours. He could think of nothing but Annette and her swollen body. She had been unbearably pathetic as she sat there at the table crying her eyes out. It was his child she bore in her womb. He began to feel drowsy, and then with a start he was once more wide awake, for suddenly it came to him, it came to him with the shattering suddenness of gun-fire: he was in love with her. It was such a surprise, such a shock that he couldn't cope with it. Of course he'd thought of her a lot, but never in that way, he'd thought it would be a great joke if he made her fall in love with him, it would be a triumph if the time came when she offered what he had taken by force; but not for a moment had it occurred to him that she was anything to him but a woman like another. She wasn't his type. She wasn't very pretty. There was nothing to her. Why should he have all of a sudden this funny feeling for her? It wasn't a pleasant feeling either, it was a pain. But he knew what it was all right; it was love, and it made him feel happier than he had ever felt in his life. He wanted to take her in his arms, he wanted to pet her, he wanted to kiss those tear-stained eyes of hers. He didn't desire her, he thought, as a man desires a woman, he wanted to comfort her, wanted her to smile at him – strange, he had never seen her smile, he wanted to see her eyes – fine eyes they were, beautiful eyes – soft with tenderness.

For three days he could not leave Soissons and for three days, three days and three nights, he thought of Annette and the child she would bear. Then he was able to go to the farm. He wanted to see Madame Périer by herself, and luck was with him, for he met her on the road some way from the house. She had been gathering sticks in the wood and was going home with a great bundle on her back. He stopped his motor-cycle. He knew that the friendliness she showed him was due only to the provisions he brought with him, but he didn't care; it was enough that she was mannerly, and that she was prepared to be so as long as she could get something out of him. He told her he wanted to talk to her and asked her to put her bundle down. She did as he bade. It was a grey, cloudy day, but not cold.

"I know about Annette," he said.

She started.

"How did you find out? She was set on your not knowing."

"She told me."

"That was a pretty job of work you did that evening."

"I didn't know. Why didn't you tell me sooner?"

She began to talk, not bitterly, not blaming him even, but as though it were a misfortune of nature, like a cow dying in giving birth to a calf or a sharp spring frost nipping the fruit trees and ruining the crop, a misfortune that human kind must accept with resignation and humility. After that dreadful night Annette had been in bed for days with a high fever. They thought she was going out of her mind. She would scream for hours on end. There were no doctors to be got. The village doctor had been called to the colours. Even in Soissons there were only two doctors left, old men both of them, and how could they get to the farm even if it had been possible to send for them? They weren't allowed to leave the town. Even when the fever went down Annette was too ill to leave her bed, and when she got up she was so weak, so pale, it was pitiful. The shock had been terrible, and when a month went by, and another month, without her being unwell she paid no attention. She had always been irregular. It was Madame Périer who first suspected that something was wrong. She questioned Annette. They were terrified, both of them, but they weren't certain and they said nothing to Périer. When the third month came it was impossible to doubt any longer. Annette was pregnant.

They had an old Citroën in which before the war Madame Périer had taken the farm produce into the market at Soissons two mornings a week, but since the German occupation they had had nothing to sell that made the journey worth while. Petrol was almost unobtainable. But now they got it out and drove into town. The only cars to be seen were the military cars of the Germans. German soldiers lounged about. There were German signs in the streets, and on public buildings proclamations in French signed by the Officer Commanding. Many shops were closed. They went to the old doctor they knew, and he confirmed their suspicions. But he was a devout Catholic and would not help them. When they wept he shrugged his shoulders.

"You're not the only one," he said. "*Il faut souffrir.*"

They knew about the other doctor too and went to see him. They rang the bell and for a long time no one answered. At last the door was opened by a sad-faced woman in black, but when they asked to see the doctor she began to cry. He had been arrested by the Germans because he was a freemason, and was held as a hostage. A bomb had exploded in a café frequented by German officers and two had been killed and several wounded. If the guilty were not handed over before a certain date he was to be shot. The woman seemed kindly and Madame Périer told her of their trouble.

"The brutes," she said. She looked at Annette with compassion. "My poor child."

She gave them the address of a midwife in the town and told them to say that they had come from her. The midwife gave them some medicine. It made Annette so ill that she thought she was going to die, but it had no further effect. Annette was still pregnant.

That was the story that Madame Périer told Hans. For a while he was silent.

"It's Sunday tomorrow," he said then. "I shall have nothing to do. I'll come and we'll talk. I'll bring something nice."

"We have no needles. Can you bring some?"

"I'll try."

She hoisted the bundle of sticks on her back and trudged down the road. Hans went back to Soissons. He dared not use his motor-cycle, so next day he hired a push-bike. He tied his parcel of food on the carrier. It was a larger parcel than usual because he had put a bottle of champagne into it. He got to the farm when the gathering darkness made it certain that they would all be home from work. It was warm and cosy in the kitchen when he walked in. Madame Périer was cooking and her husband was reading a *Paris-Soir*. Annette was darning stockings.

"Look, I've brought you some needles," he said, as he undid his parcel. "And here's some material for you, Annette."

"I don't want it."

"Don't you?" he grinned. "You'll have to begin making things for the baby."

"That's true, Annette," said her mother, "and we have nothing." Annette did not look up from her sewing. Madame Périer's greedy eyes ran over the contents of the parcel. "A bottle of champagne."

174

Hans chuckled.

"I'll tell you what that's for presently. I've had an idea." He hesitated for a moment, then drew up a chair and sat down facing Annette. "I don't know quite how to begin. I'm sorry for what I did that night, Annette. It wasn't my fault, it was the circumstances. Can't you forgive me?"

She threw him a look of hatred.

"Never. Why don't you leave me alone? Isn't it enough that you've ruined my life?"

"Well, that's just it. Perhaps I haven't. When I knew you were going to have a baby it had a funny effect on me. It's all different now. It's made me so proud."

"Proud?" she flung at him viciously.

"I want you to have the baby, Annette. I'm glad you couldn't get rid of it."

"How dare you say that?"

"But listen to me. I've been thinking of nothing else since I knew. The war will be over in six months. We shall bring the English to their knees in the spring. They haven't got a chance. And then I shall be demobilized and I'll marry you."

"You? Why?"

He blushed under his tan. He could not bring himself to say it in French, so he said it in German. He knew she understood it.

"*Ich liebe dich.*"

"What does he say?" asked Madame Périer.

"He says he loves me."

Annette threw back her head and broke into a peal of harsh laughter. She laughed louder and louder and she couldn't stop and tears streamed from her eyes. Madame Périer slapped her sharply on both cheeks.

"Don't pay any attention," she said to Hans. "It's hysteria. Her condition, you know."

Annette gasped. She gained control over herself.

"I brought the bottle of champagne to celebrate our engagement," said Hans.

"That's the bitterest thing of all," said Annette, "that we were beaten by fools, by such fools."

Hans went on speaking in German.

"I didn't know I loved you till that day when I found out that you were going to have a baby. It came like a clap of thunder, but I think I've loved you all the time."

"What does he say?" asked Madame Périer.

"Nothing of importance."

He fell back into French. He wanted Annette's parents to hear what he had to say.

"I'd marry you now, only they wouldn't let me. And don't think I'm nothing at all. My father's well-to-do and we're well thought of in our commune. I'm the eldest son and you'd want for nothing."

"Are you a Catholic?" asked Madame Périer.

"Yes, I'm a Catholic."

"That's something."

"It's pretty, the country where we live, and the soil's good. There's not better farming land between Munich and Innsbruck, and it's our own. My grandfather bought it after the war of 'seventy. And we've got a car and a radio, and we're on the telephone."

Annette turned to her father.

"He has all the tact in the world, this gentleman," she cried ironically. She eyed Hans. "It would be a nice position for me, the foreigner from the conquered country with a child born out of wedlock. It offers me a chance of happiness, doesn't it? A fine chance."

Périer, a man of few words, spoke for the first time.

"No. I don't deny that it's a fine gesture you're making. I went through the last war and we all did things we wouldn't have done in peace time. Human nature is human nature. But now that our son is dead, Annette is all we have. We can't let her go."

"I thought you might feel that way," said Hans, "and I've got my answer to that. I'll stay here."

Annette gave him a quick look.

"What do you mean?" asked Madame Périer.

"I've got another brother. He can stay and help my father. I like this country. With energy and initiative a man could make a good thing of your farm. When the war's over a lot of Germans will be settling here. It's well known that you haven't got enough men in France to work the land you've got. A fellow gave us a lecture the other day at Soissons. He said that a third of the farms were left uncultivated because there aren't the men to work them."

Périer and his wife exchanged glances and Annette saw that they were wavering. That was what they'd wanted since their son had died, a son-in-law who was strong and hefty and could take over when they grew too old to do more than potter about.

"That changes the case," said Madame Périer. "It's a proposition to consider."

"Hold your tongue," cried Annette roughly. She leant forward and fixed her burning eyes on the German. "I'm engaged to a teacher who worked in the boys' school in the town where I taught, we were to be married after the war. He's not strong and big like you, or handsome; he's small and frail. His only beauty is the intelligence that shines in his face, his only strength is the greatness of his soul. He's not a barbarian, he's civilized; he has a thousand years of civilization behind him. I love him. I love him with all my heart and soul."

Hans's face grew sullen. It had never occurred to him that Annette might care for anyone else.

"Where is he now?"

"Where do you suppose he is? In Germany. A prisoner and starving. While you eat the fat of our land. How many times have I got to tell you that I hate you? You ask me to forgive you. Never. You want to make reparation. You fool." She threw her head back and there was a look of intolerable anguish on her face. "Ruined. Oh, he'll forgive me. He's tender. But I'm tortured by the thought that one day the suspicion may come to him that perhaps I hadn't been forced – that perhaps I'd given myself to you for butter and cheese and silk stockings. I shouldn't be the only one. And what would our life be with that child between us, your child, a German child? Big like you, and blond like you, and blue-eyed like you. Oh, my God, why do I have to suffer this?"

She got up and went swiftly out of the kitchen. For a minute the three were left in silence. Hans looked ruefully at his bottle of champagne. He sighed and rose to his feet. When he went out Madame Périer accompanied him.

"Did you mean it when you said you would marry her?" she asked him, speaking in a low voice.

"Yes. Every word. I love her."

"And you wouldn't take her away? You'd stay here and work on the farm?"

"I promise you."

"Evidently my old man can't last for ever. At home you'd have to share with your brother. Here you'd share with nobody."

"There's that too."

"We never were in favour of Annette marrying that teacher, but our son was alive then and he said, if she wants to marry him, why shouldn't she? Annette was crazy about him. But now that our son's dead, poor boy, it's different. Even if she wanted to, how could she work the farm alone?"

"It would be a shame if it was sold. I know how one feels about one's own land."

They had reached the road. She took his hand and gave it a little squeeze.

"Come again soon."

Hans knew that she was on his side. It was a comfort to him to think that as he rode back to Soissons. It was a bother that Annette was in love with somebody else. Fortunately he was a prisoner; long before he was likely to be released the baby would be born. That might change her: you could never tell with a woman. Why, in his village there'd been a woman who was so much in love with her husband that it had been a joke, and then she had a baby and after that she couldn't bear the sight of him. Well, why shouldn't the contrary happen too? And now that he'd offered to marry her she must see that he was a decent sort of fellow. God, how pathetic she'd looked with her head flung back, and how well she'd spoken! What language! An actress on the stage couldn't have expressed herself better, and yet it had all sounded so natural. You had to admit that, these French people knew how to talk. Oh, she was clever. Even when she lashed him with that bitter tongue it was a joy to listen to her. He hadn't had a bad education himself, but he couldn't hold a candle to her. Culture, that's what she had.

"I'm a donkey," he said out loud as he rode along. She'd said he was big and strong and handsome. Would she have said that if it hadn't meant something to her? And she'd talked of the baby having fair hair and blue eyes like his own. If that didn't mean that his colouring had made an impression on her he was a Dutchman. He chuckled. "Give me time. Patience, and let nature go to work."

The weeks went by. The CO at Soissons was an elderly, easy-going fellow and in view of what the spring had in store for them he was content not to drive his men too hard. The German papers told them that England was being wrecked by the Luftwaffe and the people were in a panic. Submarines were sinking British ships by the score and the country was starving. Revolution was imminent. Before summer it would be all over and the Germans would be masters of the world. Hans wrote home and told his parents that he was going to marry a French girl and with her a fine farm. He proposed that his brother should borrow money to buy him out of his share of the family property so that he could increase the size of his own holding while land, owing to the war and the exchange, could still be bought for a song. He went over the farm with Périer. The old man listened quietly when Hans told him his ideas: the farm would have to be restocked and as a German he would have a pull; the motor tractor was old, he would get a fine new one from Germany, and a motor plough. To make a farm pay you had to take advantage of modern inventions. Madame Périer told him afterwards that her husband had said he wasn't a bad lad and seemed to know a lot. She was very friendly with him now and insisted that he should share their midday meal with them on Sundays. She translated his name into French and called him Jean. He was always ready to give a hand, and as time went on and Annette could do less and less it was useful to have a man about who didn't mind doing a job of work.

Annette remained fiercely hostile. She never spoke to him except to answer his direct questions and as soon as it was possible went to her own room. When it was so cold that she couldn't stay there she sat by the side of the kitchen stove, sewing or reading, and took no more notice of him than if he hadn't been there. She was in radiant health. There was colour in her cheeks and in Hans's eyes she was beautiful. Her approaching maternity had given her a strange dignity and he was filled with exultation when he gazed upon her. Then one day when he was on his way to the farm he saw Madame Périer in the road waving to him to stop. He put his brakes on hard.

"I've been waiting for an hour. I thought you'd never come. You must go back. Pierre is dead."

"Who's Pierre?"

"Pierre Gavin. The teacher Annette was going to marry."

Hans's heart leapt. What luck! Now he'd have his chance.

"Is she upset?"

"She's not crying. When I tried to say something she bit my head off. If she saw you today she's capable of sticking a knife into you."

"It's not my fault if he died. How did you hear?"

"A prisoner, a friend of his, escaped through Switzerland and he wrote to Annette. We got the letter this morning. There was a mutiny in the camp because they weren't given enough to eat, and the ringleaders were shot. Pierre was one of them."

Hans was silent. He could only think it served the man right. What did they think that a prison camp was – the Ritz?

"Give her time to get over the shock," said Madame Périer. "When she's calmer I'll talk to her. I'll write you a letter when you can come again."

"All right. You will help me, won't you?"

"You can be sure of that. My husband and I, we're agreed. We talked it over and we came to the conclusion that the only thing to do was to accept the situation. He's no fool, my husband, and he says the best chance for France now is to collaborate. And take it all in all I don't dislike you. I shouldn't wonder if you didn't make Annette a better husband than that teacher. And with the baby coming and all."

"I want it to be a boy," said Hans.

"It's going to be a boy. I know for certain. I've seen it in the coffee grounds and I've put out the cards. The answer is a boy every time."

"I almost forgot, here are some papers for you," said Hans, as he turned his cycle and prepared to mount.

He handed her three numbers of *Paris-Soir*. Old Périer read every evening. He read that the French must be realistic and accept the new order that Hitler was going to create in Europe. He read that the German submarines were sweeping the sea. He read that the General Staff had organized to the last detail the campaign that would bring England to her knees and that the Americans were too unprepared, too soft and too divided to come to her help. He read that

France must take the heaven-sent opportunity and by loyal collaboration with the Reich regain her honoured position in the new Europe. And it wasn't Germans who wrote it all; it was Frenchmen. He nodded his head with approval when he read that the plutocrats and the Jews would be destroyed and the poor man in France would at last come into his own. They were quite right, the clever fellows who said that France was essentially an agricultural country and its backbone was its industrious farmers. Good sense, that was.

One evening, when they were finishing their supper, ten days after the news had come of Pierre Gavin's death, Madame Périer, by arrangement with her husband, said to Annette:

"I wrote a letter to Hans a few days ago telling him to come here tomorrow."

"Thank you for the warning. I shall stay in my room."

"Oh, come, daughter, the time has passed for foolishness. You must be realistic. Pierre is dead. Hans loves you and wants to marry you. He's a fine-looking fellow. Any girl would be proud of him as a husband. How can we restock the farm without his help? He's going to buy a tractor and a plough with his own money. You must let bygones be bygones."

"You're wasting your breath, mother. I earned my living before, I can earn my living again. I hate him. I hate his vanity and his arrogance. I could kill him: his death wouldn't satisfy me. I should like to torture him as he's tortured me. I think I should die happy if I could find a way to wound him as he's wounded me."

"You're being very silly, my poor child."

"Your mother's right, my girl," said Périer. "We've been defeated and we must accept the consequences. We've got to make the best arrangement we can with the conquerors. We're cleverer than they are and if we play our cards well we shall come out on top. France was rotten. It's the Jews and the plutocrats who ruined the country. Read the papers and you'll see for yourself!"

"Do you think I believe a word in that paper? Why do you think he brings it to you except that it's sold to the Germans? The men who write in it – traitors, traitors. Oh God, may I live to see them torn to pieces by the mob. Bought, bought, every one of them – bought with German money. The swine."

Madame Périer was getting exasperated.

"What have you got against the boy? He took you by force – yes, he was drunk at the time. It's not the first time that's happened to a woman and it won't be the last time. He hit your father and he bled like a pig, but does your father bear him malice?"

"It was an unpleasant incident, but I've forgotten it," said Périer.

Annette burst into harsh laughter.

"You should have been a priest. You forgive injuries with a spirit truly Christian."

"And what is there wrong about that?" asked Madame Périer angrily. "Hasn't he done everything he could to make amends? Where would your father have got his tobacco all these months if it hadn't been for him? If we haven't gone hungry it's owing to him."

"If you'd had any pride, if you'd had any sense of decency, you'd have thrown his presents in his face."

"You've profited by them, haven't you?"

"Never. Never."

"It's a lie and you know it. You've refused to eat the cheese he brought and the butter and the sardines. But the soup you've eaten, you know I put the meat in it that he brought; and the salad you ate tonight, if you didn't have to eat it dry, it's because he brought me oil."

Annette sighed deeply. She passed her hand over her eyes.

"I know. I tried not to, I couldn't help myself, I was so hungry. Yes, I knew his meat went into the soup and I ate it. I knew the salad was made with his oil. I wanted to refuse it; I had such a longing for it, it wasn't I that ate it, it was a ravenous beast within me."

"That's neither here nor there. You ate it."

"With shame. With despair. They broke our strength first with their tanks and their planes, and now when we're defenceless they're breaking our spirit by starving us."

"You get nowhere by being theatrical, my girl. For an educated woman you have really no sense. Forget the past and give a father to your child, to say nothing of a good workman for the farm who'll be worth two hired men. That is sense."

Annette shrugged her shoulders wearily and they lapsed into silence. Next day Hans came. Annette gave him a sullen look, but neither spoke nor moved. Hans smiled.

"Thank you for not running away," he said.

"My parents asked you to come and they've gone down to the village. It suits me because I want to have a definite talk with you. Sit down."

He took off his coat and his helmet and drew a chair to the table.

"My parents want me to marry you. You've been clever; with your presents, with your promises, you've got round them. They believe all they read in the papers you bring them. I want to tell you that I will never marry you. I wouldn't have thought it possible that I could hate a human being as I hate you."

"Let me speak in German. You understand enough to know what I'm saying."

"I ought to. I taught it. For two years I was governess to two little girls in Stuttgart."

He broke into German, but she went on speaking French.

"It's not only that I love you, I admire you. I admire your distinction and your grace. There's something about you I don't understand. I respect you. Oh, I can see that you don't want to marry me now even if it were possible. But Pierre is dead."

"Don't speak of him," she cried violently. "That would be the last straw."

"I only want to tell you that for your sake I'm sorry he died."

"Shot in cold blood by his German jailers."

"Perhaps in time you'll grieve for him less. You know, when someone you love dies, you think you'll never get over it, but you do. Won't it be better then to have a father for your child?"

"Even if there were nothing else do you think I could ever forget that you are a German and I'm a Frenchwoman? If you weren't as stupid as only a German can be you'd see that that child must be a reproach to me as long as I live. Do you think I have no friends? How could I ever look them in the face with the child I had with a German soldier? There's only one thing I ask you; leave me alone with my disgrace. Go, go – for God's sake go and never come again."

"But he's my child too. I want him."

"You?" she cried in astonishment. "What can a by-blow that you got in a moment of savage drunkenness mean to you?"

"You don't understand. I'm so proud and so happy. It was when I knew you were going to have a baby that I knew I loved you. At first I couldn't believe it; it was such a surprise to me. Don't you see what I mean? That child that's going to be born means everything in the world to me. Oh, I don't know how to put it; it's put feeling in my heart that I don't understand myself."

She looked at him intently and there was a strange gleam in her eyes. You would have said it was a look of triumph. She gave a short laugh.

"I don't know whether I more loathe the brutality of you Germans or despise your sentimentality."

He seemed not to have heard what she said.

"I think of him all the time."

"You've made up your mind it'll be a boy?"

"I know it'll be a boy. I want to hold him in my arms and I want to teach him to walk. And then when he grows older I'll teach him all I know. I'll teach him to ride and I'll teach him to shoot. Are there fish in your brook? I'll teach him to fish. I'm going to be the proudest father in the world."

She stared at him with hard, hard eyes. Her face was set and stern. An idea, a terrible idea was forming itself in her mind.

He gave her a disarming smile.

"Perhaps when you see how much I love our boy, you'll come to love me too. I'll make you a good husband, my pretty."

She said nothing. She merely kept on gazing at him sullenly.

"Haven't you one kind word for me?" he said.

She flushed. She clasped her hands tightly together.

"Others may despise me. I will never do anything that can make me despise myself. You are my enemy and you will always be my enemy. I only live to see the deliverance of France. It'll come, perhaps not next year or the year after, perhaps not for thirty years, but it'll come. The rest of them can do what they like, I will never come to terms with the invaders of my country. I hate you and I hate this child that you've given me. Yes, we've been defeated. Before the end comes you'll see that we haven't been conquered. Now go. My mind's made up and nothing on God's earth can change it."

He was silent for a minute or two.

"Have you made arrangements for a doctor? I'll pay all the expenses."

"Do you suppose we want to spread our shame through the whole countryside? My mother will do all that's necessary."

"But supposing there's an accident?"

"And supposing you mind your own business!"

He sighed and rose to his feet. When he closed the door behind him she watched him walk down the pathway that led to the road. She realized with rage that some of the things he said had aroused in her heart a feeling that she had never felt for him before.

"O God, give me strength," she cried.

Then, as he walked along, the dog, an old dog they'd had for years, ran up to him barking angrily. He had tried for months to make friends with the dog, but it had never responded to his advances; when he tried to pat it, it backed away growling and showing its teeth. And now as the dog ran towards him, irritably giving way to his feeling of frustration, Hans gave it a savage brutal kick and the dog was flung into the bushes and limped yelping away.

"The beast," she cried. "Lies, lies, lies. And I was weak enough to be almost sorry for him."

There was a looking-glass hanging by the side of the door and she looked at herself in it. She drew herself up and smiled at her reflection. But rather than a smile it was a fiendish grimace.

It was now March. There was a bustle of activity in the garrison at Soissons. There were inspections and there was intensive training. Rumour was rife. There was no doubt they were going somewhere, but the rank and file could only guess where. Some thought they were being got ready at last for the invasion of England, others were of opinion that they would be sent to the Balkans, and others again talked of the Ukraine. Hans was kept busy. It was not till the second Sunday afternoon that he was able to get out to the farm. It was a cold grey day, with sleet that looked as though it might turn to snow falling in sudden windy flurries. The country was grim and cheerless.

"You!" cried Madame Périer when he went in. "We thought you were dead."

"I couldn't come before. We're off any day now. We don't know when."

"The baby was born this morning. It's a boy."

Hans's heart gave a great leap in his breast. He hung his arms round the old woman and kissed her on both cheeks.

"A Sunday child, he ought to be lucky. Let's open the bottle of champagne. How's Annette?"

"She's as well as can be expected. She had a very easy time. She began to have pains last night and by five o'clock this morning it was all over."

Old Périer was smoking his pipe sitting as near the stove as he could get. He smiled quietly at the boy's enthusiasm.

"One's first child, it has an effect on one," he said.

"He has quite a lot of hair and it's as fair as yours; and blue eyes just like you said he'd have," said Madame Périer. "I've never seen a lovelier baby. He'll be just like his papa."

"Oh, my God, I'm so happy," cried Hans. "How beautiful the world is! I want to see Annette."

"I don't know if she'll see you. I don't want to upset her on account of the milk."

"No, no, don't upset her on my account. If she doesn't want to see me it doesn't matter. But let me see the baby just for a minute."

"I'll see what I can do. I'll try to bring it down."

Madame Périer went out and they heard her heavy tread clumping up the stairs. But in a moment they heard her clattering down again. She burst into the kitchen.

"They're not there. She isn't in her room. The baby's gone."

Périer and Hans cried out and without thinking what they were doing all three of them scampered upstairs. The harsh light of the winter afternoon cast over the shabby furniture, the iron bed, the cheap wardrobe, the chest of drawers, a dismal squalor. There was no one in the room.

"Where is she?" screamed Madame Périer. She ran into the narrow passage, opening doors, and called the girl's name. "Annette, Annette. Oh, what madness!"

"Perhaps in the sitting-room."

They ran downstairs to the unused parlour. An icy air met them as they opened the door. They opened the door of a storeroom.

"She's gone out. Something awful has happened."

"How could she have got out?" asked Hans, sick with anxiety.

"Through the front door, you fool."

Périer went up to it and looked.

"That's right. The bolt's drawn back."

"Oh, my God, my God, what madness," cried Madame Périer. "It'll kill her."

"We must look for her," said Hans. Instinctively, because that was the way he always went in and out, he ran back into the kitchen and the others followed him. "Which way?"

"The brook," the old woman gasped.

He stopped as though turned to stone with horror. He stared at the old woman aghast.

"I'm frightened," she cried. "I'm frightened."

Hans flung open the door, and as he did so Annette walked in. She had nothing on but her nightdress and a flimsy rayon dressing-gown. It was pink, with pale blue flowers. She was soaked, and her hair, dishevelled, clung damply to her head and hung down her shoulders in bedraggled wisps. She was deathly white. Madame Périer sprang towards her and took her in her arms.

"Where have you been? Oh, my poor child, you're wet through. What madness!"

But Annette pushed her away. She looked at Hans.

"You've come at the right moment, you."

"Where's the baby?" cried Madame Périer.

"I had to do it at once. I was afraid if I waited I shouldn't have the courage."

"Annette, what have you done?"

"I've done what I had to do. I took it down to the brook and held it under water till it was dead."

Hans gave a great cry, the cry of an animal wounded to death; he covered his face with his hands, and staggering like a drunken man flung out of the door. Annette sank into a chair, and leaning her forehead on her two fists burst into passionate weeping.

BEFORE THE PARTY

MRS SKINNER LIKED to be in good time. She was already dressed, in black silk as befitted her age and the mourning she wore for her son-in-law, and now she put on her toque. She was a little uncertain about it, since the egrets' feathers which adorned it might very well arouse in some of the friends she would certainly meet at the party acid expostulations; and of course it was shocking to kill those beautiful white birds, in the mating season too, for the sake of their feathers; but there they were, so pretty and stylish, and it would have been silly to refuse them, and it would have hurt her son-in-law's feelings. He had brought them all the way from Borneo and he expected her to be so pleased with them. Kathleen had made herself rather unpleasant about them, she must wish she hadn't now, after what had happened, but Kathleen had never really liked Harold. Mrs Skinner, standing at her dressing-table, placed the toque on her head, it was after all the only nice hat she had, and put in a pin with a large jet knob. If anybody spoke to her about the ospreys she had her answer.

"I know it's dreadful," she would say, "and I wouldn't dream of buying them, but my poor son-in-law brought them back the last time he was home on leave."

That would explain her possession of them and excuse their use. Everyone had been very kind. Mrs Skinner took a clean handkerchief from a drawer and sprinkled a little eau de Cologne on it. She never used scent, and she had always thought it rather fast, but eau de Cologne was so refreshing. She was very nearly ready now, and her eyes wandered out of the window behind her looking-glass. Canon Heywood had a beautiful day for his garden-party. It was warm and the sky was blue; the trees had not yet lost the fresh green of the spring. She smiled as she saw her little granddaughter in the strip of garden behind the house busily raking her very own flower-bed. Mrs Skinner wished Joan were not quite so pale, it was a mistake to have kept her so long in the tropics; and she was so grave for her age, you never saw her run about; she played quiet games of her own invention and watered her garden. Mrs Skinner gave the front of her dress a little pat, took up her gloves, and went downstairs.

Kathleen was at the writing-table in the window busy with lists she was making, for she was honorary secretary of the Ladies' Golf Club, and when there were competitions had a good deal to do. But she too was ready for the party.

"I see you've put on your jumper after all," said Mrs Skinner.

They had discussed at luncheon whether Kathleen should wear her jumper or her black chiffon. The jumper was black and white, and Kathleen thought it rather smart, but it was hardly mourning. Millicent, however, was in favour of it.

"There's no reason why we should all look as if we'd just come from a funeral," she said. "Harold's been dead eight months."

To Mrs Skinner it seemed rather unfeeling to talk like that. Millicent was strange since her return from Borneo.

"You're not going to leave off your weeds yet, darling?" she asked.

Millicent did not give a direct answer.

"People don't wear mourning in the way they used," she said. She paused a little and when she went on there was a tone in her voice which Mrs Skinner thought quite peculiar. It was plain that Kathleen noticed it too, for she gave her sister a curious look. "I'm sure Harold wouldn't wish me to wear mourning for him indefinitely."

"I dressed early because I wanted to say something to Millicent," said Kathleen in reply to her mother's observation.

"Oh?"

Kathleen did not explain. But she put her lists aside and with knitted brows read for the second time a letter from a lady who complained that the committee had most unfairly marked down her handicap from twenty-four to eighteen. It requires a good deal of tact to be honorary secretary to a ladies' golf club. Mrs Skinner began to put on her new gloves. The sun-blinds kept the room cool and dark. She looked at the great wooden hornbill, gaily painted, which Harold had left in her safekeeping; and it seemed a little odd and barbaric to her, but he had set much store on it. It had some religious significance and Canon Heywood had been greatly struck by it. On the wall, over the sofa, were Malay weapons, she forgot what they were called, and here and there on occasional tables pieces of silver and brass which Harold at various times had sent to them. She had liked Harold and involuntarily her eyes sought his photograph which stood on the piano with photographs of her two daughters, her grandchild, her sister, and her sister's son.

"Why, Kathleen, where's Harold's photograph?" she asked.

Kathleen looked round. It no longer stood in its place.

"Someone's taken it away," said Kathleen.

Surprised and puzzled, she got up and went over to the piano. The photographs had been rearranged so that no gap should show.

"Perhaps Millicent wanted to have it in her bedroom," said Mrs Skinner.

"I should have noticed it. Besides, Millicent has several photographs of Harold. She keeps them locked up."

Mrs Skinner had thought it very peculiar that her daughter should have no photographs of Harold in her room. Indeed she had spoken of it once, but Millicent had made no reply. Millicent had been strangely silent since she came back from Borneo, and had not encouraged the sympathy Mrs Skinner would have been so willing to show her. She seemed unwilling to speak of her great loss. Sorrow took people in different ways. Her husband had said the best thing was to leave her alone. The thought of him turned her ideas to the party they were going to.

"Father asked if I thought he ought to wear a top-hat," she said. "I said I thought it was just as well to be on the safe side."

It was going to be quite a grand affair. They were having ices, strawberry and vanilla, from Boddy, the confectioner, but the Heywoods were making the iced coffee at home. Everyone would be there. They had been asked to meet the Bishop of Hong Kong, who was staying with the Canon, an old college friend of his, and he was going to speak on the Chinese missions. Mrs Skinner, whose daughter had lived in the East for eight years and whose son-in-law had been Resident of a district in Borneo, was in a flutter of interest. Naturally it meant more to her than to people who had never had anything to do with the Colonies and that sort of thing.

"What can they know of England who only England know?" as Mr Skinner said.

He came into the room at that moment. He was a lawyer, as his father had been before him, and he had offices in Lincoln's Inn Fields. He went up to London every morning and came down every evening. He was only able to accompany his wife and daughters to the Canon's garden-party because the Canon had very wisely chosen a Saturday to have it on. Mr Skinner looked very well in his tail-coat and pepper-and-salt trousers. He was not exactly dressy, but he was neat. He looked like a respectable family solicitor, which indeed he was; his firm never touched work that was not perfectly above board, and if a client went to him with some trouble that was not quite nice, Mr Skinner would look grave.

"I don't think this is the sort of case that we very much care to undertake," he said. "I think you'd do better to go elsewhere."

He drew towards him his writing-block and scribbled a name and address on it. He tore off a sheet of paper and handed it to his client.

"If I were you I think I would go and see these people. If you mention my name I believe they'll do anything they can for you."

Mr Skinner was clean-shaven and very bald. His pale lips were tight and thin, but his blue eyes were shy. He had no colour in his cheeks and his face was much lined.

"I see you've put on your new trousers," said Mrs Skinner.

"I thought it would be a good opportunity," he answered. "I was wondering if I should wear a buttonhole."

"I wouldn't, father," said Kathleen. "I don't think it's awfully good form."

"A lot of people will be wearing them," said Mrs Skinner.

"Only clerks and people like that," said Kathleen. "The Heywoods have had to ask everybody, you know. And besides, we are in mourning."

"I wonder if there'll be a collection after the Bishop's address," said Mr Skinner.

"I should hardly think so," said Mrs Skinner.

"I think it would be rather bad form," agreed Kathleen.

"It's as well to be on the safe side," said Mr Skinner. "I'll give for all of us. I was wondering if ten shillings would be enough or if I must give a pound."

"If you give anything I think you ought to give a pound, father," said Kathleen.

"I'll see when the time comes. I don't want to give less than anyone else, but on the other hand I see no reason to give more than I need."

Kathleen put away her papers in the drawer of the writing-table and stood up. She looked at her wrist-watch.

"Is Millicent ready?" asked Mrs Skinner.

"There's plenty of time. We're only asked at four, and I don't think we ought to arrive much before half past. I told Davis to bring the car round at four-fifteen."

Generally Kathleen drove the car, but on grand occasions like this Davis, who was the gardener, put on his uniform and acted as chauffeur. It looked better when you drove up, and naturally Kathleen didn't much want to drive herself when she was wearing her new jumper. The sight of her mother forcing her fingers one by one into her new gloves reminded her that she must put on her own. She smelt them to see if any odour of the cleaning still clung to them. It was very slight. She didn't believe anyone would notice.

At last the door opened and Millicent came in. She wore her widow's weeds. Mrs Skinner never could get used to them, but of course she knew that Millicent must wear them for a year. It was a pity they didn't suit her; they suited some people. She had tried on Millicent's bonnet once, with its white band and long veil, and thought she looked very well in it. Of course she hoped dear Alfred would survive her, but if he didn't she would never go out of weeds. Queen Victoria never had. It was different for Millicent; Millicent was a much younger woman; she was only thirty-six: it was very sad to be a widow at thirty-six. And there wasn't much chance of her marrying again. Kathleen wasn't very likely to marry now, she was thirty-five; last time Millicent and Harold had come home she had suggested that they should have Kathleen to stay with them; Harold had seemed willing enough, but Millicent said it wouldn't do. Mrs Skinner didn't know why not. It would give her a chance. Of course they didn't want to get rid of her, but a girl ought to marry, and somehow all the men they knew at home were married already. Millicent said the climate was trying. It was true she was a bad colour. No one would think now that Millicent had been the prettier of the two. Kathleen had fined down as she grew older, of course some people said she was too thin, but now that she had cut her hair, with her cheeks red from playing golf in all weathers, Mrs Skinner thought her quite pretty. No one could say that of poor Millicent; she had lost her figure completely; she had never been tall, and now that she had filled out she looked stocky. She was a good deal too fat; Mrs Skinner supposed it was due to the tropical heat that prevented her from taking exercise. Her skin was sallow and muddy; and her blue eyes, which had been her best feature, had gone quite pale.

"She ought to do something about her neck," Mrs Skinner reflected. "She's becoming dreadfully jowly."

She had spoken of it once or twice to her husband. He remarked that Millicent wasn't as young as she was; that might be, but she needn't let herself go altogether. Mrs Skinner made up her mind to talk to her daughter seriously, but of course she must respect her grief, and she would wait till the year was up. She was just as glad to have this reason to put off a conversation the thought of which made her slightly nervous. For Millicent was certainly changed. There was something sullen in her face which made her mother not quite at home with her. Mrs Skinner liked to say aloud all the thoughts that passed through her head, but Millicent when you made a remark (just to say something, you know) had an awkward habit of not answering, so that you wondered whether she had heard. Sometimes Mrs Skinner found it so irritating, that not to be quite sharp with Millicent she had to remind herself that poor Harold had only been dead eight months.

The light from the window fell on the widow's heavy face as she advanced silently, but Kathleen stood with her back to it. She watched her sister for a moment.

"Millicent, there's something I want to say to you," she said. "I was playing golf with Gladys Heywood this morning."

"Did you beat her?" asked Millicent.

Gladys Heywood was the Canon's only unmarried daughter.

"She told me something about you which I think you ought to know."

Millicent's eyes passed beyond her sister to the little girl watering flowers in the garden.

"Have you told Annie to give Joan her tea in the kitchen, mother?" she said.

"Yes, she'll have it when the servants have theirs."

Kathleen looked at her sister coolly.

"The Bishop spent two or three days at Singapore on his way home," she went on. "He's very fond of travelling. He's been to Borneo, and he knows a good many of the people that you know."

"He'll be interested to see you, dear," said Mrs Skinner. "Did he know poor Harold?"

"Yes, he met him at Kuala Solor. He remembers him very well. He says he was shocked to hear of his death."

Millicent sat down and began to put on her black gloves. It seemed strange to Mrs Skinner that she received these remarks with complete silence.

"Oh, Millicent," she said, "Harold's photo has disappeared. Have you taken it?"

"Yes, I put it away."

"I should have thought you'd like to have it out."

Once more Millicent said nothing. It really was an exasperating habit.

Kathleen turned slightly in order to face her sister.

"Millicent, why did you tell us that Harold died of fever?"

The widow made no gesture, she looked at Kathleen with steady eyes, but her sallow skin darkened with a flush. She did not reply.

"What *do* you mean, Kathleen?" asked Mr Skinner, with surprise.

"The Bishop says that Harold committed suicide."

Mrs Skinner gave a startled cry, but her husband put out a deprecating hand.

"Is it true, Millicent?"

"It is."

"But why didn't you tell us?"

Millicent paused for an instant. She fingered idly a piece of Brunei brass which stood on the table by her side. That too had been a present from Harold.

"I thought it better for Joan that her father should be thought to have died of fever. I didn't want her to know anything about it."

"You've put us in an awfully awkward position," said Kathleen, frowning a little. "Gladys Heywood said she thought it rather nasty of me not to have told her the truth. I had the greatest difficulty in getting her to believe that I knew absolutely nothing about it. She said her father was rather put out. He says, after all the years we've known one another, and considering that he married you, and the terms we've been on, and all that, he does think we might have had confidence in him. And at all events, if we didn't want to tell him the truth we needn't have told him a lie."

"I must say I sympathize with him there," said Mr Skinner, acidly.

"Of course I told Gladys that we weren't to blame. We only told them what you told us."

"I hope it didn't put you off your game," said Millicent.

"Really, my dear, I think that is a most improper observation," exclaimed her father.

He rose from his chair, walked over to the empty fireplace, and from force of habit stood in front of it with parted coat-tails.

"It was my business," said Millicent, "and if I chose to keep it to myself I didn't see why I shouldn't."

"It doesn't look as if you had any affection for your mother if you didn't even tell her," said Mrs Skinner.

Millicent shrugged her shoulders.

"You might have known it was bound to come out," said Kathleen.

"Why? I didn't expect that two gossiping old parsons would have nothing else to talk about than me."

"When the Bishop said he'd been to Borneo it's only natural that the Heywoods should ask him if he knew you and Harold."

"All that's neither here nor there," said Mr Skinner. "I think you should certainly have told us the truth, and we could have decided what was the best thing to do. As a solicitor I can tell you that in the long run it only makes things worse if you attempt to hide them."

"Poor Harold," said Mrs Skinner, and the tears began to trickle down her raddled cheeks. "It seems dreadful. He was always a good son-in-law to me. Whatever induced him to do such a dreadful thing?"

"The climate."

"I think you'd better give us all the facts, Millicent," said her father.

"Kathleen will tell you."

Kathleen hesitated. What she had to say really was rather dreadful. It seemed terrible that such things should happen to a family like theirs.

"The Bishop says he cut his throat."

Mrs Skinner gasped and she went impulsively up to her bereaved daughter. She wanted to fold her in her arms.

"My poor child," she sobbed.

But Millicent withdrew herself.

"Please don't fuss me, mother. I really can't stand being mauled about."

"Really, Millicent," said Mr Skinner, with a frown.

He did not think she was behaving very nicely.

195

Mrs Skinner dabbed her eyes carefully with her handkerchief and with a sigh and a little shake of the head returned to her chair. Kathleen fidgeted with the long chain she wore round her neck.

"It does seem rather absurd that I should have to be told the details of my brother-in-law's death by a friend. It makes us all look such fools. The Bishop wants very much to see you, Millicent; he wants to tell you how much he feels for you." She paused, but Millicent did not speak. "He says that Millicent had been away with Joan and when she came back she found poor Harold lying dead on his bed."

"It must have been a great shock," said Mr Skinner.

Mrs Skinner began to cry again, but Kathleen put her hand gently on her shoulder.

"Don't cry, mother," she said. "It'll make your eyes red and people will think it so funny."

They were all silent while Mrs Skinner, drying her eyes, made a successful effort to control herself. It seemed very strange to her that at this very moment she should be wearing in her toque the ospreys that poor Harold had given her.

"There's something else I ought to tell you," said Kathleen.

Millicent looked at her sister again, without haste, and her eyes were steady, but watchful. She had the look of a person who is waiting for a sound which he is afraid of missing.

"I don't want to say anything to wound you, dear," Kathleen went on, "but there's something else and I think you ought to know it. The Bishop says that Harold drank."

"Oh, my dear, how dreadful!" cried Mrs Skinner. "What a shocking thing to say. Did Gladys Heywood tell you? What did you say?"

"I said it was entirely untrue."

"This is what comes of making secrets of things," said Mr Skinner, irritably. "It's always the same. If you try and hush a thing up all sorts of rumours get about which are ten times worse than the truth."

"They told the Bishop in Singapore that Harold had killed himself while he was suffering from delirium tremens. I think for all our sakes you ought to deny that, Millicent."

"It's such a dreadful thing to have said about anyone who's dead," said Mrs Skinner. "And it'll be so bad for Joan when she grows up."

"But what is the foundation of this story, Millicent?" asked her father. "Harold was always very abstemious."

"Here," said the widow.

"Did he drink?"

"Like a fish."

The answer was so unexpected, and the tone so sardonic, that all three of them were startled.

"Millicent, how can you talk like that of your husband when he's dead?" cried her mother, clasping her neatly gloved hands. "I can't understand you. You've been so strange since you came back. I could never have believed that a girl of mine could take her husband's death like that."

"Never mind about that, mother," said Mr Skinner. "We can go into all that later."

He walked to the window and looked out at the sunny little garden, and then walked back into the room. He took his pince-nez out of his pocket, and though he had no intention of putting them on, wiped them with his handkerchief. Millicent looked at him and in her eyes, unmistakably, was a look of irony which was quite cynical. Mr Skinner was vexed. He had finished his week's work and he was a free man till Monday morning. Though he had told his wife that this garden-party was a great nuisance and he would much sooner have tea quietly in his own garden, he had been looking forward to it. He did not care very much about Chinese missions, but it would be interesting to meet the Bishop. And now this! It was not the kind of thing he cared to be mixed up in; it was most unpleasant to be told on a sudden that his son-in-law was a drunkard and a suicide. Millicent was thoughtfully smoothing her white cuffs. Her coolness irritated him; but instead of addressing her he spoke to his younger daughter.

"Why don't you sit down, Kathleen? Surely there are plenty of chairs in the room."

Kathleen drew forward a chair and without a word seated herself. Mr Skinner stopped in front of Millicent and faced her.

"Of course I see why you told us Harold had died of fever. I think it was a mistake, because that sort of thing is bound to come out sooner or later. I don't know how far what the Bishop has told the Heywoods coincides with the facts, but if you will take my advice you will tell us everything as circumstantially as you can, then we can see. We can't hope that it will go no further now that Canon Heywood and Gladys know. In a place like this people are bound to talk. It will make it easier for all of us if we at all events know the exact truth."

Mrs Skinner and Kathleen thought he put the matter very well. They waited for Millicent's reply. She had listened with an impassive face; that sudden flush had disappeared and it was once more, as usual, pasty and sallow.

"I don't think you'll much like the truth if I tell it you," she said.

"You must know that you can count on our sympathy and understanding," said Kathleen gravely.

Millicent gave her a glance and the shadow of a smile flickered across her set mouth. She looked slowly at the three of them. Mrs Skinner had an uneasy impression that she looked at them as though they were mannequins at a dressmaker's. She seemed to live in a different world from theirs and to have no connexion with them.

"You know, I wasn't in love with Harold when I married him," she said reflectively.

Mrs Skinner was on the point of making an exclamation when a rapid gesture of her husband, barely indicated, but after so many years of married life perfectly significant, stopped her. Millicent went on. She spoke with a level voice, slowly, and there was little change of expression in her tone.

"I was twenty-seven, and no one else seemed to want to marry me. It's true he was forty-four, and it seemed rather old, but he had a very good position, hadn't he? I wasn't likely to get a better chance."

Mrs Skinner felt inclined to cry again, but she remembered the party.

"Of course I see now why you took his photograph away," she said dolefully.

"Don't, mother," exclaimed Kathleen.

It had been taken when he was engaged to Millicent and was a very good photograph of Harold. Mrs Skinner had always thought him quite a fine man. He was heavily built, tall and perhaps a little too fat, but he held himself well, and his presence was imposing. He was inclined to be bald, even then, but men did go bald very early nowadays, and he said that topees, sun-helmets, you know, were very bad for the hair. He had a small dark moustache, and his face was deeply burned by the sun. Of course his best feature was his eyes; they were brown and large, like Joan's. His conversation was interesting. Kathleen said he was pompous, but Mrs Skinner didn't think him so, she didn't mind it if a man laid down the law; and when she saw, as she very soon did, that he was attracted by Millicent she began to like him very much. He was always very attentive to Mrs Skinner, and she listened as though she were really interested when he spoke of his district, and told her of the big game he had killed. Kathleen said he had a pretty good opinion of himself, but Mrs Skinner came of a generation which accepted without question the good opinion that men had of themselves. Millicent saw very soon which way the wind blew, and though she said nothing to her mother, her mother knew that if Harold asked her she was going to accept him.

Harold was staying with some people who had been thirty years in Borneo and they spoke well of the country. There was no reason why a woman shouldn't live there comfortably; of course the children had to come home when they were seven; but Mrs Skinner thought it unnecessary to trouble about that yet. She asked Harold to dine, and she told him they were always in to tea. He seemed to be at a loose end, and when his visit to his old friends was drawing to a close, she told him they would be very much pleased if he would come and spend a fortnight with them. It was towards the end of this that Harold and Millicent became engaged. They had a very pretty wedding, they went to Venice for their honeymoon, and then they started for the East. Millicent wrote from various ports at which the ship touched. She seemed happy.

"People were very nice to me at Kuala Solor," she said. Kuala Solor was the chief town of the state of Sembulu. "We stayed with the Resident and everyone asked us to dinner. Once or twice I heard men ask Harold to have a drink, but he refused; he said he had turned over a new leaf now he was a married man. I didn't know why they laughed. Mrs Gray, the Resident's wife, told me they were all so glad Harold was married. She said it was dreadfully lonely for a bachelor on one of the outstations. When we left Kuala Solor Mrs Gray said good-bye to me so funnily that I was quite surprised. It was as if she was solemnly putting Harold in my charge."

They listened to her in silence. Kathleen never took her eyes off her sister's impassive face; but Mr Skinner stared straight in front of him at the Malay arms, krises and parangs, which hung on the wall above the sofa on which his wife sat.

"It wasn't till I went back to Kuala Solor a year and a half later, that I found out why their manner had seemed so odd." Millicent gave a queer little sound like the echo of a scornful laugh. "I knew then a good deal that I hadn't known before. Harold came to England that time in order to marry. He didn't much mind who it was. Do you remember how we spread ourselves out to catch him, mother? We needn't have taken so much trouble."

"I don't know what you mean, Millicent," said Mrs Skinner, not without acerbity, for the insinuation of scheming did not please her. "I saw he was attracted by you."

Millicent shrugged her heavy shoulders.

"He was a confirmed drunkard. He used to go to bed every night with a bottle of whisky and empty it before morning. The Chief Secretary told him he'd have to resign unless he stopped drinking. He said he'd give him one more chance. He could take his leave then and go to England. He advised him to marry so that when he got back he'd have someone to look after him. Harold married me because he wanted a keeper. They took bets in Kuala Solor on how long I'd make him stay sober."

"But he was in love with you," Mrs Skinner interrupted. "You don't know how he used to speak to me about you, and at that time you're speaking of, when you went to Kuala Solor to have Joan, he wrote me such a charming letter about you."

Millicent looked at her mother again and a deep colour dyed her sallow skin. Her hands, lying on her lap, began to tremble a little. She thought of those first months of her married life. The government launch took them to the mouth of the river, and they spent the night at the bungalow which Harold said jokingly was their seaside residence. Next day they went up-stream in a prahu. From the novels she had read she expected the rivers of Borneo to be dark and strangely sinister, but the sky was blue, dappled with little white clouds, and the green of the mangroves and the nipahs, washed by the flowing water, glistened in the sun. On each side stretched the pathless jungle, and in the distance, silhouetted against the sky, was the rugged outline of a mountain. The air in the early morning was fresh and buoyant. She seemed to enter upon a friendly, fertile land, and she had a sense of spacious freedom. They watched the banks for monkeys sitting on the branches of the tangled trees, and once Harold pointed out something that looked like a log and said it was a crocodile. The Assistant Resident, in ducks and a topee, was at the landing-stage to meet them, and a dozen trim little soldiers were lined up to do them honour. The Assistant Resident was introduced to her. His name was Simpson.

"By Jove, sir," he said to Harold. "I'm glad to see you back. It's been deuced lonely without you."

The Resident's bungalow, surrounded by a garden in which grew wildly all manner of gay flowers, stood on the top of a low hill. It was a trifle shabby and the furniture was sparse, but the rooms were cool and of generous size.

"The kampong is down there," said Harold, pointing.

Her eyes followed his gesture, and from among the coconut trees rose the beating of a gong. It gave her a queer little sensation in the heart.

Though she had nothing much to do the days passed easily enough. At dawn a boy brought them their tea and they lounged about the veranda, enjoying the fragrance of the morning (Harold in a singlet and a sarong, she in a dressing-gown) till it was time to dress for breakfast. Then Harold went to his office and she spent an hour or two learning Malay. After tiffin he went back to his office while she slept. A cup of tea revived them both, and they went for a walk or played golf on the nine-hole links which Harold had made on a level piece of cleared jungle below the bungalow. Night fell at six and Mr Simpson came along to have a drink. They chatted till their late dinner hour, and sometimes Harold and Mr Simpson played chess. The balmy evenings were enchanting. The fireflies turned the bushes just below the veranda into coldly-sparkling, tremulous beacons, and flowering trees scented the air with sweet odours. After dinner they read the papers which had left London six weeks before and presently went to bed. Millicent enjoyed being a married woman, with a house of her own, and she was pleased with the native servants, in their gay sarongs, who went about the bungalow, with bare feet, silent but friendly. It gave her a pleasant sense of importance to be the wife of

the Resident. Harold impressed her by the fluency with which
he spoke the language, by his air of command, and by his dignity.
She went into the court-house now and then to hear him try cases.
The multifariousness of his duties and the competent way in
which he performed them aroused her respect. Mr Simpson told
her that Harold understood the natives as well as any man in the
country. He had the combination of firmness, tact, and good-
humour which was essential in dealing with that timid, revengeful,
and suspicious race. Millicent began to feel a certain admiration for
her husband.

They had been married nearly a year when two English naturalists
came to stay with them for a few days on their way to the interior.
They brought a pressing recommendation from the governor, and
Harold said he wanted to do them proud. Their arrival was an
agreeable change. Millicent asked Mr Simpson to dinner (he lived
at the Fort and only dined with them on Sunday nights) and after
dinner the men sat down to play bridge. Millicent left them presently
and went to bed, but they were so noisy that for some time she could
not get to sleep. She did not know at what hour she was awakened by
Harold staggering into the room. She kept silent. He made up his
mind to have a bath before getting into bed; the bath-house was just
below their room, and he went down the steps that led to it.
Apparently he slipped, for there was a great clatter, and he began to
swear. Then he was violently sick. She heard him sluice the buckets
of water over himself and in a little while, walking very cautiously
this time, he crawled up the stairs and slipped into bed. Millicent
pretended to be asleep. She was disgusted. Harold was drunk. She
made up her mind to speak about it in the morning. What would the
naturalists think of him? But in the morning Harold was so dignified
that she hadn't quite the determination to refer to the matter. At
eight Harold and she, with their two guests, sat down to breakfast.
Harold looked round the table.

"Porridge," he said. "Millicent, your guests might manage a little
Worcester sauce for breakfast, but I don't think they'll much fancy
anything else. Personally I shall content myself with a whisky and
soda."

The naturalists laughed, but shamefacedly.

"Your husband's a terror," said one of them.

"I should not think I had properly performed the duties of hospitality if I sent you sober to bed on the first night of your visit," said Harold, with his round, stately way of putting things.

Millicent, smiling acidly, was relieved to think that her guests had been as drunk as her husband. The next evening she sat up with them and the party broke up at a reasonable hour. But she was glad when the strangers went on with their journey. Their life resumed its placid course. Some months later Harold went on a tour of inspection of his district and came back with a bad attack of malaria. This was the first time she had seen the disease of which she had heard so much, and when he recovered it did not seem strange to her that Harold was very shaky. She found his manner peculiar. He would come back from the office and stare at her with glazed eyes; he would stand on the veranda, swaying slightly, but still dignified, and make long harangues about the political situation in England; losing the thread of his discourse, he would look at her with an archness which his natural stateliness made somewhat disconcerting and say:

"Pulls you down dreadfully, this confounded malaria. Ah, little woman, you little know the strain it puts upon a man to be an empire builder."

She thought that Mr Simpson began to look worried, and once or twice, when they were alone, he seemed on the point of saying something to her which his shyness at the last moment prevented. The feeling grew so strong that it made her nervous, and one evening when Harold, she knew not why, had remained later than usual at the office she tackled him.

"What have you got to say to me, Mr Simpson?" she broke out suddenly.

He blushed and hesitated.

"Nothing. What makes you think I have anything in particular to say to you?"

Mr Simpson was a thin, weedy youth of four and twenty, with a fine head of waving hair which he took great pains to plaster down very flat. His wrists were swollen and scarred with mosquito bites. Millicent looked at him steadily.

"If it's something to do with Harold don't you think it would be kinder to tell me frankly?"

He grew scarlet now. He shuffled uneasily on his rattan chair. She insisted.

"I'm afraid you'll think it awful cheek," he said at last. "It's rotten of me to say anything about my chief behind his back. Malaria's a rotten thing, and after one's had a bout of it one feels awfully down and out."

He hesitated again. The corners of his mouth sagged as if he were going to cry. To Millicent he seemed like a little boy.

"I'll be as silent as the grave," she said with a smile, trying to conceal her apprehension. "Do tell me."

"I think it's a pity your husband keeps a bottle of whisky at the office. He's apt to take a nip more often than he otherwise would."

Mr Simpson's voice was hoarse with agitation. Millicent felt a sudden coldness shiver through her. She controlled herself, for she knew that she must not frighten the boy if she were to get out of him all there was to tell. He was unwilling to speak. She pressed him, wheedling, appealing to his sense of duty, and at last she began to cry. Then he told her that Harold had been drunk more or less for the last fortnight, the natives were talking about it, and they said that soon he would be as bad as he had been before his marriage. He had been in the habit of drinking a good deal too much then, but details of that time, notwithstanding all her attempts, Mr Simpson resolutely declined to give her.

"Do you think he's drinking now?" she asked.

"I don't know."

Millicent felt herself on a sudden hot with shame and anger. The Fort, as it was called because the rifles and the ammunition were kept there, was also the court-house. It stood opposite the Resident's bungalow in a garden of its own. The sun was just about to set and she did not need a hat. She got up and walked across. She found Harold sitting in the office behind the large hall in which he administered justice. There was a bottle of whisky in front of him. He was smoking cigarettes and talking to three or four Malays who stood in front of him listening with obsequious and at the same time scornful smiles. His face was red.

The natives vanished.

"I came to see what you were doing," she said.

He rose, for he always treated her with elaborate politeness, and lurched. Feeling himself unsteady he assumed an elaborate stateliness of demeanour.

"Take a seat, my dear, take a seat. I was detained by press of work."

She looked at him with angry eyes.

"You're drunk," she said.

He stared at her, his eyes bulging a little, and a haughty look gradually traversed his large and fleshy face.

"I haven't the remotest idea what you mean," he said.

She had been ready with a flow of wrathful expostulation, but suddenly she burst into tears. She sank into a chair and hid her face. Harold looked at her for an instant, then the tears began to trickle down his own cheeks; he came towards her with outstretched arms and fell heavily on his knees. Sobbing, he clasped her to him.

"Forgive me, forgive me," he said. "I promise you it shall not happen again. It was that damned malaria."

"It's so humiliating," she moaned.

He wept like a child. There was something very touching in the self-abasement of that big dignified man. Presently Millicent looked up. His eyes, appealing and contrite, sought hers.

"Will you give me your word of honour that you'll never touch liquor again?"

"Yes, yes. I hate it."

It was then she told him that she was with child. He was overjoyed.

"That is the one thing I wanted. That'll keep me straight."

They went back to the bungalow. Harold bathed himself and had a nap. After dinner they talked long and quietly. He admitted that before he married her he had occasionally drunk more than was good for him; in outstations it was easy to fall into bad habits. He agreed to everything that Millicent asked. And during the months before it was necessary for her to go to Kuala Solor for her confinement, Harold was an excellent husband, tender, thoughtful, proud, and affectionate; he was irreproachable. A launch came to fetch her. She was to leave him for six weeks, and he promised faithfully to drink nothing during her absence. He put his hands on her shoulders.

"I never break a promise," he said in his dignified way. "But even without it, can you imagine that while you are going through so much, I should do anything to increase your troubles?"

Joan was born. Millicent stayed at the Resident's, and Mrs Gray, his wife, a kindly creature of middle age, was very good to her. The two women had little to do during the long hours they were alone but to talk, and in course of time Millicent learnt everything there was to know of her husband's alcoholic past. The fact which she found most difficult to reconcile herself to was that Harold had been told that the only condition upon which he would be allowed to keep his post was that he should bring back a wife. It caused in her a dull feeling of resentment. And when she discovered what a persistent drunkard he had been, she felt vaguely uneasy. She had a horrid fear that during her absence he would not have been able to resist the craving. She went home with her baby and a nurse. She spent a night at the mouth of the river and sent a messenger in a canoe to announce her arrival. She scanned the landing-stage anxiously as the launch approached it. Harold and Mr Simpson were standing there. The trim little soldiers were lined up. Her heart sank, for Harold was swaying slightly, like a man who seeks to keep his balance on a rolling ship, and she knew he was drunk.

It wasn't a very pleasant home-coming. She had almost forgotten her mother and father and her sister who sat there silently listening to her. Now she roused herself and became once more aware of their presence. All that she spoke of seemed very far away.

"I knew that I hated him then," she said. "I could have killed him."

"Oh, Millicent, don't say that," cried her mother. "Don't forget that he's dead, poor man."

Millicent looked at her mother, and for a moment a scowl darkened her impassive face. Mr Skinner moved uneasily.

"Go on," said Kathleen.

"When he found out that I knew all about him he didn't bother very much more. In three months he had another attack of DTs."

"Why didn't you leave him?" said Kathleen.

"What would have been the good of that? He would have been dismissed from the service in a fortnight. Who was to keep me and Joan? I had to stay. And when he was sober I had nothing to complain of. He wasn't in the least in love with me, but he was fond of me; I hadn't married him because I was in love with him, but because I wanted to be married. I did everything I could to keep liquor from him; I managed to get Mr Gray to prevent whisky being sent from Kuala Solor, but he got it from the Chinese. I watched him as a cat watches a mouse. He was too cunning for me. In a little while he had another outbreak. He neglected his duties. I was afraid complaints would be made. We were two days from Kuala Solor and that was our safeguard, but I suppose something was said, for Mr Gray wrote a private letter of warning to me. I showed it to Harold. He stormed and blustered, but I saw he was frightened, and for two or three months he was quite sober. Then he began again. And so it went on till our leave became due.

"Before we came to stay here I begged and prayed him to be careful. I didn't want any of you to know what sort of a man I had married. All the time he was in England he was all right and before we sailed I warned him. He'd grown to be very fond of Joan, and very proud of her, and she was devoted to him. She always liked him better than she liked me. I asked him if he wanted to have his child grow up, knowing that he was a drunkard, and I found out that at last I'd got a hold on him. The thought terrified him. I told him that *I* wouldn't allow it, and if he ever let Joan see him drunk I'd take her away from him at once. Do you know, he grew quite pale when I said it. I fell on my knees that night and thanked God, because I'd found a way of saving my husband.

"He told me that if I would stand by him he would have another try. We made up our minds to fight the thing together. And he tried so hard. When he felt as though he *must* drink he came to me. You know he was inclined to be rather pompous; with me he was so humble, he was like a child; he depended on me. Perhaps he didn't love me when he married me, but he loved me then, me and Joan. I'd hated him, because of the humiliation, because when he was drunk and tried to be dignified and impressive he was loathsome; but now I got a strange feeling in my heart. It wasn't love, but it was a queer, shy tenderness. He was something more than my husband, he was like a child that I'd carried under my heart for long and weary months. He was so proud of me and, you know, I was proud too. His long speeches didn't irritate me any more, and I only thought his stately ways rather funny and charming. At last we won. For two years he never touched a drop. He lost his craving entirely. He was even able to joke about it.

"Mr Simpson had left us then and we had another young man called Francis.

"'I'm a reformed drunkard, you know, Francis,' Harold said to him once. 'If it hadn't been for my wife I'd have been sacked long ago. I've got the best wife in the world, Francis.'

"You don't know what it meant to me to hear him say that. I felt that all I'd gone through was worth while. I was so happy."

She was silent. She thought of the broad, yellow and turbid river on whose banks she had lived so long. The egrets, white and gleaming in the tremulous sunset, flew down the stream in a flock, flew low and swift, and scattered. They were like a ripple of snowy notes, sweet and pure and spring-like, which an unseen hand drew forth, a divine arpeggio, from an unseen harp. They fluttered along between the green banks, wrapped in the shadows of evening, like the happy thoughts of a contented mind.

"Then Joan fell ill. For three weeks we were very anxious. There was no doctor nearer than Kuala Solor and we had to put up with the treatment of a native dispenser. When she grew well again I took her down to the mouth of the river in order to give her a breath of sea air. We stayed there a week. It was the first time I had been separated from Harold since I went away to have Joan. There was a fishing village, on piles, not far from us, but really we were quite alone. I thought a great deal about Harold, so tenderly, and all at once I knew that I loved him. I was so glad when the prahu came to fetch us back, because I wanted to tell him. I thought it would mean a good deal to him. I can't tell you how happy I was. As we rowed up-stream the headman told me that Mr Francis had had to go up-country to arrest a woman who had murdered her husband. He had been gone a couple of days.

"I was surprised that Harold was not on the landing-stage to meet me; he was always very punctilious about that sort of thing; he used to say that husband and wife should treat one another as politely as they treated acquaintances; and I could not imagine what business had prevented him. I walked up the little hill on which the bungalow stood. The ayah brought Joan behind me. The bungalow was strangely silent. There seemed to be no servants about, and I could not make it out; I wondered if Harold hadn't expected me so soon and was out. I went up the steps. Joan was thirsty and the ayah took her to the servants' quarters to give her something to drink. Harold was not in the sitting-room. I called him, but there was no answer. I was disappointed because I should have liked him to be there. I went into our bedroom. Harold wasn't out after all; he was lying on the bed asleep. I was really very much amused, because he always pretended he never slept in the afternoon. He said it was an unnecessary habit that we white people got into. I went up to the bed softly. I thought I would have a joke with him. I opened the mosquito curtains. He was lying on his back, with nothing on but a sarong, and there was an empty whisky bottle by his side. He was drunk.

"It had begun again. All my struggles for so many years were wasted. My dream was shattered. It was all hopeless. I was seized with rage."

Millicent's face grew once again darkly red and she clenched the arms of the chair she sat in.

"I took him by the shoulders and shook him with all my might. 'You beast,' I cried, 'you beast.' I was so angry I don't know what I did, I don't know what I said. I kept on shaking him. You don't know how loathsome he looked, that large fat man, half naked; he hadn't shaved for days, and his face was bloated and purple. He was breathing heavily. I shouted at him, but he took no notice. I tried to drag him out of bed, but he was too heavy. He lay there like a log. 'Open your eyes,' I screamed. I shook him again. I hated him. I hated him all the more because for a week I'd loved him with all my heart. He'd let me down. He'd let me down. I wanted to tell him what a filthy beast he was. I could make no impression on him. 'You shall open your eyes,' I cried. I was determined to make him look at me."

The widow licked her dry lips. Her breath seemed hurried. She was silent.

"If he was in that state I should have thought it best to have let him go on sleeping," said Kathleen.

"There was a parang on the wall by the side of the bed. You know how fond Harold was of curios."

"What's a parang?" said Mrs Skinner.

"Don't be silly, mother," her husband replied irritably. "There's one on the wall immediately behind you."

He pointed to the Malay sword on which for some reason his eyes had been unconsciously resting. Mrs Skinner drew quickly into the corner of the sofa, with a little frightened gesture, as though she had been told that a snake lay curled up beside her.

"Suddenly the blood spurted out from Harold's throat. There was a great red gash right across it."

"Millicent," cried Kathleen, springing up and almost leaping towards her, "what in God's name do you mean?"

Mrs Skinner stood staring at her with wide startled eyes, her mouth open.

"The parang wasn't on the wall any more. It was on the bed. Then Harold opened his eyes. They were just like Joan's."

"I don't understand," said Mr Skinner. "How could he have committed suicide if he was in the state you describe?"

Kathleen took her sister's arm and shook her angrily.

"Millicent, for God's sake explain."

Millicent released herself.

"The parang was on the wall, I told you. I don't know what happened. There was all the blood, and Harold opened his eyes. He died almost at once. He never spoke, but he gave a sort of gasp."

At last Mr Skinner found his voice.

"But, you wretched woman, it was murder."

Millicent, her face mottled with red, gave him such a look of scornful hatred that he shrank back. Mrs Skinner cried out.

"Millicent, you didn't do it, did you?"

Then Millicent did something that made them all feel as though their blood were turned to ice in their veins. She chuckled.

"I don't know who else did," she said.

"My God," muttered Mr Skinner.

Kathleen had been standing bolt upright with her hands to her heart, as though its beating were intolerable.

"And what happened then?" she said.

"I screamed. I went to the window and flung it open. I called for the ayah. She came across the compound with Joan. 'Not Joan,' I cried. 'Don't let her come.' She called the cook and told him to take the child. I cried to her to hurry. And when she came I showed her

Harold. 'The Tuan's killed himself!' I cried. She gave a scream and ran out of the house.

"No one would come near. They were all frightened out of their wits. I wrote a letter to Mr Francis, telling him what had happened and asking him to come at once."

"How do you mean you told him what had happened?"

"I said, on my return from the mouth of the river, I'd found Harold with his throat cut. You know, in the tropics you have to bury people quickly. I got a Chinese coffin, and the soldiers dug a grave behind the Fort. When Mr Francis came, Harold had been buried for nearly two days. He was only a boy. I could do anything I wanted with him. I told him I'd found the parang in Harold's hand and there was no doubt he'd killed himself in an attack of delirium tremens. I showed him the empty bottle. The servants said he'd been drinking hard ever since I left to go to the sea. I told the same story at Kuala Solor. Everyone was very kind to me, and the government granted me a pension."

For a little while nobody spoke. At last Mr Skinner gathered himself together.

"I am a member of the legal profession. I'm a solicitor. I have certain duties. We've always had a most respectable practice. You've put me in a monstrous position."

He fumbled, searching for the phrases that played at hide and seek in his scattered wits. Millicent looked at him with scorn.

"What are you going to do about it?"

"It was murder, that's what it was; do you think I can possibly connive at it?"

"Don't talk nonsense, father," said Kathleen sharply. "You can't give up your own daughter."

"You've put me in a monstrous position," he repeated.

Millicent shrugged her shoulders again.

"You made me tell you. And I've borne it long enough by myself. It was time that all of you bore it too."

At that moment the door was opened by the maid.

"Davis has brought the car round, sir," she said.

Kathleen had the presence of mind to say something, and the maid withdrew.

"We'd better be starting," said Millicent.

"I can't go to the party now," cried Mrs Skinner, with horror. "I'm far too upset. How can we face the Heywoods? And the Bishop will want to be introduced to you."

Millicent made a gesture of indifference. Her eyes held their ironical expression.

"We must go, mother," said Kathleen. "It would look so funny if we stayed away." She turned on Millicent furiously. "Oh, I think the whole thing is such frightfully bad form."

Mrs Skinner looked helplessly at her husband. He went to her and gave her his hand to help her up from the sofa.

"I'm afraid we must go, mother," he said.

"And me with the ospreys in my toque that Harold gave me with his own hands," she moaned.

He led her out of the room, Kathleen followed close on their heels, and a step or two behind came Millicent.

"You'll get used to it, you know," she said quietly. "At first I thought of it all the time, but now I forget it for two or three days together. It's not as if there was any danger."

They did not answer. They walked through the hall and out of the front door. The three ladies got into the back of the car and Mr Skinner seated himself beside the driver. They had no self-starter; it was an old car, and Davis went to the bonnet to crank it up. Mr Skinner turned round and looked petulantly at Millicent.

"I ought never to have been told," he said. "I think it was most selfish of you."

Davis took his seat and they drove off to the Canon's garden-party.

THE YELLOW STREAK

THE TWO PRAHUS were dropping easily down-stream, one a few yards ahead of the other, and in the first sat the two white men. After seven weeks on the rivers they were glad to know that they would lodge that night in a civilized house. To Izzart, who had been in Borneo since the war, the Dyak houses and their feasts were of course an old story; but Campion, though new to the country and at first amused by the strangeness, hankered too now for chairs to sit on and a bed to sleep in. The Dyaks were hospitable, but no one could say that there was much comfort to be found in their houses, and there was a monotony in the entertainment they offered a guest which presently grew somewhat wearisome. Every evening, as the travellers reached the landing-place, the headman, bearing a flag, and the more important members of the household came down to the river to fetch them. They were led up to the long-house – a village really under one roof, built on piles, to which access was obtained by climbing up the trunk of a tree rudely notched into steps – and to the beating of drums and gongs walked up and down the whole length of it in long procession. On both sides serried throngs of brown people sat on their haunches and stared silently as the white men passed. Clean mats were unrolled and the guests seated themselves. The headman brought a live chicken and, holding it by the legs, waved it three times over their heads, called the spirits loudly to witness and uttered an invocation. Then various persons brought eggs. Arak was drunk. A girl, a very small shy thing with the grace of a flower but with something hieratic in her immobile face, held a cup to the white man's lips till it was empty and then a great shout arose. The men began to dance, one after the other, each treading his little measure, with his shield and his parang, to the accompaniment of drum and gong. After this had gone on for some time the visitors were taken into one of the rooms that led off the long platform on which was led the common life of the household and found their supper prepared for them. The girls fed them with Chinese spoons. Then everyone grew a little drunk and they all talked till the early hours of the morning.

But now their journey was done and they were on their way to the coast. They had started at dawn. The river then was very shallow and ran clear and bright over a shingly bottom; the trees leaned over it so that above there was only a strip of blue sky; but now it had broadened out, and the men were poling no longer but paddling. The trees, bamboos, wild sago like huge bunches of ostrich feathers, trees with enormous leaves and trees with feathery foliage like the acacia, coconut trees and areca palms, with their long straight white stems, the trees on the banks were immensely and violently luxuriant. Here and there, gaunt and naked, was the bare skeleton of a tree struck by lightning or dead of old age, and its whiteness against all that green was vivid. Here and there, rival kings of the forest, tall trees soared above the common level of the jungle. Then there were the parasites; in the fork of two branches great tufts of lush green leaves, or flowering creepers that covered the spreading foliage like a bride's veil; sometimes they wound round a tall trunk, a sheath of splendour, and threw long flowering arms from branch to branch. There was something thrilling in the passionate wildness of that eager growth; it had the daring abandon of the nomad rioting in the train of the god.

The day wore on, and now the heat was no longer so oppressive. Campion looked at the shabby silver watch on his wrist. It could not be long now before they reached their destination.

"What sort of a chap is Hutchinson?" he asked.

"I don't know him. I believe he's a very good sort."

Hutchinson was the Resident in whose house they were to spend the night, and they had sent on a Dyak in a canoe to announce their arrival.

"Well, I hope he's got some whisky. I've drunk enough arak to last me a lifetime."

Campion was a mining engineer whom the Sultan on his way to England had met at Singapore, and finding him at a loose end had commissioned to go to Sembulu and see whether he could discover any mineral which might be profitably worked. He sent Willis, the Resident at Kuala Solor, instructions to afford him every facility, and Willis had put him in the care of Izzart because Izzart spoke both Malay and Dyak like a native. This was the third trip they had made into the interior, and now Campion was to go home with his reports. They were to catch the *Sultan Ahmed*, which was due to pass the mouth of the river at dawn on the next day but one, and with any luck they should reach Kuala Solor on the same afternoon. They were both glad to get back to it. There was tennis and golf there, and the club with its billiard tables, food which was relatively good, and the comforts of civilization. Izzart was glad, too, that he would have other society than Campion's. He gave him a sidelong glance. He was a little man with a big, bald head, and though certainly fifty, strong and wiry; he had quick, shining blue eyes and a stubbly, grey moustache. He was seldom without an old briar pipe between his broken and discoloured teeth. He was neither clean nor neat, his khaki shorts were ragged and his singlet torn; he was wearing now a battered topee. He had knocked about the world since he was eighteen and had been in South Africa, in China and in Mexico. He was good company; he could tell a story well, and he was prepared to drink and drink again with anyone he met. They had got on very well together, but Izzart had never felt quite at home with him. Though they joked and laughed together, got drunk together, Izzart felt that there was no intimacy between them; for all the cordiality of their relations they remained nothing but acquaintances. He was very sensitive to the impression he made on others, and behind Campion's joviality he had felt a certain coolness; those shining blue eyes had summed him up; and it vaguely irritated Izzart that Campion had formed an opinion of him, and he did not quite know what it was. He was exasperated by the possibility that this common little man did not think entirely well of him. He desired to be liked and admired. He wanted to be popular. He wished the people he met to take an inordinate fancy to him, so that he could either reject them or a trifle condescendingly bestow his friendship on them. His inclination was to be familiar with all and sundry, but he was held back by the fear of a rebuff; sometimes he had been uneasily conscious that his effusiveness surprised the persons he lavished it on.

By some chance he had never met Hutchinson, though of course he knew all about him just as Hutchinson knew all about *him*, and they would have many common friends to talk of. Hutchinson had been at Winchester, and Izzart was glad that he could tell him that he had been at Harrow...

The prahu rounded a bend in the river and suddenly, standing on a slight eminence, they saw the bungalow. In a few minutes they caught sight of the landing-stage and on it, among a little group of natives, a figure in white waving to them.

Hutchinson was a tall, stout man with a red face. His appearance led you to expect that he was breezy and self-confident, so that it was not a little surprising to discover quickly that he was diffident and even a trifle shy. When he shook hands with his guests – Izzart introduced himself and then Campion – and led them up the pathway to the bungalow, though he was plainly anxious to be civil it was not hard to see that he found it difficult to make conversation. He took them out on to the veranda and here they found on the table glasses and whisky and soda. They made themselves comfortable on long chairs. Izzart, conscious of Hutchinson's slight embarrassment with strangers, expanded; he was very hearty and voluble. He began to speak of their common acquaintances at Kuala Solor, and he managed very soon to slip in casually the information that he had been at Harrow.

"You were at Winchester, weren't you?" he asked.

"Yes."

"I wonder if you knew George Parker. He was in my regiment. He was at Winchester. I daresay he was younger than you."

Izzart felt that it was a bond between them that they had been at these particular schools, and it excluded Campion, who obviously had enjoyed no such advantage. They drank two or three whiskies. Izzart in half an hour began to call his host Hutchie. He talked a good deal about "my regiment" in which he had got his company during the war, and what good fellows his brother officers were. He mentioned two or three names which could hardly be unknown to Hutchinson. They were not the sort of people that Campion was likely to have come across, and he was not sorry to administer to him a neat snub when he claimed acquaintance with someone he spoke of.

"Billie Meadows? I knew a fellow called Billie Meadows in Sinaloa many years ago," said Campion.

"Oh, I shouldn't think it could be the same," said Izzart, with a smile. "Billie's by way of being a peer of the realm. He's the Lord Meadows who races. Don't you remember, he owned Spring Carrots?"

Dinner time was approaching, and after a wash and brush-up they drank a couple of gin pahits. They sat down. Hutchinson had not been to Kuala Solor for the best part of a year, and had not seen another white man for three months. He was anxious to make the most of his visitors. He could give them no wine, but there was plenty of whisky and after dinner he brought out a precious bottle of Benedictine. They were very gay. They laughed and talked a great deal. Izzart was getting on famously. He thought he had never liked a fellow more than Hutchinson, and he pressed him to come down to Kuala Solor as soon as he could. They would have a wonderful beano. Campion was left out of the conversation by Izzart with the faintly malicious intention of putting him in his place, and by Hutchinson through shyness; and presently, after yawning a good deal, he said he would go to bed. Hutchinson showed him to his room, and when he returned Izzart said to him:

"You don't want to turn in yet, do you?"

"Not on your life. Let's have another drink."

They sat and talked. They both grew a little drunk. Presently Hutchinson told Izzart that he lived with a Malay girl, and had a couple of children by her. He had told them to keep out of sight while Campion was there.

"I expect she's asleep now," said Hutchinson, with a glance at the door which Izzart knew led into his room, "but I'd like you to see the kiddies in the morning."

Just then a faint wail was heard and Hutchinson with a "Hullo, the little devil's awake", went to the door and opened it. In a moment or two he came out of the room with a child in his arms. A woman followed him.

"He's cutting his teeth," said Hutchinson. "It makes him restless."

The woman wore a sarong and a thin white jacket and she was barefoot. She was young, with fine dark eyes, and she gave Izzart when he spoke to her a bright and pleasant smile. She sat down and lit a cigarette. She answered the civil questions Izzart put to her without embarrassment, but also without effusion. Hutchinson asked her if she would have a whisky and soda, but she refused. When the two men began to talk again in English she sat on quite quietly, faintly rocking herself in her chair, and occupied with none could tell what calm thoughts.

"She's a very good girl," said Hutchinson. "She looks after the house and she's no trouble. Of course it's the only thing to do in a place like this."

"I shall never do it myself," said Izzart. "After all, one may want to get married and then it means all sorts of botherations."

"But who wants to get married? What a life for a white woman. I wouldn't ask a white woman to live here for anything in the world."

"Of course it's a matter of taste. If I have any kiddies I'm going to see that they have a white mother."

Hutchinson looked down at the little dark-skinned child he held in his arms. He gave a faint smile.

"It's funny how you get to like them," he said. "When they're your own it doesn't seem to matter that they've got a touch of the tar-brush."

The woman gave the child a look, and getting up said she would take it back to bed.

"I should think we'd better all turn in," said Hutchinson. "God knows what the time is."

Izzart went to his room and threw open the shutters which his boy Hassan, whom he was travelling with, had closed. Blowing out the candle so that it should not attract the mosquitoes, he sat down at the window and looked at the soft night. The whisky he had drunk made him feel very wide awake, and he was not inclined to go to bed. He took off his ducks, put on a sarong and lit a cheroot. His good-humour was gone. It was the sight of Hutchinson looking fondly at the half-caste child which had upset him.

"They've got no right to have them," he said to himself. "They've got no chance in the world. Ever."

He passed his hands reflectively along his bare and hairy legs. He shuddered a little. Though he had done everything he could to develop the calves, his legs were like broomsticks. He hated them. He was uneasily conscious of them all the time. They were like a native's. Of course they were the very legs for a top-boot. In his uniform he had looked very well. He was a tall, powerful man, over six feet high, and he had a neat black moustache and neat black hair. His dark eyes were fine and mobile. He was a good-looking fellow and he knew it, and he dressed well, shabbily when shabbiness was good form, and smartly when the occasion demanded. He had loved the army, and it was a bitter blow to him when, at the end of the war, he could not remain in it. His ambitions were simple. He wanted to have two thousand a year, give smart little dinners, go to parties, and wear a uniform. He hankered after London.

Of course his mother lived there, and his mother cramped his style. He wondered how on earth he could produce her if ever he got engaged to the girl of good family (with a little money) whom he was looking for to make his wife. Because his father had been dead so long and during the later part of his career was stationed in the most remote of the Malay States, Izzart felt fairly sure that no one in Sembulu knew anything about her, but he lived in terror lest someone, running across her in London, should write over to tell people that she was a half-caste. She had been a beautiful creature when Izzart's father, an engineer in the government service, had married her; but now she was a fat old woman with grey hair who sat about all day smoking cigarettes. Izzart was twelve years old when his father died and then he could speak Malay much more fluently than English. An aunt offered to pay for his education and Mrs Izzart accompanied her son to England. She lived habitually in furnished apartments, and her rooms with their Oriental draperies and Malay silver were overheated and stuffy. She was for ever in trouble with her landladies because she would leave cigarette-ends about. Izzart hated the way she made friends with them: she would be shockingly familiar with them for a time, then there would be a falling-out, and after a violent scene she would flounce out of the house. Her only amusement was the pictures, and to these she went every day in the week. At home she wore an old and tawdry dressing-gown, but when she went out she dressed herself – but, oh, how untidily – in extravagant colours, so that it was a mortification to her dapper son. He quarrelled with her frequently, she made him impatient and he was ashamed of her; and yet he felt for her a deep tenderness; it was almost a physical bond between them, something stronger than the ordinary feeling of mother and son, so that notwithstanding the failings that exasperated him she was the only person in the world with whom he felt entirely at home.

It was owing to his father's position and his own knowledge of Malay, for his mother always spoke it to him, that after the war, finding himself with nothing to do, he had managed to enter the service of the Sultan of Sembulu. He had been a success. He played games well, he was strong and a good athlete; in the rest-house at Kuala Solor were the cups which he had won at Harrow for running and jumping, and to these he had added since others for golf and tennis. With his abundant fund of small-talk he was an asset at parties and his cheeriness made things go. He ought to have been happy and he was wretched. He wanted so much to be popular, and he had an impression, stronger than ever at this moment, that popularity escaped him. He wondered whether by any chance the men at Kuala Solor with whom he was so hail-fellow-well-met suspected that he had native blood in him. He knew very well what to expect if they ever found out. They wouldn't say he was gay and friendly then, they would say he was damned familiar; and they would say he was inefficient and careless, as the half-castes were, and when he talked of marrying a white woman they would snigger. Oh, it was so unfair! What difference could it make, that drop of native blood in his veins, and yet because of it they would always be on the watch for the expected failure at the critical moment. Everyone knew that you couldn't rely on Eurasians, sooner or later they would let you down; he knew it too, but now he asked himself whether they didn't fail because failure was expected of them. They were never given a chance, poor devils.

But a cock crew loudly. It must be very late and he was beginning to feel chilly. He got into bed. When Hassan brought him his tea next morning he had a racking headache, and when he went into breakfast he could not look at the porridge and the bacon and eggs which were set before him. Hutchinson too was feeling none too well.

"I fancy we made rather a night of it," said his host, with a smile to conceal his faint embarrassment.

"I feel like hell," said Izzart.

"I'm going to breakfast off a whisky and soda myself," added Hutchinson.

Izzart asked for nothing better, and it was with distaste that they watched Campion eat with healthy appetite a substantial meal. Campion chaffed them.

"By God, Izzart, you're looking green about the gills," he said. "I never saw such a filthy colour."

Izzart flushed. His swarthiness was always a sensitive point with him. But he forced himself to give a cheery laugh.

"You see, I had a Spanish grandmother," he answered, "and when I'm under the weather it always comes out. I remember at Harrow I fought a boy and licked him, because he called me a damned half-caste."

"You are dark," said Hutchinson. "Do Malays ever ask you if you have any native blood in you?"

"Yes, damn their impudence."

A boat with their kit had started early in the morning in order to get to the mouth of the river before them, and tell the skipper of the *Sultan Ahmed*, if by chance he arrived before he was due, that they were on their way. Campion and Izzart were to set out immediately after tiffin in order to arrive at the place where they were to spend the night before the Bore passed. A Bore is a tidal wave that, by reason of a peculiarity in the lie of the land, surges up certain rivers, and there happened to be one on the river on which they were travelling. Hutchinson had talked to them of it the night before and Campion, who had never seen such a thing, was much interested.

"This is one of the best in Borneo. It's worth looking at," said Hutchinson.

He told them how the natives, waiting the moment, rode it and were borne up the river on its crest at a breathless and terrifying speed. He had done it once himself.

"Never no more for me," he said. "I was scared out of my wits."

"I should like to try it once," said Izzart.

"It's exciting enough, but my word, when you're in a flimsy dugout and you know that if the native doesn't get the right moment you'll be flung in that seething torrent and you won't have a chance in a million . . . no, it's not my idea of sport."

"I've shot a good many rapids in my day," said Campion.

"Rapids be damned. You wait till you see the Bore. It's one of the most terrifying things I know. D'you know that at least a dozen natives are drowned in it in this river alone every year?"

They lounged about on the veranda most of the morning and Hutchinson showed them the court-house. Then gin pahits were served. They drank two or three. Izzart began to feel himself, and when at length tiffin was ready he found that he had an excellent appetite. Hutchinson had boasted of his Malay curry and when the steaming, succulent dishes were placed before them they all set to ravenously. Hutchinson pressed them to drink.

"You've got nothing to do but sleep. Why shouldn't you get drunk?"

He could not bear to let them go so soon, it was good after so long to have white men to talk to, and he lingered over the meal. He urged them to eat. They would have a filthy meal that night at the long-house and nothing to drink but arak. They had better make hay while the sun shone. Campion suggested once or twice that they should start, but Hutchinson, and Izzart too, for now he was feeling very happy and comfortable, assured him there was plenty of time. Hutchinson sent for his precious bottle of Benedictine. They had made a hole in it last night; they might as well finish it before they went.

When at last he walked down with them to the river they were all very merry and none of them was quite steady on his legs. Over the middle of the boat was an attap awning, and under this Hutchinson had had a mattress laid. The crew were prisoners who had been marched down from the jail to row the white men, and they wore dingy sarongs with the prison mark. They waited at their oars. Izzart and Campion shook hands with Hutchinson and threw themselves down on the mattress. The boat pushed off. The turbid river, wide and placid, glistened in the heat of that brilliant afternoon like polished brass. In the distance ahead of them they could see the bank with its tangle of green trees. They felt drowsy, but Izzart at least found a curious enjoyment in resisting for a little while the heaviness that was creeping over him, and he made up his mind that he would not let himself fall asleep till he had finished his cheroot. At last the stub began to burn his fingers and he flung it into the river.

"I'm going to have a wonderful snooze," he said.

"What about the Bore?" asked Campion.

"Oh, that's all right. We needn't worry about that."

He gave a long and noisy yawn. His limbs felt like lead. He had one moment in which he was conscious of his delicious drowsiness and then he knew nothing more. Suddenly he was awakened by Campion shaking him.

"I say, what's that?"

"What's what?"

He spoke irritably, for sleep was still heavy upon him, but with his eyes he followed Campion's gesture. He could hear nothing, but a good way off he saw two or three white-crested waves following one another. They did not look very alarming.

"Oh, I suppose that's the Bore."

"What are we going to do about it?" cried Campion.

Izzart was scarcely yet quite awake. He smiled at the concern in Campion's voice.

"Don't worry. These fellows know all about it. They know exactly what to do. We may get a bit splashed."

But while they were saying these few words the Bore came nearer, very quickly, with a roar like the roar of an angry sea, and Izzart saw that the waves were much higher than he had thought. He did not like the look of them and he tightened his belt so that his shorts should not slip down if the boat were upset. In a moment the waves were upon them. It was a great wall of water that seemed to tower over them, and it might have been ten or twelve feet high, but you could measure it only with your horror. It was quite plain that no boat could weather it. The first wave dashed over them, drenching them all, half filling the boat with water, and then immediately another wave struck them. The boatmen began to shout. They pulled madly at their oars and the steersman yelled an order. But in that surging torrent they were helpless, and it was frightening to see how soon they lost all control of the boat. The force of the water turned it broadside on and it was carried along, helter skelter, upon the crest of the Bore. Another great wave dashed over them and the boat began to sink. Izzart and Campion scrambled out of the covered place in which they had been lying and suddenly the boat gave way under their feet and they found themselves struggling in the water. It surged and stormed around them. Izzart's first impulse was to swim for the shore, but his boy, Hassan, shouted to him to cling to the boat. For a minute or two they all did this.

"Are you all right?" Campion shouted to him.

"Yes, enjoying the bath," said Izzart.

He imagined that the waves would pass by as the Bore ascended the river, and in a few minutes at the outside they would find themselves in calm water once more. He forgot that they were being carried along on its crest. The waves dashed over them. They clung to the gunwale and the base of the structure which supported the attap awning. Then a larger wave caught the boat as it turned over, falling upon them so that they lost their hold; there seemed nothing but a slippery bottom to cling to and Izzart's hands slithered helplessly on the greasy surface. But the boat continued to turn and he made a desperate grab at the gunwale, only to feel it slip out of his hands as the turn went on, then he caught the framework of the awning, and still it turned, turned slowly right round and once more he sought for a hand-hold on the bottom. The boat went round and round with a horrible regularity. He thought this must be because everyone was clinging to one side of it, and he tried to make the crew go round to the other. He could not make them understand. Everyone was shouting and the waves beat against them with a dull and angry roar. Each time the boat rolled over on them Izzart was pushed under water, only to come up again as the gunwale and the framework of the awning gave him something to cling to. The struggle was awful. Presently he began to get terribly out of breath, and he felt his strength leaving him. He knew that he could not hold on much longer, but he did not feel frightened, for his fatigue by now was so great that he did not very much care what happened. Hassan was by his side and he told him he was growing very tired. He thought the best thing was to make a dash for the shore, it did not look more than sixty yards away, but Hassan begged him not to. Still they were being carried along amid those seething, pounding waves. The boat went round and round and they scrambled over it like squirrels in a cage. Izzart swallowed a lot of water. He felt he was very nearly done. Hassan could not help him, but it was a comfort that he was there, for Izzart knew that his boy, used to the water all his life, was a powerful swimmer. Then, Izzart did not know why, for a minute or two the boat held bottom downwards, so that he was able to hold on to the gunwale. It was a precious thing to be able to get his breath. At that moment two dug-outs, with Malays in them riding the Bore, passed swiftly by them. They shouted for help, but the Malays averted their faces and went on. They saw the white men, and did not want to be concerned in any trouble that might befall them. It was agonizing to see them go past, callous and indifferent in their safety. But on a sudden the boat rolled round again, round and round, slowly, and the miserable, exhausting scramble repeated itself. It took the heart out of you. But the short respite had helped Izzart, and he was able to struggle a little longer. Then once more he found himself so terribly out of breath that he thought his chest would burst. His strength was all gone, and he did not know now whether he had enough to try to swim for the shore. Suddenly he heard a cry.

"Izzart, Izzart. Help. Help."

It was Campion's voice. It was a scream of agony. It sent a shock all through Izzart's nerves. Campion, Campion, what did he care for Campion? Fear seized him, a blind animal fear, and it gave him a new strength. He did not answer.

"Help me, quick, quick," he said to Hassan.

Hassan understood him at once. By a miracle one of the oars was floating quite close to them and he pushed it into Izzart's reach. He placed a hand under Izzart's arm and they struck away from the boat. Izzart's heart was pounding and his breath came with difficulty. He felt horribly weak. The waves beat in his face. The bank looked dreadfully far away. He did not think he could ever reach it. Suddenly the boy cried that he could touch bottom and Izzart put down his legs; but he could feel nothing; he swam a few more exhausted strokes, his eyes fixed on the bank, and then, trying again, felt his feet sink into thick mud. He was thankful. He floundered on and there was the bank within reach of his hands, black mud in which he sank to his knees; he scrambled up, desperate to get out of the cruel water, and when he came to the top he found a little flat with tall rank grass all about it. He and Hassan sank down on it and lay for a while stretched out like dead men. They were so tired that they could not move. They were covered with black mud from head to foot.

But presently Izzart's mind began to work, and a pang of anguish on a sudden shook him. Campion was drowned. It was awful. He did not know how he was going to explain the disaster when he got back to Kuala Solor. They would blame him for it; he ought to have remembered the Bore and told the steersman to make for the bank and tie up the boat when he saw it coming. It wasn't his fault, it was the steersman's, he knew the river; why in God's name hadn't he had the sense to get into safety? How could he have expected that it was possible to ride that horrible torrent? Izzart's limbs shook as he remembered the wall of seething water that rushed down upon them. He must get the body and take it back to Kuala Solor. He wondered whether any of the crew were drowned too. He felt too weak to move, but Hassan now rose and wrung the water out of his sarong; he looked over the river and quickly turned to Izzart.

"Tuan, a boat is coming."

The lalang grass prevented Izzart from seeing anything.

"Shout to them," he said.

Hassan slipped out of view and made his way along the branch of a tree that overhung the water; he cried out and waved. Presently Izzart heard voices. There was a rapid conversation between the boy and the occupants of the boat, and then the boy came back.

"They saw us capsize, Tuan," he said, "and they came as soon as the Bore passed. There's a long-house on the other side. If you will cross the river they will give us sarongs and food and we can sleep there."

Izzart for a moment felt that he could not again trust himself on the face of the treacherous water.

"What about the other tuan?" he asked.

"They do not know."

"If he's drowned they must find the body."

"Another boat has gone up-stream."

Izzart did not know what to do. He was numb. Hassan put his arm round his shoulder and raised him to his feet. He made his way through the thick grass to the edge of the water, and there he saw a dug-out with two Dyaks in it. The river now once more was calm and sluggish; the great wave had passed on and no one would have dreamed that so short a while before the placid surface was like a stormy sea. The Dyaks repeated to him what they had already told the boy. Izzart could not bring himself to speak. He felt that if he said a word he would burst out crying. Hassan helped him to get in, and the Dyaks began to pull across. He fearfully wanted something to smoke, but his cigarettes and his matches, both in a hip-pocket, were soaking. The passage of the river seemed endless. The night fell and when they reached the bank the first stars were shining. He stepped ashore and one of the Dyaks took him up to the long-house. But Hassan seized the paddle he had dropped and with the other pushed out into the stream. Two or three men and some children came down to meet Izzart and he climbed to the house amid a babel of conversation. He went up the ladder and was led with greetings and excited comment to the space where the young men slept. Rattan mats were hurriedly laid to make him a couch and he sank down on them. Someone brought him a jar of arak and he took a long drink; it was rough and fiery, burning his throat, but it warmed his heart. He slipped off his shirt and trousers and put on a dry sarong which someone lent him. By chance he caught sight of the yellow new moon lying on her back, and it gave him a keen, almost a sensual, pleasure. He could not help thinking that he might at that moment be a corpse floating up the river with the tide. The moon had never looked to him more lovely. He began to feel hungry and he asked for rice. One of the women went into a room to prepare it. He was more himself now, and he began to think again of the explanations he would make at Kuala Solor. No one could really blame him because he had gone to sleep; he certainly wasn't drunk, Hutchinson would bear him out there, and how was he to suspect that the steersman would be such a damned fool? It was just rotten luck. But he couldn't think of Campion without a shudder. At last a platter of rice was brought him, and he was just about to start eating when a man ran hurriedly along and came up to him.

"The tuan's come," he cried.

"What tuan?"

He jumped up. There was a commotion about the doorway and he stepped forward. Hassan was coming quickly towards him out of the darkness, and then he heard a voice.

"Izzart. Are you there?"

Campion advanced towards him.

"Well, here we are again. By God, that was a pretty near thing, wasn't it? You seem to have made yourself nice and comfortable. My heavens, I could do with a drink."

His dank clothes clung round him, and he was muddy and dishevelled. But he was in excellent spirits.

"I didn't know where the hell they were bringing me. I'd made up my mind that I should have to spend the night on the bank. I thought you were drowned."

"Here's some arak," said Izzart.

Campion put his mouth to the jar and drank and spluttered and drank again.

"Muck, but by God it's strong." He looked at Izzart with a grin of his broken and discoloured teeth. "I say, old man, you look as though you'd be all the better for a wash."

"I'll wash later."

"All right, so will I. Tell them to get me a sarong. How did you get out?" He did not wait for an answer. "I thought I was done for. I owe my life to these two sportsmen here." He indicated with a cheery nod two of the Dyak prisoners whom Izzart vaguely recognized as having been part of their crew. "They were hanging on to that blasted boat on each side of me and somehow they cottoned on to it that I was down and out. I couldn't have lasted another minute. They made signs to me that we could risk having a shot at getting to the bank, but I didn't think I had the strength. By George, I've never been so blown in all my life. I don't know how they managed it, but somehow they got hold of the mattress we'd been lying on, and they made it into a roll. They're sportsmen they are. I don't know why they didn't just save themselves without bothering about me. They gave it me. I thought it a damned poor lifebelt, but I saw the force of the proverb about a drowning man clutching at a straw. I caught hold of the damned thing and between them somehow or other they dragged me ashore."

The danger from which he had escaped made Campion excited and voluble; but Izzart hardly listened to what he said. He heard once more, as distinctly as though the words rang now through the air, Campion's agonized cry for help, and he felt sick with terror. The blind panic raced down his nerves. Campion was talking still, but was he talking to conceal his thoughts? Izzart looked into those bright blue eyes and sought to read the sense behind the flow of words. Was there a hard glint in them or something of cynical mockery? Did he know that Izzart, leaving him to his fate, had cut and run? He flushed deeply. After all, what was there that he could have done? At such a moment it was each for himself and the devil take the hindmost. But what would they say in Kuala Solor if Campion told them that Izzart had deserted him? He ought to have stayed, he wished now with all his heart that he had, but then, then it was stronger than himself, he couldn't. Could anyone blame him? No one who had seen that fierce and seething torrent. Oh, the water and the exhaustion, so that he could have cried!

"If you're as hungry as I am you'd better have a tuck in at this rice," he said.

Campion ate voraciously, but when Izzart had taken a mouthful or two he found that he had no appetite. Campion talked and talked. Izzart listened suspiciously. He felt that he must be alert and he drank more arak. He began to feel a little drunk.

"I shall get into the devil of a row at KS," he said tentatively.

"I don't know why."

"I was told off to look after you. They won't think it was very clever of me to let you get nearly drowned."

"It wasn't your fault. It was the fault of the damned fool of a steersman. After all, the important thing is that we're saved. By George, I thought I was finished once. I shouted out to you. I don't know if you heard me."

"No, I didn't hear anything. There was such a devil of a row, wasn't there?"

"Perhaps you'd got away before. I don't know exactly when you did get away."

Izzart looked at him sharply. Was it his fancy that there was an odd look in Campion's eyes?

"There was such an awful confusion," he said. "I was just about down and out. My boy threw me over an oar. He gave me to understand you were all right. He told me you'd got ashore."

The oar! He ought to have given Campion the oar and told Hassan, the strong swimmer, to give *him* his help. Was it his fancy again that Campion gave him a quick and searching glance?

"I wish I could have been of more use to you," said Izzart.

"Oh, I'm sure you had enough to do to look after yourself," answered Campion.

The headman brought them cups of arak, and they both drank a great deal. Izzart's head began to spin and he suggested that they should turn in. Beds had been prepared for them and mosquito nets fixed. They were to set out at dawn on the rest of their journey down the river. Campion's bed was next to his, and in a few minutes he heard him snoring. He had fallen asleep the moment he lay down. The young men of the long-house and the prisoners of the boat's crew went on talking late into the night. Izzart's head now was aching horribly and he could not think. When Hassan roused him as day broke it seemed to him that he had not slept at all. Their clothes had been washed and dried, but they were bedraggled objects as they walked along the narrow pathway to the river where the prahu was waiting for them. They rowed leisurely. The morning was lovely and the great stretch of placid water gleamed in the early light.

"By George, it's fine to be alive," said Campion.

He was grubby and unshaved. He took long breaths, and his twisted mouth was half open with a grin. You could tell that he found the air singularly good to breathe. He was delighted with the blue sky and the sunshine and the greenness of the trees. Izzart hated him. He was sure that this morning there was a difference in his manner. He did not know what to do. He had a mind to throw himself on his mercy. He had behaved like a cad, but he was sorry, he would give anything to have the chance again, but anyone might have done what he did, and if Campion gave him away he was ruined. He could never stay in Sembulu; his name would be mud in Borneo and the Straits Settlements. If he made his confession to Campion he could surely get Campion to promise to hold his tongue. But would he keep his promise? He looked at him, a shifty little man: how could he be relied on? Izzart thought of what he had said the night before. It wasn't the truth, of course, but who could know that? At all events who could prove that he hadn't honestly thought that Campion was safe? Whatever Campion said, it was only his word against Izzart's; he could laugh and shrug his shoulders and say that Campion had lost his head and didn't know what he was talking about. Besides, it wasn't certain that Campion hadn't accepted his story; in that frightful struggle for life he could be very sure of nothing. He had a temptation to go back to the subject, but he was afraid if he did that he would excite suspicion in Campion's mind. He *must* hold his tongue. That was his only chance of safety. And when they got to KS he would get in his story first.

"I should be completely happy now," said Campion, "if I only had something to smoke."

"We shall be able to get some stinkers on board."

Campion gave a little laugh.

"Human beings are very unreasonable," he said. "At the first moment I was so glad to be alive that I thought of nothing else, but now I'm beginning to regret the loss of my notes and my photographs and my shaving tackle."

Izzart formulated the thought which had lurked at the back of his mind, but which all through the night he had refused to admit into his consciousness.

"I wish to God he'd been drowned. Then I'd have been safe."

"There she is," cried Campion suddenly.

Izzart looked round. They were at the mouth of the river and there was the *Sultan Ahmed* waiting for them. Izzart's heart sank: he had forgotten that she had an English skipper and that he would have to be told the story of their adventure. What would Campion say? The skipper was called Bredon, and Izzart had met him often at Kuala Solor. He was a little bluff man, with a black moustache, and a breezy manner.

"Hurry up," he called out to them, as they rowed up, "I've been waiting for you since dawn." But when they climbed on board his face fell. "Hullo, what's the matter with you?"

"Give us a drink and you shall hear all about it," said Campion, with his crooked grin.

"Come along."

They sat down under the awning. On a table were glasses, a bottle of whisky and soda-water. The skipper gave an order and in a few minutes they were noisily under way.

"We were caught in the Bore," said Izzart.

He felt he must say something. His mouth was horribly dry notwithstanding the drink.

"Were you, by Jove? You're lucky not to have been drowned. What happened?"

He addressed himself to Izzart because he knew him, but it was Campion who answered. He related the whole incident, accurately, and Izzart listened with strained attention. Campion spoke in the plural when he told the early part of the story, and then, as he came to the moment when they were thrown into the water, changed to the singular. At first it was what they had done and now it was what happened to *him*. He left Izzart out of it. Izzart did not know whether to be relieved or alarmed. Why did he not mention him? Was it because in that mortal struggle for life he had thought of nothing but himself or – did he *know*?

"And what happened to you?" said Captain Bredon, turning to Izzart.

Izzart was about to answer when Campion spoke.

"Until I got over to the other side of the river I thought he was drowned. I don't know how he got out. I expect he hardly knows himself."

"It was touch and go," said Izzart with a laugh.

Why had Campion said that? He caught his eye. He was sure now that there was a gleam of amusement in it. It was awful not to be certain. He was frightened. He was ashamed. He wondered if he could not so guide the conversation, either now or later, as to ask Campion whether that was the story he was going to tell in Kuala Solor. There was nothing in it to excite anyone's suspicions. But if nobody else knew, Campion knew. He could have killed him.

"Well, I think you're both of you damned lucky to be alive," said the skipper.

It was but a short run to Kuala Solor, and as they steamed up the Sembulu river Izzart moodily watched the banks. On each side were the mangroves and the nipahs washed by the water, and behind, the dense green of the jungle; here and there, among fruit trees, were Malay houses on piles. Night fell as they docked. Goring, of the police, came on board and shook hands with them. He was living at the rest-house just then, and as he set about his work of seeing the native passengers he told them they would find another man, Porter by name, staying there too. They would all meet at dinner. The boys took charge of their kit, and Campion and Izzart strolled along. They bathed and changed, and at half past eight the four of them assembled in the common-room for gin pahits.

"I say, what's this Bredon tells me about your being nearly drowned?" said Goring as he came in.

Izzart felt himself flush, but before he could answer Campion broke in, and it seemed certain to Izzart that he spoke in order to give the story as he chose. He felt hot with shame. Not a word was spoken in disparagement of him, not a word was said of him at all; he wondered if those two men who listened, Goring and Porter, thought it strange that he should be left out. He looked at Campion intently as he proceeded with his narration; he told it rather humorously; he did not disguise the danger in which they had been, but he made a joke of it, so that the two listeners laughed at the quandary in which they found themselves.

"A thing that's tickled me since," said Campion, "is that when I got over to the other bank I was black with mud from head to foot. I felt I really ought to jump in the river and have a wash, but you know I felt I'd been in that damned river as much as ever I wanted, and I said to myself: No, by George, I'll go dirty. And when I got into the long-house and saw Izzart as black as I was, I knew he'd felt just like I did."

They laughed and Izzart forced himself to laugh too. He noticed that Campion had told the story in precisely the same words as he had used when he told it to the skipper of the *Sultan Ahmed*. There could be only one explanation of that; he knew, he knew everything, and had made up his mind exactly what story to tell. The ingenuity with which Campion gave the facts and yet left out what must be to Izzart's discredit was devilish. But why was he holding his hand? It wasn't in him not to feel contempt and resentment for the man who had callously deserted him in that moment of dreadful peril. Suddenly, in a flash of inspiration Izzart understood: he was keeping the truth to tell to Willis, the Resident. Izzart had gooseflesh as he thought of confronting Willis. He could deny, but would his denials serve him? Willis was no fool, and he would get at Hassan; Hassan could not be trusted to be silent; Hassan would give him away. Then he would be done for. Willis would suggest that he had better go home.

He had a racking headache, and after dinner he went to his room, for he wanted to be alone so that he could devise a plan of action. And then a thought came to him which made him go hot and cold: he knew that the secret which he had guarded so long was a secret to nobody. He was on a sudden certain of it. Why should he have those bright eyes and that swarthy skin? Why should he speak Malay with such ease and have learned Dyak so quickly? Of course they knew. What a fool he was ever to think that they believed that story of his, about the Spanish grandmother! They must have laughed up their sleeves when he told it, and behind his back they had called him a damned nigger. And now another thought came to him, torturing, and he asked himself whether it was on account of that wretched drop of native blood in him that when he heard Campion cry out his nerve failed him. After all, anyone might at that moment have been seized with panic; and why in God's name should he sacrifice his life to save a man's whom he cared nothing for? It was insane. But of course in KS they would say it was only what they expected; they would make no allowances.

At last he went to bed, but when, after tossing about recklessly for God knows how long, he fell asleep, he was awakened by a fearful dream; he seemed to be once more in that raging torrent, with the boat turning, turning; and then there was the desperate clutching at the gunwale, and the agony as it slipped out of his hands, and the water that roared over him. He was wide awake before dawn. His only chance was to see Willis and get his story in first; and he thought over carefully what he was going to say, and chose the very words he meant to use.

He got up early, and in order not to see Campion went out without breakfast. He walked along the high road till such time as he knew the Resident would be in his office, and then walked back again. He sent in his name and was ushered into Willis's room. He was a little elderly man with thin grey hair and a long yellow face.

"I'm glad to see you back safe and sound," he said, shaking hands with Izzart. "What's this I hear about your being nearly drowned?"

Izzart, in clean ducks, his topee spotless, was a fine figure of a man. His black hair was neatly brushed, and his moustache was trimmed. He had an upright and soldierly bearing.

"I thought I'd better come and tell you at once, sir, as you told me to look after Campion."

"Fire away."

Izzart told his story. He made light of the danger. He gave Willis to understand that it had not been very great. They would never have been upset if they had not started so late.

"I tried to get Campion away earlier, but he'd had two or three drinks and the fact is, he didn't want to move."

"Was he tight?"

"I don't know about that," smiled Izzart good-humouredly. "I shouldn't say he was cold sober."

He went on with his story. He managed to insinuate that Campion had lost his head a little. Of course it was a very frightening business to a man who wasn't a decent swimmer: he, Izzart, had been more concerned for Campion than for himself; he knew the only chance was to keep cool, and the moment they were upset he saw that Campion had got the wind up.

"You can't blame him for that," said the Resident.

"Of course I did everything I possibly could for him, sir, but the fact is, there wasn't anything much I could do."

"Well, the great thing is that you both escaped. It would have been very awkward for all of us if he'd been drowned."

"I thought I'd better come and tell you the facts before you saw Campion, sir. I fancy he's inclined to talk rather wildly about it. There's no use exaggerating."

"On the whole your stories agree pretty well," said Willis, with a little smile.

Izzart looked at him blankly.

"Haven't you seen Campion this morning? I heard from Goring that there'd been some trouble, and I looked in last night on my way home from the Fort after dinner. You'd already gone to bed."

Izzart felt himself trembling, and he made a great effort to preserve his composure.

"By the way, you got away first, didn't you?"

"I don't really know, sir. You see, there was a lot of confusion."

"You must have if you got over to the other side before he did."

"I suppose I did then."

"Well, thanks for coming to tell me," said Willis, rising from his chair.

As he did so he knocked some books on the floor. They fell with a sudden thud. The unexpected sound made Izzart start violently, and he gave a gasp. The Resident looked at him quickly.

"I say, your nerves are in a pretty state."

Izzart could not control his trembling.

"I'm very sorry, sir," he murmured.

"I expect it's been a shock. You'd better take it easy for a few days. Why don't you get the doctor to give you something?"

"I didn't sleep very well last night."

The Resident nodded as though he understood. Izzart left the room, and as he passed out some man he knew stopped and congratulated him on his escape. They all knew of it. He walked back to the rest-house. And as he walked, he repeated to himself the story he had told the Resident. Was it really the same story that Campion had told? He had never suspected that the Resident had already heard it from Campion. What a fool he had been to go to bed! He should never have let Campion out of his sight. Why had the Resident listened without telling him that he already knew? Now Izzart cursed himself for having suggested that Campion was drunk and had lost his head. He had said this in order to discredit him, but he knew now that it was a stupid thing to do. And why had Willis said that about his having got away first? Perhaps he was holding his hand too; perhaps he was going to make inquiries; Willis was very shrewd. But what exactly had Campion said? He must know that; at whatever cost he must know. Izzart's mind was seething, so that he felt he could hardly keep a hold on his thoughts, but he must keep calm. He felt like a hunted animal. He did not believe that Willis liked him; once or twice in the office he had blamed him because he was careless; perhaps he was just waiting till he got all the facts. Izzart was almost hysterical.

He entered the rest-house and there, sitting on a long chair, with his legs stretched out, was Campion. He was reading the papers which had arrived during their absence in the jungle. Izzart felt a blind rush of hatred well up in him as he looked at the little, shabby man who held him in the hollow of his hand.

"Hullo," said Campion, looking up. "Where have you been?"

To Izzart it seemed that there was in his eyes a mocking irony. He clenched his hands, and his breath came fast.

"What have you been saying to Willis about me?" he asked abruptly.

The tone in which he put the unexpected question was so harsh that Campion gave him a glance of faint surprise.

"I don't think I've been saying anything very much about you. Why?"

"He came here last night."

Izzart looked at him intently. His brows were drawn together in an angry frown as he tried to read Campion's thoughts.

"I told him you'd gone to bed with a headache. He wanted to know about our mishap."

"I've just seen him."

Izzart walked up and down the large and shaded room; now, though it was still early, the sun was hot and dazzling. He felt himself in a net. He was blind with rage; he could have seized Campion by the throat and strangled him, and yet, because he did not know what he had to fight against, he felt himself powerless. He was tired and ill, and his nerves were shaken. On a sudden the anger which had given him a sort of strength left him, and he was filled with despondency. It was as though water and not blood ran through his veins; his heart sank and his knees seemed to give way. He felt that if he did not take care, he would begin to cry. He was dreadfully sorry for himself.

"Damn you, I wish to God I'd never set eyes on you," he cried pitifully.

"What on earth's the matter?" asked Campion, with astonishment.

"Oh, don't pretend. We've been pretending for two days, and I'm fed up with it." His voice rose shrilly, it sounded odd in that robust and powerful man. "I'm fed up with it. I cut and run. I left you to drown. I know I behaved like a skunk. I couldn't help it."

Campion rose slowly from his chair.

"What *are* you talking about?"

His tone was so genuinely surprised that it gave Izzart a start. A cold shiver ran down his spine.

"When you called for help I was panic-stricken. I just caught hold of an oar and got Hassan to help me get away."

"That was the most sensible thing you could do."

"I couldn't help you. There wasn't a thing I could do."

"Of course not. It was damned silly of me to shout. It was waste of breath, and breath was the very thing I wanted."

"Do you mean to say you didn't know?"

"When those fellows got me the mattress, I thought you were still clinging to the boat. I had an idea that I got away before you did."

Izzart put both his hands to his head, and gave a hoarse cry of despair.

"My God, what a fool I've been."

The two men stood for a while staring at one another. The silence seemed endless.

"What are you going to do now?" asked Izzart at last.

"Oh, my dear fellow, don't worry. I've been frightened too often myself to blame anyone who shows the white feather. I'm not going to tell a soul."

"Yes, but you *know*."

"I promise you, you can trust me. Besides, my job's done here and I'm going home. I want to catch the next boat to Singapore." There was a pause, and Campion looked for a while reflectively at Izzart. "There's only one thing I'd like to ask you: I've made a good many friends here, and there are one or two things I'm a little sensitive about; when you tell the story of our upset, I should be grateful if you wouldn't make out that I had behaved badly. I wouldn't like the fellows here to think that I'd lost my nerve."

Izzart flushed darkly. He remembered what he had said to the Resident. It almost looked as though Campion had been listening over his shoulder. He cleared his throat.

"I don't know why you think I should do that."

Campion chuckled good-naturedly, and his blue eyes were gay with amusement.

"The yellow streak," he replied, and then, with a grin that showed his broken and discoloured teeth: "Have a cheroot, dear boy."

THE VESSEL OF WRATH

THERE ARE FEW books in the world that contain more meat than the *Sailing Directions* published by the Hydrographic Department by order of the Lords Commissioners of the Admiralty. They are handsome volumes, bound (very flimsily) in cloth of different colours, and the most expensive of them is cheap. For four shillings you can buy the *Yangtse Kiang Pilot*, "containing a description of, and sailing directions for, the Yangtse Kiang from the Wusung River to the highest navigable point, including the Han Kiang, the Kialing Kiang, and the Min Kiang"; and for three shillings you can get Part III of the *Eastern Archipelago Pilot*, "comprising the NE end of Celebes, Molucca and Gilolo passages, Banda and Arafura Seas, and North, West, and South-West coasts of New Guinea". But it is not very safe to do so if you are a creature of settled habits that you have no wish to disturb or if you have an occupation that holds you fast to one place. These business-like books take you upon enchanted journeys of the spirit; and their matter-of-fact style, the admirable order, the concision with which the material is set before you, the stern sense of the practical that informs every line, cannot dim the poetry that, like the spice-laden breeze that assails your senses with a more than material languor when you approach some of those magic islands of the Eastern seas, blows with so sweet a fragrance through the printed pages. They tell you the anchorages and the landing-places, what supplies you can get at each spot, and where you can get water; they tell you the lights and buoys, tides, winds, and weather that you will find there. They give you brief information about the population and the trade. And it is strange when you think how sedately it is all set down, with no words wasted, that so much else is given you besides. What? Well, mystery and beauty, romance and the glamour of the unknown. It is no common book that offers you casually turning its pages such a paragraph as this: "Supplies. A few jungle fowl are preserved, the island is also the resort of vast numbers of sea birds. Turtle are found in the lagoon, as well as quantities of various fish, including grey mullet, shark, and dog-fish; the seine cannot be used with any effect; but there is a fish which may be taken on a rod. A small store of tinned provisions and spirits is kept in a hut for the relief of shipwrecked persons. Good water may be obtained from a well near the landing-place." Can the imagination want more material than this to go on a journey through time and space?

In the volume from which I have copied this passage, the compilers with the same restraint have described the Alas Islands. They are composed of a group or chain of islands, "for the most part low and wooded, extending about 75 miles east and west, and 40 miles north and south". The information about them, you are told, is very slight; there are channels between the different groups, and several vessels have passed through them, but the passages have not been thoroughly explored, and the positions of many of the dangers not yet determined; it is therefore advisable to avoid them. The population of the group is estimated at about 8,000, of whom 200 are Chinese and 400 Mohammedans. The rest are heathen. The principal island is called Baru, it is surrounded by a reef, and here lives a Dutch Contrôleur. His white house with its red roof on the top of a little hill is the most prominent object that the vessels of the Royal Netherlands Steam Packet Company see when every other month on their way up to Macassar and every four weeks on their way down to Merauke in Dutch New Guinea they touch at the island.

At a certain moment of the world's history the Contrôleur was Mynheer Evert Gruyter and he ruled the people who inhabited the Alas Islands with firmness tempered by a keen sense of the ridiculous. He had thought it a very good joke to be placed at the age of twenty-seven in a position of such consequence, and at thirty he was still amused by it. There was no cable communication between his islands and Batavia, and the mail arrived after so long a delay that even if he asked advice, by the time he received it, it was useless, and so he equably did what he thought best and trusted to his good fortune to keep out of trouble with the authorities. He was very short, not more than five feet four in height, and extremely fat; he was of a florid complexion. For coolness' sake he kept his head shaved and his face was hairless. It was round and red. His eyebrows were so fair that you hardly saw them; and he had little twinkling blue eyes. He knew that he had no dignity, but for the sake of his position made up for it by dressing very dapperly. He never went to his office, nor sat in court, nor walked abroad but in spotless white. His stengah-shifter, with its bright brass buttons, fitted him very tightly and displayed the shocking fact that, young though he was, he had a round and protruding belly. His good-humoured face shone with sweat and he constantly fanned himself with a palm-leaf fan.

But in his house Mr Gruyter preferred to wear nothing but a sarong and then with his white podgy little body he looked like a fat funny boy of sixteen. He was an early riser and his breakfast was always ready for him at six. It never varied. It consisted of a slice of papaia, three cold fried eggs, Edam cheese, sliced thin, and a cup of black coffee. When he had eaten it, he smoked a large Dutch cigar, read the papers if he had not read them through and through already, and then dressed to go down to his office.

One morning while he was thus occupied his head boy came into his bedroom and told him that Tuan Jones wanted to know if he could see him. Mr Gruyter was standing in front of a looking-glass. He had his trousers on and was admiring his smooth chest. He arched his back in order to throw it out and throw in his belly and with a good deal of satisfaction gave his breast three or four resounding slaps. It was a manly chest. When the boy brought the message he looked at his own eyes in the mirror and exchanged a slightly ironic smile with them. He asked himself what the devil his visitor could want. Evert Gruyter spoke English, Dutch, and Malay with equal facility, but he thought in Dutch. He liked to do this. It seemed to him a pleasantly ribald language.

"Ask the tuan to wait and say I shall come directly." He put on his tunic, over his naked body, buttoned it up, and strutted into the sitting-room. The Rev. Owen Jones got up.

"Good morning, Mr Jones," said the Contrôleur. "Have you come in to have a peg with me before I start my day's work?"

Mr Jones did not smile.

"I've come to see you upon a very distressing matter, Mr Gruyter," he answered.

The Contrôleur was not disconcerted by his visitor's gravity nor depressed by his words. His little blue eyes beamed amiably.

"Sit down, my dear fellow, and have a cigar."

Mr Gruyter knew quite well that the Rev. Owen Jones neither drank nor smoked, but it tickled something prankish in his nature to offer him a drink and a smoke whenever they met. Mr Jones shook his head.

Mr Jones was in charge of the Baptist Mission on the Alas Islands. His headquarters were at Baru, the largest of them, with the greatest population, but he had meeting-houses under the care of native helpers in several other islands of the group. He was a tall, thin, melancholy man, with a long face, sallow and drawn, of about forty. His brown hair was already white on the temples and it receded from the forehead. This gave him a look of somewhat vacuous intellectuality. Mr Gruyter both disliked and respected him. He disliked him because he was narrow-minded and dogmatic. Himself a cheerful pagan who liked the good things of the flesh and was determined to get as many of them as his circumstances permitted, he had no patience with a man who disapproved of them all. He thought the customs of the country suited its inhabitants and had no patience with the missionary's energetic efforts to destroy a way of life that for centuries had worked very well. He respected him because he was honest, zealous, and good. Mr Jones, an Australian of Welsh descent, was the only qualified doctor in the group and it was a comfort to know that if you fell ill you need not rely only on a Chinese practitioner, and none knew better than the Contrôleur how useful to all Mr Jones's skill had been and with what charity he had given it.

On the occasion of an epidemic of influenza the missionary had done the work of ten men and no storm short of a typhoon could prevent him from crossing to one island or another if his help was needed.

He lived with his sister in a little white house about half a mile from the village, and when the Contrôleur had arrived came on board to meet him and begged him to stay till he could get his own house in order. The Contrôleur had accepted and soon saw for himself with what simplicity the couple lived. It was more than he could stand. Tea at three sparse meals a day, and when he lit his cigar Mr Jones politely but firmly asked him to be good enough not to smoke, since both his sister and he strongly disapproved of it. In twenty-four hours Mr Gruyter moved into his own house. He fled, with panic in his heart, as though from a plague-stricken city. The Contrôleur was fond of a joke and he liked to laugh; to be with a man who took your nonsense in deadly earnest and never even smiled at your best story was more than flesh and blood could stand. The Rev. Owen Jones was a worthy man, but as a companion he was impossible. His sister was worse. Neither had a sense of humour, but whereas the missionary was of a melancholy turn, doing his duty so conscientiously, with the obvious conviction that everything in the world was hopeless, Miss Jones was resolutely cheerful. She grimly looked on the bright side of things. With the ferocity of an avenging angel she sought out the good in her fellow-men. Miss Jones taught in the mission school and helped her brother in his medical work. When he did operations she gave the anaesthetic and was matron, dresser, and nurse of the tiny hospital which on his own initiative Mr Jones had added to the mission. But the Contrôleur was an obstinate little fellow and he never lost his capacity of extracting amusement from the Rev. Owen's dour struggle with the infirmities of human nature, and Miss Jones's ruthless optimism. He had to get his fun where he could. The Dutch boats came in three times in two months for a few hours and then he could have a good old crack with the captain and chief engineer, and once in a blue moon a pearling lugger came in from Thursday Island or Port Darwin and for two or three days he had a grand time. They were rough fellows, the pearlers, for the most part, but they were full of guts, and they had plenty of liquor on board, and good stories to tell, and the Contrôleur had them up to his house and gave them a fine dinner, and the party was only counted a success if they were all too drunk to get back on the lugger again that night. But beside the missionary the only white man who lived on Baru was Ginger Ted, and he, of course, was a disgrace to civilization. There was not a single thing to be said in his favour. He cast discredit on the white race. All the same, but for Ginger Ted the Contrôleur sometimes thought he would find life on the island of Baru almost more than he could bear.

Oddly enough it was on account of this scamp that Mr Jones, when he should have been instructing the pagan young in the mysteries of the Baptist faith, was paying Mr Gruyter this early visit.

"Sit down, Mr Jones," said the Contrôleur. "What can I do for you?"

"Well, I've come to see you about the man they call Ginger Ted. What are you going to do now?"

"Why, what's happened?"

"Haven't you heard? I thought the sergeant would have told you."

"I don't encourage the members of my staff to come to my private house unless the matter is urgent," said the Contrôleur rather grandly. "I am unlike you, Mr Jones, I only work in order to have leisure, and I like to enjoy my leisure without disturbance."

But Mr Jones did not care much for small talk and he was not interested in general reflections.

"There was a disgraceful row in one of the Chinese shops last night. Ginger Ted wrecked the place and half killed a Chinaman."

"Drunk again, I suppose," said the Contrôleur placidly.

"Naturally. When is he anything else? They sent for the police and he assaulted the sergeant. They had to have six men to get him to the jail."

"He's a hefty fellow," said the Contrôleur.

"I suppose you'll send him to Macassar."

Evert Gruyter returned the missionary's outraged look with a merry twinkle. He was no fool and he knew already what Mr Jones was up to. It gave him considerable amusement to tease him a little.

"Fortunately my powers are wide enough to enable me to deal with the situation myself," he answered.

"You have power to deport anyone you like, Mr Gruyter, and I'm sure it would save a lot of trouble if you got rid of the man altogether."

"I have the power of course, but I am sure you would be the last person to wish me to use it arbitrarily."

"Mr Gruyter, the man's presence here is a public scandal. He's never sober from morning till night; it's notorious that he has relations with one native woman after another."

"That is an interesting point, Mr Jones. I had always heard that alcoholic excess, though it stimulated sexual desire, prevented its gratification. What you tell me about Ginger Ted does not seem to bear out this theory."

The missionary flushed a dull red.

"These are physiological matters which at the moment I have no wish to go into," he said, frigidly. "The behaviour of this man does incalculable damage to the prestige of the white race, and his example seriously hampers the efforts that are made in other quarters to induce the people of these islands to lead a less vicious life. He's an out-and-out bad lot."

"Pardon my asking, but have you made any attempts to reform him?"

"When he first drifted here I did my best to get in touch with him. He repelled all my advances. When there was that first trouble I went to him and talked to him straight from the shoulder. He swore at me."

"No one has a greater appreciation than I of the excellent work that you and other missionaries do on these islands, but are you sure that you always exercise your calling with all the tact possible?"

The Contrôleur was rather pleased with this phrase. It was extremely courteous and yet contained a reproof that he thought worth administering. The missionary looked at him gravely. His sad brown eyes were full of sincerity.

"Did Jesus exercise tact when he took a whip and drove the money-changers from the Temple? No, Mr Gruyter. Tact is the subterfuge the lax avail themselves of to avoid doing their duty."

Mr Jones's remark made the Contrôleur feel suddenly that he wanted a bottle of beer. The missionary leaned forward earnestly.

"Mr Gruyter, you know this man's transgressions just as well as I do. It's unnecessary for me to remind you of them. There are no excuses for him. Now he really has overstepped the limit. You'll never have a better chance than this. I beg you to use the power you have and turn him out once for all."

The Contrôleur's eyes twinkled more brightly than ever. He was having a lot of fun. He reflected that human beings were much more amusing when you did not feel called upon in dealing with them to allot praise or blame.

"But, Mr Jones, do I understand you right? Are you asking me to give you an assurance to deport this man before I've heard the evidence against him and listened to his defence?"

"I don't know what his defence can be."

The Contrôleur rose from his chair and really he managed to get quite a little dignity into his five feet four inches.

"I am here to administer justice according to the laws of the Dutch Government. Permit me to tell you that I am exceedingly surprised that you should attempt to influence me in my judicial functions."

The missionary was a trifle flustered. It had never occurred to him that this little whipper-snapper of a boy, ten years younger than himself, would dream of adopting such an attitude. He opened his mouth to explain and apologize, but the Contrôleur raised a podgy little hand.

"It is time for me to go to my office, Mr Jones. I wish you good morning."

The missionary, taken aback, bowed and without another word walked out of the room. He would have been surprised to see what the Contrôleur did when his back was turned. A broad grin broke on his lips and he put his thumb to his nose and cocked a snook at the Rev. Owen Jones.

A few minutes later he went down to his office. His head clerk, who was a Dutch half-caste, gave him his version of the previous night's row. It agreed pretty well with Mr Jones's. The court was sitting that day.

"Will you take Ginger Ted first, sir?" asked the clerk.

"I see no reason to do that. There are two or three cases held over from the last sitting. I will take him in his proper order."

245

"I thought perhaps as he was a white man you would like to see him privately, sir."

"The majesty of the law knows no difference between white and coloured, my friend," said Mr Gruyter, somewhat pompously.

The court was a big square room with wooden benches on which, crowded together, sat natives of all kinds, Polynesians, Bugis, Chinese, Malays, and they all rose when a door was opened and a sergeant announced the arrival of the Contrôleur. He entered with his clerk and took his place on a little dais at a table of varnished pitch pine. Behind him was a large engraving of Queen Wilhelmina. He dispatched half a dozen cases and then Ginger Ted was brought in. He stood in the dock, handcuffed, with a warder on either side of him. The Contrôleur looked at him with a grave face, but he could not keep the amusement out of his eyes.

Ginger Ted was suffering from a hangover. He swayed a little as he stood and his eyes were vacant. He was a man still young, thirty perhaps, of somewhat over the middle height, rather fat, with a bloated red face and a shock of curly red hair. He had not come out of the tussle unscathed. He had a black eye and his mouth was cut and swollen. He wore khaki shorts, very dirty and ragged, and his singlet had been almost torn off his back. A great rent showed the thick mat of red hair with which his chest was covered, but showed also the astonishing whiteness of his skin. The Contrôleur looked at the charge sheet. He called the evidence. When he had heard it, when he had seen the Chinaman whose head Ginger Ted had broken with a bottle, when he had heard the agitated story of the sergeant who had been knocked flat when he tried to arrest him, when he had listened to the tale of the havoc wrought by Ginger Ted who in his drunken fury had smashed everything he could lay hands on he turned and addressed the accused in English.

"Well, Ginger, what have you got to say for yourself?"

"I was blind. I don't remember a thing about it. If they say I half killed 'im I suppose I did. I'll pay the damage if they'll give me time."

"You will, Ginger," said the Contrôleur, "but it's me who'll give you time."

He looked at Ginger Ted for a minute in silence. He was an unappetizing object. A man who had gone completely to pieces. He was horrible. It made you shudder to look at him and if Mr Jones had

not been so officious, at that moment the Contrôleur would certainly have ordered him to be deported.

"You've been a trouble ever since you came to the islands,
Ginger. You're a disgrace. You're incorrigibly idle. You've been
picked up in the street dead drunk time and time again. You've
kicked up row after row. You're hopeless. I told you the last time you
were brought here that if you were arrested again I should deal with
you severely. You've gone the limit this time and you're for it.
I sentence you to six months' hard labour."

"Me?"

"You."

"By God, I'll kill you when I come out."

He burst into a string of oaths both filthy and blasphemous.
Mr Gruyter listened scornfully. You can swear much better in
Dutch than in English and there was nothing that Ginger Ted said
that he could not have effectively capped.

"Be quiet," he ordered. "You make me tired."

The Contrôleur repeated his sentence in Malay and the prisoner
was led struggling away.

Mr Gruyter sat down to tiffin in high good-humour. It was
astonishing how amusing life could be if you exercised a little
ingenuity. There were people in Amsterdam, and even in Batavia
and Surabaya, who looked upon his island home as a place of exile.
They little knew how agreeable it was and what fun he could extract
from unpromising material. They asked him whether he did not miss
the club and the races and the cinema, the dances that were held once
a week at the Casino and the society of Dutch ladies. Not at all. He
liked comfort. The substantial furniture of the room in which he sat
had a satisfying solidity. He liked reading French novels of a frivolous
nature and he appreciated the sensation of reading one after the other
without the uneasiness occasioned by the thought that he was
wasting his time. It seemed to him a great luxury to waste time.
When his young man's fancy turned to thoughts of love his head boy
brought to the house a little dark-skinned bright-eyed creature in a
sarong. He took care to form no connexion of a permanent nature.
He thought that change kept the heart young. He enjoyed freedom
and was not weighed down by a sense of responsibility. He did not
mind the heat. It made a sluice over with cold water half a dozen

times a day a pleasure that had almost an aesthetic quality. He played the piano. He wrote letters to his friends in Holland. He felt no need for the conversation of intellectual persons. He liked a good laugh, but he could get that out of a fool just as well as out of a professor of philosophy. He had a notion that he was a very wise little man.

Like all good Dutchmen in the Far East he began his lunch with a small glass of Hollands gin. It has a musty acrid flavour, and the taste for it must be acquired, but Mr Gruyter preferred it to any cocktail. When he drank it he felt besides that he was upholding the traditions of his race. Then he had *rijsttafel*. He had it every day. He heaped a soup-plate high with rice, and then, his three boys waiting on him, helped himself to the curry that one handed him, to the fried egg that another brought, and to the condiment presented by the third. Then each one brought another dish, of bacon, or bananas, or pickled fish, and presently his plate was piled high in a huge pyramid. He stirred it all together and began to eat. He ate slowly and with relish. He drank a bottle of beer.

He did not think while he was eating. His attention was applied to the mass in front of him and he consumed it with a happy concentration. It never palled on him. And when he had emptied the great plate it was a compensation to think that next day he would have *rijsttafel* again. He grew tired of it as little as the rest of us grow tired of bread. He finished his beer and lit his cigar. The boy brought him a cup of coffee. He leaned back in his chair then and allowed himself the luxury of reflection.

It tickled him to have sentenced Ginger Ted to the richly deserved punishment of six months' hard labour, and he smiled when he thought of him working on the roads with the other prisoners. It would have been silly to deport from the island the one man with whom he could occasionally have a heart-to-heart talk, and besides, the satisfaction it would have given the missionary would have been bad for that gentleman's character. Ginger Ted was a scamp and a scallywag, but the Contrôleur had a kindly feeling for him. They had drunk many a bottle of beer in one another's company, and when the pearl fishers from Port Darwin came in and they all made a night of it, they had got gloriously tight together. The Contrôleur liked the reckless way in which Ginger Ted squandered the priceless treasure of life.

Ginger Ted had wandered in one day on the ship that was going up from Merauke to Macassar. The captain did not know how he had found his way there, but he had travelled steerage with the natives, and he stopped off at the Alas Islands because he liked the look of them. Mr Gruyter had a suspicion that their attraction consisted perhaps in their being under the Dutch flag and so out of British jurisdiction. But his papers were in order, so there was no reason why he should not stay. He said that he was buying pearl-shell for an Australian firm, but it soon appeared that his commercial undertakings were not serious. Drink, indeed, took up so much of his time that he had little left over for other pursuits. He was in receipt of two pounds a week, paid monthly, which came regularly to him from England. The Contrôleur guessed that this sum was paid only so long as he kept well away from the persons who sent it. It was anyway too small to permit him any liberty of movement. Ginger Ted was reticent. The Contrôleur discovered that he was an Englishman, this he learnt from his passport, which described him as Edward Wilson, and that he had been in Australia. But why he had left England and what he had done in Australia he had no notion. Nor could he ever quite tell to what class Ginger Ted belonged. When you saw him in a filthy singlet and a pair of ragged trousers, a battered topee on his head, with the pearl fishers and heard his conversation, coarse, obscene, and illiterate, you thought he must be a sailor before the mast who had deserted his ship, or a labourer, but when you saw his handwriting you were surprised to find that it was that of a man not without at least some education, and on occasion when you got him alone, if he had had a few drinks but was not yet drunk, he would talk of matters that neither a sailor nor a labourer would have been likely to know anything about. The Contrôleur had a certain sensitiveness and he realized that Ginger Ted did not speak to him as an inferior to a superior but as an equal. Most of his remittance was mortgaged before he received it, and the Chinamen to whom he owed money were standing at his elbow when the monthly letter was delivered to him, but with what was left he proceeded to get drunk. It was then that he made trouble, for when drunk he grew violent and was then likely to commit acts that brought him into the hands of the police. Hitherto Mr Gruyter had contented himself with keeping him in jail till he was sober and giving him a talking to. When he was out of money he cadged what drink he could from anyone who would give it him. Rum, brandy, arak, it was all the same to him. Two or three times Mr Gruyter had got him work on plantations run by Chinese in one or other of the islands, but he could not stick to it, and in a few weeks was back again at Baru on the beach. It was a miracle how he kept body and soul together. He had, of course, a way with him. He picked up the various dialects spoken on the islands, and knew how to make the natives laugh. They despised him, but they respected his physical strength, and they liked his company. He was as a result never at a loss for a meal or a mat to sleep on. The strange thing was, and it was this that chiefly outraged the Rev. Owen Jones, that he could do anything he liked with a woman. The Contrôleur could not imagine what it was they saw in him. He was casual with them and rather brutal. He took what they gave him, but seemed incapable of gratitude. He used them for his pleasure and then flung them indifferently away. Once or twice this had got him into trouble, and Mr Gruyter had had to sentence an angry father for sticking a knife in Ginger Ted's back one night, and a Chinese woman had sought to poison herself by swallowing opium because he had deserted her. Once Mr Jones came to the Contrôleur in a great state because the beachcomber had seduced one of his converts. The Contrôleur agreed that it was very deplorable, but could only advise Mr Jones to keep a sharp eye on these young persons. The Contrôleur liked it less when he discovered that a girl whom he fancied a good deal himself and had been seeing for several weeks had all the time been according her favours also to Ginger Ted. When he thought of this particular incident he smiled again at the thought of Ginger Ted doing six months' hard labour. It is seldom in this life that in the process of doing your bounden duty you can get back on a fellow who has played you a dirty trick.

A few days later Mr Gruyter was taking a walk, partly for exercise and partly to see that some job he wanted done was being duly proceeded with, when he passed a gang of prisoners working under the charge of a warder. Among them he saw Ginger Ted. He wore the prison sarong, a dingy tunic called in Malay a *baju,* and his own battered topee. They were repairing the road, and Ginger Ted was wielding a heavy pick. The way was narrow and the Contrôleur saw that he must pass within a foot of him. He remembered his threats. He knew that Ginger Ted was a man of violent passion, and the language he had used in the dock made it plain that he had not seen what a good joke it was of the Contrôleur's to sentence him to six months' hard labour. If Ginger Ted suddenly attacked him with the pick, nothing on God's earth could save him. It was true that the warder would immediately shoot him down, but meanwhile the Contrôleur's head would be bashed in. It was with a funny little feeling in the pit of his stomach that Mr Gruyter walked through the gang of prisoners. They were working in pairs a few feet from one another. He set his mind on neither hastening his pace nor slackening it. As he passed Ginger Ted, the man swung his pick into the ground and looked up at the Contrôleur and as he caught his eye winked. The Contrôleur checked the smile that rose to his lips and with official dignity strode on. But that wink, so lusciously full of sardonic humour, filled him with satisfaction. If he had been the Caliph of Baghdad instead of a junior official in the Dutch Civil Service, he could forthwith have released Ginger Ted, sent slaves to bath and perfume him, and having clothed him in a golden robe entertained him to a sumptuous repast.

Ginger Ted was an exemplary prisoner and in a month or two the Contrôleur, having occasion to send a gang to do some work on one of the outlying islands, included him in it. There was no jail there, so the ten fellows he sent, under the charge of a warder, were billeted on the natives and after their day's work lived like free men. The job was sufficient to take up the rest of Ginger Ted's sentence. The Contrôleur saw him before he left.

"Look here, Ginger," he said to him, "here's ten guilder for you so that you can buy yourself tobacco when you're gone."

"Couldn't you make it a bit more? There's eight pounds a month coming in regularly."

"I think that's enough. I'll keep the letters that come for you, and when you get back you'll have a tidy sum. You'll have enough to take you anywhere you want to go."

"I'm very comfortable here," said Ginger Ted.

"Well, the day you come back, clean yourself up and come over to my house. We'll have a bottle of beer together."

"That'll be fine. I guess I'll be ready for a good crack then."

Now chance steps in. The island to which Ginger Ted had been sent was called Maputiti, and like all the rest of them it was rocky, heavily wooded, and surrounded by a reef. There was a village among coconuts on the sea-shore opposite the opening of the reef and another village on a brackish lake in the middle of the island. Of this some of the inhabitants had been converted to Christianity. Communication with Baru was effected by a launch that touched at the various islands at irregular intervals. It carried passengers and produce. But the villagers were seafaring folk, and if they had to communicate urgently with Baru, manned a prahu and sailed the fifty miles or so that separated them from it. It happened that when Ginger Ted's sentence had but another fortnight to run the Christian headman of the village on the lake was taken suddenly ill. The native remedies availed him nothing and he writhed in agony. Messengers were sent to Baru imploring the missionary's help; but as ill luck would have it Mr Jones was suffering at the moment from an attack of malaria. He was in bed and unable to move. He talked the matter over with his sister.

"It sounds like acute appendicitis," he told her.

"You can't go, Owen," she said.

"I can't let the man die."

Mr Jones had a temperature of a hundred and four. His head was aching like mad. He had been delirious all night. His eyes were shining strangely and his sister felt that he was holding on to his wits by a sheer effort of will.

"You couldn't operate in the state you're in."

"No, I couldn't. Then Hassan must go."

Hassan was the dispenser.

"You couldn't trust Hassan. He'd never dare to do an operation on his own responsibility. And they'd never let him. I'll go. Hassan can stay here and look after you."

"You can't remove an appendix."

"Why not? I've seen you do it. I've done lots of minor operations."

Mr Jones felt he didn't quite understand what she was saying. "Is the launch in?"

"No, it's gone to one of the islands. But I can go in the prahu the men came in."

"You? I wasn't thinking of you. You can't go."

"I'm going, Owen."

"Going where?" he said.

She saw that his mind was wandering already. She put her hand soothingly on his dry forehead. She gave him a dose of medicine. He muttered something and she realized that he did not know where he was. Of course she was anxious about him, but she knew that his illness was not dangerous, and she could leave him safely to the mission boy who was helping her nurse him and to the native dispenser. She slipped out of the room. She put her toilet things, a night-dress, and a change of clothes into a bag. A little chest with surgical instruments, bandages, and antiseptic dressings was kept always ready. She gave them to the two natives who had come over from Maputiti, and telling the dispenser what she was going to do gave him instructions to inform her brother when he was able to listen. Above all he was not to be anxious about her. She put on her topee and sallied forth. The mission was about half a mile from the village. She walked quickly. At the end of the jetty the prahu was waiting. Six men manned it. She took her place in the stern and they set off with a rapid stroke. Within the reef the sea was calm, but when they crossed the bar they came upon a long swell. But this was not the first journey of the sort Miss Jones had taken and she was confident of the seaworthiness of the boat she was in. It was noon and the sun beat down from a sultry sky. The only thing that harassed her was that they could not arrive before dark, and if she found it necessary to operate at once she could count only on the light of hurricane lamps.

Miss Jones was a woman of hard on forty. Nothing in her appearance would have prepared you for such determination as she had just shown. She had an odd drooping gracefulness, which suggested that she might be swayed by every breeze; it was almost an affectation; and it made the strength of character which you soon discovered in her seem positively monstrous. She was flat-chested, tall, and extremely thin. She had a long sallow face and she was much afflicted with prickly heat. Her lank brown hair was drawn back straight from her forehead. She had rather small eyes, grey in colour, and because they were somewhat too close they gave her face a shrewish look. Her nose was long and thin and a trifle red. She suffered a good deal from indigestion. But this infirmity availed nothing against her ruthless determination to look upon the bright side of things. Firmly persuaded that the world was evil and men unspeakably vicious, she extracted any little piece of decency she could find in them with the modest pride with which a conjurer extracts a rabbit from a hat. She was quick, resourceful, and competent. When she arrived on the island she saw that there was not a moment to lose if she was to save the headman's life. Under the greatest difficulties, showing a native how to give the anaesthetic, she operated, and for the next three days nursed the patient with anxious assiduity. Everything went very well and she realized that her brother could not have made a better job of it. She waited long enough to take out the stitches and then prepared to go home. She could flatter herself that she had not wasted her time. She had given medical attention to such as needed it, she had strengthened the small Christian community in its faith, admonished such as were lax, and cast the good seed in places where it might be hoped under divine providence to take root.

The launch, coming from one of the other islands, put in somewhat late in the afternoon, but it was full moon and they expected to reach Baru before midnight. They brought her things down to the wharf and the people who were seeing her off stood about repeating their thanks. Quite a little crowd collected. The launch was loaded with sacks of copra, but Miss Jones was used to its strong smell and it did not incommode her. She made herself as comfortable a place to sit in as she could, and waiting for the launch to start, chatted with her grateful flock. She was the only passenger. Suddenly a group of natives emerged from the trees that embowered the little village on the lagoon and she saw that among them was a white man. He wore a prison sarong and a baju. He had long red hair. She at once recognized Ginger Ted. A policeman was with him. They shook hands and Ginger Ted shook hands with the villagers who accompanied him. They bore bundles of fruit and a jar which Miss Jones guessed contained native spirit, and these they put in the launch. She discovered to her surprise that Ginger Ted was coming with her. His term was up and instructions had arrived that he was to be returned to Baru in the launch. He gave her a glance, but did not nod – indeed Miss Jones turned away her head – and stepped in. The mechanic started his engine and in a moment they were jug-jugging through the channel in the lagoon. Ginger Ted clambered on to a pile of sacks and lit a cigarette.

Miss Jones ignored him. Of course she knew him very well. Her heart sank when she thought that he was going to be once more in Baru, creating a scandal and drinking, a peril to the women and a thorn in the flesh of all decent people. She knew the steps her brother had taken to have him deported and she had no patience with the Contrôleur, who would not see a duty that stared him so plainly in the face. When they had crossed the bar and were in the open sea Ginger Ted took the stopper out of the jar of arak and putting his mouth to it took a long pull. Then he handed the jar to the two mechanics who formed the crew. One was a middle-aged man and the other a youth.

"I do not wish you to drink anything while we are on the journey," said Miss Jones sternly to the elder one.

He smiled at her and drank.

"A little arak can do no one any harm," he answered. He passed the jar to his companion, who drank also.

"If you drink again I shall complain to the Contrôleur," said Miss Jones.

The elder man said something she could not understand, but which she suspected was very rude, and passed the jar back to Ginger Ted. They went along for an hour or more. The sea was like glass and the sun set radiantly. It set behind one of the islands and for a few minutes changed it into a mystic city of the skies. Miss Jones turned round to watch it and her heart was filled with gratitude for the beauty of the world.

"And only man is vile," she quoted to herself.

They went due east. In the distance was a little island which she knew they passed close by. It was uninhabited. A rocky islet thickly grown with virgin forest. The boatman lit his lamps. The night fell and immediately the sky was thick with stars. The moon had not yet risen. Suddenly there was a slight jar and the launch began to vibrate strangely. The engine rattled. The head mechanic, calling to his mate to take the helm, crept under the housing. They seemed to be going more slowly. The engine stopped. She asked the youth what was the matter, but he did not know. Ginger Ted got down from the top of

255

the copra sacks and slipped under the housing. When he reappeared she would have liked to ask him what had happened, but her dignity prevented her. She sat still and occupied herself with her thoughts. There was a long swell and the launch rolled slightly. The mechanic emerged once more into view and started the engine. Though it rattled like mad they began to move. The launch vibrated from stem to stern. They went very slowly. Evidently something was amiss, but Miss Jones was exasperated rather than alarmed. The launch was supposed to do six knots, but now it was just crawling along; at that rate they would not get into Baru till long, long after midnight. The mechanic, still busy under the housing, shouted out something to the man at the helm. They spoke in Bugi, of which Miss Jones knew very little. But after a while she noticed that they had changed their course and seemed to be heading for the little uninhabited island a good deal to the lee of which they should have passed.

"Where are we going?" she asked the helmsman with sudden misgiving.

He pointed to the islet. She got up and went to the housing and called to the man to come out.

"You're not going there? Why? What's the matter?"

"I can't get to Baru," he said.

"But you must. I insist. I order you to go to Baru."

The man shrugged his shoulders. He turned his back on her and slipped once more under the housing. Then Ginger Ted addressed her.

"One of the blades of the propeller has broken off. He thinks he can get as far as that island. We shall have to stay the night there and he'll put on a new propeller in the morning when the tide's out."

"I can't spend the night on an uninhabited island with three men," she cried.

"A lot of women would jump at it."

"I insist on going to Baru. Whatever happens we must get there tonight."

"Don't get excited, old girl. We've got to beach the boat to put a new propeller on, and we shall be all right on the island."

"How dare you speak to me like that! I think you're very insolent."

256

"You'll be OK. We've got plenty of grub and we'll have a snack when we land. You have a drop of arak and you'll feel like a house on fire."

"You're an impertinent man. If you don't go to Baru I'll have you all put in prison."

"We're not going to Baru. We can't. We're going to that island and if you don't like it you can get out and swim."

"Oh, you'll pay for this."

"Shut up, you old cow," said Ginger Ted.

Miss Jones gave a gasp of anger. But she controlled herself. Even out there, in the middle of the ocean, she had too much dignity to bandy words with that vile wretch. The launch, the engine rattling horribly, crawled on. It was pitch dark now, and she could no longer see the island they were making for. Miss Jones, deeply incensed, sat with lips tight shut and a frown on her brow; she was not used to being crossed. Then the moon rose and she could see the bulk of Ginger Ted sprawling on the top of the piled sacks of copra. The glimmer of his cigarette was strangely sinister. Now the island was vaguely outlined against the sky. They reached it and the boatman ran the launch on to the beach. Suddenly Miss Jones gave a gasp. The truth had dawned on her and her anger changed to fear. Her heart beat violently. She shook in every limb. She felt dreadfully faint. She saw it all. Was the broken propeller a put-up job or was it an accident? She could not be certain; anyhow, she knew that Ginger Ted would seize the opportunity. Ginger Ted would rape her. She knew his character. He was mad about women. That was what he had done, practically, to the girl at the mission, such a good little thing she was and an excellent sempstress; they would have prosecuted him for that and he would have been sentenced to years of imprisonment only very unfortunately the innocent child had gone back to him several times and indeed had only complained of his ill usage when he left her for somebody else. They had gone to the Contrôleur about it, but he had refused to take any steps, saying in that coarse way of his that even if what the girl said was true, it didn't look very much as though it had been an altogether unpleasant experience. Ginger Ted was a scoundrel. And she was a white woman. What chance was there that he would spare her? None. She knew men. But she must pull herself together. She must keep her wits about her. She must have courage. She was determined to sell her virtue dearly, and if he killed her – well, she would rather die than yield. And if she died she would rest in the arms of Jesus. For a moment a great light blinded her eyes and she saw the mansions of her Heavenly Father. They were a grand and sumptuous mixture of a picture palace and a railway station. The mechanics and Ginger Ted jumped out of the launch and, waist-deep in water, gathered round the broken propeller. She took advantage of their preoccupation to get her case of surgical instruments out of the box. She took out the four scalpels it contained and secreted them in her clothing. If Ginger Ted touched her she would not hesitate to plunge a scalpel in his heart.

"Now then, miss, you'd better get out," said Ginger Ted. "You'll be better off on the beach than in the boat."

She thought so too. At least here she would have freedom of action. Without a word she clambered over the copra sacks. He offered her his hand.

"I don't want your help," she said coldly.

"You can go to hell," he answered.

It was a little difficult to get out of the boat without showing her legs, but by the exercise of considerable ingenuity she managed it.

"Damned lucky we've got something to eat. We'll make a fire and then you'd better have a snack and a nip of arak."

"I want nothing. I only want to be left alone."

"It won't hurt me if you go hungry."

She did not answer. She walked, with head erect, along the beach. She held the largest scalpel in her closed fist. The moon allowed her to see where she was going. She looked for a place to hide. The thick forest came down to the very edge of the beach; but, afraid of its darkness (after all, she was but a woman), she dared not plunge into its depth. She did not know what animals lurked there or what dangerous snakes. Besides, her instinct told her that it was better to keep those three bad men in sight; then if they came towards her she would be prepared. Presently she found a little hollow. She looked round. They seemed to be occupied with their own efforts and they could not see her. She slipped in. There was a rock between them and her so that she was hidden from them and yet could watch them. She saw them go to and from the boat carrying things.

She saw them build a fire. It lit them luridly and she saw them sit around it and eat, and she saw the jar of arak passed from one to the other. They were all going to get drunk. What would happen to her then? It might be that she could cope with Ginger Ted, though his strength terrified her, but against three she would be powerless. A mad idea came to her to go to Ginger Ted and fall on her knees before him and beg him to spare her. He must have some spark of decent feeling in him and she had always been so convinced that there was good even in the worst of men. He must have had a mother. Perhaps he had a sister. Ah, but how could you appeal to a man blinded with lust and drunk with arak? She began to feel terribly weak. She was afraid she was going to cry. That would never do. She needed all her self-control. She bit her lip. She watched them, like a tiger watching his prey; no, not like that, like a lamb watching three hungry wolves. She saw them put more wood on the fire, and Ginger Ted, in his sarong, silhouetted by the flames. Perhaps after he had had his will of her he would pass her on to the others. How could she go back to her brother when such a thing had happened to her? Of course he would be sympathetic, but would he ever feel quite the same to her again? It would break his heart. And perhaps he would think that she ought to have resisted more. For his sake perhaps it would be better if she said nothing about it. Naturally the men would say nothing. It would mean twenty years in prison for them. But then supposing she had a baby. Miss Jones instinctively clenched her hands with horror and nearly cut herself with the scalpel. Of course it would only infuriate them if she resisted.

"What shall I do?" she cried. "What have I done to deserve this?"

She flung herself down on her knees and prayed to God to save her. She prayed long and earnestly. She reminded God that she was a virgin and just mentioned, in case it had slipped the divine memory, how much St Paul had valued that excellent state. And then she peeped round the rock again. The three men appeared to be smoking and the fire was dying down. Now was the time that Ginger Ted's lewd thoughts might be expected to turn to the woman who was at his mercy. She smothered a cry, for suddenly he got up and walked in her direction. She felt all her muscles grow taut, and though her heart was beating furiously she clenched the scalpel firmly in her hand. But it was for another purpose that Ginger Ted had got up. Miss Jones blushed and looked away. He strolled slowly back to the others and sitting down again raised the jar of arak to his lips. Miss Jones, crouching behind the rock, watched with straining eyes. The conversation round the fire grew less and presently she divined, rather than saw, that the two natives wrapped themselves in blankets and composed themselves to slumber. She understood. This was the moment Ginger Ted had been waiting for. When they were fast asleep he would get up cautiously and without a sound, in order not to wake the others, creep stealthily towards her. Was it that he was unwilling to share her with them or did he know that his deed was so dastardly that he did not wish them to know of it? After all, he was a white man and she was a white woman. He could not have sunk so low as to allow her to suffer the violence of natives. But his plan, which was so obvious to her, had given her an idea; when she saw him coming she would scream, she would scream so loudly that it would wake the two mechanics. She remembered now that the elder, though he had only one eye, had a kind face. But Ginger Ted did not move. She was feeling terribly tired. She began to fear that she would not have the strength now to resist him. She had gone through too much. She closed her eyes for a minute.

When she opened them it was broad daylight. She must have fallen asleep and, so shattered was she by emotion, have slept till long after dawn. It gave her quite a turn. She sought to rise, but something caught in her legs. She looked and found that she was covered with two empty copra sacks. Someone had come in the night and put them over her. Ginger Ted! She gave a little scream. The horrible thought flashed through her mind that he had outraged her in her sleep. No. It was impossible. And yet he had had her at his mercy. Defenceless. And he had spared her. She blushed furiously. She raised herself to her feet, feeling a little stiff, and arranged her disordered dress. The scalpel had fallen from her hand and she picked it up. She took the two copra sacks and emerged from her hiding-place. She walked towards the boat. It was floating in the shallow water of the lagoon.

"Come on, Miss Jones," said Ginger Ted. "We've finished. I was just going to wake you up."

She could not look at him, but she felt herself as red as a turkey cock.

"Have a banana?" he said.

Without a word she took it. She was very hungry, and ate it with relish.

"Step on this rock and you'll be able to get in without wetting your feet."

Miss Jones felt as though she could sink into the ground with shame, but she did as he told her. He took hold of her arm – good heavens! his hand was like an iron vice, never, never could she have struggled with him – and helped her into the launch. The mechanic started the engine and they slid out of the lagoon. In three hours they were at Baru.

That evening, having been officially released, Ginger Ted went to the Contrôleur's house. He wore no longer the prison uniform but the ragged singlet and the khaki shorts in which he had been arrested. He had had his hair cut and it fitted his head now like a little curly red cap. He was thinner. He had lost his bloated flabbiness and looked younger and better. Mr Gruyter, a friendly grin on his round face, shook hands with him and asked him to sit down. The boy brought two bottles of beer.

"I'm glad to see you hadn't forgotten my invitation, Ginger," said the Contrôleur.

"Not likely. I've been looking forward to this for six months."

"Here's luck, Ginger Ted."

"Same to you, Contrôleur."

They emptied their glasses and the Contrôleur clapped his hands. The boy brought two more bottles.

"Well, you don't bear me any malice for the sentence I gave you, I hope."

"No bloody fear. I was mad for a minute, but I got over it. I didn't have half a bad time, you know. Nice lot of girls on that island, Contrôleur. You ought to give 'em a look over one of these days."

"You're a bad lot, Ginger."

"Terrible."

"Good beer, isn't it?"

"Fine."

"Let's have some more."

Ginger Ted's remittance had been arriving every month and the Contrôleur now had fifty pounds for him. When the damage he had done to the Chinaman's shop was paid for there would still be over thirty.

"That's quite a lot of money, Ginger. You ought to do something useful with it."

"I mean to," answered Ginger. "Spend it."

The Contrôleur sighed.

"Well, that's what money's for, I guess."

The Contrôleur gave his guest the news. Not much had happened during the last six months. Time on the Alas Islands did not matter very much and the rest of the world did not matter at all.

"Any wars anywhere?" asked Ginger Ted.

"No. Not that I've noticed. Harry Jervis found a pretty big pearl. He says he's going to ask a thousand quid for it."

"I hope he gets it."

"And Charlie McCormack's married."

"He always was a bit soft."

Suddenly the boy appeared and said Mr Jones wished to know if he might come in. Before the Contrôleur could give an answer Mr Jones walked in.

"I won't detain you long," he said. "I've been trying to get hold of this good man all day and when I heard he was here I thought you wouldn't mind my coming."

"How is Miss Jones?" asked the Contrôleur politely. "None the worse for her night in the open, I trust."

"She's naturally a bit shaken. She had a temperature and I've insisted on her going to bed, but I don't think it's serious."

The two men had got up on the missionary's entrance, and now the missionary went up to Ginger Ted and held out his hand.

"I want to thank you. You did a great and noble thing. My sister is right, one should always look for the good in their fellow-men; I am afraid I misjudged you in the past: I beg your pardon."

He spoke very solemnly. Ginger Ted looked at him with amazement. He had not been able to prevent the missionary taking his hand. He still held it.

"What the hell are you talking about?"

"You had my sister at your mercy and you spared her. I thought you were all evil and I am ashamed. She was defenceless. She was in your power. You had pity on her. I thank you from the bottom of my heart. Neither my sister nor I will ever forget. God bless and guard you always."

Mr Jones's voice shook a little and he turned his head away. He released Ginger Ted's hand and strode quickly to the door. Ginger Ted watched him with a blank face.

"What the blazes does he mean?" he asked.

The Contrôleur laughed. He tried to control himself, but the more he did the more he laughed. He shook and you saw the folds of his fat belly ripple under the sarong. He leaned back in his long chair and rolled from side to side. He did not laugh only with his face, he laughed with his whole body, and even the muscles of his podgy legs shook with mirth. He held his aching ribs. Ginger Ted looked at him frowning, and because he did not understand what the joke was he grew angry. He seized one of the empty beer bottles by the neck.

"If you don't stop laughing, I'll break your bloody head open," he said.

The Contrôleur mopped his face. He swallowed a mouthful of beer. He sighed and groaned because his sides were hurting him.

"He's thanking you for having respected the virtue of Miss Jones," he spluttered at last.

"Me?" cried Ginger Ted.

The thought took quite a long time to travel through his head, but when at last he got it he flew into a violent rage. There flowed from his mouth such a stream of blasphemous obscenities as would have startled a marine.

"That old cow," he finished. "What does he take me for?"

"You have the reputation of being rather hot stuff with the girls, Ginger," giggled the little Contrôleur.

"I wouldn't touch her with the fag-end of a barge-pole. It never entered my head. The nerve. I'll wring his blasted neck. Look here, give me my money, I'm going to get drunk."

"I don't blame you," said the Contrôleur.

"That old cow," repeated Ginger Ted. "That old cow."

He was shocked and outraged. The suggestion really shattered his sense of decency.

The Contrôleur had the money at hand and having got Ginger Ted to sign the necessary papers gave it to him.

"Go and get drunk, Ginger Ted," he said, "but I warn you, if you get into mischief it'll be twelve months next time."

"I shan't get into mischief," said Ginger Ted sombrely. He was suffering from a sense of injury. "It's an insult," he shouted at the Contrôleur. "That's what it is, it's a bloody insult."

He lurched out of the house, and as he went he muttered to himself: "Dirty swine, dirty swine." Ginger Ted remained drunk for a week. Mr Jones went to see the Contrôleur again.

"I'm very sorry to hear that poor fellow has taken up his evil course again," he said. "My sister and I are dreadfully disappointed. I'm afraid it wasn't very wise to give him so much money at once."

"It was his own money. I had no right to keep it back."

"Not a legal right, perhaps, but surely a moral right."

He told the Contrôleur the story of that fearful night on the island. With her feminine instinct, Miss Jones had realized that the man, inflamed with lust, was determined to take advantage of her, and, resolved to defend herself to the last, had armed herself with a scalpel. He told the Contrôleur how she had prayed and wept and how she had hidden herself. Her agony was indescribable, and she knew that she could never have survived the shame. She rocked to and fro and every moment she thought he was coming. And there was no help anywhere and at last she had fallen asleep; she was tired out, poor thing, she had undergone more than any human being could stand, and then when she awoke she found that he had covered her with copra sacks. He had found her asleep, and surely it was her innocence, her very helplessness that had moved him, he hadn't the heart to touch her; he covered her gently with two copra sacks and crept silently away.

"It shows you that deep down in him there is something sterling. My sister feels it's our duty to save him. We must do something for him."

"Well, in your place I wouldn't try till he's got through all his money," said the Contrôleur, "and then if he's not in jail you can do what you like."

But Ginger Ted didn't want to be saved. About a fortnight after his release from prison he was sitting on a stool outside a Chinaman's shop looking vacantly down the street when he saw Miss Jones coming along. He stared at her for a minute and once more amazement seized him. He muttered to himself and there can be little doubt that his mutterings were disrespectful. But then he noticed that Miss Jones had seen him and he quickly turned his head away; he was conscious, notwithstanding, that she was looking at him. She was walking briskly, but she sensibly diminished her pace as she approached him. He thought she was going to stop and speak to him. He got up quickly and went into the shop. He did not venture to come out for at least five minutes. Half an hour later Mr Jones himself came along and he went straight up to Ginger Ted with outstretched hand.

"How do you do, Mr Edward? My sister told me I should find you here."

Ginger Ted gave him a surly look and did not take the proffered hand. He made no answer.

"We'd be so very glad if you'd come to dinner with us next Sunday. My sister's a capital cook and she'll make you a real Australian dinner."

"Go to hell," said Ginger Ted.

"That's not very gracious," said the missionary, but with a little laugh to show that he was not affronted. "You go and see the Contrôleur from time to time, why shouldn't you come and see us? It's pleasant to talk to white people now and then. Won't you let bygones be bygones? I can assure you of a very cordial welcome."

"I haven't got clothes fit to go out in," said Ginger Ted sulkily.

"Oh, never mind about that. Come as you are."

"I won't."

"Why not? You must have a reason."

Ginger Ted was a blunt man. He had no hesitation in saying what we should all like to when we receive unwelcome invitations.

"I don't want to."

"I'm sorry. My sister will be very disappointed."

Mr Jones, determined to show that he was not in the least offended, gave him a breezy nod and walked on. Forty-eight hours later there mysteriously arrived at the house in which Ginger Ted lodged a parcel containing a suit of ducks, a tennis shirt, a pair of socks, and some shoes. He was unaccustomed to receiving presents and next time he saw the Contrôleur asked him if it was he who had sent the things.

"Not on your life," replied the Contrôleur. "I'm perfectly indifferent to the state of your wardrobe."

"Well, then, who the hell can have?"

"Search me."

It was necessary from time to time for Miss Jones to see Mr Gruyter on business and shortly after this she came to see him one morning in his office. She was a capable woman and though she generally wanted him to do something he had no mind to, she did not waste his time. He was a little surprised then to discover that she had come on a very trivial errand. When he told her that he could not take cognizance of the matter in question, she did not as was her habit try to convince him, but accepted his refusal as definite. She got up to go and then as though it were an afterthought said:

"Oh, Mr Gruyter, my brother is very anxious that we should have the man they call Ginger Ted to supper with us and I've written him a little note inviting him for the day after tomorrow. I think he's rather shy, and I wonder if you'd come with him."

"That's very kind of you."

"My brother feels that we ought to do something for the poor fellow."

"A woman's influence and all that sort of thing," said the Contrôleur demurely.

"Will you persuade him to come? I'm sure he will if you make a point of it, and when he knows the way he'll come again. It seems such a pity to let a young man like that go to pieces altogether."

The Contrôleur looked up at her. She was several inches taller than he. He thought her very unattractive. She reminded him strangely of wet linen hung on a clothes-line to dry. His eyes twinkled, but he kept a straight face.

"I'll do my best," he said.

"How old is he?" she asked.

"According to his passport he's thirty-one."

"And what is his real name?"

"Wilson."

"Edward Wilson," she said softly.

"It's astonishing that after the life he's led he should be so strong," murmured the Contrôleur. "He has the strength of an ox."

"Those red-headed men sometimes are very powerful," said Miss Jones, but spoke as though she were choking.

"Quite so," said the Contrôleur.

Then for no obvious reason Miss Jones blushed. She hurriedly said goodbye to the Contrôleur and left his office.

"*Godverdomme!*" said the Contrôleur.

He knew now who had sent Ginger Ted the new clothes.

He met him during the course of the day and asked him whether he had heard from Miss Jones. Ginger Ted took a crumpled ball of paper out of his pocket and gave it to him. It was the invitation. It ran as follows:

Dear Mr Wilson

My brother and I would be so very glad if you would come and have supper with us next Thursday at 7.30. The Contrôleur has kindly promised to come. We have some new records from Australia which I am sure you will like. I am afraid I was not very nice to you last time we met, but I did not know you so well then, and I am big enough to admit it when I have committed an error. I hope you will forgive me and let me be your friend, Yours sincerely, Martha Jones

The Contrôleur noticed that she addressed him as Mr Wilson and referred to his own promise to go, so that when she told him she had already invited Ginger Ted she had a little anticipated the truth.

"What are you going to do?"

"I'm not going, if that's what you mean. Damned nerve."

"You must answer the letter."

"Well, I won't."

"Now look here, Ginger, you put on those new clothes and you come as a favour to me. I've got to go and, damn it all, you can't leave me in the lurch. It won't hurt you just once."

Ginger Ted looked at the Contrôleur suspiciously, but his face was serious and his manner sincere: he could not guess that within him the Dutchman bubbled with laughter.

"What the devil do they want me for?"

"I don't know. The pleasure of your society, I suppose."

"Will there be any booze?"

"No, but come up to my house at seven, and we'll have a tiddly before we go."

"Oh, all right," said Ginger Ted sulkily.

The Contrôleur rubbed his little fat hands with joy. He was expecting a great deal of amusement from the party. But when Thursday came and seven o'clock, Ginger Ted was dead drunk and Mr Gruyter had to go alone. He told the missionary and his sister the plain truth. Mr Jones shook his head.

"I'm afraid it's no good, Martha, the man's hopeless."

For a moment Miss Jones was silent and the Contrôleur saw two tears trickle down her long thin nose. She bit her lip.

"No one is hopeless. Everyone has some good in him. I shall pray for him every night. It would be wicked to doubt the power of God."

Perhaps Miss Jones was right in this, but the divine providence took a very funny way of effecting its ends. Ginger Ted began to drink more heavily than ever. He was so troublesome that even Mr Gruyter lost patience with him. He made up his mind that he could not have the fellow on the island any more and resolved to deport him on the next boat that touched at Baru. Then a man died under mysterious circumstances after having been for a trip to one of the islands and the Contrôleur learnt that there had been several deaths on the same island. He sent the Chinese who was the official doctor of the group to look into the matter, and very soon received intelligence that the deaths were due to cholera. Two more took place at Baru and the certainty was forced upon him that there was an epidemic.

The Contrôleur cursed freely. He cursed in Dutch, he cursed in English, and he cursed in Malay. Then he drank a bottle of beer and smoked a cigar. After that he took thought. He knew the Chinese doctor would be useless. He was a nervous little man from Java and the natives would refuse to obey his orders. The Contrôleur was efficient and knew pretty well what must be done, but he could not do everything single-handed. He did not like Mr Jones, but just then he was thankful that he was at hand, and he sent for him at once. He was accompanied by his sister.

"You know what I want to see you about, Mr Jones," he said abruptly.

"Yes. I've been expecting a message from you. That is why my sister has come with me. We are ready to put all our resources at your disposal. I need not tell you that my sister is as competent as a man."

"I know. I shall be very glad of her assistance."

They set to without further delay to discuss the steps that must be taken. Hospital huts would have to be erected and quarantine stations. The inhabitants of the various villages on the islands must be forced to take proper precautions. In a good many cases the infected villages drew their water from the same well as the unin-fected, and in each case this difficulty would have to be dealt with according to circumstances. It was necessary to send round people to give orders and make sure that they were carried out. Negligence must be ruthlessly punished. The worst of it was that the natives would not obey other natives, and orders given by native policemen, themselves unconvinced of their efficacy, would certainly be disre-garded. It was advisable for Mr Jones to stay at Baru, where the population was largest and his medical attention most wanted; and what with the official duties that forced him to keep in touch with headquarters, it was impossible for Mr Gruyter to visit all the other islands himself. Miss Jones must go; but the natives of some of the outlying islands were wild and treacherous; the Contrôleur had had a good deal of trouble with them. He did not like the idea of exposing her to danger.

"I'm not afraid," she said.

"I daresay. But if you have your throat cut I shall get into trouble, and besides, we're so short-handed I don't want to risk losing your help."

"Then let Mr Wilson come with me. He knows the natives better than anyone and can speak all their dialects."

"Ginger Ted?" The Contrôleur stared at her. "He's just getting over an attack of DTs."

"I know," she answered.

"You know a great deal, Miss Jones."

Even though the moment was so serious Mr Gruyter could not but smile. He gave her a sharp look, but she met it coolly.

"There's nothing like responsibility for bringing out what there is in a man, and I think something like this may be the making of him."

"Do you think it would be wise to trust yourself for days at a time to a man of such infamous character?" said the missionary.

"I put my trust in God," she answered gravely.

"Do you think he'd be any use?" asked the Contrôleur. "You know what he is."

"I'm convinced of it." Then she blushed. "After all, no one knows better than I that he's capable of self-control."

The Contrôleur bit his lip.

"Let's send for him."

He gave a message to the sergeant and in a few minutes Ginger Ted stood before them. He looked ill. He had evidently been much shaken by his recent attack and his nerves were all to pieces. He was in rags and he had not shaved for a week. No one could have looked more disreputable.

"Look here, Ginger," said the Contrôleur, "it's about this cholera business. We've got to force the natives to take precautions and we want you to help us."

"Why the hell should I?"

"No reason at all. Except philanthropy."

"Nothing doing, Contrôleur. I'm not a philanthropist."

"That settles that. That was all. You can go."

But as Ginger Ted turned to the door Miss Jones stopped him.

"It was my suggestion, Mr Wilson. You see, they want me to go to Labobo and Sakunchi, and the natives there are so funny I was afraid to go alone. I thought if you came I should be safer."

He gave her a look of extreme distaste.

"What do you suppose I care if they cut your throat?"

Miss Jones looked at him and her eyes filled with tears. She began to cry. He stood and watched her stupidly.

"There's no reason why you should." She pulled herself together and dried her eyes. "I'm being silly. I shall be all right. I'll go alone."

"It's damned foolishness for a woman to go to Labobo."

She gave him a little smile.

"I daresay it is, but you see, it's my job and I can't help myself. I'm sorry if I offended you by asking you. You must forget about it. I daresay it wasn't quite fair to ask you to take such a risk."

For quite a minute Ginger Ted stood and looked at her. He shifted from one foot to the other. His surly face seemed to grow black.

"Oh, hell, have it your own way," he said at last. "I'll come with you. When d'you want to start?"

They set out next day, with drugs and disinfectants, in the Government launch. Mr Gruyter as soon as he had put the necessary work in order was to start off in a prahu in the other direction. For four months the epidemic raged. Though everything possible was done to localize it, one island after another was attacked. The Contrôleur was busy from morning to night. He had no sooner got back to Baru from one or other of the islands to do what was necessary there than he had to set off again. He distributed food and medicine. He cheered the terrified people. He supervised everything. He worked like a dog. He saw nothing of Ginger Ted, but he heard from Mr Jones that the experiment was working out beyond all hopes. The scamp was behaving himself. He had a way with the natives; and by cajolery, firmness, and on occasion the use of his fist, managed to make them take the steps necessary for their own safety. Miss Jones could congratulate herself on the success of the scheme. But the Contrôleur was too tired to be amused. When the epidemic had run its course he rejoiced because out of a population of eight thousand only six hundred had died.

Finally he was able to give the district a clean bill of health.

One evening he was sitting in his sarong on the veranda of his house and he read a French novel with the happy consciousness that once more he could take things easy. His head boy came in and told him that Ginger Ted wished to see him. He got up from his chair and shouted to him to come in. Company was just what he wanted. It had crossed the Contrôleur's mind that it would be pleasant to get drunk that night, but it is dull to get drunk alone, and he had regretfully put the thought aside. And heaven had sent Ginger Ted in the nick of time. By God, they would make a night of it. After four months they deserved a bit of fun. Ginger Ted entered. He was wearing a clean suit of white ducks. He was shaved. He looked another man.

"Why, Ginger, you look as if you'd been spending a month at a health resort instead of nursing a pack of natives dying of cholera. And look at your clothes. Have you just stepped out of a bandbox?"

Ginger Ted smiled rather sheepishly. The head boy brought two bottles of beer and poured them out.

"Help yourself, Ginger," said the Contrôleur as he took his glass.

"I don't think I'll have any, thank you."

The Contrôleur put down his glass and looked at Ginger Ted with amazement.

"Why, what's the matter? Aren't you thirsty?"

"I don't mind having a cup of tea."

"A cup of what?"

"I'm on the wagon. Martha and I are going to be married."

"Ginger!"

The Contrôleur's eyes popped out of his head. He scratched his shaven pate.

"You can't marry Miss Jones," he said. "No one could marry Miss Jones."

"Well, I'm going to. That's what I've come to see you about. Owen's going to marry us in chapel, but we want to be married by Dutch law as well."

"A joke's a joke, Ginger. What's the idea?"

"She wanted it. She fell for me that night we spent on the island when the propeller broke. She's not a bad old girl when you get to know her. It's her last chance, if you understand what I mean, and I'd like to do something to oblige her. And she wants someone to take care of her, there's no doubt about that."

"Ginger, Ginger, before you can say knife she'll make you into a damned missionary."

"I don't know that I'd mind that so much if we had a little mission of our own. She says I'm a bloody marvel with the natives. She says I can do more with a native in five minutes than Owen can do in a year. She says she's never known anyone with the magnetism I have. It seems a pity to waste a gift like that."

The Contrôleur looked at him without speaking and slowly nodded his head three or four times. She'd nobbled him all right.

"I've converted seventeen already," said Ginger Ted.

"You? I didn't know you believed in Christianity."

"Well, I don't know that I did exactly, but when I talked to 'em and they just came into the fold like a lot of blasted sheep, well, it gave me quite a turn. Blimey, I said, I daresay there's something in it after all."

"You should have raped her, Ginger. I wouldn't have been hard on you. I wouldn't have given you more than three years' and three years' is soon over."

"Look here, Contrôleur, don't you ever let on that the thought never entered my head. Women are touchy, you know, and she'd be as sore as hell if she knew that."

"I guessed she'd got her eye on you, but I never thought it would come to this." The Contrôleur in an agitated manner walked up and down the veranda. "Listen to me, old boy," he said after an interval of reflection, "we've had some grand times together and a friend's a friend. I'll tell you what I'll do, I'll lend you the launch and you can go and hide on one of the islands till the next ship comes along and then I'll get 'em to slow down and take you on board. You've only got one chance now and that's to cut and run."

Ginger Ted shook his head.

"It's no good, Contrôleur, I know you mean well, but I'm going to marry the blasted woman, and that's that. You don't know the joy of bringing all them bleeding sinners to repentance, and Christ! that girl can make a treacle pudding. I haven't eaten a better one since I was a kid."

The Contrôleur was very much disturbed. The drunken scamp was his only companion on the islands and he did not want to lose him. He discovered that he had even a certain affection for him. Next day he went to see the missionary.

"What's this I hear about your sister marrying Ginger Ted?" he asked him. "It's the most extraordinary thing I've ever heard in my life."

"It's true nevertheless."

"You must do something about it. It's madness."

"My sister is of full age and entitled to do as she pleases."

"But you don't mean to tell me you approve of it. You know Ginger Ted. He's a bum and there are no two ways about it. Have you told her the risk she's running? I mean, bringing sinners to repentance and all that sort of thing's all right, but there are limits. And does the leopard ever change his spots?"

Then for the first time in his life the Contrôleur saw a twinkle in the missionary's eye.

"My sister is a very determined woman, Mr Gruyter," he replied. "From that night they spent on the island he never had a chance."

The Contrôleur gasped. He was as surprised as the prophet when the Lord opened the mouth of the ass, and she said unto Balaam, What have I done unto thee, that thou hast smitten me these three times? Perhaps Mr Jones was human after all.

"*Allejezus!*" muttered the Contrôleur.

Before anything more could be said Miss Jones swept into the room. She was radiant. She looked ten years younger. Her cheeks were flushed and her nose was hardly red at all.

"Have you come to congratulate me, Mr Gruyter?" she cried, and her manner was sprightly and girlish. "You see, I was right after all. Everyone has some good in them. You don't know how splendid Edward has been all through this terrible time. He's a hero. He's a saint. Even I was surprised."

"I hope you'll be very happy, Miss Jones."

"I know I shall. Oh, it would be wicked of me to doubt it. For it is the Lord who has brought us together."

"Do you think so?"

"I know it. Don't you see? Except for the cholera Edward would never have found himself. Except for the cholera we should never have learnt to know one another. I have never seen the hand of God more plainly manifest."

The Contrôleur could not but think that it was rather a clumsy device to bring those two together that necessitated the death of six hundred innocent persons, but not being well versed in the ways of omnipotence he made no remark.

"You'll never guess where we're going for our honeymoon," said Miss Jones, perhaps a trifle archly.

"Java."

"No, if you'll lend us the launch, we're going to that island where we were marooned. It has very tender recollections for both of us. It was there that I first guessed how fine and good Edward was. It's there I want him to have his reward."

The Contrôleur caught his breath. He left quickly, for he thought that unless he had a bottle of beer at once he would have a fit. He was never so shocked in his life.

THE FORCE OF CIRCUMSTANCE

SHE WAS SITTING on the veranda waiting for her husband to come in for luncheon. The Malay boy had drawn the blinds when the morning lost its freshness, but she had partly raised one of them so that she could look at the river. Under the breathless sun of midday it had the white pallor of death. A native was paddling along in a dugout so small that it hardly showed above the surface of the water. The colours of the day were ashy and wan. They were but the various tones of the heat. (It was like an Eastern melody, in the minor key, which exacerbates the nerves by its ambiguous monotony; and the ear awaits impatiently a resolution, but waits in vain.) The cicadas sang their grating song with a frenzied energy; it was as continual and monotonous as the rustling of a brook over the stones; but on a sudden it was drowned by the loud singing of a bird, mellifluous and rich; and for an instant, with a catch at her heart, she thought of the English blackbird.

Then she heard her husband's step on the gravel path behind the bungalow, the path that led to the court-house in which he had been working, and she rose from her chair to greet him. He ran up the short flight of steps, for the bungalow was built on piles, and at the door the boy was waiting to take his topee. He came into the room which served them as a dining-room and parlour, and his eyes lit up with pleasure as he saw her.

"Hulloa, Doris. Hungry?"

"Ravenous."

"It'll only take me a minute to have a bath and then I'm ready."

"Be quick," she smiled.

He disappeared into his dressing-room and she heard him whistling cheerily while, with the carelessness with which she was always remonstrating, he tore off his clothes and flung them on the floor. He was twenty-nine, but he was still a school-boy; he would never grow up. That was why she had fallen in love with him, perhaps, for no amount of affection could persuade her that he was good-looking. He was a little round man, with a red face like the full moon, and blue eyes. He was rather pimply. She had examined him carefully and had been forced to confess to him that he had not a single feature which she could praise. She had told him often that he wasn't her type at all.

"I never said I was a beauty," he laughed.

"I can't think what it is I see in you."

But of course she knew perfectly well. He was a gay, jolly little man, who took nothing very solemnly, and he was constantly laughing. He made her laugh too. He found life an amusing rather than a serious business, and he had a charming smile. When she was with him she felt happy and good-tempered. And the deep affection which she saw in those merry blue eyes of his touched her. It was very satisfactory to be loved like that. Once, sitting on his knees, during their honeymoon she had taken his face in her hands and said to him:

"You're an ugly, little fat man, Guy, but you've got charm. I can't help loving you."

A wave of emotion swept over her and her eyes filled with tears. She saw his face contorted for a moment with the extremity of his feeling and his voice was a little shaky when he answered.

"It's a terrible thing for me to have married a woman who's mentally deficient," he said.

She chuckled. It was the characteristic answer which she would have liked him to make.

It was hard to realize that nine months ago she had never even heard of him. She had met him at a small place by the seaside where she was spending a month's holiday with her mother. Doris was a secretary to a member of parliament. Guy was home on leave. They were staying at the same hotel, and he quickly told her all about himself. He was born in Sembulu, where his father had served for thirty years under the second Sultan, and on leaving school he had entered the same service. He was devoted to the country.

"After all, England's a foreign land to me," he told her. "My home's Sembulu."

276

And now it was her home too. He asked her to marry him at the end of the month's holiday. She had known he was going to, and had decided to refuse him. She was her widowed mother's only child and she could not go so far away from her, but when the moment came she did not quite know what happened to her, she was carried off her feet by an unexpected emotion, and she accepted him. They had been settled now for four months in the little outstation of which he was in charge. She was very happy.

She told him once that she had quite made up her mind to refuse him.

"Are you sorry you didn't?" he asked, with a merry smile in his twinkling blue eyes.

"I should have been a perfect fool if I had. What a bit of luck that fate or chance or whatever it was stepped in and took the matter entirely out of my hands!"

Now she heard Guy clatter down the steps to the bath-house. He was a noisy fellow and even with bare feet he could not be quiet. But he uttered an exclamation. He said two or three words in the local dialect and she could not understand. Then she heard someone speaking to him, not aloud, but in a sibilant whisper. Really it was too bad of people to waylay him when he was going to have his bath. He spoke again and though his voice was low she could hear that he was vexed. The other voice was raised now; it was a woman's. Doris supposed it was someone who had a complaint to make. It was like a Malay woman to come in that surreptitious way. But she was evidently getting very little from Guy, for she heard him say: Get out. That at all events she understood, and then she heard him bolt the door. There was a sound of the water he was throwing over himself (the bathing arrangements still amused her, the bath-houses were under the bedrooms, on the ground; you had a large tub of water and you sluiced yourself with a little tin pail) and in a couple of minutes he was back again in the dining-room. His hair was still wet. They sat down to luncheon.

"It's lucky I'm not a suspicious or a jealous person," she laughed. "I don't know that I should altogether approve of your having animated conversations with ladies while you're having your bath."

His face, usually so cheerful, had borne a sullen look when he came in, but now it brightened.

"I wasn't exactly pleased to see her."

"So I judged by the tone of your voice. In fact, I thought you were rather short with the young person."

"Damned cheek, waylaying me like that!"

"What did she want?"

"Oh, I don't know. It's a woman from the kampong. She's had a row with her husband or something."

"I wonder if it's the same one who was hanging about this morning."

He frowned a little.

"Was there someone hanging about?"

"Yes, I went into your dressing-room to see that everything was nice and tidy, and then I went down to the bath-house. I saw someone slink out of the door as I went down the steps and when I looked out I saw a woman standing there."

"Did you speak to her?"

"I asked her what she wanted and she said something, but I couldn't understand."

"I'm not going to have all sorts of stray people prowling about here," he said. "They've got no right to come."

He smiled, but Doris, with the quick perception of a woman in love, noticed that he smiled only with his lips, not as usual with his eyes also, and wondered what it was that troubled him.

"What have you been doing this morning?" he asked.

"Oh, nothing much. I went for a little walk."

"Through the kampong?"

"Yes. I saw a man send a chained monkey up a tree to pick coconuts, which rather thrilled me."

"It's rather a lark, isn't it?"

"Oh, Guy, there were two little boys watching him who were much whiter than the others. I wondered if they were half-castes. I spoke to them, but they didn't know a word of English."

"There are two or three half-caste children in the kampong," he answered.

"Who do they belong to?"

"Their mother is one of the village girls."

"Who is their father?"

"Oh, my dear, that's the sort of question we think it a little dangerous to ask out here." He paused. "A lot of fellows have native wives, and then when they go home or marry they pension them off and send them back to their village."

Doris was silent. The indifference with which he spoke seemed a little callous to her. There was almost a frown on her frank, open, pretty English face when she replied.

"But what about the children?"

"I have no doubt they're properly provided for. Within his means, a man generally sees that there's enough money to have them decently educated. They get jobs as clerks in a government office, you know; they're all right."

She gave him a slightly rueful smile.

"You can't expect me to think it's a very good system."

"You mustn't be too hard," he smiled back.

"I'm not hard. But I'm thankful you never had a Malay wife. I should have hated it. Just think if those two little brats were yours."

The boy changed their plates. There was never much variety in their menu. They started luncheon with river fish, dull and insipid, so that a good deal of tomato ketchup was needed to make it palatable, and then went on to some kind of stew. Guy poured Worcester Sauce over it.

"The old Sultan didn't think it was a white woman's country," he said presently. "He rather encouraged people to – keep house with native girls. Of course things have changed now. The country's perfectly quiet and I suppose we know better how to cope with the climate."

"But, Guy, the eldest of those boys wasn't more than seven or eight and the other was about five."

"It's awfully lonely on an outstation. Why, often one doesn't see another white man for six months on end. A fellow comes out here when he's only a boy." He gave her that charming smile of his which transfigured his round, plain face. "There are excuses, you know."

She always found that smile irresistible. It was his best argument. Her eyes grew once more soft and tender.

"I'm sure there are." She stretched her hand across the little table and put it on his. "I'm very lucky to have caught you so young.

Honestly, it would upset me dreadfully if I were told that you had lived like that."

He took her hand and pressed it.

"Are you happy here, darling?"

"Desperately."

She looked very cool and fresh in her linen frock. The heat did not distress her. She had no more than the prettiness of youth, though her brown eyes were fine; but she had a pleasing frankness of expression, and her dark, short hair was neat and glossy. She gave you the impression of a girl of spirit and you felt sure that the member of parliament for whom she worked had in her a very competent secretary.

"I loved the country at once," she said. "Although I'm alone so much I don't think I've ever once felt lonely."

Of course she had read novels about the Malay Archipelago and she had formed an impression of a sombre land with great ominous rivers and a silent, impenetrable jungle. When a little coasting steamer set them down at the mouth of the river, where a large boat, manned by a dozen Dyaks, was waiting to take them to the station, her breath was taken away by the beauty, friendly rather than awe-inspiring, of the scene. It had a gaiety, like the joyful singing of birds in the trees, which she had never expected. On each bank of the river were mangroves and nipah palms, and behind them the dense green of the forest. In the distance stretched blue mountains, range upon range, as far as the eye could see. She had no sense of confinement nor of gloom, but rather of openness and wide spaces where the exultant fancy could wander with delight. The green glittered in the sunshine and the sky was blithe and cheerful. The gracious land seemed to offer her a smiling welcome.

They rowed on, hugging a bank, and high overhead flew a pair of doves. A flash of colour, like a living jewel, dashed across their path. It was a kingfisher. Two monkeys, with their dangling tails, sat side by side on a branch. On the horizon, over there on the other side of the broad and turbid river, beyond the jungle, was a row of little white clouds, the only clouds in the sky, and they looked like a row of ballet-girls, dressed in white, waiting at the back of the stage, alert and merry, for the curtain to go up. Her heart was filled with joy; and now, remembering it all, her eyes rested on her husband with a grateful, assured affection.

And what fun it had been to arrange their living-room! It was very big. On the floor, when she arrived, was torn and dirty matting; on the walls of unpainted wood hung (much too high up) photogravures of Academy pictures, Dyak shields, and parangs. The tables were covered with Dyak cloth in sombre colours, and on them stood pieces of Brunei brass-ware, much in need of cleaning, empty cigarette tins, and bits of Malay silver. There was a rough wooden shelf with cheap editions of novels and a number of old travel books in battered leather; and another shelf was crowded with empty bottles. It was a bachelor's room, untidy but stiff; and though it amused her she found it intolerably pathetic. It was a dreary, comfortless life that Guy had led there, and she threw her arms round his neck and kissed him.

"You poor darling," she laughed.

She had deft hands and she soon made the room habitable. She arranged this and that, and what she could not do with she turned out. Her wedding-presents helped. Now the room was friendly and comfortable. In glass vases were lovely orchids and in great bowls huge masses of flowering shrubs. She felt an inordinate pride because it was her house (she had never in her life lived in anything but a poky flat) and she had made it charming for him.

"Are you pleased with me?" she asked when she had finished.

"Quite," he smiled.

The deliberate understatement was much to her mind. How jolly it was that they should understand each other so well! They were both of them shy of displaying emotion, and it was only at rare moments that they used with one another anything but ironic banter.

They finished luncheon and he threw himself into a long chair to have a sleep. She went towards her room. She was a little surprised that he drew her to him as she passed and, making her bend down, kissed her lips. They were not in the habit of exchanging embraces at odd hours of the day.

"A full tummy is making you sentimental, my poor lamb," she chaffed him.

"Get out and don't let me see you again for at least two hours."

"Don't snore."

She left him. They had risen at dawn and in five minutes were fast asleep.

Doris was awakened by the sound of her husband's splashing in the bath-house. The walls of the bungalow were like a sounding board and not a thing that one of them did escaped the other. She felt too lazy to move, but she heard the boy bring the tea things in, so she jumped up and ran down into her own bath-house. The water, not cold but cool, was deliciously refreshing. When she came into the sitting-room Guy was taking the rackets out of the press, for they played tennis in the short cool of the evening. The night fell at six.

The tennis-court was two or three hundred yards from the bungalow and after tea, anxious not to lose time, they strolled down to it.

"Oh, look," said Doris, "there's that girl that I saw this morning."

Guy turned quickly. His eyes rested for a moment on a native woman, but he did not speak.

"What a pretty sarong she's got," said Doris. "I wonder where it comes from."

They passed her. She was slight and small, with the large, dark, starry eyes of her race and a mass of raven hair. She did not stir as they went by, but stared at them strangely. Doris saw then that she was not quite so young as she had at first thought. Her features were a trifle heavy and her skin was dark, but she was very pretty. She held a small child in her arms. Doris smiled a little as she saw it, but no answering smile moved the woman's lips. Her face remained impassive. She did not look at Guy, she looked only at Doris, and he walked on as though he did not see her. Doris turned to him.

"Isn't that baby a duck?"

"I didn't notice."

She was puzzled by the look of his face. It was deathly white, and the pimples which not a little distressed her were more than commonly red.

"Did you notice her hands and feet? She might be a duchess."

"All natives have good hands and feet," he answered, but not jovially as was his wont; it was as though he forced himself to speak.

But Doris was intrigued.

"Who is she, d'you know?"

"She's one of the girls in the kampong."

They had reached the court now. When Guy went up to the net to see that it was taut he looked back. The girl was still standing where they had passed her. Their eyes met.

"Shall I serve?" said Doris.

"Yes, you've got the balls on your side."

He played very badly. Generally he gave her fifteen and beat her, but today she won easily. And he played silently. Generally he was a noisy player, shouting all the time, cursing his foolishness when he missed a ball and chaffing her when he placed one out of her reach.

"You're off your game, young man," she cried.

"Not a bit," he said.

He began to slam the balls, trying to beat her, and sent one after the other into the net. She had never seen him with that set face. Was it possible that he was a little out of temper because he was not playing well? The light fell, and they ceased to play. The woman whom they had passed stood in exactly the same position as when they came and once more, with expressionless face, she watched them go.

The blinds on the veranda were raised now, and on the table between their two long chairs were bottles and soda-water. This was the hour at which they had the first drink of the day and Guy mixed a couple of gin slings. The river stretched widely before them, and on the further bank the jungle was wrapped in the mystery of the approaching night. A native was silently rowing upstream, standing at the bow of the boat, with two oars.

"I played like a fool," said Guy, breaking a silence. "I'm feeling a bit under the weather."

"I'm sorry. You're not going to have fever, are you?"

"Oh, no. I shall be all right tomorrow."

Darkness closed in upon them. The frogs croaked loudly and now and then they heard a few short notes from some singing bird of the night. Fireflies flitted across the veranda and they made the trees that surrounded it look like Christmas trees lit with tiny candles. They sparkled softly. Doris thought she heard a little sigh. It vaguely disturbed her. Guy was always so full of gaiety.

"What is it, old man?" she said gently. "Tell mother."

"Nothing. Time for another drink," he answered breezily.

Next day he was as cheerful as ever and the mail came. The coasting steamer passed the mouth of the river twice a month, once on its way to the coalfields and once on its way back. On the outward journey it brought mail, which Guy sent a boat down to fetch. Its arrival was the excitement of their uneventful lives. For the first day or two they skimmed rapidly all that had come, letters, English papers and papers from Singapore, magazines and books, leaving for the ensuing weeks a more exact perusal. They snatched the illustrated papers from one another. If Doris had not been so absorbed she might have noticed that there was a change in Guy. She would have found it hard to describe and harder still to explain. There was in his eyes a sort of watchfulness and in his mouth a slight droop of anxiety.

Then, perhaps a week later, one morning when she was sitting in the shaded room studying a Malay grammar (for she was industriously learning the language) she heard a commotion in the compound. She heard the house boy's voice, he was speaking angrily, the voice of another man, perhaps it was the water-carrier's, and then a woman's, shrill and vituperative. There was a scuffle. She went to the window and opened the shutters. The water-carrier had hold of a woman's arm and was dragging her along, while the house boy was pushing her from behind with both hands. Doris recognized her at once as the woman she had seen one morning loitering in the compound and later in the day outside the tennis-court. She was holding a baby against her breast. All three were shouting angrily.

"Stop," cried Doris. "What are you doing?"

At the sound of her voice the water-carrier let go suddenly and the woman, still pushed from behind, fell to the ground. There was a sudden silence and the house boy looked sullenly into space. The water-carrier hesitated a moment and then slunk away. The woman raised herself slowly to her feet, arranged the baby on her arm, and stood impassive, staring at Doris. The boy said something to her which Doris could not have heard even if she had understood: the woman by no change of face showed that his words meant anything to her; but she slowly strolled away. The boy followed her to the gate of the compound. Doris called to him as he walked back, but he pretended not to hear. She was growing angry now and she called more sharply.

"Come here at once," she cried.

Suddenly, avoiding her wrathful glance, he came towards the bungalow. He came in and stood at the door. He looked at her sulkily.

"What were you doing with that woman?" she asked abruptly.

"Tuan say she no come here."

"You mustn't treat a woman like that. I won't have it. I shall tell the tuan exactly what I saw."

The boy did not answer. He looked away, but she felt that he was watching her through his long eyelashes. She dismissed him.

"That'll do."

Without a word he turned and went back to the servants' quarters. She was exasperated and she found it impossible to give her attention once more to the Malay exercises. In a little while the boy came in to lay the cloth for luncheon. On a sudden he went to the door.

"What is it?" she asked.

"Tuan just coming."

He went out to take Guy's hat from him. His quick ears had caught the footsteps before they were audible to her. Guy did not as usual come up the steps immediately; he paused, and Doris at once surmised that the boy had gone down to meet him in order to tell him of the morning's incident. She shrugged her shoulders. The boy evidently wanted to get his story in first. But she was astonished when Guy came in. His face was ashy.

"Guy, what on earth's the matter?"

He flushed a sudden hot red.

"Nothing. Why?"

She was so taken aback that she let him pass into his room without a word of what she had meant to speak of at once. It took him longer than usual to have his bath and change his clothes and luncheon was served when he came in.

"Guy," she said, as they sat down, "that woman we saw the other day was here again this morning."

"So I've heard," he answered.

"The boys were treating her brutally. I had to stop them. You must really speak to them about it."

Though the Malay understood every word she said, he made no sign that he heard. He handed her the toast.

"She's been told not to come here. I gave instructions that if she showed herself again she was to be turned out."

"Were they obliged to be so rough?"

"She refused to go. I don't think they were any rougher than they could help."

"It was horrible to see a woman treated like that. She had a baby in her arms."

"Hardly a baby. It's three years old."

"How d'you know?"

"I know all about her. She hasn't the least right to come here pestering everybody."

"What does she want?"

"She wants to do exactly what she did. She wants to make a disturbance."

For a little while Doris did not speak. She was surprised at her husband's tone. He spoke tersely. He spoke as though all this were no concern of hers. She thought him a little unkind. He was nervous and irritable.

"I doubt if we shall be able to play tennis this afternoon," he said. "It looks to me as though we were going to have a storm."

The rain was falling when she awoke and it was impossible to go out. During tea Guy was silent and abstracted. She got her sewing and began to work. Guy sat down to read such of the English papers as he had not yet gone through from cover to cover; but he was restless; he walked up and down the large room and then went out on the veranda. He looked at the steady rain. What was he thinking of? Doris was vaguely uneasy.

It was not till after dinner that he spoke. During the simple meal he had exerted himself to be his usual gay self, but the exertion was apparent. The rain had ceased and the night was starry. They sat on the veranda. In order not to attract insects they had put out the lamp in the sitting-room. At their feet, with a mighty, formidable sluggishness, silent, mysterious, and fatal, flowed the river. It had the terrible deliberation and the relentlessness of destiny.

"Doris, I've got something to say to you," he said suddenly.

His voice was very strange. Was it her fancy that he had difficulty in keeping it quite steady? She felt a little pang in her heart because he was in distress, and she put her hand gently into his. He drew it away.

"It's rather a long story. I'm afraid it's not a very nice one and I find it rather difficult to tell. I'm going to ask you not to interrupt me, or to say anything, till I've finished."

In the darkness she could not see his face, but she felt that it was haggard. She did not answer. He spoke in a voice so low that it hardly broke the silence of the night.

"I was only eighteen when I came out here. I came straight from school. I spent three months in Kuala Solor, and then I was sent to a station up the Sembulu river. Of course there was a Resident there and his wife. I lived in the court-house, but I used to have my meals with them and spend the evening with them. I had an awfully good time. Then the fellow who was here fell ill and had to go home. We were short of men on account of the war and I was put in charge of this place. Of course I was very young, but I spoke the language like a native, and they remembered my father. I was as pleased as punch to be on my own."

He was silent while he knocked the ashes out of his pipe and refilled it. When he lit a match, Doris, without looking at him, noticed that his hand was unsteady.

"I'd never been alone before. Of course at home there'd been father and mother and generally an assistant. And then at school naturally there were always fellows about. On the way out, on the boat, there were people all the time, and at KS, and the same at my first post. The people there were almost like my own people. I seemed always to live in a crowd. I like people. I'm a noisy blighter. I like to have a good time. All sorts of things make me laugh and you must have somebody to laugh with. But it was different here. Of course it was all right in the day time; I had my work and I could talk to the Dyaks. Although they were head-hunters in those days, and now and then I had a bit of trouble with them, they were an awfully decent lot of fellows. I got on very well with them. Of course I should have liked a white man to gas to, but they were better than nothing, and it was easier for me because they didn't look upon me quite as a stranger. I liked the work too. It was rather lonely in the evening to sit on the veranda and drink a gin and bitters by myself, but I could read. And the boys were about. My own boy was called Abdul. He'd known my father. When I got tired of reading I could give him a shout and have a bit of a jaw with him.

"It was the nights that did for me. After dinner the boys shut up and went away to sleep in the kampong. I was all alone. There wasn't a sound in the bungalow except now and then the croak of the chik-chak. It used to come out of the silence, suddenly, so that it made me jump. Over in the kampong I heard the sound of a gong or fire-crackers. They were having a good time, they weren't so far away, but I had to stay where I was. I was tired of reading. I couldn't have been more of a prisoner if I'd been in jail. Night after night it was the same. I tried drinking three or four whiskies, but it's poor fun drinking alone, and it didn't cheer me up; it only made me feel rather rotten next day. I tried going to bed immediately after dinner, but I couldn't sleep. I used to lie in bed, getting hotter and hotter, and more wide awake, till I didn't know what to do with myself. By George, those nights were long. D'you know, I got so low, I was so sorry for myself that sometimes – it makes me laugh now when I think of it, but I was only nineteen and a half – sometimes I used to cry.

"Then, one evening, after dinner, Abdul had cleared away and was just going off, when he gave a little cough. He said, wasn't I lonely in the house all night by myself? 'Oh, no, that's all right,' I said. I didn't want him to know what a damned fool I was, but I expect he knew all right. He stood there without speaking, and I knew he wanted to say something to me. 'What is it?' I said. 'Spit it out.' Then he said that if I'd like to have a girl to come and live with me he knew one who was willing. She was a very good girl and he could recommend her. She'd be no trouble and it would be someone to have about the bungalow. She'd mend my things for me . . . I felt awfully low. It had been raining all day and I hadn't been able to get any exercise. I knew I shouldn't sleep for hours. It wouldn't cost me very much money, he said, her people were poor and they'd be quite satisfied with a small present. Two hundred Straits dollars. 'You look,' he said. 'If you don't like her you send her away.' I asked him where she was. 'She's here,' he said. 'I call her.' He went to the door. She'd been waiting on the steps with her mother. They came in and sat down on the floor. I gave them some sweets. She was shy, of course, but cool enough, and when I said something to her she gave me a smile. She was very young, hardly more than a child, they said she was fifteen. She was awfully pretty, and she had her best clothes on. We began to talk. She didn't say much, but she laughed a lot when I chaffed her. Abdul said I'd find she had plenty to say for herself when she got to know me. He told her to come and sit by me. She giggled and refused, but her mother told her to come, and I made room for her on the chair. She blushed and laughed, but she came, and then she snuggled up to me. The boy laughed too. 'You see, she's taken to you already,' he said. 'Do you want her to stay?' he asked. 'Do you want to?' I said to her. She hid her face, laughing, on my shoulder. She was very soft and small. 'Very well,' I said, 'let her stay.'"

Guy leaned forward and helped himself to a whisky and soda.

"May I speak now?" asked Doris.

"Wait a minute, I haven't finished yet. I wasn't in love with her, not even at the beginning. I only took her so as to have somebody about the bungalow. I think I should have gone mad if I hadn't, or else taken to drink. I was at the end of my tether. I was too young to be quite alone. I was never in love with anyone but you." He hesitated a moment. "She lived here till I went home last year on leave. It's the woman you've seen hanging about."

"Yes, I guessed that. She had a baby in her arms. Is that your child?"

"Yes. It's a little girl."

"Is it the only one?"

"You saw the two small boys the other day in the kampong. You mentioned them."

"She has three children then?"

"Yes."

"It's quite a family you've got."

She felt the sudden gesture which her remark forced from him, but she did not speak.

"Didn't she know that you were married till you suddenly turned up here with a wife?" asked Doris.

"She knew I was going to be married."

"When?"

"I sent her back to the village before I left here. I told her it was all over. I gave her what I'd promised. She always knew it was only a temporary arrangement. I was fed up with it. I told her I was going to marry a white woman."

"But you hadn't even seen me then."

"No, I know. But I'd made up my mind to marry when I was home." He chuckled in his old manner. "I don't mind telling you that I was getting rather despondent about it when I met you. I fell in love with you at first sight and then I knew it was either you or nobody."

"Why didn't you tell me? Don't you think it would have been only fair to give me a chance of judging for myself? It might have occurred to you that it would be rather a shock to a girl to find out that her husband had lived for ten years with another girl and had three children."

"I couldn't expect you to understand. The circumstances out here are peculiar. It's the regular thing. Five men out of six do it. I thought perhaps it would shock you and I didn't want to lose you. You see, I was most awfully in love with you. I am now, darling. There was no reason that you should ever know. I didn't expect to come back here. One seldom goes back to the same station after home leave. When we came here I offered her money if she'd go to some other village. First she said she would and then she changed her mind."

"Why have you told me now?"

"She's been making the most awful scenes. I don't know how she found out that you knew nothing about it. As soon as she did she began to blackmail me. I've had to give her an awful lot of money. I gave orders that she wasn't to be allowed in the compound. This morning she made that scene just to attract your attention. She wanted to frighten me. It couldn't go on like that. I thought the only thing was to make a clean breast of it."

There was a long silence as he finished. At last he put his hand on hers.

"You do understand, Doris, don't you? I know I've been to blame."

She did not move her hand. He felt it cold beneath his.

"Is she jealous?"

"I daresay there were all sorts of perks when she was living here, and I don't suppose she much likes not getting them any longer. But she was never in love with me any more than I was in love with her. Native women never do really care for white men, you know."

"And the children?"

"Oh, the children are all right. I've provided for them. As soon as the boys are old enough I shall send them to school at Singapore."

"Do they mean nothing to you at all?"

He hesitated.

"I want to be quite frank with you. I should be sorry if anything happened to them. When the first one was expected I thought I'd be much fonder of it than I ever had been of its mother. I suppose I should have been if it had been white. Of course, when it was a baby it was rather funny and touching, but I had no particular feeling that it was mine. I think that's what it is; you see, I have no sense of their belonging to me. I've reproached myself sometimes, because it seemed rather unnatural, but the honest truth is that they're no more to me than if they were somebody else's children. Of course a lot of slush is talked about children by people who haven't got any."

Now she had heard everything. He waited for her to speak, but she said nothing. She sat motionless.

"Is there anything more you want to ask me, Doris?" he said at last.

"No, I've got rather a headache. I think I shall go to bed." Her voice was as steady as ever. "I don't quite know what to say. Of course it's been all very unexpected. You must give me a little time to think."

"Are you very angry with me?"

"No. Not at all. Only – only I must be left to myself for a while. Don't move. I'm going to bed."

She rose from her long chair and put her hand on his shoulder.

"It's so very hot tonight. I wish you'd sleep in your dressing-room. Good night."

She was gone. He heard her lock the door of her bedroom.

She was pale next day and he could see that she had not slept. There was no bitterness in her manner, she talked as usual, but without ease; she spoke of this and that as though she were making conversation with a stranger. They had never had a quarrel, but it seemed to Guy that so would she talk if they had had a disagreement and the subsequent reconciliation had left her still wounded. The look in her eyes puzzled him; he seemed to read in them a strange fear. Immediately after dinner she said:

"I'm not feeling very well tonight. I think I shall go straight to bed."

"Oh, my poor darling, I'm so sorry," he cried.

"It's nothing. I shall be all right in a day or two."

"I shall come in and say good night to you later."

"No, don't do that. I shall try and get straight off to sleep."

"Well, then, kiss me before you go."

He saw that she flushed. For an instant she seemed to hesitate; then, with averted eyes, she leaned towards him. He took her in his arms and sought her lips, but she turned her face away and he kissed her cheek. She left him quickly and again he heard the key turn softly in the lock of her door. He flung himself heavily on the chair. He tried to read, but his ear was attentive to the smallest sound in his wife's room. She had said she was going to bed, but he did not hear her move. The silence in there made him unaccountably nervous. Shading the lamp with his hand he saw that there was a glimmer under her door; she had not put out her light. What on earth was she doing? He put down his book. It would not have surprised him if she had been angry and had made him a scene or if she had cried; he could have coped with that; but her calmness frightened him. And then what was that fear which he had seen so plainly in her eyes? He thought once more over all he had said to her on the previous night. He didn't know how else he could have put it. After all, the chief point was that he'd done the same as everybody else, and it was all over long before he met her. Of course as things turned out he had been a fool, but anyone could be wise after the event. He put his hand to his heart. Funny how it hurt him there.

"I suppose that's the sort of thing people mean when they say they're heartbroken," he said to himself. "I wonder how long it's going on like this?"

Should he knock at the door and tell her he must speak to her? It was better to have it out. He *must* make her understand. But the silence scared him. Not a sound! Perhaps it was better to leave her alone. Of course it had been a shock. He must give her as long as she wanted. After all, she knew how devotedly he loved her. Patience, that was the only thing; perhaps she was fighting it out with herself; he must give her time; he must have patience. Next morning he asked her if she had slept better.

"Yes, much," she said.

"Are you very angry with me?" he asked piteously.

She looked at him with candid, open eyes.

"Not a bit."

"Oh, my dear, I'm so glad. I've been a brute and a beast. I know it's been hateful for you. But do forgive me. I've been so miserable."

"I do forgive you. I don't even blame you."

He gave her a little rueful smile, and there was in his eyes the look of a whipped dog.

"I haven't much liked sleeping by myself the last two nights."

She glanced away. Her face grew a trifle paler.

"I've had the bed in my room taken away. It took up so much space. I've had a little camp bed put there instead."

"My dear, what are you talking about?"

Now she looked at him steadily.

"I'm not going to live with you as your wife again."

"Never?"

She shook her head. He looked at her in a puzzled way. He could hardly believe he had heard aright and his heart began to beat painfully.

"But that's awfully unfair to me, Doris."

"Don't you think it was a little unfair to me to bring me out here in the circumstances?"

"But you just said you didn't blame me."

"That's quite true. But the other's different. I can't do it."

"But how are we going to live together like that?"

She stared at the floor. She seemed to ponder deeply.

"When you wanted to kiss me on the lips last night I – it almost made me sick."

"Doris."

She looked at him suddenly and her eyes were cold and hostile.

"That bed I slept on, is that the bed in which she had her children?" She saw him flush deeply. "Oh, it's horrible. How could you?" She wrung her hands, and her twisting, tortured fingers looked like little writhing snakes. But she made a great effort and controlled herself. "My mind is quite made up. I don't want to be unkind to you, but there are some things that you can't ask me to do. I've thought it all over. I've been thinking of nothing else since you told me, night and day, till I'm exhausted. My first instinct was to get up and go. At once. The steamer will be here in two or three days."

"Doesn't it mean anything to you that I love you?"

"Oh, I know you love me. I'm not going to do that. I want to give us both a chance. I have loved you so, Guy." Her voice broke, but she did not cry. "I don't want to be unreasonable. Heaven knows, I don't want to be unkind. Guy, will you give me time?"

"I don't know quite what you mean."

"I just want you to leave me alone. I'm frightened by the feelings that I have."

He had been right then; she was afraid.

"What feelings?"

"Please don't ask me. I don't want to say anything to wound you. Perhaps I shall get over them. Heaven knows, I want to. I'll try, I promise you. I'll try. Give me six months. I'll do everything in the world for you, but just that one thing." She made a little gesture of appeal. "There's no reason why we shouldn't be happy enough together. If you really love me you'll – you'll have patience."

He sighed deeply.

"Very well," he said. "Naturally I don't want to force you to do anything you don't like. It shall be as you say."

He sat heavily for a little, as though, on a sudden grown old, it was an effort to move; then he got up.

"I'll be getting along to the office."

He took his topee and went out.

A month passed. Women conceal their feelings better than men and a stranger visiting them would never have guessed that Doris was in any way troubled. But in Guy the strain was obvious; his round, good-natured face was drawn, and in his eyes was a hungry, harassed look. He watched Doris. She was gay and she chaffed him as she had been used to do; they played tennis together; they chatted about one thing and another. But it was evident that she was merely playing a part, and at last, unable to contain himself, he tried to speak again of his connexions with the Malay woman.

"Oh, Guy, there's no object in going back on all that," she answered breezily. "We've said all we had to say about it and I don't blame you for anything."

"Why do you punish me then?"

"My poor boy, I don't want to punish you. It's not my fault if . . . " she shrugged her shoulders. "Human nature is very odd."

"I don't understand."

"Don't try."

The words might have been harsh, but she softened them with a pleasant, friendly smile. Every night when she went to bed she leaned over Guy and lightly kissed his cheek. Her lips only touched it. It was as though a moth had just brushed his face in its flight.

A second month passed, then a third, and suddenly the six months which had seemed so interminable were over. Guy asked himself whether she remembered. He gave a strained attention now to everything she said, to every look on her face and to every gesture of her hands. She remained impenetrable. She had asked him to give her six months; well, he had.

The coasting steamer passed the mouth of the river, dropped their mail, and went on its way. Guy busily wrote the letters which it would pick up on the return journey. Two or three days passed by. It was a Tuesday and the prahu was to start at dawn on Thursday to await the steamer. Except at meal time when Doris exerted herself to make conversation they had not of late talked very much together; and after dinner as usual they took their books and began to read; but when the boy had finished clearing away and was gone for the night Doris put down hers.

"Guy, I have something I want to say to you," she murmured.

His heart gave a sudden thud against his ribs and he felt himself change colour.

"Oh, my dear, don't look like that, it's not so very terrible," she laughed.

But he thought her voice trembled a little.

"Well?"

"I want you to do something for me."

"My darling, I'll do anything in the world for you."

He put out his hand to take hers, but she drew it away.

"I want you to let me go home."

"You?" he cried, aghast. "When? Why?"

"I've borne it as long as I can. I'm at the end of my tether."

"How long do you want to go for? For always?"

"I don't know. I think so." She gathered determination. "Yes, for always."

"Oh, my God!"

His voice broke and she thought he was going to cry.

"Oh, Guy, don't blame me. It really is not my fault. I can't help myself."

"You asked me for six months. I accepted your terms. You can't say I've made a nuisance of myself."

"No, no."

"I've tried not to let you see what a rotten time I was having."

"I know. I'm very grateful to you. You've been awfully kind to me. Listen, Guy, I want to tell you again that I don't blame you for a single thing you did. After all, you were only a boy, and you did no more than the others; I know what the loneliness is here. Oh, my dear, I'm so dreadfully sorry for you. I knew all that from the beginning. That's why I asked you for six months. My common sense tells me that I'm making a mountain out of a molehill. I'm unreasonable; I'm being unfair to you. But, you see, common sense has nothing to do with it; my whole soul is in revolt. When I see the woman and her children in the village I just feel my legs shaking. Everything in this house; when I think of that bed I slept in it gives me goose-flesh . . . You don't know what I've endured."

"I think I've persuaded her to go away. And I've applied for a transfer."

"That wouldn't help. She'll be there always. You belong to them, you don't belong to me. I think perhaps I could have stood it if there'd only been one child, but three; and the boys are quite big boys. For ten years you lived with her." And now she came out with what she had been working up to. She was desperate. "It's a physical thing, I can't help it, it's stronger than I am. I think of those thin black arms of hers round you and it fills me with a physical nausea. I think of you holding those little black babies in your arms. Oh, it's loathsome. The touch of you is odious to me. Each night, when I've kissed you, I've had to brace myself up to it. I've had to clench my hands and force myself to touch your cheek." Now she was clasping and unclasping her fingers in a nervous agony, and her voice was out of control. "I know it's I who am to blame now. I'm a silly, hysterical woman. I thought I'd get over it. I can't, and now I never shall. I've brought it all on myself; I'm willing to take the consequences; if you say I must stay here, I'll stay, but if I stay I shall die. I beseech you to let me go."

And now the tears which she had restrained so long overflowed and she wept broken-heartedly. He had never seen her cry before.

"Of course I don't want to keep you here against your will," he said hoarsely.

Exhausted, she leaned back in her chair. Her features were all twisted and awry. It was horribly painful to see the abandonment of grief on that face which was habitually so placid.

"I'm so sorry, Guy. I've broken your life, but I've broken mine too. And we might have been so happy."

"When do you want to go? On Thursday?"

"Yes."

She looked at him piteously. He buried his face in his hands. At last he looked up.

"I'm tired out," he muttered.

"May I go?"

"Yes."

For two minutes perhaps they sat there without a word. She started when the chik-chak gave its piercing, hoarse, and strangely human cry. Guy rose and went out on to the veranda. He leaned against the rail and looked at the softly flowing water. He heard Doris go into her room.

Next morning, up earlier than usual, he went to her door and knocked.

"Yes?"

"I have to go up-river today. I shan't be back till late."

"All right."

She understood. He had arranged to be away all day in order not to be about while she was packing. It was heartbreaking work. When she had packed her clothes she looked round the sitting-room at the things that belonged to her. It seemed dreadful to take them. She left everything but the photograph of her mother. Guy did not come in till ten o'clock at night.

"I'm sorry I couldn't get back to dinner," he said. "The headman at the village I had to go to had a lot of things for me to attend to."

She saw his eyes wander about the room and notice that her mother's photograph no longer stood in its place.

"Is everything quite ready?" he asked. "I've ordered the boatman to be at the steps at dawn."

"I told the boy to wake me at five."

"I'd better give you some money." He went to his desk and wrote out a cheque. He took some notes from a drawer. "Here's some cash to take you as far as Singapore and at Singapore you'll be able to change the cheque."

"Thank you."

"Would you like me to come to the mouth of the river with you?"

"Oh, I think it would be better if we said good-bye here."

"All right. I think I shall turn in. I've had a long day and I'm dead beat."

He did not even touch her hand. He went into his room. In a few minutes she heard him throw himself on his bed. For a little while she sat looking for the last time round that room in which she had been so happy and so miserable. She sighed deeply. She got up and went into her own room. Everything was packed except the one or two things she needed for the night.

It was dark when the boy awakened them. They dressed hurriedly and when they were ready breakfast was waiting for them. Presently they heard the boat row up to the landing-stage below the bungalow, and then the servants carried down her luggage. It was a poor pretence they made of eating. The darkness thinned away and the river was ghostly. It was not yet day, but it was no longer night. In the silence the voices of the natives at the landing-stage were very clear. Guy glanced at his wife's untouched plate.

"If you've finished we might stroll down. I think you ought to be starting."

She did not answer. She rose from the table. She went into her room to see that nothing had been forgotten and then side by side with him walked down the steps. A little winding path led them to the river. At the landing-stage the native guards in their smart uniform were lined up and they presented arms as Guy and Doris passed. The head boatman gave her his hand as she stepped into the boat. She turned and looked at Guy. She wanted desperately to say one last word of comfort, once more to ask for his forgiveness, but she seemed to be struck dumb.

He stretched out his hand.

"Well, good-bye, I hope you'll have a jolly journey."

They shook hands.

Guy nodded to the head boatman and the boat pushed off. The dawn now was creeping along the river mistily, but the night lurked still in the dark trees of the jungle. He stood at the landing-stage till the boat was lost in the shadows of the morning. With a sigh he turned away. He nodded absent-mindedly when the guard once more presented arms. But when he reached the bungalow he called the boy. He went round the room picking out everything that had belonged to Doris.

"Pack all these things up," he said. "It's no good leaving them about."

Then he sat down on the veranda and watched the day advance gradually like a bitter, an unmerited, and an overwhelming sorrow. At last he looked at his watch. It was time for him to go to the office.

In the afternoon he could not sleep, his head ached miserably, so he took his gun and went for a tramp in the jungle. He shot nothing, but he walked in order to tire himself out. Towards sunset he came back and had two or three drinks, and then it was time to dress for dinner. There wasn't much use in dressing now; he might just as well be comfortable; he put on a loose native jacket and a sarong. That was what he had been accustomed to wear before Doris came. He was barefoot. He ate his dinner listlessly and the boy cleared away and went. He sat down to read the *Tatler*. The bungalow was very silent. He could not read and let the paper fall on his knees. He was exhausted. He could not think and his mind was strangely vacant. The chik-chak was noisy that night and its hoarse and sudden cry seemed to mock him. You could hardly believe that this reverberating sound came from so small a throat. Presently he heard a discreet cough.

"Who's there?" he cried.

There was a pause. He looked at the door. The chik-chak laughed harshly. A small boy sidled in and stood on the threshold. It was a little half-caste boy in a tattered singlet and a sarong. It was the elder of his two sons.

"What do you want?" said Guy.

The boy came forward into the room and sat down, tucking his legs away under him.

"Who told you to come here?"

"My mother sent me. She says, do you want anything?"

Guy looked at the boy intently. The boy said nothing more. He sat and waited, his eyes cast down shyly. Then Guy in deep and bitter reflection buried his face in his hands. What was the use? It was finished. Finished! He surrendered. He sat back in his chair and sighed deeply.

"Tell your mother to pack up her things and yours. She can come back."

"When?" asked the boy, impassively.

Hot tears trickled down Guy's funny, round spotty face.

"Tonight."

THE ALIEN CORN

I HAD KNOWN the Blands a long time before I discovered that they had any connexion with Ferdy Rabenstein. Ferdy must have been nearly fifty when I first knew him and at the time of which I write he was well over seventy. He had altered little. His hair, coarse but abundant and curly, was white, but he had kept his figure and held himself as gallantly as ever. It was not hard to believe that in youth he had been as beautiful as people said. He had still his fine Semitic profile and the lustrous black eyes that had caused havoc in so many a Gentile breast. He was very tall, lean, with an oval face and a clear skin. He wore his clothes very well and in evening dress, even now, he was one of the handsomest men I had ever seen. He wore then large black pearls in his shirt-front and platinum and sapphire rings on his fingers. Perhaps he was rather flashy, but you felt it was so much in character that it would have ill become him to be anything else.

"After all, I am an Oriental," he said. "I can carry a certain barbaric magnificence."

I have often thought that Ferdy Rabenstein would make an admirable subject for a biography. He was not a great man, but within the limits he set himself he made of his life a work of art. It was a masterpiece in little, like a Persian miniature, and derived its interest from its perfection. Unfortunately the materials are scanty. They would consist of letters that may very well have been destroyed and the recollections of people who are old now and will soon be dead. His memory is extraordinary, but he would never write his memoirs, for he looks upon his past as a source of purely private entertainment; and he is a man of the most perfect discretion. Nor do I know anyone who could do justice to the subject but Max Beerbohm. There is no one else in this hard world of today who can look upon the trivial with such tender sympathy and wring such a delicate pathos from futility. I wonder that Max, who must have known Ferdy much better than I, and long before, was never tempted to exercise his exquisite fancy on such a theme. He was born for Max to write about. And who should have illustrated the elegant book that I see in my mind's eye but Aubrey Beardsley? Thus would have been erected a monument of triple brass and the ephemera imprisoned to succeeding ages in the amber's translucency.

Ferdy's conquests were social and his venue was the great world. He was born in South Africa and did not come to England till he was twenty. For some time he was on the Stock Exchange, but on the death of his father he inherited a considerable fortune, and retiring from business devoted himself to the life of a man about town. At that period English society was still a closed body and it was not easy for a Jew to force its barriers, but to Ferdy they fell like the walls of Jericho. He was handsome, he was rich, he was a sportsman and he was good company. He had a house in Curzon Street, furnished with the most beautiful French furniture, and a French chef, and a brougham. It would be interesting to know the first steps in his wonderful career: they are lost in the dark abysm of time. When I first met him he had been long established as one of the smartest men in London: this was at a very grand house in Norfolk to which I had been asked as a promising young novelist by the hostess who took an interest in letters, but the company was very distinguished and I was overawed. We were sixteen, and I felt shy and alone among these Cabinet Ministers, great ladies, and peers of the realm who talked of people and things of which I knew nothing. They were civil to me, but indifferent, and I was conscious that I was somewhat of a burden to my hostess. Ferdy saved me. He sat with me, walked with me, and talked with me. He discovered that I was a writer and we discussed the drama and the novel: he learnt that I had lived much on the Continent and he talked to me pleasantly of France, Germany, and Spain. He seemed really to seek my society. He gave me the flattering impression that he and I stood apart from the other members of the company and by our conversation upon affairs of the spirit made that of the rest of them, the political situation, the scandal of somebody's divorce, and the growing disinclination of pheasants to be killed, seem a little ridiculous. But if Ferdy had at the bottom of his heart a feeling of ever so faint a contempt for the hearty British gentry that surrounded us I am sure that it was only to me that he allowed an inkling of it to appear, and looking back I cannot but wonder whether it was not after all a suave and very delicate compliment that he paid me. I think of course that he liked to exercise his charm and I daresay the obvious pleasure his conversation gave me gratified him, but he could have had no motive for taking so much trouble over an obscure novelist other than his real interest in art and letters. I felt that he and I at bottom were equally alien in that company, I because I was a writer and he because he was a Jew, but I envied the ease with which he bore himself. He was completely at home. Everyone called him Ferdy. He seemed to be always in good spirits. He was never at a loss for a quip, a jest, or a repartee. They liked him in that house because he made them laugh, but never made them uncomfortable by talking over their heads. He brought a faint savour of Oriental romance into their lives, but so cleverly that they only felt more English. You could never be dull when he was by and with him present you were safe from the fear of the devastating silences that sometimes overwhelm a British company. A pause looked inevitable and Ferdy Rabenstein had broken into a topic that interested everyone. An invaluable asset

to any party. He had an inexhaustible fund of Jewish stories. He was a
very good mimic and he assumed the Yiddish accent and reproduced
the Jewish gestures to perfection; his head sank into his body, his face
grew cunning, his voice oily, and he was a rabbi or an old clothes
merchant or a smart commercial traveller or a fat procuress in
Frankfort. It was as good as a play. Because he was himself a Jew
and insisted on it you laughed without reserve, but for my own part
not without an under-current of discomfort. I was not quite sure of
a sense of humour that made such cruel fun of his own race. I
discovered afterwards that Jewish stories were his speciality and
I seldom met him anywhere without hearing him tell sooner or
later the last he had heard.

But the best story he told me on this occasion was not a Jewish
one. It struck me so that I have never forgotten it, but for one reason
or another I have never had occasion to tell it again. I give it here
because it is a curious little incident concerning persons whose names
at least will live in the social history of the Victorian Era and I think it
would be a pity if it were lost. He told me then that once when quite
a young man he was staying in the country in a house where
Mrs Langtry, at that time at the height of her beauty and astounding
reputation, was also a guest. It happened to be within driving
distance of that in which lived the Duchess of Somerset, who had
been Queen of Beauty at the Eglinton Tournament, and knowing
her slightly, it occurred to him that it would be interesting to bring
the two women together. He suggested to Mrs Langtry, who was
willing, and forthwith wrote to the Duchess asking if he might bring
the celebrated beauty to call on her. It was fitting, he said, that the
loveliest woman of this generation (this was in the 'eighties) should
pay her respects to the loveliest woman of the last. "Bring her by all
means," answered the Duchess, "but I warn you that it will be a
shock to her." They drove over in a carriage and pair, Mrs Langtry in
a close-fitting blue bonnet with long satin strings, which showed the
fine shape of her head and made her blue eyes even bluer, and were
received by a little ugly old hag who looked with irony out of her
beady eyes at the radiant beauty who had come to see her. They had
tea, they talked, and they drove home again. Mrs Langtry was very
silent and when Ferdy looked at her he saw that she was quietly
weeping. When they got back to the house she went to her room

and would not come down to dinner that night. For the first time she had realized that beauty dies.

Ferdy asked me for my address and a few days after I got back to London invited me to dinner. There were only six of us, an American woman married to an English peer, a Swedish painter, an actress, and a well-known critic. We ate very good food and drank excellent wine. The conversation was easy and intelligent. After dinner Ferdy was persuaded to play the piano. He only played Viennese waltzes, I discovered later that they were his speciality, and the light, tuneful, and sensual music seemed to accord well with his discreet flamboyance. He played without affectation, with a lilt, and he had a graceful touch. This was the first of a good many dinners I had with him, he would ask me two or three times a year, and as time passed I met him more and more frequently at other people's houses. I rose in the world and perhaps he came down a little. Of late years I had sometimes found him at parties where other Jews were and I fancied that I read in his shining liquid eyes, resting for a moment on these members of his race, a certain good-natured amusement at the thought of what the world was coming to. There were people who said he was a snob, but I do not think he was; it just happened that in his early days he had never met any but the great. He had a real passion for art and in his commerce with those that produced it was at his best. With them he had never that faint air of persiflage which when he was with very grand persons made you suspect that he was never quite the dupe of their grandeur. His taste was perfect and many of his friends were glad to avail themselves of his knowledge. He was one of the first to value old furniture and he rescued many a priceless piece from the attics of ancestral mansions and gave it an honourable place in the drawing-room. It amused him to saunter round the auction rooms and he was always willing to give his advice to great ladies who desired at once to acquire a beautiful thing and make a profitable investment. He was rich and good-natured. He liked to patronize the arts and would take a great deal of trouble to get commissions for some young painter whose talent he admired or an engagement to play at a rich man's house for a violinist who could in no other way get a hearing. But he never let his rich man down. His taste was too good to deceive and civil though he might be to the mediocre he would not lift a finger to help them. His own musical parties, very small and carefully chosen, were a treat.

He never married.

"I am a man of the world," he said, "and I flatter myself that I have no prejudices, *tous les goûts sont dans la nature*, but I do not think I could bring myself to marry a Gentile. There's no harm in going to the opera in a dinner jacket, but it just would never occur to me to do so."

"Then why didn't you marry a Jewess?"

(I did not hear this conversation, but the lively and audacious creature who thus tackled him told me of it.)

"Oh, my dear, our women are so prolific. I could not bear the thought of peopling the world with a little Ikey and a little Jacob and a little Rebecca and a little Leah and a little Rachel."

But he had had affairs of note and the glamour of past romance still clung to him. He was in his youth of an amorous complexion. I have met old ladies who told me that he was irresistible, and when in reminiscent mood they talked to me of this woman and that who had completely lost her head over him, I divined that, such was his beauty, they could not find it in their hearts to blame them. It was interesting to hear of great ladies that I had read of in the memoirs of the day or had met as respectable dowagers garrulous over their grandsons at Eton or making a mess of a hand at bridge and bethink myself that they had been consumed with sinful passion for the handsome Jew. Ferdy's most notorious amour was with the Duchess of Hereford, the loveliest, the most gallant and dashing of the beauties of the end of Queen Victoria's reign. It lasted for twenty years. He had doubtless flirtations meanwhile, but their relations were stable and recognized. It was proof of his marvellous tact that when at last they ended he exchanged an ageing mistress for a loyal friend. I remember meeting the pair not so very long ago at luncheon. She was an old woman, tall and of a commanding presence, but with a mask of paint on a ravaged face. We were lunching at the Carlton and Ferdy, our host, came a few minutes late. He offered us a cocktail and the Duchess told him we had already had one.

"Ah, I wondered why your eyes were so doubly bright," he said.

The old raddled woman flushed with pleasure.

My youth passed, I grew middle-aged, I wondered how soon I must begin to describe myself as elderly; I wrote books and plays, I travelled, I underwent experiences, I fell in love and out of it; and still I kept meeting Ferdy at parties. War broke out and was waged, millions of men were killed, and the face of the world was changed. Ferdy did not like the war. He was too old to take part in it, and his German name was awkward, but he was discreet and took care not to expose himself to humiliation. His old friends were faithful to him and he lived in a dignified but not too strict seclusion. But then peace came and with courage he set himself to making the best of changed conditions. Society was mixed now, parties were rowdy, but Ferdy fitted himself to the new life. He still told his funny Jewish stories, he still played charmingly the waltzes of Strauss, he still went round auction rooms and told the new rich what they ought to buy. I went to live abroad, but whenever I was in London I saw Ferdy and now there was something a little uncanny in him. He did not give in. He had never known a day's illness. He seemed never to grow tired. He still dressed beautifully. He was interested in everybody. His mind was alert and people asked him to dinner, not for old times' sake, but because he was worth his salt. He still gave charming little concerts at his house in Curzon Street.

It was when he invited me to one of these that I made the discovery that started the recollections of him I have here set down. We were dining at a house in Hill Street, a large party, and the women having gone upstairs Ferdy and I found ourselves side by side. He told me that Lea Makart was coming to play for him on the following Friday evening and he would be glad if I would come.

"I'm awfully sorry," I said, "but I'm going down to the Blands."

"What Blands?"

"They live in Sussex at a place called Tilby."

"I didn't know you knew them."

He looked at me rather strangely. He smiled. I didn't know what amused him.

"Oh, yes, I've known them for years. It's a very nice house to stay at."

"Adolf is my nephew."

"Sir Adolphus?"

"It suggests one of the bucks of the Regency, doesn't it? But I will not conceal from you that he was named Adolf."

"Everyone I know calls him Freddy."

"I know, and I understand that Miriam, his wife, only answers to the name of Muriel."

"How does he happen to be your nephew?"

"Because Hannah Rabenstein, my sister, married Alfons Bleikogel, who ended life as Sir Alfred Bland, first Baronet, and Adolf, their only son, in due course became Sir Adolphus Bland, second Baronet."

"Then Freddy Bland's mother, the Lady Bland who lives in Portland Place, is your sister?"

"Yes, my sister Hannah. She was the eldest of the family. She's eighty, but in full possession of her faculties and a remarkable woman."

"I've never met her."

"I think your friends the Blands would just as soon you didn't. She has never lost her German accent."

"Do you never see them?" I asked.

"I haven't spoken to them for twenty years. I am such a Jew and they are so English." He smiled. "I could never remember that their names were Freddy and Muriel. I used to come out with an Adolf or a Miriam at awkward moments. And they didn't like my stories. It was better that we should not meet. When the war broke out and I would not change my name it was the last straw. It was too late, I could never have accustomed my friends to think of me as anything but Ferdy Rabenstein; I was quite content. I was not ambitious to be a Smith, a Brown or a Robinson."

Though he spoke facetiously, there was in his tone the faintest possible derision and I felt, hardly felt even, the sensation was so shadowy, that, as it had often vaguely seemed to me before, there was in the depth of his impenetrable heart a cynical contempt for the Gentiles he had conquered.

"Then you don't know the two boys?" I said.

"No."

"The eldest is called George, you know. I don't think he's so clever as Harry, the other one, but he's an engaging youth. I think you'd like him."

"Where is he now?"

"Well, he's just been sent down from Oxford. I suppose he's at home. Harry's still at Eton."

"Why don't you bring George to lunch with me?"

"I'll ask him. I should think he'd love to come."

"It has reached my ears that he's been a little troublesome."

"Oh, I don't know. He wouldn't go into the army, which is what they wanted. They rather fancied the Guards. And so he went to Oxford instead. He didn't work and he spent a great deal of money and he painted the town red. It was all quite normal."

"What was he sent down for?"

"I don't know. Nothing of any consequence."

At that moment our host rose and we went upstairs. When Ferdy bade me good night he asked me not to forget about his great-nephew.

"Ring me up," he said. "Wednesday would suit me. Or Friday."

Next day I went down to Tilby. It was an Elizabethan mansion standing in a spacious park, in which roamed fallow deer, and from its windows you had wide views of rolling downs. It seemed to me that as far as the eye could reach the land belonged to the Blands. His tenants must have found Sir Adolphus a wonderful landlord, for I never saw farms kept in such order, the barns and cow-sheds were spick and span and the pigsties were a picture; the public-houses looked like Old English water-colours and the cottages he had built on the estate combined admirably picturesqueness and convenience. It must have cost him a pot of money to run the place on these lines. Fortunately he had it. The park with its grand old trees (and its nine-hole golf course) was tended like a garden, and the wide-stretching gardens were the pride of the neighbour-hood. The magnificent house, with its steep roofs and mullioned windows, had been restored by the most celebrated architect in England and furnished by Lady Bland, with taste and knowledge, in a style that perfectly fitted it.

"Of course it's very simple," she said. "Just an English house in the country."

The dining-room was adorned with old English sporting pictures and the Chippendale chairs were of incredible value. In the drawing-room were portraits by Reynolds and Gainsborough and landscapes by Old Crome and Richard Wilson. Even in my bedroom with its four-post bed were water-colours by Birket Foster. It was very beautiful and a treat to stay there, but though it would have distressed Muriel Bland beyond anything to know it, it entirely missed oddly enough the effect she had sought. It did not give you for a moment the impression of an English house. You had the feeling that every object had been bought with a careful eye to the general scheme. You missed the full Academy portraits that hung in the dining-room beside a Carlo Dolci that an ancestor had brought back from the grand tour, and the water-colours painted by a great-aunt that cluttered up the drawing-room so engagingly. There was no ugly Victorian sofa that had always been there and that it never occurred to anybody to take away and no needlework chairs that an unmarried daughter had so painstakingly worked at about the time of the Great Exhibition. There was beauty but no sentiment.

And yet how comfortable it was and how well looked after you were! And what a cordial greeting the Blands gave you! They seemed really to like people. They were generous and kindly. They were never happier than when they were entertaining the county, and though they had not owned the property for more than twenty years they had established themselves firmly in the favour of their neighbours. Except perhaps in their splendour and the competent way in which the estate was run there was nothing to suggest that they had not been settled there for centuries.

Freddy had been at Eton and Oxford. He was now in the early fifties. He was quiet in manner, courtly, very clever, I imagine, but a trifle reserved. He had great elegance, but it was not an English elegance; he had grey hair and a short pointed grey beard, fine dark eyes and an aquiline nose. He was just above middle height; I don't think you would have taken him for a Jew, but rather for a foreign diplomat of some distinction. He was a man of character, but gave you, strangely enough, notwithstanding the success he had had in life, an impression of faint melancholy. His successes had been financial and political; in the world of sport, for all his perseverance, he had never shone. For many years he had followed hounds, but he was a bad rider and I think it must have been a relief to him when he could persuade himself that middle age and pressure of business forced him to give up hunting. He had excellent shooting and gave grand parties for it, but he was a poor shot; and despite the course in his park he never succeeded in being more than an indifferent golfer. He knew only too well how much these things meant in England and his incapacity was a bitter disappointment to him. However George would make up for it.

George was scratch at golf, and though tennis was not his game he played much better than the average; the Blands had had him taught to shoot as soon as he was old enough to hold a gun and he was a fine shot; they had put him on a pony when he was two, and Freddy, watching him mount his horse, knew that out hunting when the boy came to a fence he felt exhilaration and not that sickening feeling in the pit of his stomach, which, though he had chased the fox with such grim determination, had always made the sport a torture to him. George was so tall and slim, his curly hair, of a palish brown, was so fine, his eyes were so blue, he was the perfect type of the young Englishman. He had the engaging candour of the breed. His nose was straight, though perhaps a trifle fleshy, and his lips were perhaps a little full and sensual, but he had beautiful teeth, and his smooth skin was like ivory. George was the apple of his father's eye. He did not like Harry, his second son, so well. He was rather stocky, broad-shouldered and strong for his age, but his black eyes, shining with cleverness, his coarse dark hair, and his big nose revealed his race. Freddy was severe with him, and often impatient, but with George he was all indulgence. Harry would go into the business, he had brains and push, but George was the heir. George would be an English gentleman.

George had offered to motor me down in the roadster his father had given him as a birthday present. He drove very fast and we arrived before the rest of the guests. The Blands were sitting on the lawn and tea was laid out under a magnificent cedar.

"By the way," I said presently, "I saw Ferdy Rabenstein the other day and he wants me to bring George to lunch with him."

I had not mentioned the invitation to George on the way because I thought that if there had been a family coldness I had better address his parents as well.

"Who in God's name is Ferdy Rabenstein?" said George.

How brief is human glory! A generation back such a question would have seemed grotesque.

"He's by way of being your great-uncle," I replied.

A glance had passed from father to mother when I first spoke.

"He's a horrid old man," said Muriel.

"I don't think it's in the least necessary for George to resume relationships that were definitely severed before he was born," said Freddy with decision.

"Anyhow I've delivered the message," said I, feeling somewhat snubbed.

"I don't want to see the old blighter," said George.

The conversation was broken off by the arrival of other guests and in a little while George went off to play golf with one of his Oxford friends.

It was not till next day that the matter was referred to again. I had played an unsatisfactory round with Freddy Bland in the morning and several sets of what is known as country-house tennis in the afternoon and was sitting alone with Muriel on the terrace. In England we have so much bad weather that it is only fair that a beautiful day should be more beautiful than anywhere in the world and this June evening was perfect. The blue sky was cloudless and the air was balmy; before us stretched green rolling downs, and woods, and in the distance you saw the red roofs of a little village church. It was a day when to be alive was sufficient happiness. Detached lines of poetry hovered vaguely in my memory. Muriel and I had been chatting desultorily.

"I hope you didn't think it rather horrid of us to refuse to let George lunch with Ferdy," she said suddenly. "He's such a fearful snob, isn't he?"

"D'you think so? He's always been very nice to me."

"We haven't been on speaking terms for twenty years. Freddy never forgave him for his behaviour during the war. So unpatriotic, I thought, and one really must draw the line somewhere. You know, he absolutely refused to drop his horrible German name. With Freddy in Parliament and running munitions and all that sort of thing it was quite impossible. I don't know why he should want to see George. He can't mean anything to him."

"He's an old man. George and Harry are his great-nephews. He must leave his money to someone."

"We'd rather not have his money," said Muriel coldly.

Of course I didn't care a row of pins whether George went to lunch with Ferdy Rabenstein, and I was quite willing to let the matter drop, but evidently the Blands had talked it over and Muriel felt that some explanation was due to me.

"Of course you know that Freddy has Jewish blood in him," she said.

She looked at me sharply. Muriel was rather a big blonde woman and she spent a great deal of time trying to keep down the corpulence to which she was predisposed. She had been very pretty when young, and even now was a comely person; but her round blue eyes, slightly prominent, her fleshy nose, the shape of her face and the back of her neck, her exuberant manner, betrayed her race. No Englishwoman, however fair-haired, ever looked like that. And yet her observation was designed to make me take it for granted that she was a Gentile. I answered discreetly:

"So many people have nowadays."

"I know. But there's no reason to dwell on it, is there? After all, we're absolutely English; no one could be more English than George, in appearance and manner and everything; I mean, he's such a fine sportsman and all that sort of thing, I can't see any object of his knowing Jews just because they happen to be distant connexions of his."

"It's very difficult in England now not to know Jews, isn't it?"

"Oh, I know, in London one does meet a good many, and I think some of them are very nice. They're so artistic. I don't go so far as to say that Freddy and I deliberately avoid them, of course I wouldn't do that, but it just happens that we don't really know any of them very well. And down here, there simply aren't any to know."

I could not but admire the convincing manner in which she spoke. It would not have surprised me to be told that she really believed every word she said.

"You say that Ferdy might leave George his money. Well, I don't believe it's so very much anyway; it was quite a comfortable fortune before the war, but that's nothing nowadays. Besides we're hoping that George will go in for politics when he's a little older, and I don't think it would do him any good in the constituency to inherit money from a Mr Rabenstein."

"Is George interested in politics?" I asked, to change the conversation.

"Oh, I do hope so. After all, there's the family constituency waiting for him. It's a safe Conservative seat and one can't expect Freddy to go on with the grind of the House of Commons indefinitely."

Muriel was grand. She talked already of the constituency as though twenty generations of Blands had sat for it. Her remark, however, was my first intimation that Freddy's ambition was not satisfied.

"I suppose Freddy would go to the House of Lords when George was old enough to stand."

"We've done a good deal for the party," said Muriel.

Muriel was a Catholic and she often told you that she had been educated in a convent – "Such sweet women, those nuns, I always said that if I had a daughter I should have sent her to a convent too" – but she liked her servants to be Church of England, and on Sunday evenings we had what was called supper because the fish was cold and there was ice-cream, so that they could go to church, and we were waited on by two footmen instead of four. It was still light when we finished and Freddy and I, smoking our cigars, walked up and down the terrace in the gloaming. I suppose Muriel had told him of her conversation with me, and it may be that his refusal to let George see his great-uncle still troubled him, but being subtler than she he attacked the question more indirectly. He told me that he had been very much worried about George. It had been a great disappointment that he had refused to go into the army.

"I should have thought he'd have loved the life," he said.

"And he would certainly have looked marvellous in his Guards uniform."

"He would, wouldn't he?" returned Freddy, ingenuously. "I wonder he could resist that."

He had been completely idle at Oxford; although his father had given him a very large allowance, he had got monstrously into debt; and now he had been sent down. But though he spoke so tartly I could see that he was not a little proud of his scapegrace son, he loved him with oh, such an unEnglish love, and in his heart it flattered him that George had cut such a dash.

"Why should you worry?" I said. "You don't really care if George has a degree or not."

Freddy chuckled.

"No, I don't suppose I do really. I always think the only important thing about Oxford is that people know you were there, and I dare say that George isn't any wilder than the other young men in his set. It's the future I'm thinking of. He's so damned idle. He doesn't seem to want to do anything but have a good time."

"He's young, you know."

"He's not interested in politics, and though he's so good at games he's not even very keen on sport. He seems to spend most of his time strumming the piano."

"That's a harmless amusement."

"Oh, yes, I don't mind that, but he can't go on loafing indefinitely. You see, all this will be his one day." Freddy gave a sweeping gesture that seemed to embrace the whole county, but I knew that he did not own it all yet. "I'm very anxious that he should be fit to assume his responsibilities. His mother is very ambitious for him, but I only want him to be an English gentleman."

Freddy gave me a sidelong glance as though he wanted to say something but hesitated in case I thought it ridiculous; but there is one advantage in being a writer that, since people look upon you as of no account, they will often say things to you that they would not to their equals. He thought he would risk it.

"You know, I've got an idea that nowhere in the world now is the Greek ideal of life so perfectly cultivated as by the English country gentleman living on his estates. I think his life has the beauty of a work of art."

I could not but smile when I reflected that it was impossible for the English country gentleman in these days to do anything of the sort without a packet of money safely invested in American Bonds, but I smiled with sympathy. I thought it rather touching that this Jewish financier should cherish so romantic a dream.

"I want him to be a good landlord. I want him to take his part in the affairs of the country. I want him to be a thorough sportsman."

"Poor mutt," I thought, but said: "Well, what are your plans for George now?"

"I think he has a fancy for the diplomatic service. He's suggested going to Germany to learn the language."

"A very good idea, I should have thought."

"For some reason he's got it into his head that he wants to go to Munich."

"A nice place."

Next day I went back to London and shortly after my arrival rang up Ferdy.

"I'm sorry, but George isn't able to come to lunch on Wednesday."

"What about Friday?"

"Friday's no good either." I thought it useless to beat about the bush. "The fact is, his people aren't keen on his lunching with you."

There was a moment's silence. Then:

"I see. Well, will you come on Wednesday anyway?"

"Yes, I'd like to," I answered.

So on Wednesday at half past one I strolled round to Curzon Street. Ferdy received me with the somewhat elaborate graciousness that he cultivated. He made no reference to the Blands. We sat in the drawing-room and I could not help reflecting what an eye for beautiful objects that family had. The room was more crowded than the fashion of today approves, and the gold snuff-boxes in vitrines, the French china, appealed to a taste that was not mine; but they were no doubt choice pieces; and the Louis XV suite, with its beautiful *petit point*, must have been worth an enormous lot of money. The pictures on the walls by Lancret, Pater, and Watteau did not greatly interest me, but I recognized their intrinsic excellence. It was a proper setting for this aged man of the world. It fitted his period. Suddenly the door opened and George was announced. Ferdy saw my surprise and gave me a little smile of triumph.

"I'm very glad you were able to come after all," he said as he shook George's hand.

I saw him in a glance take in his great-nephew whom he saw today for the first time. George was very well dressed. He wore a short black coat, striped trousers, and the grey double-breasted waistcoat which at that time was the mode. You could only wear it with elegance if you were tall and thin and your belly was slightly concave. I felt sure that Ferdy knew exactly who George's tailor was and what haberdasher he went to and approved of them. George, so smart and trim, wearing his clothes so beautifully, certainly looked very handsome. We went down to luncheon. Ferdy had the social graces at his fingers' ends and he put the boy at his ease, but I saw that he was carefully appraising him; then, I do not know why, he began to tell some of his Jewish stories. He told them with gusto and with his wonderful mimicry. I saw George flush, and though he laughed at them, I could see that it was with embarrassment. I wondered what on earth had induced Ferdy to be so tactless. But he was watching George and he told story after story. It looked as though he would never stop. I wondered if for some reason I could not grasp he was taking a malicious pleasure in the boy's obvious discomfiture. At last we went upstairs and to make things easier I asked Ferdy to play the piano. He played us three or four little waltzes. He had lost none of his exquisite lightness nor his sense of their lilting rhythm. Then he turned to George.

"Do you play?" he asked him.

"A little."

"Won't you play something?"

"I'm afraid I only play classical music. I don't think it would interest you."

Ferdy smiled slightly, but did not insist. I said it was time for me to go and George accompanied me.

"What a filthy old Jew," he said as soon as we were in the street. "I hated those stories of his."

"They're his great stunt. He always tells them."

"Would you if you were a Jew?"

I shrugged my shoulders.

"How is it you came to lunch after all?" I asked George.

He chuckled. He was a light-hearted creature, with a sense of humour, and he shook off the slight irritation his great-uncle had caused him.

"He went to see Granny. You don't know Granny, do you?"

"No."

"She treats daddy like a kid in Etons. Granny said I was to go to lunch with great-uncle Ferdy and what Granny says goes."

"I see."

A week or two later George went to Munich to learn German. I happened then to go on a journey and it was not till the following spring that I was again in London. Soon after my arrival I found myself sitting next to Muriel Bland at dinner. I asked after George.

"He's still in Germany," she said.

"I see in the papers that you're going to have a great beano at Tilby for his coming of age."

"We're going to entertain the tenants and they're making George a presentation."

She was less exuberant than usual, but I did not pay much attention to the fact. She led a strenuous life and it might be that she was tired. I knew she liked to talk of her son, so I continued.

"I suppose George has been having a grand time in Germany," I said.

She did not answer for a moment and I gave her a glance. I was surprised to see that her eyes were filled with tears.

"I'm afraid George has gone mad," she said.

"What *do* you mean?"

"We've been so frightfully worried. Freddy's so angry, he won't even discuss it. I don't know what we're going to do."

Of course it immediately occurred to me that George, who, I supposed, like most young Englishmen sent to learn the language, had been put with a German family, had fallen in love with the daughter of the house and wanted to marry her. I had a pretty strong suspicion that the Blands were intent on his making a very grand marriage.

"Why, what's happened?" I asked.

"He wants to become a pianist."

"A what?"

"A professional pianist."

"What on earth put that idea in his head?"

"Heaven knows. We didn't know anything about it. We thought he was working for his exam. I went out to see him. I thought I'd like to know that he was getting on all right. Oh, my dear. He looks like nothing on earth. And he used to be so smart; I could have cried. He told me he wasn't going in for the exam. and had never had any intention of doing so; he'd only suggested the diplomatic service so that we'd let him go to Germany and he'd be able to study music."

"But has he any talent?"

"Oh, that's neither here nor there. Even if he had the genius of Paderewski we couldn't have George traipsing around the country playing at concerts. No one can deny that I'm very artistic, and so is Freddy, we love music and we've always known a lot of artists, but George will have a very great position, it's out of the question. We've set our hearts on his going into Parliament. He'll be very rich one day. There's nothing he can't aspire to."

"Did you point all that out to him?"

"Of course I did. He laughed at me. I told him he'd break his father's heart. He said his father could always fall back on Harry. Of course I'm devoted to Harry, and he's as clever as a monkey, but it was always understood that he was to go into the business; even though I am his mother I can see that he hasn't got the advantages that George has. Do you know what he said to me? He said that if his father would settle five pounds a week on him he would resign everything in Harry's favour and Harry could be his father's heir and succeed to the baronetcy and everything. It's too ridiculous. He said that if the Crown Prince of Romania could abdicate a throne he didn't see why he couldn't abdicate a baronetcy. But you can't do that. Nothing can prevent him from being third baronet and if Freddy should be granted a peerage from succeeding to it at Freddy's death. Do you know, he even wants to drop the name of Bland and take some horrible German name."

I could not help asking what.

"Bleikogel or something like that," she answered.

That was a name I recognized. I remembered Ferdy telling me that Hannah Rabenstein had married Alfons Bleikogel who became eventually Sir Alfred Bland, first Baronet. It was all very strange. I wondered what had happened to the charming and so typically English boy whom I had seen only a few months before.

"Of course when I came home and told Freddy he was furious. I've never seen him so angry. He foamed at the mouth. He wired to George to come back immediately and George wired back to say he couldn't on account of his work."

"Is he working?"

"From morning till night. That's the maddening part of it. He never did a stroke of work in his life. Freddy used to say he was born idle."

"H'm."

"Then Freddy wired to say that if he didn't come he'd stop his allowance and George wired back: 'Stop it.' That put the lid on. You don't know what Freddy can be when his back is up."

I knew that Freddy had inherited a large fortune, but I knew also that he had immensely increased it, and I could well imagine that behind the courteous and amiable Squire of Tilby there was a ruthless man of affairs. He had been used to having his own way and I could believe that when crossed he would be hard and cruel.

"We'd been making George a very handsome allowance, but you know how frightfully extravagant he was. We didn't think he'd be able to hold out long and in point of fact within a month he wrote to Ferdy and asked him to lend him a hundred pounds. Ferdy went to my mother-in-law, she's his sister, you know, and asked her what it meant. Though they hadn't spoken for twenty years Freddy went to see him and begged him not to send George a penny, and he promised he wouldn't. I don't know how George has been making both ends meet. I'm sure Freddy's right, but I can't help being rather worried. If I hadn't given Freddy my word of honour that I wouldn't send him anything I think I'd have slipped a few notes in a letter in case of accident. I mean, it's awful to think that perhaps he hasn't got enough to eat."

"It'll do him no harm to go short for a bit."

"We were in an awful hole, you know. We'd made all sorts of preparations for his coming of age, and I'd issued hundreds of invitations. Suddenly George said he wouldn't come. I was simply frantic. I wrote and wired. I would have gone over to Germany only Freddy wouldn't let me. I practically went down on my bended knees to George. I begged him not to put us in such a humiliating position. I mean, it's the sort of thing it's so difficult to explain. Then my mother-in-law stepped in. You don't know her, do you? She's an extraordinary old woman. You'd never think she was Freddy's mother. She was German originally, but of very good family."

319

"Oh?"

"To tell you the truth I'm rather frightened of her. She tackled
Freddy and then she wrote to George herself. She said that if he'd
come home for his twenty-first birthday she'd pay any debts he had
in Munich and we'd all give a patient hearing to anything he had to
say. He agreed to that and we're expecting him one day next week.
But I'm not looking forward to it, I can tell you."

She gave a deep sigh. When we were walking upstairs after dinner
Freddy addressed me.

"I see Muriel has been telling you about George. The damned
fool! I have no patience with him. Fancy wanting to be a pianist. It's
so ungentlemanly."

"He's very young, you know," I said soothingly.

"He's had things too easy for him. I've been much too indulgent.
There's never been a thing he wanted that I haven't given him. I'll
learn him."

The Blands had a discreet apprehension of the uses of advertisement
and I gathered from the papers that the celebrations at Tilby of
George's twenty-first birthday were conducted in accordance with
the usage of English county families. There was a dinner-party and a
ball for the gentry and a collation and a dance in marquees on the
lawn for the tenants. Expensive bands were brought down from
London. In the illustrated papers were pictures of George surrounded by his family being presented with a solid silver tea-set by
the tenantry. They had subscribed to have his portrait painted, but
since his absence from the country had made it impossible for him to
sit, the tea-service had been substituted. I read in the columns of the
gossip writers that his father had given him a hunter, his mother a
gramophone that changed its own records, his grandmother the
dowager Lady Bland an *Encyclopaedia Britannica*, and his great-uncle
Ferdinand Rabenstein a *Virgin and Child* by Pellegrino da Modena.
I could not help observing that these gifts were bulky and not readily
convertible into cash. From Ferdy's presence at the festivities
I concluded that George's unaccountable vagary had effected a
reconciliation between uncle and nephew. I was right. Ferdy did
not at all like the notion of his great-nephew becoming a professional
pianist. At the first hint of danger to its prestige the family drew

together and a united front was presented to oppose George's designs. Since I was not there I only know from hearsay what happened when the birthday celebrations were over. Ferdy told me something and so did Muriel, and later George gave me his version. The Blands had very much the impression that when George came home and found himself occupying the centre of the stage, when, surrounded by splendour, he saw for himself once more how much it meant to be the heir of a great estate, he would weaken. They surrounded him with love. They flattered him. They hung on his words. They counted on the goodness of his heart and thought that if they were very kind to him he would not have the courage to cause them pain. They seemed to take it for granted that he had no intention of going back to Germany and in conversation included him in all their plans. George did not say very much. He seemed to be enjoying himself. He did not open a piano. Things looked as though they were going very well. Peace descended on the troubled house. Then one day at luncheon when they were discussing a garden-party to which they had all been asked for one day of the following week, George said pleasantly:

"Don't count on me. I shan't be here."

"Oh, George, why not?" asked his mother.

"I must get back to my work. I'm leaving for Munich on Monday."

There was an awful pause. Everyone looked for something to say, but was afraid of saying the wrong thing, and at last it seemed impossible to break it. Luncheon was finished in silence. Then George went into the garden and the others, old Lady Bland and Ferdy, Muriel and Sir Adolphus, into the morning-room. There was a family council. Muriel wept. Freddy flew into a temper. Presently from the drawing-room they heard the sound of someone playing a nocturne of Chopin. It was George. It was as though now he had announced his decision he had gone for comfort, rest, and strength to the instrument he loved. Freddy sprang to his feet.

"Stop that noise," he cried. "I won't have him play the piano in my house."

Muriel rang for a servant and gave him a message.

"Will you tell Mr Bland that her ladyship has a bad headache and would he mind not playing the piano."

Ferdy, the man of the world, was deputed to have a talk with George. He was authorized to make him certain promises if he would give up the idea of becoming a pianist. If he did not wish to go into the diplomatic service his father would not insist, but if he would stand for Parliament he was prepared to pay his election expenses, give him a flat in London, and make him an allowance of five thousand a year. I must say it was a handsome offer. I do not know what Ferdy said to the boy. I suppose he painted to him the life that a young man could lead in London on such an income. I am sure he made it very alluring. It availed nothing. All George asked was five pounds a week to be able to continue his studies and to be left alone. He was indifferent to the position that he might some day enjoy. He didn't want to hunt. He didn't want to shoot. He didn't want to be a Member of Parliament. He didn't want to be a millionaire. He didn't want to be a baronet. He didn't want to be a peer. Ferdy left him defeated and in a state of considerable exasperation.

After dinner that evening there was a battle royal. Freddy was a quick-tempered man, unused to opposition, and he gave George the rough side of his tongue. I gather that it was very rough indeed. The women who sought to restrain his violence were sternly silenced. Perhaps for the first time in his life Freddy would not listen to his mother. George was obstinate and sullen. He had made up his mind and if his father didn't like it he could lump it. Freddy was peremptory. He forbade George to go back to Germany. George answered that he was twenty-one and his own master. He would go where he chose. Freddy swore he would not give him a penny.

"All right, I'll earn money."

"You! You've never done a stroke of work in your life. What do you expect to do to earn money?"

"Sell old clothes," grinned George.

There was a gasp from all of them. Muriel was so taken aback that she said a stupid thing.

"Like a Jew?"

"Well, aren't I a Jew? And aren't you a Jewess and isn't daddy a Jew? We're all Jews, the whole gang of us, and everyone knows it and what the hell's the good of pretending we're not?"

Then a very dreadful thing happened. Freddy burst suddenly into tears. I'm afraid he didn't behave very much like Sir Adolphus Bland,

Bart, MP, and the good old English gentleman he so much wanted to be, but like an emotional Adolf Bleikogel who loved his son and wept with mortification because the great hopes he had set on him were brought to nothing and the ambition of his life was frustrated. He cried noisily with great loud sobs and pulled his beard and beat his breast and rocked to and fro. Then they all began to cry, old Lady Bland and Muriel, and Ferdy, who sniffed and blew his nose and wiped the tears streaming down his face, and even George cried. Of course it was very painful, but to our rough Anglo-Saxon temperament I am afraid it must seem also a trifle ridiculous. No one tried to console anybody else. They just sobbed and sobbed. It broke up the party.

But it had no result on the situation. George remained obdurate. His father would not speak to him. There were more scenes. Muriel sought to excite his pity; he was deaf to her piteous entreaties, he did not seem to mind if he broke her heart, he did not care two hoots if he killed his father. Ferdy appealed to him as a sportsman and a man of the world. George was flippant and indeed personally offensive. Old Lady Bland with her guttural German accent and strong common sense argued with him, but he would not listen to reason. It was she, however, who at last found a way out. She made George acknowledge that it was no use to throw away all the beautiful things the world laid at his feet unless he had talent. Of course he thought he had, but he might be mistaken. It was not worth while to be a second-rate pianist. His only excuse, his only justification, was genius. If he had genius his family had no right to stand in his way.

"You can't expect me to show genius already," said George. "I shall have to work for years."

"Are you sure you are prepared for that?"

"It's my only wish in the world. I'll work like a dog. I only want to be given my chance."

This was the proposition she made. His father was determined to give him nothing and obviously they could not let the boy starve. He had mentioned five pounds a week. Well, she was willing to give him that herself. He could go back to Germany and study for two years. At the end of that time he must come back and they would get some competent and disinterested person to hear him play, and if then that person said he showed promise of becoming a first-rate pianist no further obstacles would be placed in his way. He would be given every advantage, help, and encouragement. If on the other hand that person decided that his natural gifts were not such as to ensure ultimate success he must promise faithfully to give up all thoughts of making music his profession and in every way accede to his father's wishes. George could hardly believe his ears.

"Do you mean that, Granny?"

"I do."

"But will daddy agree?"

"I vill see dat he does," she answered.

George seized her in his arms and impetuously kissed her on both cheeks.

"Darling," he cried.

"An, but de promise?"

He gave her his solemn word of honour that he would faithfully abide by the terms of the arrangement. Two days later he went back to Germany. Though his father consented unwillingly to his going, and indeed could not help doing so, he would not be reconciled to him and when he left refused to say good-bye to him.

I imagine that in no manner could he have caused himself such pain. I permit myself a trite remark. It is strange that men, inhabitants for so short a while of an alien and inhuman world, should go out of their way to cause themselves so much unhappiness.

George had stipulated that during his two years of study his family should not visit him, so that when Muriel heard some months before he was due to come home that I was passing through Munich on my way to Vienna, whither business called me, it was not unnatural that she should ask me to look him up. She was anxious to have first-hand information about him. She gave me George's address and I wrote ahead, telling him I was spending a day in Munich, and asked him to lunch with me. His answer awaited me at the hotel. He said he worked all day and could not spare the time to lunch with me, but if I would come to his studio about six he would like to show me that and if I had nothing better to do would love to spend the evening with me. So soon after six I went to the address he gave me. He lived on the second floor of a large block of flats and when I came to his door I heard the sound of piano-playing. It stopped when I rang and

George opened the door for me. I hardly recognized him. He had grown very fat. His hair was extremely long, it curled all over his head in picturesque confusion; and he had certainly not shaved for three days. He wore a grimy pair of Oxford bags, a tennis shirt, and slippers. He was not very clean and his finger-nails were rimmed with black. It was a startling change from the spruce, slim youth so elegantly dressed in such beautiful clothes that I had last seen. I could not but think it would be a shock to Ferdy to see him now. The studio was large and bare; on the walls were three or four unframed canvases of a highly cubist nature, there were several arm-chairs much the worse for wear, and a grand piano. Books were littered about and old newspapers and art magazines. It was dirty and untidy and there was a frowzy smell of stale beer and stale smoke.

"Do you live here alone?" I asked.

"Yes, I have a woman who comes in twice a week and cleans up. But I make my own breakfast and lunch."

"Can you cook?"

"Oh, I only have bread and cheese and a bottle of beer for lunch. I dine at a *Bierstube*."

It was pleasant to discover that he was very glad to see me. He seemed in great spirits and extremely happy. He asked after his relations and we talked of one thing and another. He had a lesson twice a week and for the rest of the time practised. He told me that he worked ten hours a day.

"That's a change," I said.

He laughed.

"Daddy said I was born tired. I wasn't really lazy. I didn't see the use of working at things that bored me."

I asked him how he was getting on with the piano. He seemed to be satisfied with his progress and I begged him to play to me.

"Oh, not now, I'm all in, I've been at it all day. Let's go out and dine and come back here later and then I'll play. I generally go to the same place, there are several students I know there, and it's rather fun."

Presently we set out. He put on socks and shoes and a very old golf coat, and we walked together through the wide quiet streets. It was a brisk cold day. His step was buoyant. He looked round him with a sigh of delight.

"I love Munich," he said. "It's the only city in the world where there's art in the very air you breathe. After all, art is the only thing that matters, isn't it? I loathe the idea of going home."

"All the same I'm afraid you'll have to."

"I know. I'll go all right, but I'm not going to think about it till the time comes."

"When you do, you might do worse than get a haircut. If you don't mind my saying so you look almost too artistic to be convincing."

"You English, you're such Philistines," he said.

He took me to a rather large restaurant in a side street, crowded even at that early hour with people dining, and furnished heavily in the German medieval style. A table covered with a red cloth, well away from the air, was reserved for George and his friends and when we went to it four or five youths were at it. There was a Pole studying Oriental languages, a student of philosophy, a painter (I suppose the author of George's cubist pictures), a Swede, and a young man who introduced himself to me, clicking his heels, as Hans Reiting, *Dichter*, namely Hans Reiting, poet. Not one of them was more than twenty-two and I felt a trifle out of it. They all addressed George as *du* and I noticed that his German was extremely fluent. I had not spoken it for some time and mine was rusty, so that I could not take much part in the lively conversation. But nevertheless I thoroughly enjoyed myself. They ate sparingly, but drank a good deal of beer. They talked of art and women. They were very revolutionary and, though gay, very much in earnest. They were contemptuous of everyone you had ever heard of, and the only point on which they all agreed was that in this topsy-turvy world only the vulgar could hope for success. They argued points of technique with animation, and contradicted one another, and shouted and were obscene. They had a grand time.

At about eleven George and I walked back to his studio. Munich is a city that frolics demurely and except about the Marienplatz the streets were still and empty. When we got in he took off his coat and said:

"Now I'll play to you."

I sat in one of the dilapidated arm-chairs and a broken spring stuck into my behind, but I made myself as comfortable as I could. George played Chopin. I know very little of music and that is one of the reasons for which I have found this story difficult to write. When I go to a concert at the Queen's Hall and in the intervals read the programme it is all Greek to me. I know nothing of harmony and counterpoint. I shall never forget how humiliated I felt once when, having come to Munich for a Wagner Festival, I went to a wonderful performance of *Tristan und Isolde* and never heard a note of it. The first few bars sent me off and I began to think of what I was writing, my characters leapt into life and I heard their long conversations, I suffered their pains and was a party to their joy; the years swept by and all sorts of things happened to me, the spring brought me its rapture and in the winter I was cold and hungry; and I loved and I hated and I died. I suppose there were intervals in which I walked round and round the garden and probably ate *Schinken-Brödchen* and drank beer, but I have no recollection of them. The only thing I know is that when the curtain for the last time fell I woke with a start. I had had a wonderful time, but I could not help thinking it was very stupid of me to come such a long way and spend so much money if I couldn't pay attention to what I heard and saw.

I knew most of the things George played. They were the familiar pieces of concert programmes. He played with a great deal of dash. Then he played Beethoven's *Appassionata*. I used to play it myself when I played the piano (very badly) in my far distant youth and I still knew every note of it. Of course it is a classic and a great work, it would be foolish to deny it, but I confess that at this time of day it leaves me cold. It is like *Paradise Lost*, splendid, but a trifle stolid. This too George played with vigour. He sweated profusely. At first I could not make out what was the matter with his playing, something did not seem to me quite right, and then it struck me that the two hands did not exactly synchronize, so that there was ever so slight an interval between the bass and the treble; but I repeat, I am ignorant of these things; what disconcerted me might have been merely the effect of his having drunk a good deal of beer that evening or indeed only my fancy. I said all I could think of to praise him.

"Of course I know I need a lot more work. I'm only a beginner, but I know I can do it. I feel it in my bones. It'll take me ten years, but then I shall be a pianist."

He was tired and came away from the piano. It was after midnight and I suggested going, but he would not hear of it. He opened a couple of bottles of beer and lit his pipe. He wanted to talk.

"Are you happy here?" I asked him.

"Very," he answered gravely. "I'd like to stay for ever. I've never had such fun in my life. This evening, for instance. Wasn't it grand?"

"It was very jolly. But one can't go on leading the student's life. Your friends here will grow older and go away."

"Others'll come. There are always students here and people like that."

"Yes, but you'll grow older too. Is there anything more lamentable than the middle-aged man who tries to go on living the undergraduate's life? The old fellow who wants to be a boy among boys, and tries to persuade himself that they'll accept him as one of themselves – how ridiculous he is. It can't be done."

"I feel so at home here. My poor father wants me to be an English gentleman. It gives me goose-flesh. I'm not a sportsman. I don't care a damn for hunting and shooting and playing cricket. I was only acting."

"You gave a very natural performance."

"It wasn't till I came here that I knew it wasn't real. I loved Eton, and Oxford was a riot, but all the same I knew I didn't belong. I played the part all right, because acting's in my blood, but there was always something in me that wasn't satisfied. The house in Grosvenor Square is a freehold and daddy paid a hundred and eighty thousand pounds for Tilby; I don't know if you understand what I mean, I felt they were just furnished houses we'd taken for the season and one of these days we'd pack up and the real owners would come back."

I listened to him attentively, but I wondered how much he was describing what he had obscurely felt and how much he imagined now in his changed circumstances that he had felt.

"I used to hate hearing great-uncle Ferdy tell his Jewish stories. I thought it so damned mean. I understand now; it was a safety valve. My God, the strain of being a man about town. It's easier for daddy, he can play the old English squire at Tilby, but in the City he can be himself. He's all right. I've taken the make-up off and my stage clothes and at last I can be my real self too. What a relief! You know, I don't like English people. I never really know where I am with you. You're so dull and conventional. You never let yourselves go. There's no freedom in you, freedom of the soul, and you're such funks. There's nothing in the world you're so frightened of as doing the wrong thing."

"Don't forget that you're English yourself, George," I murmured. He laughed.

"I? I'm not English. I haven't got a drop of English blood in me. I'm a Jew and you know it, and a German Jew into the bargain. I don't want to be English. I want to be a Jew. My friends are Jews. You don't know how much more easy I feel with them. I can be myself. We did everything we could to avoid Jews at home; mummy, because she was blonde, thought she could get away with it and pretended she was a Gentile. What rot! D'you know, I have a lot of fun wandering about the Jewish parts of Munich and looking at the people. I went to Frankfort once, there are a lot of them there, and I walked about and looked at the frowzy old men with their hooked noses and the fat women with their false hair. I felt such a sympathy for them, I felt I belonged to them, I could have kissed them. When they looked at me I wondered if they knew that I was one of them. I wish to God I knew Yiddish. I'd like to become friends with them, and go into their houses and eat Kosher food and all that sort of thing. I wanted to go to a synagogue, but I was afraid I'd do the wrong thing and be kicked out. I like the smell of the Ghetto and the sense of life, and the mystery and the dust and the squalor and the romance. I shall never get the longing for it out of my head now. That's the real thing. All the rest is only pretence."

"You'll break your father's heart," I said.

"It's his or mine. Why can't he let me go? There's Harry. Harry would love to be squire of Tilby. He'd be an English gentleman all right. You know, mummy's set her heart on my marrying a Christian. Harry would love to. He'll found the good old English family all right. After all, I ask so little. I only want five pounds a week, and they can keep the title and the park and the Gainsboroughs and the whole bag of tricks."

"Well, the fact remains that you gave your solemn word of honour to go back after two years."

"I'll go back all right," he said sullenly. "Lea Makart has promised to come and hear me play."

"What'll you do if she says you're no good?"

"Shoot myself," he said gaily.

"What nonsense," I answered in the same tone.

"Do *you* feel at home in England?"

"No," I said, "but then I don't feel at home anywhere else."

But he was quite naturally not interested in me.

"I loathe the idea of going back. Now that I know what life has to offer I wouldn't be an English country gentleman for anything in the world. My God, the boredom of it!"

"Money's a very nice thing and I've always understood it's very pleasant to be an English peer."

"Money means nothing to me. I want none of the things it can buy, and I don't happen to be a snob."

It was growing very late and I had to get up early next day. It seemed unnecessary for me to pay too much attention to what George said. It was the sort of nonsense a young man might very well indulge in when thrown suddenly among painters and poets. Art is strong wine and needs a strong head to carry it. The divine fire burns most efficiently in those who temper its fury with horse sense. After all, George was not twenty-three yet. Time teaches. And when all was said and done his future was no concern of mine. I bade him good night and walked back to my hotel. The stars were shining in the indifferent sky. I left Munich in the morning.

I did not tell Muriel on my return to London what George had said to me, or what he looked like, but contented myself with assuring her that he was well and happy, working very hard, and seemed to be leading a virtuous and sober life. Six months later he came home. Muriel asked me to go down to Tilby for the week-end; Ferdy was bringing Lea Makart to hear George play and he particularly wished me to be there. I accepted. Muriel met me at the station.

"How did you find George?" I asked.

"He's very fat, but he seems in great spirits. I think he's pleased to be back again. He's been very sweet to his father."

"I'm glad of that."

"Oh, my dear, I do hope Lea Makart will say he's no good. It'll be such a relief to all of us."

"I'm afraid it'll be a terrible disappointment to him."

"Life is full of disappointments." said Muriel crisply. "But one learns to put up with them."

I gave her a smile of amusement. We were sitting in a Rolls, and there was a footman as well as a chauffeur on the box. She wore a string of pearls that had probably cost forty thousand pounds. I recollected that in the birthday honours Sir Adolphus Bland had not been one of the three gentlemen on whom the King had been pleased to confer a peerage.

Lea Makart was able to make only a flying visit. She was playing that evening at Brighton and would motor over to Tilby on the Sunday morning for luncheon. She was returning to London the same day because she had a concert in Manchester on the Monday. George was to play in the course of the afternoon.

"He's practising very hard," his mother told me. "That's why he didn't come with me to meet you."

We turned in at the park gates and drove up the imposing avenue of elms that led to the house. I found that there was no party.

I met the dowager Lady Bland for the first time. I had always been curious to see her. I had had in my mind's eye a somewhat sensational picture of an old, old Jewish woman who lived alone in her grand house in Portland Place, and, with a finger in every pie, ruled her family with a despotic hand. She did not disappoint me. She was of commanding presence, rather tall, and stout without being corpulent. Her countenance was markedly Hebraic. She wore a rather heavy moustache and a wig of a peculiarly metallic brown. Her dress was very grand, of black brocade, and she had a row of large diamond stars on her breast and round her neck a chain of diamonds. Diamond rings gleamed on her wrinkled hands. She spoke in a rather harsh voice and with a strong German accent. When I was introduced to her she fixed me with shining eyes. She summed me up with despatch and to my fancy at all events made no attempt to conceal from me that the judgement she formed was unfavourable.

"You have known my brother Ferdinand for many years, is it not so?" she said, rolling a guttural R. "My brother Ferdinand has always moved in very good society. Where is Sir Adolphus, Muriel? Does he know your guest is arrived? And will you not send for George? If he does not know his pieces by now he will not know them by tomorrow."

Muriel explained that Freddy was finishing a round of golf with his secretary and that she had had George told I was there. Lady Bland looked as though she thought Muriel's replies highly unsatisfactory and turned again to me.

"My daughter-in-law tells me you have been in Italy?"

"Yes, I've only just come back."

"It is a beautiful country. How is the King?"

I said I did not know.

"I used to know him when he was a little boy. He was not very strong then. His mother, Queen Margherita, was a great friend of mine. They thought he would never marry. The Duchess of Aosta was very angry when he fell in love with that Princess of Montenegro."

She seemed to belong to some long-past period of history, but she was very alert and I imagine that little escaped her beady eyes. Freddy, very spruce in plus-fours, presently came in. It was amusing and yet a little touching to see this grey-bearded man, as a rule somewhat domineering, so obviously on his best behaviour with the old lady. He called her Mamma. Then George came in. He was as fat as ever, but he had taken my advice and had his hair cut; he was losing his boyish looks, but he was a powerful and well-set-up young man. It was good to see the pleasure he took in his tea. He ate quantities of sandwiches and great hunks of cake. He had still a boy's appetite. His father watched him with a tender smile and as I looked at him I could not be surprised at the attachment which they all so obviously felt for him. He had an ingenuousness, a charm, and an enthusiasm which were certainly very pleasant. There was about him a generosity of demeanour, a frankness, and a natural cordiality which could not but make people take to him. I do not know whether it was owing to a hint from his grandmother or merely of his own good nature, but it was plain that he was going out of his way to be nice to his father; and in his father's soft eyes, in the way he hung upon the boy's words, in his pleased, proud, and happy look, you felt how bitterly the estrangement of the last two years had weighed on him. He adored George.

★ ★ ★

We played golf in the morning, a three-ball match, since Muriel, having to go to Mass, could not join us, and at one Ferdy arrived in Lea Makart's car. We sat down to luncheon. Of course Lea Makart's reputation was well known to me. She was acknowledged to be the greatest woman pianist in Europe. She was a very old friend of Ferdy's, who with his interest and patronage had greatly helped her at the beginning of her career, and it was he who had arranged for her to come and give her opinion of George's chances. At one time I went as often as I could to hear her play. She had no affectations; she played as a bird sings, without any appearance of effort, very naturally, and the silvery notes dripped from her light fingers in a curiously spontaneous manner, so that it gave you the impression that she was improvising those complicated rhythms. They used to tell me that her technique was wonderful. I could never make up my mind how much the delight her playing gave me was due to her person. In those days she was the most ethereal thing you could imagine, and it was surprising that a creature so sylphlike should be capable of so much power. She was very slight, pale, with enormous eyes and magnificent black hair, and at the piano she had a child-like wistfulness that was most appealing. She was very beautiful in a hardly human way and when she played, a little smile on her closed lips, she seemed to be remembering things she had heard in another world. Now, however, a woman in the early forties, she was sylphlike no more; she was stout and her face had broadened; she had no longer that lovely remoteness, but the authority of her long succession of triumphs. She was brisk, business-like, and somewhat overwhelming. Her vitality lit her with a natural spotlight as his sanctity surrounds the saint with a halo. She was not interested in anything very much but her own affairs, but since she had humour and knew the world she was able to invest them with gaiety. She held the conversation, but did not absorb it. George talked little. Every now and then she gave him a glance, but did not try to draw him in. I was the only Gentile at the table. All but old Lady Bland spoke perfect English, yet I could not help feeling that they did not speak like English people; I think they rounded their vowels more than we do, they certainly spoke louder, and the words seemed not to fall, but to gush from their lips. I think if I had been in another room where I could hear the tone but not the words of their speech I should have thought it was in a foreign language that they were conversing. The effect was slightly disconcerting.

Lea Makart wished to set out for London at about six, so it was arranged that George should play at four. Whatever the result of the audition, I felt that I, a stranger in the circle which her departure must render exclusively domestic, would be in the way and so, pretending an early engagement in town next morning, I asked her if she would take me with her in her car.

At a little before four we all wandered into the drawing-room. Old Lady Bland sat on a sofa with Ferdy; Freddy, Muriel, and I made ourselves comfortable in arm-chairs; and Lea Makart sat by herself. She chose instinctively a high-backed Jacobean chair that had somewhat the air of a throne, and in a yellow dress, with her olive skin, she looked very handsome. She had magnificent eyes. She was very much made up and her mouth was scarlet.

George gave no sign of nervousness. He was already seated at the piano when I went in with his father and mother, and he watched us quietly settling ourselves down. He gave me the shadow of a smile. When he saw that we were all at our ease he began to play. He played Chopin. He played two waltzes that were familiar to me, a polonaise and an *étude*. He played with a great deal of brio. I wish I knew music well enough to give an exact description of his playing. It had strength, and a youthful exuberance, but I felt that he missed what to me is the peculiar charm of Chopin, the tenderness, the nervous melancholy, the wistful gaiety and the slightly faded romance that reminds me always of an Early Victorian keepsake. And again I had the vague sensation, so slight that it almost escaped me, that the two hands did not quite synchronize. I looked at Ferdy and saw him give his sister a look of faint surprise. Muriel's eyes were fixed on the pianist, but presently she dropped them and for the rest of the time stared at the floor. His father looked at him too, and his eyes were steadfast, but unless I was much mistaken he went pale and his face betrayed something like dismay. Music was in the blood of all of them, all their lives they had heard the greatest pianists in the world, and they judged with instinctive precision. The only person whose face betrayed no emotion was Lea Makart. She listened very attentively. She was as still as an image in a niche.

At last he stopped and turning round on his seat faced her. He did not speak.

"What is it you want me to tell you?" she asked.

They looked into one another's eyes.

"I want you to tell me whether I have any chance of becoming in time a pianist in the first rank."

"Not in a thousand years."

For a moment there was dead silence. Freddy's head sank and he looked down at the carpet at his feet. His wife put out her hand and took his. But George continued to look steadily at Lea Makart.

"Ferdy has told me the circumstances," she said at last. "Don't think I'm influenced by them. Nothing of this is very important." She made a great sweeping gesture that took in the magnificent room with the beautiful things it contained and all of us. "If I thought you had in you the makings of an artist I shouldn't hesitate to beseech you to give up everything for art's sake. Art is the only thing that matters. In comparison with art, wealth and rank and power are not worth a straw." She gave us a look so sincere that it was void of insolence. "We are the only people who count. We give the world significance. You are only our raw material."

I was not too pleased to be included with the rest under that heading, but that is neither here nor there.

"Of course I can see that you've worked very hard. Don't think it's been wasted. It will always be a pleasure to you to be able to play the piano and it will enable you to appreciate great playing as no ordinary person can hope to do. Look at your hands. They're not a pianist's hands."

Involuntarily I glanced at George's hands. I had never noticed them before. I was astounded to see how podgy they were and how short and stumpy the fingers.

"Your ear is not quite perfect. I don't think you can ever hope to be more than a very competent amateur. In art the difference between the amateur and the professional is immeasurable."

George did not reply. Except for his pallor no one would have known that he was listening to the blasting of all his hopes. The silence that fell was quite awful. Lea Makart's eyes suddenly filled with tears.

"But don't take my opinion alone," she said. "After all, I'm not infallible. Ask somebody else. You know how good and generous Paderewski is. I'll write to him about you and you can go down and play to him. I'm sure he'll hear you."

George now gave a little smile. He had very good manners and whatever he was feeling did not want to make the situation too difficult for others.

"I don't think that's necessary, I am content to accept your verdict. To tell you the truth it's not so very different from my master's in Munich."

He got up from the piano and lit a cigarette. It eased the strain. The others moved a little in their chairs. Lea Makart smiled at George.

"Shall I play to you?" she said.

"Yes, do."

She got up and went to the piano. She took off the rings with which her fingers were laden. She played Bach. I do not know the names of the pieces, but I recognized the stiff ceremonial of the frenchified little German courts and the sober, thrifty comfort of the burghers, and the dancing on the village green, the green trees that looked like Christmas trees, and the sunlight on the wide German country, and a tender cosiness; and in my nostrils there was a warm scent of the soil and I was conscious of a sturdy strength that seemed to have its roots deep in mother earth, and of an elemental power that was timeless and had no home in space. She played beautifully, with a soft brilliance that made you think of the full moon shining at dusk in the summer sky. With another part of me I watched the others and I saw how intensely they were conscious of the experience. They were rapt. I wished with all my heart that I could get from music the wonderful exaltation that possessed them. She stopped, a smile hovered on her lips, and she put on her rings. George gave a little chuckle.

"That clinches it, I fancy," he said.

The servants brought in tea and after tea Lea Makart and I bade the company farewell and got into the car. We drove up to London. She talked all the way, if not brilliantly at all events with immense gusto; she told me of her early years in Manchester and of the struggle of her beginnings. She was very interesting. She never even mentioned George; the episode was of no consequence, it was finished and she thought of it no more.

We little knew what was happening at Tilby. When we left George went out on the terrace and presently his father joined him. Freddy had won the day, but he was not happy. With his more than feminine sensitiveness he felt all that George was feeling, and George's anguish simply broke his heart. He had never loved his son more than then. When he appeared George greeted him with a little smile. Freddy's voice broke. In a sudden and overwhelming emotion he found it in him to surrender the fruits of his victory.

"Look here, old boy," he said, "I can't bear to think that you've had such a disappointment. Would you like to go back to Munich for another year and then see?"

George shook his head.

"No, it wouldn't be any good. I've had my chance. Let's call it a day."

"Try not to take it too hard."

"You see, the only thing in the world I want is to be a pianist. And there's nothing doing. It's a bit thick if you come to think of it."

George, trying so hard to be brave, smiled wanly.

"Would you like to go round the world? You can get one of your Oxford pals to go with you and I'll pay all the expenses. You've been working very hard for a long time."

"Thanks awfully, daddy, we'll talk about it. I'm just going for a stroll now."

"Shall I come with you?"

"I'd rather go alone."

Then George did a strange thing. He put his arm round his father's neck, and kissed him on the lips. He gave a funny little moved laugh and walked away. Freddy went back to the drawing-room. His mother, Ferdy, and Muriel were sitting there.

"Freddy, why don't you marry the boy?" said the old lady. "He is twenty-three. It would take his mind off his troubles and when he is married and has a baby he will soon settle down like everybody else."

"Whom is he to marry, mamma?" asked Sir Adolphus, smiling.

"That's not so difficult. Lady Frielinghausen came to see me the other day with her daughter Violet. She is a very nice maiden and she will have money of her own. Lady Frielinghausen gave me to understand that her Sir Jacob would come down very handsome if Violet made a good match."

Muriel flushed.

"I hate Lady Frielinghausen. George is much too young to marry. He can afford to marry anyone he likes."

Old Lady Bland gave her daughter a strange look.

"You are a very foolish girl, Miriam," she said, using the name Muriel had long discarded. "As long as I am here I shall not allow you to commit a foolishness."

She knew as well as if Muriel had said it in so many words that she wanted George to marry a Gentile, but she knew also that so long as she was alive neither Freddy nor his wife would dare to suggest it.

But George did not go for a walk. Perhaps because the shooting season was about to open he took it into his head to go into the gun-room. He began to clean the gun that his mother had given him on his twentieth birthday. No one had used it since he went to Germany. Suddenly the servants were startled by a report. When they went into the gun-room they found George lying on the floor shot through the heart. Apparently the gun had been loaded and George while playing about with it had accidentally shot himself. One reads of such accidents in the paper often.

VIRTUE

THERE ARE FEW things better than a good Havana. When I was young and very poor and smoked a cigar only when somebody gave me one, I determined that if ever I had money I would smoke a cigar every day after luncheon and after dinner. This is the only resolution of my youth that I have kept. It is the only ambition I have achieved that has never been embittered by disillusion. I like a cigar that is mild, but full-flavoured, neither so small that it is finished before you have become aware of it nor so large as to be irksome, rolled so that it draws without consciousness of effort on your part, with a leaf so firm that it doesn't become messy on your lips, and in such condition that it keeps its savour to the very end. But when you have taken the last pull and put down the shapeless stump and watched the final cloud of smoke dwindle blue in the surrounding air it is impossible, if you have a sensitive nature, not to feel a certain melancholy at the thought of all the labour, the care and pains that have gone, the thought, the trouble, the complicated organization that have been required to provide you with half an hour's delight. For this men have sweltered long years under tropical suns and ships have scoured the seven seas. These reflections become more poignant still when you are eating a dozen oysters (with half a bottle of dry white wine), and they become almost unbearable when it comes to a lamb cutlet. For these are animals and there is something that inspires awe in the thought that since the surface of the earth became capable of supporting life from generation to generation for millions upon millions of years creatures have come into exist-ence to end at last upon a plate of crushed ice or on a silver grill. It may be that a sluggish fancy cannot grasp the dreadful solemnity of eating an oyster and evolution has taught us that the bivalve has through the ages kept itself to itself in a manner that inevitably alienates sympathy. There is an aloofness in it that is offensive to the aspiring spirit of man and a self-complacency that is obnoxious to his vanity. But I do not know how anyone can look upon a lamb cutlet without thoughts too deep for tears: here man himself has taken a hand and the history of the race is bound up with the tender morsel on your plate.

And sometimes even the fate of human beings is curious to consider. It is strange to look upon this man or that, the quiet ordinary persons of every day, the bank clerk, the dustman, the middle-aged girl in the second row of the chorus, and think of the interminable history behind them and of the long, long series of hazards by which from the primeval slime the course of events has brought them at this moment to such and such a place. When such tremendous vicissitudes have been needed to get them here at all one would have thought some huge significance must be attached to them; one would have thought that what befell them must matter a little to the Life Spirit or whatever else it is that has produced them. An accident befalls them. The thread is broken. The story that began with the world is finished abruptly and it looks as though it meant nothing at all. A tale told by an idiot. And is it not odd that this event, of an importance so dramatic, may be brought about by a cause so trivial?

An incident of no moment, that might easily not have happened, has consequences that are incalculable. It looks as though blind chance ruled all things. Our smallest actions may affect profoundly the whole lives of people who have nothing to do with us. The story I have to tell would never have happened if one day I had not walked across the street. Life is really very fantastic and one has to have a peculiar sense of humour to see the fun of it.

I was strolling down Bond Street one spring morning and having nothing much to do till lunch-time thought I would look in at Sotheby's, the auction rooms, to see whether there was anything on show that interested me. There was a block in the traffic and I threaded my way through the cars. When I reached the other side I ran into a man I had known in Borneo coming out of a hatter's.

"Hullo, Morton," I said. "When did you come home?"

"I've been back about a week."

He was a District Officer. The Governor had given me a letter of introduction to him and I wrote and told him I meant to spend a week at the place he lived at and should like to put up at the government rest-house. He met me on the ship when I arrived and asked me to stay with him. I demurred. I did not see how I could spend a week with a total stranger, I did not want to put him to the expense of my board, and besides I thought I should have more freedom if I were on my own. He would not listen to me.

"I've got plenty of room," he said, "and the rest-house is beastly. I haven't spoken to a white man for six months and I'm fed to the teeth with my own company."

But when Morton had got me and his launch had landed us at the bungalow and he had offered me a drink he did not in the least know what to do with me. He was seized on a sudden with shyness, and his conversation, which had been fluent and ready, ran dry. I did my best to make him feel at home (it was the least I could do, considering that it was his own house) and asked him if he had any new records. He turned on the gramophone and the sound of ragtime gave him confidence.

His bungalow overlooked the river and his living-room was a large veranda. It was furnished in the impersonal fashion that characterized the dwellings of government officials who were moved here and there at little notice according to the exigencies of the service. There were native hats as ornaments on the walls and the horns of animals, blow-pipes, and spears. In the book-shelf were detective novels and old magazines. There was a cottage piano with yellow keys. It was very untidy, but not uncomfortable.

Unfortunately I cannot very well remember what he looked like. He was young, twenty-eight, I learnt later, and he had a boyish and attractive smile. I spent an agreeable week with him. We went up and down the river and we climbed a mountain. We had tiffin one day with some planters who lived twenty miles away and every evening we went to the club. The only members were the manager of a kutch factory and his assistants, but they were not on speaking terms with one another and it was only on Morton's representations that they must not let him down when he had a visitor that we could get up a rubber of bridge. The atmosphere was strained. We came back to dinner, listened to the gramophone, and went to bed. Morton had little office work and one would have thought the time hung heavy on his hands, but he had energy and high spirits; it was his first post of the sort and he was happy to be independent. His only anxiety was lest he should be transferred before he had finished a road he was building. This was the joy of his heart. It was his own idea and he had wheedled the government into giving him the money to make it; he had surveyed the country himself and traced the path. He had solved unaided the technical problems that presented themselves. Every morning, before he went to his office, he drove out in a rickety old Ford to where the coolies were working and watched the progress that had been made since the day before. He thought of nothing else. He dreamt of it at night. He reckoned that it would be finished in a year and he did not want to take his leave till then. He could not have worked with more zest if he had been a painter or a sculptor creating a work of art. I think it was this eagerness that made me take a fancy to him. I liked his zeal. I liked his ingenuousness. And I was impressed by the passion for achievement that made him indifferent to the solitariness of his life, to promotion, and even to the thought of going home. I forget how long the road was, fifteen or twenty miles, I think, and I forget what purpose it was to serve. I don't believe Morton cared very much. His passion was the artist's and his triumph was the triumph of man over nature. He learnt as he went along. He had the jungle to contend against, torrential rains that destroyed the labour of weeks, accidents of topography; he had to collect his labour and hold it together; he had inadequate funds. His imagination sustained him. His labours gained a sort of epic quality and the vicissitudes of the work were a great saga that unrolled itself with an infinity of episodes.

His only complaint was that the day was too short. He had office duties, he was judge and tax collector, father and mother (at twenty-eight) of the people in his district; he had now and then to make tours that took him away from home. Unless he was on the spot nothing was done. He would have liked to be there twenty-four hours a day driving the reluctant coolies to further effort. It so happened that shortly before I arrived an incident had occurred that filled him with jubilation. He had offered a contract to a Chinese to make a certain section of the road and the Chinese had asked more than Morton could afford to pay. Notwithstanding interminable discussions they had been unable to arrive at an agreement and Morton with rage in his heart saw his work held up. He was at his wits' end. Then going down to his office one morning, he heard that there had been a row in one of the Chinese gambling houses the night before. A coolie had been badly wounded and his assailant was under arrest. This assailant was the contractor. He was brought into court, the evidence was clear, and Morton sentenced him to eighteen months' hard labour.

"Now he'll have to build the blasted road for nothing," said Morton, his eyes glistening when he told me the story.

We saw the fellow at work one morning, in the prison sarong, unconcerned. He was taking his misfortune in good part.

"I've told him I'll remit the rest of his sentence when the road's finished," said Morton, "and he's as pleased as Punch. Bit of a snip for me, eh, what?"

When I left Morton I asked him to let me know when he came to England and he promised to write to me as soon as he landed. On the spur of the moment one gives these invitations and one is perfectly sincere about them. But when one is taken at one's word a slight dismay seizes one. People are so different at home from what they are abroad. There they are easy, cordial, and natural. They have interesting things to tell you. They are immensely kind. You are anxious when your turn comes to do something in return for the hospitality you have received. But it is not easy. The persons who were so entertaining in their own surroundings are very dull in yours. They are constrained and shy. You introduce them to your friends and your friends find them a crashing bore. They do their best to be civil, but sigh with relief when the strangers go and the conversation can once more run easily in its accustomed channels. I think the residents in far places early in their careers understand the situation pretty well, as the result maybe of bitter and humiliating experiences, for I have found that they seldom take advantage of the invitation which on some outstation on the edge of the jungle has been so cordially extended to them and by them as cordially accepted. But Morton was different. He was a young man and single. It is generally the wives that are the difficulty; other women look at their drab clothes, in a glance take in their provincial air, and freeze them with their indifference. But a man can play bridge and tennis, and dance. Morton had charm. I had had no doubt that in a day or two he would find his feet.

"Why didn't you let me know you were back?" I asked him.

"I thought you wouldn't want to be bothered with me," he smiled.

"What nonsense!"

Of course now as we stood in Bond Street on the kerb and chatted for a minute he looked strange to me. I had never seen him in anything but khaki shorts and tennis shirt, except when we got back from the club at night and he put on a pyjama jacket and a sarong for dinner. It is as comfortable a form of evening dress as has ever been devised. He looked a bit awkward in his blue serge suit. His face against a white collar was very brown.

"How about the road?" I asked him.

"Finished. I was afraid I'd have to postpone my leave, we struck one or two snags towards the end, but I made 'em hustle and the day before I left I drove the Ford to the end and back without stopping."

I laughed. His pleasure was charming.

"What have you been doing with yourself in London?"

"Buying clothes."

"Been having a good time?"

343

"Marvellous. A bit lonely, you know, but I don't mind that. I've been to a show every night. The Palmers, you know, I think you met them in Sarawak, were going to be in town and we were going to do the play together, but they had to go to Scotland because her mother's ill."

His words, said so breezily, cut me to the quick. His was the common experience. It was heartbreaking. For months, for long months before it was due, these people planned their leave, and when they got off the ship they were in such spirits they could hardly contain themselves. London. Shops and clubs and theatres and restaurants. London. They were going to have the time of their lives. London. It swallowed them. A strange turbulent city, not hostile but indifferent, and they were lost in it. They had no friends. They had nothing in common with the acquaintances they made. They were more lonely than in the jungle. It was a relief when at a theatre they ran across someone they had known in the East (and perhaps been bored stiff by or disliked) and they could fix up an evening together and have a good laugh and tell one another what a grand time they were having and talk of common friends and at last confide to one another a little shyly that they would not be sorry when their leave was up and they were once again in harness. They went to see their families and of course they were glad to see them, but it wasn't the same as it had been, they did feel a bit out of it, and when you came down to brass tacks the life people led in England was deadly. It was grand fun to come home, but you couldn't live there any more, and sometimes you thought of your bungalow overlooking the river and your tours of the district and what a lark it was to run over once in a blue moon to Sandakan or Kuching or Singapore.

And because I remembered what Morton had looked forward to when, the road finished and off his chest, he went on leave, I could not but feel a pang when I thought of him dining by himself in a dismal club where he knew nobody or alone in a restaurant in Soho and then going off to see a play with no one by his side with whom he could enjoy it and no one to have a drink with during the interval. And at the same time I reflected that even if I had known he was in London I could have done nothing much for him, for during the last week I had not had a moment free. That very evening I was dining with friends and going to a play, and the next day I was going abroad.

"What are you doing tonight?" I asked him.

"I'm going to the Pavilion. It's packed jammed full, but there's a fellow over the road who's wonderful and he's got me a ticket that had been returned. You can often get one seat, you know, when you can't get two."

"Why don't you come and have supper with me? I'm taking some people to the Haymarket and we're going on to Ciro's afterwards."

"I'd love to."

We arranged to meet at eleven and I left him to keep an engagement.

I was afraid the friends I had asked him to meet would not amuse Morton very much, for they were distinctly middle-aged, but I could not think of anyone young that at this season of the year I should be likely to get hold of at the last moment. None of the girls I knew would thank me for asking her to supper to dance with a shy young man from Malaya. I could trust the Bishops to do their best for him, and after all it must be jollier for him to have supper in a club with a good band where he could see pretty women dancing than to go home to bed at eleven because he had nowhere else in the world to go. I had known Charlie Bishop first when I was a medical student. He was then a thin fellow with sandy hair and blunt features; he had fine eyes, dark and gleaming, but he wore spectacles. He had a round, merry, red face. He was very fond of the girls. I suppose he had a way with him, for, with no money and no looks, he managed to pick up a succession of young persons who gratified his roving desires. He was clever and bumptious, argumentative and quick-tempered. He had a caustic tongue. Looking back, I should say he was a rather disagreeable young man, but I do not think he was a bore. Now, half-way through the fifties, he was inclined to be stout and he was very bald, but his eyes behind the gold-rimmed spectacles were still bright and alert. He was dogmatic and somewhat conceited, argumentative still and caustic, but he was good-natured and amusing. After you have known a person so long his idiosyncrasies cease to trouble you. You accept them as you accept your own physical defects. He was by profession a pathologist and now and then he sent me a slim book he had just published. It was severe and extremely technical and grimly illustrated with photographs of bacteria. I did not read it. I gathered from what I sometimes heard that Charlie's views on the subjects with which he dealt were unsound. I do not believe that he was very popular with the other members of his profession, he made no secret of the fact that he looked upon them as a set of incompetent idiots; but he had his job, it brought him in six or eight hundred a year, I think, and he was completely indifferent to other people's opinion of him.

I liked Charlie Bishop because I had known him for thirty years, but I liked Margery, his wife, because she was very nice. I was extremely surprised when he told me he was going to be married. He was hard on forty at the time and so fickle in his affections that I had made up my mind he would remain single. He was very fond of women, but he was not in the least sentimental, and his aims were loose. His views on the female sex would in these idealistic days be thought crude. He knew what he wanted and he asked for it, and if he couldn't get it for love or money he shrugged his shoulders and went his way. To be brief, he did not look to women to gratify his ideal but to provide him with fornication. It was odd that though small and plain he found so many who were prepared to grant his wishes. For his spiritual needs he found satisfaction in unicellular organisms. He had always been a man who spoke to the point, and when he told me he was going to marry a young woman called Margery Hobson I did not hesitate to ask him why. He grinned.

"Three reasons. First, she won't let me go to bed with her without. Second, she makes me laugh like a hyena. And third, she's alone in the world, without a single relation, and she must have someone to take care of her."

"The first reason is just swank and the second is eyewash. The third is the real one and it means that she's got you by the short hairs."

His eyes gleamed softly behind his large spectacles.

"I shouldn't be surprised if you weren't dead right."

"She's not only got you by the short hairs but you're as pleased as Punch that she has."

"Come and lunch tomorrow and have a look at her. She's easy on the eye."

Charlie was a member of a cock-and-hen club which at that time I used a good deal and we arranged to lunch there. I found Margery a very attractive young woman. She was then just under thirty. She was a lady. I noticed the fact with satisfaction, but with a certain astonishment, for it had not escaped my notice that Charlie was attracted as a rule by women whose breeding left something to be desired. She was not beautiful, but comely, with fine dark hair and fine eyes, a good colour and a look of health. She had a pleasant frankness and an air of candour that were very taking. She looked honest, simple, and dependable. I took an immediate liking to her. She was easy to talk to and though she did not say anything very brilliant she understood what other people were talking about; she was quick to see a joke and she was not shy. She gave you the impression of being competent and business-like. She had a happy placidity that suggested a good temper and an excellent digestion.

They seemed extremely pleased with one another. I had asked myself when I first saw her why Margery was marrying this irritable little man, baldish already and by no means young, but I discovered very soon that it was because she was in love with him. They chaffed one another a good deal and laughed a lot and every now and then their eyes met more significantly and they seemed to exchange a little private message. It was really rather touching.

A week later they were married at a registrar's office. It was a very successful marriage. Looking back now after sixteen years I could not but chuckle sympathetically at the thought of the lark they had made of their life together. I had never known a more devoted couple. They had never had very much money. They never seemed to want any. They had no ambitions. Their life was a picnic that never came to an end. They lived in the smallest flat I ever saw, in Panton Street, a small bedroom, a small sitting-room, and a bathroom that served also as a kitchen. But they had no sense of home, they ate their meals in restaurants, and only had breakfast in the flat. It was merely a place to sleep in. It was comfortable, though a third person coming in for a whisky and soda crowded it, and Margery with the help of a char-woman kept it as neat as Charlie's untidiness permitted, but there was not a single thing in it that had a personal note. They had a tiny car and whenever Charlie had a holiday they took it across the Channel and started off, with a bag each for all their luggage, to drive wherever the fancy took them. Breakdowns never disturbed them, bad weather was part of the fun, a puncture was no end of a joke, and if they lost their way and had to sleep out in the open they thought they were having the time of their lives.

Charlie continued to be irascible and contentious, but nothing he did ever disturbed Margery's lovely placidity. She could calm him with a word. She still made him laugh. She typed his monographs on obscure bacteria and corrected the proofs of his articles in the scientific magazines. Once I asked them if they ever quarrelled.

"No," she said, "we never seem to have anything to quarrel about. Charlie has the temper of an angel."

"Nonsense," I said, "he's an overbearing, aggressive, and can-tankerous fellow. He always has been."

She looked at him and giggled and I saw that she thought I was being funny.

"Let him rave," said Charlie. "He's an ignorant fool and he uses words of whose meaning he hasn't the smallest idea."

They were sweet together. They were very happy in one another's company and were never apart if they could help it. Even after the long time they had been married Charlie used to get into the car every day at luncheon-time to come west and meet Margery at a restaurant. People used to laugh at them, not unkindly, but perhaps with a little catch in the throat, because when they were asked to go and spend a week-end in the country Margery would write to the hostess and say they would like to come if they could be given a double bed. They had slept together for so many years that neither of them could sleep alone. It was often a trifle awkward. Husbands and wives as a rule not only demanded separate rooms, but were inclined to be peevish if asked to share the same bathroom. Modern houses were not arranged for domestic couples, but among their friends it became an understood thing that if you wanted the Bishops you must give them a room with a double bed. Some people of course thought it a little indecent, and it was never convenient, but they were a pleasant pair to have to stay and it was worth while to put up with their crankiness. Charlie was always full of spirits and in his caustic way extremely amusing, and Margery was peaceful and easy. They were no trouble to entertain. Nothing pleased them more than to be left to go out together for a long ramble in the country.

When a man marries, his wife sooner or later estranges him from his old friends, but Margery on the contrary increased Charlie's intimacy with them. By making him more tolerant she made him a more agreeable companion. They gave you the impression not of a married couple, but, rather amusingly, of two middle-aged bachelors living together; and when Margery, as was the rule, found herself the only woman among half a dozen men, ribald, argumentative, and gay, she was not a bar to good-fellowship but an asset. Whenever I was in England I saw them. They generally dined at the club of which I have spoken and if I happened to be alone I joined them.

When we met that evening for a snack before going to the play I told them I had asked Morton to come to supper.

"I'm afraid you'll find him rather dull," I said. "But he's a very decent sort of boy and he was awfully kind to me when I was in Borneo."

"Why didn't you let me know sooner?" cried Margery. "I'd have brought a girl along."

"What do you want a girl for?" said Charlie. "There'll be you."

"I don't think it can be much fun for a young man to dance with a woman of my advanced years," said Margery.

"Rot. What's your age got to do with it?" He turned to me. "Have you ever danced with anyone who danced better?"

I had, but she certainly danced very well. She was light on her feet and she had a good sense of rhythm.

"Never," I said heartily.

Morton was waiting for us when we reached Ciro's. He looked very sunburned in his evening clothes. Perhaps it was because I knew that they had been wrapped away in a tin box with mothballs for four years that I felt he did not look quite at home in them. He was certainly more at ease in khaki shorts. Charlie Bishop was a good talker and liked to hear himself speak. Morton was shy. I gave him a cocktail and ordered some champagne. I had a feeling that he would be glad to dance, but was not quite sure whether it would occur to him to ask Margery. I was acutely conscious that we all belonged to another generation.

"I think I should tell you that Mrs Bishop is a beautiful dancer," I said.

"Is she?" He flushed a little. "Will you dance with me?"

She got up and they took the floor. She was looking peculiarly nice that evening, not at all smart, and I do not think her plain black dress had cost more than six guineas, but she looked a lady. She had the advantage of having extremely good legs and at that time skirts were still being worn very short. I suppose she had a little make-up on, but in contrast with the other women there she looked very natural. Shingled hair suited her; it was not even touched with white and it had an attractive sheen. She was not a pretty woman, but her kindliness, her wholesome air, her good health gave you, if not the illusion that she was, at least the feeling that it didn't at all matter. When she came back to the table her eyes were bright and she had a heightened colour.

"How does he dance?" asked her husband.

"Divinely."

"You're very easy to dance with," said Morton.

Charlie went on with his discourse. He had a sardonic humour and he was interesting because he was himself so interested in what he said. But he spoke of things that Morton knew nothing about and though he listened with a civil show of interest I could see that he was too much excited by the gaiety of the scene, the music, and the champagne to give his attention to conversation. When the music struck up again his eyes immediately sought Margery's. Charlie caught the look and smiled.

"Dance with him, Margery. Good for my figure to see you take exercise."

They set off again and for a moment Charlie watched her with fond eyes.

"Margery's having the time of her life. She loves dancing and it makes me puff and blow. Not a bad youth."

My little party was quite a success and when Morton and I, having taken leave of the Bishops, walked together towards Piccadilly Circus he thanked me warmly. He had really enjoyed himself. I said good-bye to him. Next morning I went abroad.

I was sorry not to have been able to do more for Morton and I knew that when I returned he would be on his way back to Borneo. I gave him a passing thought now and then, but by the autumn when I got home he had slipped my memory. After I had been in London a week or so I happened to drop in one night at the club to which Charlie Bishop also belonged. He was sitting with three or four men

I knew and I went up. I had not seen any of them since my return. One of them, a man called Bill Marsh, whose wife, Janet, was a great friend of mine, asked me to have a drink.

"Where have you sprung from?" asked Charlie. "Haven't seen you about lately."

I noticed at once that he was drunk. I was astonished. Charlie had always liked his liquor, but he carried it well and never exceeded. In years gone by, when we were very young, he got tight occasionally, but probably more than anything to show what a great fellow he was, and it is unfair to bring up against a man the excesses of his youth. But I remembered that Charlie had never been very nice when he was drunk: his natural aggressiveness was exaggerated then and he talked too much and too loud; he was very apt to be quarrelsome. He was very dogmatic now, laying down the law and refusing to listen to any of the objections his rash statements called forth. The others knew he was drunk and were struggling between the irritation his cantankerousness aroused in them and the good-natured tolerance which they felt his condition demanded. He was not an agreeable object. A man of that age, bald and fattish, with spectacles, is disgusting drunk. He was generally rather dapper, but he was untidy now and there was tobacco ash all over him. Charlie called the waiter and ordered another whisky. The waiter had been at the club for thirty years.

"You've got one in front of you, sir."

"Mind your own damned business," said Charlie Bishop. "Bring me a double whisky right away or I'll report you to the secretary for insolence."

"Very good, sir," said the waiter.

Charlie emptied his glass at a gulp, but his hand was unsteady and he spilled some of the whisky over himself.

"Well, Charlie, old boy, we'd better be toddling along," said Bill Marsh. He turned to me. "Charlie's staying with us for a bit."

I was more surprised still. But I felt that something was wrong and thought it safer not to say anything.

"I'm ready," said Charlie. "I'll just have another drink before I go. I shall have a better night if I do."

It did not look to me as though the party would break up for some time, so I got up and announced that I meant to stroll home.

"I say," said Bill, as I was about to go, "you wouldn't come and dine with us tomorrow night, would you, just me and Janet and Charlie?"

"Yes, I'll come with pleasure," I said.

It was evident that something was up.

The Marshes lived in a terrace on the East side of Regent's Park. The maid who opened the door for me asked me to go in to Mr Marsh's study. He was waiting for me there.

"I thought I'd better have a word with you before you went upstairs," he said as he shook hands with me. "You know Margery's left Charlie?"

"No!"

"He's taken it very hard. Janet thought it was so awful for him alone in that beastly little flat that we asked him to stay here for a bit. We've done everything we could for him. He's been drinking like a fish. He hasn't slept a wink for a fortnight."

"But she hasn't left him for good?"

I was astounded.

"Yes. She's crazy about a fellow called Morton."

"Morton. Who's he?"

It never struck me it was my friend from Borneo.

"Damn it all, you introduced him and a pretty piece of work you did. Let's go upstairs. I thought I'd better put you wise."

He opened the door and we went out. I was thoroughly confused.

"But look here," I said.

"Ask Janet. She knows the whole thing. It beats me. I've got no patience with Margery, and he must be a mess."

He preceded me into the drawing-room. Janet Marsh rose as I entered and came forward to greet me. Charlie was sitting at the window, reading the evening paper; he put it aside as I went up to him and shook his hand. He was quite sober and he spoke in his usual rather perky manner, but I noticed that he looked very ill. We had a glass of sherry and went down to dinner. Janet was a woman of spirit. She was tall and fair and good to look at. She kept the conversation going with alertness. When she left us to drink a glass of port it was with instructions not to stay more than ten minutes. Bill, as a rule somewhat taciturn, exerted himself now to talk. I tumbled to the game. I was hampered by my ignorance of what exactly had happened, but it was plain that the Marshes wanted to prevent Charlie from brooding, and I did my best to interest him. He seemed willing to play his part, he was always fond of holding forth, and he discussed, from the pathologist's standpoint, a murder that was just then absorbing the public. But he spoke without life. He was an empty shell, and one had the feeling that though for the sake of his host he forced himself to speak, his thoughts were elsewhere. It was a relief when a knocking on the floor above indicated to us that Janet was getting impatient. This was an occasion when a woman's presence eased the situation. We went upstairs and played family bridge. When it was time for me to go Charlie said he would walk with me as far as the Marylebone Road.

"Oh, Charlie, it's so late, you'd much better go to bed," said Janet.

"I shall sleep better if I have a stroll before turning in," he replied.

She gave him a worried look. You cannot forbid a middle-aged professor of pathology from going for a little walk if he wants to. She glanced brightly at her husband.

"I daresay it'll do Bill no harm."

I think the remark was tactless. Women are often a little too managing. Charlie gave her a sullen look.

"There's absolutely no need to drag Bill out," he said with some firmness.

"I haven't the smallest intention of coming," said Bill, smiling. "I'm tired out and I'm going to hit the hay."

I fancy we left Bill Marsh and his wife to a little argument.

"They've been frightfully kind to me," said Charlie, as we walked along by the railings. "I don't know what I should have done without them. I haven't slept for a fortnight."

I expressed regret but did not ask the reason, and we walked for a little in silence. I presumed that he had come with me in order to talk to me of what had happened, but I felt that he must take his own time. I was anxious to show my sympathy, but afraid of saying the wrong things; I did not want to seem eager to extract confidences from him. I did not know how to give him a lead. I was sure he did not want one. He was not a man given to beating about the bush. I imagined that he was choosing his words. We reached the corner.

"You'll be able to get a taxi at the church," he said. "I'll walk on a bit further. Good night."

He nodded and slouched off. I was taken aback. There was nothing for me to do but to stroll on till I found a cab. I was having my bath next morning when a telephone call dragged me out of it, and with a towel round my wet body I took up the receiver. It was Janet.

"Well, what do you think of it all?" she said. "You seem to have kept Charlie up pretty late last night. I heard him come home at three."

"He left me at the Marylebone Road," I answered. "He said nothing to me at all."

"Didn't he?"

There was something in Janet's voice that suggested that she was prepared to have a long talk with me. I suspected she had a telephone by the side of her bed.

"Look here," I said quickly. "I'm having my bath."

"Oh, have you got a telephone in your bathroom?" she answered eagerly, and I think with envy.

"No, I haven't." I was abrupt and firm. "And I'm dripping all over the carpet."

"Oh!" I felt disappointment in her tone and a trace of irritation. "Well, when can I see you? Can you come here at twelve?"

It was inconvenient, but I was not prepared to start an argument.

"Yes, good-bye."

I rang off before she could say anything more. In heaven when the blessed use the telephone they will say what they have to say and not a word beside.

I was devoted to Janet, but I knew that there was nothing that thrilled her more than the misfortunes of her friends. She was only too anxious to help them, but she wanted to be in the thick of their difficulties. She was the friend in adversity. Other people's business was meat and drink to her. You could not enter upon a love affair without finding her somehow your confidante nor be mixed up in a divorce case without discovering that she too had a finger in the pie. Withal she was a very nice woman. I could not help then chuckling in my heart when at noon I was shown into Janet's drawing-room and observed the subdued eagerness with which she received me. She was very much upset by the catastrophe that had befallen the Bishops, but it was exciting, and she was tickled to death to have someone fresh whom she could tell all about it. Janet had just that business-like expectancy that a mother has when she is discussing with the family doctor her married daughter's first confinement. Janet was conscious that the matter was very serious, and she would not for a moment have been thought to regard it flippantly, but she was determined to get every ounce of value out of it.

"I mean, no one could have been more horrified than I was when Margery told me she'd finally made up her mind to leave Charlie," she said, speaking with the fluency of a person who has said the same thing in the same words a dozen times at least. "They were the most devoted couple I'd ever known. It was a perfect marriage. They got on like a house on fire. Of course Bill and I are devoted to one another, but we have awful rows now and then. I mean, I could kill him sometimes."

"I don't care a hang about your relations with Bill," I said. "Tell me about the Bishops. That's what I've come here for."

"I simply felt I must see you. After all you're the only person who can explain it."

"Oh, God, don't go on like that. Until Bill told me last night I didn't know a thing about it."

"That was my idea. It suddenly dawned on me that perhaps you didn't know and I thought you might put your foot in it too awfully."

"Supposing you began at the beginning," I said.

"Well, you're the beginning. After all you started the trouble. You introduced the young man. That's why I was so crazy to see you. You know all about him. I never saw him. All I know is what Margery has told me about him."

"At what time are you lunching?" I asked.

"Half past one."

"So am I. Get on with the story."

But my remark had given Janet an idea.

"Look here, will you get out of your luncheon if I get out of mine? We could have a snack here. I'm sure there's some cold meat in the house, and then we needn't hurry. I don't have to be at the hairdresser's till three."

"No, no, no," I said. "I hate the notion of that. I shall leave here at twenty minutes past one at the latest."

"Then I shall just have to race through it. What do you think of Gerry?"

"Who's Gerry?"

"Gerry Morton. His name's Gerald."

"How should I know that?"

"You stayed with him. Weren't there any letters lying about?"

"I daresay, but I didn't happen to read them," I answered somewhat tartly.

"Oh, don't be so stupid. I meant the envelopes. What's he like?"

"All right. Rather the Kipling type, you know. Very keen on his work. Hearty. Empire-builder and all that sort of thing."

"I don't mean that," cried Janet, not without impatience. "I mean, what does he look like?"

"More or less like everybody else, I think. Of course I should recognize him if I saw him again, but I can't picture him to myself very distinctly. He looks clean."

"Oh, my God," said Janet. "Are you a novelist or are you not? What's the colour of his eyes?"

"I don't know."

"You must know. You can't spend a week with anyone without knowing if their eyes are blue or brown. Is he fair or dark?"

"Neither."

"Is he tall or short?"

"Average, I should say."

"Are you trying to irritate me?"

"No. He's just ordinary. There's nothing in him to attract your attention. He's neither plain nor good-looking. He looks quite decent. He looks a gentleman."

"Margery says he has a charming smile and a lovely figure."

"I daresay."

"He's absolutely crazy about her."

"What makes you think that?" I asked dryly.

"I've seen his letters."

"Do you mean to say she's shown them to you?"

"Why, of course."

It is always difficult for a man to stomach the want of reticence that women betray in their private affairs. They have no shame. They will talk to one another without embarrassment of the most intimate matters. Modesty is a masculine virtue. But though a man may know this theoretically, each time he is confronted with women's lack of reserve he suffers a new shock. I wondered what Morton would think if he knew that not only were his letters read by Janet Marsh as well as by Margery, but that she had been kept posted from day to day with the progress of his infatuation. According to Janet he had fallen in love with Margery at first sight. The morning after they had met at my little supper party at Ciro's he had rung up and asked her to come and have tea with him at some place where they could dance. While I listened to Janet's story I was conscious of course that she was giving me Margery's view of the circumstances and I kept an open mind. I was interested to observe that Janet's sympathies were with Margery. It was true that when Margery left her husband it was her idea that Charlie should come to them for two or three weeks rather than stay on in miserable loneliness in the deserted flat and she had been extraordinarily kind to him. She lunched with him almost every day, because he had been accustomed to lunch every day with Margery; she took him for walks in Regent's Park and made Bill play golf with him on Sundays. She listened with wonderful patience to the story of his unhappiness and did what she could to console him. She was terribly sorry for him. But all the same she was definitely on Margery's side and when I expressed my disapproval of her she came down on me like a thousand of bricks. The affair thrilled her. She had been in it from the beginning when Margery, smiling, flattered, and a little doubtful, came and told her that she had a young man to the final scene when Margery, exasperated and distraught, announced that she could not stand the strain any more and had packed her things and moved out of the flat.

"Of course, at first I couldn't believe my ears," she said. "You know how Charlie and Margery were. They simply lived in one another's pockets. One couldn't help laughing at them, they were so devoted to one another. I never thought him a very nice little man and heaven knows he wasn't very attractive physically, but one couldn't help liking him because he was so awfully nice to Margery. I rather envied her sometimes. They had no money and they lived in a hugger-mugger sort of way, but they were frightfully happy. Of course I never thought anything would come of it. Margery was rather amused. 'Naturally I don't take it very seriously,' she told me, 'but it is rather fun to have a young man at my time of life. I haven't had any flowers sent me for years. I had to tell him not to send any more because Charlie would think it so silly. He doesn't know a soul in London and he loves dancing and he says I dance like a dream. It's miserable for him going to the theatre by himself all the time and we've done two or three matinées together. It's pathetic to see how grateful he is when I say I'll go out with him.' 'I must say,' I said, 'he sounds rather a lamb.' 'He is,' she said. 'I knew you'd understand. You don't blame me, do you?' 'Of course not, darling,' I said, 'surely you know me better than that. I'd do just the same in your place.' "

Margery made no secret of her outings with Morton and her husband chaffed her good-naturedly about her beau. But he thought him a very civil, pleasant-spoken young man and was glad that Margery had someone to play with while he was busy. It never occurred to him to be jealous. The three of them dined together several times and went to a show. But presently Gerry Morton begged Margery to spend an evening with him alone; she said it was impossible, but he was persuasive, he gave her no peace; and at last she went to Janet and asked her to ring up Charlie one day and ask him to come to dinner and make a fourth at bridge. Charlie would never go anywhere without his wife, but the Marshes were old friends, and Janet made a point of it. She invented some cock-and-bull story that made it seem important that he should consent. Next day Margery and she met. The evening had been wonderful. They had dined at Maidenhead and danced there and then had driven home through the summer night.

"He says he's crazy about me," Margery told her.

"Did he kiss you?" asked Janet.

"Of course," Margery chuckled. "Don't be silly, Janet. He is awfully sweet and, you know, he has such a nice nature. Of course I don't believe half the things he says to me."

"My dear, you're not going to fall in love with him."

"I have," said Margery.

"Darling, isn't it going to be rather awkward?"

"Oh, it won't last. After all he's going back to Borneo in the autumn."

"Well, one can't deny that it's made you look years younger."

"I know, and I feel years younger."

Soon they were meeting every day. They met in the morning and walked in the Park together or went to a picture gallery. They separated for Margery to lunch with her husband and after lunch met again and motored into the country or to some place on the river. Margery did not tell her husband. She very naturally thought he would not understand.

"How was it you never met Morton?" I asked Janet.

"Oh, she didn't want me to. You see, we belong to the same generation, Margery and I. I can quite understand that."

"I see."

"Of course I did everything I could. When she went out with Gerry she was always supposed to be with me."

I am a person who likes to cross a "t" and dot an "i".

"Were they having an affair?" I asked.

"Oh, no. Margery isn't that sort of woman at all."

"How do you know?"

"She would have told me."

"I suppose she would."

"Of course I asked her. But she denied it point-blank and I'm sure she was telling me the truth. There's never been anything of that sort between them at all."

"It seems rather odd to me."

"Well, you see, Margery is a very good woman."

I shrugged my shoulders.

"She was absolutely loyal to Charlie. She wouldn't have deceived him for anything in the world. She couldn't bear the thought of having any secret from him. As soon as she knew she was in love with Gerry she wanted to tell Charlie. Of course I begged her not to. I told her it wouldn't do any good and it would only make Charlie miserable. And after all, the boy was going away in a couple of months, it didn't seem much good to make a lot of fuss about a thing that couldn't possibly last."

But Gerry's imminent departure was the cause of the crash. The Bishops had arranged to go abroad as usual and proposed to motor through Belgium, Holland, and the North of Germany. Charlie was busy with maps and guides. He collected information from friends about hotels and roads. He looked forward to his holiday with the bubbling excitement of a schoolboy. Margery listened to him discussing it with a sinking heart. They were to be away four weeks and in September Gerry was sailing. She could not bear to lose so much of the short time that remained to them and the thought of the motor tour filled her with exasperation. As the interval grew shorter and shorter she grew more and more nervous. At last she decided that there was only one thing to do.

"Charlie, I don't want to come on this trip," she interrupted him suddenly, one day when he was talking to her of some restaurant he had just heard of. "I wish you'd get someone else to go with you."

He looked at her blankly. She was startled at what she had said and her lips trembled a little.

"Why, what's the matter?"

"Nothing's the matter. I don't feel like it. I want to be by myself for a bit."

"Are you ill?"

She saw the sudden fear in his eyes. His concern drove her beyond her endurance.

"No. I've never been better in my life. I'm in love."

"You? Whom with?"

"Gerry."

He looked at her in amazement. He could not believe his ears. She mistook his expression.

"It's no good blaming me. I can't help it. He's going away in a few weeks. I'm not going to waste the little time he has left."

He burst out laughing.

"Margery, how can you make such a damned fool of yourself? You're old enough to be his mother."

She flushed.

"He's just as much in love with me as I am with him."

"Has he told you so?"

"A thousand times."

"He's a bloody liar, that's all."

He chuckled. His fat stomach rippled with mirth. He thought it a huge joke. I daresay Charlie did not treat his wife in the proper way. Janet seemed to think he should have been tender and compassionate. *He should have understood.* I saw the scene that was in her mind's eye, the stiff upper lip, the silent sorrow, and the final renunciation. Women are always sensitive to the beauty of the self-sacrifice of others. Janet would have sympathized also if he had flown into a violent passion, broken one or two pieces of furniture (which he would have had to replace), or given Margery a sock in the jaw. But to laugh at her was unpardonable. I did not point out that it is very difficult for a rather stout and not very tall professor of pathology, aged fifty-five, to act all of a sudden like a cave-man. Anyhow, the excursion to Holland was given up and the Bishops stayed in London through August. They were not very happy. They lunched and dined together every day because they had been in the habit of doing so for so many years and the rest of the time Margery spent with Gerry. The hours she passed with him made up for all she had to put up with and she had to put up with a good deal. Charlie had a ribald and sarcastic humour and he made himself very funny at her expense and at Gerry's. He persisted in refusing to take the matter seriously. He was vexed with Margery for being so silly, but apparently it never occurred to him that she might have been unfaithful to him. I commented upon this to Janet.

"He never suspected it even," she said. "He knew Margery much too well."

The weeks passed and at last Gerry sailed. He went from Tilbury and Margery saw him off. When she came back she cried for forty-eight hours. Charlie watched her with increasing exasperation. His nerves were much frayed.

"Look here, Margery," he said at last, "I've been very patient with you, but now you must pull yourself together. This is getting past a joke."

"Why can't you leave me alone?" she cried. "I've lost everything that made life lovely to me."

"Don't be such a fool," he said.

I do not know what else he said. But he was unwise enough to tell her what he thought of Gerry and I gather that the picture he drew was virulent. It started the first violent scene they had ever had. She had borne Charlie's jibes when she knew that she would see Gerry in an hour or next day, but now that she had lost him for ever she could bear them no longer. She had held herself in for weeks: now she flung her self-control to the winds. Perhaps she never knew exactly what she said to Charlie. He had always been irascible and at last he hit her. They were both frightened when he had. He seized a hat and flung out of the flat. During all that miserable time they had shared the same bed, but when he came back, in the middle of the night, he found that she had made herself up a shake-down on the sofa in the sitting-room.

"You can't sleep there," he said. "Don't be so silly. Come to bed."

"No, I won't, let me alone."

For the rest of the night they wrangled, but she had her way and now made up her bed every night on the sofa. But in that tiny flat they could not get away from one another; they could not even get out of sight or out of hearing of one another. They had lived in such intimacy for so many years that it was an instinct for them to be together. He tried to reason with her. He thought her incredibly stupid and argued with her interminably in the effort to show her how wrong-headed she was. He could not leave her alone. He would not let her sleep, and he talked half through the night till they were both exhausted. He thought he could talk her out of love. For two or three days at a time they would not speak to one another. Then one day, coming home, he found her crying bitterly; the sight of her tears distracted him; he told her how much he loved her and sought to move her by the recollection of all the happy years they had spent together. He wanted to let bygones be bygones. He promised never to refer to Gerry again. Could they not forget the nightmare they had been through? But the thought of all that a reconciliation implied revolted her. She told him she had a racking headache and asked him to give her a sleeping draught. She pretended to be still asleep when he went out next morning, but the moment he was gone she packed up her things and left. She had a few trinkets that she had inherited and by selling them she got a little money. She took a room at a cheap boarding-house and kept her address a secret from Charlie.

It was when he found she had left him that he went all to pieces. The shock of her flight broke him. He told Janet that his loneliness was intolerable. He wrote to Margery imploring her to come back, and asked Janet to intercede for him; he was willing to promise anything; he abased himself. Margery was obdurate.

"Do you think she'll ever go back?" I asked Janet.

"She says not."

I had to leave then, for it was nearly half past one and I was bound for the other end of London.

Two or three days later I got a telephone message from Margery asking if I could see her. She suggested coming to my rooms. I asked her to tea. I tried to be nice to her; her affairs were no business of mine, but in my heart I thought her a very silly woman and I daresay my manner was cold. She had never been handsome and the passing years had changed her little. She had still those fine dark eyes and her face was astonishingly unlined. She was very simply dressed and if she wore make-up it was so cunningly put on that I did not perceive it. She had still the charm she had always had of perfect naturalness and of a kindly humour.

"I want you to do something for me if you will," she began without beating about the bush.

"What is it?"

"Charlie is leaving the Marshes today and going back to the flat. I'm afraid his first few days there will be rather difficult; it would be awfully nice of you if you'd ask him to dinner or something."

"I'll have a look at my book."

"I'm told he's been drinking heavily. It's such a pity. I wish you could give him a hint."

"I understand he's had some domestic worries of late," I said, perhaps acidly.

Margery flushed. She gave me a pained look. She winced as though I had struck her.

"Of course you've known him ever so much longer than you've known me. It's natural that you should take his part."

"My dear, to tell you the truth I've known him all these years chiefly on your account. I have never very much liked him, but I thought you were awfully nice."

She smiled at me and her smile was very sweet. She knew that I meant what I said.

"Do you think I was a good wife to him?"

"Perfect."

"He used to put people's backs up. A lot of people didn't like him, but I never found him difficult."

"He was awfully fond of you."

"I know. We had a wonderful time together. For sixteen years we were perfectly happy." She paused and looked down. "I had to leave him. It became quite impossible. That cat-and-dog life we were leading was too awful."

"I never see why two persons should go on living together if they don't want to."

"You see, it was awful for us. We'd always lived in such close intimacy. We could never get away from one another. At the end I hated the sight of him."

"I don't suppose the situation was easy for either of you."

"It wasn't my fault that I fell in love. You see, it was quite a different love from the one I'd felt for Charlie. There was always something maternal in that and protective. I was so much more reasonable than he was. He was unmanageable, but I could always manage him. Gerry was different." Her voice grew soft and her face was transfigured with glory. "He gave me back my youth. I was a girl to him and I could depend on his strength and be safe in his care."

"He seemed to me a very nice lad," I said slowly. "I imagine he'll do well. He was very young for the job he had when I ran across him. He's only twenty-nine now, isn't he?"

She smiled softly. She knew quite well what I meant.

"I never made any secret of my age to him. He says it doesn't matter."

I knew this was true. She was not the woman to have lied about her age. She had found a sort of fierce delight in telling him the truth about herself.

"How old are you?"

"Forty-four."

"What are you going to do now?"

"I've written to Gerry and told him I've left Charlie. As soon as I hear from him I'm going out to join him."

I was staggered.

"You know, it's a very primitive little colony he's living in. I'm afraid you'll find your position rather awkward."

"He made me promise that if I found my life impossible after he left I'd go to him."

"Are you sure you're wise to attach so much importance to the things a young man says when he's in love?"

Again that really beautiful look of exaltation came into her face.

"Yes, when the young man happens to be Gerry."

My heart sank. I was silent for a moment. Then I told her the story of the road Gerry Morton had built. I dramatized it, and I think I made it rather effective.

"What did you tell me that for?" she asked when I finished.

"I thought it rather a good story."

She shook her head and smiled.

"No, you wanted to show me that he was very young and enthusiastic, and so keen on his work that he hadn't much time to waste on other interests. I wouldn't interfere with his work. You don't know him as I do. He's incredibly romantic. He looks upon himself as a pioneer. I've caught from him something of his excitement at the idea of taking part in the opening up of a new country. It *is* rather splendid, isn't it? It makes life here seem very humdrum and commonplace. But of course it's very lonely there. Even the companionship of a middle-aged woman may be worth having."

"Are you proposing to marry him?" I asked.

"I leave myself in his hands. I want to do nothing that he does not wish."

She spoke with so much simplicity, there was something so touching in her self-surrender, that when she left me I no longer felt angry with her. Of course I thought her very foolish, but if the folly of men made one angry one would pass one's life in a state of chronic ire. I thought all would come right. She said Gerry was romantic. He was, but the romantics in this workaday world only get away with their nonsense because they have at bottom a shrewd sense of reality: the mugs are the people who take their vapourings at their face value. The English are romantic; that is why other nations think them hypocritical; they are not: they set out in all sincerity for the Kingdom of God, but the journey is arduous and they have reason to pick up any gilt-edged investment that offers itself by the way. The British soul, like Wellington's armies, marches on its belly. I supposed that Gerry would go through a bad quarter of an hour when he received Margery's letter. My sympathies were not deeply engaged in the matter and I was only curious to see how he would extricate himself from the pass he was in. I thought Margery would suffer a bitter disappointment; well, that would do her no great harm, and then she would go back to her husband and I had no doubt the pair of them, chastened, would live in peace, quiet, and happiness for the rest of their lives.

The event was different. It happened that it was quite impossible for me to make any sort of engagement with Charlie Bishop for some days, but I wrote to him and asked him to dine with me one evening in the following week. I proposed, though with misgiving, that we should go to a play; I knew he was drinking like a fish, and when tight he was noisy. I hoped he would not make a nuisance of himself in the theatre. We arranged to meet at our club and dine at seven because the piece we were going to began at a quarter past eight. I arrived. I waited. He did not come. I rang up his flat, but could get no reply, so concluded that he was on his way. I hate missing the beginning of a play and I waited impatiently in the hall so that when he came we could go straight upstairs. To save time I had ordered dinner. The clock pointed to half past seven, then a quarter to eight; I did not see why I should wait for him any longer, so walked up to the dining-room and ate my dinner alone. He did not appear. I put a call through from the dining-room to the Marshes and presently was told by a waiter that Bill Marsh was at the end of the wire.

"I say, do you know anything about Charlie Bishop?" I said. "We were dining together and going to a play and he hasn't turned up."

"He died this afternoon."

"What?"

My exclamation was so startled that two or three people within earshot looked up. The dining-room was full and the waiters were hurrying to and fro. The telephone was on the cashier's desk and a wine waiter came up with a bottle of hock and two long-stemmed glasses on a tray and gave the cashier a chit. The portly steward showing two men to a table jostled me.

"Where are you speaking from?" asked Bill.

I suppose he heard the clatter that surrounded me. When I told him he asked me if I could come round as soon as I had finished my dinner. Janet wanted to speak to me.

"I'll come at once," I said.

I found Janet and Bill sitting in the drawing-room. He was reading the paper and she was playing patience. She came forward swiftly when the maid showed me in. She walked with a sort of spring, crouching a little, on silent feet, like a panther stalking his prey. I saw at once that she was in her element. She gave me her hand and turned her face away to hide her eyes brimming with tears. Her voice was low and tragic.

"I brought Margery here and put her to bed. The doctor has given her a sedative. She's all in. Isn't it awful?" She gave a sound that was something between a gasp and a sob. "I don't know why these things always happen to me."

The Bishops had never kept a servant but a charwoman went in every morning, cleaned the flat, and washed up the breakfast things. She had her own key. That morning she had gone in as usual and done the sitting-room. Since his wife had left him Charlie's hours had been irregular and she was not surprised to find him asleep. But the time passed and she knew he had his work to go to. She went to the bedroom door and knocked. There was no answer. She thought she heard him groaning. She opened the door softly. He was lying in bed, on his back, and was breathing stertorously. He did not wake. She called him. Something about him frightened her. She went to the flat on the same landing. It was occupied by a journalist. He was still in bed when she rang, and opened the door to her in pyjamas.

"Beg pardon, sir," she said, "but would you just come and 'ave a look at my gentleman. I don't think he's well."

The journalist walked across the landing and into Charlie's flat. There was an empty bottle of veronal by the bed.

"I think you'd better fetch a policeman," he said.

A policeman came and rang through to the police station for an ambulance. They took Charlie to Charing Cross Hospital. He never recovered consciousness. Margery was with him at the end.

"Of course there'll have to be an inquest," said Janet. "But it's quite obvious what happened. He'd been sleeping awfully badly for the last three or four weeks and I suppose he'd been taking veronal. He must have taken an overdose by accident."

"Is that what Margery thinks?" I asked.

"She's too upset to think anything, but I told her I was positive he hadn't committed suicide. I mean, he wasn't that sort of a man. Am I right, Bill?"

"Yes, dear," he answered.

"Did he leave any letter?"

"No, nothing. Oddly enough Margery got a letter from him this morning, well, hardly a letter, just a line. 'I'm so lonely without you, darling.' That's all. But of course that means nothing and she's promised to say nothing about it at the inquest. I mean, what is the use of putting ideas in people's heads? Everyone knows that you never can tell with veronal, I wouldn't take it myself for anything in the world, and it was quite obviously an accident. Am I right, Bill?"

"Yes, dear," he answered.

I saw that Janet was quite determined to believe that Charlie Bishop had not committed suicide, but how far in her heart she believed what she wanted to believe I was not sufficiently expert in female psychology to know. And of course it might be that she was right. It is unreasonable to suppose that a middle-aged scientist should kill himself because his middle-aged wife leaves him and it is extremely plausible that, exasperated by sleeplessness, and in all probability far from sober, he took a larger dose of the sleeping-draught than he realized. Anyhow that was the view the coroner took of the matter. It was indicated to him that of late Charles Bishop had given way to habits of intemperance which had caused his wife to leave him, and it was quite obvious that nothing was further from his thoughts than to put an end to himself. The coroner expressed his sympathy with the widow and commented very strongly on the dangers of sleeping-draughts.

I hate funerals, but Janet begged me to go to Charlie's. Several of his colleagues at the hospital had intimated their desire to come, but at Margery's wish they were dissuaded; and Janet and Bill, Margery and I were the only persons who attended it. We were to fetch the hearse from the mortuary and they offered to call for me on their way. I was on the look-out for the car and when I saw it drive up went downstairs, but Bill got out and met me just inside the door.

"Half a minute," he said. "I've got something to say to you. Janet wants you to come back afterwards and have tea. She says it's no good Margery moping and after tea we'll play a few rubbers of bridge. Can you come?"

"Like this?" I asked.

I had a tail coat on and a black tie and my evening dress trousers.

"Oh, that's all right. It'll take Margery's mind off."

"Very well."

But we did not play bridge after all. Janet, with her fair hair, was very smart in her deep mourning and she played the part of the sympathetic friend with amazing skill. She cried a little, wiping her eyes delicately so as not to disturb the black on her eyelashes, and when Margery sobbed broken-heartedly put her arm tenderly through hers. She was a very present help in trouble. We returned to the house. There was a telegram for Margery. She took it and went upstairs. I presumed it was a message of condolence from one of Charlie's friends who had just heard of his death. Bill went to change and Janet and I went up to the drawing-room and got the bridge table out. She took off her hat and put it on the piano.

"It's no good being hypocritical," she said. "Of course Margery has been frightfully upset, but she must pull herself together now. A rubber of bridge will help her to get back to her normal state. Naturally I'm dreadfully sorry about poor Charlie, but as far as he was concerned I don't believe he'd ever have got over Margery's leaving him and one can't deny that it has made things much easier for her. She wired to Gerry this morning."

"What about?"

"To tell him about poor Charlie."

At that moment the maid came to the room.

"Will you go up to Mrs Bishop, please, ma'am? She wants to see you."

"Yes, of course."

She went out of the room quickly and I was left alone. Bill joined me presently and we had a drink. At last Janet came back.

She handed a telegram to me. It read as follows:

For God's sake await letter. Gerry

"What do you think it means?" she asked me.

"What it says," I replied.

"Idiot! Of course I've told Margery that it doesn't mean anything, but she's rather worried. It must have crossed her cable telling him that Charles was dead. I don't think she feels very much like bridge after all. I mean, it would be rather bad form to play on the very day her husband has been buried."

"Quite," I said.

"Of course he may wire in answer to the cable. He's sure to do that, isn't he? The only thing we can do now is to sit tight and wait for his letter."

I saw no object in continuing the conversation. I left. In a couple of days Janet rang me up to tell me that Margery had received a telegram of condolence from Morton. She repeated it to me:

Dreadfully distressed to hear sad news. Deeply
sympathize with your great grief. Love. Gerry

"What do you think of it?" she asked me.

"I think it's very proper."

"Of course he couldn't say he was as pleased as Punch, could he?"

"Not with any delicacy."

"And he did put in *love*."

I imagined how those women had examined the two telegrams from every point of view and scrutinized every word to press from it every possible shade of meaning. I almost heard their interminable conversations.

"I don't know what'll happen to Margery if he lets her down now," Janet went on. "Of course it remains to be seen if he's a gentleman."

"Rot," I said and rang off quickly.

In the course of the following days I dined with the Marshes a couple of times. Margery looked tired. I guessed that she awaited the letter that was on the way with sickening anxiety. Grief and fear had worn her to a shadow, she seemed very fragile now and she had acquired a spiritual look that I had never seen in her before. She was very gentle, very grateful for every kindness shown her, and in her smile, unsure and a little timid, was an infinite pathos. Her helplessness was very appealing. But Morton was several thousand miles away. Then one morning Janet rang me up.

"The letter has come. Margery says I can show it to you. Will you come round?"

Her tense voice told me everything. When I arrived Janet gave it to me. I read it. It was a very careful letter and I guessed that Morton had written it a good many times. It was very kind and he had evidently taken great pains to avoid saying anything that could possibly wound Margery; but what transpired was his terror. It was obvious that he was shaking in his shoes. He had felt apparently that the best way to cope with the situation was to be mildly facetious and he made very good fun of the white people in the colony. What would they say if Margery suddenly turned up? He would be given the order of the boot pretty damn quick. People thought the East was free and easy; it wasn't, it was more suburban than Clapham. He loved Margery far too much to bear the thoughts of those horrible women out there turning up their noses at her. And besides he had been sent to a station ten days from anywhere; she couldn't live in his bungalow exactly and of course there wasn't a hotel, and his work took him out into the jungle for days at a time. It was no place for a woman anyhow. He told her how much she meant to him, but she mustn't bother about him and he couldn't help thinking it would be better if she went back to her husband. He would never forgive himself if he thought he had come between her and Charlie. Yes, I am quite sure it had been a difficult letter to write.

"Of course he didn't know then that Charlie was dead. I've told Margery that changes everything."

"Does she agree with you?"

"I think she's being rather unreasonable. What do you make of the letter?"

"Well, it's quite plain that he doesn't want her."

"He wanted her badly enough two months ago."

"It's astonishing what a change of air and a change of scene will do for you. It must seem to him already like a year since he left London. He's back among his old friends and his old interests. My dear, it's no good Margery kidding herself; the life there has taken him back and there's no place for her."

"I've advised her to ignore the letter and go straight out to him."

"I hope she's too sensible to expose herself to a very terrible rebuff."

"But then what's to happen to her? Oh, it's too cruel. She's the best woman in the world. She has real goodness."

"It's funny if you come to think of it, it's her goodness that has caused all the trouble. Why on earth didn't she have an affair with Morton? Charlie would have known nothing about it and wouldn't have been a penny the worse. She and Morton could have had a grand time and when he went away they could have parted with the consciousness that a pleasant episode had come to a graceful end. It would have been a jolly recollection, and she could have gone back to Charlie satisfied and rested and continued to make him the excellent wife she had always been."

Janet pursed her lips. She gave me a look of disdain.

"There is such a thing as virtue, you know."

"Virtue be damned. A virtue that only causes havoc and unhappiness is worth nothing. You can call it virtue if you like. I call it cowardice."

"The thought of being unfaithful to Charlie while she was living with him revolted her. There are women like that, you know."

"Good gracious, she could have remained faithful to him in spirit while she was being unfaithful to him in the flesh. That is a feat of legerdemain that women find it easy to accomplish."

"What an odious cynic you are."

"If it's cynical to look truth in the face and exercise common sense in the affairs of life, then certainly I'm a cynic and odious if you like. Let's face it, Margery's a middle-aged woman, Charlie was fifty-five and they'd been married for sixteen years. It was natural enough that she should lose her head over a young man who made a fuss of her. But don't call it love. It was physiology. She was a fool to take anything he said seriously. It wasn't himself speaking, it was his starved sex, he'd suffered from sexual starvation, at least as far as white women are concerned, for four years; it's monstrous that she should seek to ruin his life by holding him to the wild promises he made then. It was an accident that Margery took his fancy; he wanted her, and because he couldn't get her wanted her more. I daresay he thought it love; believe me, it was only letch. If they'd gone to bed together Charlie would be alive today. It's her damned virtue that caused the whole trouble."

"How stupid you are. Don't you see that she couldn't help herself? She just doesn't happen to be a loose woman."

"I prefer a loose woman to a selfish one and a wanton to a fool."

"Oh, shut up. I didn't ask you to come here in order to make yourself absolutely beastly."

"What did you ask me to come here for?"

"Gerry is your friend. You introduced him to Margery. If she's in the soup it's on his account. But you are the cause of the whole trouble. It's your duty to write to him and tell him he must do the right thing by her."

"I'm damned if I will," I said.

"Then you'd better go."

I started to do so.

"Well, at all events it's a mercy that Charlie's life was insured," said Janet.

Then I turned on her.

"And you have the nerve to call me a cynic."

I will not repeat the opprobrious word I flung at her as I slammed the door behind me. But Janet is all the same a very nice woman. I often think it would be great fun to be married to her.

THE BUM

GOD KNOWS HOW often I had lamented that I had not half the time I needed to do half the things I wanted. I could not remember when last I had had a moment to myself. I had often amused my fancy with the prospect of just one week's complete idleness. Most of us when not busy working are busy playing; we ride, play tennis or golf, swim or gamble; but I saw myself doing nothing at all. I would lounge through the morning, dawdle through the afternoon, and loaf through the evening. My mind would be a slate and each passing hour a sponge that wiped out the scribblings written on it by the world of sense. Time, because it is so fleeting, time, because it is beyond recall, is the most precious of human goods and to squander it is the most delicate form of dissipation in which man can indulge. Cleopatra dissolved in wine a priceless pearl, but she gave it to

Antony to drink; when you waste the brief golden hours you take the beaker in which the gem is melted and dash its contents to the ground. The gesture is grand and like all grand gestures absurd. That of course is its excuse. In the week I promised myself I should naturally read, for to the habitual reader reading is a drug of which he is the slave; deprive him of printed matter and he grows nervous, moody, and restless; then, like the alcoholic bereft of brandy who will drink shellac or methylated spirit, he will make do with the advertisements of a paper five years old; he will make do with a telephone directory. But the professional writer is seldom a disinterested reader. I wished my reading to be but another form of idleness. I made up my mind that if ever the happy day arrived when I could enjoy untroubled leisure I would complete an enterprise that had always tempted me, but which hitherto, like an explorer making reconnaissances into an undiscovered country, I had done little more than enter upon: I would read the entire works of Nick Carter.

But I had always fancied myself choosing my moment with surroundings to my liking, not having it forced upon me; and when I was suddenly faced with nothing to do and had to make the best of it (like a steamship acquaintance whom in the wide waste of the Pacific Ocean you have invited to stay with you in London and who turns up without warning and with all his luggage) I was not a little taken aback. I had come to Vera Cruz from Mexico City to catch one of the Ward Company's white cool ships to Yucatan; and found to my dismay that, a dock strike having been declared overnight, my ship would not put in. I was stuck in Vera Cruz. I took a room in the Hotel Diligencias overlooking the *plaza*, and spent the morning looking at the sights of the town. I wandered down side streets and peeped into quaint courts. I sauntered through the Parish church; it is picturesque with its gargoyles and flying buttresses, and the salt wind and the blazing sun have patined its harsh and massive walls with the mellowness of age; its cupola is covered with white and blue tiles. Then I found that I had seen all that was to be seen and I sat down in the coolness of the arcade that surrounded the square and ordered a drink. The sun beat down on the *plaza* with a merciless splendour. The coco-palms drooped dusty and bedraggled. Great black buzzards perched on them for a moment uneasily, swooped to the ground to gather some bit of offal, and then with lumbering wings flew up to the church tower. I watched the people crossing the square; negroes, Indians, Creoles, and Spanish, the motley people of the Spanish Main; and they varied in colour from ebony to ivory. As the morning wore on, the tables around me filled up, chiefly with men, who had come to have a drink before luncheon, for the most part in white ducks, but some notwithstanding the heat in the dark clothes of professional respectability. A small band, a guitarist, a blind fiddler, and a harpist, played ragtime and after every other tune the guitarist came round with a plate. I had already bought the local paper and I was adamant to the newsvendors who pertinaciously sought to sell me more copies of the same sheet. I refused, oh, twenty times at least, the solicitations of grimy urchins who wanted to shine my spotless shoes; and having come to the end of my small change I could only shake my head at the beggars who importuned me. They gave one no peace. Little Indian women, in shapeless rags, each one with a baby tied in the shawl on her back, held out skinny hands and in a whimper recited a dismal screed; blind men were led up to my table by small boys; the maimed, the halt, the deformed exhibited the sores and the monstrosities with which nature or accident had afflicted them; and half naked, underfed children whined endlessly their demand for coppers. But these kept their eyes open for the fat policeman who would suddenly dart out on them with a thong and give them a sharp cut on the back or over the head. Then they would scamper, only to return again when, exhausted by the exercise of so much energy, he relapsed into lethargy.

But suddenly my attention was attracted by a beggar who, unlike the rest of them and indeed the people sitting round me, swarthy and black-haired, had hair and beard of a red so vivid that it was startling. His beard was ragged and his long mop of hair looked as though it had not been brushed for months. He wore only a pair of trousers and a cotton singlet, but they were tatters, grimy and foul, that barely held together. I have never seen anyone so thin; his legs, his naked arms were but skin and bone, and through the rents of his singlet you saw every rib of his wasted body; you could count the bones of his dust-covered feet. Of that starveling band he was easily the most abject. He was not old, he could not well have been more than forty, and I could not but ask myself what had brought him to this pass. It was absurd to think that he would not have worked if work he had been able to get. He was the only one of the beggars who did not speak. The rest of them poured forth their litany of woe and if it did not bring the alms they asked continued until an impatient word from you chased them away. He said nothing. I suppose he felt that his look of destitution was all the appeal he needed. He did not even hold out his hand, he merely looked at you, but with such wretchedness in his eyes, such despair in his attitude, it was dreadful; he stood on and on, silent and immobile, gazing steadfastly, and then, if you took no notice of him, he moved slowly to the next table. If he was given nothing he showed neither disappointment nor anger. If someone offered him a coin he stepped forward a little, stretched out his claw-like hand, took it without a word of thanks, and impassively went his way. I had nothing to give him and when he came to me, so that he should not wait in vain, I shook my head.

"*Dispense Usted por Dios*," I said, using the polite Castillian formula with which the Spaniards refuse a beggar.

But he paid no attention to what I said. He stood in front of me, for as long as he stood at the other tables, looking at me with tragic eyes. I have never seen such a wreck of humanity. There was something terrifying in his appearance. He did not look quite sane. At length he passed on.

It was one o'clock and I had lunch. When I awoke from my siesta it was still very hot, but towards evening a breath of air coming in through the windows which I had at last ventured to open tempted me into the *plaza*. I sat down under my arcade and ordered a long drink. Presently people in greater numbers filtered into the open space from the surrounding streets, the tables in the restaurants round it filled up, and in the kiosk in the middle the band began to play. The crowd grew thicker. On the free benches people sat huddled together like dark grapes clustered on a stalk. There was a lively hum of conversation. The big black buzzards flew screeching overhead, swooping down when they saw something to pick up, or scurrying away from under the feet of the passers-by. As twilight descended they swarmed, it seemed from all parts of the town, towards the church tower; they circled heavily about it and hoarsely crying, squabbling, and jangling, settled themselves uneasily to roost. And again bootblacks begged me to have my shoes cleaned, newsboys pressed dank papers upon me, beggars whined their plaintive demand for alms. I saw once more that strange, red-bearded fellow and watched him stand motionless, with the crushed and piteous air, before one table after another. He did not stop before mine. I supposed he remembered me from the morning and having failed to get anything from me then thought it useless to try again. You do not often see a red-haired Mexican, and because it was only in Russia that I had seen men of so destitute a mien I asked myself if he was by chance a Russian. It accorded well enough with the Russian feckless-ness that he should have allowed himself to sink to such a depth of degradation. Yet he had not a Russian face; his emaciated features were clear-cut, and his blue eyes were not set in the head in a Russian manner; I wondered if he could be a sailor, English, Scandinavian, or American, who had deserted his ship and by degrees sunk to this pitiful condition. He disappeared. Since there was nothing else to do, I stayed on till I got hungry, and when I had eaten came back. I sat on till the thinning crowd suggested it was bed-time. I confess that the day had seemed long and I wondered how many similar days I should be forced to spend there.

But I woke after a little while and could not get to sleep again. My room was stifling. I opened the shutters and looked out at the church. There was no moon, but the bright stars faintly lit its outline. The buzzards were closely packed on the cross above the cupola and on the edges of the tower, and now and then they moved a little. The effect was uncanny. And then, I have no notion why, that red scarecrow recurred to my mind and I had suddenly a strange feeling that I had seen him before. It was so vivid that it drove away from me the possibility of sleep. I felt sure that I had come across him, but when and where I could not tell. I tried to picture the surroundings in which he might take his place, but I could see no more than a dim figure against a background of fog. As the dawn approached it grew a little cooler and I was able to sleep.

I spent my second day at Vera Cruz as I had spent the first. But I watched for the coming of the red-haired beggar, and as he stood at the tables near mine I examined him with attention. I felt certain now that I had seen him somewhere. I even felt certain that I had known him and talked to him, but I still could recall none of the circumstances. Once more he passed my table without stopping and when his eyes met mine I looked in them for some gleam of recollection. Nothing. I wondered if I had made a mistake and thought I had seen him in the same way as sometimes, by some queer motion of the brain, in the act of doing something you are convinced that you are repeating an action that you have done at some past time. I could not get out of my head the impression that at some moment he had entered into my life. I racked my brains. I was sure now that he was either English or American. But I was shy of addressing him. I went over in my mind the possible occasions when I might have met him. Not to be able to place him exasperated me as it does when you try to remember a name that is on the tip of your tongue and yet eludes you. The day wore on.

Another day came, another morning, another evening. It was Sunday and the *plaza* was more crowded than ever. The tables under the arcade were packed. As usual the red-haired beggar came along, a terrifying figure in his silence, his threadbare rags, and his pitiful distress. He was standing in front of a table only two from mine, mutely beseeching, but without a gesture. Then I saw the policeman who at intervals tried to protect the public from the importunities of all these beggars sneak round a column and give him a resounding whack with his thong. His thin body winced, but he made no protest and showed no resentment; he seemed to accept the stinging blow as in the ordinary course of things, and with his slow movements slunk away into the gathering night of the plaza. But the cruel stripe had whipped my memory and suddenly I remembered.

Not his name, that escaped me still, but everything else. He must have recognized me, for I have not changed very much in twenty years, and that was why after that first morning he had never paused in front of my table. Yes, it was twenty years since I had known him. I was spending a winter in Rome and every evening I used to dine in a restaurant in the Via Sistina where you got excellent macaroni and a good bottle of wine. It was frequented by a little band of English and American art students, and one or two writers; and we used to stay late into the night engaged in interminable arguments upon art and literature. He used to come in with a young painter who was a friend of his. He was only a boy then, he could not have been more than twenty-two; and with his blue eyes, straight nose, and red hair he was pleasing to look at. I remembered that he spoke a great deal of Central America, he had had a job with the American Fruit

Company, but had thrown it over because he wanted to be a writer. He was not popular among us because he was arrogant and we were none of us old enough to take the arrogance of youth with tolerance. He thought us poor fish and did not hesitate to tell us so. He would not show us his work, because our praise meant nothing to him and he despised our censure. His vanity was enormous. It irritated us; but some of us were uneasily aware that it might perhaps be justified. Was it possible that the intense consciousness of genius that he had, rested on no grounds? He had sacrificed everything to be a writer. He was so certain of himself that he infected some of his friends with his own assurance.

I recalled his high spirits, his vitality, his confidence in the future, and his disinterestedness. It was impossible that it was the same man, and yet I was sure of it. I stood up, paid for my drink, and went out into the *plaza* to find him. My thoughts were in a turmoil. I was aghast. I had thought of him now and then and idly wondered what had become of him. I could never have imagined that he was reduced to this frightful misery. There are hundreds, thousands of youths who enter upon the hard calling of the arts with extravagant hopes; but for the most part they come to terms with their mediocrity and find somewhere in life a niche where they can escape starvation. This was awful. I asked myself what had happened. What hopes deferred had broken his spirit, what disappointments shattered him, and what lost illusions ground him to the dust? I asked myself if nothing could be done. I walked round the *plaza*. He was not in the arcades. There was no hope of finding him in the crowd that circled round the bandstand. The light was waning and I was afraid I had lost him. Then I passed the church and saw him sitting on the steps. I cannot describe what a lamentable object he looked. Life had taken him, rent him on its racks, torn him limb from limb, and then flung him, a bleeding wreck, on the stone steps of that church. I went up to him.

"Do you remember Rome?" I said.

He did not move. He did not answer. He took no more notice of me than if I were not standing before him. He did not look at me. His vacant blue eyes rested on the buzzards that were screaming and tearing at some object at the bottom of the steps. I did not know what to do. I took a yellow-backed note out of my pocket and pressed it in his hand. He did not give it a glance. But his hand moved a little, the thin claw-like fingers closed on the note and scrunched it up; he made it into a little ball and then edging it on to his thumb flicked it into the air so that it fell among the jangling buzzards. I turned my head instinctively and saw one of them seize it in his beak and fly off followed by two others screaming behind it. When I looked back the man was gone.

I stayed three more days in Vera Cruz. I never saw him again.

THE TREASURE

RICHARD HARENGER WAS a happy man. Notwithstanding what the pessimists, from Ecclesiastes onwards, have said, this is not so rare a thing to find in this unhappy world, but Richard Harenger knew it, and that is a very rare thing indeed. The golden mean which the ancients so highly prized is out of fashion, and those who follow it must put up with polite derision from those who see no merit in self-restraint and no virtue in common sense. Richard Harenger shrugged a polite and amused shoulder. Let others live dangerously, let others burn with a hard gemlike flame, let others stake their fortunes on the turn of a card, walk the tightrope that leads to glory or the grave, or hazard their lives for a cause, a passion, or an adventure. He neither envied the fame their exploits brought them nor wasted his pity on them when their efforts ended in disaster.

But it must not be inferred from this that Richard Harenger was a selfish or a callous man. He was neither. He was considerate and of a generous disposition. He was always ready to oblige a friend and he was sufficiently well off to be able to indulge himself in the pleasure of helping others. He had some money of his own and he occupied in the Home Office a position that brought him an adequate stipend. The work suited him. It was regular, responsible, and pleasant. Every day when he left the office he went to his club to play bridge for a couple of hours, and on Saturdays and Sundays he played golf. He went abroad for his holidays, staying at good hotels, and visited churches, galleries, and museums. He was a regular first-nighter.

He dined out a good deal. His friends liked him. He was easy to talk to. He was well-read, knowledgeable, and amusing. He was besides of a personable exterior, not remarkably handsome, but tall, slim, and erect of carriage, with a lean, intelligent face; his hair was growing thin, for he was now approaching the age of fifty, but his brown eyes retained their smile, and his teeth were all his own. He had from nature a good constitution and he had always taken care of himself. There was no reason in the world why he should not be a happy man, and if there had been in him a trace of self-complacency he might have claimed that he deserved to be.

He had the good fortune even to sail safely through those peril-ous, unquiet straits of marriage in which so many wise and good men have made shipwreck. Married for love in the early twenties, his wife and he, after some years of almost perfect felicity, had drifted grad-ually apart. Neither of them wished to marry anyone else, so there was no question of divorce (which indeed Richard Harenger's situation in the government service made undesirable), but for con-venience's sake, with the help of the family lawyer, they arranged a separation which left them free to lead their lives as each one wished without interference from the other. They parted with mutual expressions of respect and good will.

Richard Harenger sold his house in St John's Wood and took a flat within convenient walking distance of Whitehall. It had a sitting-room which he lined with his books, a dining-room into which his Chippendale furniture just fitted, a nice-sized bedroom for himself, and beyond the kitchen a couple of maids' rooms. He brought his cook, whom he had had for many years, from St John's Wood, but needing no longer so large a staff dismissed the rest of the servants and applied at a registry office for a house-parlourmaid. He knew exactly what he wanted and he explained his needs to the superintendent of the agency with precision. He wanted a maid who was not too young, first because young women are flighty and secondly because, though he was of mature age and a man of principle, people would talk, the porter and the tradesmen if nobody else, and both for the sake of his own reputation and that of the young person he con-sidered that the applicant should have reached years of discretion. Besides that he wanted a maid who could clean silver well. He had always had a fancy for old silver, and it was reasonable to demand that the forks and spoons that had been used by a woman of quality under the reign of Queen Anne should be treated with tenderness and respect. He was of a hospitable nature and liked to give at least once a week little dinners of not less than four people and not more than eight. He could trust his cook to send in a meal that his guests would take pleasure in eating and he desired his parlourmaid to wait with neatness and dispatch. Then he needed a perfect valet. He dressed well, in a manner that suited his age and condition, and he liked his clothes to be properly looked after. The parlourmaid he was looking for must be able to press trousers and iron a tie, and he was very particular that his shoes should be well shone. He had small feet and he took a good deal of trouble to have well-cut shoes. He had a large supply and he insisted that they should be treed up the moment he took them off. Finally the flat must be kept clean and tidy. It was of course understood that any applicant for the post must be of irreproachable character, sober, honest, reliable, and of a pleasing exterior. In return for this he was prepared to offer good wages, reasonable liberty, and ample holidays. The superintendent listened without batting an eyelash and, telling him that she was quite sure she could suit him, sent him a string of candidates which proved that she had not paid the smallest attention to a word he said. He saw them all personally. Some were obviously inefficient, some looked fast, some were too old, others too young, some lacked the presence he thought essential; there was not one to whom he was inclined even to give a trial. He was a kindly, polite man and he declined their services with a smile and a pleasant expression of regret. He did not lose patience. He was prepared to interview house-parlourmaids till he found one who was suitable.

Now it is a funny thing about life, if you refuse to accept anything but the best you very often get it: if you utterly decline to make do with what you can get, then somehow or other you are very likely to get what you want. It is as though fate said, this man's a perfect fool, he's asking for perfection, and then just out of her feminine wilfulness flung it in his lap. One day the porter of the flats said to Richard Harenger out of a blue sky:

"I hear you're lookin' for a house-parlourmaid, sir. There's someone I know lookin' for a situation as might do."

"Can you recommend her personally?"

Richard Harenger had the sound opinion that one servant's recommendation of another was worth much more than that of an employer.

"I can vouch for her respectability. She's been in some very good situations."

"I shall be coming in to dress about seven. If that's convenient to her I could see her then."

"Very good, sir. I'll see that she's told."

He had not been in more than five minutes when the cook, having answered a ring at the front door, came in and told him that the person the porter had spoken to him about had called.

"Show her in," he said.

He turned on some more light so that he could see what the applicant looked like and, getting up, stood with his back to the fireplace. A woman came in and stood just inside the door in a respectful attitude.

"Good evening," he said. "What is your name?"

"Pritchard, sir."

"How old are you?"

"Thirty-five, sir."

"Well, that's a reasonable age."

He gave his cigarette a puff and looked at her reflectively. She was on the tall side, nearly as tall as he, but he guessed that she wore high heels. Her black dress fitted her station. She held herself well. She had good features and a rather high colour.

"Will you take off your hat?" he asked.

She did so and he saw that she had pale brown hair. It was neatly and becomingly dressed. She looked strong and healthy. She was neither fat nor thin. In a proper uniform she would look very presentable. She was not inconveniently handsome, but she was certainly a comely, in another class of life you might almost have said a handsome, woman. He proceeded to ask her a number of questions. Her answers were satisfactory. She had left her last place for an adequate reason. She had been trained under a butler and appeared to be well acquainted with her duties. In her last place she had been head parlourmaid of three, but she did not mind undertaking the work of the flat single-handed. She had valeted a gentleman before who had sent her to a tailor's to learn how to press clothes. She was a little shy, but neither timid nor ill-at-ease. Richard asked her his questions in his amiable, leisurely way and she answered them with modest composure. He was considerably impressed. He asked her what references she could give. They seemed extremely satisfactory.

"Now look here," he said, "I'm very much inclined to engage you. But I hate changes, I've had my cook for twelve years: if you suit me and the place suits you I hope you'll stay. I mean, I don't want you to come to me in three or four months and say that you're leaving to get married."

"There's not much fear of that, sir. I'm a widow. I don't believe marriage is much catch for anyone in my position, sir. My husband never did a stroke of work from the day I married him to the day he died, and I had to keep him. What I want now is a good home."

"I'm inclined to agree with you," he smiled. "Marriage is a very good thing, but I think it's a mistake to make a habit of it."

She very properly made no reply to this, but waited for him to announce his decision. She did not seem anxious about it. He reflected that if she was as competent as she appeared she must be well aware that she would have no difficulty in finding a place. He told her what wages he was offering and these seemed to be satisfactory to her. He gave her the necessary information about the place, but she gave him to understand that she was already apprised of this, and he received the impression, which amused rather than disconcerted him, that she had made certain inquiries about him before applying for the situation. It showed prudence on her part and good sense.

"When would you be able to come in if I engaged you? I haven't got anybody at the moment. The cook's managing as best she can with a char, but I should like to get settled as soon as possible."

"Well, sir, I was going to give myself a week's holiday, but if it's a matter of obliging a gentleman I don't mind giving that up. I could come in tomorrow if it was convenient."

Richard Harenger gave her his attractive smile.

"I shouldn't like you to do without a holiday that I daresay you've been looking forward to. I can very well go on like this for another week. Go and have your holiday and come to me when it's over."

"Thank you very much, sir. Would it do if I came in tomorrow week?"

"Quite well."

When she left, Richard Harenger felt he had done a good day's work. It looked as though he had found exactly what he was after. He rang for the cook and told her he had engaged a house-parlourmaid at last.

"I think you'll like her, sir," she said. "She came in and 'ad a talk with me this afternoon. I could see at once she knew her duties. And she's not one of them flighty ones."

"We can but try, Mrs Jeddy. I hope you gave me a good character."

"Well, I said you was particular, sir. I said you was a gentleman as liked things just so."

"I admit that."

"She said she didn't mind that. She said she liked a gentleman as knew what was what. She said there's no satisfaction in doing things proper if nobody notices. I expect you'll find she'll take a rare lot of pride in her work."

"That's what I want her to do. I think we might go farther and fare worse."

"Well, sir, there is that to it, of course. And the proof of the pudding's the eating. But if you ask my opinion I think she's going to be a real treasure."

And that is precisely what Pritchard turned out. No man was ever better served. The way she shone shoes was marvellous, and he set out of a fine morning for his walk to the office with a more jaunty step because you could almost see yourself reflected in them. She looked after his clothes with such attention that his colleagues began to chaff him about being the best-dressed man in the Civil Service. One day, coming home unexpectedly, he found a line of socks and handkerchiefs hung up to dry in the bathroom. He called Pritchard.

"D'you wash my socks and handkerchiefs yourself, Pritchard? I should have thought you had enough to do without that."

"They do ruin them so at the laundry, sir. I prefer to do them at home if you have no objection."

She knew exactly what he should wear on every occasion, and without asking him was aware whether she should put out a dinner jacket and a black tie in the evening or a dress coat and a white one. When he was going to a party where decorations were to be worn he found his neat little row of medals automatically affixed to the lapel of his coat. He soon ceased to choose every morning from his wardrobe the tie he wanted, for he found that she put out for him without fail the one he would have himself selected. Her taste was perfect. He supposed she read his letters, for she always knew what his movements were, and if he had forgotten at what hour he had an engagement he had no need to look in his book, for Pritchard could tell him. She knew exactly what tone to use with persons with whom she conversed on the telephone. Except with tradesmen, with whom she was apt to be peremptory, she was always polite, but there was a distinct difference in her manner if she was addressing one of Mr Harenger's literary friends or the wife of a Cabinet Minister. She knew by instinct with whom he wished to speak and with whom he didn't. From his sitting-room he sometimes heard her with placid sincerity assuring a caller that he was out, and then she would come in and tell him that So-and-So had rung up, but she thought he wouldn't wish to be disturbed.

"Quite right, Pritchard," he smiled.

"I knew she only wanted to bother you about that concert," said Pritchard.

His friends made appointments with him through her, and she would tell him what she had done on his return in the evening.

"Mrs Soames rang up, sir, and asked if you would lunch with her on Thursday, the eighth, but I said you were very sorry but you were lunching with Lady Versinder. Mr Oakley rang up and asked if you'd go to a cocktail party at the Savoy next Tuesday at six. I said you would if you possibly could, but you might have to go to the dentist's."

"Quite right."

"I thought you could see when the time came, sir."

She kept the flat like a new pin. On one occasion soon after she entered his service, Richard coming back from a holiday took out a book from his shelves and at once noticed that it had been dusted. He rang the bell.

"I forgot to tell you when I went away under no circumstances ever to touch my books. When books are taken out to be dusted they're never put back in the right place. I don't mind my books being dirty, but I hate not being able to find them."

"I'm very sorry, sir," said Pritchard. "I know some gentlemen are very particular and I took care to put back every book exactly where I took it from."

Richard Harenger gave his books a glance. So far as he could see every one was in its accustomed place. He smiled.

"I apologize, Pritchard."

"They were in a muck, sir. I mean, you couldn't open one without getting your hands black with dust."

She certainly kept his silver as he had never had it kept before. He felt called upon to give her a special word of praise.

"Most of it's Queen Anne and George I, you know," he explained.

"Yes, I know, sir. When you've got something good like that to look after it's a pleasure to keep it like it should be."

"You certainly have a knack for it. I never knew a butler who kept his silver as well as you do."

"Men haven't the patience women have," she replied modestly. As soon as he thought Pritchard had settled down in the place he resumed the little dinners he was fond of giving once a week. He had already discovered that she knew how to wait at table but it was with a warm sense of complacency that he realized then how competently she could manage a party. She was quick, silent, and watchful. A guest had hardly felt the need of something before Pritchard was at his elbow offering him what he wanted. She soon learned the tastes of his more intimate friends and remembered that one liked water instead of soda with his whisky and that another particularly fancied the knuckle end of a leg of lamb. She knew exactly how cold a hock should be not to ruin its taste and how long claret should have stood in the room to bring out its bouquet. It was a pleasure to see her pour out a bottle of burgundy in such a fashion as not to disturb the grounds. On one occasion she did not serve the wine Richard had ordered. He somewhat sharply pointed this out to her.

"I opened the bottle, sir, and it was slightly corked. So I got the Chambertin, as I thought it was safer."

"Quite right, Pritchard."

Presently he left this matter entirely in her hands, for he discovered that she knew perfectly what wines his guests would like. Without orders from him she would provide the best in his cellar and his oldest brandy if she thought they were the sort of people who knew what they were drinking. She had no belief in the palate of women, and when they were of the party was apt to serve the champagne which had to be drunk before it went off. She had the English servant's instinctive knowledge of social differences, and neither rank nor money blinded her to the fact that someone was not a gentleman, but she had favourites among his friends, and when someone she particularly liked was dining, with the air of a cat that has swallowed a canary she would pour out for him a bottle of a wine that Harenger kept for very special occasions. It amused him.

"You've got on the right side of Pritchard, old boy," he exclaimed. "There aren't many people she gives this wine to."

Pritchard became an institution. She was known very soon to be the perfect parlourmaid. People envied Harenger the possession of her as they envied nothing else that he had. She was worth her weight in gold. Her price was above rubies. Richard Harenger beamed with self-complacency when they praised her.

"Good masters make good servants," he said gaily.

One evening, when they were sitting over their port and she had left the room, they were talking about her.

"It'll be an awful blow when she leaves you."

"Why should she leave me? One or two people have tried to get her away from me, but she turned them down. She knows where she's well off."

"She'll get married one of these days."

"I don't think she's that sort."

"She's a good-looking woman."

"Yes, she has quite a decent presence."

"What are you talking about? She's a very handsome creature. In another class of life she'd be a well-known society beauty with her photograph in all the papers."

At that moment Pritchard came in with the coffee. Richard Harenger looked at her. After seeing her every day, off and on, for four years it was now – my word, how time flies – he had really forgotten what she looked like. She did not seem to have changed much since he had first seen her. She was no stouter than then, she still had the high colour, and her regular features bore the same expression which was at once intent and vacuous. The black uniform suited her. She left the room.

"She's a paragon and there's no doubt about it."

"I know she is," answered Harenger. "She's perfection. I should be lost without her. And the strange thing is that I don't very much like her."

"Why not?"

"I think she bores me a little. You see, she has no conversation. I've often tried to talk to her. She answers when I speak to her, but that's all. In four years she's never volunteered a remark of her own. I know absolutely nothing about her. I don't know if she likes me or if she's completely indifferent to me. She's an automaton. I respect her, I appreciate her, I trust her. She has every quality in the world and I've often wondered why it is that with all that I'm so completely indifferent to her. I think it must be that she is entirely devoid of charm."

They left it at that.

Two or three days after this, since it was Pritchard's night out and he had no engagement, Richard Harenger dined by himself at his club. A page-boy came to him and told him that they had just rung up from his flat to say that he had gone out without his keys and should they be brought along to him in a taxi? He put his hand to his pocket. It was a fact. By a singular chance he had forgotten to replace them when he had changed into a blue serge suit before coming out to dinner. His intention had been to play bridge, but it was an off-night at the club and there seemed little chance of a decent game; it occurred to him that it would be a good opportunity to see a picture that he had heard talked about, so he sent back the message by the page that he would call for the keys himself in half an hour.

He rang at the door of his flat and it was opened by Pritchard. She had the keys in her hand.

"What are you doing here, Pritchard?" he asked. "It's your night out, isn't it?"

"Yes, sir. But I didn't care about going, so I told Mrs Jeddy she could go instead."

"You ought to get out when you have the chance," he said, with his usual thoughtfulness. "It's not good for you to be cooped up here all the time."

"I get out now and then on an errand, but I haven't been out in the evening for the last month."

"Why on earth not?"

"Well, it's not very cheerful going out by yourself, and somehow I don't know anyone just now that I'm particularly keen on going out with."

"You ought to have a bit of fun now and then. It's good for you."

"I've got out of the habit of it somehow."

"Look here, I'm just going to the cinema. Would you like to come along with me?"

He spoke in kindliness, on the spur of the moment, and the moment he had said the words half regretted them.

"Yes, sir, I'd like to," said Pritchard.

"Run along then and put on a hat."

"I shan't be a minute."

She disappeared and he went into the sitting-room and lit a cigarette. He was a little amused at what he was doing, and pleased too; it was nice to be able to make someone happy with so little trouble to himself. It was characteristic of Pritchard that she had shown neither surprise nor hesitation. She kept him waiting about five minutes, and when she came back he noticed that she had changed her dress. She wore a blue frock in what he supposed was artificial silk, a small black hat with a blue brooch on it, and a silver fox round her neck. He was a trifle relieved to see that she looked neither shabby nor showy. It would never occur to anyone who happened to see them that this was a distinguished official in the Home Office taking his housemaid to the pictures.

"I'm sorry to have kept you waiting, sir."

"It doesn't matter at all," he said graciously.

He opened the front door for her and she went out before him. He remembered the familiar anecdote of Louis XIV and the courtier and appreciated the fact that she had not hesitated to precede him. The cinema for which they were bound was at no great distance from Mr Harenger's flat and they walked there. He talked about the weather and the state of the roads and Adolf Hitler. Pritchard made suitable replies. They arrived just as Mickey the Mouse was starting and this put them in a good humour. During the four years she had been in his service Richard Harenger had hardly ever seen Pritchard even smile, and now it diverted him vastly to hear her peal upon peal of joyous laughter. He enjoyed her pleasure. Then the principal attraction was thrown on the screen. It was a good picture and they both watched it with breathless excitement. Taking his cigarette-case out to help himself he automatically offered it to Pritchard.

"Thank you, sir," she said, taking one.

He lit it for her. Her eyes were on the screen and she was almost unconscious of his action. When the picture was finished they streamed out with the crowd into the street. They walked back towards the flat. It was a fine starry night.

"Did you like it?" he said.

"Like anything, sir. It was a real treat."

A thought occurred to him.

"By the way, did you have any supper tonight?"

"No, sir, I didn't have time."

"Aren't you starving?"

"I'll have a bit of bread and cheese when I get in and I'll make meself a cup of cocoa."

"That sounds rather grim." There was a feeling of gaiety in the air, and the people who poured past them, one way and another, seemed filled with a pleasant elation. In for a penny, in for a pound, he said to himself. "Look here, would you like to come and have a bit of supper with me somewhere?"

"If you'd like to, sir."

"Come on."

He hailed a cab. He was feeling very philanthropic and it was not a feeling that he disliked at all. He told the driver to go to a restaurant in Oxford Street which was gay, but at which he was confident there was no chance of meeting anyone he knew. There was an orchestra and people danced. It would amuse Pritchard to see them. When they sat down a waiter came up to them.

"They've got a set supper here," he said, thinking that was what she would like. "I suggest we have that. What would you like to drink? A little white wine?"

"What I really fancy is a glass of ginger beer," she said.

Richard Harenger ordered himself a whisky and soda. She ate the supper with hearty appetite, and though Harenger was not hungry, to put her at her ease he ate too. The picture they had just seen gave them something to talk about. It was quite true what they had said the other night, Pritchard was not a bad-looking woman, and even if someone had seen them together he would not have minded. It would make rather a good story for his friends when he told them how he had taken the incomparable Pritchard to the cinema and then afterwards to supper. Pritchard was looking at the dancers with a faint smile on her lips.

"Do you like dancing?" he said.

"I used to be a rare one for it when I was a girl. I never danced much after I was married. My husband was a bit shorter than me and somehow I never think it looks well unless the gentleman's taller, if you know what I mean. I suppose I shall be getting too old for it soon."

Richard was certainly taller than his parlourmaid. They would look all right. He was fond of dancing and he danced well. But he hesitated. He did not want to embarrass Pritchard by asking her to dance with him. It was better not to go too far perhaps. And yet what did it matter? It was a drab life she led. She was so sensible, if she thought it a mistake he was pretty sure she would find a decent excuse.

"Would you like to take a turn, Pritchard?" he said, as the band struck up again.

"I'm terribly out of practice, sir."

"What does that matter?"

"If you don't mind, sir," she answered coolly, rising from her seat.

She was not in the least shy. She was only afraid that she would not be able to follow his step. They moved on to the floor. He found she danced very well.

"Why, you dance perfectly, Pritchard," he said.

"It's coming back to me."

Although she was a big woman she was light on her feet and she had a natural sense of rhythm. She was very pleasant to dance with. He gave a glance at the mirrors that lined the walls and he could not help reflecting that they looked very well together. Their eyes met in the mirror; he wondered whether she was thinking that too. They had two more dances and then Richard Harenger suggested that they should go. He paid the bill and they walked out. He noticed that she threaded her way through the crowd without a trace of self-consciousness. They got into a taxi and in ten minutes were at home.

"I'll go up the back way, sir," said Pritchard.

"There's no need to do that. Come up in the lift with me."

He took her up, giving the night-porter an icy glance, so that he should not think it strange that he came back at that somewhat late hour with his parlourmaid, and with his latch-key let her into the flat.

"Well, good night, sir," she said. "Thank you very much. It's been a real treat for me."

"Thank *you*, Pritchard. I should have had a very dull evening by myself. I hope you've enjoyed your outing."

"That I have, sir, more than I can say."

It had been a success. Richard Harenger was satisfied with himself. It was a kindly thing for him to have done. It was a very agreeable sensation to give anyone so much real pleasure. His benevolence warmed him and for a moment he felt a great love in his heart for the whole human race.

"Good night, Pritchard," he said, and because he felt happy and good he put his arm round her waist and kissed her on the lips.

Her lips were very soft. They lingered on his and she returned his kiss. It was the warm, hearty embrace of a healthy woman in the prime of life. He found it very pleasant and he held her to him a little more closely. She put her arms round his neck.

As a general rule he did not wake till Pritchard came in with his letters, but next morning he woke at half past seven. He had a curious sensation that he did not recognize. He was accustomed to sleep with two pillows under his head and he suddenly grew aware of the fact that he had only one. Then he remembered and with a start looked round. The other pillow was beside his own. Thank God, no sleeping head rested there, but it was plain that one had. His heart sank. He broke out into a cold sweat.

"My God, what a fool I've been!" he cried out loud.

How could he have done anything so stupid? What on earth had come over him? He was the last man to play about with servant girls. What a disgraceful thing to do! At his age and in his position. He had not heard Pritchard slip away. He must have been asleep. It wasn't even as if he'd liked her very much. She wasn't his type. And, as he had said the other night, she rather bored him. Even now he only knew her as Pritchard. He had no notion what her first name was. What madness! And what was to happen now? The position was impossible. It was obvious he couldn't keep her, and yet to send her away for what was his fault as much as hers seemed shockingly unfair. How idiotic to lose the best parlourmaid a man ever had just for an hour's folly!

"It's that damned kindness of heart of mine," he groaned.

He would never find anyone else to look after his clothes so admirably or clean the silver so well. She knew all his friends' telephone numbers and she understood wine. But of course she must go. She must see for herself that after what had happened things could never be the same. He would make her a handsome present and give her an excellent reference. At any minute she would be coming in now. Would she be arch, would she be familiar? Or would she put on airs? Perhaps even she wouldn't trouble to come in with his letters. It would be awful if he had to ring the bell and Mrs Jeddy came in and said: Pritchard's not up yet, sir, she's having a lie in after last night.

"What a fool I've been! What a contemptible cad!"

There was a knock at the door. He was sick with anxiety.

"Come in."

Richard Harenger was a very unhappy man.

Pritchard came in as the clock struck. She wore the print dress she was in the habit of wearing during the early part of the day.

"Good morning, sir," she said.

"Good morning."

She drew the curtains and handed him his letters and the papers. Her face was impassive. She looked exactly as she always looked. Her movements had the same competent deliberation that they always had. She neither avoided Richard's glance nor sought it.

"Will you wear your grey, sir? It came back from the tailor's yesterday."

"Yes."

He pretended to read his letters, but he watched her from under his eyelashes. Her back was turned to him. She took his vest and drawers and folded them over a chair. She took the studs out of the shirt he had worn the day before and studded a clean one. She put out some clean socks for him and placed them on the seat of a chair with the suspenders to match by the side. Then she put out his grey suit and attached the braces to the back buttons of the trousers. She opened his wardrobe and after a moment's reflection chose a tie to go with the suit. She collected on her arm the suit of the day before and picked up the shoes.

"Will you have breakfast now, sir, or will you have your bath first?"

"I'll have breakfast now," he said.

"Very good, sir."

With her slow quiet movements, unruffled, she left the room. Her face bore that rather serious, deferential, vacuous look it always bore. What had happened might have been a dream. Nothing in Pritchard's demeanour suggested that she had the smallest recollection of the night before. He gave a sigh of relief. It was going to be all right. She need not go, she need not go. Pritchard was the perfect parlourmaid. He knew that never by word nor gesture would she ever refer to the fact that for a moment their relations had been other than those of master and servant. Richard Harenger was a very happy man.

THE COLONEL'S LADY

ALL THIS HAPPENED two or three years before the outbreak of the war.

The Peregrines were having breakfast. Though they were alone and the table was long they sat at opposite ends of it. From the walls George Peregrine's ancestors, painted by the fashionable painters of the day, looked down upon them. The butler brought in the morning post. There were several letters for the colonel, business letters, *The Times*, and a small parcel for his wife Evie. He looked at his letters and then, opening *The Times*, began to read it. They finished breakfast and rose from the table. He noticed that his wife hadn't opened the parcel.

"What's that?" he asked.

"Only some books."

"Shall I open it for you?"

"If you like."

He hated to cut string and so with some difficulty untied the knots.

"But they're all the same," he said when he had unwrapped the parcel. "What on earth d'you want six copies of the same book for?" He opened one of them. "Poetry." Then he looked at the title page. *When Pyramids Decay*, he read, by E. K. Hamilton. Eva Katherine Hamilton: that was his wife's maiden name. He looked at her with smiling surprise. "Have you written a book, Evie? You are a slyboots."

"I didn't think it would interest you very much. Would you like a copy?"

"Well, you know poetry isn't much in my line, but – yes, I'd like a copy; I'll read it. I'll take it along to my study. I've got a lot to do this morning."

He gathered up *The Times*, his letters, and the book, and went out. His study was a large and comfortable room, with a big desk, leather arm-chairs, and what he called "trophies of the chase" on the walls. On the bookshelves were works of reference, books on farming, gardening, fishing, and shooting, and books on the last war, in which he had won an MC and a DSO. For before his marriage he had been in the Welsh Guards. At the end of the war he retired and settled down to the life of a country gentleman in the spacious house, some twenty miles from Sheffield, which one of his forebears had built in the reign of George III. George Peregrine had an estate of some fifteen hundred acres which he managed with ability; he was a Justice of the Peace and performed his duties conscientiously. During the season he rode to hounds two days a week. He was a good shot, a golfer, and though now a little over fifty could still play a hard game of tennis. He could describe himself with propriety as an all-round sportsman.

He had been putting on weight lately, but was still a fine figure of a man; tall, with grey curly hair, only just beginning to grow thin on the crown, frank blue eyes, good features, and a high colour. He was a public-spirited man, chairman of any number of local organizations and, as became his class and station, a loyal member of the Conservative Party. He looked upon it as his duty to see to the welfare of the people on his estate and it was a satisfaction to him to know that Evie could be trusted to tend the sick and succour the poor. He had built a cottage hospital on the outskirts of the village and paid the wages of a nurse out of his own pocket. All he asked of the recipients of his bounty was that at elections, county or general, they should vote for his candidate. He was a friendly man, affable to his inferiors, considerate with his tenants, and popular with the neighbouring gentry. He would have been pleased and at the same time slightly embarrassed if someone had told him he was a jolly good fellow. That was what he wanted to be. He desired no higher praise.

It was hard luck that he had no children. He would have been an excellent father, kindly but strict, and would have brought up his sons as gentlemen's sons should be brought up, sent them to Eton, you know, taught them to fish, shoot, and ride. As it was, his heir was a nephew, son of his brother killed in a motor accident, not a bad boy, but not a chip off the old block, no, sir, far from it; and would you believe it, his fool of a mother was sending him to a co-educational school. Evie had been a sad disappointment to him. Of course she was a lady, and she had a bit of money of her own; she managed the house uncommonly well and she was a good hostess. The village people adored her. She had been a pretty little thing when he married her, with a creamy skin, light brown hair, and a trim figure, healthy too, and not a bad tennis player; he couldn't understand why she'd had no children; of course she was faded now, she must be getting on for five and forty; her skin was drab, her hair had lost its sheen, and she was as thin as a rail. She was always neat and suitably dressed, but she didn't seem to bother how she looked, she wore no make-up and didn't even use lipstick; sometimes at night when she dolled herself up for a party you could tell that once she'd been quite attractive, but ordinarily she was – well, the sort of woman you simply didn't notice. A nice woman, of course, a good wife, and it wasn't her fault if she was barren, but it was tough on a fellow who wanted an heir of his own loins; she hadn't any vitality, that's what was the matter with her. He supposed he'd been in love with her when he asked her to many him, at least sufficiently in love for a man who wanted to marry and settle down, but with time he discovered that they had nothing much in common. She didn't care about hunting, and fishing bored her. Naturally they'd drifted apart. He had to do her the justice to admit that she'd never bothered him. There'd been no scenes. They had no quarrels. She seemed to take it for granted that he should go his own way. When he went up to London now and then she never wanted to come with him. He had a girl there, well, she wasn't exactly a girl, she was thirty-five if she was a day, but she was blonde and luscious and he only had to wire ahead of time and they'd dine, do a show, and spend the night together. Well, a man, a healthy normal man had to have some fun in his life. The thought crossed his mind that if Evie hadn't been such a good woman she'd have been a better wife; but it was not the sort of thought that he welcomed and he put it away from him.

George Peregrine finished his *Times* and being a considerate fellow rang the bell and told the butler to take it to Evie. Then he looked at his watch. It was half past ten and at eleven he had an appointment with one of his tenants. He had half an hour to spare.

"I'd better have a look at Evie's book," he said to himself.

He took it up with a smile. Evie had a lot of highbrow books in her sitting-room, not the sort of books that interested him, but if they amused her he had no objection to her reading them. He noticed that the volume he now held in his hand contained no more than ninety pages. That was all to the good. He shared Edgar Allan Poe's opinion that poems should be short. But as he turned the pages he noticed that several of Evie's had long lines of irregular length and didn't rhyme. He didn't like that. At his first school, when he was a little boy, he remembered learning a poem that began: *The boy stood on the burning deck*, and later, at Eton, one that started: *Ruin seize thee, ruthless king*; and then there was *Henry V*; they'd had to take that, one half. He stared at Evie's pages with consternation.

"That's not what I call poetry," he said.

Fortunately it wasn't all like that. Interspersed with the pieces that looked so odd, lines of three or four words and then a line of ten or fifteen, there were little poems, quite short, that rhymed, thank God, with the lines all the same length. Several of the pages were just headed with the word *Sonnet*, and out of curiosity he counted the lines; there were fourteen of them. He read them. They seemed all right, but he didn't quite know what they were all about. He repeated to himself: *Ruin seize thee, ruthless king*.

"Poor Evie," he sighed.

At that moment the farmer he was expecting was ushered into the study, and putting the book down he made him welcome. They embarked on their business.

"I read your book, Evie," he said as they sat down to lunch. "Jolly good. Did it cost you a packet to have it printed?"

"No, I was lucky. I sent it to a publisher and he took it."

"Not much money in poetry, my dear," he said in his good-natured, hearty way.

"No, I don't suppose there is. What did Bannock want to see you about this morning?"

Bannock was the tenant who had interrupted his reading of Evie's poems.

"He's asked me to advance the money for a pedigree bull he wants to buy. He's a good man and I've half a mind to do it."

George Peregrine saw that Evie didn't want to talk about her book and he was not sorry to change the subject. He was glad she had used her maiden name on the title page; he didn't suppose anyone would ever hear about the book, but he was proud of his own unusual name and he wouldn't have liked it if some damned penny-a-liner had made fun of Evie's effort in one of the papers.

During the few weeks that followed he thought it tactful not to ask Evie any questions about her venture into verse, and she never referred to it. It might have been a discreditable incident that they had silently agreed not to mention. But then a strange thing happened. He had to go to London on business and he took Daphne out to dinner. That was the name of the girl with whom he was in the habit of passing a few agreeable hours whenever he went to town.

"Oh, George," she said, "is that your wife who's written a book they're all talking about?"

"What on earth d'you mean?"

"Well, there's a fellow I know who's a critic. He took me out to dinner the other night and he had a book with him. 'Got anything for me to read?' I said. 'What's that?' 'Oh, I don't think that's your cup of tea,' he said. 'It's poetry. I've just been reviewing it.' 'No poetry for me,' I said. 'It's about the hottest stuff I ever read,' he said. 'Selling like hot cakes. And it's damned good.'"

"Who's the book by?" asked George.

"A woman called Hamilton. My friend told me that wasn't her real name. He said her real name was Peregrine. 'Funny,' I said, 'I know a fellow called Peregrine.' 'Colonel in the army,' he said. 'Lives near Sheffield.'"

'I'd just as soon you didn't talk about me to your friends," said George with a frown of vexation.

"Keep your shirt on, dearie. Who d'you take me for? I just said: 'It's not the same one.'" Daphne giggled. "My friend said: 'They say he's a regular Colonel Blimp.'"

George had a keen sense of humour.

"You could tell them better than that," he laughed. "If my wife had written a book I'd be the first to know about it, wouldn't I?"

"I suppose you would."

Anyhow the matter didn't interest her and when the colonel began to talk of other things she forgot about it. He put it out of his mind too. There was nothing to it, he decided, and that silly fool of a critic had just been pulling Daphne's leg. He was amused at the thought of her tackling that book because she had been told it was hot stuff and then finding it just a lot of bosh cut up into unequal lines.

He was a member of several clubs and next day he thought he'd lunch at one in St James's Street. He was catching a train back to Sheffield early in the afternoon. He was sitting in a comfortable arm-chair having a glass of sherry before going into the dining-room when an old friend came up to him.

"Well, old boy, how's life?" he said. "How d'you like being the husband of a celebrity?"

George Peregrine looked at his friend. He thought he saw an amused twinkle in his eyes.

"I don't know what you're talking about," he answered.

"Come off it, George. Everyone knows E. K. Hamilton is your wife. Not often a book of verse has a success like that. Look here, Henry Dashwood is lunching with me. He'd like to meet you."

"Who the devil is Henry Dashwood and why should he want to meet me?"

"Oh, my dear fellow, what do you do with yourself all the time in the country? Henry's about the best critic we've got. He wrote a wonderful review of Evie's book. D'you mean to say she didn't show it you?"

Before George could answer his friend had called a man over. A tall, thin man, with a high forehead, a beard, a long nose, and a stoop, just the sort of man whom George was prepared to dislike at first sight. Introductions were effected. Henry Dashwood sat down.

"Is Mrs Peregrine in London by any chance? I should very much like to meet her," he said.

"No, my wife doesn't like London. She prefers the country," said George stiffly.

"She wrote me a very nice letter about my review. I was pleased. You know, we critics get more kicks than halfpence. I was simply bowled over by her book. It's so fresh and original, very modern without being obscure. She seems to be as much at her ease in free verse as in the classical metres." Then because he was a critic he thought he should criticize. "Sometimes her ear is a trifle at fault, but you can say the same of Emily Dickinson. There are several of those short lyrics of hers that might have been written by Landor."

All this was gibberish to George Peregrine. The man was nothing but a disgusting highbrow. But the colonel had good manners and he answered with proper civility: Henry Dashwood went on as though he hadn't spoken.

"But what makes the book so outstanding is the passion that throbs in every line. So many of these young poets are so anaemic, cold, bloodless, dully intellectual, but here you have real naked, earthy passion; of course deep, sincere emotion like that is tragic – ah, my dear Colonel, how right Heine was when he said that the poet makes little songs out of his great sorrows. You know, now and then, as I read and re-read those heart-rending pages I thought of Sappho."

This was too much for George Peregrine and he got up.

"Well, it's jolly nice of you to say such nice things about my wife's little book. I'm sure she'll be delighted. But I must bolt, I've got to catch a train and I want to get a bite of lunch."

"Damned fool," he said irritably to himself as he walked upstairs to the dining-room.

He got home in time for dinner and after Evie had gone to bed he went into his study and looked for her book. He thought he'd just glance through it again to see for himself what they were making such a fuss about, but he couldn't find it. Evie must have taken it away.

"Silly," he muttered.

He'd told her he thought it jolly good. What more could a fellow be expected to say? Well, it didn't matter. He lit his pipe and read the *Field* till he felt sleepy. But a week or so later it happened that he had to go into Sheffield for the day. He lunched there at his club. He had nearly finished when the Duke of Haverel came in. This was the great local magnate and of course the colonel knew him, but only to say how d'you do to; and he was surprised when the Duke stopped at his table.

"We're so sorry your wife couldn't come to us for the week-end," he said, with a sort of shy cordiality. "We're expecting rather a nice lot of people."

George was taken aback. He guessed that the Haverels had asked him and Evie over for the week-end and Evie, without saying a word to him about it, had refused. He had the presence of mind to say he was sorry too.

"Better luck next time," said the Duke pleasantly and moved on.

Colonel Peregrine was very angry and when he got home he said to his wife:

"Look here, what's this about our being asked over to Haverel? Why on earth did you say we couldn't go? We've never been asked before and it's the best shooting in the county."

"I didn't think of that. I thought it would only bore you."

"Damn it all, you might at least have asked me if I wanted to go."

"I'm sorry."

He looked at her closely. There was something in her expression that he didn't quite understand. He frowned.

"I suppose *I* was asked?" he barked.

Evie flushed a little.

"Well, in point of fact you weren't."

"I call it damned rude of them to ask you without asking me."

"I suppose they thought it wasn't your sort of party. The Duchess is rather fond of writers and people like that, you know. She's having Henry Dashwood, the critic, and for some reason he wants to meet me."

"It was damned nice of you to refuse, Evie."

"It's the least I could do," she smiled. She hesitated a moment. "George, my publishers want to give a little dinner party for me one day towards the end of the month and of course they want you to come too."

"Oh, I don't think that's quite my mark. I'll come up to London with you if you like. I'll find someone to dine with."

Daphne.

"I expect it'll be very dull, but they're making rather a point of it. And the day after, the American publisher who's taken my book is giving a cocktail party at Claridge's. I'd like you to come to that if you wouldn't mind."

"Sounds like a crashing bore, but if you really want me to come I'll come."

"It would be sweet of you."

George Peregrine was dazed by the cocktail party. There were a lot of people. Some of them didn't look so bad, a few of the women were decently turned out, but the men seemed to him pretty awful. He was introduced to everyone as Colonel Peregrine, E. K. Hamilton's husband, you know. The men didn't seem to have anything to say to him, but the women gushed.

"You *must* be proud of your wife. Isn't it *wonderful*? You know, I read it right through at a sitting, I simply couldn't put it down, and when I'd finished I started again at the beginning and read it right through a second time. I was simply *thrilled*."

The English publisher said to him:

"We've not had a success like this with a book of verse for twenty years. I've never seen such reviews."

The American publisher said to him:

"It's swell. It'll be a smash hit in America. You wait and see."

The American publisher had sent Evie a great spray of orchids. Damned ridiculous, thought George. As they came in, people were taken up to Evie, and it was evident that they said flattering things to her, which she took with a pleasant smile and a word or two of thanks. She was a trifle flushed with the excitement, but seemed quite at her ease. Though he thought the whole thing a lot of stuff and nonsense George noted with approval that his wife was carrying it off in just the right way.

"Well, there's one thing," he said to himself, "you can see she's a lady and that's a damned sight more than you can say of anyone else here."

He drank a good many cocktails. But there was one thing that bothered him. He had a notion that some of the people he was introduced to looked at him in rather a funny sort of way, he couldn't quite make out what it meant, and once when he strolled by two women who were sitting together on a sofa he had the impression that they were talking about him and after he passed he was almost certain they tittered. He was very glad when the party came to an end.

In the taxi on their way back to their hotel Evie said to him:

"You were wonderful, dear. You made quite a hit. The girls simply raved about you: they thought you so handsome."

"Girls," he said bitterly. "Old hags."

"Were you bored, dear?"

"Stiff."

She pressed his hand in a gesture of sympathy.

"I hope you won't mind if we wait and go down by the afternoon train. I've got some things to do in the morning."

"No, that's all right. Shopping?"

"I do want to buy one or two things, but I've got to go and be photographed. I hate the idea, but they think I ought to be. For America, you know."

He said nothing. But he thought. He thought it would be a shock to the American public when they saw the portrait of the homely, desiccated little woman who was his wife. He'd always been under the impression that they liked glamour in America.

He went on thinking, and next morning when Evie had gone out he went to his club and up to the library. There he looked up recent numbers of *The Times Literary Supplement*, the *New Statesman*, and the *Spectator*. Presently he found reviews of Evie's book. He didn't read them very carefully, but enough to see that they were extremely favourable. Then he went to the bookseller's in Piccadilly where he occasionally bought books. He'd made up his mind that he had to read this damned thing of Evie's properly, but he didn't want to ask her what she'd done with the copy she'd given him. He'd buy one for himself. Before going in he looked in the window and the first thing he saw was a display of *When Pyramids Decay*. Damned silly title! He went in. A young man came forward and asked if he could help him.

"No, I'm just having a look round." It embarrassed him to ask for Evie's book and he thought he'd find it for himself and then take it to the salesman. But he couldn't see it anywhere and at last, finding the young man near him, he said in a carefully casual tone: "By the way, have you got a book called *When Pyramids Decay*?"

"The new edition came in this morning. I'll get a copy."

In a moment the young man returned with it. He was a short, rather stout young man, with a shock of untidy carroty hair and spectacles. George Peregrine, tall, upstanding, very military, towered over him.

"Is this a new edition then?" he asked.

"Yes, sir. The fifth. It might be a novel the way it's selling."

George Peregrine hesitated a moment.

"Why d'you suppose it's such a success? I've always been told no one reads poetry."

"Well, it's good, you know. I've read it meself." The young man, though obviously cultured, had a slight Cockney accent, and George quite instinctively adopted a patronizing attitude. "It's the story they like. Sexy, you know, but tragic."

George frowned a little. He was coming to the conclusion that the young man was rather impertinent. No one had told him anything about there being a story in the damned book and he had not gathered that from reading the reviews. The young man went on:

"Of course it's only a flash in the pan, if you know what I mean. The way I look at it, she was sort of inspired like by a personal experience, like Housman was with *The Shropshire Lad*. She'll never write anything else."

"How much is the book?" said George coldly to stop his chatter. "You needn't wrap it up, I'll just slip it into my pocket."

The November morning was raw and he was wearing a greatcoat.

At the station he bought the evening papers and magazines and he and Evie settled themselves comfortably in opposite corners of a first-class carriage and read. At five o'clock they went along to the restaurant car to have tea and chatted a little. They arrived. They drove home in the car which was waiting for them. They bathed, dressed for dinner, and after dinner Evie, saying she was tired out, went to bed. She kissed him, as was her habit, on the forehead. Then he went into the hall, took Evie's book out of his greatcoat pocket and going into the study began to read it. He didn't read verse very easily and though he read with attention, every word of it, the impression he received was far from clear. Then he began at the beginning again and read it a second time. He read with increasing malaise, but he was not a stupid man and when he had finished he had a distinct understanding of what it was all about. Part of the book was in free verse, part in conventional metres, but the story it related was coherent and plain to the meanest intelligence. It was the story of a passionate love affair between an older woman, married, and a young man. George Peregrine made out the steps of it as easily as if he had been doing a sum in simple addition.

Written in the first person, it began with the tremulous surprise of the woman, past her youth, when it dawned upon her that the young man was in love with her. She hesitated to believe it. She thought she must be deceiving herself. And she was terrified when on a sudden she discovered that she was passionately in love with him. She told herself it was absurd; with the disparity of age between them nothing but unhappiness could come to her if she yielded to her emotion. She tried to prevent him from speaking but the day came when he told her that he loved her and forced her to tell him that she loved him too. He begged her to run away with him. She couldn't leave her husband, her home; and what life could they look forward to, she an ageing woman, he so young? How could she expect his love to last? She begged him to have mercy on her. But his love was impetuous. He wanted her, he wanted her with all his heart, and at last, trembling, afraid, desirous, she yielded to him. Then there was a period of ecstatic happiness. The world, the dull, humdrum world of every day, blazed with glory. Love songs flowed from her pen. The woman worshipped the young, virile body of her lover. George flushed darkly when she praised his broad chest and slim flanks, the beauty of his legs and the flatness of his belly.

Hot stuff, Daphne's friend had said. It was that all right. Disgusting.

There were sad little pieces in which she lamented the emptiness of her life when as must happen he left her, but they ended with a cry that all she had to suffer would be worth it for the bliss that for a while had been hers. She wrote of the long, tremulous nights they passed together and the languor that lulled them to sleep in one another's arms. She wrote of the rapture of brief stolen moments when, braving all danger, their passion overwhelmed them and they surrendered to its call.

She thought it would be an affair of a few weeks, but miraculously it lasted. One of the poems referred to three years having gone by without lessening the love that filled their hearts. It looked as though he continued to press her to go away with him, far away, to a hill town in Italy, a Greek island, a walled city in Tunisia, so that they could be together always, for in another of the poems she besought him to let things be as they were. Their happiness was precarious. Perhaps it was owing to the difficulties they had to encounter and the rarity of their meetings that their love had retained for so long its first enchanting ardour. Then on a sudden the young man died. How, when or where George could not discover. There followed a long, heartbroken cry of bitter grief, grief she could not indulge in, grief that had to be hidden. She had to be cheerful, give dinner-parties and go out to dinner, behave as she had always behaved, though the light had gone out of her life and she was bowed down with anguish. The last poem of all was a set of four short stanzas in which the writer, sadly resigned to her loss, thanked the dark powers that rule man's destiny that she had been privileged at least for a while to enjoy the greatest happiness that we poor human beings can ever hope to know.

It was three o'clock in the morning when George Peregrine finally put the book down. It had seemed to him that he heard Evie's voice in every line, over and over again he came upon turns of phrase he had heard her use, there were details that were as familiar to him as to her: there was no doubt about it; it was her own story she had told, and it was as plain as anything could be that she had had a lover and her lover had died. It was not anger so much that he felt, nor horror or dismay, though he was dismayed and he was horrified, but amazement. It was as inconceivable that Evie should have had a love affair, and a wildly passionate one at that, as that the trout in a glass case over the chimney piece in his study, the finest he had ever caught, should suddenly wag its tail. He understood now the meaning of the amused look he had seen in the eyes of that man he had spoken to at the club, he understood why Daphne when she was talking about the book had seemed to be enjoying a private joke, and why those two women at the cocktail party had tittered when he strolled past them.

He broke out into a sweat. Then on a sudden he was seized with fury and he jumped up to go and awake Evie and ask her sternly for an explanation. But he stopped at the door. After all, what proof had he? A book. He remembered that he'd told Evie he thought it jolly good. True, he hadn't read it, but he'd pretended he had. He would look a perfect fool if he had to admit that.

"I must watch my step," he muttered.

He made up his mind to wait for two or three days and think it all over. Then he'd decide what to do. He went to bed, but he couldn't sleep for a long time.

"Evie," he kept on saying to himself. "Evie, of all people."

They met at breakfast next morning as usual. Evie was as she always was, quiet, demure, and self-possessed, a middle-aged woman who made no effort to look younger than she was, a woman who had nothing of what he still called It. He looked at her as he hadn't looked at her for years. She had her usual placid serenity. Her pale blue eyes were untroubled. There was no sign of guilt on her candid brow. She made the same little casual remarks she always made.

"It's nice to get back to the country again after those two hectic days in London. What are you going to do this morning?"

It was incomprehensible.

Three days later he went to see his solicitor. Henry Blane was an old friend of George's as well as his lawyer. He had a place not far from Peregrine's and for years they had shot over one another's preserves. For two days a week he was a country gentleman and for the other five a busy lawyer in Sheffield. He was a tall, robust fellow, with a boisterous manner and a jovial laugh, which suggested that he liked to be looked upon essentially as a sportsman and a good fellow and only incidentally as a lawyer. But he was shrewd and worldly-wise.

"Well, George, what's brought you here today?" he boomed as the colonel was shown into his office. "Have a good time in London? I'm taking my missus up for a few days next week. How's Evie?"

"It's about Evie I've come to see you," said Peregrine, giving him a suspicious look. "Have you read her book?"

His sensitivity had been sharpened during those last days of troubled thought and he was conscious of a faint change in the lawyer's expression. It was as though he were suddenly on his guard.

"Yes, I've read it. Great success, isn't it? Fancy Evie breaking out into poetry. Wonders will never cease."

George Peregrine was inclined to lose his temper.

"It's made me look a perfect damned fool."

"Oh, what nonsense, George! There's no harm in Evie's writing a book. You ought to be jolly proud of her."

"Don't talk such rot. It's her own story. You know it and everyone else knows it. I suppose I'm the only one who doesn't know who her lover was."

"There is such a thing as imagination, old boy. There's no reason to suppose the whole thing isn't made up."

"Look here, Henry, we've known one another all our lives. We've had all sorts of good times together. Be honest with me. Can you look me in the face and tell me you believe it's a made-up story?"

Harry Blane moved uneasily in his chair. He was disturbed by the distress in old George's voice.

"You've got no right to ask me a question like that. Ask Evie."

"I daren't," George answered after an anguished pause. "I'm afraid she'd tell me the truth."

There was an uncomfortable silence.

"Who was the chap?"

Harry Blane looked at him straight in the eye.

"I don't know, and if I did I wouldn't tell you."

"You swine. Don't you see what a position I'm in? Do you think it's very pleasant to be made absolutely ridiculous?"

The lawyer lit a cigarette and for some moments silently puffed it.

"I don't see what I can do for you," he said at last.

"You've got private detectives you employ, I suppose. I want you to put them on the job and let them find everything out."

"It's not very pretty to put detectives on one's wife, old boy; and besides, taking for granted for a moment that Evie had an affair, it was a good many years ago and I don't suppose it would be possible to find out a thing. They seem to have covered their tracks pretty carefully."

"I don't care. You put the detectives on. I want to know the truth."

"I won't, George. If you're determined to do that you'd better consult someone else. And look here, even if you got evidence that Evie had been unfaithful to you what would you do with it? You'd look rather silly divorcing your wife because she'd committed adultery ten years ago."

"At all events I could have it out with her."

"You can do that now, but you know just as well as I do that if you do she'll leave you. D'you want her to do that?"

George gave him an unhappy look.

"I don't know. I always thought she'd been a damned good wife to me. She runs the house perfectly, we never have any servant trouble; she's done wonders with the garden and she's splendid with all the village people. But damn it, I have my self-respect to think of. How can I go on living with her when I know that she was grossly unfaithful to me?"

"Have you always been faithful to her?"

"More or less, you know. After all, we've been married for nearly twenty-four years and Evie was never much for bed."

The solicitor slightly raised his eyebrows, but George was too intent on what he was saying to notice.

"I don't deny that I've had a bit of fun now and then. A man wants it. Women are different."

"We only have men's word for that," said Harry Blane, with a faint smile.

"Evie's absolutely the last woman I'd have suspected of kicking over the traces. I mean, she's a very fastidious, reticent woman. What on earth made her write the damned book?"

"I suppose it was a very poignant experience and perhaps it was a relief to her to get it off her chest like that."

"Well, if she had to write it why the devil didn't she write it under an assumed name?"

"She used her maiden name. I suppose she thought that was enough, and it would have been if the book hadn't had this amazing boom."

George Peregrine and the lawyer were sitting opposite one another with a desk between them. George, his elbow on the desk, his cheek on his hand, frowned at his thought.

"It's so rotten not to know what sort of a chap he was. One can't even tell if he was by way of being a gentleman. I mean, for all I know he may have been a farm-hand or a clerk in a lawyer's office."

Harry Blane did not permit himself to smile and when he answered there was in his eyes a kindly, tolerant look.

"Knowing Evie so well I think the probabilities are that he was all right. Anyhow I'm sure he wasn't a clerk in my office."

"It's been a shock to me," the colonel sighed. "I thought she was fond of me. She couldn't have written that book unless she hated me."

"Oh, I don't believe that. I don't think she's capable of hatred."

"You're not going to pretend that she loves me?"

"No."

"Well, what does she feel for me?"

Harry Blane leaned back in his swivel chair and looked at George reflectively.

"Indifference, I should say."

The colonel gave a little shudder and reddened.

"After all, you're not in love with her, are you?"

George Peregrine did not answer directly.

"It's been a great blow to me not to have any children, but I've never let her see that I think she's let me down. I've always been kind to her. Within reasonable limits I've tried to do my duty by her."

The lawyer passed a large hand over his mouth to conceal the smile that trembled on his lips.

"It's been such an awful shock to me," Peregrine went on. "Damn it all, even ten years ago Evie was no chicken and God knows, she wasn't much to look at. It's so ugly." He sighed deeply. "What would *you* do in my place?"

"Nothing."

George Peregrine drew himself bolt upright in his chair and he looked at Harry with the stern set face that he must have worn when he inspected his regiment.

"I can't overlook a thing like this. I've been made a laughing-stock. I can never hold up my head again."

"Nonsense," said the lawyer sharply, and then in a pleasant, kindly manner, "listen, old boy: the man's dead; it all happened a long while back. Forget it. Talk to people about Evie's book, rave about it, tell 'em how proud you are of her. Behave as though you had so much confidence in her, you *knew* she could never have been unfaithful to you. The world moves so quickly and people's memories are so short. They'll forget."

"I shan't forget."

"You're both middle-aged people. She probably does a great deal more for you than you think and you'd be awfully lonely without her. I don't think it matters if you don't forget. It'll be all to the good if you can get it into that thick head of yours that there's a lot more in Evie than you ever had the gumption to see."

"Damn it all, you talk as if I was to blame."

"No, I don't think you were to blame, but I'm not so sure that Evie was either. I don't suppose she wanted to fall in love with this boy. D'you remember those verses right at the end? The impression they gave me was that though she was shattered by his death, in a strange sort of way she welcomed it. All through she'd been aware of the fragility of the tie that bound them. He died in the full flush of his first love and had never known that love so seldom endures; he'd only known its bliss and beauty. In her own bitter grief she found solace in the thought that he'd been spared all sorrow."

"All that's a bit above my head, old boy. I see more or less what you mean."

George Peregrine stared unhappily at the inkstand on the desk. He was silent and the lawyer looked at him with curious, yet sympathetic, eyes.

"Do you realize what courage she must have had never by a sign to show how dreadfully unhappy she was?" he said gently.

Colonel Peregrine sighed.

"I'm broken. I suppose you're right; it's no good crying over spilt milk and it would only make things worse if I made a fuss."

"Well?"

George Peregrine gave a pitiful little smile.

"I'll take your advice. I'll do nothing. Let them think me a damned fool and to hell with them. The truth is, I don't know what I'd do without Evie. But I'll tell you what, there's one thing I shall never understand till my dying day: what in the name of heaven did the fellow ever see in her?"

THE HUMAN ELEMENT

I SEEM NEVER to find myself in Rome but at the dead season. I pass through in August or September on my way somewhere or other and spend a couple of days revisiting places or pictures that are endeared to me by old associations. It is very hot then and the inhabitants of the city spend their day interminably strolling up and down the Corso. The Caffè Nazionale is crowded with people sitting at little tables for long hours with an empty cup of coffee in front of them and a glass of water. In the Sistine Chapel you see blond and sunburned Germans, in knickerbockers and shirts open at the neck, who have walked down the dusty roads of Italy with knapsacks on their shoulders; and in St Peter's little groups of the pious, tired but eager, who have come on pilgrimage (at an inclusive rate) from some distant country. They are under the charge of a priest and they speak strange tongues. The Hotel Plaza then is cool and restful. The public rooms are dark, silent and spacious. In the lounge at tea-time the only persons are a young, smart officer and a woman with fine eyes, drinking iced lemonade, and they talk intimately, in low tones, with the unwearying fluency of their race. You go up to your room and read and write letters and come down again two hours later and they are still talking. Before dinner a few people saunter into the bar, but for the rest of the day it is empty and the barman has time to tell you of his mother in Switzerland and his experiences in New York. You discuss life and love and the high cost of liquor.

And on this occasion too I found that I had the hotel almost to myself. When the reception clerk took me to my room he told me that they were pretty full, but when, having bathed and changed, I came down again to the hall, the liftman, an old acquaintance, informed me that there were not more than a dozen people staying there. I was tired after a long and hot journey down Italy and had made up my mind to dine quietly in the hotel and go to bed early. It was late when I went into the dining-room, vast and brightly lit, but not more than three or four tables were occupied. I looked round me with satisfaction. It is very agreeable to find yourself alone in a great city which is yet not quite strange to you and in a large empty hotel. It gives you a delectable sense of freedom. I felt the wings of my spirit give a little flutter of delight. I had paused for ten minutes in the bar and had a dry Martini. I ordered myself a bottle of good red wine. My limbs were weary, but my soul responded wonderfully to food and drink and I began to feel a singular lightness of heart. I ate my soup and my fish and pleasant thoughts filled my mind. Scraps of dialogue occurred to me and my fancy played happily with the persons of a novel I was then at work on. I rolled a phrase on my tongue and it tasted better than the wine. I began to think of the difficulty of describing the looks of people in such a way as to make the reader see them as you see them. To me it has always been one of the most difficult things in fiction. What does the reader really get when you describe a face feature by feature? I should think nothing. And yet the plan some writers adopt of taking a salient characteristic, a crooked smile or shifty eyes, and emphasizing that, though effective, avoids rather than solves the problem. I looked about me and wondered how I would describe the people at the tables round me. There was one man by himself just opposite and for practice I asked myself in what way I should treat him. He was a tall, spare fellow, and what I believe is generally called loose-limbed. He wore a dinner jacket and a boiled shirt. He had a rather long face and pale eyes; his hair was fairish and wavy, but it was growing thin, and the baldness of his temples gave him a certain nobility of brow. His features were undistinguished. His mouth and nose were like everybody else's; he was clean-shaven; his skin was naturally pale, but at the moment sunburned. His appearance suggested an intellectual but slightly commonplace distinction. He looked as though he might have been a lawyer or a don who played a pretty game of golf. I felt that he had good taste and was well-read and would be a very agreeable guest at a luncheon-party in Chelsea. But how the devil one was to describe him so as in a few lines to give a vivid, interesting, and accurate picture I could not imagine. Perhaps it would be better to let all the rest go and dwell only on that rather fatigued distinction which on the whole was the most definite impression he gave. I looked at him reflectively. Suddenly he leaned forwards and gave me a stiff but courtly little bow. I have a ridiculous habit of flushing when I am taken aback and now I felt my cheeks redden. I was startled. I had been staring at him for several minutes as though he were a dummy. He must have thought me extremely rude. I nodded with a good deal of embarrassment and looked away. Fortunately at that moment the waiter was handing me a dish. To the best of my belief I had never seen the fellow before. I asked myself whether his bow was due to my insistent stare, which made him think that he had met me somewhere, or whether I had really run across him and completely forgotten. I have a bad memory for faces and I had in this case the excuse that he looked exactly like a great many other people. You saw a dozen of him at every golf course round London on a fine Sunday.

He finished his dinner before me. He got up, but on his way out stopped at my table. He stretched out his hand.

"How d'you do?" he said. "I didn't recognize you when you first came in. I wasn't meaning to cut you."

He spoke in a pleasant voice with the tones cultivated at Oxford and copied by many who have never been there. It was evident that he knew me and evident too that he had no notion that I did not also know him. I had risen and since he was a good deal taller than I he looked down on me. He held himself with a sort of languor. He stooped a little, which added to the impression he gave me of having about him an air that was vaguely apologetic. His manner was a trifle condescending and at the same time a trifle shy.

"Won't you come and have your coffee with me?" he said. "I'm quite alone."

"Yes, I shall be glad to."

He left me and I still had no notion who he was or where I had met him. I had noticed one curious thing about him. Not once during the few sentences we exchanged, when we shook hands, or when with a nod he left me, did even the suspicion of a smile cross his face. Seeing him more closely I observed that he was in his way good-looking; his features were regular, his grey eyes were handsome, he had a slim figure; but it was a way that I found uninteresting. A silly woman would say he looked romantic. He reminded you of one of the knights of Burne-Jones though he was on a larger scale and there was no suggestion that he suffered from the chronic colitis that afflicted those unfortunate creatures. He was the sort of man whom you expected to look wonderful in fancy dress till you saw him in it and then you found that he looked absurd.

Presently I finished my dinner and went into the lounge. He was sitting in a large arm-chair and when he saw me he called a waiter. I sat down. The waiter came up and he ordered coffee and liqueurs. He spoke Italian very well. I was wondering by what means I could find out who he was without offending him. People are always a little disconcerted when you do not recognize them, they are so important to themselves, it is a shock to discover of what small importance they are to others. The excellence of his Italian recalled him to me. I remembered who he was and remembered at the same time that I did not like him. His name was Humphrey Carruthers. He was in the Foreign Office and he had a position of some importance. He was in charge of I know not what department. He had been attached to various embassies and I supposed that a sojourn in Rome accounted for his idiomatic Italian. It was stupid of me not to have seen at once that he was connected with the diplomatic service. He had all the marks of the profession. He had the supercilious courtesy that is so well calculated to put up the backs of the general public and the aloofness due to the consciousness the diplomat has that he is not as other men are, joined with the shyness occasioned by his uneasy feeling that other men do not quite realize it. I had known Carruthers for a good many years, but had met him infrequently, at luncheon-parties where I said no more than how do you do to him and at the opera where he gave me a cool nod. He was generally thought intelligent; he was certainly cultured. He could talk of all the right things. It was inexcusable of me not to have remembered him, for he had lately acquired a very considerable reputation as a writer of short stories. They had appeared first in one or other of those magazines that are founded now and then by well-disposed persons to give the intelligent reader something worthy of his attention and that die when their proprietors have lost as much money as they want to; and in their discreet and handsomely printed pages had excited as much attention as an exiguous circulation permitted. Then they were published in book form. They created a sensation. I have seldom read such unanimous praise in the weekly papers. Most of them gave the book a column and the Literary Supplement of *The Times* reviewed it not among the common ruck of novels but in a place by itself cheek by jowl with the memoirs of a distinguished statesman. The critics welcomed Humphrey Carruthers as a new star in the firmament. They praised his distinction, his subtlety, his delicate irony, and his insight. They praised his style, his sense of beauty, and his atmosphere. Here at last was a writer who had raised the short story from the depths into which in English-speaking countries it had fallen and here was work to which an Englishman could point with pride; it bore comparison with the best compositions in this manner of Finland, Russia, and Czecho-Slovakia.

Three years later Humphrey Carruthers brought out his second book and the critics commented on the interval with satisfaction. Here was no hack prostituting his talent for money! The praise it received was perhaps a little cooler than that which welcomed his first volume, the critics had had time to collect themselves, but it was enthusiastic enough to have delighted any common writer who earns his living by his pen and there was no doubt that his position in the world of letters was secure and honourable. The story that attracted most commendation was called *The Shaving Mop* and all the best critics pointed out with what beauty the author in three or four pages had laid bare the tragic soul of a barber's assistant.

But his best-known story, which was also his longest, was called *Week End*. It gave its title to his first book. It narrated the adventures of a number of people who left Paddington Station on Saturday afternoon to stay with friends at Taplow and on Monday morning returned to London. It was so delicate that it was a little difficult to know exactly what happened. A young man, parliamentary secretary to a Cabinet Minister, very nearly proposed to a baronet's daughter, but didn't. Two or three others went on the river in a punt. They all talked a great deal in an allusive way, but none of them ever finished a sentence and what they meant was very subtly indicated by dots and dashes. There were a good many descriptions of flowers in the garden and a sensitive picture of the Thames under the rain. It was all seen through the eyes of the German governess and everyone agreed that Carruthers had conveyed her outlook on the situation with quite delicious humour.

I read both Humphrey Carruthers's books. I think it part of the writer's business to make himself aware of what is being written by his contemporaries. I am very willing to learn and I thought I might discover in them something that would be useful to me. I was disappointed. I like a story to have a beginning, a middle, and an end. I have a weakness for a point. I think atmosphere is all very well, but atmosphere without anything else is like a frame without a picture; it has not much significance. But it may be that I could not see the merit of Humphrey Carruthers on account of defects in myself, and if I have described his two most successful stories without enthusiasm the cause perhaps lies in my own wounded vanity. For I was perfectly conscious that Humphrey Carruthers looked upon me as a writer of no account. I am convinced that he had never read a word I had written. The popularity I enjoyed was sufficient to persuade him that there was no occasion for him to give me any of his attention. For a moment, such was the stir he created, it looked as though he might himself be faced with that ignominy, but it soon appeared that his exquisite work was above the heads of the public. One can never tell how large the intelligentsia is, but one can tell fairly well how many of its members are prepared to pay money to patronize the arts they cherish. The plays that are of too fine a quality to attract the patrons of the commercial theatre can count on an audience of ten thousand, and the books that demand from their readers more comprehension than can be expected from the common herd sell twelve hundred copies. For the intelligentsia, notwithstanding their sensitiveness to beauty, prefer to go to the theatre on the nod and to get a book from the library.

I am sure this did not distress Carruthers. He was an artist. He was also a clerk in the Foreign Office. His reputation as a writer was distinguished; he was not interested in the vulgar, and to sell well would possibly have damaged his career. I could not surmise what had induced him to invite me to have coffee with him. It is true he was alone, but I should have supposed he found his thoughts excellent company, and I could not believe he imagined that I had anything to say that would interest him. Nevertheless I could not but see that he was doing his dreary best to be affable. He reminded me of where we had last met and we talked for a moment of common friends in London. He asked me how I came to be in Rome at this season and I told him. He volunteered the information that he had arrived that morning from Brindisi. Our conversation did not go easily and I made up my mind that as soon as I civilly could I would get up and leave him. But presently I had an odd sensation, I hardly know what caused it, that he was conscious of this and was desperately anxious not to give me the opportunity. I was surprised. I gathered my wits about me. I noticed that whenever I paused he broke in with a new topic. He was trying to find something to interest me so that I should stay. He was straining every nerve to be agreeable. Surely he could not be lonely; with his diplomatic connexions he must know plenty of people with whom he could have spent the evening. I wondered indeed that he was not dining at the Embassy; even though it was summer there must be someone there he knew. I noticed also that he never smiled. He talked with a sort of harsh eagerness as though he were afraid of a moment's silence and the sound of his voice shut out of his mind something that tortured him. It was very strange. Though I did not like him, though he meant nothing to me and to be with him irked me somewhat, I was against my will a trifle interested. I gave him a searching glance. I wondered if it was my fancy that I saw in those pale eyes of his the cowed look of a hunted dog and, notwithstanding his neat features and his expression so civilly controlled, in his aspect something that suggested the grimace of a soul in pain. I could not understand. A dozen absurd notions flashed through my mind. I was not particularly sympathetic: like an old war horse scenting the fray I roused myself. I had been feeling very tired, but now I grew alert. My sensibilities put out tentacles. I was suddenly alive to every expression of his face and every gesture. I put aside the thought that had come to me that he had written a play and wanted my advice. These exquisite persons succumb strangely to the glamour of the footlights and they are not averse from getting a few tips from the craftsman whose competence they superciliously despise. No, it was not that. A single man in Rome, of aesthetic leanings, is liable to get into trouble, and I asked myself whether Carruthers had got into some difficulty to extricate himself from which the Embassy was the last place he could go to. The idealist, I have noticed, is apt at times to be imprudent in the affairs of the flesh. He sometimes finds love in places which the police inconveniently visit. I tittered in my heart. Even the gods laugh when a prig is caught in an equivocal situation.

Suddenly Carruthers said something that staggered me.

"I'm so desperately unhappy," he muttered.

He said it without warning. He obviously meant it. There was in his tone a sort of gasp. It might very well have been a sob. I cannot describe what a shock it was to me to hear him say those words. I felt as you do when you turn a corner of the street and on a sudden a great blast of wind meets you, takes your breath away, and nearly blows you off your feet. It was so unexpected. After all I hardly knew the fellow. We were not friends. I did not like him; he did not like me. I have never looked on him as quite human. It was amazing that a man so self-controlled, so urbane, accustomed to the usages of polite society, should break in upon a stranger with such a confession. I am naturally reticent. I should be ashamed, whatever I was suffering, to disclose my pain to another. I shivered. His weakness outraged me. For a moment I was filled with a passion of anger. How dared he thrust the anguish of his soul on me? I very nearly cried:

"What the hell do I care?"

But I didn't. He was sitting huddled up in the big arm-chair. The solemn nobility of his features, which reminded one of the marble statue of a Victorian statesman, had strangely crumpled and his face sagged. He looked almost as though he were going to cry. I hesitated. I faltered. I had flushed when he spoke and now I felt my face go white. He was a pitiable object.

"I'm awfully sorry," I said.

"Do you mind if I tell you about it?"

"No."

It was not the moment for many words. I suppose Carruthers was in the early forties. He was a well-made man, athletic in his way, and with a confident bearing. Now he looked twenty years older and strangely shrivelled. He reminded me of the dead soldiers I had seen during the war and how oddly small death had made them. I was embarrassed and looked away, but I felt his eyes claiming mine and I looked back.

"Do you know Betty Welldon-Burns?" he asked me.

"I used to meet her sometimes in London years ago. I've not seen her lately."

"She lives in Rhodes now, you know. I've just come from there. I've been staying with her."

"Oh?"

He hesitated.

"I'm afraid you'll think it awfully strange of me to talk to you like this. I'm at the end of my tether. If I don't talk to somebody I shall go off my head."

He had ordered double brandies with the coffee and now calling the waiter he ordered himself another. We were alone in the lounge. There was a little shaded lamp on the table between us. Because it was a public room he spoke in a low voice. The place gave one oddly enough a sense of intimacy. I cannot repeat all that Carruthers said to me in the words he said it; it would be impossible for me to remember them; it is more convenient for me to put it in my own fashion. Sometimes he could not bring himself to say a thing right out and I had to guess at what he meant. Sometimes he had not understood, and it seemed to me that in certain ways I saw the truth more clearly than he. Betty Welldon-Burns had a very keen sense of humour and he had none. I perceived a good deal that had escaped him.

I had met her a good many times, but I knew her chiefly from hearsay. In her day she had made a great stir in the little world of London and I had heard of her often before I met her. This was at a dance in Portland Place soon after the war. She was then already at the height of her celebrity. You could not open an illustrated paper without seeing in it a portrait of her, and her mad pranks were a staple of conversation. She was twenty-four. Her mother was dead, her father, the Duke of St Erth, old and none too rich, spent most of the year in his Cornish castle and she lived in London with a widowed aunt. At the outbreak of the war she went to France. She was just eighteen. She was a nurse in a hospital at the Base and then drove a car. She acted in a theatrical tour designed to amuse the troops; she posed in *tableaux* at home for charitable purposes, held auctions for this object and that, and sold flags in Piccadilly. Every one of her activities was widely advertised and in every new role she was profusely photographed. I suppose that she managed to have a very good time. But now that the war was over she was having her fling with a vengeance. Just then everybody a little lost his head. The young, relieved of the burden that for five years had oppressed them, indulged in one wild escapade after another. Betty took part in them all. Sometimes, for one reason or another, an account of them found its way into the newspapers and her name was always in the headlines. At that time night clubs were in the first flush of their success and she was to be seen at them every night. She lived a life of hectic gaiety. It can only be described in a hackneyed phrase, because it was a hackneyed thing. The British public in its odd way took her to its heart and Lady Betty was a sufficient description of her throughout the British islands. Women mobbed her when she went to a wedding and the gallery applauded her at first nights as though she were a popular actress. Girls copied the way she did her hair and manufacturers of soap and face cream paid her money to use her photograph to advertise their wares.

Of course dull, stodgy people, the people who remembered and regretted the old order, disapproved of her. They sneered at her constant appearance in the limelight. They said she had an insane passion for self-advertisement. They said she was fast. They said she drank too much. They said she smoked too much. I will admit that nothing I had heard of her had predisposed me to think very well of her. I held cheap the women who seemed to look upon the war as an occasion to enjoy themselves and be talked about. I am bored by the papers in which you see photographs of persons in society walking in Cannes or playing golf at St Andrews. I have always found the Bright Young People extremely tedious. The gay life seems dull and stupid to the onlooker, but the moralist is unwise to judge it harshly. It is as absurd to be angry with the young things who lead it as with a litter of puppies scampering aimlessly around, rolling one another over and chasing their tails. It is well to bear it with fortitude if they cause havoc in the flower beds or break a piece of china. Some of them will be drowned because their points are not up to the mark and the rest will grow up into well-behaved dogs. Their unruliness is due only to the vitality of youth.

And it was vitality that was Betty's most shining characteristic. The urge of life flowed through her with a radiance that dazzled you. I do not think I shall ever forget the impression she made on me at the party at which I first saw her. She was like a maenad. She danced with an abandon that made you laugh, so obvious was her intense enjoyment of the music and the movement of her young limbs. Her hair was brown, slightly disordered by the vigour of her gestures, but her eyes were deep blue, and her skin was milk and roses. She was a great beauty, but she had none of the coldness of great beauty. She laughed constantly and when she was not laughing she smiled and her eyes danced with the joy of living. She was like a milkmaid on the farmstead of the gods. She had the strength and health of the people; and yet the independence of her bearing, a sort of noble frankness of carriage, suggested the great lady. I do not quite know how to put the feeling she gave me, that though so simple and unaffected she was not unconscious of her station. I fancied that if occasion arose she could get on her dignity and be very grand indeed. She was charming to everybody because, probably without being quite aware of it, in the depths of her heart she felt that the rest of the world was perfectly insignificant. I understood why the factory girls in the East End adored her and why half a million people who had never seen her except in a photograph looked upon her with the intimacy of personal friendship. I was introduced to her and she spent a few minutes talking to me. It was extraordinarily flattering to see the interest she showed in you; you knew she could not really be so pleased to meet you as she seemed or so delighted with what you said, but it was very attractive. She had the gift of being able to jump over the first difficult phases of acquaintance and you had not known her for five minutes before you felt you had known her all her life. She was snatched away from me by someone who wanted to dance with her and she surrendered herself to her partner's arms with just the same eager happiness as she had shown when she sank into a chair by my side. I was surprised when I met her at luncheon a fortnight later to find that she remembered exactly what we had talked about during those noisy ten minutes at the dance. A young woman with all the social graces.

I mentioned the incident to Carruthers.

"She was no fool," he said. "Very few people knew how intelligent she was. She wrote some very good poetry. Because she was so gay, because she was so reckless and never cared a damn for anybody, people thought she was scatter-brained. Far from it. She was as clever as a monkey. You would never have thought she'd had the time to read all the things she had. I don't suppose anyone knew that side of her as well as I did. We used to take walks together, in the country at week-ends, and in London we'd drive out to Richmond Park and walk there, and talk. She loved flowers and trees and grass. She was interested in everything. She had a lot of information and a lot of sense. There was nothing she couldn't talk about. Sometimes when we'd been for a walk in the afternoon and we met at a night club and she'd had a couple of glasses of champagne, that was enough to make her completely buffy, you know, and she was the life and soul of the party, I couldn't help thinking how amazed the rest of them would be if they knew how seriously we'd been talking only a few hours before. It was an extraordinary contrast. There seemed to be two entirely different women in her."

Carruthers said all this without a smile. He spoke with the melancholy he might have used if he had been speaking of some person snatched from the pleasant company of the living by untimely death. He gave a deep sigh.

"I was madly in love with her. I proposed to her half a dozen times. Of course I knew I hadn't a chance. I was only a very junior clerk at the FO, but I couldn't help myself. She refused me, but she was always frightfully nice about it. It never made any difference to our friendship. You see, she really liked me. I gave her something that other people didn't. I always thought that she was really fonder of me than of anybody. I was crazy about her."

"I don't suppose you were the only one," I said, having to say something.

"Far from it. She used to get dozens of love letters from men she'd never seen or heard of, farmers in Africa, miners, and policemen in Canada. All sorts of people proposed to her. She could have married anyone she liked."

"Even royalty, one heard."

"Yes, she said she couldn't stand the life. And then she married Jimmie Welldon-Burns."

"People were rather surprised, weren't they?"

"Did you ever know him?"

"No, I don't think so. I may have met him, but he left no impression on me."

"He wouldn't. He was the most insignificant fellow that ever breathed. His father was a big manufacturer up in the North. He'd made a lot of money during the war and bought a baronetcy. I believe he hadn't an aitch to his name. Jimmie was at Eton with me, they'd tried hard to make a gentleman of him, and in London after the war he was about a good deal. He was always willing to throw a party. No one ever paid any attention to him. He just paid the bill. He was the most crashing bore. You know, rather prim, terribly polite; he made you rather uncomfortable because he was so anxious not to do the wrong thing. He always wore his clothes as though he'd just put them on for the first time and they were a little too tight for him."

When Carruthers innocently opened his *Times* one morning and casting his eyes down the fashionable intelligence of the day saw that a marriage had been arranged between Elizabeth, only daughter of the Duke of St Erth, and James, eldest son of Sir John Welldon-Burns, Bart, he was dumbfounded. He rang Betty up and asked if it was true.

"Of course," she said.

He was so shocked that for the moment he found nothing to say. She went on speaking.

"He's bringing his family to luncheon today to meet father. I daresay it'll be a bit grim. You might stand me a cocktail at Claridge's to fortify me, will you?"

"At what time?" he asked.

"One."

"All right. I'll meet you there."

He was waiting for her when she came in. She walked with a sort of spring as though her eager feet itched to break into a dance. She was smiling. Her eyes shone with the joy that suffused her because she was alive and the world was such a pleasant place to live in. People recognizing her whispered to one another as she came in. Carruthers really felt that she brought sunshine and the scent of flowers into the sober but rather overwhelming splendour of Claridge's lounge. He did not wait to say how do you do to her.

"Betty, you can't do it," he said. "It's simply out of the question."

"Why?"

"He's awful."

"I don't think he is. I think he's rather nice."

A waiter came up and took their order. Betty looked at Carruthers with those beautiful blue eyes of hers that managed to be at the same time so gay and so tender.

"He's such a frightful bounder, Betty."

"Oh, don't be so silly, Humphrey. He's just as good as anybody else. I think you're rather a snob."

"He's so dull."

"No, he's rather quiet. I don't know that I want a husband who's too brilliant. I think he'll make a very good background. He's quite good-looking and he has nice manners."

"My God, Betty."

"Oh, don't be idiotic, Humphrey."

"Are you going to pretend you're in love with him?"

"I think it would be tactful, don't you?"

"Why are you going to marry him?"

She looked at him coolly.

"He's got pots of money. I'm nearly twenty-six."

There was nothing much more to be said. He drove her back to her aunt's house. She had a very grand marriage, with dense crowds lining the approach to St Margaret's, Westminster, presents from practically all the royal family, and the honeymoon was passed on the yacht her father-in-law had lent them. Carruthers applied for a post abroad and was sent to Rome (I was right in guessing that he had thus acquired his admirable Italian) and later to Stockholm. Here he was counsellor and here he wrote the first of his stories.

Perhaps Betty's marriage had disappointed the British public who expected much greater things of her, perhaps it was only that as a young married woman she no longer appealed to the popular sense of romance; the fact was plain that she soon lost her place in the public eye. You ceased to hear very much about her. Not long after the marriage it was rumoured that she was going to have a baby and a little later that she had had a miscarriage. She did not drop out of society, I suppose she continued to see her friends, but her activities were no longer spectacular. She was certainly but seldom seen any more in those raffish assemblies where the members of a tarnished aristocracy hob-nob with the hangers-on of the arts and flatter themselves that they are being at once smart and cultured. People said she was settling down. They wondered how she was getting on with her husband and no sooner did they do this than they concluded that she was not getting on very well. Presently gossip said that Jimmie was drinking too much and then, a year or two later, one heard that he had contracted tuberculosis. The Welldon-Burnses spent a couple of winters in Switzerland. Then the news spread that they had separated and Betty had gone to live in Rhodes. An odd place to choose.

"It must be deadly," her friends said.

A few of them went to stay with her now and then and came back with reports of the beauty of the island and the leisurely charm of the life. But of course it was very lonely. It seemed strange that Betty, with her brilliance and her energy, should be content to settle there. She had bought a house. She knew no one but a few Italian officials, there was indeed no one to know; but she seemed perfectly happy. Her visitors could not make it out. But the life of London is busy and memories are short. People ceased to concern themselves with her. She was forgotten. Then, a few weeks before I met Humphrey Carruthers in Rome, *The Times* announced the death of Sir James Welldon-Burns, second baronet. His younger brother succeeded him in the title. Betty had never had a child.

Carruthers continued to see her after the marriage. Whenever he came to London they lunched together. She had the ability to take up a friendship after a long separation as though no passage of time had intervened, so that there was never any strangeness in their meetings. Sometimes she asked him when he was going to marry.

"You're getting on, you know, Humphrey. If you don't marry soon you'll get rather old-maidish."

"D'you recommend marriage?"

It was not a very kindly thing to say, because like everyone else he had heard that she was not getting on too well with her husband, but her remark piqued him.

"On the whole. I think probably an unsatisfactory marriage is better than no marriage at all."

"You know quite well that nothing would induce me to marry and you know why."

"Oh, my dear, you're not going to pretend that you're still in love with me?"

"I am."

"You are a damned fool."

"I don't care."

She smiled at him. Her eyes always had that look, partly bantering, partly tender, that gave him such a happy pain in his heart. Funny, he could almost localize it.

"You're rather sweet, Humphrey. You know I'm devoted to you, but I wouldn't marry you even if I were free."

When she left her husband and went to live in Rhodes Carruthers ceased to see her. She never came to England. They maintained an active correspondence.

"Her letters were wonderful," he said. "You seemed to hear her talking. They were just like her. Clever and witty, inconsequent and yet so shrewd."

He suggested coming to Rhodes for a few days, but she thought he had better not. He understood why. Everyone knew he had been madly in love with her. Everyone knew he was still. He did not know in what circumstances exactly the Welldon-Burnses had separated. It might be that there had been a good deal of bad feeling. Betty might think that his presence on the island would compromise her.

"She wrote a charming letter to me when my first book came out. You know I dedicated it to her. She was surprised that I had done anything so good. Everyone was very nice about it, and she was delighted with that. I think her pleasure was the chief thing that pleased me. After all I'm not a professional writer, you know: I don't attach much importance to literary success."

Fool, I thought, and liar. Did he think I had not noticed the self-satisfaction that consumed him on account of the favourable reception of his books? I did not blame him for feeling that, nothing could be more pardonable, but why be at such pains to deny it. But it was doubtless true that it was mostly for Betty's sake that he relished the notoriety they had brought him. He had a positive achievement to offer her. He could lay at her feet now not only his love, but a distinguished reputation. Betty was not very young any more, she

428

was thirty-six; her marriage, her sojourn abroad, had changed things; she was no longer surrounded by suitors; she had lost the halo with which the public admiration had surrounded her. The distance between them was no longer insuperable. He alone had remained faithful through the years. It was absurd that she should continue to bury her beauty, her wit, her social grace in an island in the corner of the Mediterranean. He knew she was fond of him. She could hardly fail to be touched by his long devotion. And the life he had to offer her now was one that he knew would appeal to her. He made up his mind to ask her once more to marry him. He was able to get away towards the end of July. He wrote and said that he was going to spend his leave in the Greek islands and if she would be glad to see him he would stop off at Rhodes for a day or two where he had heard the Italians had opened a very good hotel. He put his suggestion in this casual way out of delicacy. His training at the Foreign Office had taught him to eschew abruptness. He never willingly put himself in a position from which he could not if necessary withdraw with tact. Betty sent him a telegram in reply. She said it was too marvellous that he was coming to Rhodes and of course he must come and stay with her, for at least a fortnight, and he was to wire what boat he was coming by.

He was in a state of wild excitement when at last the ship he had taken at Brindisi steamed, soon after sunrise, into the neat and pretty harbour of Rhodes. He had hardly slept a wink all night and getting up early had watched the island loom grandly out of the dawn and the sun rise over the summer sea. Boats came out as the ship dropped her anchor. The gangway was lowered. Humphrey, leaning over the rail, watched the doctor and the port officials and the hotel couriers swarm up it. He was the only Englishman on board. His nationality was obvious. A man came on deck and immediately walked up to him.

"Are you Mr Carruthers?"

"Yes."

He was about to smile and put out his hand, but he perceived in the twinkling of an eye that the person who addressed him, an Englishman like himself, was not a gentleman. Instinctively his manner, remaining exceedingly polite, became a trifle stiff. Of course

Carruthers did not tell me this, but I see the scene so clearly that I have no hesitation in describing it.

"Her ladyship hopes you don't mind her not coming to meet you, but the boat got in so early and it's more than an hour's drive to where we live."

"Oh, of course. Her ladyship well?"

"Yes, thank you. Got your luggage ready?"

"Yes."

"If you'll show me where it is I'll tell one of these fellows to put it in a boat. You won't have any difficulty at the Customs. I've fixed that up all right, and then we'll get off. Have you had breakfast?"

"Yes, thank you."

The man was not quite sure of his aitches. Carruthers wondered who he was. You could not say he was uncivil, but he was certainly a little offhand. Carruthers knew that Betty had rather a large estate; perhaps he was her agent. He seemed very competent. He gave the porters instructions in fluent Greek and when they got in the boat and the boatmen asked for more money than he gave them, he said something that made them laugh and they shrugged their shoulders satisfied. The luggage was passed through the Customs without examination, Humphrey's guide shaking hands with the officials, and they went into a sunny place where a large yellow car was standing.

"Are you going to drive me?" asked Carruthers.

"I'm her ladyship's chauffeur."

"Oh, I see. I didn't know."

He was not dressed like a chauffeur. He wore white duck trousers and espadrilles on his bare feet, a white tennis shirt, with no tie and open at the neck, and a straw hat. Carruthers frowned. Betty oughtn't to let her chauffeur drive the car like that. It was true that he had had to get up before daybreak and it looked like being a hot drive up to the villa. Perhaps under ordinary conditions he wore uniform. Though not so tall as Carruthers, who was six feet one in his socks, he was not short; but he was broad-shouldered and squarely built, so that he looked stocky. He was not fat, but plump rather; he looked as though he had a hearty appetite and ate well. Young still, thirty perhaps or thirty-one, he had already a massive look and one day would be very beefy. Now he was a hefty fellow.

He had a broad face deeply sunburned, a short thickish nose, and a somewhat sullen look. He wore a short fair moustache. Oddly enough Carruthers had a vague feeling that he had seen him before.

"Have you been with her ladyship long?" he asked.

"Well, I have, in a manner of speaking."

Carruthers became a trifle stiffer. He did not quite like the manner in which the chauffeur spoke. He wondered why he did not say "sir" to him. He was afraid Betty had let him get a little above himself. It was like her to be a bit careless about such things. But it was a mistake. He'd give her a hint when he got a chance. Their eyes met for an instant and he could have sworn that there was a twinkle of amusement in the chauffeur's. Carruthers could not imagine why. He was not aware that there was anything amusing in him.

"That, I suppose, is the old city of the Knights," he said distantly, pointing to the battlemented walls.

"Yes. Her ladyship'll take you over. We get a rare lot of tourists here in the season."

Carruthers wished to be affable. He thought it would be nicer of him to offer to sit by the chauffeur rather than behind by himself and was just going to suggest it when the matter was taken out of his hands. The chauffeur told the porters to put Carruthers' bags at the back, and settling himself at the wheel said: "Now if you'll hop in we'll get along."

Carruthers sat down beside him and they set off along a white road that ran by the sea. In a few minutes they were in the open country. They drove in silence. Carruthers was a little on his dignity. He felt that the chauffeur was inclined to be familiar and he did not wish to give him occasion to be so. He flattered himself that he had a manner with him that puts his inferiors in their place. He thought with sardonic grimness that it would not be long before the chauffeur would be calling him "sir". But the morning was lovely; the white road ran between olive groves and the farmhouses they passed now and then, with their white walls and flat roofs, had an Oriental look that took the fancy. And Betty was waiting for him. The love in his heart disposed him to kindliness towards all men and lighting himself a cigarette he thought it would be a generous act to offer the chauffeur one too. After all, Rhodes was very far away from England

431

and the age was democratic. The chauffeur accepted the gift and stopped the car to light up.

"Have you got the baccy?" he asked suddenly.

"Have I got what?"

The chauffeur's face fell.

"Her ladyship wired to you to bring two pounds of Player's Navy Cut. That's why I fixed it up with the Customs people not to open your luggage."

"I never got the wire."

"Damn!"

"What on earth does her ladyship want with two pounds of Player's Navy Cut?"

He spoke with hauteur. He did not like the chauffeur's exclamation. The fellow gave him a sidelong glance in which Carruthers read a certain insolence.

"We can't get it here," he said briefly.

He threw away with what looked very like exasperation the Egyptian cigarette Carruthers had given him and started off again. He looked sulky. He said nothing more. Carruthers felt that his efforts at sociability had been a mistake. For the rest of the journey he ignored the chauffeur. He adopted the frigid manner that he had used so successfully as secretary at the Embassy when a member of the British public came to him for assistance. For some time they had been running up hill and now they came to a long low wall and then to an open gate. The chauffeur turned in.

"Have we arrived?" cried Carruthers.

"Sixty-five kilometres in fifty-seven minutes," said the chauffeur, a smile suddenly showing his fine white teeth. "Not so bad considering the road."

He sounded his klaxon shrilly. Carruthers was breathless with excitement. They drove up a narrow road through an olive grove, and came to a low, white, rambling house. Betty was standing at the door. He jumped out of the car and kissed her on both cheeks. For a moment he could not speak. But subconsciously he noticed that at the door stood an elderly butler in white ducks and a couple of footmen in the fustanellas of their country. They were smart and picturesque. Whatever Betty permitted her chauffeur it was evident that the house was run in the civilized style suited to her station. She led him through the hall, a large apartment with whitewashed walls in which he was vaguely conscious of handsome furniture, into the drawing-room. This was also large and low, with the same whitewashed walls, and he had immediately an impression of comfort and luxury.

"The first thing you must do is to come and look at my view," she said.

"The first thing I must do is to look at you."

She was dressed in white. Her arms, her face, her neck, were deeply burned by the sun; her eyes were bluer than he had ever seen them and the whiteness of her teeth was startling. She looked extremely well. She was very trim and neat. Her hair was waved, her nails were manicured; he had had a moment's anxiety that in the easy life she led on this romantic isle she had let herself go.

"Upon my word you look eighteen, Betty. How do you manage it?"

"Happiness," she smiled.

It gave him a momentary pang to hear her say this. He did not want her to be too happy. He wanted to give her happiness. But now she insisted on taking him out on the terrace. The drawing-room had five long windows that led out to it and from the terrace the olive-clad hill tumbled steeply to the sea. There was a tiny bay below in which a white boat, mirrored on the calm water, lay at anchor. On a further hill, round the corner, you saw the white houses of a Greek village and beyond it a huge grey crag surmounted by the battlements of a medieval castle.

"It was one of the strongholds of the Knights," she said. "I'll take you up there this evening."

The scene was quite lovely. It took your breath away. It was peaceful and yet it had a strange air of life. It moved you not to contemplation, but stirred you to activity.

"You've got the tobacco all right, I suppose."

He started.

"I'm afraid I haven't. I never got your wire."

"But I wired to the Embassy and I wired to the Excelsior."

"I stayed at the Plaza."

"What a bore! Albert'll be furious."

433

"Who is Albert?"

"He drove you out. Player's is the only tobacco he likes and he can't get it here."

"Oh, the chauffeur." He pointed to the boat that lay gleaming beneath them. "Is that the yacht I've heard about?"

"Yes."

It was a large caïque that Betty had bought, fitted with a motor auxiliary and smartened up. In it she wandered about the Greek islands. She had been as far north as Athens and as far south as Alexandria.

"We'll take you for a trip if you can spare the time," she said. "You ought to see Cos while you're here."

"Who runs it for you?"

"Of course I have a crew, but Albert chiefly. He's very clever with motors and all that."

He did not know why it gave him a vague discomfort to hear her speak of the chauffeur again. Carruthers wondered if she did not leave too much in his hands. It was a mistake to give a servant too much leeway.

"You know, I couldn't help thinking I'd seen Albert before somewhere. But I can't place him."

She smiled brightly, her eyes shining, with that sudden gaiety of hers that gave her face its delightful frankness.

"You ought to remember him. He was the second footman at Aunt Louise's. He must have opened the door to you hundreds of times."

Aunt Louise was the aunt with whom Betty had lived before her marriage.

"Oh, is that who he is? I suppose I must have seen him there without noticing him. How does he happen to be here?"

"He comes from our place at home. When I married he wanted to come with me, so I took him. He was Jimmie's valet for some time and then I sent him to some motor works, he was mad about cars, and eventually I took him on as my chauffeur. I don't know what I should do without him now."

"Don't you think it's rather a mistake to get too dependent on a servant?"

"I don't know. It never occurred to me."

Betty showed him the rooms that had been got ready for him, and when he had changed they strolled down to the beach. A dinghy was waiting for them and they rowed out to the caïque and bathed from there. The water was warm and they sunned themselves on the deck. The caïque was roomy, comfortable, and luxurious. Betty showed him over and they came upon Albert tinkering with the engines. He was in filthy overalls, his hands were black and his face was smeared with grease.

"What's the matter, Albert?" said Betty.

He raised himself and faced her respectfully.

"Nothing, m'lady. I was just 'aving a look round."

"There are only two things Albert loves in the world. One is the car and the other's the yacht. Isn't that true, Albert?"

She gave him a gay smile and Albert's rather stolid face lit up. He showed his beautiful white teeth.

"That's true, m'lady."

"He sleeps on board, you know. We rigged up a very nice cabin for him aft."

Carruthers fell into the life very easily. Betty had bought the estate from a Turkish pasha exiled to Rhodes by Abdul Hamid and she had added a wing to the picturesque house. She had made a wild garden of the olive grove that surrounded it. It was planted with rosemary and lavender and asphodel, broom that she had had sent from England and the roses for which the island was famous. In the spring, she told him, the ground was carpeted with anemones. But when she showed him her property, telling him her plans and what alterations she had in mind, Carruthers could not help feeling a little uneasy.

"You talk as though you were going to live here all your life," he said.

"Perhaps I am," she smiled.

"What nonsense! At your age."

"I'm getting on for forty, old boy," she answered lightly.

He discovered with satisfaction that Betty had an excellent cook and it gratified his sense of propriety to dine with her in the splendid dining-room, with its Italian furniture, and be waited on by the dignified Greek butler and the two handsome footmen in their flamboyant uniforms. The house was furnished with taste; the rooms contained nothing that was not essential, but every piece was good. Betty lived in considerable state. When, the day after his arrival, the Governor with several members of his staff came over to dinner she displayed all the resources of the household. The Governor entering the house passed between a double row of flunkeys magnificent in their starched petticoats, embroidered jackets, and velvet caps. It was almost a bodyguard. Carruthers liked the grand style. The dinner-party was very gay. Betty's Italian was fluent and Carruthers spoke it perfectly. The young officers in the Governor's suite were uncommonly smart in their uniforms. They were very attentive to Betty and she treated them with easy cordiality. She chaffed them. After dinner the gramophone was turned on and they danced with her one after the other.

When they were gone Carruthers asked her:

"Aren't they all madly in love with you?"

"I don't know about that. They hint occasionally at alliances permanent or otherwise, but they take it very good-naturedly when I decline with thanks."

They were not serious. The young ones were callow and the not so young were fat and bald. Whatever they might feel about her Carruthers could not for a moment believe that Betty would make a fool of herself with a middle-class Italian. But a day or two later a curious thing happened. He was in his rooms dressing for dinner; he heard a man's voice outside in the passage, he could not hear what was said or what language was spoken, and then ringing out suddenly Betty's laughter. It was a charming laugh, rippling and gay, like a young girl's, and it had a joyous abandon that was infectious. But whom could she be laughing with? It was not the way you would laugh with a servant. It had a curious intimacy. It may seem strange that Carruthers read all this into a peal of laughter, but it must be remembered that Carruthers was very subtle. His stories were remarkable for such touches.

When they met presently on the terrace and he was shaking a cocktail he sought to gratify his curiosity.

"What were you laughing your head off over just now? Has anyone been here?"

"No."

She looked at him with genuine surprise.

"I thought one of your Italian officers had come to pass the time of day."

"No."

Of course the passage of years had had its effect on Betty. She was beautiful, but her beauty was mature. She had always had assurance, but now she had repose; her serenity was a feature, like her blue eyes and her candid brow, that was part of her beauty. She seemed to be at peace with all the world; it rested you to be with her as it rested you to lie among the olives within sight of the wine-coloured sea. Though she was as gay and witty as ever, the seriousness which once he had been alone to know was now patent. No one could accuse her any longer of being scatter-brained; it was impossible not to perceive the fineness of her character. It had even nobility. That was not a trait it was usual to find in the modern woman and Carruthers said to himself that she was a throw-back; she reminded him of the great ladies of the eighteenth century. She had always had a feeling for literature, the poems she wrote as a girl were graceful and melodious, and he was more interested than surprised when she told him that she had undertaken a solid historical work. She was getting materials together for an account of the Knights of St John in Rhodes. It was a story of romantic incidents. She took Carruthers to the city and showed him the noble battlements and together they wandered through austere and stately buildings. They strolled up the silent Street of the Knights with the lovely stone façades and the great coats of arms that recalled a dead chivalry. She had a surprise for him there. She had bought one of the old houses and with affectionate care had restored it to its old state. When you entered the little courtyard, with its carved stone stairway, you were taken back into the middle ages. It had a tiny walled garden in which a fig-tree grew and roses. It was small and secret and silent. The old knights had been in contact with the East long enough to have acquired Oriental ideas of privacy.

"When I'm tired of the villa I come here for two or three days and picnic. It's a relief sometimes not to be surrounded by people."

"But you're not alone here?"

"Practically."

There was a little parlour austerely furnished.

"What is this?" said Carruthers pointing with a smile to a copy of the *Sporting Times* that lay on a table.

"Oh, that's Albert's. I suppose he left it here when he came to meet you. He has the *Sporting Times* and the *News of the World* sent him every week. That is how he keeps abreast of the great world."

She smiled tolerantly. Next to the parlour was a bedroom with nothing much in it but a large bed.

"The house belonged to an Englishman. That's partly why I bought it. He was a Sir Giles Quern, and one of my ancestors married a Mary Quern who was a cousin of his. They were Cornish people."

Finding that she could not get on with her history without such a knowledge of Latin as would enable her to read the medieval documents with ease, Betty had set about learning the classical language. She troubled to acquire only the elements of grammar and then started, with a translation by her side, to read the authors that interested her. It is a very good method of learning a language and I have often wondered that it is not used in schools. It saves all the endless turning over of dictionaries and the fumbling search for meaning. After nine months Betty could read Latin as fluently as most of us can read French. It seemed a trifle ridiculous to Carruthers that this lovely, brilliant creature should take her work so seriously and yet he was moved; he would have liked to snatch her in his arms and kiss her, not at that moment as a woman, but as a precocious child whose cleverness suddenly enchants you. But later he reflected upon what she had told him. He was of course a very clever man, otherwise he could not have attained the position he held in the Foreign Office, and it would be silly to claim that those two books of his could have made so much stir without some merit; if I have made him look a bit of a fool it is only because I did not happen to like him, and if I have derided his stories it is merely because stories of that sort seem to me rather silly. He had tact and insight. He had a conviction that there was but one way to win her. She was in a groove and happy in it, her plans were definite; but her life at Rhodes was so well-ordered, so complete and satisfying, that for that very reason its hold over her could be combated. His chance was to arouse in her the restlessness that lies deep in the heart of the English. So he talked to Betty of England and London, their common friends and the painters, writers, and musicians with whom his literary success had brought him acquaintance. He talked of the Bohemian parties in Chelsea, and of the opera, of trips to Paris *en bande* for a fancy-dress ball, or to Berlin to see the new plays. He recalled to her imagination a life rich and easy, varied, cultured, intelligent, and highly civilized. He tried to make her feel that she was stagnating in a backwater. The world was hurrying on, from one new and interesting phase to another, and she was standing still. They were living in a thrilling age and she was missing it. Of course he did not tell her this; he left her to infer it. He was amusing and spirited, he had an excellent memory for a good story, he was whimsical and gay. I know I have not made Humphrey Carruthers witty any more than I have shown Lady Betty brilliant. The reader must take my word for it that they were. Carruthers was generally reckoned an entertaining companion, and that is half the battle; people were willing to find him amusing and they vowed the things he said were marvellous. Of course his wit was social. It needed a particular company, who understood his allusions and shared his exclusive sense of humour. There are a score of journalists in Fleet Street who could knock spots off the most famous of the society wits; it is their business to be witty and brilliance is in their day's work. There are a few of the society beauties whose photographs appear in the papers who could get a job at three pounds a week in the chorus of a song-and-dance show. Amateurs must be judged with tolerance. Carruthers knew that Betty enjoyed his society. They laughed a great deal together. The days passed in a flash.

"I shall miss you terribly when you go," she said in her frank way. "It's been a treat having you here. You are a sweet, Humphrey."

"Have you only just discovered it?"

He patted himself on the back. His tactics had been right. It was interesting to see how well his simple plan had worked. Like a charm. The vulgar might laugh at the Foreign Office, but there was no doubt it taught you how to deal with difficult people. Now he had but to choose his opportunity. He felt that Betty had never been more attached to him. He would wait till the end of his visit. Betty was emotional. She would be sorry that he was going. Rhodes would seem very dull without him. Whom would she have to talk to when he was gone? After dinner they usually sat on the terrace looking at the starry sea; the air was warm and balmy and vaguely scented: it was then he would ask her to marry him, on the eve of his departure. He felt it in his bones that she would accept him.

One morning when he had been in Rhodes a little over a week, he happened to be coming upstairs as Betty was walking along the passage.

"You've never shown me your room, Betty," he said.

"Haven't I? Come in and have a look now. It's rather nice."

She turned back and he followed her in. It was over the drawing-room and nearly as large. It was furnished in the Italian style, and as is the present way more like a sitting-room than a bedroom. There were fine Paninis on the walls and one or two handsome cabinets. The bed was Venetian and beautifully painted.

"That's a couch of rather imposing dimensions for a widow lady," he said facetiously.

"It is enormous, isn't it? But it was so lovely, I had to buy it. It cost a fortune."

His eye took in the bed-table by the side. There were two or three books on it, a box of cigarettes, and on an ash-tray a briar pipe. Funny! What on earth had Betty got a pipe by her bed for?

"Do look at this *cassone*. Isn't the painting marvellous? I almost cried when I found it."

"I suppose that cost a fortune too."

"I daren't tell you what I paid."

When they were leaving the room he cast another glance at the bed-table. The pipe had vanished.

It was odd that Betty should have a pipe in her bedroom, she certainly didn't smoke one herself, and if she had would have made no secret of it, but of course there were a dozen reasonable explanations. It might be a present she was making to somebody, one of the Italians or even Albert, he had not been able to see if it was new or old, or it might be a pattern that she was going to ask him to take home to have others of the same sort sent out to her. After the moment's perplexity, not altogether unmingled with amusement, he put the matter out of his mind. They were going for a picnic that day, taking their luncheon with them, and Betty was driving him herself. They had arranged to go for a cruise of a couple of days before he left so that he should see Patmos and Cos, and Albert was busy with the engines of the caïque. They had a wonderful day. They visited a ruined castle and climbed a mountain on which grew asphodel, hyacinth, and narcissus, and returned dead beat. They separated not long after dinner and Carruthers went to bed. He read for a little and then turned out his light. But he could not sleep. It was hot under his mosquito-net. He turned and tossed. Presently he thought he would go down to the little beach at the foot of the hill and bathe. It was not more than three minutes' walk. He put on his espadrilles and took a towel. The moon was full and he saw it shining on the sea through the olive-trees. But he was not alone to have thought that this radiant night would be lovely to bathe in, for just before he came out on to the beach sounds reached his ears. He muttered a little damn of vexation, some of Betty's servants were bathing, and he could not very well disturb them. The olive-trees came almost to the water's edge and undecided he stood in their shelter. He heard a voice that gave him a sudden start.

"Where's my towel?"

English. A woman waded out of the water and stood for a moment at its edge. From the darkness a man came forward with nothing but a towel round his loins. The woman was Betty. She was stark naked. The man wrapped a bath-robe round her and began drying her vigorously. She leaned on him while she put on first one shoe and then the other and to support her he placed his arm round her shoulders. The man was Albert.

Carruthers turned and fled up the hill. He stumbled blindly. Once he nearly fell. He was gasping like a wounded beast. When he got into his room he flung himself on the bed and clenched his fists and the dry, painful sobs that tore his chest broke into tears. He evidently had a violent attack of hysterics. It was all clear to him, clear with the ghastly vividness with which on a stormy night a flash of lightning can disclose a ravaged landscape, clear, horribly clear. The way the man had dried her and the way she leaned against him pointed not to passion, but to a long-continued intimacy and the pipe by the bedside, the pipe had a hideously conjugal air. It suggested the pipe a man might smoke while he was reading in bed before going to sleep. The *Sporting Times*! That was why she had that little house in the Street of the Knights, so that they could spend two or three days together in domestic familiarity. They were like an old married couple. Humphrey asked himself how long the hateful thing had lasted and suddenly he knew the answer; for years. Ten, twelve, fourteen; it had started when the young footman first came to London, he was a boy then and it was obvious enough that it was not he who had made the advances; all through those years when she was the idol of the British public, when everyone adored her and she could have married anyone she liked, she was living with the second footman at her aunt's house. She took him with her when she married. Why had she made that surprising marriage? And the still-born child that came before its time. Of course that was why she had married Jimmie Welldon-Burns, because she was going to have a child by Albert. Oh, shameless, shameless! And then, when Jimmie's health broke down she had made him take Albert as his valet. And what had Jimmie known and what had he suspected? He drank, that was what had started his tuberculosis; but why had he started drinking? Perhaps it was to still a suspicion that was so ugly that he could not face it. And it was to live with Albert that she had left Jimmie and it was to live with Albert that she had settled in Rhodes. Albert, his hands with their broken nails stained by his work on the motors, coarse of aspect and stocky, rather like a butcher with his high colour and clumsy strength, Albert not even very young any more and running to fat, uneducated and vulgar, with his common way of speaking. Albert, Albert, how could she?

Carruthers got up and drank some water. He threw himself into a chair. He could not bear his bed. He smoked cigarette after cigarette. He was a wreck in the morning. He had not slept at all. They brought him in his breakfast; he drank the coffee but could eat nothing. Presently there was a brisk knock on his door.

"Coming down to bathe, Humphrey?"

That cheerful voice sent the blood singing through his head. He braced himself and opened the door.

"I don't think I will today. I don't feel very well."

She gave him a look.

"Oh, my dear, you look all in. What's the matter with you?"

"I don't know. I think I must have got a touch of the sun."

His voice was dead and his eyes were tragic. She looked at him more closely. She did not say anything for a moment. He thought she went pale. He *knew*. Then a faintly mocking smile crossed her eyes; she thought the situation comic.

"Poor old boy, go and lie down, I'll send you in some aspirin. Perhaps you'll feel better at luncheon."

He lay in his darkened room. He would have given anything to get away then so that he need not set eyes on her again, but there was no means of that, the ship that was to take him back to Brindisi did not touch at Rhodes till the end of the week. He was a prisoner. And the next day they were to go to the islands. There was no escape from her there; in the caïque they would be in one another's pockets all day long. He couldn't face that. He was so ashamed. But she wasn't ashamed. At that moment when it had been plain to her that nothing was hidden from him any longer she had smiled. She was capable of telling him all about it. He could not bear that. That was too much. After all she couldn't be certain that he knew, at best she could only suspect; if he behaved as if nothing had happened, if at luncheon and during the days that remained he was as gay and jolly as usual she would think she had been mistaken. It was enough to know what he knew, he would not suffer the crowning humiliation of hearing from her own lips the disgraceful story. But at luncheon the first thing she said was:

"Isn't it a bore. Albert says something's gone wrong with the motor, we shan't be able to go on our trip after all. I daren't trust to sail at this time of the year. We might be becalmed for a week."

She spoke lightly and he answered in the same casual fashion.

"Oh, I'm sorry, but still I don't really care. It's so lovely here, I really didn't much want to go."

He told her that the aspirin had done him good and he felt much better; to the Greek butler and the two footmen in fustanellas it must have seemed that they talked as vivaciously as usual. That night the British consul came to dinner and the night after some Italian officers. Carruthers counted the days, he counted the hours. Oh, if the moment would only come when he could step on the ship and be free from the horror that every moment of the day obsessed him! He was growing so tired. But Betty's manner was so self-possessed that sometimes he asked himself if she really knew that he was aware of her secret. Was it the truth that she had told about the caïque and not, as had at once struck him, an excuse; and was it an accident that a succession of visitors prevented them from ever being alone together? The worst of having so much tact was that you never quite knew whether other people were acting naturally or being tactful too. When he looked at her, so easy and calm, so obviously happy, he could not believe the odious truth. And yet he had seen with his own eyes. And the future. What would her future be? It was horrible to think of. Sooner or later the truth must become notorious. And to think of Betty a mock and an outcast, in the power of a coarse and common man, growing older, losing her beauty; and the man was five years younger than she. One day he would take a mistress, one of her own maids, perhaps, with whom he would feel at home as he had never felt with the great lady, and what could she do then? What humiliation then must she be prepared to put up with! He might be cruel to her. He might beat her. Betty. Betty.

Carruthers wrung his hands. And on a sudden an idea came to him that filled him with a painful exaltation; he put it away from him, but it returned; it would not let him be. He must save her, he had loved her too much and too long to let her sink, sink as she was sinking; a passion of self-sacrifice welled up in him. Notwithstanding everything, though his love now was dead and he felt for her an almost physical repulsion, he would marry her. He laughed mirthlessly. What would his life be? He couldn't help that. He didn't matter. It was the only thing to do. He felt wonderfully uplifted, and yet very humble, for he was awed at the thoughts of the heights which the divine spirit of man could reach.

His ship was to sail on Saturday and on Thursday when the guests who had been dining left them, he said:

"I hope we're going to be alone tomorrow."

"As a matter of fact I've asked some Egyptians who spend the summer here. She's a sister of the ex-Khedive and very intelligent. I'm sure you'll like her."

"Well, it's my last evening. Couldn't we spend it alone?"

She gave him a glance. There was a faint amusement in her eyes, but his were grave.

"If you like. I can put them off."

"Then do."

★ ★ ★

444

He was to start early in the morning and his luggage was packed. Betty had told him not to dress, but he had answered that he preferred to. For the last time they sat down to dinner facing one another. The dining-room, with its shaded lights, was bare and formal, but the summer night flooding in through the great open windows gave it a sober richness. It had the effect of the private refectory in a convent to which a royal lady had retired in order to devote the remainder of her life to a piety not too austere. They had their coffee on the terrace. Carruthers drank a couple of liqueurs. He was feeling very nervous.

"Betty, my dear, I've got something I want to say to you," he began.

"Have you? I wouldn't say it if I were you."

She answered gently. She remained perfectly calm, watching him shrewdly, but with the glimmer of a smile in her blue eyes.

"I must."

She shrugged her shoulders and was silent. He was conscious that his voice trembled a little and he was angry with himself.

"You know I've been madly in love with you for many years. I don't know how many times I've asked you to marry me. But, after all, things change and people change too, don't they? We're neither of us so young as we were. Won't you marry me now, Betty?"

She gave him the smile that had always been such an attractive thing in her; it was so kindly, so frank, and still, still so wonderfully innocent.

"You're very sweet, Humphrey. It's awfully nice of you to ask me again. I can't tell you how touched I am. But you know, I'm a creature of habit, I've got in the habit of saying no to you now, and I can't change it."

"Why not?"

There was something aggressive in his tone, something almost ominous, that made her give him a quick look. Her face blanched with sudden anger, but she immediately controlled herself.

"Because I don't want to," she smiled.

"Are you going to marry anyone else?"

"I? No. Of course not."

For a moment she seemed to draw herself up as though a wave of ancestral pride swept through her and then she began to laugh. But whether she laughed at the thought that had passed through her mind or because something in Humphrey's proposal had amused her none but she could have told.

"Betty. I implore you to marry me."

"Never."

"You can't go on living this life."

He put into his voice all the anguish of his heart and his face was drawn and tortured. She smiled affectionately.

"Why not? Don't be such a donkey. You know I adore you, Humphrey, but you are rather an old woman."

"Betty. Betty."

Did she not see that it was for her sake that he wanted it? It was not love that made him speak, but human pity and shame. She got up.

"Don't be tiresome, Humphrey. You'd better go to bed, you know you have to be up with the lark. I shan't see you in the morning. Good-bye and God bless you. It's been wonderful having you here."

She kissed him on both cheeks. Next morning, early, for he had to be on board at eight, when Carruthers stepped out of the front door he found Albert waiting for him in the car. He wore a singlet, duck trousers, and a beret basque. Carruthers' luggage was in the back. He turned to the butler.

"Put my bags beside the chauffeur," he said. "I'll sit behind."

Albert made no remark. Carruthers got in and they drove off. When they arrived at the harbour, porters ran up. Albert got out of the car. Carruthers looked down at him from his greater height.

"You need not see me on board. I can manage perfectly well by myself. Here's a tip for you."

He gave him a five-pound note. Albert flushed. He was taken aback, he would have liked to refuse it, but did not know how to and the servility of years asserted itself. Perhaps he did not know what he said.

"Thank you, sir."

Carruthers gave him a curt nod and walked away. He had forced Betty's lover to call him "sir". It was as though he had struck her a blow across that smiling mouth of hers and flung in her face an opprobrious word. It filled him with a bitter satisfaction.

★ ★ ★

446

He shrugged his shoulders and I could see that even this small triumph now seemed vain. For a little while we were silent. There was nothing for me to say. Then he began again.

"I daresay you think it's very strange that I should tell you all this. I don't care. You know, I feel as if nothing mattered any more. I feel as if decency no longer existed in the world. Heaven knows, I'm not jealous. You can't be jealous unless you love and my love is dead. It was killed in a flash. After all those years. I can't think of her now without horror. What destroys me, what makes me so frightfully unhappy is to think of her unspeakable degradation."

So it has been said that it was not jealousy that caused Othello to kill Desdemona, but an agony that the creature that he believed angelic should be proved impure and worthless. What broke his noble heart was that virtue should so fall.

"I thought there was no one like her. I admired her so much. I admired her courage and her frankness, her intelligence and her love of beauty. She's just a sham and she's never been anything else."

"I wonder if that's true. Do you think any of us are all of a piece? Do you know what strikes me? I should have said that Albert was only the instrument, her toll to the solid earth, so to speak; that left her soul at liberty to range the empyrean. Perhaps the mere fact that he was so far below her gave her a sense of freedom in her relations with him that she would have lacked with a man of her own class. The spirit is very strange, it never soars so high as when the body has wallowed for a period in the gutter."

"Oh, don't talk such rot," he answered angrily.

"I don't think it is rot. I don't put it very well, but the idea's sound."

"Much good it does me. I'm broken and done for. I'm finished."

"Oh, nonsense. Why don't you write a story about it?"

"I?"

"You know, that's the great pull a writer has over other people. When something has made him terribly unhappy, and he's tortured and miserable, he can put it all into a story and it's astonishing what a comfort and relief it is."

"It would be monstrous. Betty was everything in the world to me. I couldn't do anything so caddish."

He paused for a little and I saw him reflect. I saw that notwithstanding the horror that my suggestion caused him he did for one minute look at the situation from the standpoint of the writer. He shook his head.

"Not for her sake, for mine. After all I have some self-respect. Besides, there's no story there."

FOOTPRINTS IN THE JUNGLE

THERE IS NO place in Malaya that has more charm than Tanah Merah. It lies on the sea, and the sandy shore is fringed with casuarinas. The government offices are still in the old Raad Huis that the Dutch built when they owned the land, and on the hill stand the grey ruins of the fort by aid of which the Portuguese maintained their hold over the unruly natives. Tanah Merah has a history and in the vast labyrinthine houses of the Chinese merchants, backing on the sea so that in the cool of the evening they may sit in their loggias and enjoy the salt breeze, families dwell that have been settled in the country for three centuries. Many have forgotten their native language and hold intercourse with one another in Malay and pidgin English. The imagination lingers here gratefully, for in the Federated Malay States the only past is within the memory for the most part of the fathers of living men.

Tanah Merah was for long the busiest mart of the Middle East and its harbour was crowded with shipping when the clipper and the junk still sailed the China seas. But now it is dead. It has the sad and romantic air of all places that have once been of importance and live now on the recollection of a vanished grandeur. It is a sleepy little town and strangers that come to it, losing their native energy, insensibly drop into its easy and lethargic ways. Successive rubber booms bring it no prosperity and the ensuing slumps hasten its decay.

The European quarter is very silent. It is trim and neat and clean. The houses of the white men – government servants and agents of companies – stand round an immense padang, agreeable and roomy bungalows shaded by great cassias, and the padang is vast and green and well cared for, like the lawn of a cathedral close, and

448

indeed there is in the aspect of this corner of Tanah Merah something quiet and delicately secluded that reminds you of the precincts of Canterbury.

The club faces the sea; it is a spacious but shabby building; it has an air of neglect and when you enter you feel that you intrude. It gives you the impression that it is closed really, for alterations and repairs, and that you have taken indiscreet advantage of an open door to go where you are not wanted. In the morning you may find there a couple of planters who have come in from their estates on business and are drinking a gin-sling before starting back again; and latish in the afternoon a lady or two may perhaps be seen looking with a furtive air through old numbers of the *Illustrated London News*. At nightfall a few men saunter in and sit about the billiard-room watching the play and drinking sukas. But on Wednesdays there is a little more animation. On that day the gramophone is set going in the large room upstairs and people come in from the surrounding country to dance. There are sometimes no less than a dozen couples and it is even possible to make up two tables of bridge.

It was on one of these occasions that I met the Cartwrights. I was staying with a man called Gaze who was head of the police and he came into the billiard-room, where I was sitting, and asked me if I would make up a four. The Cartwrights were planters and they came in to Tanah Merah on Wednesdays because it gave their girl a chance of a little fun. They were very nice people, said Gaze, quiet and unobtrusive, and played a very pleasant game of bridge. I followed Gaze into the card-room and was introduced to them. They were already seated at a table and Mrs Cartwright was shuffling the cards. It inspired me with confidence to see the competent way in which she did it. She took half the pack in each hand, and her hands were large and strong, deftly inserted the corners of one half under the corners of the other, and with a click and a neat bold gesture cascaded the cards together.

It had all the effect of a conjuring trick. The card-player knows that it can be done perfectly only after incessant practice. He can be fairly sure that anyone who can so shuffle a pack of cards loves cards for their own sake.

"Do you mind if my husband and I play together?" asked Mrs Cartwright. "It's no fun for us to win one another's money."

"Of course not."

We cut for deal and Gaze and I sat down.

Mrs Cartwright drew an ace and while she dealt, quickly and neatly, chatted with Gaze of local affairs. But I was aware that she took stock of me. She looked shrewd, but good-natured.

She was a woman somewhere in the fifties (though in the East, where people age quickly, it is difficult to tell their ages), with white hair very untidily arranged, and a constant gesture with her was an impatient movement of the hand to push back a long wisp of hair that kept falling over her forehead. You wondered why she did not, by the use of a hairpin or two, save herself so much trouble. Her blue eyes were large, but pale and a little tired; her face was lined and sallow; I think it was her mouth that gave it the expression which I felt was characteristic of caustic but tolerant irony. You saw that here was a woman who knew her mind and was never afraid to speak it. She was a chatty player (which some people object to strongly, but which does not disconcert me, for I do not see why you should behave at the card-table as though you were at a memorial service) and it was soon apparent that she had an effective knack of badinage. It was pleasantly acid, but it was amusing enough to be offensive only to a fool. If now and then she uttered a remark so sarcastic that you wanted all your sense of humour to see the fun in it, you could not but quickly see that she was willing to take as much as she gave. Her large, thin mouth broke into a dry smile and her eyes shone brightly when by a lucky chance you brought off a repartee that turned the laugh against her.

I thought her a very agreeable person. I liked her frankness. I liked her quick wit. I liked her plain face. I never met a woman who obviously cared so little how she looked. It was not only her head that was untidy, everything about her was slovenly; she wore a high-necked silk blouse, but for coolness had unbuttoned the top buttons and showed a gaunt and withered neck; the blouse was crumpled and none too clean, for she smoked innumerable cigarettes and covered herself with ash. When she got up for a moment to speak to somebody I saw that her blue skirt was rather ragged at the hem and badly needed a brush, and she wore heavy, low-heeled boots. But none of this mattered. Everything she wore was perfectly in character.

And it was a pleasure to play bridge with her. She played very quickly, without hesitation, and she had not only knowledge but flair. Of course she knew Gaze's game, but I was a stranger and she soon took my measure. The team-work between her husband and herself was admirable; he was sound and cautious, but knowing him, she was able to be bold with assurance and brilliant with safety. Gaze was a player who founded a foolish optimism on the hope that his opponents would not have the sense to take advantage of his errors, and the pair of us were no match for the Cartwrights. We lost one rubber after another, and there was nothing to do but smile and look as if we liked it.

"I don't know what's the matter with the cards," said Gaze at last, plaintively. "Even when we have every card in the pack we go down."

"It can't be anything to do with your play," answered Mrs Cartwright, looking him full in the face with those pale blue eyes of hers, "it must be bad luck pure and simple. Now if you hadn't had your hearts mixed up with your diamonds in that last hand you'd have saved the game."

Gaze began to explain at length how the misfortune, which had cost us dear, occurred, but Mrs Cartwright, with a deft flick of the hand, spread out the cards in a great circle so that we should cut for deal. Cartwright looked at the time.

"This will have to be the last, my dear," he said.

"Oh, will it?" She glanced at her watch and then called to a young man who was passing through the room. "Oh, Mr Bullen, if you're going upstairs tell Olive that we shall be going in a few minutes." She turned to me. "It takes us the best part of an hour to get back to the estate and poor Theo has to be up at the crack of dawn."

"Oh, well, we only come in once a week," said Cartwright, "and it's the one chance Olive gets of being gay and abandoned."

I thought Cartwright looked tired and old. He was a man of middle height, with a bald, shiny head, a stubbly grey moustache, and gold-rimmed spectacles. He wore white ducks and a black-and-white tie. He was rather neat and you could see he took much more pains with his clothes than his untidy wife. He talked little, but it was plain that he enjoyed his wife's caustic humour and sometimes he made quite a neat retort. They were evidently very good friends.

It was pleasing to see so solid and tolerant an affection between two people who were almost elderly and must have lived together for so many years.

It took but two hands to finish the rubber and we had just ordered a final gin and bitters when Olive came down.

"Do you really want to go already, Mumsey?" she asked.

Mrs Cartwright looked at her daughter with fond eyes.

"Yes, darling. It's nearly half past eight. It'll be ten before we get our dinner."

"Damn our dinner," said Olive gaily.

"Let her have one more dance before we go," suggested Cartwright.

"Not one. You must have a good night's rest."

Cartwright looked at Olive with a smile.

"If your mother has made up her mind, my dear, we may just as well give in without any fuss."

"She's a determined woman," said Olive, lovingly stroking her mother's wrinkled cheek.

Mrs Cartwright patted her daughter's hand, and kissed it.

Olive was not very pretty, but she looked extremely nice. She was nineteen or twenty, I suppose, and she had still the plumpness of her age; she would be more attractive when she had fined down a little. She had none of the determination that gave her mother's face so much character, but resembled her father; she had his dark eyes and slightly aquiline nose, and his look of rather weak good nature. It was plain that she was strong and healthy. Her cheeks were red and her eyes bright. She had a vitality that he had long since lost. She seemed to be the perfectly normal English girl, with high spirits, a great desire to enjoy herself, and an excellent temper.

When we separated, Gaze and I set out to walk to his house.

"What did you think of the Cartwrights?" he asked me.

"I liked them. They must be a great asset in a place like this."

"I wish they came oftener. They live a very quiet life."

"It must be dull for the girl. The father and mother seem very well satisfied with one another's company."

"Yes, it's been a great success."

"Olive is the image of her father, isn't she?"

Gaze gave me a sidelong glance.

"Cartwright isn't her father. Mrs Cartwright was a widow when he married her. Olive was born four months after her father's death."

"Oh!"

I drew out the sound in order to put in it all I could of surprise, interest, and curiosity. But Gaze said nothing and we walked the rest of the way in silence. The boy was waiting at the door as we entered the house and after a last gin pahit we sat down to dinner.

At first Gaze was inclined to be talkative. Owing to the restriction of the output of rubber there had sprung up a considerable activity among the smugglers and it was part of his duty to circumvent their knavishness. Two junks had been captured that day and he was rubbing his hands over his success. The go-downs were full of confiscated rubber and in a little while it was going to be solemnly burnt. But presently he fell into silence and we finished without a word. The boys brought in coffee and brandy and we lit our cheroots. Gaze leaned back in his chair. He looked at me reflectively and then looked at his brandy. The boys had left the room and we were alone.

"I've known Mrs Cartwright for over twenty years," he said slowly. "She wasn't a bad-looking woman in those days. Always untidy, but when she was young it didn't seem to matter so much. It was rather attractive. She was married to a man called Bronson. Reggie Bronson. He was a planter. He was manager of an estate up in Selantan and I was stationed at Alor Lipis. It was a much smaller place than it is now; I don't suppose there were more than twenty people in the whole community, but they had a jolly little club, and we used to have a very good time. I remember the first time I met Mrs Bronson as though it was yesterday. There were no cars in those days and she and Bronson had ridden in on their bicycles. Of course then she didn't look so determined as she looks now. She was much thinner, she had a nice colour, and her eyes were very pretty – blue, you know – and she had a lot of dark hair. If she'd only taken more trouble with herself she'd have been rather stunning. As it was she was the best-looking woman there."

I tried to construct in my mind a picture of what Mrs Cartwright – Mrs Bronson as she was then – looked like from what she was now and from Gaze's not very graphic description. In the solid woman, with her well-covered bones, who sat rather heavily at the bridge-table, I tried to see a slight young thing with buoyant movements and graceful, easy gestures. Her chin now was square and her nose decided, but the roundness of youth must have masked this: she must have been charming with a pink-and-white skin and her hair, carelessly dressed, brown and abundant. At that period she wore a long skirt, a tight waist, and a picture hat. Or did women in Malaya still wear the topees that you see in old numbers of the illustrated papers?

"I hadn't seen her for – oh, nearly twenty years," Gaze went on. "I knew she was living somewhere in the FMS, but it was a surprise when I took this job and came here to run across her in the club just as I had up in Selantan so many years before. Of course she's an elderly woman now and she's changed out of all recognition. It was rather a shock to see her with a grown-up daughter, it made me realize how the time had passed; I was a young fellow when I met her last and now, by Jingo, I'm due to retire on the age limit in two or three years. Bit thick, isn't it?"

Gaze, a rueful grin on his ugly face, looked at me with faint indignation, as though I could help the hurrying march of the years as they trod upon one another's heels.

"I'm no chicken myself," I replied.

"You haven't lived out East all your life. It ages one before one's time. One's an elderly man at fifty and at fifty-five one's good for nothing but the scrap-heap."

But I did not want Gaze to wander off into a disquisition on old age.

"Did you recognize Mrs Cartwright when you saw her again?" I asked.

"Well, I did and I didn't. At the first glance I thought I knew her, but couldn't quite place her. I thought perhaps she was someone I'd met on board ship when I was going on leave and had known only by sight. But the moment she spoke I remembered at once. I remembered the dry twinkle in her eyes and the crisp sound of her voice. There was something in her voice that seemed to mean: You're a bit of a damned fool, my lad, but you're not a bad sort and upon my soul I rather like you."

"That's a good deal to read into the sound of a voice," I smiled.

"She came up to me in the club and shook hands with me. 'How do you do, Major Gaze? Do you remember me?' she said.

"'Of course I do.'

"'A lot of water has passed under the bridge since we met last. We're none of us as young as we were. Have you seen Theo?'

"For a moment I couldn't think whom she meant. I suppose I looked rather stupid, because she gave a little smile, that chaffing smile that I knew so well, and explained.

"'I married Theo, you know. It seemed the best thing to do. I was lonely and he wanted it.'

"'I heard you married him,' I said. 'I hope you've been very happy.'

"'Oh, very. Theo's a perfect duck. He'll be here in a minute. He'll be so glad to see you.'

"I wondered. I should have thought I was the last man Theo would wish to see. I shouldn't have thought she would wish it very much either. But women are funny."

"Why shouldn't she wish to see you?" I asked.

"I'm coming to that later," said Gaze. "Then Theo turned up. I don't know why I call him Theo; I never called him anything but Cartwright, I never thought of him as anything but Cartwright. Theo was a shock. You know what he looks like now; I remembered him as a curly-headed youngster, very fresh and clean-looking. He was always neat and dapper, he had a good figure, and he held himself well, like a man who's used to taking a lot of exercise. Now I come to think of it he wasn't bad-looking, not in a big, massive way, but graceful, you know, and lithe. When I saw this bowed, cadaverous, bald-headed old buffer with spectacles I could hardly believe my eyes. I shouldn't have known him from Adam. He seemed pleased to see me, at least, interested; he wasn't effusive, but he'd always been on the quiet side and I didn't expect him to be.

"'Are you surprised to find us here?' he asked me.

"'Well, I hadn't the faintest notion where you were.'

"'We've kept track of your movements more or less. We've seen your name in the paper every now and then. You must come out one day and have a look at our place. We've been settled there a good many years, and I suppose we shall stay there till we go home for good. Have you ever been back to Alor Lipis?'

455

"'No, I haven't,' I said.

"'It was a nice little place. I'm told it's grown. I've never been back.'

"'It hasn't got the pleasantest recollections for us,' said Mrs Cartwright.

"I asked them if they'd have a drink and we called the boy. I daresay you noticed that Mrs Cartwright likes her liquor; I don't mean that she gets tight or anything like that, but she drinks her stengah like a man. I couldn't help looking at them with a certain amount of curiosity. They seemed perfectly happy; I gathered that they hadn't done at all badly, and I found out later that they were quite well off. They had a very nice car, and when they went on leave they denied themselves nothing. They were on the best of terms with one another. You know how jolly it is to see two people who've been married a great many years obviously better pleased with their own company than anyone else's. Their marriage had evidently been a great success. And they were both of them devoted to Olive and very proud of her. Theo especially."

"Although she was only his step-daughter?" I said.

"Although she was only his step-daughter," answered Gaze. "You'd think that she would have taken his name. But she hadn't. She called him Daddy, of course, he was the only father she'd ever known, but she signed her letters, Olive Bronson."

"What was Bronson like, by the way?"

"Bronson? He was a great big fellow, very hearty, with a loud voice and a bellowing laugh, beefy, you know, and a fine athlete. There was not very much to him, but he was as straight as a die. He had a red face and red hair. Now I come to think of it I remember that I never saw a man sweat as much as he did. Water just poured off him, and when he played tennis he always used to bring a towel on the court with him."

"It doesn't sound very attractive."

"He was a handsome chap. He was always fit. He was keen on that. He hadn't much to talk about but rubber and games, tennis, you know, and golf and shooting; and I don't suppose he read a book from year's end to year's end. He was the typical public-school boy. He was about thirty-five when I first knew him, but he had the mind of a boy of eighteen. You know how many fellows when they come out East seem to stop growing."

I did indeed. One of the most disconcerting things to the traveller is to see stout, middle-aged gentlemen, with bald heads, speaking and acting like schoolboys. You might almost think that no idea has entered their heads since they first passed through the Suez Canal. Though married and the fathers of children, and perhaps in control of a large business, they continue to look upon life from the stand-point of the sixth form.

"But he was no fool," Gaze went on. "He knew his work from A to Z. His estate was one of the best managed in the country and he knew how to handle his labour. He was a damned good sort, and if he did get on your nerves a little you couldn't help liking him. He was generous with his money, and always ready to do anybody a good turn. That's how Cartwright happened to turn up in the first instance."

"Did the Bronsons get on well together?"

"Oh, yes, I think so. I'm sure they did. He was good-natured and she was very jolly and gay. She was very outspoken, you know. She can be damned amusing when she likes even now, but there's generally a sting lurking in the joke; when she was a young woman and married to Bronson it was just pure fun. She had high spirits and liked having a good time. She never cared a hang what she said, but it went with her type, if you understand what I mean; there was something so open and frank and careless about her that you didn't care what she said to you. They seemed very happy.

"Their estate was about five miles from Alor Lipis. They had a trap and they used to drive in most evenings about five. Of course it was a very small community and men were in the majority. There were only about six women. The Bronsons were a god-send. They bucked things up the moment they arrived. We used to have very jolly times in that little club. I've often thought of them since and I don't know that on the whole I've ever enjoyed myself more than I did when I was stationed there. Between six and eight-thirty the club at Alor Lipis twenty years ago was about as lively a place as you could find between Aden and Yokohama.

"One day Mrs Bronson told us that they were expecting a friend to stay with them and a few days later they brought Cartwright along.

It appeared that he was an old friend of Bronson's, they'd been at school together, Marlborough, or some place like that, and they'd first come out East on the same ship. Rubber had taken a toss and a lot of fellows had lost their jobs. Cartwright was one of them. He'd been out of work for the greater part of a year and he hadn't anything to fall back on. In those days planters were even worse paid than they are now and a man had to be very lucky to put by something for a rainy day. Cartwright had gone to Singapore. They all go there when there's a slump, you know. It's awful then, I've seen it; I've known of planters sleeping in the street because they hadn't the price of a night's lodging. I've known them stop strangers outside the Europe and ask for a dollar to get a meal, and I think Cartwright had had a pretty rotten time.

"At last he wrote to Bronson and asked him if he couldn't do something for him. Bronson asked him to come and stay till things got better, at least it would be free board and lodging, and Cartwright jumped at the chance, but Bronson had to send him the money to pay his railway fare. When Cartwright arrived at Alor Lipis he hadn't ten cents in his pocket. Bronson had a little money of his own, two or three hundred a year, I think, and though his salary had been cut, he'd kept his job, so that he was better off than most planters. When Cartwright came Mrs Bronson told him that he was to look upon the place as his home and stay as long as he liked."

"It was very nice of her, wasn't it?" I remarked.

"Very."

Gaze lit himself another cheroot and filled his glass. It was very still and but for the occasional croak of the chik-chak the silence was intense. We seemed to be alone in the tropical night and heaven only knows how far from the habitations of men. Gaze did not speak for so long that at last I was forced to say something.

"What sort of a man was Cartwright at that time?" I asked. "Younger, of course, and you told me rather nice-looking; but in himself?"

"Well, to tell you the truth, I never paid much attention to him. He was pleasant and unassuming. He's very quiet now, as I daresay you noticed; well, he wasn't exactly lively then. But he was perfectly inoffensive. He was fond of reading and he played the piano rather nicely. You never minded having him about, he was never in the way, but you never bothered very much about him. He danced well and the women rather liked that, but he also played billiards quite decently and he wasn't bad at tennis. He fell into our little groove very naturally. I wouldn't say that he ever became wildly popular, but everyone liked him. Of course we were sorry for him, as one is for a man who's down and out, but there was nothing we could do, and, well, we just accepted him and then forgot that he hadn't always been there. He used to come in with the Bronsons every evening and pay for his drinks like everyone else, I suppose Bronson had lent him a bit of money for current expenses, and he was always very civil. I'm rather vague about him, because really he didn't make any particular impression on me; in the East one meets such a lot of people, and he seemed very much like anybody else. He did everything he could to get something to do, but he had no luck; the fact is, there were no jobs going, and sometimes he seemed rather depressed about it. He was with the Bronsons for over a year. I remember his saying to me once:

"'After all I can't live with them for ever. They've been most awfully good to me, but there are limits.'

"'I should think the Bronsons would be very glad to have you,' I said. 'It's not particularly gay on a rubber estate, and as far as your food and drink go, it must make precious little difference if you're there or not.'"

Gaze stopped once more and looked at me with a sort of hesitation.

"What's the matter?" I asked.

"I'm afraid I'm telling you this story very badly," he said. "I seem to be just rambling on. I'm not a damned novelist, I'm a policeman, and I'm just telling you the facts as I saw them at the time; and from my point of view all the circumstances are important; it's important, I mean, to realize what sort of people they were."

"Of course. Fire away."

"I remember someone, a woman, I think it was, the doctor's wife, asking Mrs Bronson if she didn't get tired sometimes of having a stranger in the house. You know, in places like Alor Lipis there isn't very much to talk about, and if you didn't talk about your neighbours there'd be nothing to talk about at all.

"'Oh, no,' she said, 'Theo's no trouble.' She turned to her husband, who was sitting there mopping his face. 'We like having him, don't we?'

"'He's all right,' said Bronson.

"'What does he do with himself all day long?'

"'Oh, I don't know,' said Mrs Bronson. 'He walks round the estate with Reggie sometimes, and he shoots a bit. He talks to me.'

"'He's always glad to make himself useful,' said Bronson. 'The other day when I had a go of fever, he took over my work and I just lay in bed and had a good time.'"

"Hadn't the Bronsons any children?" I asked.

"No," Gaze answered. "I don't know why, they could well have afforded it."

Gaze leant back in his chair. He took off his glasses and wiped them. They were very strong and hideously distorted his eyes. Without them he wasn't so homely. The chik-chak on the ceiling gave its strangely human cry. It was like the cackle of an idiot child.

"Bronson was killed," said Gaze suddenly.

"Killed?"

"Yes, murdered. I shall never forget that night. We'd been playing tennis, Mrs Bronson and the doctor's wife, Theo Cartwright and I; and then we played bridge. Cartwright had been off his game and when we sat down at the bridge-table Mrs Bronson said to him: 'Well, Theo, if you play bridge as rottenly as you played tennis we shall lose our shirts.'

"We'd just had a drink, but she called the boy and ordered another round.

"'Put that down your throat,' she said to him, 'and don't call without top honours and an outside trick.'

"Bronson hadn't turned up, he'd cycled in to Kabulong to get the money to pay his coolies their wages and was to come along to the club when he got back. The Bronsons' estate was nearer Alor Lipis than it was to Kabulong, but Kabulong was a more important place commercially, and Bronson banked there.

"'Reggie can cut in when he turns up,' said Mrs Bronson.

"'He's late, isn't he?' said the doctor's wife.

"'Very. He said he wouldn't get back in time for tennis, but would be here for a rubber. I have a suspicion that he went to the club at Kabulong instead of coming straight home and is having drinks, the ruffian.'

"'Oh, well, he can put away a good many without their having much effect on him,' I laughed.

"'He's getting fat, you know. He'll have to be careful.'

"We sat by ourselves in the card-room and we could hear the crowd in the billiard-room talking and laughing. They were all on the merry side. It was getting on to Christmas Day and we were all letting ourselves go a little. There was going to be a dance on Christmas Eve.

"I remembered afterwards that when we sat down the doctor's wife asked Mrs Bronson if she wasn't tired.

"'Not a bit,' she said. 'Why should I be?'

"I didn't know why she flushed.

"'I was afraid the tennis might have been too much for you,' said the doctor's wife.

"'Oh, no,' answered Mrs Bronson, a trifle abruptly, I thought, as though she didn't want to discuss the matter.

"I didn't know what they meant, and indeed it wasn't till later that I remembered the incident.

"We played three or four rubbers and still Bronson didn't turn up.

"'I wonder what's happened to him,' said his wife. 'I can't think why he should be so late.'

"Cartwright was always silent, but this evening he had hardly opened his mouth. I thought he was tired and asked him what he'd been doing.

"'Nothing very much,' he said. 'I went out after tiffin to shoot pigeon.'

"'Did you have any luck?' I asked.

"'Oh, I got half a dozen. They were very shy.'

"But now he said: 'If Reggie got back late, I daresay he thought it wasn't worth while to come here. I expect he's had a bath and when we get in we shall find him asleep in his chair.'

"'It's a good long ride from Kabulong,' said the doctor's wife.

"'He doesn't take the road, you know,' Mrs Bronson explained. 'He takes the short cut through the jungle.'

"'Can he get along on his bicycle?' I asked.

"'Oh, yes, it's a very good track. It saves about a couple of miles.'

"We had just started another rubber when the bar-boy came in and said there was a police-sergeant outside who wanted to speak to me.

"'What does he want?' I asked.

"The boy said he didn't know, but he had two coolies with him.

"'Curse him,' I said. 'I'll give him hell if I find he's disturbed me for nothing.'

"I told the boy I'd come and I finished playing the hand. Then I got up.

"'I won't be a minute,' I said. 'Deal for me, will you?' I added to Cartwright.

"I went out and found the sergeant with two Malays waiting for me on the steps. I asked him what the devil he wanted. You can imagine my consternation when he told me that the Malays had come to the police-station and said there was a white man lying dead on the path that led through the jungle to Kabulong. I immediately thought of Bronson.

"'Dead?' I cried.

"'Yes, shot. Shot through the head. A white man with red hair.'

"Then I knew it was Reggie Bronson, and indeed, one of them naming his estate said he'd recognized him as the man. It was an awful shock. And there was Mrs Bronson in the card-room waiting impatiently for me to sort my cards and make a bid. For a moment I really didn't know what to do. I was frightfully upset. It was dreadful to give her such a terrible and unexpected blow without a word of preparation, but I found myself quite unable to think of any way to soften it. I told the sergeant and the coolies to wait and went back into the club. I tried to pull myself together. As I entered the card-room Mrs Bronson said: 'You've been an awful long time.' Then she caught sight of my face. 'Is anything the matter?' I saw her clench her fists and go white. You'd have thought she had a presentiment of evil.

"'Something dreadful has happened,' I said, and my throat was all closed up so that my voice sounded even to myself hoarse and uncanny. 'There's been an accident. Your husband's been wounded.'

"She gave a long gasp, it was not exactly a scream, it reminded me oddly of a piece of silk torn in two.

"'Wounded?'

"She leapt to her feet and with her eyes starting from her head stared at Cartwright. The effect on him was ghastly, he fell back in his chair and went as white as death.

"'Very, very badly, I'm afraid,' I added.

"I knew that I must tell her the truth, and tell it then, but I couldn't bring myself to tell it all at once.

"'Is he,' her lips trembled so that she could hardly form the words, 'is he – conscious?'

"I looked at her for a moment without answering. I'd have given a thousand pounds not to have to.

"'No, I'm afraid he isn't.'

"Mrs Bronson stared at me as though she were trying to see right into my brain.

"'Is he dead?'

"I thought the only thing was to get it out and have done with it.

"'Yes, he was dead when they found him.'

"Mrs Bronson collapsed into her chair and burst into tears.

"'Oh, my God,' she muttered. 'Oh, my God.'

"The doctor's wife went to her and put her arms round her. Mrs Bronson with her face in her hands swayed to and fro weeping hysterically. Cartwright, with that livid face, sat quite still, his mouth open, and stared at her. You might have thought he was turned to stone.

"'Oh, my dear, my dear,' said the doctor's wife, 'you must try and pull yourself together.' Then, turning to me, 'Get her a glass of water and fetch Harry.'

"Harry was her husband and he was playing billiards. I went in and told him what had happened.

"'A glass of water be damned,' he said. 'What she wants is a good long peg of brandy.'

"We took it in to her and forced her to drink it and gradually the violence of her emotion exhausted itself. In a few minutes the doctor's wife was able to take her into the ladies' lavatory to wash her face. I'd made up my mind now what had better be done. I could see that Cartwright wasn't good for much; he was all to pieces. I could understand that it was a fearful shock to him, for after all Bronson was his greatest friend and had done everything in the world for him.

" 'You look as though you'd be all the better for a drop of brandy yourself, old man,' I said to him.

"He made an effort.

" 'It's shaken me, you know,' he said. 'I ... I didn't ...' He stopped as though his mind was wandering; he was still fearfully pale; he took out a packet of cigarettes and struck a match, but his hand was shaking so that he could hardly manage it.

" 'Yes, I'll have a brandy.'

" 'Boy,' I shouted, and then to Cartwright: 'Now, are you fit to take Mrs Bronson home?'

" 'Oh, yes,' he answered.

" 'That's good. The doctor and I will go along with the coolies and some police to where the body is.'

" 'Will you bring him back to the bungalow?' asked Cartwright.

" 'I think he'd better be taken straight to the mortuary,' said the doctor before I could answer. 'I shall have to do a PM.'

"When Mrs Bronson, now so much calmer that I was amazed, came back, I told her what I suggested. The doctor's wife, kind woman, offered to go with her and spend the night at the bungalow, but Mrs Bronson wouldn't hear of it. She said she would be perfectly all right, and when the doctor's wife insisted – you know how bent some people are on forcing their kindness on those in trouble – she turned on her almost fiercely.

" 'No, no, I must be alone,' she said. 'I really must. And Theo will be there.'

"They got into the trap. Theo took the reins and they drove off. We started after them, the doctor and I, while the sergeant and the coolies followed. I had sent my seis to the police-station with instructions to send two men to the place where the body was lying. We soon passed Mrs Bronson and Cartwright.

" 'All right?' I called.

" 'Yes,' he answered.

"For some time the doctor and I drove without saying a word; we were both of us deeply shocked. I was worried as well. Somehow or other I'd got to find the murderers and I foresaw that it would be no easy matter.

" 'Do you suppose it was gang robbery?' said the doctor at last.

"He might have been reading my thoughts.

"'I don't think there's a doubt of it,' I answered. 'They knew he'd gone into Kabulong to get the wages and lay in wait for him on the way back. Of course he should never have come alone through the jungle when everyone knew he had a packet of money with him.'

"'He'd done it for years,' said the doctor. 'And he's not the only one.'

"'I know. The question is, how we're going to get hold of the fellows that did it.'

"'You don't think the two coolies who say they found him could have had anything to do with it?'

"'No. They wouldn't have the nerve. I think a pair of Chinks might think out a trick like that, but I don't believe Malays would. They'd be much too frightened. Of course we'll keep an eye on them. We shall soon see if they seem to have any money to fling about.'

"'It's awful for Mrs Bronson,' said the doctor. 'It would have been bad enough at any time, but now she's going to have a baby . . .'

"'I didn't know that,' I said, interrupting him.

"'No, for some reason she wanted to keep it dark. She was rather funny about it, I thought.'

"I recollected then that little passage between Mrs Bronson and the doctor's wife. I understood why that good woman had been so anxious that Mrs Bronson should not overtire herself.

"'It's strange her having a baby after being married so many years.'

"'It happens, you know. But it was a surprise to her. When first she came to see me and I told her what was the matter she fainted, and then she began to cry. I should have thought she'd be as pleased as Punch. She told me that Bronson didn't like children and he'd be awfully bored at the idea, and she made me promise to say nothing about it till she had had a chance of breaking it to him gradually.'

"I reflected for a moment.

"'He was the kind of breezy, hearty cove whom you'd expect to be as keen as mustard on having kids.'

"'You never can tell. Some people are very selfish and just don't want the bother.'

"'Well, how did he take it when she did tell him? Wasn't he rather bucked?'

"'I don't know that she ever told him. Though she couldn't have waited much longer; unless I'm very much mistaken she ought to be confined in about five months.'

"'Poor devil,' I said. 'You know, I've got a notion that he'd have been most awfully pleased to know.'

"We drove in silence for the rest of the way and at last came to the point at which the short cut to Kabulong branched off from the road. Here we stopped and in a minute or two my trap, in which were the police-sergeant and the two Malays, came up. We took the head-lamps to light us on our way. I left the doctor's seis to look after the ponies and told him that when the policemen came they were to follow the path till they found us. The two coolies, carrying the lamps, walked ahead, and we followed them. It was a fairly broad track, wide enough for a small cart to pass, and before the road was built it had been the highway between Kabulong and Alor Lipis. It was firm to the foot and good walking. The surface here and there was sandy and in places you could see quite plainly the mark of a bicycle wheel. It was the track Bronson had left on his way to Kabulong.

"We walked twenty minutes, I should think, in single file, and on a sudden the coolies, with a cry, stopped sharply. The sight had come upon them so abruptly that notwithstanding they were expecting it they were startled. There, in the middle of the pathway lit dimly by the lamps the coolies carried, lay Bronson; he'd fallen over his bicycle and lay across it in an ungainly heap. I was too shocked to speak, and I think the doctor was, too. But in our silence the din of the jungle was deafening; those damned cicadas and the bull-frogs were making enough row to wake the dead. Even under ordinary circumstances the noise of the jungle at night is uncanny; because you feel that at that hour there should be utter silence it has an odd effect on you, that ceaseless and invisible uproar that beats upon your nerves. It surrounds you and hems you in. But just then, believe me, it was terrifying. That poor fellow lay dead and all round him the restless life of the jungle pursued its indifferent and ferocious course.

"He was lying face downwards. The sergeant and the coolies looked at me as though awaiting an order. I was a young fellow then and I'm afraid I felt a little frightened. Though I couldn't see the face I had no doubt that it was Bronson, but I felt that I ought to turn the body over to make sure. I suppose we all have our little squeamishnesses; you know, I've always had a horrible distaste for touching dead bodies. I've had to do it fairly often now, but it still makes me feel slightly sick.

"'It's Bronson, all right,' I said.

"The doctor – by George, it was lucky for me he was there – the doctor bent down and turned the head. The sergeant directed the lamp on the dead face.

"'My God, half his head's been shot away,' I cried.

"'Yes.'

"The doctor stood up straight and wiped his hands on the leaves of a tree that grew beside the path.

"'Is he quite dead?' I asked.

"'Oh, yes. Death must have been instantaneous. Whoever shot him must have fired at pretty close range.'

"'How long has he been dead, d'you think?'

"'Oh, I don't know, several hours.'

"'He would have passed here about five o'clock, I suppose, if he was expecting to get to the club for a rubber at six.'

"'There's no sign of any struggle,' said the doctor.

"'No, there wouldn't be. He was shot as he was riding along.'

"I looked at the body for a little while. I couldn't help thinking how short a time ago it was since Bronson, noisy and loud-voiced, had been so full of hearty life.

"'You haven't forgotten that he had the coolies' wages on him,' said the doctor.

"'No, we'd better search him.'

"'Shall we turn him over?'

"'Wait a minute. Let us just have a look at the ground first.'

"I took the lamp and as carefully as I could looked all about me. Just where he had fallen the sandy pathway was trodden and confused; there were our footprints and the footprints of the coolies who had found him. I walked two or three paces and then saw quite clearly the mark of his bicycle wheels; he had been riding straight and steadily. I followed it to the spot where he had fallen, to just before that, rather, and there saw very distinctly the prints on each side of

467

the wheels of his heavy boots. He had evidently stopped there and put his feet to the ground, then he'd started off again, there was a great wobble of the wheel, and he'd crashed.

"'Now let's search him,' I said.

"The doctor and the sergeant turned the body over and one of the coolies dragged the bicycle away. They laid Bronson on his back. I supposed he would have had the money partly in notes and partly in silver. The silver would have been in a bag attached to the bicycle and a glance told me that it was not there. The notes he would have put in a wallet. It would have been a good thick bundle. I felt him all over, but there was nothing; then I turned out the pockets, they were all empty except the right trouser pocket, in which there was a little small change.

"'Didn't he always wear a watch?' asked the doctor.

"'Yes, of course he did.'

"I remembered that he wore the chain through the buttonhole in the lapel of his coat and the watch and some seals and things in his handkerchief pocket. But watch and chain were gone.

"'Well, there's not much doubt now, is there?' I said.

"It was clear that he had been attacked by gang robbers who knew he had money on him. After killing him they had stripped him of everything. I suddenly remembered the footprints that proved that for a moment he had stood still. I saw exactly how it had been done. One of them had stopped him on some pretext and then, just as he started off again, another, slipping out of the jungle behind him, had emptied the two barrels of a gun into his head.

"'Well,' I said to the doctor, 'it's up to me to catch them, and I'll tell you what, it'll be a real pleasure to me to see them hanged.'

"Of course there was an inquest. Mrs Bronson gave evidence, but she had nothing to say that we didn't know already. Bronson had left the bungalow about eleven, he was to have tiffin at Kabulong and was to be back between five and six. He asked her not to wait for him, he said he would just put the money in the safe and come straight to the club. Cartwright confirmed this. He had lunched alone with Mrs Bronson and after a smoke had gone out with a gun to shoot pigeon. He had got in about five, a little before perhaps, had a bath and changed to play tennis. He was shooting not far from the place where Bronson was killed, but never heard a shot. That, of course, meant nothing; what with the cicadas and the frogs and the other sounds of the jungle, he would have had to be very near to hear anything; and besides, Cartwright was probably back in the bungalow before Bronson was killed. We traced Bronson's movements. He had lunched at the club, he had got money at the bank just before it closed, had gone back to the club and had one more drink, and then started off on his bicycle. He had crossed the river by the ferry; the ferryman remembered distinctly seeing him, but was positive that no one else with a bicycle had crossed. That looked as though the murderers were not following, but lying in wait for him. He rode along the main road for a couple of miles and then took the path which was a short cut to his bungalow.

"It looked as though he had been killed by men who knew his habits, and suspicion, of course, fell immediately on the coolies of his estate. We examined them all – pretty carefully – but there was not a scrap of evidence to connect any of them with the crime. In fact, most of them were able satisfactorily to account for their actions and those who couldn't seemed to me for one reason and another out of the running. There were a few bad characters among the Chinese at Alor Lipis and I had them looked up. But somehow I didn't think it was the work of the Chinese; I had a feeling that Chinese would have used revolvers and not a shotgun. Anyhow, I could find out nothing there. So then we offered a reward of a thousand dollars to anyone who could put us in the way of discovering the murderers. I thought there were a good many people to whom it would appeal to do a public service and at the same time earn a tidy sum. But I knew that an informer would take no risks, he wouldn't want to tell what he knew till he knew he could tell it safely, and I armed myself with patience. The reward had brightened the interest of my police and I knew they would use every means they had to bring the criminals to trial. In a case like this they could do more than I.

"But it was strange, nothing happened; the reward seemed to tempt no one. I cast my net a little wider. There were two or three kampongs along the road and I wondered if the murderers were there; I saw the headmen, but got no help from them. It was not that they would tell me nothing, I was sure they had nothing to tell. I talked to the bad hats, but there was absolutely nothing to connect them with the murder. There was not the shadow of a clue.

"'Very well, my lads,' I said to myself, as I drove back to Alor Lipis, 'there's no hurry; the rope won't spoil by keeping.'

"The scoundrels had got away with a considerable sum, but money is no good unless you spend it. I felt I knew the native temperament enough to be sure that the possession of it was a constant temptation. The Malays are an extravagant race, and a race of gamblers, and the Chinese are gamblers, too; sooner or later someone would start flinging his money about, and then I should want to know where it came from. With a few well-directed questions I thought I could put the fear of God into the fellow and then, if I knew my business, it shouldn't be hard to get a full confession.

"The only thing now was to sit down and wait till the hue and cry had died down and the murderers thought the affair was forgotten. The itch to spend those ill-gotten dollars would grow more and more intolerable till at last it could be resisted no longer. I would go about my business, but I meant never to relax my watch, and one day, sooner or later, my time must come.

"Cartwright took Mrs Bronson down to Singapore. The company Bronson had worked for asked him if he would care to take Bronson's place, but he said, very naturally, that he didn't like the idea of it; so they put another man in and told Cartwright that he could have the job that Bronson's successor had vacated. It was the management of the estate that Cartwright lives on now. He moved in at once. Four months after this Olive was born at Singapore, and a few months later, when Bronson had been dead just over a year, Cartwright and Mrs Bronson were married. I was surprised; but on thinking it over I couldn't help confessing that it was very natural. After the trouble Mrs Bronson had leant much on Cartwright and he had arranged everything for her; she must have been lonely, and rather lost, and I daresay she was grateful for his kindness, he did behave like a brick; and so far as he was concerned I imagined he was sorry for her, it was a dreadful position for a woman, she had nowhere to go, and all they'd gone through must have been a tie between them. There was every reason for them to marry and it was probably the best thing for them both.

"It looked as though Bronson's murderers would never be caught, for that plan of mine didn't work; there was no one in the district who spent more money than he could account for, and if anyone had that hoard buried away under his floor he was showing a self-control that was superhuman. A year had passed and to all intents and purposes the thing was forgotten. Could anyone be so prudent as after so long not to let a little money dribble out? It was incredible. I began to think that Bronson had been killed by a couple of wandering Chinese who had got away, to Singapore perhaps, where there would be small chance of catching them. At last I gave it up. If you come to think of it, as a rule, it's just those crimes, crimes of robbery, in which there is least chance of getting the culprit; for there's nothing to attach suspicion to him, and if he's caught it can only be by his own carelessness. It's different with crimes of passion or vengeance, then you can find out who had a motive to put the victim out of the way.

"It's no use grizzling over one's failures, and bringing my common sense to bear I did my best to put the matter out of my mind. No one likes to be beaten, but beaten I was and I had to put as good a face on it as I could. And then a Chinaman was caught trying to pawn poor Bronson's watch.

"I told you that Bronson's watch and chain had been taken, and of course Mrs Bronson was able to give us a fairly accurate description of it. It was a half-hunter, by Benson, there was a gold chain, three or four seals, and a sovereign purse. The pawnbroker was a smart fellow and when the Chinaman brought the watch he recognized it at once. On some pretext he kept the man waiting and sent for a policeman. The man was arrested and immediately brought to me. I greeted him like a long-lost brother. I was never so pleased to see anyone in my life. I have no feeling about criminals, you know; I'm rather sorry for them, because they're playing a game in which their opponents hold all the aces and kings; but when I catch one it gives me a little thrill of satisfaction, like bringing off a neat finesse at bridge. At last the mystery was going to be cleared up, for if the Chinaman hadn't done the thing himself we were pretty sure through him to trace the murderers. I beamed on him.

"I asked him to account for his possession of the watch. He said he had bought it from a man he didn't know. That was very thin. I explained the circumstances briefly and told him he would be charged with murder. I meant to frighten him and I did. He said then that he'd found the watch.

"'Found it?' I said. 'Fancy that. Where?'

"His answer staggered me; he said he'd found it in the jungle. I laughed at him; I asked him if he thought watches were likely to be left lying about in the jungle; then he said he'd been coming along the pathway that led from Kabulong to Alor Lipis, and had gone into the jungle and caught sight of something gleaming and there was the watch. That was odd. Why should he have said he found the watch just there? It was either true or excessively astute. I asked him where the chain and the seals were, and he produced them immediately. I'd got him scared, and he was pale and shaking; he was a knock-kneed little fellow and I should have been a fool not to see that I hadn't got hold of the murderer there. But his terror suggested that he knew something.

"I asked him when he'd found the watch.

"'Yesterday,' he said.

"I asked him what he was doing on the short-cut from Kabulong to Alor Lipis. He said he'd been working in Singapore and had gone to Kabulong because his father was ill, and that he himself had come to Alor Lipis to work. A friend of his father, a carpenter by trade, had given him a job. He gave me the name of the man with whom he had worked in Singapore and the name of the man who had engaged him at Alor Lipis. All he said seemed plausible and could so easily be verified that it was hardly likely to be false. Of course it occurred to me that if he had found the watch as he said, it must have been lying in the jungle for more than a year. It could hardly be in very good condition; I tried to open it, but couldn't. The pawn-broker had come to the police-station and was waiting in the next room. Luckily he was also something of a watch-maker. I sent for him and asked him to look at the watch; when he opened it he gave a little whistle, the works were thick with rust.

"'This watch no good,' he said, shaking his head. 'Him never go now.'

"I asked him what had put it in such a state, and without a word from me he said that it had been long exposed to wet. For the moral effect I had the prisoner put in a cell and I sent for his employer. I sent a wire to Kabulong and another to Singapore. While I waited I did my best to put two and two together. I was inclined to believe the man's story true; his fear might be ascribed to no more guilt than consisted in his having found something and tried to sell it. Even quite innocent persons are apt to be nervous when they're in the hands of the police; I don't know what there is about a policeman, people are never very much at their ease in his company. But if he really had found the watch where he said, someone had thrown it there. Now that was funny. Even if the murderers had thought the watch a dangerous thing to possess, one would have expected them to melt down the gold case; that would be a very simple thing for any native to do; and the chain was of so ordinary a pattern they could hardly have thought it possible to trace that. There were chains like it in every jeweller's shop in the country. Of course there was the possibility that they had plunged into the jungle and having dropped the watch in their hurry had been afraid to go back and look for it. I didn't think that very likely: the Malays are used to keeping things tucked away in their sarongs, and the Chinese have pockets in their coats. Besides, the moment they got into the jungle they knew there was no hurry; they probably waited and divided the swag then and there.

"In a few minutes the man I had sent for came to the police-station and confirmed what the prisoner had said, and in an hour I got an answer from Kabulong. The police had seen his father, who told them that the boy had gone to Alor Lipis to get a job with a carpenter. So far everything he had said seemed true. I had him brought in again, and told him I was going to take him to the place where he said he had found the watch and he must show me the exact spot. I handcuffed him to a policeman, though it was hardly necessary, for the poor devil was shaking with fright, and took a couple of men besides. We drove out to where the track joined the road and walked along it; within five yards of the place where Bronson was killed the Chinaman stopped."

" 'Here,' he said.

"He pointed to the jungle and we followed him in. We went in about ten yards and he pointed to a chink between two large boulders and said that he found the watch there. It could only have been by the merest chance that he noticed it, and if he really had found it there it looked very much as though someone had put it there to hide it."

Gaze stopped and gave me a reflective look.

"What would you have thought then?" he asked.

"I don't know," I answered.

"Well, I'll tell you what I thought. I thought that if the watch was there the money might be there, too. It seemed worth while having a look. Of course, to look for something in the jungle makes looking for a needle in a bundle of hay a drawing-room pastime. I couldn't help that. I released the Chinaman, I wanted all the help I could get, and set him to work. I set my three men to work, and I started in myself. We made a line – there were five of us – and we searched from the road; for fifty yards on each side of the place at which Bronson was murdered and for a hundred yards in we went over the ground foot by foot. We routed among dead leaves and peered in bushes, we looked under boulders and in the hollows of trees. I knew it was a foolish thing to do, for the chances against us were a thousand to one; my only hope was that anyone who had just committed a murder would be rattled and if he wanted to hide anything would hide it quickly; he would choose the first obvious hiding-place that offered itself. That is what he had done when he hid the watch. My only reason for looking in so circumscribed an area was that as the watch had been found so near the road, the person who wanted to get rid of the things must have wanted to get rid of them quickly.

"We worked on. I began to grow tired and cross. We were sweating like pigs. I had a maddening thirst and nothing in the world to drink. At last I came to the conclusion that we must give it up as a bad job, for that day at least, when suddenly the Chinaman – he must have had sharp eyes, that young man – uttered a guttural cry. He stooped down and from under the winding root of a tree drew out a messy, mouldering, stinking thing. It was a pocket-book that had been out in the rain for a year, that had been eaten by ants and beetles and God knows what, that was sodden and foul, but it was a pocket-book all right, Bronson's, and inside were the shapeless, mushed-up, fetid remains of the Singapore notes he had got from the bank at Kabulong. There was still the silver and I was convinced that it was hidden somewhere about, but I wasn't going to bother about that. I had found out something very important; whoever had murdered Bronson had made no money out of it.

"Do you remember my telling you that I'd noticed the print of Bronson's feet on each side of the broad line of the pneumatic tyre, where he had stopped, and presumably spoken to someone? He was a heavy man and the prints were well marked. He hadn't just put his feet on the soft sand and taken them off, but must have stopped at least for a minute or two. My explanation was that he had stopped to chat with a Malay or a Chinaman, but the more I thought of it the less I liked it. Why the devil should he? Bronson wanted to get home, and though a jovial chap, he certainly was not hail-fellow-well-met with the natives. His relations towards them were those of master and servants. Those footprints had always puzzled me. And now the truth flashed across me. Whoever had murdered Bronson hadn't murdered him to rob and if he'd stopped to talk with someone it could only be with a friend. I knew at last who the murderer was."

I have always thought the detective story a most diverting and ingenious variety of fiction, and have regretted that I never had the skill to write one, but I have read a good many, and I flatter myself it is rarely that I have not solved the mystery before it was disclosed to me; and now for some time I had foreseen what Gaze was going to say, but when at last he said it I confess that it gave me, notwithstanding, somewhat of a shock.

"The man he met was Cartwright. Cartwright was pigeon-shooting. He stopped and asked him what sport he had had, and as he rode on Cartwright raised his gun and discharged both barrels into his head. Cartwright took the money and the watch in order to make it look like the work of gang robbers and hurriedly hid them in the jungle, then made his way along the edge till he got to the road, went back to the bungalow, changed into his tennis things, and drove with Mrs Bronson to the club.

"I remembered how badly he'd played tennis, and how he'd collapsed when, in order to break the news more gently to Mrs Bronson, I said Bronson was wounded and not dead. If he was only wounded he might have been able to speak. By George, I bet that was a bad moment. The child was Cartwright's. Look at Olive: why, you saw the likeness yourself. The doctor had said that Mrs Bronson was upset when he told her she was going to have a baby and made him promise not to tell Bronson. Why? Because Bronson knew that he couldn't be the father of the child."

"Do you think that Mrs Bronson knew what Cartwright had done?" I asked.

"I'm sure of it. When I look back on her behaviour that evening at the club I am convinced of it. She was upset, but not because Bronson was killed; she was upset because I said he was wounded; on my telling her that he was dead when they found him she burst out crying, but from relief. I know that woman. Look at that square chin of hers and tell me that she hasn't got the courage of the devil. She has a will of iron. She made Cartwright do it. She planned every detail and every move. He was completely under her influence; he is now."

"But do you mean to tell me that neither you nor anyone else ever suspected that there was anything between them?"

"Never. Never."

"If they were in love with one another and knew that she was going to have a baby, why didn't they just bolt?"

"How could they? It was Bronson who had the money; she hadn't a bean and neither had Cartwright. He was out of a job. Do you think he would have got another with that story round his neck? Bronson had taken him in when he was starving and he'd stolen his wife from him. They wouldn't have had a dog's chance. They couldn't afford to let the truth come out, their only chance was to get Bronson out of the way, and they got him out of the way."

"They might have thrown themselves on his mercy."

"Yes, but I think they were ashamed. He'd been so good to them, he was such a decent chap, I don't think they had the heart to tell him the truth. They preferred to kill him."

There was a moment's silence while I reflected over what Gaze said.

"Well, what did you do about it?" I asked.

"Nothing. What was there to do? What was the evidence? That the watch and notes had been found? They might easily have been hidden by someone who was afterwards afraid to come and get them. The murderer might have been quite content to get away with the silver. The footprints? Bronson might have stopped to light a cigarette or there might have been a tree-trunk across the path and he waited while the coolies he met there by chance moved it away. Who could prove that the child that a perfectly decent, respectable woman had had four months after her husband's death was not his child? No jury would have convicted Cartwright. I held my tongue and the Bronson murder was forgotten."

"I don't suppose the Cartwrights have forgotten," I suggested.

"I shouldn't be surprised. Human memory is astonishingly short and if you want my professional opinion I don't mind telling you that I don't believe remorse for a crime ever sits very heavily on a man when he's absolutely sure he'll never be found out."

I thought once more of the pair I had met that afternoon, the thin, elderly, bald man with gold-rimmed spectacles, and that white-haired untidy woman with her frank speech and kindly, caustic smile. It was almost impossible to imagine that in the distant past they had been swayed by so turbulent a passion, for that alone made their behaviour explicable, that it had brought them in the end to such a pass that they could see no other issue than a cruel and cold-blooded murder.

"Doesn't it make you feel a little uncomfortable to be with them?" I asked Gaze. "For, without wishing to be censorious, I'm bound to say that I don't think they can be very nice people."

"That's where you're wrong. They are very nice people; they're about the pleasantest people here. Mrs Cartwright is a thoroughly good sort and a very amusing woman. It's my business to prevent crime and to catch the culprit when crime is committed, but I've known far too many criminals to think that on the whole they're worse than anybody else. A perfectly decent fellow may be driven by circumstances to commit a crime and if he's found out he's punished; but he may very well remain a perfectly decent fellow. Of course society punishes him if he breaks its laws, and it's quite right, but it's not always his actions that indicate the essential man. If you'd been a policeman as long as I have, you'd know it's not what people do that really matters, it's what they are. Luckily a policeman has nothing to do with their thoughts, only with their deeds; if he had, it would be a very different, a much more difficult matter."

Gaze flicked the ash from his cheroot and gave me his wry, sardonic, but agreeable smile.

"I'll tell you what, there's one job I *shouldn't* like," he said.

"What is that?" I asked.

"God's, at the Judgement Day," said Gaze. "No, sir."

THE BOOK-BAG

SOME PEOPLE READ for instruction, which is praiseworthy, and some for pleasure, which is innocent, but not a few read from habit, and I suppose that this is neither innocent nor praiseworthy. Of that lamentable company am I. Conversation after a time bores me, games tire me, and my own thoughts, which we are told are the unfailing resource of a sensible man, have a tendency to run dry. Then I fly to my book as the opium-smoker to his pipe. I would sooner read the catalogue of the Army and Navy Stores or Bradshaw's *Guide* than nothing at all, and indeed I have spent many delightful hours over both these works. At one time I never went out without a second-hand book-seller's list in my pocket. I know no reading more fruity. Of course to read in this way is as reprehensible as doping, and I never cease to wonder at the impertinence of great readers who, because they are such, look down on the illiterate. From the standpoint of what eternity is it better to have read a thousand books than to have ploughed a million furrows? Let us admit that reading with us is just a drug that we cannot do without – who of this band does not know the restlessness that attacks him when he has been severed from reading too long, the apprehension and irritability, and the sigh of relief which the sight of a printed page extracts from him? – and so let us be no more vainglorious than the poor slaves of the hypodermic needle or the pint-pot.

And like the dope-fiend who cannot move from place to place without taking with him a plentiful supply of his deadly balm I never venture far without a sufficiency of reading matter. Books are so necessary to me that when in a railway train I have become aware that fellow-travellers have come away without a single one I have been seized with a veritable dismay. But when I am starting on a long journey the problem is formidable. I have learnt my lesson. Once, imprisoned by illness for three months in a hill-town in Java, I came to the end of all the books I had brought with me, and knowing no Dutch was obliged to buy the schoolbooks from which intelligent Javanese, I suppose, acquired knowledge of French and German. So I read again after five-and-twenty years the frigid plays of Goethe, the fables of La Fontaine, and the tragedies of the tender and exact Racine. I have the greatest admiration for Racine, but I admit that to read his plays one after the other requires a certain effort in a person who is suffering from colitis. Since then I have made a point of travelling with the largest sack made for carrying soiled linen and filling it to the brim with books to suit every possible occasion and every mood. It weighs a ton and strong porters reel under its weight. Custom-house officials look at it askance, but recoil from it with consternation when I give them my word that it contains nothing but books. Its inconvenience is that the particular work I suddenly hanker to read is always at the bottom and it is impossible for me to get it without emptying the book-bag's entire contents upon the floor. Except for this, however, I should perhaps never have heard the singular history of Olive Hardy.

I was wandering about Malaya, staying here and there, a week or two if there was a rest-house or a hotel, and a day or so if I was obliged to inflict myself on a planter or a District Officer whose hospitality I had no wish to abuse; and at the moment I happened to be at Penang. It is a pleasant little town, with a hotel that has always seemed to me very agreeable, but the stranger finds little to do there and time hung a trifle heavily on my hands. One morning I received a letter from a man I knew only by name. This was Mark Featherstone. He was Acting Resident, in the absence on leave of the Resident, at a place called Tenggarah. There was a sultan there and it appeared that a water festival of some sort was to take place which Featherstone thought would interest me. He said that he would be glad if I would come and stay with him for a few days. I wired to tell him that I should be delighted and next day took the train to Tenggarah. Featherstone met me at the station. He was a man of about thirty-five, I should think, tall and handsome, with fine eyes and a strong, stern face. He had a wiry black moustache and bushy eyebrows. He looked more like a soldier than a government official. He was very smart in white ducks, with a white topee, and he wore his clothes with elegance. He was a little shy, which seemed odd in a strapping fellow of resolute mien, but I surmised that this was only because he was unused to the society of that strange fish, a writer, and I hoped in a little to put him at his ease.

"My boys'll look after your barang," he said. "We'll go down to the club. Give them your keys and they'll unpack before we get back."

I told him that I had a good deal of luggage and thought it better to leave everything at the station but what I particularly wanted. He would not hear of it.

"It doesn't matter a bit. It'll be safer at my house. It's always better to have one's barang with one."

"All right."

I gave my keys and the ticket for my trunk and my book-bag to a Chinese boy who stood at my host's elbow. Outside the station a car was waiting for us and we stepped in.

"Do you play bridge?" asked Featherstone.

"I do."

"I thought most writers didn't."

"They don't," I said. "It's generally considered among authors a sign of deficient intelligence to play cards."

The club was a bungalow, pleasing but unpretentious; it had a large reading-room, a billiard-room with one table, and a small card-room. When we arrived it was empty but for one or two persons reading the English weeklies, and we walked through to the tennis courts, where a couple of sets were being played. A number of people were sitting on the veranda, looking on, smoking, and sipping long drinks. I was introduced to one or two of them. But the light was failing and soon the players could hardly see the ball. Feather-stone asked one of the men I had been introduced to if he would like a rubber. He said he would. Featherstone looked about for a fourth. He caught sight of a man sitting a little by himself, paused for a second, and went up to him. The two exchanged a few words and then came towards us. We strolled in to the card-room. We had a very nice game. I did not pay much attention to the two men who made up the four. They stood me drinks and I, a temporary member of the club, returned the compliment. The drinks were very small, quarter whiskies, and in the two hours we played each of us was able to show his open-handedness without an excessive consumption of alcohol. When the advancing hour suggested that the next rubber must be the last we changed from whisky to gin pahits. The rubber came to an end. Featherstone called for the book and the winnings and losings of each one of us were set down. One of the men got up.

"Well, I must be going," he said.

"Going back to the estate?" asked Featherstone.

"Yes," he nodded. He turned to me. "Shall you be here tomorrow?"

"I hope so."

He went out of the room.

"I'll collect my mem and get along home to dinner," said the other.

"We might be going too," said Featherstone.

"I'm ready whenever you are," I replied.

We got into the car and drove to his house. It was a longish drive. In the darkness I could see nothing much, but presently I realized that we were going up a rather steep hill. We reached the Residency.

It had been an evening like any other, pleasant, but not at all exciting, and I had spent I don't know how many just like it. I did not expect it to leave any sort of impression on me.

Featherstone led me into his sitting-room. It looked comfortable, but it was a trifle ordinary. It had large basket arm-chairs covered with cretonne and on the walls were a great many framed photographs; the tables were littered with papers, magazines, and official reports, with pipes, yellow tins of straight-cut cigarettes, and pink tins of tobacco. In a row of shelves were untidily stacked a good many books, their bindings stained with damp and the ravages of white ants. Featherstone showed me my room and left me with the words:

"Shall you be ready for a gin pahit in ten minutes?"

"Easily," I said.

I had a bath and changed and went downstairs. Featherstone, ready before me, mixed our drink as he heard me clatter down the wooden staircase. We dined. We talked. The festival which I had been invited to see was the next day but one, but Featherstone told me he had arranged for me before that to be received by the Sultan.

"He's a jolly old boy," he said. "And the palace is a sight for sore eyes."

After dinner we talked a little more, Featherstone put on the gramophone, and we looked at the latest illustrated papers that had arrived from England. Then we went to bed. Featherstone came to my room to see that I had everything I wanted.

"I suppose you haven't any books with you," he said. "I haven't got a thing to read."

"Books?" I cried.

I pointed to my book-bag. It stood upright, bulging oddly, so that it looked like a humpbacked gnome somewhat the worse for liquor.

"Have you got books in there? I thought that was your dirty linen or a camp-bed or something. Is there anything you can lend me?"

"Look for yourself."

Featherstone's boys had unlocked the bag, but quailing before the sight that then discovered itself had done no more. I knew from long experience how to unpack it. I threw it over on its side, seized its leather bottom and, walking backwards, dragged the sack away from its contents. A river of books poured on to the floor. A look of stupefaction came upon Featherstone's face.

"You don't mean to say you travel with as many books as that? By George, what a snip!"

He bent down and turning them over rapidly looked at the titles. There were books of all kinds. Volumes of verse, novels, philosophical works, critical studies (they say books about books are profitless, but they certainly make very pleasant reading), biographies, history; there were books to read when you were ill and books to read when your brain, all alert, craved for something to grapple with; there were books that you had always wanted to read, but in the hurry of life at home had never found time to; there were books to read at sea when you were meandering through narrow waters on a tramp steamer, and there were books for bad weather when your whole cabin creaked and you had to wedge yourself in your bunk in order not to fall out; there were books chosen solely for their length, which you took with you when on some expedition you had to travel light, and there were the books you could read when you could read nothing else. Finally Featherstone picked out a life of Byron that had recently appeared.

"Hullo, what's this?" he said. "I read a review of it some time ago."

"I believe it's very good," I replied. "I haven't read it yet."

"May I take it? It'll do me for tonight at all events."

"Of course. Take anything you like."

"No, that's enough. Well, good night. Breakfast at eight-thirty."

When I came down next morning the head boy told me that Featherstone, who had been at work since six, would be in shortly. While I waited for him I glanced at his shelves.

"I see you've got a grand library of books on bridge," I remarked as we sat down to breakfast.

"Yes, I get every one that comes out. I'm very keen on it."

"That fellow we were playing with yesterday plays a good game."

"Which? Hardy?"

"I don't know. Not the one who said he was going to collect his wife. The other."

"Yes, that was Hardy. That was why I asked him to play. He doesn't come to the club very often."

"I hope he will tonight."

"I wouldn't bank on it. He has an estate about thirty miles away. It's a longish ride to come just for a rubber of bridge."

"Is he married?"

"No. Well, yes. But his wife is in England."

"It must be awfully lonely for those men who live by themselves on those estates," I said.

"Oh, he's not so badly off as some. I don't think he much cares about seeing people. I think he'd be just as lonely in London."

There was something in the way Featherstone spoke that struck me as a little strange. His voice had what I can only describe as a shuttered tone. He seemed suddenly to have moved away from me. It was as though one were passing along a street at night and paused for a second to look in at a lighted window that showed a comfortable room and suddenly an invisible hand pulled down a blind. His eyes, which habitually met those of the person he was talking to with frankness, now avoided mine, and I had a notion that it was not only my fancy that read in his face an expression of pain. It was drawn for a moment as it might be by a twinge of neuralgia. I could not think of anything to say and Featherstone did not speak. I was conscious that his thoughts, withdrawn from me and what we were about, were turned upon a subject unknown to me. Presently he gave a little sigh, very slight, but unmistakable, and seemed with a deliberate effort to pull himself together.

"I'm going down to the office immediately after breakfast," he said. "What are you going to do with yourself?"

"Oh, don't bother about me. I shall slack around. I'll stroll down and look at the town."

"There's not much to see."

"All the better. I'm fed up with sights."

I found that Featherstone's veranda gave me sufficient entertainment for the morning. It had one of the most enchanting views I had seen in the FMS. The Residency was built on the top of a hill and the garden was large and well cared for. Great trees gave it almost the look of an English park. It had vast lawns and there Tamils, black and emaciated, were scything with deliberate and beautiful gestures. Beyond and below, the jungle grew thickly to the bank of a broad, winding, and swiftly flowing river, and on the other side of this, as far as the eye could reach, stretched the wooded hills of Tenggarah. The contrast between the trim lawns, so strangely English, and the savage growth of the jungle beyond pleasantly titillated the fancy. I sat and read and smoked. It is my business to be curious about people and I asked myself how the peace of this scene, charged nevertheless with a tremulous and dark significance, affected Featherstone who lived with it. He knew it under every aspect: at dawn when the mist rising from the river shrouded it with a ghostly pall; in the splendour of noon; and at last when the shadowy gloaming crept softly out of the jungle, like an army making its way with caution in unknown country, and presently enveloped the green lawns and the great flowering trees and the flaunting cassias in the silent night. I wondered whether, unbeknownst to him, the tender and yet strangely sinister aspect of the scene, acting on his nerves and his loneliness, imbued him with some mystical quality so that the life he led, the life of the capable administrator, the sportsman, and the good fellow, on occasion seemed to him not quite real. I smiled at my own fancies, for certainly the conversation we had had the night before had not indicated in him any stirrings of the soul. I had thought him quite nice. He had been at Oxford and was a member of a good London club. He seemed to attach a good deal of importance to social things. He was a gentleman and slightly conscious of the fact that he belonged to a better class than most of the Englishmen his life brought him in contact with. I gathered from the various silver pots that adorned his dining-room that he excelled in games. He played tennis and billiards. When he went on leave he hunted and, anxious to keep his weight down, he dieted carefully. He talked a good deal of what he would do when he retired. He hankered after the life of a country gentleman. A little house in Leicestershire, a couple of hunters, and neighbours to play bridge with. He would have his pension and he had a little money of his own. But meanwhile he worked hard and did his work, if not brilliantly, certainly with competence. I have no doubt that he was looked upon by his superiors as a reliable officer. He was cut upon a pattern that I knew too well to find very interesting. He was like a novel that is careful, honest, and efficient, yet a little ordinary, so that you seem to have read it all before, and you turn the pages listlessly, knowing that it will never afford you a surprise or move you to excitement.

But human beings are incalculable and he is a fool who tells himself that he knows what a man is capable of.

In the afternoon Featherstone took me to see the Sultan. We were received by one of his sons, a shy, smiling youth who acted as his ADC. He was dressed in a neat blue suit, but round his waist he wore a sarong, white flowers on a yellow ground, on his head a red fez, and on his feet knobby American shoes. The palace, built in the Moorish style, was like a very big doll's house and it was painted bright yellow, which is the royal colour. We were led into a spacious room, furnished with the sort of furniture you would find in an English lodging-house at the seaside, but the chairs were covered with yellow silk. On the floor was a Brussels carpet and on the walls photographs in very grand gilt frames of the Sultan at various state functions. In a cabinet was a large collection of all kinds of fruit done entirely in crochet work. The Sultan came in with several attendants. He was a man of fifty, perhaps, short and stout, dressed in trousers and tunic of a large white-and-yellow check; round his middle he wore a very beautiful yellow sarong and on his head a white fez. He had large handsome friendly eyes. He gave us coffee to drink, sweet cakes to eat, and cheroots to smoke. Conversation was not difficult, for he was affable, and he told me that he had never been to a theatre or played cards, for he was very religious, and he had four wives and twenty-four children. The only bar to the happiness of his life seemed to be that common decency obliged him to divide his time equally between his four wives. He said that an hour with one was a month and with another five minutes. I remarked that

Professor Einstein – or was it Bergson? – had made similar observations upon time and indeed on this question had given the world much to ponder over. Presently we took our leave and the Sultan presented me with some beautiful white Malaccas.

In the evening we went to the club. One of the men we had played with the day before got up from his chair as we entered.

"Ready for a rubber?" he said.

"Where's our fourth?" I asked.

"Oh, there are several fellows here who'll be glad to play."

"What about that man we played with yesterday?" I had forgotten his name.

"Hardy? He's not here."

"It's not worth while waiting for him," said Featherstone.

"He very seldom comes to the club. I was surprised to see him last night."

I did not know why I had the impression that behind the very ordinary words of these two men there was an odd sense of embarrassment. Hardy had made no impression on me and I did not even remember what he looked like. He was just a fourth at the bridge table. I had a feeling that they had something against him. It was no business of mine and I was quite content to play with a man who at that moment joined us. We certainly had a more cheerful game than before. A good deal of chaff passed from one side of the table to the other. We played less serious bridge. We laughed. I wondered if it was only that they were less shy of the stranger who had happened in upon them or if the presence of Hardy had caused in the other two a certain constraint. At half past eight we broke up and Featherstone and I went back to dine at his house.

After dinner we lounged in arm-chairs and smoked cheroots. For some reason our conversation did not flow easily. I tried topic after topic, but could not get Featherstone to interest himself in any of them. I began to think that in the last twenty-four hours he had said all he had to say. I fell somewhat discouraged into silence. It prolonged itself, and again, I did not know why, I had a faint sensation that it was charged with a significance that escaped me. I felt slightly uncomfortable. I had that queer feeling that one sometimes has when sitting in an empty room that one is not by oneself. Presently I was conscious that Featherstone was steadily looking at me. I was sitting by a lamp, but he was in shadow so that the play of his features was hidden from me. But he had very large brilliant eyes and in the half darkness they seemed to shine dimly. They were like new boot-buttons that caught a reflected light. I wondered why he looked at me like that. I gave him a glance and catching his eyes insistently fixed upon me faintly smiled.

"Interesting book that one you lent me last night," he said suddenly, and I could not help thinking his voice did not sound quite natural. The words issued from his lips as though they were pushed from behind.

"Oh, the *Life of Byron*?" I said breezily. "Have you read it already?"

"A good deal of it. I read till three."

"I've heard it's very well done. I'm not sure that Byron interests me so much as all that. There was so much in him that was so frightfully second-rate. It makes one rather uncomfortable."

"What do you think is the real truth of that story about him and his sister?"

"Augusta Leigh? I don't know very much about it. I've never read *Astarte*."

"Do you think they were really in love with one another?"

"I suppose so. Isn't it generally believed that she was the only woman he ever genuinely loved?"

"Can you understand it?"

"I can't really. It doesn't particularly shock me. It just seems to me very unnatural. Perhaps 'unnatural' isn't the right word. It's incomprehensible to me. I can't throw myself into the state of feeling in which such a thing seems possible. You know, that's how a writer gets to know the people he writes about, by standing himself in their shoes and feeling with their hearts."

I know I did not make myself very clear, but I was trying to describe a sensation, an action of the subconscious, which from experience was perfectly familiar to me, but which no words I knew could precisely indicate. I went on:

"Of course she was only his half-sister, but just as habit kills love I should have thought habit would prevent its arising. When two persons have known one another all their lives and lived together in close contact I can't imagine how or why that sudden spark should flash that results in love. The probabilities are that they would be joined by mutual affection and I don't know anything that is more contrary to love than affection."

I could just see in the dimness the outline of a smile flicker for a moment on my host's heavy, and it seemed to me then, somewhat saturnine face.

"You only believe in love at first sight?"

"Well, I suppose I do, but with the proviso that people may have met twenty times before seeing one another. 'Seeing' has an active side and a passive one. Most people we run across mean so little to us that we never bestir ourselves to look at them. We just suffer the impression they make on us."

"Oh, but one's often heard of couples who've known one another for years and it's never occurred to one they cared two straws for each other and suddenly they go and get married. How do you explain that?"

"Well, if you're going to bully me into being logical and consistent, I should suggest that their love is of a different kind. After all, passion isn't the only reason for marriage. It may not even be the best one. Two people may marry because they're lonely or because they're good friends or for convenience's sake. Though I said that affection was the greatest enemy of love, I would never deny that it's a very good substitute. I'm not sure that a marriage founded on it isn't the happiest."

"What did you think of Tim Hardy?"

I was a little surprised at the sudden question, which seemed to have nothing to do with the subject of our conversation.

"I didn't think of him very much. He seemed quite nice. Why?"

"Did he seem to you just like everybody else?"

"Yes. Is there anything peculiar about him? If you'd told me that, I'd have paid more attention to him."

"He's very quiet, isn't he? I suppose no one who knew nothing about him would give him a second thought."

I tried to remember what he looked like. The only thing that had struck me when we were playing cards was that he had fine hands. It passed idly through my mind that they were not the sort of hands I should have expected a planter to have. But why a planter should have different hands from anybody else I did not trouble to ask myself. His were somewhat large, but very well formed with peculiarly long fingers, and the nails were of an admirable shape. They were virile and yet oddly sensitive hands. I noticed this and thought no more about it. But if you are a writer instinct and the habit of years enable you to store up impressions that you are not aware of. Sometimes of course they do not correspond with the facts and a woman for example may remain in your subconsciousness as a dark, massive, and ox-eyed creature when she is indeed rather small and of a nondescript colouring. But that is of no consequence. The impression may very well be more exact than the sober truth. And now, seeking to call up from the depths of me a picture of this man I had a feeling of some ambiguity. He was clean-shaven and his face, oval but not thin, seemed strangely pale under the tan of long exposure to the tropical sun. His features were vague. I did not know whether I remembered it or only imagined now that his rounded chin gave one the impression of a certain weakness. He had thick brown hair, just turning grey, and a long wisp fell down constantly over his forehead. He pushed it back with a gesture that had become habitual. His brown eyes were rather large and gentle, but perhaps a little sad; they had a melting softness which, I could imagine, might be very appealing.

After a pause Featherstone continued:

"It's rather strange that I should run across Tim Hardy here after all these years. But that's the way of the FMS. People move about and you find yourself in the same place as a man you'd known years before in another part of the country. I first knew Tim when he had an estate near Sibuku. Have you ever been there?"

"No. Where is it?"

"Oh, it's up north. Towards Siam. It wouldn't be worth your while to go. It's just like every other place in the FMS. But it was rather nice. It had a very jolly little club and there were some quite decent people. There was the schoolmaster and the head of the police, the doctor, the padre, and the government engineer. The usual lot, you know. A few planters. Three or four women. I was ADO. It was one of my first jobs. Tim Hardy had an estate about twenty-five miles away. He lived there with his sister. They had a bit of money of their own and he'd bought the place. Rubber was pretty good then and he wasn't doing at all badly. We rather cottoned on to one another. Of course it's a toss-up with planters. Some of them are very good fellows, but they're not exactly..." he sought for a word or a phrase that did not sound snobbish. "Well, they're not the sort of people you'd be likely to meet at home. Tim and Olive were of one's own class, if you understand what I mean."

"Olive was the sister?"

"Yes. They'd had a rather unfortunate past. Their parents had separated when they were quite small, seven or eight, and the mother had taken Olive and the father had kept Tim. Tim went to Clifton, they were West Country people, and only came home for the holidays. His father was a retired naval man who lived at Fowey. But Olive went with her mother to Italy. She was educated in Florence; she spoke Italian perfectly and French too. For all those years Tim and Olive never saw one another once, but they used to write to one another regularly. They'd been very much attached when they were children. As far as I could understand, life when their people were living together had been rather stormy with all sorts of scenes and upsets, you know the sort of thing that happens when two people who are married don't get on together, and that had thrown them on their own resources. They were left a good deal to themselves. Then Mrs Hardy died and Olive came home to England and went back to her father. She was eighteen then and Tim was seventeen. A year later the war broke out. Tim joined up and his father, who was over fifty, got some job at Portsmouth. I take it he had been a hard liver and a heavy drinker. He broke down before the end of the war and died after a lingering illness. They don't seem to have had any relations. They were the last of a rather old family; they had a fine old house in Dorsetshire that had belonged to them for a good many generations, but they had never been able to afford to live in it and it was always let. I remember seeing photographs of it. It was very much a gentleman's house, of grey stone and rather stately, with a coat of arms carved over the front door, and mullioned windows. Their great ambition was to make enough money to be able to live in it. They used to talk about it a lot. They never spoke as though either of them would marry, but always as though it were a settled thing that they would remain together. It was rather funny considering how young they were."

"How old were they then?" I asked.

"Well, I suppose he was twenty-five or twenty-six and she was a year older. They were awfully kind to me when I first went up to Sibuku. They took a fancy to me at once. You see, we had more in common than most of the people there. I think they were glad of my company. They weren't particularly popular."

"Why not?" I asked.

"They were rather reserved and you couldn't help seeing that they liked their own society better than other people's. I don't know if you've noticed it, but that always seems to put people's backs up. They resent it somehow if they have a feeling that you can get along very well without them."

"It's tiresome, isn't it?" I said.

"It was rather a grievance to the other planters that Tim was his own master and had private means. They had to put up with an old Ford to get about in, but Tim had a real car. Tim and Olive were very nice when they came to the club and they played in the tennis tournaments and all that sort of thing, but you had an impression that they were always glad to get away again. They'd dine out with people and make themselves very pleasant, but it was pretty obvious that they'd just as soon have stayed at home. If you had any sense you couldn't blame them. I don't know if you've been much to planters' houses. They're a bit dreary. A lot of gimcrack furniture and silver ornaments and tiger skins. And the food's uneatable. But the Hardys had made their bungalow rather nice. There was nothing very grand in it; it was just easy and homelike and comfortable. Their living-room was like a drawing-room in an English country house. You felt that their things meant something to them and that they had had them a long time. It was a very jolly house to stay at. The bungalow was in the middle of the estate, but it was on the brow of a little hill and you looked right over the rubber trees to the sea in the distance. Olive took a lot of trouble with her garden and it was really topping. I never saw such a show of cannas. I used to go there for weekends. It was only about half an hour's drive to the sea and we'd take our lunch with us and bathe and sail. Tim kept a small boat there. Those days were grand. I never knew one could enjoy oneself so much. It's a beautiful bit of coast and it was really extraordinarily romantic. Then in the evenings we'd play patience and chess or turn on the gramo-phone. The cooking was damned good too. It was a change from what one generally got. Olive had taught their cook to make all sorts of Italian dishes and we used to have great wallops of macaroni and risotto and gnocchi and things like that. I couldn't help envying them their life, it was so jolly and peaceful, and when they talked of what they'd do when they went back to England for good I used to tell them they'd always regret what they'd left.

" 'We've been very happy here,' said Olive.

"She had a way of looking at Tim, with a slow, sidelong glance from under her long eyelashes, that was rather engaging.

"In their own house they were quite different from what they were when they went out. They were so easy and cordial. Everybody admitted that and I'm bound to say that people enjoyed going there. They often asked people over. They had the gift of making you feel at home. It was a very happy house, if you know what I mean. Of course no one could help seeing how attached they were to one another. And whatever people said about their being stand-offish and self-centred, they were bound to be rather touched by the affection they had for one another. People said they couldn't have been more united if they were married, and when you saw how some couples got on you couldn't help thinking they made most marriages look rather like a wash-out. They seemed to think the same things at the same time. They had little private jokes that made them laugh like children. They were so charming with one another, so gay and happy, that really to stay with them was, well, a spiritual refreshment. I don't know what else you could call it. When you left them, after a couple of days at the bungalow, you felt you'd absorbed some of their peace and their sober gaiety. It was as though your soul had been sluiced with cool clear water. You felt strangely purified."

It was singular to hear Featherstone talking in this exalted strain. He looked so spruce in his smart white coat, technically known as a bum-freezer, his moustache was so trim, his thick curly hair so carefully brushed, that his high-flown language made me a trifle uncomfortable. But I realized that he was trying to express in his clumsy way a very sincerely felt emotion.

"What was Olive Hardy like?" I asked.

"I'll show you. I've got quite a lot of snapshots."

He got up from his chair and going to a shelf brought me a large album. It was the usual thing, indifferent photographs of people in groups and unflattering likenesses of single figures. They were in bathing dress or in shorts or tennis things, generally with their faces screwed up because the sun blinded them, or puckered by the distortion of laughter. I recognized Hardy, not much changed after ten years, with his wisp of hair hanging across his forehead. I remembered him better now that I saw the snapshots. In them he looked nice and fresh and young. He had an alertness of expression that was attractive and that I certainly had not noticed when I saw him. In his eyes was a sort of eagerness for life that danced and sparkled through the fading print. I glanced at the photographs of his sister. Her bathing dress showed that she had a good figure, well-developed, but slender; and her legs were long and slim.

"They look rather alike," I said.

"Yes, although she was a year older they might have been twins, they were so much alike. They both had the same oval face and that pale skin without any colour in the cheeks, and they both had those soft brown eyes, very liquid and appealing, so that you felt whatever they did you could never be angry with them. And they both had a sort of careless elegance that made them look charming whatever they wore and however untidy they were. He's lost that now, I suppose, but he certainly had it when I first knew him. They always rather reminded me of the brother and sister in *Twelfth Night*. You know whom I mean."

"Viola and Sebastian."

"They never seemed to belong quite to the present. There was something Elizabethan about them. I don't think it was only because I was very young then that I couldn't help feeling they were strangely romantic somehow. I could see them living in Illyria."

I gave one of the snapshots another glance.

"The girl looks as though she had a good deal more character than her brother," I remarked.

"She had. I don't know if you'd have called Olive beautiful, but she was awfully attractive. There was something poetic in her, a sort of lyrical quality, as it were, that coloured her movements, her acts, and everything about her. It seemed to exalt her above common cares. There was something so candid in her expression, so courageous and independent in her bearing, that – oh, I don't know, it made mere beauty just flat and dull."

"You speak as if you'd been in love with her," I interrupted.

"Of course I was. I should have thought you'd guessed that at once. I was frightfully in love with her."

"Was it love at first sight?" I smiled.

"Yes, I think it was, but I didn't know it for a month or so. When it suddenly struck me that what I felt for her – I don't know how to explain it, it was a sort of shattering turmoil that affected every bit of me – that that was love, I knew I'd felt it all along. It was not only her looks, though they were awfully alluring, the smoothness of her pale skin and the way her hair fell over her forehead and the grave sweetness of her brown eyes, it was more than that; you had a sensation of well-being when you were with her, as though you could relax and be quite natural and needn't pretend to be anything you weren't. You felt she was incapable of meanness. It was impossible to think of her as envious of other people or catty. She seemed to have a natural generosity of soul. One could be silent with her for an hour at a time and yet feel that one had had a good time."

"A rare gift," I said.

"She was a wonderful companion. If you made a suggestion to do something she was always glad to fall in with it. She was the least exacting girl I ever knew. You could throw her over at the last minute and however disppointed she was it made no difference. Next time you saw her she was just as cordial and serene as ever."

"Why didn't you marry her?"

Featherstone's cheroot had gone out. He threw the stub away and deliberately lit another. He did not answer for a while. It may seem strange to persons who live in a highly civilized state that he should confide these intimate things to a stranger; it did not seem strange to me. I was used to it. People who live so desperately alone, in the remote places of the earth, find it a relief to tell someone whom in all probability they will never meet again the story that has burdened perhaps for years their waking thoughts and their dreams at night. And I have an inkling that the fact of your being a writer attracts their confidence. They feel that what they tell you will excite your interest in an impersonal way that makes it easier for them to discharge their souls. Besides, as we all know from our own experience, it is never unpleasant to talk about oneself.

494

"Why didn't you marry her?" I had asked him.

"I wanted to badly enough," Featherstone answered at length. "But I hesitated to ask her. Although she was always so nice to me and so easy to get on with, and we were such good friends, I always felt that there was something a little mysterious in her. Although she was so simple, so frank and natural, you never quite got over the feeling of an inner kernel of aloofness, as if deep in her heart she guarded, not a secret, but a sort of privacy of the soul that not a living person would ever be allowed to know. I don't know if I make myself clear."

"I think so."

"I put it down to her upbringing. They never talked of their mother, but somehow I got the impression that she was one of those neurotic, emotional women who wreck their own happiness and are a pest to everyone connected with them. I had a suspicion that she'd led rather a hectic life in Florence and it struck me that Olive owed her beautiful serenity to a disciplined effort of her own will, and that her aloofness was a sort of citadel she'd built to protect herself from the knowledge of all sorts of shameful things. But of course that aloofness was awfully captivating. It was strangely exciting to think that if she loved you, and you were married to her, you would at last pierce right into the hidden heart of that mystery; and you felt that if you could share that with her it would be as it were a consummation of all you'd ever desired in your life. Heaven wouldn't be in it. You know, I felt about it just like Bluebeard's wife about the forbidden chamber in the castle. Every room was open to me, but I should never rest till I had gone into that last one that was locked against me."

My eye was caught by a chik-chak, a little brown house lizard with a large head, high up on the wall. It is a friendly little beast and it is good to see it in a house. It watched a fly. It was quite still. On a sudden it made a dart and then as the fly flew away fell back with a sort of jerk into a strange immobility.

"And there was another thing that made me hesitate. I couldn't bear the thought that if I proposed to her and she refused me she wouldn't let me come to the bungalow in the same old way. I should have hated that, I enjoyed going there so awfully. It made me so happy to be with her. But you know, sometimes one can't help oneself. I did ask her at last, but it was almost by accident. One evening, after dinner, when we were sitting on the veranda by ourselves, I took her hand. She withdrew it at once.

"'Why did you do that?' I asked her.

"'I don't very much like being touched,' she said. She turned her head a little and smiled. 'Are you hurt? You mustn't mind, it's just a funny feeling I have. I can't help it.'

"'I wonder if it's ever occurred to you that I'm frightfully fond of you,' I said.

"I expect I was terribly awkward about it, but I'd never proposed to anyone before." Featherstone gave a little sound that was not quite a chuckle and not quite a sigh. "For the matter of that, I've never proposed to anyone since. She didn't say anything for a minute. Then she said:

"'I'm very glad, but I don't think I want you to be anything more than that.'

"'Why not?' I asked.

"'I could never leave Tim.'

"'But supposing he marries?'

"'He never will.'

"I'd gone so far then that I thought I'd better go on. But my throat was so dry that I could hardly speak. I was shaking with nervousness.

"'I'm frightfully in love with you, Olive. I want to marry you more than anything in the world.'

"She put her hand very gently on my arm. It was like a flower falling to the ground.

"'No, dear, I can't,' she said.

"I was silent. It was difficult for me to say what I wanted to. I'm naturally rather shy. She was a girl. I couldn't very well tell her that it wasn't quite the same thing living with a husband and living with a brother. She was normal and healthy; she must want to have babies; it wasn't reasonable to starve her natural instincts. It was such waste of her youth. But it was she who spoke first.

"'Don't let's talk about this any more,' she said. 'D'you mind? It did strike me once or twice that perhaps you cared for me. Tim noticed it. I was sorry because I was afraid it would break up our friendship. I don't want it to do that, Mark. We do get on so well together, the three of us, and we have such jolly times. I don't know what we should do without you now.'

"'I thought of that too,' I said.

"'D'you think it need?' she asked me.

"'My dear, I don't want it to,' I said. 'You must know how much I love coming here. I've never been so happy anywhere before!'

"'You're not angry with me?'

"'Why should I be? It's not your fault. It only means that you're not in love with me. If you were you wouldn't care a hang about Tim.'

"'You are rather sweet,' she said.

"She put her arm round my neck and kissed me lightly on the cheek. I had a notion that in her mind it settled our relation. She adopted me as a second brother.

"A few weeks later Tim went back to England. The tenant of their house in Dorset was leaving and though there was another in the offing, he thought he ought to be on the spot to conduct negotiations. And he wanted some new machinery for the estate. He thought he'd get it at the same time. He didn't expect to be gone more than three months and Olive made up her mind not to go. She knew hardly anyone in England, and it was practically a foreign country to her, she didn't mind being left alone, and she wanted to look after the estate. Of course they could have put a manager in charge, but that wasn't the same thing. Rubber was falling and in case of accidents it was just as well that one or other of them should be there. I promised Tim I'd look after her and if she wanted me she could always call me up. My proposal hadn't changed anything. We carried on as though nothing had happened. I don't know whether she'd told Tim. He made no sign that he knew. Of course I loved her as much as ever, but I kept it to myself. I have a good deal of self-control, you know. I had a sort of feeling I hadn't a chance. I hoped eventually my love would change into something else and we could just be wonderful friends. It's funny, it never has, you know. I suppose I was hit too badly ever to get quite over it.

"She went down to Penang to see Tim off and when she came back I met her at the station and drove her home. I couldn't very well stay at the bungalow while Tim was away, but I went over every Sunday and had tiffin and we'd go down to the sea and have a bathe.

People tried to be kind to her and asked her to stay with them, but she wouldn't. She seldom left the estate. She had plenty to do. She read a lot. She was never bored. She seemed quite happy in her own company, and when she had visitors it was only from a sense of duty. She didn't want them to think her ungracious. But it was an effort and she told me she heaved a sigh of relief when she saw the last of them and could again enjoy without disturbance the peaceful loneliness of the bungalow. She was a very curious girl. It was strange that at her age she should be so indifferent to parties and the other small gaieties the station afforded. Spiritually, if you know what I mean, she was entirely self-supporting. I don't know how people found out that I was in love with her; I thought I'd never given myself away in anything, but I had hints here and there that they knew. I gathered they thought Olive hadn't gone home with her brother on my account. One woman, a Mrs Sergison, the policeman's wife, actually asked me when they were going to be able to congratulate me. Of course I pretended I didn't know what she was talking about, but it didn't go down very well. I couldn't help being amused. I meant so little to Olive in that way that I really believe she'd entirely forgotten that I'd asked her to marry me. I can't say she was unkind to me, I don't think she could have been unkind to anyone; but she treated me with just the casualness with which a sister might treat a younger brother. She was two or three years older than I. She was always terribly glad to see me, but it never occurred to her to put herself out for me; she was almost amazingly intimate with me, but unconsciously, you know, as you might be with a person you'd known so well all your life that you never thought of putting on frills with him. I might not have been a man at all, but an old coat that she wore all the time because it was easy and comfortable and she didn't mind what she did in it. I should have been crazy not to see that she was a thousand miles away from loving me.

"Then one day, three or four weeks before Tim was due back, when I went to the bungalow I saw she'd been crying. I was startled. She was always so composed. I'd never seen her upset over anything.

"'Hullo, what's the matter?' I said.

"'Nothing.'

"'Come off it, darling,' I said. 'What have you been crying about?'

"She tried to smile.

"'I wish you hadn't got such sharp eyes,' she said. 'I think I'm being silly. I've just had a cable from Tim to say he's postponed his sailing.'

"'Oh, my dear, I am sorry,' I said. 'You must be awfully disappointed.'

"'I've been counting the days. I want him back so badly.'

"'Does he say why he's postponing?' I asked.

"'No, he says he's writing. I'll show you the cable.'

"I saw that she was very nervous. Her slow quiet eyes were filled with apprehension and there was a little frown of anxiety between her brows. She went into her bedroom and in a moment came back with the cable. I felt that she was watching me anxiously as I read. So far as I remember it ran: *Darling, I cannot sail on the seventh after all. Please forgive me. Am writing fully. Fondest love. Tim.*

"'Well, perhaps the machinery he wanted isn't ready and he can't bring himself to sail without it,' I said.

"'What could it matter if it came by a later ship? Anyhow, it'll be hung up at Penang.'

"'It may be something about the house.'

"'If it is why doesn't he say so? He must know how frightfully anxious I am.'

"'It wouldn't occur to him,' I said. 'After all, when you're away you don't realize that the people you've left behind don't know something that you take as a matter of course.'

"She smiled again, but now more happily.

"'I daresay you're right. In point of fact Tim is a little like that. He's always been rather slack and casual. I daresay I've been making a mountain out of a molehill. I must just wait patiently for his letter.'

"Olive was a girl with a lot of self-control and I saw her by an effort of will pull herself together. The little line between her eyebrows vanished and she was once more her serene, smiling, and kindly self. She was always gentle: that day she had a mildness so heavenly that it was shattering. But for the rest of the time I could see that she kept her restlessness in check only by the deliberate exercise of her common sense. It was as though she had a foreboding of ill. I was with her the day before the mail was due. Her anxiety was all the more pitiful to see because she took such pains to hide it. I was always busy on mail day, but I promised to go up to the estate later on and hear the news. I was just thinking of starting when Hardy's seis came along in the car with a message from the amah asking me to go at once to her mistress. The amah was a decent, elderly woman to whom I had given a dollar or two and said that if anything went wrong on the estate she was to let me know at once. I jumped into my car. When I arrived I found the amah waiting for me on the steps.

" 'A letter came this morning,' she said.

"I interrupted her. I ran up the steps. The sitting-room was empty.

" 'Olive,' I called.

"I went into the passage and suddenly I heard a sound that froze my heart. The amah had followed me and now she opened the door of Olive's room. The sound I had heard was the sound of Olive crying. I went in. She was lying on her bed, on her face, and her sobs shook her from head to foot. I put my hand on her shoulder.

" 'Olive, what is it?' I asked.

" 'Who's that?' she cried. She sprang to her feet suddenly, as though she were scared out of her wits. And then: 'Oh, it's you,' she said. She stood in front of me, with her head thrown back and her eyes closed, and the tears streamed from them. It was dreadful. 'Tim's married,' she gasped, and her face screwed up in a sort of grimace of pain.

"I must admit that for one moment I had a thrill of exultation, it was like a little electric shock tingling through my heart; it struck me that now I had a chance, she might be willing to marry me; I know it was terribly selfish of me; you see, the news had taken me by surprise; but it was only for a moment, after that I was melted by her awful distress and the only thing I felt was deep sorrow because she was unhappy. I put my arm round her waist.

" 'Oh, my dear, I'm so sorry,' I said. 'Don't stay here. Come into the sitting-room and sit down and we'll talk about it. Let me give you something to drink.'

"She let me lead her into the next room and we sat down on the sofa. I told the amah to fetch the whisky and syphon and I mixed her a good strong stengah and made her drink a little. I took her in my arms and rested her head on my shoulder. She let me do what I liked with her. The great tears streamed down her poor face.

" 'How could he?' she moaned. 'How could he?'

" 'My darling,' I said, 'it was bound to happen sooner or later. He's a young man. How could you expect him never to marry? It's only natural.'

" 'No, no, no,' she gasped.

"Tight-clenched in her hand I saw that she had a letter and I guessed that it was Tim's.

" 'What does he say?' I asked.

"She gave a frightened movement and clutched the letter to her heart as though she thought I would take it from her.

" 'He says he couldn't help himself. He says he had to. What does it mean?'

" 'Well, you know, in his way he's just as attractive as you are. He has so much charm. I suppose he just fell madly in love with some girl and she with him.'

" 'He's so weak,' she moaned.

" 'Are they coming out?' I asked.

" 'They sailed yesterday. He says it won't make any difference. He's insane. How *can* I stay here?'

"She began to cry hysterically. It was torture to see that girl, usually so calm, utterly shattered by her emotion. I had always felt that her lovely serenity masked a capacity for deep feeling. But the abandon of her distress simply broke me up. I held her in my arms and kissed her, her eyes and her wet cheek and her hair. I don't think she knew what I was doing. I was hardly conscious of it myself. I was so deeply moved.

" 'What shall I do?' she wailed.

" 'Why won't you marry me?' I said.

"She tried to withdraw herself from me, but I wouldn't let her go.

" 'After all, it would be a way out,' I said.

" 'How can I marry you?' she moaned. 'I'm years older than you are.'

" 'Oh, what nonsense, two or three. What do I care?'

" 'No, no.'

" 'Why not?' I said.

" 'I don't love you,' she said.

" 'What does that matter? I love you.'

501

"I don't know what I said. I told her that I'd try to make her happy. I said I'd never ask anything from her but what she was prepared to give me. I talked and talked. I tried to make her see reason. I felt that she didn't want to stay there, in the same place as Tim, and I told her that I'd be moved soon to some other district. I thought that might tempt her. She couldn't deny that we'd always got on awfully well together. After a time she did seem to grow a little quieter. I had a feeling that she was listening to me. I had even a sort of feeling that she knew that she was lying in my arms and that it comforted her. I made her drink a drop more whisky. I gave her a cigarette. At last I thought I might be just mildly facetious.

" 'You know, I'm not a bad sort really,' I said. 'You might do worse.'

" 'You don't know me,' she said. 'You know nothing whatever about me.'

" 'I'm capable of learning,' I said.

"She smiled a little.

" 'You're awfully kind, Mark,' she said.

" 'Say yes, Olive,' I begged.

"She gave a deep sigh. For a long time she stared at the ground. But she did not move and I felt the softness of her body in my arms. I waited. I was frightfully nervous and the minutes seemed endless.

" 'All right,' she said at last, as though she were not conscious that any time had passed between my prayer and her answer.

"I was so moved that I had nothing to say. But when I wanted to kiss her lips, she turned her face away, and wouldn't let me. I wanted us to be married at once, but she was quite firm that she wouldn't. She insisted on waiting till Tim came back. You know how sometimes you see so clearly into people's thoughts that you're more certain of them than if they'd spoken them; I saw that she couldn't quite believe that what Tim had written was true and that she had a sort of miserable hope that it was all a mistake and he wasn't married after all. It gave me a pang, but I loved her so much, I just bore it. I was willing to bear anything. I adored her. She wouldn't even let me tell anyone that we were engaged. She made me promise not to say a word till Tim's return. She said she couldn't bear the thought of the congratulations and all that. She wouldn't even let me make any announcement of Tim's marriage. She was obstinate about it. I had a notion that she felt if the fact were spread about it gave it a certainty that she didn't want it to have.

"But the matter was taken out of her hands. News travels mysteriously in the East. I don't know what Olive had said in the amah's hearing when first she received the news of Tim's marriage; anyhow, the Hardys' seis told the Sergisons and Mrs Sergison attacked me the next time I went into the club.

"'I hear Tim Hardy's married,' she said.

"'Oh?' I answered, unwilling to commit myself.

"She smiled at my blank face, and told me that her amah having told her the rumour she had rung up Olive and asked her if it was true. Olive's answer had been rather odd. She had not exactly confirmed it, but said that she had received a letter from Tim telling her he was married.

"'She's a strange girl,' said Mrs Sergison. 'When I asked her for details she said she had none to give and when I said: "Aren't you thrilled?" she didn't answer.'

"'Olive's devoted to Tim, Mrs Sergison,' I said. 'His marriage has naturally been a shock to her. She knows nothing about Tim's wife. She's nervous about her.'

"'And when are you two going to be married?' she asked me abruptly.

"'What an embarrassing question!' I said, trying to laugh it off.

"She looked at me shrewdly.

"'Will you give me your word of honour that you're not engaged to her?'

"I didn't like to tell her a deliberate lie, nor to ask her to mind her own business, and I'd promised Olive faithfully that I would say nothing till Tim got back. I hedged.

"'Mrs Sergison,' I said, 'when there's anything to tell I promise that you'll be the first person to hear it. All I can say to you now is that I do want to marry Olive more than anything in the world.'

"'I'm very glad that Tim's married,' she answered. 'And I hope she'll marry you very soon. It was a morbid and unhealthy life that they led up there, those two, they kept far too much to themselves and they were far too much absorbed in one another.'

"I saw Olive practically every day. I felt that she didn't want me to make love to her, and I contented myself with kissing her when

I came and when I went. She was very nice to me, kindly and thoughtful; I knew she was glad to see me and sorry when it was time for me to go. Ordinarily, she was apt to fall into silence but during this time she talked more than I had ever heard her talk before. But never of the future and never of Tim and his wife. She told me a lot about her life in Florence and her mother. She had led a strange lonely life, mostly with servants and governesses, while her mother, I suspected, engaged in one affair after another with vague Italian counts and Russian princes. I guessed that by the time she was fourteen there wasn't much she didn't know. It was natural for her to be quite unconventional: in the only world she knew till she was eighteen conventions weren't mentioned because they didn't exist. Gradually, Olive seemed to regain her serenity and I should have thought that she was beginning to accustom herself to the thought of Tim's marriage if it hadn't been that I couldn't but notice how pale and tired she looked. I made up my mind that the moment he arrived I'd press her to marry me at once. I could get short leave whenever I asked for it, and by the time that was up I thought I could manage a transfer to some other post. What she wanted was change of air and fresh scenes.

"We knew, of course, within a day when Tim's ship would reach Penang, but it was a question whether she'd get in soon enough for him to catch the train and I wrote to the P & O agent asking him to telegraph as soon as he had definite news. When I got the wire and took it up to Olive I found that she'd just received one from Tim. The ship had docked early and he was arriving next day. The train was supposed to get in at eight o'clock in the morning, but it was liable to be anything from one to six hours late, and I bore with me an invitation from Mrs Sergison asking Olive to come back with me to stay the night with her so that she would be on the spot and need not go to the station till the news came through that the train was coming.

"I was immensely relieved. I thought that when the blow at last fell Olive wouldn't feel it so much. She had worked herself up into such a state that I couldn't help thinking that she must have a reaction now. She might take a fancy to her sister-in-law. There was no reason why they shouldn't all three get on very well together. To my surprise Olive said she wasn't coming down to the station to meet them.

" 'They'll be awfully disappointed,' I said.

" 'I'd rather wait here,' she answered. She smiled a little. 'Don't argue with me, Mark, I've quite made up my mind.'

" 'I've ordered breakfast in my house,' I said.

" 'That's all right. You meet them and take them to your house and give them breakfast, and then they can come along here afterwards. Of course I'll send the car down.'

" 'I don't suppose they'll want to breakfast if you're not there,' I said.

" 'Oh, I'm sure they will. If the train gets in on time they wouldn't have thought of breakfasting before it arrived and they'll be hungry. They won't want to take this long drive without anything to eat.'

"I was puzzled. She had been looking forward so intensely to Tim's coming, it seemed strange that she should want to wait all by herself while the rest of us were having a jolly breakfast. I supposed she was nervous and wanted to delay as long as possible meeting the strange woman who had come to take her place. It seemed unreasonable, I couldn't see that an hour sooner or an hour later could make any difference, but I knew women were funny, and anyhow I felt Olive wasn't in the mood for me to press it.

" 'Telephone when you're starting so that I shall know when to expect you,' she said.

" 'All right,' I said, 'but you know I shan't be able to come with them. It's my day for going to Lahad.'

"This was a town that I had to go to once a week to take cases. It was a good way off and one had to ferry across a river, which took some time, so that I never got back till late. There were a few Europeans there and a club. I generally had to go on there for a bit to be sociable and see that things were getting along all right.

" 'Besides,' I added, 'with Tim bringing his wife home for the first time I don't suppose he'll want me about. But if you'd like to ask me to dinner I'll be glad to come to that.'

"Olive smiled.

" 'I don't think it'll be my place to issue any more invitations, will it?' she said. 'You must ask the bride.'

"She said this so lightly that my heart leaped. I had a feeling that at last she had made up her mind to accept the altered circumstances and, what was more, was accepting them with cheerfulness. She asked me to stay to dinner. Generally I left about eight and dined at home. She was very sweet, almost tender, and I was happier than I'd been for weeks. I had never been more desperately in love with her. I had a couple of gin pahits and I think I was in rather good form at dinner. I know I made her laugh. I felt that at last she was casting away the load of misery that had oppressed her. That was why I didn't let myself be very much disturbed by what happened at the end.

"'Don't you think it's about time you were leaving a presumably maiden lady?' she said.

"She spoke in a manner that was so quietly gay that I answered without hesitation:

"'Oh, my dear, if you think you've got a shred of reputation left you deceive yourself. You're surely not under the impression that the ladies of Sibuku don't know that I've been coming to see you every day for a month. The general feeling is that if we're not married it's high time we were. Don't you think it would be just as well if I broke it to them that we're engaged?'

"'Oh, Mark, you mustn't take our engagement very seriously,' she said.

"I laughed.

"'How else do you expect me to take it? It is serious.'

"She shook her head a little.

"'No. I was upset and hysterical that day. You were being very sweet to me. I said yes because I was too miserable to say no. But now I've had time to collect myself. Don't think me unkind. I made a mistake. I've been very much to blame. You must forgive me.'

"'Oh, darling, you're talking nonsense. You've got nothing against me.'

"She looked at me steadily. She was quite calm. She had even a little smile at the back of her eyes.

"'I can't marry you. I can't marry anyone. It was absurd of me ever to think I could.'

"I didn't answer at once. She was in a queer state and I thought it better not to insist.

"'I suppose I can't drag you to the altar by main force,' I said.

"I held out my hand and she gave me hers. I put my arm round her, and she made no attempt to withdraw. She suffered me to kiss her as usual on her cheek.

"Next morning I met the train. For once in a way it was punctual. Tim waved to me as his carriage passed the place where I was standing, and by the time I had walked up he had already jumped out and was handing down his wife. He grasped my hand warmly.

"'Where's Olive?' he said, with a glance along the platform. 'This is Sally.'

"I shook hands with her and at the same time explained why Olive was not there.

"'It was frightfully early, wasn't it?' said Mrs Hardy.

"I told them that the plan was for them to come and have a bit of breakfast at my house and then drive home.

"'I'd love a bath,' said Mrs Hardy.

"'You shall have one,' I said.

"She was really an extremely pretty little thing, very fair, with enormous blue eyes and a lovely little straight nose. Her skin, all milk and roses, was exquisite. A little of the chorus girl type, of course, and you may happen to think that rather namby-pamby, but in that style she was enchanting. We drove to my house, they both had a bath and Tim a shave; I just had two minutes alone with him. He asked me how Olive had taken his marriage. I told him she'd been upset.

"'I was afraid so,' he said, frowning a little. He gave a short sigh. 'I couldn't do anything else.'

"I didn't understand what he meant. At that moment Mrs Hardy joined us and slipped her arm through her husband's. He took her hand in his and gently pressed it. He gave her a look that had in it something pleased and humorously affectionate, as though he didn't take her quite seriously, but enjoyed his sense of proprietorship and was proud of her beauty. She really was lovely. She was not at all shy, she asked me to call her Sally before we'd known one another ten minutes, and she was quick in the uptake. Of course, just then she was excited at arriving. She'd never been East and everything thrilled her. It was quite obvious that she was head over heels in love with Tim. Her eyes never left him and she hung on his words. We had a jolly breakfast and then we parted. They got into their car to go home and I into mine to go to Lahad. I promised to go straight to the estate from there and in point of fact it was out of my way to pass by my house. I took a change with me. I didn't see why Olive shouldn't like Sally very much, she was frank and gay, and ingenuous; she was extremely young, she couldn't have been more than nineteen, and her wonderful prettiness couldn't fail to appeal to Olive. I was just as glad to have had a reasonable excuse to leave the three of them by themselves for the day, but as I started out from Lahad I had a notion that by the time I arrived they would all be pleased to see me. I drove up to the bungalow and blew my horn two or three times, expecting someone to appear. Not a soul. The place was in total darkness. I was surprised. It was absolutely silent. I couldn't make it out. They must be in. Very odd, I thought. I waited a moment, then got out of the car and walked up the steps. At the top of them I stumbled over something. I swore and bent down to see what it was; it had felt like a body. There was a cry and I saw it was the amah. She shrank back cowering as I touched her and broke into loud wails.

" 'What the hell's the matter?' I cried, and then I felt a hand on my arm and heard a voice: Tuan, Tuan. I turned and in the darkness recognized Tim's head boy. He began to speak in little frightened gasps. I listened to him with horror. What he told me was unspeakable. I pushed him aside and rushed into the house. The sitting-room was dark. I turned on the light. The first thing I saw was Sally huddled up in an arm-chair. She was startled by my sudden appearance and cried out. I could hardly speak. I asked her if it was true. When she told me it was I felt the room suddenly going round and round me. I had to sit down. As the car that bore Tim and Sally drove up the road that led to the house and Tim sounded the claxon to announce their arrival and the boys and the amah ran out to greet them there was the sound of a shot. They ran to Olive's room and found her lying in front of the looking-glass in a pool of blood. She had shot herself with Tim's revolver.

" 'Is she dead?' I said.

" 'No, they sent for the doctor, and he took her to the hospital.'

"I hardly knew what I was doing. I didn't even trouble to tell Sally where I was going. I got up and staggered to the door. I got into the car and told my seis to drive like hell to the hospital. I rushed in. I asked where she was. They tried to bar my way, but I pushed them aside. I knew where the private rooms were. Someone clung to my arm, but I shook him off. I vaguely understood that the doctor had given instructions that no one was to go into the room. I didn't care about that. There was an orderly at the door; he put out his arm to prevent me from passing. I swore at him and told him to get out of my way. I suppose I made a row, I was beside myself; the door was opened and the doctor came out.

" 'Who's making all this noise?' he said. 'Oh, it's you. What do you want?'

" 'Is she dead?' I asked.

" 'No. But she's unconscious. She never regained consciousness. It's only a matter of an hour or two.'

" 'I want to see her.'

" 'You can't.'

" 'I'm engaged to her.'

" 'You?' he cried, and even at that moment I was aware that he looked at me strangely. 'That's all the more reason.'

"I didn't know what he meant. I was stupid with horror.

" 'Surely you can do something to save her,' I cried.

"He shook his head.

" 'If you saw her you wouldn't wish it,' he said.

"I stared at him aghast. In the silence I heard a man's convulsive sobbing.

" 'Who's that?' I asked.

" 'Her brother.'

"Then I felt a hand on my arm. I looked round and saw it was Mrs Sergison.

" 'My poor boy,' she said, 'I'm so sorry for you.'

" 'What on earth made her do it?' I groaned.

" 'Come away, my dear,' said Mrs Sergison. 'You can do no good here.'

" 'No, I must stay,' I said.

" 'Well, go and sit in my room,' said the doctor.

"I was so broken that I let Mrs Sergison take me by the arm and lead me into the doctor's private room. She made me sit down. I couldn't bring myself to realize that it was true. I thought it was a horrible nightmare from which I must awake. I don't know how long we sat there. Three hours. Four hours. At last the doctor came in.

" 'It's all over,' he said.

"Then I couldn't help myself, I began to cry. I didn't care what they thought of me. I was so frightfully unhappy.

"We buried her next day.

"Mrs Sergison came back to my house and sat with me for a while. She wanted me to go to the club with her. I hadn't the heart. She was very kind, but I was glad when she left me by myself. I tried to read, but the words meant nothing to me. I felt dead inside. My boy came in and turned on the lights. My head was aching like mad. Then he came back and said that a lady wished to see me. I asked who it was. He wasn't quite sure, but he thought it must be the new wife of the tuan at Putatan. I couldn't imagine what she wanted. I got up and went to the door. He was right. It was Sally. I asked her to come in. I noticed that she was deathly white. I felt sorry for her. It was a frightful experience for a girl of that age and for a bride a miserable homecoming. She sat down. She was very nervous. I tried to put her at her ease by saying conventional things. She made me very uncomfortable because she stared at me with those enormous blue eyes of hers, and they were simply ghastly with horror. She interrupted me suddenly.

"'You're the only person here I know,' she said. 'I had to come to you. I want you to get me away from here.'

"I was dumbfounded.

"'What *do* you mean?' I said.

"'I don't want you to ask me any questions. I just want you to get me away. At once. I want to go back to England!'

"'But you can't leave Tim like that just now,' I said. 'My dear, you must pull yourself together. I know it's been awful for you. But think of Tim. If you have any love for him the least you can do is to try and make him a little less unhappy.'

"'Oh, you don't know,' she cried. 'I can't tell you. It's too horrible. I beseech you to help me. If there's a train tonight let me get on it. If I can only get to Penang I can get a ship. I can't stay in this place another night. I shall go mad.'

"I was absolutely bewildered.

"'Does Tim know?' I asked her.

"'I haven't seen Tim since last night. I'll never see him again. I'd rather die.'

"I wanted to gain a little time.

"'But how can you go without your things? Have you got any luggage?'

"'What does that matter?' she cried impatiently. 'I've got what I want for the journey.'

"'Have you any money?'

"'Enough. Is there a train tonight?'

"'Yes,' I said. 'It's due just after midnight.'

"'Thank God. Will you arrange everything? Can I stay here till then?'

"'You're putting me in a frightful position,' I said. 'I don't know what to do for the best. You know, it's an awfully serious step you're taking.'

"'If you knew everything you'd know it was the only possible thing to do.'

"'It'll create an awful scandal here. I don't know what people'll say. Have you thought of the effect on Tim?' I was worried and unhappy. 'God knows I don't want to interfere in what isn't my business. But if you want me to help you I ought to know enough to feel justified in doing so. You must tell me what's happened.'

"'I can't. I can only tell you that I know everything.'

"She hid her face with her hands and shuddered. Then she gave herself a shake as though she were recoiling from some frightful sight.

"'He had no right to marry me. It was monstrous.'

"And as she spoke her voice rose shrill and piercing. I was afraid she was going to have an attack of hysterics. Her pretty doll-like face was terrified and her eyes stared as though she could never close them again.

"'Don't you love him any more?' I asked.

"'After that?'

"'What will you do if I refuse to help you?' I said.

"'I suppose there's a clergyman here or a doctor. You can't refuse to take me to one of them.'

"'How did you get here?'

"'The head boy drove me. He got a car from somewhere.'

"'Does Tim know you've gone?'

"'I left a letter for him.'

"'He'll know you're here.'

" 'He won't try to stop me. I promise you that. He daren't. For God's sake don't you try either. I tell you I shall go mad if I stay here another night.'

"I sighed. After all she was of an age to decide for herself."

I, the writer of this, hadn't spoken for a long time.

"Did you know what she meant?" I asked Featherstone.

He gave me a long, haggard look.

"There was only one thing she could mean. It was unspeakable. Yes, I knew all right. It explained everything. Poor Olive. Poor sweet. I suppose it was unreasonable of me, at that moment I only felt a horror of that little pretty fair-haired thing with her terrified eyes. I hated her. I didn't say anything for a while. Then I told her I'd do as she wished. She didn't even say thank you. I think she knew what I felt about her. When it was dinner-time I made her eat something and then she asked me if there was a room she could go and lie down in till it was time to go to the station. I showed her into my spare room and left her. I sat in the sitting-room and waited. My God, I don't think the time has ever passed so slowly for me. I thought twelve would never strike. I rang up the station and was told the train wouldn't be in till nearly two. At midnight she came back to the sitting-room and we sat there for an hour and a half. We had nothing to say to one another and we didn't speak. Then I took her to the station and put her on the train."

"Was there an awful scandal?"

Featherstone frowned.

"I don't know. I applied for short leave. After that I was moved to another post. I heard that Tim had sold his estate and bought another. But I didn't know where. It was a shock to me at first when I found him here."

Featherstone, getting up, went over to a table and mixed himself a whisky and soda. In the silence that fell now I heard the monotonous chorus of the croaking frogs. And suddenly the bird that is known as the fever-bird, perched in a tree close to the house, began to call. First, three notes in a descending, chromatic scale, then five, then four. The varying notes of the scale succeeded one another with maddening persistence. One was compelled to listen and to count them, and because one did not know how many there would be it tortured one's nerves.

"Blast that bird," said Featherstone. "That means no sleep for me tonight."

THE BACK OF BEYOND

GEORGE MOON WAS sitting in his office. His work was finished, and he lingered there because he hadn't the heart to go down to the club. It was getting on towards tiffin time, and there would be a good many fellows hanging about the bar. Two or three of them would offer him a drink. He could not face their heartiness. Some he had known for thirty years. They had bored him, and on the whole he disliked them, but now that he was seeing them for the last time it gave him a pang. Tonight they were giving him a farewell dinner. Everyone would be there and they were presenting him with a silver tea-service that he did not in the least want. They would make speeches in which they would refer eulogistically to his work in the colony, express their regret at his departure, and wish him long life to enjoy his well-earned leisure. He would reply suitably. He had prepared a speech in which he surveyed the changes that had taken place in the FMS since first, a raw cadet, he had landed at Singapore. He would thank them for their loyal co-operation with him during the term which it had been his privilege to serve as Resident at Timbang Belud, and draw a glowing picture of the future that awaited the country as a whole and Timbang Belud in particular. He would remind them that he had known it as a poverty-stricken village with a few Chinese shops and left it now a prosperous town with paved streets down which ran trams, with stone houses, a rich Chinese settlement, and a clubhouse second in splendour only to that of Singapore. They would sing "For he's a jolly good fellow" and "Auld Lang Syne". Then they would dance and a good many of the younger men would get drunk. The Malays had already given him a farewell party and the Chinese an interminable feast. Tomorrow a vast concourse would see him off at the station and that would be the end of him. He wondered what they would say of him. The Malays and the Chinese would say that he had been stern, but acknowledge that he had been just. The planters had not liked him. They thought him hard because he would not let them ride roughshod over their labour. His subordinates had feared him. He drove them. He had no patience with slackness or inefficiency. He had never spared himself and saw no reason why he should spare others. They thought him inhuman. It was true that there was nothing come-hither in him. He could not throw off his official position when he went to the club and laugh at bawdy stories, chaff and be chaffed. He was conscious that his arrival cast a gloom, and to play bridge with him (he liked to play every day from six to eight) was looked upon as a privilege rather than an entertainment. When at some other table a young man's four as the evening wore on grew hilarious, he caught glances thrown in his direction and sometimes an older member would stroll up to the noisy ones and in an undertone advise them to be quiet. George Moon sighed a little. From an official standpoint his career had been a success, he had been the youngest Resident ever appointed in the FMS, and for exceptional services a CMG had been conferred upon him; but from the human it had perhaps been otherwise. He had earned respect, respect for his ability, industry, and trustworthiness, but he was too clear-sighted to think for a moment that he had inspired affection. No one would regret him. In a few months he would be forgotten.

He smiled grimly. He was not sentimental. He had enjoyed his authority, and it gave him an austere satisfaction to know that he had kept everyone up to the mark. It did not displease him to think that he had been feared rather than loved. He saw his life as a problem in higher mathematics, the working-out of which had required intense application of all his powers, but of which the result had not the least practical consequence. Its interest lay in its intricacy and its beauty in its solution. But like pure beauty it led nowhither. His future was blank. He was fifty-five, and full of energy, and to himself his mind seemed as alert as ever, his experience of men and affairs was wide: all that remained to him was to settle down in a country town in England or in a cheap part of the Riviera and play bridge with elderly ladies and golf with retired colonels. He had met, when on leave, old chiefs of his, and had observed with what difficulty they adapted themselves to the change in their circumstances. They had looked forward to the freedom that would be theirs when they retired and had pictured the charming uses to which they would put their leisure. Mirage. It was not very pleasant to be obscure after having dwelt in a spacious Residency, to make do with a couple of maids when you had been accustomed to the service of half a dozen Chinese boys and, above all, it was not pleasant to realize that you did not matter a row of beans to anyone when you had grown used to the delicate flattery of knowing that a word of praise could delight and a frown humiliate all sorts and conditions of men.

George Moon stretched out his hand and helped himself to a cigarette from the box on his desk. As he did so he noticed all the little lines on the back of his hand and the thinness of his shrivelled fingers. He frowned with distaste. It was the hand of an old man. There was in his office a Chinese mirror-picture that he had bought long ago and that he was leaving behind. He got up and looked at himself in it. He saw a thin yellow face, wrinkled and tight-lipped, thin grey hair, and grey tired eyes. He was tallish, very spare, with narrow shoulders, and he held himself erect. He had always played polo and even now could beat most of the younger men at tennis. When you talked to him he kept his eyes fixed on your face, listening attentively, but his expression did not change, and you had no notion what effect your words had on him. Perhaps he did not realize how disconcerting this was. He seldom smiled.

An orderly came in with a name written on a chit. George Moon looked at it and told him to show the visitor in. He sat down once more in his chair and looked with his cold eyes at the door through which in a moment the visitor would come. It was Tom Saffary, and he wondered what he wanted. Presumably something to do with the festivity that night. It had amused him to hear that Tom Saffary was the head of the committee that had organized it, for their relations during the last year had been far from cordial. Saffary was a planter and one of his Tamil overseers had lodged a complaint against him for assault. The Tamil had been grossly insolent to him and Saffary had given him a thrashing. George Moon realized that the provocation was great, but he had always set his face against the planters taking the law in their own hands, and when the case was tried he sentenced Saffary to a fine. But when the court rose, to show that there was no ill-feeling he asked Saffary to luncheon: Saffary, resentful of what he thought an unmerited affront, curtly refused and since then had declined to have any social relations with the Resident. He answered when George Moon, casually, but resolved not to be affronted, spoke to him; but would play neither bridge nor tennis with him. He was manager of the largest rubber estate in the district, and George Moon asked himself sardonically whether he had arranged the dinner and collected subscriptions for the presentation because he thought his dignity required it or whether, now that his Resident was leaving, it appealed to his sentimentality to make a noble gesture. It tickled George Moon's frigid sense of humour to think that it would fall to Tom Saffary to make the principal speech of the evening, in which he would enlarge upon the departing Resident's admirable qualities and voice the community's regret at their irreparable loss.

Tom Saffary was ushered in. The Resident rose from his chair, shook hands with him and thinly smiled.

"How do you do? Sit down. Won't you have a cigarette?"

"How do you do?"

Saffary took the chair to which the Resident motioned him, and the Resident waited for him to state his business. He had a notion that his visitor was embarrassed. He was a big, burly, stout fellow, with a red face and a double chin, curly black hair, and blue eyes. He was a fine figure of a man, strong as a horse, but it was plain he did himself too well. He drank a good deal and ate too heartily. But he was a good business man and a hard worker. He ran his estate efficiently. He was popular in the community. He was generally known as a good chap. He was free with his money and ready to lend a helping hand to anyone in distress. It occurred to the Resident that Saffary had come in order before the dinner to compose the difference between them. The emotion that might have occasioned such a desire excited in the Resident's sensibility a very faint, good-humoured contempt. He had no enemies because individuals did not mean enough to him for him to hate any of them, but if he had, he thought, he would have hated them to the end.

"I daresay you're a bit surprised to see me here this morning, and I expect, as it's your last day and all that, you're pretty busy."

George Moon did not answer, and the other went on.

"I've come on rather an awkward business. The fact is that my wife and I won't be able to come to the dinner tonight, and after that unpleasantness we had together last year I thought it only right to come and tell you that it has nothing to do with that. I think you treated me very harshly; it's not the money I minded, it was the indignity, but bygones are bygones. Now that you're leaving I don't want you to think that I bear any more ill-feeling towards you."

"I realized that when I heard that you were chiefly responsible for the send-off you're giving me," answered the Resident civilly. "I'm sorry that you won't be able to come tonight."

"I'm sorry, too. It's on account of Knobby Clarke's death." Saffary hesitated for a moment. "My wife and I were very much upset by it."

"It was very sad. He was a great friend of yours, wasn't he?"

"He was the greatest friend I had in the colony."

Tears shone in Tom Saffary's eyes. Fat men are very emotional, thought George Moon.

"I quite understand that in that case you should have no heart for what looks like being a rather uproarious party," he said kindly. "Have you heard anything of the circumstances?"

"No, nothing but what appeared in the paper."

"He seemed all right when he left here."

"As far as I know he'd never had a day's illness in his life."

"Heart, I suppose. How old was he?"

"Same age as me. Thirty-eight."

"That's young to die."

Knobby Clarke was a planter and the estate he managed was next door to Saffary's. George Moon had liked him. He was a rather ugly man, sandy, with high cheek-bones and hollow temples, large pale eyes in deep sockets and a big mouth. But he had an attractive smile and an easy manner. He was amusing and could tell a good story. He had a careless good-humour that people found pleasing. He played games well. He was no fool. George Moon would have said he was somewhat colourless. In the course of his career he had known a good many men like him. They came and went. A fortnight before, he had left for England on leave and the Resident knew that the Saffarys had given a large dinner-party on his last night. He was married and his wife of course went with him.

"I'm sorry for her," said George Moon. "It must have been a terrible blow. He was buried at sea, wasn't he?"

"Yes. That's what it said in the paper."

The news had reached Timbang the night before. The Singapore papers arrived at six, just as people were getting to the club, and a good many men waited to play bridge or billiards till they had had a glance at them. Suddenly one fellow had called out:

"I say, do you see this? Knobby's dead."

"Knobby who? Not Knobby Clarke?"

There was a three-line paragraph in a column of general intelligence:

Messrs Star, Mosley and Co. have received a cable informing them that Mr Harold Clarke of Timbang Batu died suddenly on his way home and was buried at sea.

A man came up and took the paper from the speaker's hand, and incredulously read the note for himself. Another peered over his shoulder. Such as happened to be reading the paper turned to the page in question and read the three different lines.

"By George," cried one.

"I say, what tough luck," said another.

"He was as fit as a fiddle when he left here."

A shiver of dismay pierced those hearty, jovial, careless men, and each one for a moment remembered that he too was mortal. Other members came in and as they entered, braced by the thought of the six o'clock drink, and eager to meet their friends, they were met by the grim tidings.

"I say, have you heard? Poor Knobby Clarke's dead."

"No? I say, how awful!"

"Rotten luck, isn't it?"

"Rotten."

"Damned good sort."

"One of the best."

"It gave me quite a turn when I saw it in the paper just by chance."

"I don't wonder."

One man with the paper in his hand went into the billiard-room to break the news. They were playing off the handicap for the Prince of Wales's Cup. That august personage had presented it to the club on the occasion of his visit to Timbang Belud. Tom Saffary was playing against a man called Douglas, and the Resident, who had been beaten in the previous round, was seated with about a dozen others watching the game. The marker was monotonously calling out the score. The newcomer waited for Saffary to finish his break and then called out to him.

"I say, Tom, Knobby's dead."

"Knobby? It's not true."

The other handed him the paper. Three or four gathered round to read with him.

"Good God!"

There was a moment's awed silence. The paper was passed from hand to hand. It was odd that none seemed willing to believe till he saw it for himself in black and white.

"Oh, I am sorry."

"I say, it's awful for his wife," said Tom Saffary. "She was going to have a baby. My poor missus'll be upset."

"Why, it's only a fortnight since he left here."

"He was all right then."

"In the pink."

Saffary, his fat red face sagging a little, went over to a table and, seizing his glass, drank deeply.

"Look here, Tom," said his opponent, "would you like to call the game off?"

"Can't very well do that." Saffary's eye sought the score board and he saw that he was ahead. "No, let's finish. Then I'll go home and break it to Violet."

Douglas had his shot and made fourteen. Tom Saffary missed an easy in-off, but left nothing. Douglas played again, but did not score and again Saffary missed a shot that ordinarily he could have been sure of. He frowned a little. He knew his friends had betted on him pretty heavily and he did not like the idea of failing them. Douglas made twenty-two. Saffary emptied his glass and by an effort of will that was quite patent to the sympathetic onlookers settled down to concentrate on the game. He made a break of eighteen and when he just failed to do a long Jenny they gave him a round of applause. He was sure of himself now and began to score quickly. Douglas was playing well too, and the match grew exciting to watch. The few minutes during which Saffary's attention wandered had allowed his opponent to catch up with him, and now it was anybody's game.

"Spot two hundred and thirty-five," called the Malay, in his queer clipped English. "Plain two hundred and twenty-eight. Spot to play."

Douglas made eight, and then Saffary, who was plain, drew up to two hundred and forty. He left his opponent a double balk. Douglas hit neither ball, and so gave Saffary another point.

"Spot two hundred and forty-three," called the marker. "Plain two hundred and forty-one. Plain to play."

Saffary played three beautiful shots off the red and finished the game.

"A popular victory," the bystanders cried.

"Congratulations, old man," said Douglas.

"Boy," called Saffary, "ask these gentlemen what they'll have. Poor old Knobby."

He sighed heavily. The drinks were brought and Saffary signed the chit. Then he said he'd be getting along. Two others had already begun to play.

"Sporting of him to go on like that," said someone when the door was closed on Saffary.

"Yes, it shows grit."

"For a while I thought his game had gone all to pieces."

"He pulled himself together in grand style. He knew there were a lot of bets on him. He didn't want to let his backers down."

"Of course it's a shock, a thing like that."

"They were great pals. I wonder what he died of."

"Good shot, sir."

George Moon, remembering this scene, thought it strange that Tom Saffary, who on hearing of his friend's death had shown such self-control, should now apparently take it so hard. It might be that just as in the war a man when hit often did not know it till some time afterwards, Saffary had not realized how great a blow to him Harold Clarke's death was till he had had time to think it over. It seemed to him, however, more probable that Saffary, left to himself, would have carried on as usual, seeking sympathy for his loss in the company of his fellows, but that his wife's conventional sense of propriety had insisted that it would be bad form to go to a party when the grief they were suffering from made it only decent for them to eschew for a little festive gatherings. Violet Saffary was a nice little woman, three or four years younger than her husband; not very pretty, but pleasant to look at and always becomingly dressed; amiable, ladylike, and unassuming. In the days when he had been on friendly terms with the Saffarys the Resident had from time to time dined with them. He had found her agreeable, but not very amusing. They had never talked but of commonplace things. Of late he had seen little of her. When they chanced to meet she always gave him a friendly smile, and on occasion he said one or two civil words to her. But it was only by an effort of memory that he distinguished her from half a dozen of the other ladies in the community whom his official position brought him in contact with.

Saffary had presumably said what he had come to say and the Resident wondered why he did not get up and go. He sat heaped up in his chair oddly, so that it gave you the feeling that his skeleton had ceased to support him and his considerable mass of flesh was falling in on him. He looked dully at the desk that separated him from the Resident. He sighed deeply.

"You must try not to take it too hard, Saffary," said George Moon. "You know how uncertain life is in the East. One has to resign oneself to losing people one's fond of."

Saffary's eyes slowly moved from the desk, and he fixed them on George Moon's. They stared unwinking. George Moon liked people to look him in the eyes. Perhaps he felt that when he thus held their vision he held them in his power. Presently two tears formed themselves in Saffary's blue eyes and slowly ran down his cheeks. He had a strangely puzzled look. Something had frightened him. Was it death? No. Something that he thought worse. He looked cowed. His mien was cringing so that he made you think of a dog unjustly beaten.

"It's not that," he faltered. "I could have borne that."

George Moon did not answer. He held that big, powerful man with his cold level gaze and waited. He was pleasantly conscious of his absolute indifference. Saffary gave a harassed glance at the papers on the desk.

"I'm afraid I'm taking up too much of your time."

"No, I have nothing to do at the moment."

Saffary looked out of the window. A little shudder passed between his shoulders. He seemed to hesitate.

"I wonder if I might ask your advice," he said at last.

"Of course," said the Resident, with the shadow of a smile, "that's one of the things I'm here for."

"It's a purely private matter."

"You may be quite sure that I shan't betray any confidence you place in me."

"No, I know you wouldn't do that, but it's rather an awkward thing to speak about, and I shouldn't feel very comfortable meeting you afterwards. But you're going away tomorrow, and that makes it easier, if you understand what I mean."

"Quite."

Saffary began to speak, in a low voice, sulkily, as though he were ashamed, and he spoke with the awkwardness of a man unused to words. He went back and said the same thing over again. He got mixed up. He started a long, elaborate sentence and then broke off abruptly because he did not know how to finish it. George Moon listened in silence, his face a mask, smoking, and he only took his eyes off Saffary's face to reach for another cigarette from the box in front of him and light it from the stub of that which he was just finishing. And while he listened he saw, as it were a background, the monotonous round of the planter's life. It was like an accompaniment of muted strings that threw into sharper relief the calculated dissonances of an unexpected melody.

With rubber at so low a price every economy had to be exercised and Tom Saffary, notwithstanding the size of the estate, had to do work which in better times he had had an assistant for. He rose before dawn and went down to the lines where the coolies were assembled. When there was just enough light to see he read out the names, ticking them off according to the answers, and assigned the various squads to their work. Some tapped, some weeded, and others tended the ditches. Saffary went back to his solid breakfast, lit his pipe, and sallied forth again to inspect the coolies' quarters. Children were playing and babies sprawling here and there. On the sidewalks Tamil women cooked their rice. Their black skins shone with oil. They were draped about in dull red cotton and wore gold ornaments in their hair. There were handsome creatures among them, upright of carriage, with delicate features and small, exquisite hands; but Saffary looked upon them only with distaste. He set out on his rounds. On his well-grown estate the trees planted in rows gave one a charming feeling of the prim forest of a German fairy-tale. The ground was thick with dead leaves. He was accompanied by a Tamil overseer, his long black hair done in a chignon, barefooted, in sarong and baju, with a showy ring on his finger. Saffary walked hard, jumping the ditches when he came to them, and soon he dripped with sweat. He examined the trees to see that they were properly tapped, and when he came across a coolie at work looked at the shavings and if they were too thick swore at him and docked him half a day's pay. When a tree was not to be tapped any more he told the overseer to take away the cup and the wire that held it to the trunk. The weeders worked in gangs.

At noon Saffary returned to the bungalow and had a drink of beer which, because there was no ice, was lukewarm. He stripped off the khaki shorts, the flannel shirt, the heavy boots and stockings in which he had been walking, and shaved and bathed. He lunched in a sarong and baju. He lay off for half an hour, and then went down to his office and worked till five; he had tea and went to the club. About eight he started back for the bungalow, dined, and half an hour after went to bed.

But last night he went home immediately he had finished his match. Violet had not accompanied him that day. When the Clarkes were there they had met at the club every afternoon, but now they had gone home she came less often. She said there was no one there who much amused her and she had heard everything everyone had to say till she was fed to the teeth. She did not play bridge and it was dull for her to wait about while he played. She told Tom he need not mind leaving her alone. She had plenty of things to do in the house.

As soon as she saw him back so early she guessed that he had come to tell her that he had won his match. He was like a child in his self-satisfaction over one of these small triumphs. He was a kindly, simple creature and she knew that his pleasure at winning was not only on his own account, but because he thought it must give her pleasure too. It was rather sweet of him to hurry home in order to tell her all about it without delay.

"Well, how did your match go?" she said as soon as he came lumbering into the sitting-room.

"I won."

"Easily?"

"Well, not as easily as I should have. I was a bit ahead, and then I stuck, I couldn't do a thing, and you know what Douglas is, not at all showy, but steady, and he pulled up with me. Then I said to myself, well, if I don't buck up I shall get a licking, I had a bit of luck here and there, and then, to cut a long story short, I beat him by seven."

"Isn't that splendid? You ought to win the cup now, oughtn't you?"

"Well, I've got three matches more. If I can get into the semi-finals I ought to have a chance."

Violet smiled. She was anxious to show him that she was as much interested as he expected her to be.

"What made you go to pieces when you did?"

His faced sagged.

"That's why I came back at once. I'd have scratched only I thought it wasn't fair on the fellows who'd backed me. I don't know how to tell you, Violet."

She gave him a questioning look.

"Why, what's the matter? Not bad news?"

"Rotten. Knobby's dead."

For a full minute she stared at him, and her face, her neat friendly little face, grew haggard with horror. At first it seemed as though she could not understand.

"What *do* you mean?" she cried.

"It was in the paper. He died on board. They buried him at sea."

Suddenly she gave a piercing cry and fell headlong to the floor. She had fainted dead away.

"Violet," he cried, and threw himself down on his knees and took her head in his arms. "Boy, boy."

A boy, startled by the terror in his master's voice, rushed in, and Saffary shouted to him to bring brandy. He forced a little between Violet's lips. She opened her eyes, and as she remembered they grew dark with anguish. Her face was screwed up like a little child's when it is just going to burst into tears. He lifted her up in his arms and laid her on the sofa. She turned her head away.

"Oh, Tom, it isn't true. It can't be true."

"I'm afraid it is."

"No, no, no."

She burst into tears. She wept convulsively. It was dreadful to hear her. Saffary did not know what to do. He knelt beside her and tried to soothe her. He sought to take her in his arms, but with a sudden gesture she repelled him.

"Don't touch me," she cried, and she said it so sharply that he was startled.

He rose to his feet.

"Try not to take it too hard, sweetie," he said. "I know it's been an awful shock. He was one of the best."

She buried her face in the cushions and wept despairingly. It tortured him to see her body shaken by those uncontrollable sobs. She was beside herself. He put his hand gently on her shoulder.

"Darling, don't give way like that. It's so bad for you."

She shook herself free from his hand.

"For God's sake leave me alone," she cried. "Oh, Hal, Hal." He had never heard her call the dead man that before. Of course his name was Harold, but everyone called him Knobby. "What shall I do?" she wailed. "I can't bear it. I can't bear it."

Saffary began to grow a trifle impatient. So much grief did seem to him exaggerated. Violet was not normally so emotional. He supposed it was the damned climate. It made women nervous and high-strung. Violet hadn't been home for four years. She was not hiding her face now. She lay, almost falling off the sofa, her mouth open in the extremity of her pain, and the tears streamed from her staring eyes. She was distraught.

"Have a little more brandy," he said. "Try to pull yourself together, darling. You can't do Knobby any good by getting in such a state."

With a sudden gesture she sprang to her feet and pushed him aside. She gave him a look of hatred.

"Go away, Tom. I don't want your sympathy. I want to be left alone."

She walked swiftly over to an arm-chair and threw herself down in it. She flung back her head and her poor white face was wrenched into a grimace of agony.

"Oh, it's not fair," she moaned. "What's to become of me now? Oh, God, I wish I were dead."

"Violet."

His voice quavered with pain. He was very nearly crying too. She stamped her foot impatiently.

"Go away, I tell you. Go away."

He started. He stared at her and suddenly gasped. A shudder passed through his great bulk. He took a step towards her and stopped, but his eyes never left her white, tortured face; he stared as though he saw in it something that appalled him. Then he dropped his head and without a word walked out of the room. He went into a little sitting-room they had at the back, but seldom used, and sank heavily into a chair. He thought. Presently the gong sounded for dinner. He had not had his bath. He gave his hands a glance. He could not be bothered to wash them. He walked slowly into the dining-room. He told the boy to go and tell Violet that dinner was ready. The boy came back and said she did not want any.

"All right. Let me have mine then," said Saffary.

He sent Violet in a plate of soup and a piece of toast, and when the fish was served he put some on a plate for her and gave it to the boy. But the boy came back with it at once.

"Mem, she say no wantchee," he said.

Saffary ate his dinner alone. He ate from habit, solidly, through the familiar courses. He drank a bottle of beer. When he had finished the boy brought him a cup of coffee and he lit a cheroot. Saffary sat still till he had finished it. He thought. At last he got up and went back into the large veranda which was where they always sat. Violet was still huddled in the chair in which he had left her. Her eyes were closed, but she opened them when she heard him come. He took a light chair and sat down in front of her.

"What *was* Knobby to you, Violet?" he said.

She gave a slight start. She turned away her eyes, but did not speak.

"I can't quite make out why you should have been so frightfully upset by the news of his death."

"It was an awful shock."

"Of course. But it seems very strange that anyone should go simply to pieces over the death of a friend."

"I don't understand what you mean," she said.

She could hardly speak the words and he saw that her lips were trembling.

"I've never heard you call him Hal. Even his wife called him Knobby."

She did not say anything. Her eyes, heavy with grief, were fixed on vacancy.

"Look at me, Violet."

She turned her head slightly and listlessly gazed at him.

"Was he your lover?"

She closed her eyes and tears flowed from them. Her mouth was strangely twisted.

"Haven't you got anything to say at all?"

She shook her head.

"You must answer me, Violet."

"I'm not fit to talk to you now," she moaned. "How can you be so heartless?"

"I'm afraid I don't feel very sympathetic at the moment. We must get this straight now. Would you like a drink of water?"

"I don't want anything."

"Then answer my question."

"You have no right to ask it. It's insulting."

"Do you ask me to believe that a woman like you who hears of the death of someone she knew is going to faint dead away and then, when she comes to, is going to cry like that? Why, one wouldn't be so upset over the death of one's only child. When we heard of your mother's death you cried of course, anyone would, and I know you were utterly miserable, but you came to me for comfort and you said you didn't know what you'd have done without me."

"This was so frightfully sudden."

"Your mother's death was sudden, too."

"Naturally I was very fond of Knobby."

"How fond? So fond that when you heard he was dead you didn't know and you didn't care what you said? Why did you say it wasn't fair? Why did you say, 'What's going to become of me now?'?"

She sighed deeply. She turned her head this way and that like a sheep trying to avoid the hands of the butcher.

"You mustn't take me for an utter fool, Violet. I tell you it's impossible that you should be so shattered by the blow if there hadn't been something between you."

"Well, if you think that, why do you torture me with questions?"

"My dear, it's no good shilly-shallying. We can't go on like this. What d'you think I'm feeling?"

She looked at him when he said this. She hadn't thought of him at all. She had been too much absorbed in her own misery to be concerned with his.

"I'm so tired," she sighed.

He leaned forward and roughly seized her wrist.

"Speak," he cried.

"You're hurting me."

"And what about me? D'you think you're not hurting me? How can you have the heart to let me suffer like this?"

He let go of her arm and sprang to his feet. He walked to the end of the room and back again. It looked as though the movement had suddenly roused him to fury. He caught her by the shoulders and dragged her to her feet. He shook her.

"If you don't tell me the truth I'll kill you," he cried.

"I wish you would," she said.

"He was your lover?"

"Yes."

"You swine."

With one hand still on her shoulder so that she could not move he swung back his other arm and with a flat palm struck her repeatedly, with all his strength, on the side of her face. She quivered under the blows, but did not flinch or cry out. He struck her again and again. All at once he felt her strangely inert, he let go of her and she sank unconscious to the floor. Fear seized him. He bent down and touched her, calling her name. She did not move. He lifted her up and put her back into the chair from which a little while before he had pulled her. The brandy that had been brought when first she fainted was still in the room and he fetched it and tried to force it down her throat. She choked and it spilt over her chin and neck. One side of her pale face was livid from the blows of his heavy hand. She sighed a little and opened her eyes. He held the glass again to her lips, supporting her head, and she sipped a little of the neat spirit. He looked at her with penitent, anxious eyes.

"I'm sorry, Violet. I didn't mean to do that. I'm dreadfully ashamed of myself. I never thought I could sink so low as to hit a woman."

Though she was feeling very weak and her face was hurting, the flicker of a smile crossed her lips. Poor Tom. He did say things like that. He felt like that. And how scandalized he would be if you asked him why a man shouldn't hit a woman. But Saffary, seeing the wan smile, put it down to her indomitable courage. By God, she's a plucky little woman, he thought. Game isn't the word.

"Give me a cigarette," she said.

He took one out of his case and put it in her mouth. He made two or three ineffectual attempts to strike his lighter. It would not work.

"Hadn't you better get a match?" she said.

For the moment she had forgotten her heart-rending grief and was faintly amused at the situation. He took a box from the table and held the lighted match to her cigarette. She inhaled the first puff with a sense of infinite relief.

"I can't tell you how ashamed I am, Violet," he said. "I'm disgusted with myself. I don't know what came over me."

"Oh, that's all right. It was very natural. Why don't you have a drink? It'll do you good."

Without a word, his shoulders all hunched up as though the burden that oppressed him were material, he helped himself to a brandy and soda. Then, still silent, he sat down. She watched the blue smoke curl into the air.

"What are you going to do?" she said at last.

He gave a weary gesture of despair.

"We'll talk about that tomorrow. You're not in a fit state tonight. As soon as you've finished your cigarette you'd better go to bed."

"You know so much, you'd better know everything."

"Not now, Violet."

"Yes, now."

She began to speak. He heard her words, but could hardly make sense of them. He felt like a man who has built himself a house with loving care and thought to live in it all his life, and then, he does not understand why, sees the housebreakers come and with their picks and heavy hammers destroy it room by room, till what was a fair dwelling-place is only a heap of rubble. What made it so awful was that it was Knobby Clarke who had done this thing. They had come out to the FMS on the same ship and had worked at first on the same estate. They call the young planter a creeper and you can tell him in the streets of Singapore by his double felt hat and his khaki coat turned up at the wrists. Callow youths who saunter about staring and are inveigled by wily Chinese into buying worthless truck from Birmingham which they send home as Eastern curios, sit in the lounges of cheap hotels drinking innumerable stengahs, and after an evening at the pictures get into rickshaws and finish the night in the Chinese quarter. Tom and Knobby were inseparable. Tom, a big, powerful fellow, simple, very honest, hard-working; and Knobby, ungainly, but curiously attractive, with his deep-set eyes, hollow cheeks, and large humorous mouth. It was Knobby who made the jokes and Tom who laughed at them. Tom married first. He met Violet when he went on leave. The daughter of a doctor killed in the war, she was governess in the house of some people who lived in the same place as his father. He fell in love with her because she was alone in the world, and his tender heart was touched by the thought of the drab life that lay before her. But Knobby married, because Tom had and he felt lost without him, a girl who had come East to spend the winter with relations. Enid Clarke had been very pretty then in her blonde way, and full-face she was pretty still, though her skin, once so clear and fresh, was already faded; but she had a very weak, small, insignificant chin and in profile reminded you of a sheep. She had pretty flaxen hair, straight, because in the heat it would not keep its wave, and china-blue eyes. Though but twenty-six, she had already a tired look. A year after marriage she had a baby, but it died when only two years old. It was after this that Tom Saffary managed to get Knobby the post of manager of the estate next his own. The two men pleasantly resumed their old familiarity, and their wives, who till then had not known one another very well, soon made friends. They copied one another's frocks and lent one another servants and crockery when they gave a party. The four of them met every day. They went everywhere together. Tom Saffary thought it grand.

The strange thing was that Violet and Knobby Clarke lived on these terms of close intimacy for three years before they fell in love with one another. Neither saw love approaching. Neither suspected that in the pleasure each took in the other's company there was anything more than the casual friendship of two persons thrown together by the circumstances of life. To be together gave them no particular happiness, but merely a quiet sense of comfort. If by chance a day passed without their meeting they felt unaccountably bored. That seemed very natural. They played games together. They danced together. They chaffed one another. The revelation came to them by what looked like pure accident. They had all been to a dance at the club and were driving home in Saffary's car. The Clarkes' estate was on the way and he was dropping them at their bungalow. Violet and Knobby sat in the back. He had had a good deal to drink, but was not drunk; their hands touched by chance, and he took hers and held it. They did not speak. They were all tired. But suddenly the exhilaration of the champagne left him and he was cold sober. They knew in a flash that they were madly in love with one another and at the same moment they realized they had never been in love before. When they reached the Clarkes' Tom said:

"You'd better hop in beside me, Violet."

"I'm too exhausted to move," she said.

Her legs seemed so weak that she thought she would never be able to stand.

When they met next day neither referred to what had happened, but each knew that something inevitable had passed. They behaved to one another as they had always done, they continued to behave so for weeks, but they felt that everything was different. At last flesh and blood could stand it no longer and they became lovers. But the physical tie seemed to them the least important element in their relation, and indeed their way of living made it impossible for them, except very seldom, to enjoy any intimate connexion. It was enough that they saw one another, though in the company of others, every day; a glance, a touch of the hand, assured them of their love, and that was all that mattered. The sexual act was no more than an affirmation of the union of their souls.

They very seldom talked of Tom or Enid. If sometimes they laughed together at their foibles it was not unkindly. It might have seemed odd to them to realize how completely these two people whom they saw so constantly had ceased to matter to them if they had given them enough thought to consider the matter. Their relations with them fell into the routine of life that nobody notices, like shaving oneself, dressing, and eating three meals a day. They felt tenderly towards them. They even took pains to please them, as you would with a bed-ridden invalid, because their own happiness was so great that in charity they must do what they could for others less fortunate. They had no scruples. They were too much absorbed in one another to be touched even for a moment by remorse. Beauty now excitingly kindled the pleasant humdrum life they had led so long.

But then an event took place that filled them with consternation. The company for which Tom worked entered into negotiations to buy extensive rubber plantations in British North Borneo and invited Tom to manage them. It was a better job than his present one, with a higher salary, and since he would have assistants under him he would not have to work so hard. Saffary welcomed the offer. Both Clarke and Saffary were due for leave and the two couples had arranged to travel home together. They had already booked their passages. This changed everything. Tom would not be able to get away for at least a year. By the time the Clarkes came back the Saffarys would be settled in Borneo. It did not take Violet and Knobby long to decide that there was only one thing to do. They had been willing enough to go on as they were, notwithstanding the hindrances to the enjoyment of their love, when they were certain of seeing one another continually; they felt that they had endless time before them and the future was coloured with a happiness that seemed to have no limit; but neither could suffer for an instant the thought of separation. They made up their minds to run away together, and then it seemed to them on a sudden that every day that passed before they could be together always and all the time was a day lost. Their love took another guise. It flamed into a devouring passion that left them no emotion to waste on others. They cared little for the pain they must cause Tom and Enid. It was unfortunate, but inevitable. They made their plans deliberately. Knobby on the pretence of business would go to Singapore and Violet, telling Tom that she was going to spend a week with friends on an estate down the line, would join him there. They would go over to Java and thence take ship to Sydney. In Sydney Knobby would look for a job. When Violet told Tom that the Mackenzies had asked her to spend a few days with them, he was pleased.

"That's grand. I think you want a change, darling," he said. "I've fancied you've been looking a bit peaked lately."

He stroked her cheek affectionately. The gesture stabbed her heart.

"You've always been awfully good to me, Tom," she said, her eyes suddenly filled with tears.

"Well, that's the least I could be. You're the best little woman in the world."

"Have you been happy with me these eight years?"

"Frightfully."

"Well, that's something, isn't it? No one can ever take that away from you."

She told herself that he was the kind of man who would soon console himself. He liked women for themselves and it would not be long after he had regained his freedom before he found someone that he would wish to marry. And he would be just as happy with his new wife as he had been with her. Perhaps he would marry Enid. Enid was one of those dependent little things that somewhat exasperated her and she did not think her capable of deep feeling. Her vanity would be hurt; her heart would not be broken. But now that the die was cast, everything settled and the day fixed, she had a qualm. Remorse beset her. She wished that it had been possible not to cause those two people such fearful distress. She faltered.

"We've had a very good time here, Tom," she said. "I wonder if it's wise to leave it all. We're giving up a certainty for we don't know what."

"My dear child, it's a chance in a million and much better money."

"Money isn't everything. There's happiness."

"I know that, but there's no reason why we shouldn't be just as happy in BNB. And besides, there was no alternative. I'm not my own master. The directors want me to go and I must, and that's all there is to it."

She sighed. There was no alternative for her either. She shrugged her shoulders. It was hateful to cause others pain; sometimes you couldn't help yourself. Tom meant no more to her than the casual man on the voyage out who was civil to you: it was absurd that she should be asked to sacrifice her life for him.

The Clarkes were due to sail for England in a fortnight and this determined the date of their elopement. The days passed. Violet was restless and excited. She looked forward with a joy that was almost painful to the peace that she anticipated when they were once on board the ship and could begin the life which she was sure would give her at last perfect happiness.

She began to pack. The friends she was supposed to be going to stay with entertained a good deal and this gave her an excuse to take quite a lot of luggage. She was starting next day. It was eleven o'clock in the morning and Tom was making his round of the estate. One of the boys came to her room and told her that Mrs Clarke was there and at the same moment she heard Enid calling her. Quickly closing the lid of her trunk, she went out on to the veranda. To her astonishment Enid came up to her, flung her arms round her neck and kissed her eagerly. She looked at Enid and saw that her cheeks, usually pale, were flushed and that her eyes were shining. Enid burst into tears.

"What on earth's the matter, darling?" she cried.

For one moment she was afraid that Enid knew everything. But Enid was flushed with delight and not with jealousy or anger.

"I've just seen Dr Harrow," she said. "I didn't want to say anything about it. I've had two or three false alarms, but this time he says it's all right."

A sudden coldness pierced Violet's heart.

"What do you mean? You're not going to ... "

She looked at Enid and Enid nodded.

"Yes, he says there's no doubt about it at all. He thinks I'm at least three months gone. Oh, my dear, I'm so wildly happy."

She flung herself again into Violet's arms and clung to her, weeping.

"Oh, darling, don't."

Violet felt herself grow pale as death and knew that if she didn't keep a tight hold of herself she would faint.

"Does Knobby know?"

"No, I didn't say a word. He was so disappointed before. He was so frightfully cut up when baby died. He's wanted me to have another so badly."

Violet forced herself to say the things that were expected of her, but Enid was not listening. She wanted to tell the whole story of her hopes and fears, of her symptoms, and then of her interview with the doctor. She went on and on.

"When are you going to tell Knobby?" Violet asked at last. "Now, when he gets in?"

"Oh, no, he's tired and hungry when he gets back from his round. I shall wait till tonight after dinner."

Violet repressed a movement of exasperation; Enid was going to make a scene of it and was choosing her moment; but after all, it was only natural. It was lucky, for it would give her the chance to see Knobby first. As soon as she was rid of her she rang him up. She knew that he always looked in at his office on his way home, and she left a message asking him to call her. She was only afraid that he would not do so till Tom was back, but she had to take a chance of that. The bell rang and Tom had not come in.

"Hal?"

"Yes."

"Will you be at the hut at three?"

"Yes. Has anything happened?"

"I'll tell you when I see you. Don't worry."

She rang off. The hut was a little shelter on Knobby's estate which she could get to without difficulty and where they occasionally met. The coolies passed it while they worked and it had no privacy; but it was a convenient place for them without exciting comment to exchange a few minutes' conversation. At three Enid would be resting and Tom at work in his office.

When Violet walked up Knobby was already there. He gave a gasp.

"Violet, how white you are."

She gave him her hand. They did not know what eyes might be watching them and their behaviour here was always such as anyone could observe.

"Enid came to see me this morning. She's going to tell you tonight. I thought you ought to be warned. She's going to have a baby."

"Violet!"

He looked at her aghast. She began to cry. They had never talked of the relations they had, he with his wife and she with her husband.

535

They ignored the subject because it was to each horribly painful. Violet knew what her own life was; she satisfied her husband's appetite, but, with a woman's strange nonchalance, because to do so gave her no pleasure, attached no importance to it; but somehow she had persuaded herself that with Hal it was different. He felt now instinctively how bitterly what she had learned wounded her. He tried to excuse himself.

"Darling, I couldn't help myself."

She cried silently and he watched her with miserable eyes.

"I know it seems beastly," he said, "but what could I do? It wasn't as if I had any reason to . . . "

She interrupted him.

"I don't blame you. It was inevitable. It's only because I'm stupid that it gives me such a frightful pain in my heart."

"Darling!"

"We ought to have gone away together two years ago. It was madness to think we could go on like this."

"Are you sure Enid's right? She thought she was in the family way three or four years ago."

"Oh, yes, she's right. She's frightfully happy. She says you wanted a child so badly."

"It's come as such an awful surprise. I don't seem able to realize it yet."

She looked at him. He was staring at the leaf-strewn earth with harassed eyes. She smiled a little.

"Poor Hal." She sighed deeply. "There's nothing to be done about it. It's the end of us."

"What do you mean?" he cried.

"Oh, my dear, you can't very well leave her now, can you? It was all right before. She would have been unhappy, but she would have got over it. But now it's different. It's not a very nice time for a woman anyhow. For months she feels more or less ill. She wants affection. She wants to be taken care of. It would be frightful to leave her to bear it all alone. We couldn't be such beasts."

"Do you mean to say you want me to go back to England with her?"

She nodded gravely.

"It's lucky you're going. It'll be easier when you get away and we don't see one another every day."

"But I can't live without you now."

"Oh, yes, you can. You must. I can. And it'll be worse for me, because I stay behind and I shall have nothing."

"Oh, Violet, it's impossible."

"My dear, it's no good arguing. The moment she told me I saw it meant that. That's why I wanted to see you first. I thought the shock might lead you to blurt out the whole truth. You know I love you more than anything in the world. She's never done me any harm. I couldn't take you away from her now. It's bad luck on both of us, but there it is, I simply wouldn't dare to do a filthy thing like that."

"I wish I were dead," he moaned.

"That wouldn't do her any good, or me either," she smiled.

"What about the future? Have we got to sacrifice our whole lives?"

"I'm afraid so. It sounds rather grim, darling, but I suppose sooner or later we shall get over it. One gets over everything."

She looked at her wrist-watch.

"I ought to be getting back. Tom will be in soon. We're all meeting at the club at five."

"Tom and I are supposed to be playing tennis." He gave her a pitiful look. "Oh, Violet, I'm so frightfully unhappy."

"I know. So am I. But we shan't do any good by talking about it."

She gave him her hand, but he took her in his arms and kissed her, and when she released herself her cheeks were wet with his tears. But she was so desperate she could not cry.

Ten days later the Clarkes sailed.

While George Moon was listening to as much of this story as Tom Saffary was able to tell him, he reflected in his cool, detached way how odd it was that these commonplace people, leading lives so monotonous, should have been convulsed by such a tragedy. Who would have thought that Violet Saffary, so neat and demure, sitting in the club reading the illustrated papers or chatting with her friends over a lemon squash, should have been eating her heart out for love of that ordinary man? George Moon remembered seeing Knobby at the club the evening before he sailed. He seemed in great spirits. Fellows envied him because he was going home. Those who had recently come back told him by no means to miss the show at the Pavilion. Drink flowed freely. The Resident had not been asked to the farewell party the Saffarys gave for the Clarkes, but he knew very well what it had been like, the good cheer, the cordiality, the chaff, and then after dinner the gramophone turned on and everyone dancing. He wondered what Violet and Clarke had felt as they danced together. It gave him an odd sensation of dismay to think of the despair that must have filled their hearts while they pretended to be so gay.

And with another part of his mind George Moon thought of his own past. Very few knew that story. After all, it had happened twenty-five years ago.

"What are you going to do now, Saffary?" he asked.

"Well, that's what I wanted you to advise me about. Now that Knobby's dead I don't know what's going to happen to Violet if I divorce her. I was wondering if I oughtn't to let her divorce me."

"Oh, you want to divorce?"

"Well, I must."

George Moon lit another cigarette and watched for a moment the smoke that curled away into the air.

"Did you ever know that I'd been married?"

"Yes, I think I'd heard. You're a widower, aren't you?"

"No, I divorced my wife. I have a son of twenty-seven. He's farming in New Zealand. I saw my wife the last time I was home on leave. We met at a play. At first we didn't recognize one another. She spoke to me. I asked her to lunch at the Berkeley."

George Moon chuckled to himself. He was alone. It was a musical comedy. He found himself sitting next to a large fat dark woman whom he vaguely thought he had seen before, but the play was just starting and he did not give her a second look. When the curtain fell after the first act she looked at him with bright eyes and spoke.

"How are you, George?"

It was his wife. She had a bold, friendly manner and was very much at her ease.

"It's a long time since we met," she said.

"It is."

"How has life been treating you?"

"Oh, all right."

"I suppose you're a Resident now. You're still in the Service, aren't you?"

"Yes. I'm retiring soon, worse luck."

"Why? You look very fit."

"I'm reaching the age limit. I'm supposed to be an old buffer and no good any more."

"You're lucky to have kept so thin. I'm terrible, aren't I?"

"You don't look as though you were wasting away."

"I know. I'm stout and I'm growing stouter all the time. I can't help it and I love food. I can't resist cream and bread and potatoes."

George Moon laughed, but not at what she said; at his own thoughts. In years gone by it had sometimes occurred to him that he might meet her, but he had never thought that the meeting would take this turn. When the play was ended and with a smile she bade him good night, he said:

"I suppose you wouldn't lunch with me one day?"

"Any day you like."

They arranged a date and duly met. He knew that she had married the man on whose account he had divorced her, and he judged by her clothes that she was in comfortable circumstances. They drank a cocktail. She ate the *hors-d'œuvre* with gusto. She was fifty if she was a day, but she carried her years with spirit. There was something jolly and careless about her, she was quick on the uptake, chatty, and she had the hearty, infectious laugh of the fat woman who has let herself go. If he had not known that her family had for a century been in the Indian Civil Service he would have thought that she had been a chorus girl. She was not flashy, but she had a sort of flamboyance of nature that suggested the stage. She was not in the least embarrassed.

"You never married again, did you?" she asked him.

"No."

"Pity. Because it wasn't a success the first time there's no reason why it shouldn't have been the second."

"There's no need for me to ask if you've been happy."

"I've got nothing to complain of. I think I've got a happy nature. Jim's always been very good to me; he's retired now, you know, and we live in the country, and I adore Betty."

"Who's Betty?"

"Oh, she's my daughter. She got married two years ago. I'm expecting to be a grandmother almost any day."

"That ages us a bit."

She gave a laugh.

"Betty's twenty-two. It was nice of you to ask me to lunch, George. After all, it would be silly to have any feelings about something that happened so long ago as all that."

"Idiotic."

"We weren't fitted to one another and it's lucky we found it out before it was too late. Of course I was foolish, but then I was very young. Have you been happy too?"

"I think I can say I've been a success."

"Oh, well, that's probably all the happiness you were capable of."

He smiled in appreciation of her shrewdness. And then, putting the whole matter aside easily, she began to talk of other things. Though the courts had given him custody of their son, he, unable to look after him, had allowed his mother to have him. The boy had emigrated at eighteen and was now married. He was a stranger to George Moon, and he was aware that if he met him in the street he would not recognize him. He was too sincere to pretend that he took much interest in him. They talked of him, however, for a while, and then they talked of actors and plays.

"Well," she said at last, "I must be running away. I've had a lovely lunch. It's been fun meeting you, George. Thanks so much."

He put her into a taxi and taking off his hat walked down Piccadilly by himself. He thought her quite a pleasant, amusing woman: he laughed to think that he had ever been madly in love with her. There was a smile on his lips when he spoke again to Tom Saffary.

"She was a damned good-looking girl when I married her. That was the trouble. Though, of course, if she hadn't been I'd never have married her. They were all after her like flies round a honeypot. We used to have awful rows. And at last I caught her out. Of course I divorced her."

"Of course."

"Yes, but I know I was a damned fool to do it." He leaned forward. "My dear Saffary, I know now that if I'd had any sense I'd have shut my eyes. She'd have settled down and made me an excellent wife."

He wished he were able to explain to his visitor how grotesque it had seemed to him when he sat and talked with that jolly, comfortable, and good-humoured woman that he should have made so much fuss about what now seemed to him to matter so little.

"But one has one's honour to think of," said Saffary.

"Honour be damned. One has one's happiness to think of. Is one's honour really concerned because one's wife hops into bed with another man? We're not crusaders, you and I, or Spanish grandees. I *liked* my wife. I don't say I haven't had other women. I have. But she had just that something that none of the others could give me. What a fool I was to throw away what I wanted more than anything in the world because I couldn't enjoy exclusive possession of it!"

"You're the last man I should ever have expected to hear speak like that."

George Moon smiled thinly at the embarrassment that was so clearly expressed on Saffary's fat troubled face.

"I'm probably the first man you've heard speak the naked truth," he retorted.

"Do you mean to say that if it were all to do over again you would act differently?"

"If I were twenty-seven again I suppose I should be as big a fool as I was then. But if I had the sense I have now I'll tell you what I'd do if I found my wife had been unfaithful to me. I'd do just what you did last night: I'd give her a damned good hiding and let it go at that."

"Are you asking me to forgive Violet?"

The Resident shook his head slowly and smiled.

"No. You've forgiven her already. I'm merely advising you not to cut off your nose to spite your face."

Saffary gave him a worried look. It disconcerted him to know that this cold precise man should see in his heart emotions which seemed so unnatural to himself that he thrust them out of his consciousness.

"You don't know the circumstances," he said. "Knobby and I were almost like brothers. I got him this job. He owed everything to me. And except for me Violet might have gone on being a governess for the rest of her life. It seemed such a waste; I couldn't help feeling sorry for her. If you know what I mean, it was pity that first made me take any notice of her. Don't you think it's a bit thick that when you've been thoroughly decent with people they should go out of their way to do the dirty on you? It's such awful ingratitude."

"Oh, my dear boy, one mustn't expect gratitude. It's a thing that no one has a right to. After all, you do good because it gives you pleasure. It's the purest form of happiness there is. To expect thanks for it is really asking too much. If you get it, well, it's like a bonus on shares on which you've already received a dividend; it's grand, but you mustn't look upon it as your due."

Saffary frowned. He was perplexed. He could not quite make it out that George Moon should think so oddly about things that it had always seemed to him there were no two ways of thinking about. After all there were limits. I mean, if you had any sense of decency you had to behave like a tuan. There was your own self-respect to think of. It was funny that George Moon should give reasons that looked so damned plausible for doing something that, well, damn it, you had to admit you'd be only too glad to do if you could see your way to it. Of course George Moon was queer. No one ever quite understood him.

"Knobby Clarke is dead, Saffary. You can't be jealous of him any more. No one knows a thing except you and me and your wife, and tomorrow I'm going away for ever. Why don't you let bygones be bygones?"

"Violet would only despise me."

George Moon smiled and, unexpectedly on that prim, fastidious face, his smile had a singular sweetness.

"I know her very little. I always thought her a very nice woman. Is she as detestable as that?"

Saffary gave a start and reddened to his ears.

"No, she's an angel of goodness. It's me who's detestable for saying that of her." His voice broke and he gave a little sob. "God knows I only want to do the right thing."

"The right thing is the kind thing."

Saffary covered his face with his hands. He could not curb the emotion that shook him.

"I seem to be giving, giving all the time, and no one does a Goddamned thing for me. It doesn't matter if my heart is broken, I must just go on." He drew the back of his hand across his eyes and sighed deeply. "I'll forgive her."

George Moon looked at him reflectively for a little.

"I wouldn't make too much of a song and dance about it, if I were you," he said. "You'll have to walk warily. She'll have a lot to forgive too."

"Because I hit her, you mean? I know, that was awful of me."

"Not a bit. It did her a power of good. I didn't mean that. You're behaving generously, old boy, and, you know, one needs a devil of a lot of tact to get people to forgive one one's generosity. Fortunately women are frivolous and they very quickly forget the benefits conferred upon them. Otherwise, of course, there'd be no living with them."

Saffary looked at him open-mouthed.

"Upon my word you're a rum 'un, Moon," he said. "Sometimes you seem as hard as nails and then you talk so that one thinks you're almost human, and then, just as one thinks one's misjudged you and you have a heart after all, you come out with something that just shocks one. I suppose that's what they call a cynic."

"I haven't deeply considered the matter," smiled George Moon, "but if to look truth in the face and not resent it when it's unpalatable, and take human nature as you find it, smiling when it's absurd and grieved without exaggeration when it's pitiful, is to be cynical, then I suppose I'm a cynic. Mostly human nature is both absurd and pitiful, but if life has taught you tolerance you find in it more to smile at than to weep."

When Tom Saffary left the room the Resident lit himself with deliberation the last cigarette he meant to smoke before tiffin. It was a new role for him to reconcile an angry husband with an erring wife and it caused him a discreet amusement. He continued to reflect upon human nature. A wintry smile hovered upon his thin and pallid lips. He recalled with what interest in the dry creeks of certain places along the coast he had often stood and watched the Jumping Johnnies. There were hundreds of them sometimes, from little things of a couple of inches long to great fat fellows as long as your foot. They were the colour of the mud they lived in. They sat and looked at you with large round eyes and then with a sudden dash buried themselves in their holes. It was extraordinary to see them scudding on their flappers over the surface of the mud. It teemed with them. They gave you a fearful feeling that the mud itself was mysteriously become alive and an atavistic terror froze your heart when you remembered that such creatures, but gigantic and terrible, were once the only inhabitants of the earth. There was something uncanny about them, but something amusing too. They reminded you very much of human beings. It was quite entertaining to stand there for half an hour and observe their gambols.

George Moon took his topee off the peg and not displeased with life stepped out into the sunshine.

MAYHEW

THE LIVES OF most men are determined by their environment. They accept the circumstances amid which fate has thrown them not only with resignation but even with good will. They are like street-cars running contentedly on their rails and they despise the sprightly flivver that dashes in and out of the traffic and speeds so jauntily across the open country. I respect them; they are good citizens, good husbands, and good fathers, and of course somebody has to pay the taxes; but I do not find them exciting. I am fascinated by the men, few enough in all conscience, who take life in their own hands and seem to mould it to their own liking. It may be that we have no such thing as free will, but at all events we have the illusion of it. At a cross-road it does seem to us that we might go either to the right or the left and, the choice once made, it is difficult to see that the whole course of the world's history obliged us to take the turning we did.

I never met a more interesting man than Mayhew. He was a lawyer in Detroit. He was an able and a successful one. By the time he was thirty-five he had a large and a lucrative practice, he had amassed a competence, and he stood on the threshold of a distinguished career. He had an acute brain, an attractive personality, and uprightness. There was no reason why he should not become, financially or politically, a power in the land. One evening he was sitting in his club with a group of friends and they were perhaps a little the worse (or the better) for liquor. One of them had recently come from Italy and he told them of a house he had seen at Capri, a house on the hill, overlooking the Bay of Naples, with a large and shady garden. He described to them the beauty of the most beautiful island in the Mediterranean.

"It sounds fine," said Mayhew. "Is that house for sale?"

"Everything is for sale in Italy."

"Let's send 'em a cable and make an offer for it."

"What in heaven's name would you do with a house in Capri?"

"Live in it," said Mayhew.

He sent for a cable form, wrote it out, and dispatched it. In a few hours the reply came back. The offer was accepted.

Mayhew was no hypocrite and he made no secret of the fact that he would never have done so wild a thing if he had been sober, but when he was he did not regret it. He was neither an impulsive nor an emotional man, but a very honest and sincere one. He would never have continued from bravado in a course that he had come to the conclusion was unwise. He made up his mind to do exactly as he had said. He did not care for wealth and he had enough money on which to live in Italy. He thought he could do more with life than spend it on composing the trivial quarrels of unimportant people. He had no definite plan. He merely wanted to get away from a life that had given him all it had to offer. I suppose his friends thought him crazy; some must have done all they could to dissuade him. He arranged his affairs, packed up his furniture, and started.

Capri is a gaunt rock of austere outline, bathed in a deep blue sea; but its vineyards, green and smiling, give it a soft and easy grace. It is friendly, remote, and debonair. I find it strange that Mayhew should have settled on this lovely island, for I never knew a man more insensible to beauty. I do not know what he sought there: happiness, freedom, or merely leisure; I know what he found. In this place which appeals so extravagantly to the senses he lived a life entirely of the spirit. For the island is rich with historic associations and over it broods always the enigmatic memory of Tiberius the Emperor. From his windows which overlooked the Bay of Naples, with the noble shape of Vesuvius changing colour with the changing light, Mayhew saw a hundred places that recalled the Romans and the Greeks. The past began to haunt him. All that he saw for the first time, for he had never been abroad before, excited his fancy; and in his soul stirred the creative imagination. He was a man of energy. Presently he made up his mind to write a history. For some time he looked about for a subject, and at last decided on the second century of the Roman Empire. It was little known and it seemed to him to offer problems analogous with those of our own day.

He began to collect books and soon he had an immense library. His legal training had taught him to read quickly. He settled down to work. At first he had been accustomed to foregather in the evening with the painters, writers, and suchlike who met in the little tavern near the Piazza, but presently he withdrew himself, for his absorption in his studies became more pressing. He had been accustomed to bathe in that bland sea and to take long walks among the pleasant vineyards, but little by little, grudging the time, he ceased to do so. He worked harder than he had ever worked in Detroit. He would start at noon and work all through the night till the whistle of the steamer that goes every morning from Capri to Naples told him that it was five o'clock and time to go to bed. His subject opened out before him, vaster and more significant, and he imagined a work that would put him for ever beside the great historians of the past. As the years went by he was to be found seldom in the ways of men. He could be tempted to come out of his house only by a game of chess or the chance of an argument. He loved to set his brain against another's. He was widely read now, not only in history, but in philosophy and science; and he was a skilful controversialist, quick, logical, and incisive. But he had good-humour and kindliness; though he took a very human pleasure in victory, he did not exult in it to your mortification.

When first he came to the island he was a big, brawny fellow, with thick black hair and a black beard, of a powerful physique; but gradually his skin became pale and waxy; he grew thin and frail. It was an odd contradiction in the most logical of men that, though a convinced and impetuous materialist, he despised the body; he looked upon it as a vile instrument which he could force to do the spirit's bidding. Neither illness nor lassitude prevented him from going on with his work. For fourteen years he toiled unremittingly. He made thousands and thousands of notes. He sorted and classified them. He had his subject at his finger ends, and at last was ready to begin. He sat down to write. He died.

The body that he, the materialist, had treated so contumeliously took its revenge on him.

That vast accumulation of knowledge is lost for ever. Vain was that ambition, surely not an ignoble one, to set his name beside those of Gibbon and Mommsen. His memory is treasured in the hearts of a few friends, fewer, alas! as the years pass on, and to the world he is unknown in death as he was in life.

And yet to me his life was a success. The pattern is good and complete. He did what he wanted, and he died when his goal was in sight and never knew the bitterness of an end achieved.

MIRAGE

I HAD BEEN wandering about the East for months and at last reached Haiphong. It is a commercial town and a dull one, but I knew that from there I could find a ship of sorts to take me to Hong-Kong. I had some days to wait and nothing to do. It is true that from Haiphong you can visit the Bay of Along, which is one of the *Sehenswurdigkeiten* of Indo-China, but I was tired of sights. I contented myself with sitting in the cafés, for here it was none too warm and I was glad to get out of tropical clothes, and reading back numbers of *L'Illustration*, or for the sake of exercise taking a brisk walk along straight, wide streets. Haiphong is traversed by canals and sometimes I got a glimpse of a scene which in its varied life, with all the native craft on the water, was multicoloured and charming. There was one canal, with tall Chinese houses on each side of it, that had a pleasant curve. The houses were whitewashed, but the whitewash was discoloured and stained; with their grey roofs they made an agreeable composition against the pale sky. The picture had the faded elegance of an old water-colour. There was nowhere an emphatic note. It was soft and a little weary and inspired one with a faint melancholy. I was reminded, I scarcely know why, of an old maid I knew in my youth, a relic of the Victorian age, who wore black silk mittens and made crochet shawls for the poor, black for widows and white for married women. She had suffered in her youth, but whether from ill-health or unrequited love, no one exactly knew.

But there was a local paper at Haiphong, a small dingy sheet with stubby type the ink of which came off on your fingers, and it gave you a political article, the wireless news, advertisements, and local intelligence. The editor, doubtless hard pressed for matter, printed the names of the persons, Europeans, natives of the country, and Chinese, who had arrived at Haiphong or left it, and mine was put in with the rest. On the morning of the day before that on which the old tub I was taking was to sail for Hong-Kong I was sitting in the café of the hotel drinking a Dubonnet before luncheon when the boy came in and said that a gentleman wished to see me. I did not know a soul in Haiphong and asked who it was. The boy said he was an Englishman and lived there, but he could not tell me his name. The boy spoke very little French and it was hard for me to under-stand what he said. I was mystified, but told him to show the visitor in. A moment later he came back followed by a white man and pointed me out to him. The man gave me a look and walked towards me. He was a very tall fellow, well over six feet high, rather fat and bloated, with a red, clean-shaven face and extremely pale blue eyes. He wore very shabby khaki shorts and a stengah-shifter unbuttoned at the neck, and a battered helmet. I concluded at once that he was a stranded beachcomber who was going to touch me for a loan and wondered how little I could hope to get off for.

He came up to me and held out a large red hand with broken, dirty nails.

"I don't suppose you remember me," he said. "My name's Grosely. I was at St Thomas's Hospital with you. I recognized your name as soon as I saw it in the paper and I thought I'd look you up."

I had not the smallest recollection of him, but I asked him to sit down and offered him a drink. By his appearance I had first thought he would ask me for ten piastres and I might have given him five, but now it looked more likely that he would ask for a hundred and I should have to think myself lucky if I could content him with fifty.

The habitual borrower always asks twice what he expects to get and it only dissatisfies him to give him what he has asked since then he is vexed with himself for not having asked more. He feels you have cheated him.

"Are you a doctor?" I asked.

"No, I was only at the bloody place a year."

He took off his sun-helmet and showed me a mop of grey hair, which much needed a brush. His face was curiously mottled and he did not look healthy. His teeth were badly decayed and at the corners of his mouth were empty spaces. When the boy came to take the orders he asked for brandy.

"Bring the bottle," he said. "*La bouteille*. Savvy?" He turned to me. "I've been living here for the last five years, but I can't get along with French somehow. I talk Tonkinese." He leaned his chair back and looked at me. "I remember you, you know. You used to go about with those twins. What was their name? I expect I've changed more than you have. I've spent the best part of my life in China. Rotten climate, you know. It plays hell with a man."

I still had not the smallest recollection of him. I thought it best to say so.

"Were you the same year as I was?" I asked.

"Yes. 'Ninety-two."

"It's a devil of a long time ago."

About sixty boys and young men entered the hospital every year; they were most of them shy and confused by the new life they were entering upon; many had never been in London before; and to me at least they were shadows that passed without any particular rhyme or reason across a white sheet. During the first year a certain number for one reason or another dropped out, and in the second year those that remained gained by degrees the beginnings of a personality. They were not only themselves, but the lectures one had attended with them, the scone and coffee one had eaten at the same table for luncheon, the dissection one had done at the same board in the same dissecting room, and *The Belle of New York* one had seen together from the pit of the Shaftesbury Theatre.

The boy brought the bottle of brandy, and Grosely, if that was really his name, pouring himself out a generous helping drank it down at a gulp without water or soda.

"I couldn't stand doctoring," he said. "I chucked it. My people got fed up with me and I went out to China. They gave me a hundred pounds and told me to shift for myself. I was damned glad to get out, I can tell you. I guess I was just about as much fed up with them as they were with me. I haven't troubled them much since."

Then from somewhere in the depths of my memory a faint hint crept into the rim, as it were, of consciousness, as on a rising tide the water slides up the sand and then withdraws to advance with the next wave in a fuller volume. I had first an inkling of some shabby little scandal that had got into the papers. Then I saw a boy's face, and so gradually the facts recurred to me; I remembered him now. I didn't believe he was called Grosely then, I think he had a one-syllabled name, but that I was uncertain of. He was a very tall lad (I began to see him quite well), thin, with a slight stoop, he was only eighteen and had grown too fast for his strength, he had curly, shining brown hair, rather large features (they did not look so large now, perhaps because his face was fat and puffy) and a peculiarly fresh complexion, very pink and white, like a girl's. I imagine people, women especially, would have thought him a very handsome boy, but to us he was only a clumsy, shuffling lout. Then I remembered that he did not often come to lectures, no, it wasn't that I remembered, there were too many students in the theatre to recollect who was there and who wasn't. I remembered the dissecting room. He had a leg at the next table to the one I was working at and he hardly ever touched it; I forget why the men who had other parts of the body complained of his neglecting the work, I suppose somehow it interfered with them. In those days a good deal of gossip went on over the dissection of a "part" and out of the distance of thirty years some of it came back to me. Someone started the story that Grosely was a very gay dog. He drank like a fish and was an awful womanizer. Most of those boys were very simple, and they had brought to the hospital the notions they had acquired at home and at school. Some were prudish and they were shocked; others, those who worked hard, sneered at him and asked how he could hope to pass his exams; but a good many were excited and impressed, he was doing what they would have liked to do if they had had the courage. Grosely had his admirers and you could often see him surrounded by a little band listening open-mouthed to stories of his adventures. Recollections now were crowding upon me. In a very little while he lost his shyness and assumed the airs of a man of the world. They must have looked absurd on this smooth-cheeked boy with his pink and white skin. Men (so they called themselves) used to tell one another of his escapades. He became quite a hero. He would make caustic remarks as he passed the museum and saw a pair of earnest students going over their anatomy together. He was at home in the public-houses of the neighbourhood and was on familiar terms with the barmaids. Looking back, I imagine that, newly arrived from the country and the tutelage of parents and schoolmasters, he was captivated by his freedom and the thrill of London. His dissipations were harmless enough. They were due only to the urge of youth. He lost his head.

But we were all very poor and we did not know how Grosely managed to pay for his garish amusements. We knew his father was a country doctor and I think we knew exactly how much he gave his son a month. It was not enough to pay for the harlots he picked up on the promenade at the Pavilion and for the drinks he stood his friends in the Criterion Bar. We told one another in awe-struck tones that he must be getting fearfully into debt. Of course he could pawn things, but we knew by experience that you could not get more than three pounds for a microscope and thirty shillings for a skeleton. We said he must be spending at least ten pounds a week. Our ideas were not very grand and this seemed to us the wildest pitch of extravagance. At last one of his friends disclosed the mystery: Grosely had discovered a wonderful system for making money. It amused and impressed us. None of us would have thought of anything so ingenious or have had the nerve to attempt it if he had. Grosely went to auctions, not Christie's, of course, but auctions in the Strand and Oxford Street, and in private houses, and bought anything portable that was going cheap. Then he took his purchase to a pawnbroker's and pawned it for ten shillings or a pound more than he had paid. He was making money, four or five pounds a week, and he said he was going to give up medicine and make a regular business of it. Not one of us had ever made a penny in his life and we regarded Grosely with admiration.

"By Jove, he's clever," we said.

"He's just about as sharp as they make them."

"That's the sort that ends up as a millionaire."

We were all very worldly-wise and what we didn't know about life at eighteen we were pretty sure wasn't worth knowing. It was a pity that when an examiner asked us a question we were so nervous that the answer often flew straight out of our head and when a nurse asked us to post a letter we blushed scarlet. It became known that the Dean had sent for Grosely and hauled him over the coals. He had threatened him with sundry penalties if he continued systematically to neglect his work. Grosely was indignant. He'd had enough of that sort of thing at school, he said, he wasn't going to let a horse-faced eunuch treat him like a boy. Damn it all, he was getting on for nineteen and there wasn't much you could teach him. The Dean had said he heard he was drinking more than was good for him. Damned cheek. He could carry his liquor as well as any man of his age, he'd been blind last Saturday and he meant to get blind next Saturday, and if anyone didn't like it he could do the other thing. Grosely's friends quite agreed with him that a man couldn't let himself be insulted like that.

But the blow fell at last and now I remembered quite well the shock it gave us all. I suppose we had not seen Grosely for two or three days, but he had been in the habit of coming to the hospital more and more irregularly, so if we thought anything about it, I imagine we merely said that he was off on one of his bats. He would turn up again in a day or so, rather pale, but with a wonderful story of some girl he had picked up and the time he had had with her. The anatomy lecture was at nine in the morning and it was a rush to get there in time. On this particular day little attention was paid to the lecturer, who, with a visible pleasure in his limpid English and admirable elocution, was describing I know not what part of the human skeleton, for there was much excited whispering along the benches and a newspaper was surreptitiously passed from hand to hand. Suddenly the lecturer stopped. He had a pedagogic sarcasm. He affected not to know the names of his students.

"I am afraid I am disturbing the gentleman who is reading the paper. Anatomy is a very tedious science and I regret that the regulations of the Royal College of Surgeons oblige me to ask you to give it enough of your attention to pass an examination in it.

Any gentleman, however, who finds this impossible is at liberty to continue his perusal of the paper outside."

The wretched boy to whom this reproof was addressed reddened to the roots of his hair and in his embarrassment tried to stuff the newspaper in his pocket. The professor of anatomy observed him coldly.

"I am afraid, sir, that the paper is a little too large to go into your pocket," he remarked. "Perhaps you would be good enough to hand it down to me?"

The newspaper was passed from row to row to the well of the theatre, and, not content with the confusion to which he had put the poor lad, the eminent surgeon, taking it, asked:

"May I inquire what it is in the paper that the gentleman in question found of such absorbing interest?"

The student who gave it to him without a word pointed out the paragraph that we had all been reading. The professor read it and we watched him in silence. He put the paper down and went on with his lecture. The headline ran *Arrest of a Medical Student.* Grosely had been brought before the police-court magistrate for getting goods on credit and pawning them. It appears that this is an indictable offence and the magistrate had remanded him for a week. Bail was refused. It looked as though his method of making money by buying things at auctions and pawning them had not in the long run proved as steady a source of income as he expected and he had found it more profitable to pawn things that he was not at the expense of paying for. We talked the matter over excitedly as soon as the lecture was over and I am bound to say that, having no property ourselves, so deficient was our sense of its sanctity we could none of us look upon his crime as a very serious one; but with the natural love of the young for the terrible there were few who did not think he would get anything from two years' hard labour to seven years' penal servitude.

I do not know why, but I did not seem to have any recollection of what happened to Grosely. I think he may have been arrested towards the end of a session and his case may have come on again when we had all separated for holidays. I did not know if it was disposed of by the police-court magistrate or whether it went up for trial. I had a sort of feeling that he was sentenced to a short term of imprisonment, six weeks perhaps, for his operations had been pretty extensive; but I knew that he had vanished from our midst and in a little while was thought of no more. It was strange to me that after all these years I should recollect so much of the incident so clearly. It was as though, turning over an album of old snapshots, I saw all at once the photograph of a scene I had quite forgotten.

But of course in that gross elderly man with grey hair and mottled red face I should never have recognized the lanky pink-cheeked boy. He looked sixty, but I knew he must be much less than that. I wondered what he had done with himself in the intervening time. It did not look as though he had excessively prospered.

"What were you doing in China?" I asked him.

"I was a tide-waiter."

"Oh, were you?"

It is not a position of great importance and I took care to keep out of my tone any note of surprise. The tide-waiters are employees of the Chinese Customs whose duty it is to board the ships and junks at the various treaty ports and I think their chief business is to prevent opium-smuggling. They are mostly retired ABs from the Royal Navy and non-commissioned officers who have finished their time. I have seen them come on board at various places up the Yangtse. They hobnob with the pilot and the engineer, but the skipper is a trifle curt with them. They learn to speak Chinese more fluently than most Europeans and often marry Chinese women.

"When I left England I swore I wouldn't go back till I'd made my pile. And I never did. They were glad enough to get anyone to be a tide-waiter in those days, any white man I mean, and they didn't ask questions. They didn't care who you were. I was damned glad to get the job, I can tell you, I was about broke to the wide when they took me on. I only took it till I could get something better, but I stayed on, it suited me, I wanted to make money and I found out that a tide-waiter could make a packet if he knew the right way to go about it. I was with the Chinese Customs for the best part of twenty-five years and when I came away I wouldn't mind betting that lots of commissioners would have been glad to have the money I had."

He gave me a sly, mean look. I had an inkling of what he meant. But there was a point on which I was willing to be reassured; if he was going to ask me for a hundred piastres (I was resigned to that sum now) I thought I might just as well take the blow at once.

"I hope you kept it," I said.

"You bet I did. I invested all my money in Shanghai and when I left China I put it all in American railway bonds. Safety first is my motto. I know too much about crooks to take any risks myself."

I liked that remark, so I asked him if he wouldn't stay and have luncheon with me.

"No, I don't think I will. I don't eat much tiffin and anyway my chow's waiting for me at home. I think I'll be getting along." He got up and he towered over me. "But look here, why don't you come along this evening and see my place? I've married a Haiphong girl. Got a baby too. It's not often I get a chance of talking to anyone about London. You'd better not come to dinner. We only eat native food and I don't suppose you'd care for that. Come along about nine, will you?"

"All right," I said.

I had already told him that I was leaving Haiphong next day. He asked the boy to bring him a piece of paper so that he might write down his address. He wrote laboriously in the hand of a boy of fourteen.

"Tell the porter to explain to your rickshaw boy where it is. I'm on the second floor. There's no bell. Just knock. Well, see you later."

He walked out and I went in to luncheon.

After dinner I called a rickshaw and with the porter's help made the boy understand where I wanted to go. I found presently that he was taking me along the curved canal the houses of which had looked to me so like a faded Victorian water-colour; he stopped at one of them and pointed to the door. It looked so shabby and the neighbourhood was so squalid that I hesitated, thinking he had made a mistake. It seemed unlikely that Grosely could live so far in the native quarter and in a house so bedraggled. I told the rickshaw boy to wait and pushing open the door saw a dark staircase in front of me. There was no one about and the street was empty. It might have been the small hours of the morning. I struck a match and fumbled my way upstairs; on the second floor I struck another match and saw a large brown door in front of me. I knocked and in a moment it was opened by a little Tonkinese woman holding a candle. She was dressed in the earth-brown of the poorer classes, with a tight little black turban on her head; her lips and the skin round them were stained red with betel and when she opened her mouth to speak I saw that she had the black teeth and black gums that so disfigure these people. She said something in her native language and then I heard Grosely's voice:

"Come along in. I was beginning to think you weren't going to turn up."

I passed through a little dark ante-chamber and entered a large room that evidently looked on the canal. Grosely was lying on a long chair and he raised his length from it as I came in. He was reading the Hong-Kong papers by the light of a paraffin-lamp that stood on a table by his side.

"Sit down," he said, "and put your feet up."

"There's no reason I should take your chair."

"Go on. I'll sit on this."

He took a kitchen chair and sitting on it put his feet on the end of mine.

"That's my wife," he said, pointing with his thumb at the Tonkinese woman who had followed me into the room. "And over there in the corner's the kid."

I followed his eyes and against the wall, lying on bamboo mats and covered with a blanket, I saw a child sleeping.

"Lively little beggar when he's awake. I wish you could have seen him. She's going to have another soon."

I glanced at her and the truth of what he said was apparent. She was very small, with tiny hands and feet, but her face was flat and the skin muddy. She looked sullen, but may only have been shy. She went out of the room and presently came back with a bottle of whisky, two glasses, and a syphon. I looked round. There was a partition at the back of dark unpainted wood, which I suppose shut off another room, and pinned against the middle of this was a portrait cut out of an illustrated paper of John Galsworthy. He looked austere, mild, and gentlemanly, and I wondered what he did there. The other walls were whitewashed, but the whitewash was dingy and stained. Pinned on to them were pages of pictures from the *Graphic* or the *Illustrated London News*.

"I put them up," said Grosely, "I thought they made the place look homelike."

"What made you put up Galsworthy? Do you read his books?"

"No, I didn't know he wrote books. I liked his face."

There were one or two torn and shabby rattan mats on the floor and in a corner a great pile of the *Hong-Kong Times*. The only furniture consisted of a wash-hand stand, two or three kitchen chairs, a table or two, and a large teak native bed. It was cheerless and sordid.

"Not a bad little place, is it?" said Grosely. "Suits me all right. Sometimes I've thought of moving, but I don't suppose I ever shall now." He gave a little chuckle. "I came to Haiphong for forty-eight hours and I've been here five years. I was on my way to Shanghai really."

He was silent. Having nothing to say I said nothing. Then the little Tonkinese woman made a remark to him, which I could not of course understand, and he answered her. He was silent again for a minute or two, but I thought he looked at me as though he wanted to ask me something. I did not know why he hesitated.

"Have you ever tried smoking opium on your travels in the East?" he inquired at last, casually.

"Yes, I did once, at Singapore. I thought I'd like to see what it was like."

"What happened?"

"Nothing very thrilling, to tell you the truth. I thought I was going to have the most exquisite emotions. I expected visions, like de Quincey's, you know. The only thing I felt was a kind of physical well-being, the same sort of feeling that you get when you've had a Turkish bath and are lying in the cooling room, and then a peculiar activity of mind so that everything I thought of seemed extremely clear."

"I know."

"I really felt that two and two are four and there could not be the smallest doubt about it. But next morning – oh God! My head reeled. I was as sick as a dog, I was sick all day, I vomited my soul out, and as I vomited I said to myself miserably: And there are people who call this fun."

Grosely leaned back in his chair and gave a low mirthless laugh.

"I expect it was bad stuff. Or you went at it too hard. They saw you were a mug and gave you dregs that had been smoked already. They're enough to turn anybody up. Would you like to have another try now? I've got some stuff here that I know's good."

"No, I think once was enough for me."

"D'you mind if I have a pipe or two? You want it in a climate like this. It keeps you from getting dysentery. And I generally have a bit of a smoke about this time."

"Go ahead," I said.

He spoke again to the woman and she, raising her voice, called out something in a raucous tone. An answer came from the room behind the wooden partition and after a minute or two an old woman came out carrying a little round tray. She was shrivelled and old and when she entered gave me an ingratiating smile of her stained mouth. Grosely got up and crossed over to the bed and lay on it. The old woman set the tray down on the bed; on it was a spirit-lamp, a pipe, a long needle, and a little round box of opium. She squatted on the bed and Grosely's wife got on it too and sat, her feet tucked up under her, with her back against the wall. Grosely watched the old woman while she put a little pellet of the drug on the needle, held it over the flame till it sizzled, and then plugged it into the pipe. She handed it to him and with a great breath he inhaled it, he held the smoke for a little while and then blew it out in a thick grey cloud. He handed her back the pipe and she started to make another. Nobody spoke. He smoked three pipes in succession and then sank back.

"By George, I feel better now. I was feeling all in. She makes a wonderful pipe, this old hag. Are you sure you won't have one?"

"Quite."

"Please yourself. Have some tea then."

He spoke to his wife, who scrambled off the bed and went out of the room. Presently she came back with a little china pot of tea and a couple of Chinese bowls.

"A lot of people smoke here, you know. It does you no harm if you don't do it to excess. I never smoke more than twenty to twenty-five pipes a day. You can go on for years if you limit yourself to that. Some of the Frenchmen smoke as many as forty or fifty a day. That's too much. I never do that, except now and then when I feel I want a binge. I'm bound to say it's never done me any harm."

We drank our tea, pale and vaguely scented and clean on the palate. Then the old woman made him another pipe and then another. His wife had got back on to the bed and soon curling herself up at his feet went to sleep. Grosely smoked two or three pipes at a time, and while he was smoking seemed intent upon nothing else, but in the intervals he was loquacious. Several times I suggested going, but he would not let me. The hours wore on. Once or twice while he smoked I dozed. He told me all about himself. He went on and on. I spoke only to give him a cue. I cannot relate what he told me in his own words. He repeated himself. He was very long-winded and he told me his story confusedly, first a late bit, then an early bit, so that I had to arrange the sequence for myself; sometimes I saw that, afraid he had said too much, he held something back; sometimes he lied and I had to make a guess at the truth from the smile he gave me or the look in his eyes. He had not the words to describe what he had felt, and I had to conjecture his meaning from slangy metaphors and hackneyed, vulgar phrases. I kept on asking myself what his real name was, it was on the tip of my tongue and it irritated me not to be able to recall it, though why it should in the least matter to me I did not know. He was somewhat suspicious of me at first and I saw that this escapade of his in London and his imprisonment had been all these years a tormenting secret. He had always been haunted by the fear that sooner or later someone would find out.

"It's funny that even now you shouldn't remember me at the hospital," he said, looking at me shrewdly. "You must have a rotten memory."

"Hang it all, it's nearly thirty years ago. Think of the thousands of people I've met since then. There's no reason why I should remember you any more than you remember me."

"That's right. I don't suppose there is."

It seemed to reassure him. At last he had smoked enough and the old woman made herself a pipe and smoked it. Then she went over to the mat on which the child was lying and huddled down beside it. She lay so still that I supposed she had fallen directly asleep. When at last I went I found my boy curled up on the footboard of the rickshaw in so deep a slumber that I had to shake him. I knew where I was and I wanted air and exercise, so I gave him a couple of piastres and told him I would walk.

It was a strange story I carried away with me.

It was with a sort of horror that I had listened to Grosely, telling me of those twenty years he had spent in China. He had made money, I do not know how much, but from the way he talked I should think something between fifteen and twenty thousand pounds, and for a tide-waiter it was a fortune. He could not have come by it honestly, and little as I knew of the details of his trade, by his sudden reticences, by his leers and hints I guessed that there was no base transaction that, if it was made worth his while, he jibbed at. I suppose that nothing paid him better than smuggling opium, and his position gave him the opportunity to do this with safety and profit. I understood that his superior officers had often had their suspicions of him, but had never been able to get such proof of his malpractices as to justify them in taking any steps. They contented themselves with moving him from one port to another, but that did not disturb him; they watched him, but he was too clever for them. I saw that he was divided between the fear of telling me too much to his discredit and the desire to boast of his own astuteness. He prided himself on the confidence the Chinese had placed in him.

"They knew they could trust me," he said, "and it gave me a pull. I never double-crossed a Chinaman once."

The thought filled him with the complacency of the honest man. The Chinese discovered that he was keen on curios and they got in the habit of giving him bits or bringing him things to buy; he never made inquiries how they had come by them and he bought them cheap. When he had got a good lot he sent them to Peking and sold them at a handsome profit. I remembered how he had started his commercial career by buying things at auctions and pawning them. For twenty years by shabby shift and petty dishonesty he added pound to pound, and everything he made he invested in Shanghai. He lived penuriously, saving half his pay; he never went on leave because he did not want to waste his money, he would not have anything to do with the Chinese women, he wanted to keep himself free from any entanglement; he did not drink. He was consumed by one ambition, to save enough to be able to go back to England and live the life from which he had been snatched as a boy. That was the only thing he wanted. He lived in China as though in a dream; he paid no attention to the life around him; its colour and strangeness, its possibilities of pleasure, meant nothing to him. There was always before him the mirage of London, the Criterion Bar, himself standing with his foot on the rail, the promenade at the Empire and the Pavilion, the picked-up harlot, the serio-comic at the music-hall, and the musical comedy at the Gaiety. This was life and love and adventure. This was romance. This was what he yearned for with all his heart. There was surely something impressive in the way in which during all those years he had lived like an anchorite with that one end in view of leading again a life that was so vulgar. It showed character.

"You see," he said to me, "even if I'd been able to get back to England on leave I wouldn't have gone. I didn't want to go till I could go for good. And then I wanted to do the thing in style."

He saw himself putting on evening clothes every night and going out with a gardenia in his buttonhole, and he saw himself going to the Derby in a long coat and a brown hat and a pair of opera glasses slung over his shoulder. He saw himself giving the girls a look over and picking out the one he fancied. He made up his mind that on the night he arrived in London he would get blind, he hadn't been drunk for twenty years; he couldn't afford to in his job, you had to keep your wits about you. He'd take care not to get drunk on the ship on the way home. He'd wait till he got to London. What a night he'd have! He thought of it for twenty years.

I do not know why Grosely left the Chinese Customs, whether the place was getting too hot for him, whether he had reached the end of his service, or whether he had amassed the sum he had fixed. But at last he sailed. He went second class; he did not intend to start spending money till he reached London. He took rooms in Jermyn Street, he had always wanted to live there, and he went straight to a tailor's and ordered himself an outfit. Slap up. Then he had a look round the town. It was different from how he remembered it, there was much more traffic and he felt confused and a little at sea. He went to the Criterion and found there was no longer a bar where he had been used to lounge and drink. There was a restaurant in Leicester Square where he had been in the habit of dining when he was in funds, but he could not find it; he supposed it had been torn down. He went to the Pavilion, but there were no women there; he was rather disgusted and went on to the Empire, he found they had done away with the Promenade. It was rather a blow. He could not quite make it out. Well, anyhow, he must be prepared for changes in twenty years, and if he couldn't do anything else he could get drunk. He had had fever several times in China and the change of climate had brought it on again, he wasn't feeling any too well, and after four or five drinks he was glad to go to bed.

That first day was only a sample of many that followed it. Everything went wrong. Grosely's voice grew peevish and bitter as he told me how one thing and another had failed him. The old places were gone, the people were different, he found it hard to make friends, he was strangely lonely; he had never expected that in a great city like London. That's what was wrong with it, London had become too big, it wasn't the jolly, intimate place it had been in the early 'nineties. It had gone to pieces. He picked up a few girls, but they weren't as nice as the girls he had known before, they weren't the fun they used to be, and he grew dimly conscious that they thought him a rum sort of cove. He was only just over forty and they looked upon him as an old man. When he tried to cotton on to a lot of young fellows standing round a bar they gave him the cold shoulder. Anyway, these young fellows didn't know how to drink. He'd show them. He got soused every night, it was the only thing to do in that damned place, but, by Jove, it made him feel rotten next day. He supposed it was the climate of China. When he was a medical student he could drink a bottle of whisky every night and be as fresh as a daisy in the morning. He began to think more about China. All sorts of things that he never knew he had noticed came back to him. It wasn't a bad life he'd led there. Perhaps he'd been a fool to keep away from those Chinese girls, they were pretty little things some of them, and they didn't put on the airs these English girls did. One could have a damned good time in China if one had the money he had. One could keep a Chinese girl and get into the club, and there'd be a lot of nice fellows to drink with and play bridge with and billiards. He remembered the Chinese shops and all the row in the streets and the coolies carrying loads and the ports with the junks in them and the rivers with pagodas on the banks. It was funny, he never thought much of China while he was there and now – well, he couldn't get it out of his mind. It obsessed him. He began to think that London was no place for a white man. It had just gone to the dogs, that was the long and short of it, and one day the thought came to him that perhaps it would be a good thing if he went back to

China. Of course it was silly, he'd worked like a slave for twenty years to be able to have a good time in London, and it was absurd to go and live in China. With his money he ought to be able to have a good time anywhere. But somehow he couldn't think of anything else but China. One day he went to the pictures and saw a scene at Shanghai. That settled it. He was fed up with London. He hated it. He was going to get out and this time he'd get out for good. He had been home a year and a half, and it seemed longer to him than all his twenty years in the East. He took a passage on a French boat sailing from Marseilles, and when he saw the coast of Europe sink into the sea he heaved a great sigh of relief. When they got to Suez and he felt the first touch of the East he knew he had done the right thing. Europe was finished. The East was the only place.

He went ashore at Djibouti and again at Colombo and Singapore, but though the ship stopped for two days at Saigon he remained on board there. He'd been drinking a good deal and he was feeling a bit under the weather. But when they reached Haiphong, where they were staying for forty-eight hours, he thought he might just as well have a look at it. That was the last stopping-place before they got to China. He was bound for Shanghai. When he got there he meant to go to a hotel and look around a bit and then get hold of a girl and a place of his own. He would buy a pony or two and race. He'd soon make friends. In the East they weren't so stiff and stand-offish as they were in London. Going ashore, he dined at the hotel and after dinner got into a rickshaw and told the boy he wanted a woman. The boy took him to the shabby tenement in which I had sat for so many hours and there were the old woman and the girl who was now the mother of his child. After a while the old woman asked him if he wouldn't like a smoke. He had never tried opium, he had always been frightened of it, but now he didn't see why he shouldn't have a go. He was feeling good that night and the girl was a jolly cuddle-some little thing; she was rather like a Chinese girl, small and pretty, like an idol. Well, he had a pipe or two, and he began to feel very happy and comfortable. He stayed all night. He didn't sleep. He just lay, feeling very restful, and thought about things.

"I stopped there till my ship went on to Hong-Kong," he said. "And when she left I just stopped on."

"How about your luggage?" I asked.

For I am perhaps unworthily interested in the manner people combine practical details with the ideal aspects of life. When in a novel penniless lovers drive in a long, swift racing car over the distant hills I have always a desire to know how they managed to pay for it; and I have often asked myself how the characters of Henry James in the intervals of subtly examining their situation coped with the physiological necessities of their bodies.

"I only had a trunk full of clothes, I was never one to want much more than I stood up in, and I went down with the girl in a rickshaw to fetch it. I only meant to stay on till the next boat came through. You see, I was so near China here I thought I'd wait a bit and get used to things, if you understand what I mean, before I went on."

I did. Those last words of his revealed him to me. I knew that on the threshold of China his courage had failed him. England had been such a terrible disappointment that now he was afraid to put China to the test too. If that failed him he had nothing. For years England had been like a mirage in the desert. But when he had yielded to the attraction, those shining pools and the palm trees and the green grass were nothing but the rolling sandy dunes. He had China, and so long as he never saw it again he kept it.

"Somehow I stayed on. You know, you'd be surprised how quickly the days pass. I don't seem to have time to do half the things I want to. After all I'm comfortable here. The old woman makes a damned good pipe, and she's a jolly little girl, my girl, and then there's the kid. A lively young beggar. If you're happy somewhere what's the good of going somewhere else?"

I looked round that large bare sordid room. There was no comfort in it and not one of the little personal things that one would have thought might have given him the feeling of home. Grosely had taken on this equivocal little apartment, which served as a house of assignation and as a place for Europeans to smoke opium in, with the old woman who kept it, just as it was, and he camped, rather than lived, there still as though next day he would pack his traps and go. After a little while he answered my question.

"I've never been so happy in my life. I often think I'll go on to Shanghai some day, but I don't suppose I ever shall. And God knows, I never want to see England again."

"Aren't you awfully lonely sometimes for people to talk to?"

"No. Sometimes a Chinese tramp comes in with an English skipper or a Scotch engineer, and then I go on board and we have a talk about old times. There's an old fellow here, a Frenchman who was in the Customs, and he speaks English; I go and see him sometimes. But the fact is I don't want anybody very much. I think a lot. It gets on my nerves when people come between me and my thoughts. I'm not a big smoker, you know, I just have a pipe or two in the morning to settle my stomach, but I don't really smoke till night. Then I think."

"What d'you think about?"

"Oh, all sorts of things. Sometimes about London and what it was like when I was a boy. But mostly about China. I think of the good times I had and the way I made my money, and I remember the fellows I used to know, and the Chinese. I had some narrow squeaks now and then, but I always came through all right. And I wonder what the girls would have been like that I might have had. Pretty little things. I'm sorry now I didn't keep one or two. It's a great country, China; I love those shops, with an old fellow sitting on his heels smoking a water-pipe, and all the shop-signs. And the temples. By George, that's the place for a man to live in. There's life."

The mirage shone before his eyes. The illusion held him. He was happy. I wondered what would be his end. Well, that was not yet. For the first time in his life perhaps he held the present in his hand.

THE LETTER

OUTSIDE ON THE quay the sun beat fiercely. A stream of motors, lorries and buses, private cars and hirelings, sped up and down the crowded thoroughfare, and every chauffeur blew his horn; rickshaws threaded their nimble path amid the throng, and the panting coolies found breath to yell at one another; coolies, carrying heavy bales, sidled along with their quick jog-trot and shouted to the passer-by to make way; itinerant vendors proclaimed their wares. Singapore is the meeting-place of a hundred peoples; and men of all colours, black Tamils, yellow Chinks, brown Malays, Armenians, Jews, and

Bengalis, called to one another in raucous tones. But inside the office of Messrs Ripley, Joyce, and Naylor it was pleasantly cool; it was dark after the dusty glitter of the street and agreeably quiet after its unceasing din. Mr Joyce sat in his private room, at the table, with an electric fan turned full on him. He was leaning back, his elbows on the arms of the chair, with the tips of the outstretched fingers of one hand resting neatly against the tips of the outstretched fingers of the other. His gaze rested on the battered volumes of the Law Reports which stood on a long shelf in front of him. On the top of a cupboard were square boxes of japanned tin, on which were painted the names of various clients.

There was a knock at the door.

"Come in."

A Chinese clerk, very neat in his white ducks, opened it.

"Mr Crosbie is here, sir."

He spoke beautiful English, accenting each word with precision, and Mr Joyce had often wondered at the extent of his vocabulary. Ong Chi Seng was a Cantonese, and he had studied law at Gray's Inn. He was spending a year or two with Messrs Ripley, Joyce, and Naylor in order to prepare himself for practice on his own account. He was industrious, obliging, and of exemplary character.

"Show him in," said Mr Joyce.

He rose to shake hands with his visitor and asked him to sit down. The light fell on him as he did so. The face of Mr Joyce remained in shadow. He was by nature a silent man, and now he looked at Robert Crosbie for quite a minute without speaking. Crosbie was a big fellow, well over six feet high, with broad shoulders, and muscular. He was a rubber-planter, hard with the constant exercise of walking over the estate, and with the tennis which was his relaxation when the day's work was over. He was deeply sunburned. His hairy hands, his feet in clumsy boots were enormous, and Mr Joyce found himself thinking that a blow of that great fist could easily kill the fragile Tamil. But there was no fierceness in his blue eyes; they were confiding and gentle; and his face, with its big, undistinguished features, was open, frank, and honest. But at this moment it bore a look of deep distress. It was drawn and haggard.

"You look as though you hadn't had much sleep the last night or two," said Mr Joyce.

"I haven't."

Mr Joyce noticed now the old felt hat, with its broad double brim, which Crosbie had placed on the table; and then his eyes travelled to the khaki shorts he wore, showing his red hairy thighs, the tennis shirt open at the neck, without a tie, and the dirty khaki jacket with the ends of the sleeves turned up. He looked as though he had just come in from a long tramp among the rubber trees. Mr Joyce gave a slight frown.

"You must pull yourself together, you know. You must keep your head."

"Oh, I'm all right."

"Have you seen your wife today?"

"No, I'm to see her this afternoon. You know, it is a damned shame that they should have arrested her."

"I think they had to do that," Mr Joyce answered in his level, soft tone.

"I should have thought they'd have let her out on bail."

"It's a very serious charge."

"It is damnable. She did what any decent woman would do in her place. Only, nine women out of ten wouldn't have the pluck. Leslie's the best woman in the world. She wouldn't hurt a fly. Why, hang it all, man, I've been married to her for twelve years, do you think I don't know her? God, if I'd got hold of the man I'd have wrung his neck, I'd have killed him without a moment's hesitation. So would you."

"My dear fellow, everybody's on your side. No one has a good word to say for Hammond. We're going to get her off. I don't suppose either the assessors or the judge will go into court without having already made up their minds to bring in a verdict of not guilty."

"The whole thing's a farce," said Crosbie violently. "She ought never to have been arrested in the first place, and then it's terrible, after all the poor girl's gone through, to subject her to the ordeal of a trial. There's not a soul I've met since I've been in Singapore, man or woman, who hasn't told me that Leslie was absolutely justified. I think it's awful to keep her in prison all these weeks."

"The law is the law. After all, she confesses that she killed the man. It is terrible, and I'm dreadfully sorry for both you and her."

"I don't matter a hang," interrupted Crosbie.

"But the fact remains that murder has been committed, and in a civilized community a trial is inevitable."

"Is it murder to exterminate noxious vermin? She shot him as she would have shot a mad dog."

Mr Joyce leaned back again in his chair and once more placed the tips of his ten fingers together. The little construction he formed looked like the skeleton of a roof. He was silent for a moment.

"I should be wanting in my duty as your legal adviser," he said at last, in an even voice, looking at his client with his cool, brown eyes, "if I did not tell you that there is one point which causes me just a little anxiety. If your wife had only shot Hammond once, the whole thing would be absolutely plain sailing. Unfortunately she fired six times."

"Her explanation is perfectly simple. In the circumstances anyone would have done the same."

"I daresay," said Mr Joyce, "and of course I think the explanation is very reasonable. But it's no good closing our eyes to the facts. It's always a good plan to put yourself in another man's place, and I can't deny that if I were prosecuting for the Crown that is the point on which I should centre my inquiry."

"My dear fellow, that's perfectly idiotic."

Mr Joyce shot a sharp glance at Robert Crosbie. The shadow of a smile hovered over his shapely lips. Crosbie was a good fellow, but he could hardly be described as intelligent.

"I daresay it's of no importance," answered the lawyer, "I just thought it was a point worth mentioning. You haven't got very long to wait now, and when it's all over I recommend you to go off somewhere with your wife on a trip, and forget all about it. Even though we are almost dead certain to get an acquittal, a trial of that sort is anxious work, and you'll both want a rest."

For the first time Crosbie smiled, and his smile strangely changed his face. You forgot the uncouthness and saw only the goodness of his soul.

"I think I shall want it more than Leslie. She's borne up wonderfully. By God, there's a plucky little woman for you."

"Yes, I've been very much struck by her self-control," said the lawyer. "I should never have guessed that she was capable of such determination."

His duties as her counsel had made it necessary for him to have a good many interviews with Mrs Crosbie since her arrest. Though things had been made as easy as could be for her, the fact remained that she was in gaol, awaiting her trial for murder, and it would not have been surprising if her nerves had failed her. She appeared to bear her ordeal with composure. She read a great deal, took such exercise as was possible, and by favour of the authorities worked at the pillow lace which had always formed the entertainment of her long hours of leisure. When Mr Joyce saw her, she was neatly dressed in cool, fresh, simple frocks, her hair was carefully arranged, and her nails were manicured. Her manner was collected. She was able even to jest upon the little inconveniences of her position. There was something casual about the way in which she spoke of the tragedy, which suggested to Mr Joyce that only her good breeding prevented her from finding something a trifle ludicrous in a situation which was eminently serious. It surprised him, for he had never thought that she had a sense of humour.

He had known her off and on for a good many years. When she paid visits to Singapore she generally came to dine with his wife and himself, and once or twice she had passed a week-end with them at their bungalow by the sea. His wife had spent a fortnight with her on the estate, and had met Geoffrey Hammond several times. The two couples had been on friendly, if not on intimate, terms, and it was on this account that Robert Crosbie had rushed over to Singapore immediately after the catastrophe and begged Mr Joyce to take charge personally of his unhappy wife's defence.

The story she told him the first time he saw her she had never varied in the smallest detail. She told it as coolly then, a few hours after the tragedy, as she told it now. She told it connectedly, in a level, even voice, and her only sign of confusion was when a slight colour came into her cheeks as she described one or two of its incidents. She was the last woman to whom one would have expected such a thing to happen. She was in the early thirties, a fragile creature, neither short nor tall, and graceful rather than pretty. Her wrists and ankles were very delicate, but she was extremely thin, and you could see the bones of her hands through the white skin, and the veins were large and blue. Her face was colourless, slightly sallow, and her lips were pale. You did not notice the colour of her eyes. She had a great deal of light brown hair, and it had a slight natural wave; it was the sort of hair that with a little touching-up would have been very pretty, but you could not imagine that Mrs Crosbie would think of resorting to any such device. She was a quiet, pleasant, unassuming woman. Her manner was engaging, and if she was not very popular it was because she suffered from a certain shyness. This was comprehensible enough, for the planter's life is lonely, and in her own house, with people she knew, she was in her quiet way charming. Mrs Joyce, after her fortnight's stay, had told her husband that Leslie was a very agreeable hostess. There was more in her, she said, than people thought; and when you came to know her you were surprised how much she had read and how entertaining she could be.

She was the last woman in the world to commit murder.

Mr Joyce dismissed Robert Crosbie with such reassuring words as he could find and, once more alone in his office, turned over the pages of the brief. But it was a mechanical action, for all its details were familiar to him. The case was the sensation of the day, and it was discussed in all the clubs, at all the dinner tables, up and down the Peninsula, from Singapore to Penang. The facts that Mrs Crosbie gave were simple. Her husband had gone to Singapore on business, and she was alone for the night. She dined by herself, late, at a quarter to nine, and after dinner sat in the sitting-room working at her lace. It opened on the veranda. There was no one in the bungalow, for the servants had retired to their own quarters at the back of the compound. She was surprised to hear a step on the gravel path in the garden, a booted step, which suggested a white man rather than a native, for she had not heard a motor drive up, and she could not imagine who could be coming to see her at that time of night. Someone ascended the few stairs that led up to the bungalow, walked across the veranda, and appeared at the door of the room in which she sat. At the first moment she did not recognize the visitor. She sat with a shaded lamp, and he stood with his back to the darkness.

"May I come in?" he said.

She did not even recognize the voice.

"Who is it?" she asked.

She worked with spectacles, and she took them off as she spoke.

"Geoff Hammond."

"Of course. Come in and have a drink."

She rose and shook hands with him cordially. She was a little surprised to see him, for though he was a neighbour neither she nor Robert had been lately on very intimate terms with him, and she had not seen him for some weeks. He was the manager of a rubber estate nearly eight miles from theirs, and she wondered why he had chosen this late hour to come and see them.

"Robert's away," she said. "He had to go to Singapore for the night."

Perhaps he thought his visit called for some explanation, for he said:

"I'm sorry. I felt rather lonely tonight, so I thought I'd just come along and see how you were getting on."

"How on earth did you come? I never heard a car."

"I left it down the road. I thought you might both be in bed and asleep."

This was natural enough. The planter gets up at dawn in order to take the roll-call of the workers, and soon after dinner he is glad to go to bed. Hammond's car was in point of fact found next day a quarter of a mile from the bungalow.

Since Robert was away there was no whisky and soda in the room. Leslie did not call the boy, who was probably asleep, but fetched it herself. Her guest mixed himself a drink and filled his pipe.

Geoff Hammond had a host of friends in the colony. He was at this time in the late thirties, but he had come out as a lad. He had been one of the first to volunteer on the outbreak of war, and had done very well. A wound in the knee caused him to be invalided out of the army after two years, but he returned to the Federated Malay States with a DSO and an MC. He was one of the best billiard-players in the colony. He had been a beautiful dancer and a fine tennis-player, but though able no longer to dance, and his tennis, with a stiff knee, was not so good as it had been, he had the gift of popularity and was universally liked. He was a tall, good-looking fellow, with attractive blue eyes and a fine head of black, curling hair. Old stagers said his only fault was that he was too fond of the girls, and after the catastrophe they shook their heads and vowed that they had always known this would get him into trouble.

He began now to talk to Leslie about the local affairs, the forth-coming races in Singapore, the price of rubber, and his chances of killing a tiger which had been lately seen in the neighbourhood. She was anxious to finish by a certain date a piece of lace on which she was working, for she wanted to send it home for her mother's birthday, and so put on her spectacles again, and drew towards her chair the little table on which stood the pillow.

"I wish you wouldn't wear those great horn-spectacles," he said. "I don't know why a pretty woman should do her best to look plain."

She was a trifle taken aback at this remark. He had never used that tone with her before. She thought the best thing was to make light of it.

"I have no pretensions to being a raving beauty, you know, and if you ask me point-blank, I'm bound to tell you that I don't care two pins if you think me plain or not."

"I don't think you're plain. I think you're awfully pretty."

"Sweet of you," she answered, ironically. "But in that case I can only think you half-witted."

He chuckled. But he rose from his chair and sat down in another by her side.

"You're not going to have the face to deny that you have the prettiest hands in the world," he said.

He made a gesture as though to take one of them. She gave him a little tap.

"Don't be an idiot. Sit down where you were before and talk sensibly, or else I shall send you home."

He did not move.

"Don't you know that I'm awfully in love with you?" he said.

She remained quite cool.

"I don't. I don't believe it for a minute, and even if it were true I don't want you to say it."

She was the more surprised at what he was saying, since during the seven years she had known him he had never paid her any particular attention. When he came back from the war they had seen a good deal of one another, and once when he was ill Robert had gone over and brought him back to their bungalow in his car. He had stayed with them for a fortnight. But their interests were dissimilar, and the acquaintance had never ripened into friendship. For the last two or three years they had seen little of him. Now and then he came over to play tennis, now and then they met him at some planter's who was giving a party, but it often happened that they did not set eyes on him for a month at a time.

Now he took another whisky and soda. Leslie wondered if he had been drinking before. There was something odd about him, and it made her a trifle uneasy. She watched him help himself with disapproval.

"I wouldn't drink any more if I were you," she said, good-humouredly still.

He emptied his glass and put it down.

"Do you think I'm talking to you like this because I'm drunk?" he asked abruptly.

"That is the most obvious explanation, isn't it?"

"Well, it's a lie. I've loved you ever since I first knew you. I've held my tongue as long as I could, and now it's got to come out. I love you, I love you, I love you."

She rose and carefully put aside the pillow.

"Good night," she said.

"I'm not going now."

At last she began to lose her temper.

"But, you poor fool, don't you know that I've never loved anyone but Robert, and even if I didn't love Robert you're the last man I should care for."

"What do I care? Robert's away."

"If you don't go away this minute I shall call the boys, and have you thrown out."

"They're out of earshot."

She was very angry now. She made a movement as though to go on to the veranda, from which the house-boy would certainly hear her, but he seized her arm.

"Let me go," she cried furiously.

"Not much. I've got you now."

She opened her mouth and called "Boy, boy," but with a quick gesture he put his hand over it. Then before she knew what he was about he had taken her in his arms and was kissing her passionately. She struggled, turning her lips away from his burning mouth.

"No, no, no," she cried. "Leave me alone. I won't."

She grew confused about what happened then. All that had been said before she remembered accurately, but now his words assailed her ears through a mist of horror and fear. He seemed to plead for her love. He broke into violent protestations of passion. And all the time he held her in his tempestuous embrace. She was helpless, for he was a strong, powerful man, and her arms were pinioned to her sides; her struggles were unavailing, and she felt herself grow weaker; she was afraid she would faint, and his hot breath on her face made her feel desperately sick. He kissed her mouth, her eyes, her cheeks, her hair. The pressure of his arms was killing her. He lifted her off her feet. She tried to kick him, but he only held her more closely. He was carrying her now. He wasn't speaking any more, but she knew that his face was pale and his eyes hot with desire. He was taking her into the bedroom. He was no longer a civilized man, but a savage. And as he ran he stumbled against a table which was in the way. His stiff knee made him a little awkward on his feet, and with the burden of the woman in his arms he fell. In a moment she had snatched herself away from him. She ran round the sofa. He was up in a flash, and flung himself towards her. There was a revolver on the desk. She was not a nervous woman, but Robert was to be away for the night, and she had meant to take it into her room when she went to bed. That was why it happened to be there. She was frantic with terror now. She did not know what she was doing. She heard a report. She saw Hammond stagger. He gave a cry. He said something, she didn't know what. He lurched out of the room on to the veranda. She was in a frenzy now, she was beside herself, she followed him out, yes, that was it, she must have followed him out, though she remembered nothing of it, she followed firing automatically, shot after shot, till the six chambers were empty. Hammond fell down on the floor of the veranda. He crumbled up into a bloody heap.

When the boys, startled by the reports, rushed up, they found her standing over Hammond with the revolver still in her hand and Hammond lifeless. She looked at them for a moment without speaking. They stood in a frightened, huddled bunch. She let the revolver fall from her hand, and without a word turned and went into the sitting-room. They watched her go into her bedroom and turn the key in the lock. They dared not touch the dead body, but looked at it with terrified eyes, talking excitedly to one another in undertones. Then the head-boy collected himself; he had been with them for many years, he was Chinese and a level-headed fellow. Robert had gone into Singapore on his motor-cycle, and the car stood in the garage. He told the seis to get it out; they must go at once to the Assistant District Officer and tell him what had happened. He picked up the revolver and put it in his pocket. The ADO, a man called Withers, lived on the outskirts of the nearest town, which was about thirty-five miles away. It took them an hour and a half to reach him. Everyone was asleep, and they had to rouse the boys. Presently Withers came out and they told him their errand. The head-boy showed him the revolver in proof of what he said. The ADO went into his room to dress, sent for his car, and in a little while was following them back along the deserted road. The dawn was just breaking as he reached the Crosbies' bungalow. He ran up the steps of the veranda, and stopped short as he saw Hammond's body lying where he fell. He touched the face. It was quite cold.

"Where's mem?" he asked the house-boy.

The Chinese pointed to the bedroom. Withers went to the door and knocked. There was no answer. He knocked again.

"Mrs Crosbie," he called.

"Who is it?"

"Withers."

There was another pause. Then the door was unlocked and slowly opened. Leslie stood before him. She had not been to bed, and wore the tea-gown in which she had dined. She stood and looked silently at the ADO.

"Your house-boy fetched me," he said. "Hammond. What have you done?"

"He tried to rape me, and I shot him."

"My God. I say, you'd better come out here. You must tell me exactly what happened."

"Not now. I can't. You must give me time. Send for my husband."

Withers was a young man, and he did not know exactly what to do in an emergency which was so out of the run of his duties. Leslie refused to say anything till at last Robert arrived. Then she told the two men the story, from which since then, though she

575

had repeated it over and over again, she had never in the slightest degree diverged.

The point to which Mr Joyce recurred was the shooting. As a lawyer he was bothered that Leslie had fired not once, but six times, and the examination of the dead man showed that four of the shots had been fired close to the body. One might almost have thought that when the man fell she stood over him and emptied the contents of the revolver into him. She confessed that her memory, so accurate for all that had preceded, failed her here. Her mind was blank. It pointed to an uncontrollable fury; but uncontrollable fury was the last thing you would have expected from this quiet and demure woman. Mr Joyce had known her a good many years, and had always thought her an unemotional person; during the weeks that had passed since the tragedy her composure had been amazing.

Mr Joyce shrugged his shoulders.

"The fact is, I suppose," he reflected, "that you can never tell what hidden possibilities of savagery there are in the most respectable of women."

There was a knock at the door.

"Come in."

The Chinese clerk entered and closed the door behind him. He closed it gently, with deliberation, but decidedly, and advanced to the table at which Mr Joyce was sitting.

"May I trouble you, sir, for a few words' private conversation?" he said.

The elaborate accuracy with which the clerk expressed himself always faintly amused Mr Joyce, and now he smiled.

"It's no trouble, Chi Seng," he replied.

"The matter on which I desire to speak to you, sir, is delicate and confidential."

"Fire away."

Mr Joyce met his clerk's shrewd eyes. As usual Ong Chi Seng was dressed in the height of local fashion. He wore very shiny patent-leather shoes and gay silk socks. In his black tie was a pearl and ruby pin, and on the fourth finger of his left hand a diamond ring. From the pocket of his neat white coat protruded a gold fountain pen and a gold pencil. He wore a gold wristwatch, and on the bridge of his nose invisible pince-nez. He gave a little cough.

"The matter has to do with the case R *v.* Crosbie, sir."

"Yes?"

"A circumstance has come to my knowledge, sir, which seems to me to put a different complexion on it."

"What circumstance?"

"It has come to my knowledge, sir, that there is a letter in existence from the defendant to the unfortunate victim of the tragedy."

"I shouldn't be at all surprised. In the course of the last seven years I have no doubt that Mrs Crosbie often had occasion to write to Mr Hammond."

Mr Joyce had a high opinion of his clerk's intelligence and his words were designed to conceal his thoughts.

"That is very probable, sir. Mrs Crosbie must have communicated with the deceased frequently, to invite him to dine with her for example, or to propose a tennis game. That was my first thought when the matter was brought to my notice. This letter, however, was written on the day of the late Mr Hammond's death."

Mr Joyce did not flicker an eyelash. He continued to look at Ong Chi Seng with the smile of faint amusement with which he generally talked to him.

"Who has told you this?"

"The circumstances were brought to my knowledge, sir, by a friend of mine."

Mr Joyce knew better than to insist.

"You will no doubt recall, sir, that Mrs Crosbie has stated that until the fatal night she had had no communication with the deceased for several weeks."

"Have you got the letter?"

"No, sir."

"What are its contents?"

"My friend gave me a copy. Would you like to peruse it, sir?"

"I should."

Ong Chi Seng took from an inside pocket a bulky wallet. It was filled with papers, Singapore dollar notes and cigarette cards. From the confusion he presently extracted a half-sheet of thin notepaper and placed it before Mr Joyce. The letter read as follows:

R will be away for the night. I absolutely must see you. I shall expect you at eleven. I am desperate, and if you don't come I won't answer for the consequences. Don't drive up.–L.

It was written in the flowing hand which the Chinese were taught at the foreign schools. The writing, so lacking in character, was oddly incongruous with the ominous words.

"What makes you think that this note was written by Mrs Crosbie?"

"I have every confidence in the veracity of my informant, sir," replied Ong Chi Seng. "And the matter can very easily be put to the proof. Mrs Crosbie will, no doubt, be able to tell you at once whether she wrote such a letter or not."

Since the beginning of the conversation Mr Joyce had not taken his eyes off the respectable countenance of his clerk. He wondered now if he discerned in it a faint expression of mockery.

"It is inconceivable that Mrs Crosbie should have written such a letter," said Mr Joyce.

"If that is your opinion, sir, the matter is of course ended. My friend spoke to me on the subject only because he thought, as I was in your office, you might like to know of the existence of this letter before a communication was made to the Deputy Public Prosecutor."

"Who has the original?" asked Mr Joyce sharply.

Ong Chi Seng made no sign that he perceived in this question and its manner a change of attitude.

"You will remember, sir, no doubt, that after the death of Mr Hammond it was discovered that he had had relations with a Chinese woman. The letter is at present in her possession."

That was one of the things which had turned public opinion most vehemently against Hammond. It came to be known that for several months he had had a Chinese woman living in his house.

For a moment neither of them spoke. Indeed everything had been said and each understood the other perfectly.

"I'm obliged to you, Chi Seng. I will give the matter my consideration."

"Very good, sir. Do you wish me to make a communication to that effect to my friend?"

"I daresay it would be as well if you kept in touch with him," Mr Joyce answered with gravity.

"Yes, sir."

The clerk noiselessly left the room, shutting the door again with deliberation, and left Mr Joyce to his reflections. He stared at the copy, in its neat, impersonal writing, of Leslie's letter. Vague suspicions troubled him. They were so disconcerting that he made an effort to put them out of his mind. There must be a simple explanation of the letter, and Leslie without doubt could give it at once, but, by heaven, an explanation was needed. He rose from his chair, put the letter in his pocket, and took his topee. When he went out Ong Chi Seng was busily writing at his desk.

"I'm going out for a few minutes, Chi Seng," he said.

"Mr George Reed is coming by appointment at twelve o'clock, sir. Where shall I say you've gone?"

Mr Joyce gave him a thin smile.

"You can say that you haven't the least idea."

But he knew perfectly well that Ong Chi Seng was aware that he was going to the gaol. Though the crime had been committed in Belanda and the trial was to take place at Belanda Bharu, since there was in the gaol no convenience for the detention of a white woman Mrs Crosbie had been brought to Singapore.

When she was led into the room in which he waited she held out her thin, distinguished hand, and gave him a pleasant smile. She was as ever neatly and simply dressed, and her abundant, pale hair was arranged with care.

"I wasn't expecting to see you this morning," she said, graciously.

She might have been in her own house, and Mr Joyce almost expected to hear her call the boy and tell him to bring the visitor a gin pahit.

"How are you?" he asked.

"I'm in the best of health, thank you." A flicker of amusement flashed across her eyes. "This is a wonderful place for a rest cure."

The attendant withdrew and they were left alone.

"Do sit down," said Leslie.

He took a chair. He did not quite know how to begin. She was so cool that it seemed almost impossible to say to her the thing he had come to say. Though she was not pretty there was something

579

agreeable in her appearance. She had elegance, but it was the elegance of good breeding in which there was nothing of the artifice of society. You had only to look at her to know what sort of people she had and what kind of surroundings she had lived in. Her fragility gave her a singular refinement. It was impossible to associate her with the vaguest idea of grossness.

"I'm looking forward to seeing Robert this afternoon," she said, in her good-humoured, easy voice. (It was a pleasure to hear her speak, her voice and her accent were so distinctive of her class.) "Poor dear, it's been a great trial to his nerves. I'm thankful it'll all be over in a few days."

"It's only five days now."

"I know. Each morning when I awake I say to myself, 'one less'." She smiled then. "Just as I used to do at school and the holidays were coming."

"By the way, am I right in thinking that you had no communication whatever with Hammond for several weeks before the catastrophe?"

"I'm quite positive of that. The last time we met was at a tennis-party at the MacFarrens. I don't think I said more than two words to him. They have two courts, you know, and we didn't happen to be in the same sets."

"And you haven't written to him?"

"Oh, no."

"Are you quite sure of that?"

"Oh, quite," she answered, with a little smile. "There was nothing I should write to him for except to ask him to dine or to play tennis, and I hadn't done either for months."

"At one time you'd been on fairly intimate terms with him. How did it happen that you had stopped asking him to anything?"

Mrs Crosbie shrugged her thin shoulders.

"One gets tired of people. We hadn't anything very much in common. Of course, when he was ill Robert and I did everything we could for him, but the last year or two he'd been quite well, and he was very popular. He had a good many calls on his time, and there didn't seem to be any need to shower invitations upon him."

"Are you quite certain that was all?"

Mrs Crosbie hesitated for a moment.

"Well, I may just as well tell you. It had come to our ears that he was living with a Chinese woman, and Robert said he wouldn't have him in the house. I had seen her myself."

Mr Joyce was sitting in a straight-backed arm-chair, resting his chin on his hand, and his eyes were fixed on Leslie. Was it his fancy that, as she made this remark, her black pupils were filled on a sudden, for the fraction of a second, with a dull red light? The effect was startling. Mr Joyce shifted in his chair. He placed the tips of his ten fingers together. He spoke very slowly, choosing his words.

"I think I should tell you that there is in existence a letter in your handwriting to Geoff Hammond."

He watched her closely. She made no movement, nor did her face change colour, but she took a noticeable time to reply.

"In the past I've often sent him little notes to ask him to something or other, or to get me something when I knew he was going to Singapore."

"This letter asks him to come and see you because Robert was going to Singapore."

"That's impossible. I never did anything of the kind."

"You'd better read it for yourself."

He took it out of his pocket and handed it to her. She gave it a glance and with a smile of scorn handed it back to him.

"That's not my handwriting."

"I know, it's said to be an exact copy of the original."

She read the words now, and as she read a horrible change came over her. Her colourless face grew dreadful to look at. It turned green. The flesh seemed on a sudden to fall away and her skin was tightly stretched over the bones. Her lips receded, showing her teeth, so that she had the appearance of making a grimace. She stared at Mr Joyce with eyes that started from their sockets. He was looking now at a gibbering death's head.

"What does it mean?" she whispered.

Her mouth was so dry that she could utter no more than a hoarse sound. It was no longer a human voice.

"That is for you to say," he answered.

"I didn't write it. I swear I didn't write it."

"Be very careful what you say. If the original is in your handwriting it would be useless to deny it."

"It would be a forgery."

"It would be difficult to prove that. It would be easy to prove that it was genuine."

A shiver passed through her lean body. But great beads of sweat stood on her forehead. She took a handkerchief from her bag and wiped the palms of her hands. She glanced at the letter again and gave Mr Joyce a sidelong look.

"It's not dated. If I had written it and forgotten all about it, it might have been written years ago. If you'll give me time, I'll try and remember the circumstances."

"I noticed there was no date. If this letter were in the hands of the prosecution they would cross-examine the boys. They would soon find out whether someone took a letter to Hammond on the day of his death."

Mrs Crosbie clasped her hands violently and swayed in her chair so that he thought she would faint.

"I swear to you that I didn't write that letter."

Mr Joyce was silent for a little while. He took his eyes from her distraught face, and looked down on the floor. He was reflecting.

"In these circumstances we need not go into the matter further," he said slowly, at last breaking the silence. "If the possessor of this letter sees fit to place it in the hands of the prosecution you will be prepared."

His words suggested that he had nothing more to say to her, but he made no movement of departure. He waited. To himself he seemed to wait a very long time. He did not look at Leslie, but he was conscious that she sat very still. She made no sound. At last it was he who spoke.

"If you have nothing more to say to me I think I'll be getting back to my office."

"What would anyone who read the letter be inclined to think that it meant?" she asked then.

"He'd know that you had told a deliberate lie," answered Mr Joyce sharply.

"When?"

"You have stated definitely that you had had no communication with Hammond for at least three months."

"The whole thing has been a terrible shock to me. The events of that dreadful night have been a nightmare. It's not very strange if one detail has escaped my memory."

"It would be unfortunate, when your memory has reproduced so exactly every particular of your interview with Hammond, that you should have forgotten so important a point as that he came to see you in the bungalow on the night of his death at your express desire."

"I hadn't forgotten. After what happened I was afraid to mention it. I thought you'd none of you believe my story if I admitted that he'd come at my invitation. I daresay it was stupid of me; but I lost my head, and after I'd said once that I'd had no communication with Hammond I was obliged to stick to it."

By now Leslie had recovered her admirable composure, and she met Mr Joyce's appraising glance with candour. Her gentleness was very disarming.

"You will be required to explain, then, *why* you asked Hammond to come and see you when Robert was away for the night."

She turned her eyes full on the lawyer. He had been mistaken in thinking them insignificant, they were rather fine eyes, and unless he was mistaken they were bright now with tears. Her voice had a little break in it.

"It was a surprise I was preparing for Robert. His birthday is next month. I knew he wanted a new gun and you know I'm dreadfully stupid about sporting things. I wanted to talk to Geoff about it. I thought I'd get him to order it for me."

"Perhaps the terms of the letter are not very clear to your recollection. Will you have another look at it?"

"No, I don't want to," she said quickly.

"Does it seem to you the sort of letter a woman would write to a somewhat distant acquaintance because she wanted to consult him about buying a gun?"

"I daresay it's rather extravagant and emotional. I do express myself like that, you know. I'm quite prepared to admit it's very silly." She smiled. "And after all, Geoff Hammond wasn't quite a distant acquaintance. When he was ill I'd nursed him like a mother. I asked him to come when Robert was away, because Robert wouldn't have him in the house."

Mr Joyce was tired of sitting so long in the same position. He rose and walked once or twice up and down the room, choosing the words he proposed to say; then he leaned over the back of the chair in which he had been sitting. He spoke slowly in a tone of deep gravity.

"Mrs Crosbie, I want to talk to you very, very seriously. This case was comparatively plain sailing. There was only one point which seemed to me to require explanation: as far as I could judge, you had fired no less than four shots into Hammond when he was lying on the ground. It was hard to accept the possibility that a delicate, frightened, and habitually self-controlled woman, of gentle nature and refined instincts, should have surrendered to an absolutely uncontrolled frenzy. But of course it was admissible. Although Geoffrey Hammond was much liked and on the whole thought highly of, I was prepared to prove that he was the sort of man who might be guilty of the crime which in justification of your act you accused him of. The fact, which was discovered after his death, that he had been living with a Chinese woman gave us something very definite to go upon. That robbed him of any sympathy which might have been felt for him. We made up our minds to make use of the odium which such a connexion cast upon him in the minds of all respectable people. I told your husband this morning that I was certain of an acquittal, and I wasn't just telling him that to give him heart. I do not believe the assessors would have left the court."

They looked into one another's eyes. Mrs Crosbie was strangely still. She was like a little bird paralysed by the fascination of a snake. He went on in the same quiet tones.

"But this letter has thrown an entirely different complexion on the case. I am your legal adviser, I shall represent you in court. I take your story as you tell it me, and I shall conduct your defence according to its terms. It may be that I believe your statements, and it may be that I doubt them. The duty of counsel is to persuade the court that the evidence placed before it is not such as to justify it in bringing in a verdict of guilty, and any private opinion he may have of the guilt or innocence of his client is entirely beside the point."

He was astonished to see in Leslie's eyes the flicker of a smile. Piqued, he went on somewhat dryly:

"You're not going to deny that Hammond came to your house at your urgent, and I may even say, hysterical invitation?"

Mrs Crosbie, hesitating for an instant, seemed to consider.

"They can prove that the letter was taken to his bungalow by one of the house-boys. He rode over on his bicycle."

"You mustn't expect other people to be stupider than you. The letter will put them on the track of suspicions which have entered nobody's head. I will not tell you what I personally thought when I saw the copy. I do not wish you to tell me anything but what is needed to save your neck."

Mrs Crosbie gave a shrill cry. She sprang to her feet, white with terror.

"You don't think they'd hang me?"

"If they came to the conclusion that you hadn't killed Hammond in self-defence, it would be the duty of the assessors to bring in a verdict of guilty. The charge is murder. It would be the duty of the judge to sentence you to death."

"But what can they prove?" she gasped.

"I don't know what they can prove. You know. I don't want to know. But if their suspicions are aroused, if they begin to make inquiries, if the natives are questioned – what is it that can be discovered?"

She crumpled up suddenly. She fell on the floor before he could catch her. She had fainted. He looked round the room for water, but there was none there, and he did not want to be disturbed. He stretched her out on the floor, and kneeling beside her waited for her to recover. When she opened her eyes he was disconcerted by the ghastly fear that he saw in them.

"Keep quite still," he said. "You'll be better in a moment."

"You won't let them hang me," she whispered.

She began to cry, hysterically, while in undertones he sought to quieten her.

"For goodness' sake pull yourself together," he said.

"Give me a minute."

Her courage was amazing. He could see the effort she made to regain her self-control, and soon she was once more calm.

"Let me get up now."

He gave her his hand and helped her to her feet. Taking her arm, he led her to the chair. She sat down wearily.

"Don't talk to me for a minute or two," she said.

"Very well."

When at last she spoke it was to say something which he did not expect. She gave a little sigh.

"I'm afraid I've made rather a mess of things," she said.

He did not answer, and once more there was a silence.

"Isn't it possible to get hold of the letter?" she said at last.

"I do not think anything would have been said to me about it if the person in whose possession it is was not prepared to sell it."

"Who's got it?"

"The Chinese woman who was living in Hammond's house." A spot of colour flickered for an instant on Leslie's cheekbones.

"Does she want an awful lot for it?"

"I imagine that she has a very shrewd idea of its value. I doubt if it would be possible to get hold of it except for a very large sum."

"Are you going to let me be hanged?"

"Do you think it's so simple as all that to secure possession of an unwelcome piece of evidence? It's no different from suborning a witness. You have no right to make any such suggestion to me."

"Then what is going to happen to me?"

"Justice must take its course."

She grew very pale. A little shudder passed through her body.

"I put myself in your hands. Of course I have no right to ask you to do anything that isn't proper."

Mr Joyce had not bargained for the little break in her voice which her habitual self-restraint made quite intolerably moving. She looked at him with humble eyes, and he thought that if he rejected their appeal they would haunt him for the rest of his life. After all, nothing could bring poor Hammond back to life again. He wondered what really was the explanation of that letter. It was not fair to conclude from it that she had killed Hammond without provocation. He had lived in the East a long time and his sense of professional honour was not perhaps so acute as it had been twenty years before. He stared at the floor. He made up his mind to do something which he knew was unjustifiable, but it stuck in his throat and he felt dully resentful towards Leslie. It embarrassed him a little to speak.

"I don't know exactly what your husband's circumstances are?"

Flushing a rosy red, she shot a swift glance at him.

"He has a good many tin shares and a small share in two or three rubber estates. I suppose he could raise money."

"He would have to be told what it was for."

She was silent for a moment. She seemed to think.

"He's in love with me still. He would make any sacrifice to save me. Is there any need for him to see the letter?"

Mr Joyce frowned a little, and, quick to notice, she went on.

"Robert is an old friend of yours. I'm not asking you to do anything for me, I'm asking you to save a rather simple, kind man who never did you any harm from all the pain that's possible."

Mr Joyce did not reply. He rose to go and Mrs Crosbie, with the grace that was natural to her, held out her hand. She was shaken by the scene, and her look was haggard, but she made a brave attempt to speed him with courtesy.

"It's so good of you to take all this trouble for me. I can't begin to tell you how grateful I am."

Mr Joyce returned to his office. He sat in his own room, quite still, attempting to do no work, and pondered. His imagination brought him many strange ideas. He shuddered a little. At last there was the discreet knock on the door which he was expecting. Ong Chi Seng came in.

"I was just going out to have my tiffin, sir," he said.

"All right."

"I didn't know if there was anything you wanted before I went, sir."

"I don't think so. Did you make another appointment for Mr Reed?"

"Yes, sir. He will come at three o'clock."

"Good."

Ong Chi Seng turned away, walked to the door, and put his long slim fingers on the handle. Then, as though on an afterthought, he turned back.

"Is there anything you wish me to say to my friend, sir?"

Although Ong Chi Seng spoke English so admirably he had still a difficulty with the letter R, and he pronounced it "fliend".

"What friend?"

"About the letter Mrs Crosbie wrote to Hammond deceased, sir."

"Oh! I'd forgotten about that. I mentioned it to Mrs Crosbie and she denies having written anything of the sort. It's evidently a forgery."

Mr Joyce took the copy from his pocket and handed it to Ong Chi Seng. Ong Chi Seng ignored the gesture.

"In that case, sir, I suppose there would be no objection if my fliend delivered the letter to the Deputy Public Prosecutor."

"None. But I don't quite see what good that would do your friend."

"My friend, sir, thought it was his duty in the interests of justice."

"I am the last man in the world to interfere with anyone who wishes to do his duty, Chi Seng."

The eyes of the lawyer and of the Chinese clerk met. Not the shadow of a smile hovered on the lips of either, but they understood each other perfectly.

"I quite understand, sir," said Ong Chi Seng, "but from my study of the case R *v.* Crosbie I am of opinion that the production of such a letter would be damaging to our client."

"I have always had a very high opinion of your legal acumen, Chi Seng."

"It had occurred to me, sir, that if I could persuade my fliend to induce the Chinese woman who has the letter to deliver it into our hands it would save a great deal of trouble."

Mr Joyce idly drew faces on his blotting-paper.

"I suppose your friend is a business man. In what circumstances do you think he would be induced to part with the letter?"

"He has not got the letter. The Chinese woman has the letter. He is only a relation of the Chinese woman. She is an ignorant woman; she did not know the value of that letter till my fliend told her."

"What value did he put on it?"

"Ten thousand dollars, sir."

"Good God! Where on earth do you suppose Mrs Crosbie can get ten thousand dollars! I tell you the letter's a forgery."

He looked up at Ong Chi Seng as he spoke. The clerk was unmoved by the outburst. He stood at the side of the desk, civil, cool, and observant.

"Mr Crosbie owns an eighth share of the Betong Rubber Estate and a sixth share of the Selantan River Rubber Estate.

I have a fliend who will lend him the money on the security of his property."

"You have a large circle of acquaintance, Chi Seng."

"Yes sir."

"Well, you can tell them all to go to hell. I would never advise Mr Crosbie to give a penny more than five thousand for a letter that can be very easily explained."

"The Chinese woman does not want to sell the letter, sir. My fliend took a long time to persuade her. It is useless to offer her less than the sum mentioned."

Mr Joyce looked at Ong Chi Seng for at least three minutes. The clerk bore the searching scrutiny without embarrassment. He stood in a respectful attitude with downcast eyes. Mr Joyce knew his man. Clever fellow, Chi Seng, he thought, I wonder how much he's going to get out of it.

"Ten thousand dollars is a very large sum."

"Mr Crosbie will certainly pay it rather than see his wife hanged, sir."

Again Mr Joyce paused. What more did Chi Seng know than he had said? He must be pretty sure of his ground if he was obviously so unwilling to bargain. That sum had been fixed because whoever it was that was managing the affair knew it was the largest amount that Robert Crosbie could raise.

"Where is the Chinese woman now?" asked Mr Joyce.

"She is staying at the house of my fliend, sir."

"Will she come here?"

"I think it more better if you go to her, sir. I can take you to the house tonight and she will give you the letter. She is a very ignorant woman, sir, and she does not understand cheques."

"I wasn't thinking of giving her a cheque. I will bring bank notes with me."

"It would only be waste of valuable time to bring less than ten thousand dollars, sir."

"I quite understand."

"I will go and tell my fliend after I have had my tiffin, sir."

"Very good. You'd better meet me outside the club at ten o'clock tonight."

"With pleasure, sir," said Ong Chi Seng.

He gave Mr Joyce a little bow and left the room. Mr Joyce went out to have luncheon, too. He went to the club and here, as he had expected, he saw Robert Crosbie. He was sitting at a crowded table, and as he passed him, looking for a place, Mr Joyce touched him on the shoulder.

"I'd like a word or two with you before you go," he said.

"Right you are. Let me know when you're ready."

Mr Joyce had made up his mind how to tackle him. He played a rubber of bridge after luncheon in order to allow time for the club to empty itself. He did not want on this particular matter to see Crosbie in his office. Presently Crosbie came into the card-room and looked on till the game was finished. The other players went on their various affairs, and the two were left alone.

"A rather unfortunate thing has happened, old man," said Mr Joyce, in a tone which he sought to render as casual as possible. "It appears that your wife sent a letter to Hammond asking him to come to the bungalow on the night he was killed."

"But that's impossible," cried Crosbie. "She's always stated that she had had no communication with Hammond. I know from my own knowledge that she hadn't set eyes on him for a couple of months."

"The fact remains that the letter exists. It's in the possession of the Chinese woman Hammond was living with. Your wife meant to give you a present on your birthday, and she wanted Hammond to help her to get it. In the emotional excitement that she suffered from after the tragedy, she forgot all about it, and having once denied having any communication with Hammond she was afraid to say that she had made a mistake. It was, of course, very unfortunate, but I daresay it was not unnatural."

Crosbie did not speak. His large, red face bore an expression of complete bewilderment, and Mr Joyce was at once relieved and exasperated by his lack of comprehension. He was a stupid man, and Mr Joyce had no patience with stupidity. But his distress since the catastrophe had touched a soft spot in the lawyer's heart; and Mrs Crosbie had struck the right note when she asked him to help her, not for her sake, but for her husband's.

"I need not tell you that it would be very awkward if this letter found its way into the hands of the prosecution. Your wife has lied, and she would be asked to explain the lie. It alters things a little if Hammond did not intrude, an unwanted guest, but came to your house by invitation. It would be easy to arouse in the assessors a certain indecision of mind."

Mr Joyce hesitated. He was face to face now with his decision. If it had been a time for humour, he could have smiled at the reflection that he was taking so grave a step, and that the man for whom he was taking it had not the smallest conception of its gravity. If he gave the matter a thought, he probably imagined that what Mr Joyce was doing was what any lawyer did in the ordinary run of business.

"My dear Robert, you are not only my client, but my friend. I think we must get hold of that letter. It'll cost a good deal of money. Except for that I should have preferred to say nothing to you about it."

"How much?"

"Ten thousand dollars."

"That's a devil of a lot. With the slump and one thing and another it'll take just about all I've got."

"Can you get it at once?"

"I suppose so. Old Charlie Meadows will let me have it on my tin shares and on those two estates I'm interested in."

"Then will you?"

"Is it absolutely necessary?"

"If you want your wife to be acquitted."

Crosbie grew very red. His mouth sagged strangely.

"But . . . " he could not find words, his face now was purple. "But I don't understand. She can explain. You don't mean to say they'd find her guilty? They couldn't hang her for putting a noxious vermin out of the way."

"Of course they wouldn't hang her. They might only find her guilty of manslaughter. She'd probably get off with two or three years."

Crosbie started to his feet and his red face was distraught with horror.

"Three years."

Then something seemed to dawn in that slow intelligence of his. His mind was darkness across which shot suddenly a flash of lightning, and though the succeeding darkness was as profound, there remained the memory of something not seen but perhaps just descried. Mr Joyce saw that Crosbie's big red hands, coarse and hard with all the odd jobs he had set them to, trembled.

"What was the present she wanted to make me?"

"She says she wanted to give you a new gun."

Once more that great red face flushed a deeper red.

"When have you got to have the money ready?"

There was something odd in his voice now. It sounded as though he spoke with invisible hands clutching at his throat.

"At ten o'clock tonight. I thought you could bring it to my office at about six."

"Is the woman coming to you?"

"No, I'm going to her."

"I'll bring the money. I'll come with you."

Mr Joyce looked at him sharply.

"Do you think there's any need for you to do that? I think it would be better if you left me to deal with this matter by myself."

"It's my money, isn't it? I'm going to come."

Mr Joyce shrugged his shoulders. They rose and shook hands. Mr Joyce looked at him curiously.

At ten o'clock they met in the empty club.

"Everything all right?" asked Mr Joyce.

"Yes. I've got the money in my pocket."

"Let's go then."

They walked down the steps. Mr Joyce's car was waiting for them in the square, silent at that hour, and as they came to it Ong Chi Seng stepped out of the shadow of a house. He took his seat beside the driver and gave him a direction. They drove past the Hotel de L'Europe and turned up by the Sailor's Home to get into Victoria Street. Here the Chinese shops were still open, idlers lounged about, and in the roadway rickshaws and motor-cars and gharries gave a busy air to the scene. Suddenly their car stopped and Chi Seng turned round.

"I think it more better if we walk here, sir," he said.

They got out and he went on. They followed a step or two behind. Then he asked them to stop.

"You wait here, sir. I go in and speak to my fliend."

He went into a shop, open to the street, where three or four Chinese were standing behind the counter. It was one of those strange shops where nothing was on view, and you wondered what it was they sold there. They saw him address a stout man in a duck suit with a large gold chain across his breast, and the man shot a quick glance out into the night. He gave Chi Seng a key and Chi Seng came out. He beckoned to the two men waiting and slid into a doorway at the side of the shop. They followed him and found themselves at the foot of a flight of stairs.

"If you wait a minute I will light a match," he said, always resourceful. "You come upstairs, please."

He held a Japanese match in front of them, but it scarcely dispelled the darkness and they groped their way up behind him. On the first floor he unlocked a door and going in lit a gas-jet.

"Come in, please," he said.

It was a small square room, with one window, and the only furniture consisted of two low Chinese beds covered with matting. In one corner was a large chest, with an elaborate lock, and on this stood a shabby tray with an opium pipe on it and a lamp. There was in the room the faint, acrid scent of the drug. They sat down and Ong Chi Seng offered them cigarettes. In a moment the door was opened by the fat Chinaman whom they had seen behind the counter. He bade them good evening in very good English, and sat down by the side of his fellow-countryman.

"The Chinese woman is just coming," said Chi Seng.

A boy from the shop brought in a tray with a teapot and cups and the Chinaman offered them a cup of tea. Crosbie refused. The Chinese talked to one another in undertones, but Crosbie and Mr Joyce were silent. At last there was the sound of a voice outside; someone was calling in a low tone; and the Chinaman went to the door. He opened it, spoke a few words, and ushered a woman in. Mr Joyce looked at her. He had heard much about her since Hammond's death, but he had never seen her. She was a stoutish person, not very young, with a broad, phlegmatic face, she was powdered and rouged and her eyebrows were a thin black line, but she gave you the impression of a woman of character.

She wore a pale blue jacket and a white skirt, her costume was not quite European nor quite Chinese, but on her feet were little

Chinese silk slippers. She wore heavy gold chains round her neck, gold bangles on her wrists, gold ear-rings, and elaborate gold pins in her black hair. She walked in slowly, with the air of a woman sure of herself, but with a certain heaviness of tread, and sat down on the bed beside Ong Chi Seng. He said something to her and nodding she gave an incurious glance at the two white men.

"Has she got the letter?" asked Mr Joyce.

"Yes, sir."

Crosbie said nothing, but produced a roll of five-hundred-dollar notes. He counted out twenty and handed them to Chi Seng.

"Will you see if that is correct?"

The clerk counted them and gave them to the fat Chinaman.

"Quite correct, sir."

The Chinaman counted them once more and put them in his pocket. He spoke again to the woman and she drew from her bosom a letter. She gave it to Chi Seng who cast his eyes over it.

"This is the right document, sir," he said, and was about to give it to Mr Joyce when Crosbie took it from him.

"Let me look at it," he said.

Mr Joyce watched him read and then held out his hand for it.

"You'd better let me have it."

Crosbie folded it up deliberately and put it in his pocket.

"No, I'm going to keep it myself. It's cost me enough money."

Mr Joyce made no rejoinder. The three Chinese watched the little passage, but what they thought about it, or whether they thought, it was impossible to tell from their impassive countenances. Mr Joyce rose to his feet.

"Do you want me any more tonight, sir?" said Ong Chi Seng.

"No." He knew that the clerk wished to stay behind in order to get his agreed share of the money, and he turned to Crosbie. "Are you ready?"

Crosbie did not answer, but stood up. The Chinaman went to the door and opened it for them. Chi Seng found a bit of candle and lit it in order to light them down, and the two Chinese accompanied them to the street. They left the woman sitting quietly on the bed smoking a cigarette. When they reached the street the Chinese left them and went once more upstairs.

"What are you going to do with that letter?" asked Mr Joyce.

"Keep it."

They walked to where the car was waiting for them and here Mr Joyce offered his friend a lift. Crosbie shook his head.

"I'm going to walk." He hesitated a little and shuffled his feet. "I went to Singapore on the night of Hammond's death partly to buy a new gun that a man I knew wanted to dispose of. Good night."

He disappeared quickly into the darkness.

Mr Joyce was quite right about the trial. The assessors went into court fully determined to acquit Mrs Crosbie. She gave evidence on her own behalf. She told her story simply and with straightforwardness. The DPP was a kindly man and it was plain that he took no great pleasure in his task. He asked the necessary questions in a deprecating manner. His speech for the prosecution might really have been a speech for the defence, and the assessors took less than five minutes to consider their popular verdict. It was impossible to prevent the great outburst of applause with which it was received by the crowd that packed the courthouse. The judge congratulated Mrs Crosbie and she was a free woman.

No one had expressed a more violent disapprobation of Hammond's behaviour than Mrs Joyce; she was a woman loyal to her friends and she had insisted on the Crosbies staying with her after the trial, for she in common with everyone else had no doubt of the result, till they could make arrangements to go away. It was out of the question for poor, dear, brave Leslie to return to the bungalow at which the horrible catastrophe had taken place. The trial was over by half past twelve and when they reached the Joyces' house a grand luncheon was awaiting them. Cocktails were ready, Mrs Joyce's million-dollar cocktail was celebrated through all the Malay States, and Mrs Joyce drank Leslie's health. She was a talkative, vivacious woman, and now she was in the highest spirits. It was fortunate, for the rest of them were silent. She did not wonder; her husband never had much to say, and the other two were naturally exhausted from the long strain to which they had been subjected. During luncheon she carried on a bright and spirited monologue. Then coffee was served.

"Now, children," she said in her gay, bustling fashion, "you must have a rest and after tea I shall take you both for a drive to the sea."

Mr Joyce, who lunched at home only by exception, had of course to go back to his office.

"I'm afraid I can't do that, Mrs Joyce," said Crosbie. "I've got to get back to the estate at once."

"Not today?" she cried.

"Yes, now. I've neglected it for too long and I have urgent business. But I shall be very grateful if you will keep Leslie until we have decided what to do."

Mrs Joyce was about to expostulate, but her husband prevented her.

"If he must go, he must, and there's an end of it."

There was something in the lawyer's tone which made her look at him quickly. She held her tongue and there was a moment's silence. Then Crosbie spoke again.

"If you'll forgive me, I'll start at once so that I can get there before dark." He rose from the table. "Will you come and see me off, Leslie?"

"Of course."

They went out of the dining-room together.

"I think that's rather inconsiderate of him," said Mrs Joyce. "He must know that Leslie wants to be with him just now."

"I'm sure he wouldn't go if it wasn't absolutely necessary."

"Well, I'll just see that Leslie's room is ready for her. She wants a complete rest, of course, and then amusement."

Mrs Joyce left the room and Joyce sat down again. In a short time he heard Crosbie start the engine of his motor-cycle and then noisily scrunch over the gravel of the garden path. He got up and went into the drawing-room. Mrs Crosbie was standing in the middle of it, looking into space, and in her hand was an open letter. He recognized it. She gave him a glance as he came in and he saw that she was deathly pale.

"He knows," she whispered.

Mr Joyce went up to her and took the letter from her hand. He lit a match and set the paper afire. She watched it burn. When he could hold it no longer he dropped it on the tiled floor and they both looked at the paper curl and blacken. Then he trod it into ashes with his foot.

"What does he know?"

She gave him a long, long stare and into her eyes came a strange look. Was it contempt or despair? Mr Joyce could not tell.

"He knows that Geoff was my lover."

Mr Joyce made no movement and uttered no sound.

"He'd been my lover for years. He became my lover almost immediately after he came back from the war. We knew how careful we must be. When we became lovers I pretended I was tired of him, and he seldom came to the house when Robert was there. I used to drive out to a place we knew and he met me, two or three times a week, and when Robert went to Singapore he used to come to the bungalow late, when the boys had gone for the night. We saw one another constantly, all the time, and not a soul had the smallest suspicion of it. And then lately, a year ago, he began to change. I didn't know what was the matter. I couldn't believe that he didn't care for me any more. He always denied it. I was frantic. I made him scenes. Sometimes I thought he hated me. Oh, if you knew what agonies I endured. I passed through hell. I knew he didn't want me any more and I wouldn't let him go. Misery! Misery! I loved him. I'd given him everything. He was my life. And then I heard he was living with a Chinese woman. I couldn't believe it. I wouldn't believe it. At last I saw her, I saw her with my own eyes, walking in the village, with her gold bracelets and her necklaces, an old, fat Chinese woman. She was older than I was. Horrible! They all knew in the kampong that she was his mistress. And when I passed her, she looked at me and I knew that she knew I was his mistress too. I sent for him. I told him I must see him. You've read the letter. I was mad to write it. I didn't know what I was doing. I didn't care. I hadn't seen him for ten days. It was a lifetime. And when last we'd parted he took me in his arms and kissed me, and told me not to worry. And he went straight from my arms to hers."

She had been speaking in a low voice, vehemently, and now she stopped and wrung her hands.

"That damned letter. We'd always been so careful. He always tore up any word I wrote to him the moment he'd read it. How was I to know he'd leave that one? He came, and I told him I knew about the Chinawoman. He denied it. He said it was only scandal. I was beside myself. I don't know what I said to him. Oh, I hated him then. I tore him limb from limb. I said everything I could to wound him. I insulted him. I could have spat in his face. And at last he turned on me. He told me he was sick and tired of me and never wanted to see me again. He said I bored him to death. And then he acknowledged that it was true about the Chinawoman. He said he'd known her for years, before the war, and she was the only woman who really meant anything to him, and the rest was just pastime. And he said he was glad I knew and now at last I'd leave him alone. And then I don't know what happened, I was beside myself, I saw red. I seized the revolver and I fired. He gave a cry and I saw I'd hit him. He staggered and rushed for the veranda. I ran after him and fired again. He fell and then I stood over him and I fired till the revolver went click, click, and I knew there were no more cartridges."

At last she stopped, panting. Her face was no longer human, it was distorted with cruelty, and rage and pain. You would never have thought that this quiet, refined woman was capable of such fiendish passion. Mr Joyce took a step backwards. He was absolutely aghast at the sight of her. It was not a face, it was a gibbering, hideous mask. Then they heard a voice calling from another room, a loud, friendly, cheerful voice. It was Mrs Joyce.

"Come along, Leslie darling, your room's ready. You must be dropping with sleep."

Mrs Crosbie's features gradually composed themselves. Those passions, so clearly delineated, were smoothed away as with your hand you would smooth crumpled paper, and in a minute the face was cool and calm and unlined. She was a trifle pale, but her lips broke into a pleasant, affable smile. She was once more the well-bred and even distinguished woman.

"I'm coming, Dorothy dear. I'm sorry to give you so much trouble."

THE OUTSTATION

THE NEW ASSISTANT arrived in the afternoon. When the Resident, Mr Warburton, was told that the prahu was in sight he put on his solar topee and went down to the landing-stage. The guard, eight little Dyak soldiers, stood to attention as he passed. He noted with satisfaction that their bearing was martial, their uniforms neat and clean, and their guns shining. They were a credit to him. From the landing-stage he watched the bend of the river round which in a moment the boat would sweep. He looked very smart in his spotless ducks and white shoes. He held under his arm a gold-headed Malacca cane which had been given him by the Sultan of Perak. He awaited the newcomer with mingled feelings. There was more work in the district than one man could properly do, and during his periodical tours of the country under his charge it had been inconvenient to leave the station in the hands of a native clerk, but he had been so long the only white man there that he could not face the arrival of another without misgiving. He was accustomed to loneliness. During the war he had not seen an English face for three years; and once when he was instructed to put up an afforestation officer he was seized with panic, so that when the stranger was due to arrive, having arranged everything for his reception, he wrote a note telling him he was obliged to go up-river, and fled; he remained away till he was informed by a messenger that his guest had left.

Now the prahu appeared in the broad reach. It was manned by prisoners, Dyaks under various sentences, and a couple of warders were waiting on the landing-stage to take them back to gaol. They were sturdy fellows, used to the river, and they rowed with a powerful stroke. As the boat reached the side a man got out from under the attap awning and stepped on shore. The guard presented arms.

"Here we are at last. By God, I'm as cramped as the devil. I've brought you your mail."

He spoke with exuberant joviality. Mr Warburton politely held out his hand.

"Mr Cooper, I presume?"

"That's right. Were you expecting anyone else?"

The question had a facetious intent, but the Resident did not smile.

"My name is Warburton. I'll show you your quarters. They'll bring your kit along."

He preceded Cooper along the narrow pathway and they entered a compound in which stood a small bungalow.

"I've had it made as habitable as I could, but of course no one has lived in it for a good many years."

It was built on piles. It consisted of a long living-room which opened on to a broad veranda, and behind, on each side of a passage, were two bedrooms.

"This'll do me all right," said Cooper.

"I daresay you want to have a bath and a change. I shall be very much pleased if you'll dine with me tonight. Will eight o'clock suit you?"

"Any old time will do for me."

The Resident gave a polite, but slightly disconcerted smile, and withdrew. He returned to the Fort where his own residence was. The impression which Allen Cooper had given him was not very favourable, but he was a fair man, and he knew that it was unjust to form an opinion on so brief a glimpse. Cooper seemed to be about thirty. He was a tall, thin fellow, with a sallow face in which there was not a spot of colour. It was a face all in one tone. He had a large, hooked nose and blue eyes. When, entering the bungalow, he had taken off his topee and flung it to a waiting boy, Mr Warburton noticed that his large skull, covered with short, brown hair, contrasted somewhat oddly with a weak, small chin. He was dressed in khaki shorts and a khaki shirt, but they were shabby and soiled; and his battered topee had not been cleaned for days. Mr Warburton reflected that the young man had spent a week on a coasting steamer and had passed the last forty-eight hours lying in the bottom of a prahu.

"We'll see what he looks like when he comes in to dinner."

He went into his room, where his things were as neatly laid out as if he had an English valet, undressed, and, walking down the stairs to the bath-house, sluiced himself with cool water. The only concession he made to the climate was to wear a white dinner jacket; but otherwise, in a boiled shirt and a high collar, silk socks and patent-leather shoes, he dressed as formally as though he were dining at his club in Pall Mall. A careful host, he went into the dining-room to see that the table was properly laid. It was gay with orchids, and the silver shone brightly. The napkins were folded into elaborate shapes. Shaded candles in silver candlesticks shed a soft light. Mr Warburton smiled his approval and returned to the sitting-room to await his guest. Presently he appeared. Cooper was wearing the khaki shorts, the khaki shirt, and the ragged jacket in which he had landed. Mr Warburton's smile of greeting froze on his face.

"Hullo, you're all dressed up," said Cooper. "I didn't know you were going to do that. I very nearly put on a sarong."

"It doesn't matter at all. I daresay your boys were busy."

"You needn't have bothered to dress on my account, you know."

"I didn't. I always dress for dinner."

"Even when you're alone?"

"Especially when I'm alone," replied Mr Warburton, with a frigid stare.

He saw a twinkle of amusement in Cooper's eyes, and he flushed an angry red. Mr Warburton was a hot-tempered man; you might have guessed that from his red face with its pugnacious features and from his red hair now growing white; his blue eyes, cold as a rule and observing, could flash with sudden wrath; but he was a man of the world and he hoped a just one. He must do his best to get on with this fellow.

"When I lived in London I moved in circles in which it would have been just as eccentric not to dress for dinner every night as not to have a bath every morning. When I came to Borneo I saw no reason to discontinue so good a habit. For three years during the war I never saw a white man. I never omitted to dress on a single occasion on which I was well enough to come in to dinner. You have not been very long in this country; believe me, there is no better way to maintain the proper pride which you should have in yourself. When a white man surrenders in the slightest degree to the influences that surround him he very soon loses his self-respect, and when he loses his self-respect you may be quite sure the natives will soon cease to respect him."

"Well, if you expect me to put on a boiled shirt and a stiff collar in this heat I'm afraid you'll be disappointed."

"When you are dining in your own bungalow you will, of course, dress as you think fit, but when you do me the pleasure of dining with me, perhaps you will come to the conclusion that it is only polite to wear the costume usual in civilized society."

Two Malay boys, in sarongs and songkoks, with smart white coats and brass buttons, came in, one bearing gin pahits, and the other a tray on which were olives and anchovies. Then they went in to dinner. Mr Warburton flattered himself that he had the best cook, a Chinese, in Borneo, and he took great trouble to have as good food as in the difficult circumstances was possible. He exercised much ingenuity in making the best of his materials.

"Would you care to look at the menu?" he said, handing it to Cooper.

It was written in French and the dishes had resounding names. They were waited on by the two boys. In opposite corners of the room two more waved immense fans, and so gave movement to the sultry air. The fare was sumptuous and the champagne excellent.

"Do you do yourself like this every day?" said Cooper.

Mr Warburton gave the menu a careless glance.

"I have not noticed that the dinner is any different from usual," he said. "I eat very little myself, but I make a point of having a proper dinner served to me every night. It keeps the cook in practice and it's good discipline for the boys."

The conversation proceeded with effort. Mr Warburton was elaborately courteous and, it may be, found a slightly malicious amusement in the embarrassment which he thereby occasioned in his companion. Cooper had not been more than a few months in Sembulu, and Mr Warburton's inquiries about friends of his in Kuala Solor were soon exhausted.

"By the way," he said presently, "did you meet a lad called Hennerley? He's come out recently, I believe."

"Oh yes, he's in the police. A rotten bounder."

"I should hardly have expected him to be that. His uncle is my friend Lord Barraclough. I had a letter from Lady Barraclough only the other day asking me to look out for him."

"I heard he was related to somebody or other. I suppose that's how he got the job. He's been to Eton and Oxford and he doesn't forget to let you know it."

"You surprise me," said Mr Warburton. "All his family have been at Eton and Oxford for a couple of hundred years. I should have expected him to take it as a matter of course."

"I thought him a damned prig."

"To what school did you go?"

"I was born in Barbados. I was educated there."

"Oh, I see."

Mr Warburton managed to put so much offensiveness into his brief reply that Cooper flushed. For a moment he was silent.

"I've had two or three letters from Kuala Solor," continued Mr Warburton, "and my impression was that young Hennerley was a great success. They say he's a first-rate sportsman."

"Oh, yes, he's very popular. He's just the sort of fellow they would like in KS. I haven't got much use for the first-rate sportsman myself. What does it amount to in the long run that a man can play golf and tennis better than other people? And who cares if he can make a break of seventy-five at billiards? They attach a damned sight too much importance to that sort of thing in England."

"Do you think so? I was under the impression that the first-rate sportsman had come out of the war certainly no worse than anyone else."

"Oh, if you're going to talk of the war then I do know what I'm talking about. I was in the same regiment as Hennerley and I can tell you that the men couldn't stick him at any price."

"How do you know?"

"Because I was one of the men."

"Oh, you hadn't got a commission."

"A fat chance I had of getting a commission. I was what was called a Colonial. I hadn't been to a public school and I had no influence. I was in the ranks the whole damned time."

Cooper frowned. He seemed to have difficulty in preventing himself from breaking out into violent invective. Mr Warburton watched him, his little blue eyes narrowed, watched him and formed his opinion. Changing the conversation, he began to speak to Cooper about the work that would be required of him, and as the clock struck ten he rose.

"Well, I won't keep you any more. I daresay you're tired by your journey."

They shook hands.

"Oh, I say, look here," said Cooper, "I wonder if you can find me a boy. The boy I had before never turned up when I was starting from KS. He took my kit on board and all that, and then disappeared. I didn't know he wasn't there till we were out on the river."

"I'll ask my head-boy. I have no doubt he can find you someone."

"All right. Just tell him to send the boy along and if I like the look of him I'll take him."

There was a moon, so that no lantern was needed. Cooper walked across from the Fort to his bungalow.

"I wonder why on earth they've sent me a fellow like that?" reflected Mr Warburton. "If that's the kind of man they're going to get out now I don't think much of it."

He strolled down his garden. The Fort was built on the top of a little hill and the garden ran down to the river's edge; on the bank was an arbour, and hither it was his habit to come after dinner to smoke a cheroot. And often from the river that flowed below him a voice was heard, the voice of some Malay too timorous to venture into the light of day, and a complaint or an accusation was softly wafted to his ears, a piece of information was whispered to him or a useful hint, which otherwise would never have come into his official ken. He threw himself heavily into a long rattan chair. Cooper! An envious, ill-bred fellow, bumptious, self-assertive, and vain. But Mr Warburton's irritation could not withstand the silent beauty of the night. The air was scented with the sweet-smelling flowers of a tree that grew at the entrance to the arbour, and the fire-flies, sparkling dimly, flew with their slow and silvery flight. The moon made a pathway on the broad river for the light feet of Sila's bride, and on the further bank a row of palm trees was delicately silhouetted against the sky. Peace stole into the soul of Mr Warburton.

He was a queer creature and he had had a singular career. At the age of twenty-one he had inherited a considerable fortune, a hundred thousand pounds, and when he left Oxford he threw himself into the gay life, which in those days (now Mr Warburton was a man of four-and-fifty) offered itself to the young man of good family. He had his flat in Mount Street, his private hansom, and his hunting-box in Warwickshire. He went to all the places where the fashionable congregate. He was handsome, amusing, and generous. He was a figure in the society of London in the early 'nineties, and society then had not lost its exclusiveness nor its brilliance. The Boer War which shook it was unthought of; the Great War which destroyed it was prophesied only by the pessimists. It was no unpleasant thing to be a rich young man in those days, and Mr Warburton's chimney-piece during the season was packed with cards for one great function after another. Mr Warburton displayed them with complacency. For Mr Warburton was a snob. He was not a timid snob, a little ashamed of being impressed by his betters, nor a snob who sought the intimacy of persons who had acquired celebrity in politics or notoriety in the arts, nor the snob who was dazzled by riches; he was the naked, unadulterated common snob who dearly loved a lord. He was touchy and quick-tempered, but he would much rather have been snubbed by a person of quality than flattered by a commoner. His name figured insignificantly in Burke's Peerage, and it was marvellous to watch the ingenuity he used to mention his distant relationship to the noble family he belonged to; but never a word did he say of the honest Liverpool manufacturer from whom, through his mother, a Miss Gubbins, he had come by his fortune. It was the terror of his fashionable life that at Cowes, maybe, or at Ascot, when he was with a duchess or even with a prince of the blood, one of these relatives would claim acquaintance with him.

His failing was too obvious not soon to become notorious, but its extravagance saved it from being merely despicable. The great whom he adored laughed at him, but in their hearts felt his adoration not unnatural. Poor Warburton was a dreadful snob, of course, but after all he was a good fellow. He was always ready to back a bill for an impecunious nobleman, and if you were in a tight corner you could safely count on him for a hundred pounds. He gave good dinners. He played whist badly, but never minded how much he lost if the company was select. He happened to be a gambler, an unlucky one, but he was a good loser, and it was impossible not to admire the coolness with which he lost five hundred pounds at a sitting. His passion for cards, almost as strong as his passion for titles, was the cause of his undoing. The life he led was expensive and his gambling losses were formidable. He began to plunge more heavily, first on horses, and then on the Stock Exchange. He had a certain simplicity of character, and the unscrupulous found him an ingenuous prey. I do not know if he ever realized that his smart friends laughed at him behind his back, but I think he had an obscure instinct that he could not afford to appear other than careless of his money. He got into the hands of money-lenders. At the age of thirty-four he was ruined.

He was too much imbued with the spirit of his class to hesitate in the choice of his next step. When a man in his set had run through his money, he went out to the colonies. No one heard Mr Warburton repine. He made no complaint because a noble friend had advised a disastrous speculation, he pressed nobody to whom he had lent money to repay it, he paid his debts (if he had only known it, the despised blood of the Liverpool manufacturer came out in him there), sought help from no one, and, never having done a stroke of work in his life, looked for a means of livelihood. He remained cheerful, unconcerned, and full of humour. He had no wish to make anyone with whom he happened to be uncomfortable by the recital of his misfortune. Mr Warburton was a snob, but he was also a gentleman.

The only favour he asked of any of the great friends in whose daily company he had lived for years was a recommendation. The able man who was at that time Sultan of Sembulu took him into his service. The night before he sailed he dined for the last time at his club.

"I hear you're going away, Warburton," the old Duke of Hereford said to him.

"Yes, I'm going to Borneo."

"Good God, what are you going there for?"

"Oh, I'm broke."

"Are you? I'm sorry. Well, let us know when you come back. I hope you have a good time."

"Oh yes. Lots of shooting, you know."

The Duke nodded and passed on. A few hours later Mr Warburton watched the coast of England recede into the mist, and he left behind everything which to him made life worth living.

Twenty years had passed since then. He kept up a busy correspondence with various great ladies and his letters were amusing and chatty. He never lost his love for titled persons and paid careful attention to the announcements in *The Times* (which reached him six weeks after publication) of their comings and goings. He perused the column which records births, deaths, and marriages, and he was always ready with his letter of congratulation or condolence. The illustrated papers told him how people looked and on his periodical visits to England, able to take up the threads as though they had never been broken, he knew all about any new person who might have appeared on the social surface. His interest in the world of fashion was as vivid as when he himself had been a figure in it. It still seemed to him the only thing that mattered.

But insensibly another interest had entered into his life. The position he found himself in flattered his vanity; he was no longer the sycophant craving the smiles of the great, he was the master whose word was law. He was gratified by the guard of Dyak soldiers who presented arms as he passed. He liked to sit in judgement on his fellow men. It pleased him to compose quarrels between rival chiefs. When the head-hunters were troublesome in the old days he set out to chastise them with a thrill of pride in his own behaviour. He was too vain not to be of dauntless courage, and a pretty story was told of his coolness in adventuring single-handed into a stockaded village and demanding the surrender of a bloodthirsty pirate. He became a skilful administrator. He was strict, just, and honest.

And little by little he conceived a deep love for the Malays. He interested himself in their habits and customs. He was never tired of listening to their talk. He admired their virtues, and with a smile and a shrug of the shoulders condoned their vices.

"In my day," he would say, "I have been on intimate terms with some of the greatest gentlemen in England, but I have never known finer gentlemen than some well-born Malays whom I am proud to call my friends."

He liked their courtesy and their distinguished manners, their gentleness and their sudden passions. He knew by instinct exactly how to treat them. He had a genuine tenderness for them. But he never forgot that he was an English gentleman, and he had no patience with the white men who yielded to native customs. He made no surrenders. And he did not imitate so many of the white men in taking a native woman to wife, for an intrigue of this nature, however sanctified by custom, seemed to him not only shocking but undignified. A man who had been called George by Albert Edward, Prince of Wales, could hardly be expected to have any connexion with a native. And when he returned to Borneo from his visits to England it was now with something like relief. His friends, like himself, were no longer young, and there was a new generation which looked upon him as a tiresome old man. It seemed to him that the England of today had lost a good deal of what he had loved in the England of his youth. But Borneo remained the same. It was home to him now. He meant to remain in service as long as was possible, and the hope in his heart was that he would die before at last he was forced to retire. He had stated in his will that wherever he died he wished his body to be brought back to Sembulu, and buried among the people he loved within the sound of the softly flowing river.

But these emotions he kept hidden from the eyes of men; and no one, seeing this spruce, stout, well-set-up man, with his clean-shaven strong face and his whitening hair, would have dreamed that he cherished so profound a sentiment.

He knew how the work of the station should be done, and during the next few days he kept a suspicious eye on his assistant. He saw very soon that he was painstaking and competent. The only fault he had to find with him was that he was brusque with the natives.

"The Malays are shy and very sensitive," he said to him. "I think you will find that you will get much better results if you take care always to be polite, patient, and kindly."

Cooper gave a short, grating laugh.

"I was born in Barbados and I was in Africa in the war. I don't think there's much about niggers that I don't know."

"I know nothing," said Mr Warburton acidly. "But we were not talking of them. We were taking of Malays."

"Aren't they niggers?"

"You are very ignorant," replied Mr Warburton.

He said no more.

On the first Sunday after Cooper's arrival he asked him to dinner. He did everything ceremoniously, and though they had met on the previous day in the office and later, on the Fort veranda where they drank a gin and bitters together at six o'clock, he sent a polite note across to the bungalow by a boy. Cooper, however unwillingly, came in evening dress and Mr Warburton, though gratified that his wish was respected, noticed with disdain that the young man's clothes were badly cut and his shirt ill-fitting. But Mr Warburton was in a good temper that evening.

"By the way," he said to him, as he shook hands, "I've talked to my head-boy about finding you someone and he recommends his nephew. I've seen him and he seems a bright and willing lad. Would you like to see him?"

"I don't mind."

"He's waiting now."

Mr Warburton called his boy and told him to send for his nephew. In a moment a tall, slender youth of twenty appeared. He had large dark eyes and a good profile. He was very neat in his sarong, a little white coat, and a fez, without a tassel, of plum-coloured velvet. He answered to the name of Abas. Mr Warburton looked on him with approval, and his manner insensibly softened as he spoke to him in fluent and idiomatic Malay. He was inclined to be sarcastic with white people, but with the Malays he had a happy mixture of condescension and kindliness. He stood in the place of the Sultan. He knew perfectly how to preserve his own dignity and at the same time put a native at his ease.

"Will he do?" said Mr Warburton, turning to Cooper.

"Yes, I daresay he's no more of a scoundrel than any of the rest of them."

Mr Warburton informed the boy that he was engaged, and dismissed him.

"You're very lucky to get a boy like that," he told Cooper. "He belongs to a very good family. They came over from Malacca nearly a hundred years ago."

"I don't much mind if the boy who cleans my shoes and brings me a drink when I want it has blue blood in his veins or not. All I ask is that he should do what I tell him and look sharp about it."

Mr Warburton pursed his lips, but made no reply.

They went in to dinner. It was excellent, and the wine was good. Its influence presently had its effect on them, and they talked not only without acrimony, but even with friendliness. Mr Warburton liked to do himself well, and on Sunday night he made it a habit to do himself even a little better than usual. He began to think he was unfair to Cooper. Of course he was not a gentleman, but that was not his fault, and when you got to know him it might be that he would turn out a very good fellow. His faults, perhaps, were faults of manner. And he was certainly good at his work, quick, conscientious, and thorough. When they reached the dessert Mr Warburton was feeling kindly disposed towards all mankind.

"This is your first Sunday, and I'm going to give you a very special glass of port. I've only got about two dozen of it left and I keep it for special occasions."

He gave his boy instructions and presently the bottle was brought. Mr Warburton watched the boy open it.

"I got this port from my old friend Charles Hollington. He'd had it for forty years, and I've had it for a good many. He was well-known to have the best cellar in England."

"Is he a wine merchant?"

"Not exactly," smiled Mr Warburton. "I was speaking of Lord Hollington of Castle Reagh. He's one of the richest peers in England. A very old friend of mine. I was at Eton with his brother."

This was an opportunity that Mr Warburton could never resist, and he told a little anecdote of which the only point seemed to be that he knew an Earl. The port was certainly very good; he drank a glass and then a second. He lost all caution. He had not talked to a white man for months. He began to tell stories. He showed himself in the company of the great. Hearing him, you would have thought that at one time ministries were formed and policies decided on his suggestion whispered into the ear of a duchess or thrown over the dinner-table to be gratefully acted on by the confidential adviser of the Sovereign. The old days at Ascot, Goodwood, and Cowes lived again for him. Another glass of port. There were the great house-parties in Yorkshire and in Scotland to which he went every year.

"I had a man called Foreman then, the best valet I ever had, and why do you think he gave me notice? You know in the Housekeeper's Room the ladies' maids and the gentlemen's gentlemen sit according to the precedence of their masters. He told me he was sick of going to party after party at which I was the only commoner. It meant that he always had to sit at the bottom of the table, and all the best bits were taken before a dish reached him. I told the story to the old Duke of Hereford, and he roared. 'By God, sir,' he said, 'if I were King of England, I'd make you a viscount just to give your man a chance.' 'Take him yourself, Duke,' I said. 'He's the best valet I've ever had.' 'Well, Warburton,' he said, 'if he's good enough for you he's good enough for me. Send him along.'"

Then there was Monte Carlo, where Mr Warburton and the Grand Duke Fyodor, playing in partnership, had broken the bank one evening; and there was Marienbad. At Marienbad Mr Warburton had played baccarat with Edward VII.

"He was only Prince of Wales then, of course. I remember him saying to me, 'George, if you draw on a five you'll lose your shirt.' He was right; I don't think he ever said a truer word in his life. He was a wonderful man. I always said he was the greatest diplomatist in Europe. But I was a young fool in those days, I hadn't the sense to take his advice. If I had, if I'd never drawn on a five, I daresay I shouldn't be here today."

Cooper was watching him. His brown eyes, deep in their sockets, were hard and supercilious, and on his lips was a mocking smile. He had heard a good deal about Mr Warburton in Kuala Solor, not a bad sort, and he ran his district like clockwork, they said, but by heaven, what a snob! They laughed at him good-naturedly, for it was impossible to dislike a man who was so generous and so kindly, and Cooper had already heard the story of the Prince of Wales and the game of baccarat. But Cooper listened without indulgence. From the beginning he had resented the Resident's manner. He was very sensitive, and he writhed under Mr Warburton's polite sarcasms. Mr Warburton had a knack of receiving a remark of which he disapproved with a devastating silence. Cooper had lived little in England and he had a peculiar dislike of the English. He resented especially the public-school boy since he always feared that he was going to patronize him. He was so much afraid of others putting on airs with him that, in order as it were to get in first, he put on such airs as to make everyone think him insufferably conceited.

"Well, at all events the war has done one good thing for us," he said at last. "It's smashed up the power of the aristocracy. The Boer War started it, and 1914 put the lid on."

"The great families of England are doomed," said Mr Warburton with the complacent melancholy of an *émigré* who remembered the court of Louis XV. "They cannot afford any longer to live in their splendid palaces and their princely hospitality will soon be nothing but a memory."

"And a damned good job too in my opinion."

"My poor Cooper, what can you know of the glory that was Greece and the grandeur that was Rome?"

Mr Warburton made an ample gesture. His eyes for an instant grew dreamy with a vision of the past.

"Well, believe me, we're fed up with all that rot. What we want is a business government by business men. I was born in a Crown Colony, and I've lived practically all my life in the colonies. I don't give a row of pins for a lord. What's wrong with England is snobbishness. And if there's anything that gets my goat it's a snob."

A snob! Mr Warburton's face grew purple and his eyes blazed with anger. That was a word that had pursued him all his life. The great ladies whose society he had enjoyed in his youth were not inclined to look upon his appreciation of themselves as unworthy, but even great ladies are sometimes out of temper and more than once Mr Warburton had had the dreadful word flung in his teeth. He knew, he could not help knowing, that there were odious people who called him a snob. How unfair it was! Why, there was no vice he found so detestable as snobbishness. After all, he liked to mix with people of his own class, he was only at home in their company, and how in heaven's name could anyone say that was snobbish? Birds of a feather.

"I quite agree with you," he answered. "A snob is a man who admires or despises another because he is of a higher social rank than his own. It is the most vulgar failing of our English middle-class."

He saw a flicker of amusement in Cooper's eyes. Cooper put up his hand to hide the broad smile that rose to his lips, and so made it more noticeable. Mr Warburton's hands trembled a little.

Probably Cooper never knew how greatly he had offended his chief. A sensitive man himself, he was strangely insensitive to the feelings of others.

Their work forced them to see one another for a few minutes now and then during the day, and they met at six to have a drink on Mr Warburton's veranda. This was an old-established custom of the country which Mr Warburton would not for the world have broken. But they ate their meals separately, Cooper in his bungalow and Mr Warburton at the Fort. After the office work was over they walked till dusk fell, but they walked apart. There were but few paths in this country where the jungle pressed close upon the plantations of the village, and when Mr Warburton caught sight of his assistant passing along with his loose stride, he would make a circuit in order to avoid him. Cooper, with his bad manners, his conceit in his own judgement, and his intolerance, had already got on his nerves; but it was not till Cooper had been on the station for a couple of months that an incident happened which turned the Resident's dislike into bitter hatred.

Mr Warburton was obliged to go up-country on a tour of inspection, and he left the station in Cooper's charge with more confidence, since he had definitely come to the conclusion that he was a capable fellow. The only thing he did not like was that he had no indulgence. He was honest, just, and painstaking, but he had no sympathy for the natives. It bitterly amused Mr Warburton to observe that this man who looked upon himself as every man's equal should look upon so many men as his own inferiors. He was hard, he had no patience with the native mind, and he was a bully. Mr Warburton very quickly realized that the Malays disliked and feared him. He was not altogether displeased. He would not have liked it very much if his assistant had enjoyed a popularity which might rival his own. Mr Warburton made his elaborate preparations, set out on his expedition, and in three weeks returned. Meanwhile the mail had arrived. The first thing that struck his eyes when he entered his sitting-room was a great pile of open newspapers. Cooper had met him, and they went into the room together. Mr Warburton turned to one of the servants who had been left behind, and sternly asked him what was the meaning of those open papers. Cooper hastened to explain.

"I wanted to read all about the Wolverhampton murder, and so I borrowed your *Times*. I brought them back again. I knew you wouldn't mind."

Mr Warburton turned on him, white with anger.

"But I do mind. I mind very much."

"I'm sorry," said Cooper, with composure. "The fact is, I simply couldn't wait till you came back."

"I wonder you didn't open my letters as well."

Cooper, unmoved, smiled at his chief's exasperation.

"Oh, that's not quite the same thing. After all, I couldn't imagine you'd mind my looking at your newspapers. There's nothing private in them."

"I very much object to anyone reading my paper before me." He went up to the pile. There were nearly thirty numbers there. "I think it extremely impertinent of you. They're all mixed up."

"We can easily put them in order," said Cooper, joining him at the table.

"Don't touch them," cried Mr Warburton.

"I say, it's childish to make a scene about a little thing like that."

"How dare you speak to me like that?"

"Oh, go to hell," said Cooper, and he flung out of the room.

Mr Warburton, trembling with passion, was left contemplating his papers. His greatest pleasure in life had been destroyed by those callous, brutal hands. Most people living in out-of-the-way places when the mail comes tear open impatiently their papers and taking the last ones first glance at the latest news from home. Not so Mr Warburton. His newsagent had instructions to write on the outside of the wrapper the date of each paper he dispatched, and when the great bundle arrived Mr Warburton looked at these dates and with his blue pencil numbered them. His head-boy's orders were to place one on the table every morning in the veranda with the early cup of tea and it was Mr Warburton's especial delight to break the wrapper as he sipped his tea, and read the morning paper. It gave him the illusion of living at home. Every Monday morning he read the Monday *Times* of six weeks back, and so went through the week. On Sunday he read the *Observer*. Like his habit of dressing for dinner it was a tie to civilization. And it was his pride that no matter how exciting the news was he had never yielded to the temptation of opening a paper before its allotted time. During the war the suspense sometimes had been intolerable, and when he read one day that a push was begun he had undergone agonies of suspense which he might have saved himself by the simple expedient of opening a later paper which lay waiting for him on a shelf. It had been the severest trial to which he had ever exposed himself, but he victoriously surmounted it. And that clumsy fool had broken open those neat tight packages because he wanted to know whether some horrid woman had murdered her odious husband.

Mr Warburton sent for his boy and told him to bring wrappers. He folded up the papers as neatly as he could, placed a wrapper round each and numbered it. But it was a melancholy task.

"I shall never forgive him," he said. "Never."

Of course his boy had been with him on his expedition; he never travelled without him, for his boy knew exactly how he liked things, and Mr Warburton was not the kind of jungle traveller who was prepared to dispense with his comforts; but in the interval since their arrival he had been gossiping in the servants' quarters. He had learnt that Cooper had had trouble with his boys. All but the youth Abas had left him. Abas had desired to go too, but his uncle had placed him there on the instructions of the Resident, and he was afraid to leave without his uncle's permission.

"I told him he had done well, Tuan," said the boy. "But he is unhappy. He says it is not a good house, and he wishes to know if he may go as the others have gone."

"No, he must stay. The Tuan must have servants. Have those who went been replaced?"

"No, Tuan, no one will go."

Mr Warburton frowned. Cooper was an insolent fool, but he had an official position and must be suitably provided with servants. It was not seemly that his house should be improperly conducted.

"Where are the boys who ran away?"

"They are in the kampong, Tuan."

"Go and see them tonight, and tell them that I expect them to be back in Tuan Cooper's house at dawn tomorrow."

"They say they will not go, Tuan."

"On my order?"

The boy had been with Mr Warburton for fifteen years, and he knew every intonation of his master's voice. He was not afraid of him, they had gone through too much together, once in the jungle the Resident had saved his life, and once, upset in some rapids, but for him the Resident would have been drowned; but he knew when the Resident must be obeyed without question.

"I will go to the kampong," he said.

Mr Warburton expected that his subordinate would take the first opportunity to apologize for his rudeness, but Cooper had the ill-bred man's inability to express regret; and when they met next morning in the office he ignored the incident. Since Mr Warburton had been away for three weeks it was necessary for them to have a somewhat prolonged interview. At the end of it, Mr Warburton dismissed him.

"I don't think there's anything else, thank you." Cooper turned to go, but Mr Warburton stopped him. "I understand you've been having some trouble with your boys."

Cooper gave a harsh laugh.

"They tried to blackmail me. They had the damned cheek to run away, all except that incompetent fellow Abas – he knew when he was well off – but I just sat tight. They've all come to heel again."

"What do you mean by that?"

"This morning they were all back on their jobs, the Chinese cook and all. There they were, as cool as cucumbers; you would have thought they owned the place. I suppose they'd come to the conclusion that I wasn't such a fool as I looked."

"By no means. They came back on my express order."

Cooper flushed slightly.

"I should be obliged if you wouldn't interfere with my private concerns."

"They're not your private concerns. When your servants run away it makes you ridiculous. You are perfectly free to make a fool of yourself, but I cannot allow you to be made a fool of. It is unseemly that your house should not be properly staffed. As soon as I heard that your boys had left you, I had them told to be back in their places at dawn. That'll do."

Mr Warburton nodded to signify that the interview was at an end. Cooper took no notice.

"Shall I tell you what I did? I called them and gave the whole bally lot the sack. I gave them ten minutes to get out of the compound."

Mr Warburton shrugged his shoulders.

"What makes you think you can get others?"

"I've told my own clerk to see about it."

Mr Warburton reflected for a moment.

"I think you behaved very foolishly. You will do well to remember in future that good masters make good servants."

"Is there anything else you want to teach me?"

"I should like to teach you manners, but it would be an arduous task, and I have not the time to waste. I will see that you get boys."

"Please don't put yourself to any trouble on my account. I'm quite capable of getting them for myself."

Mr Warburton smiled acidly. He had an inkling that Cooper disliked him as much as he disliked Cooper, and he knew that nothing is more galling than to be forced to accept the favours of a man you detest.

"Allow me to tell you that you have no more chance of getting Malay or Chinese servants here now than you have of getting an English butler or a French chef. No one will come to you except on an order from me. Would you like me to give it?"

"No."

"As you please. Good morning."

Mr Warburton watched the development of the situation with acrid humour. Cooper's clerk was unable to persuade Malay, Dyak, or Chinese to enter the house of such a master. Abas, the boy who remained faithful to him, knew how to cook only native food, and Cooper, a coarse feeder, found his gorge rise against the everlasting rice. There was no water-carrier, and in that great heat he needed several baths a day. He cursed Abas, but Abas opposed him with sullen resistance and would not do more than he chose. It was galling to know that the lad stayed with him only because the Resident insisted. This went on for a fortnight and then, one morning, he found in his house the very servants whom he had previously dismissed. He fell into a violent rage, but he had learnt a little sense, and this time, without a word, he let them stay. He swallowed his humiliation, but the impatient contempt he had felt for Mr Warburton's idiosyncrasies changed into a sullen hatred: the Resident with this malicious stroke had made him the laughing-stock of all the natives.

The two men now held no communication with one another. They broke the time-honoured custom of sharing, notwithstanding personal dislike, a drink at six o'clock with any white man who happened to be at the station. Each lived in his own house as though the other did not exist. Now that Cooper had fallen into the work, it was necessary for them to have little to do with one another in the office. Mr Warburton used his orderly to send any message he had to give his assistant, and his instructions he sent by formal letter. They saw one another constantly, that was inevitable, but did not exchange half a dozen words in a week. The fact that they could not avoid catching sight of one another got on their nerves. They brooded over their antagonism, and Mr Warburton, taking his daily walk, could think of nothing but how much he detested his assistant.

And the dreadful thing was that in all probability they would remain thus, facing each other in deadly enmity, till Mr Warburton went on leave. It might be three years. He had no reason to send in a complaint to headquarters: Cooper did his work very well, and at that time men were hard to get. True, vague complaints reached him and hints that the natives found Cooper harsh. There was certainly a feeling of dissatisfaction among them. But when Mr Warburton looked into specific cases, all he could say was that Cooper had shown severity where mildness would not have been misplaced, and had been unfeeling when he himself would have been sympathetic. He had done nothing for which he could be taken to task. But Mr Warburton watched him. Hatred will often make a man clear-sighted, and he had a suspicion that Cooper was using the natives without consideration, yet keeping within the law, because he felt that thus he could exasperate his chief. One day perhaps he would go too far. None knew better than Mr Warburton how irritable the incessant heat could make a man and how difficult it was to keep one's self-control after a sleepless night. He smiled softly to himself. Sooner or later Cooper would deliver himself into his hand.

When at last the opportunity came, Mr Warburton laughed aloud. Cooper had charge of the prisoners; they made roads, built sheds, rowed when it was necessary to send the prahu up or down stream, kept the town clean, and otherwise usefully employed themselves. If well-behaved they even on occasion served as house-boys. Cooper kept them hard at it. He liked to see them work. He took pleasure in devising tasks for them; and seeing quickly enough that they were being made to do useless things the prisoners worked badly. He punished them by lengthening their hours. This was contrary to the regulations, and as soon as it was brought to the attention of Mr Warburton, without referring the matter back to his subordinate, he gave instructions that the old hours should be kept; Cooper, going out for his walk, was astounded to see the prisoners strolling back to the gaol; he had given instructions that they were not to knock off till dusk. When he asked the warder in charge why they had left off work he was told that it was the Resident's bidding.

White with rage he strode to the Fort. Mr Warburton, in his spotless white ducks and his neat topee, with a walking-stick in his hand, followed by his dogs, was on the point of starting out on his afternoon stroll. He had watched Cooper go, and knew that he had taken the road by the river. Cooper jumped up the steps and went straight up to the Resident.

"I want to know what the hell you mean by countermanding my order that the prisoners were to work till six," he burst out, beside himself with fury.

Mr Warburton opened his cold blue eyes very wide and assumed an expression of great surprise.

"Are you out of your mind? Are you so ignorant that you do not know that that is not the way to speak to your official superior?"

"Oh, go to hell. The prisoners are my pidgin, and you've got no right to interfere. You mind your business and I'll mind mine. I want to know what the devil you mean by making a damned fool of me. Everyone in the place will know that you've countermanded my order."

Mr Warburton kept very cool.

"You had no power to give the order you did. I countermanded it because it was harsh and tyrannical. Believe me, I have not made half such a damned fool of you as you have made of yourself."

"You disliked me from the first moment I came here. You've done everything you could to make the place impossible for me because I wouldn't lick your boots for you. You got your knife into me because I wouldn't flatter you."

Cooper, spluttering with rage, was nearing dangerous ground, and Mr Warburton's eyes grew on a sudden colder and more piercing.

"You are wrong. I thought you were a cad, but I was perfectly satisfied with the way you did your work."

"You snob. You damned snob. You thought me a cad because I hadn't been to Eton. Oh, they told me in KS what to expect. Why, don't you know that you're the laughing-stock of the whole country? I could hardly help bursting into a roar of laughter when you told your celebrated story about the Prince of Wales. My God, how they shouted at the club when they told it. By God, I'd rather be the cad I am than the snob you are."

He got Mr Warburton on the raw.

"If you don't get out of my house this minute I shall knock you down," he cried.

The other came a little closer to him and put his face in his.

"Touch me, touch me," he said. "By God, I'd like to see you hit me. Do you want me to say it again? Snob. Snob."

Cooper was three inches taller than Mr Warburton, a strong, muscular young man. Mr Warburton was fat and fifty-four. His clenched fist shot out. Cooper caught him by the arm and pushed him back.

"Don't be a damned fool. Remember I'm not a gentleman. I know how to use my hands."

He gave a sort of hoot, and grinning all over his pale, sharp face jumped down the veranda steps. Mr Warburton, his heart in his anger pounding against his ribs, sank exhausted into a chair. His body tingled as though he had prickly heat. For one horrible moment he thought he was going to cry. But suddenly he was conscious that his head-boy was on the veranda and instinctively regained control of himself. The boy came forward and filled him a glass of whisky and soda. Without a word Mr Warburton took it and drank it to the dregs.

"What do you want to say to me?" asked Mr Warburton, trying to force a smile on to his strained lips.

"Tuan, the assistant Tuan is a bad man. Abas wishes again to leave him."

"Let him wait a little. I shall write to Kuala Solor and ask that Tuan Cooper should go elsewhere."

"Tuan Cooper is not good with the Malays."

"Leave me."

The boy silently withdrew. Mr Warburton was left alone with his thoughts. He saw the club at Kuala Solor, the men sitting round the table in the window in their flannels, when the night had driven them in from golf and tennis, drinking whiskies and gin pahits, and laughing when they told the celebrated story of the Prince of Wales and himself at Marienbad. He was hot with shame and misery. A snob! They all thought him a snob. And he had always thought them very good fellows, he had always been gentleman enough to let it make no difference to him that they were of very second-rate position. He hated them now. But his hatred for them was nothing compared with his hatred for Cooper. And if it had come to blows Cooper could have thrashed him. Tears of mortification ran down his red, fat face. He sat there for a couple of hours smoking cigarette after cigarette, and he wished he were dead.

At last the boy came back and asked him if he would dress for dinner. Of course! He always dressed for dinner. He rose wearily from his chair and put on his stiff shirt and the high collar. He sat down at the prettily decorated table, and was waited on as usual by the two boys while two others waved their great fans. Over there in the bungalow, two hundred yards away, Cooper was eating a filthy meal clad only in a sarong and a baju. His feet were bare and while he ate he probably read a detective story. After dinner Mr Warburton sat down to write a letter. The Sultan was away, but he wrote, privately and confidentially, to his representative. Cooper did his work very well, he said, but the fact was that he couldn't get on with him. They were getting dreadfully on each other's nerves and he would look upon it as a very great favour if Cooper could be transferred to another post.

He dispatched the letter next morning by special messenger. The answer came a fortnight later with the month's mail. It was a private note, and ran as follows:

My dear Warburton,

I do not want to answer your letter officially, and so I am writing you a few lines myself. Of course if you insist I will put the matter up to the Sultan, but I think you would be much wiser to drop it. I know Cooper is a rough diamond, but he is capable, and he had a pretty thin time in the war, and I think he should be given every chance. I think you are a little too much inclined to attach importance to a man's social position. You must remember that times have changed. Of course it's a very good thing for a man to be a gentleman, but it's better that he should be competent and hard-working. I think if you'll exercise a little tolerance you'll get on very well with Cooper.

Yours very sincerely,
Richard Temple

The letter dropped from Mr Warburton's hand. It was easy to read between the lines. Dick Temple, whom he had known for twenty years, Dick Temple who came from quite a good county family, thought him a snob, and for that reason had no patience with his request. Mr Warburton felt on a sudden discouraged with life. The world of which he was a part had passed away and the future belonged to a meaner generation. Cooper represented it and Cooper he hated with all his heart. He stretched out his hand to fill his glass, and at the gesture his head-boy stepped forward.

"I didn't know you were there."

The boy picked up the official letter. Ah, that was why he was waiting.

"Does Tuan Cooper go, Tuan?"

"No."

"There will be a misfortune."

For a moment the words conveyed nothing to his lassitude. But only for a moment. He sat up in his chair and looked at the boy. He was all attention.

"What do you mean by that?"

"Tuan Cooper is not behaving rightly with Abas."

Mr Warburton shrugged his shoulders. How should a man like Cooper know how to treat servants? Mr Warburton knew the type: he would be grossly familiar with them at one moment and rude and inconsiderate the next.

"Let Abas go back to his family."

"Tuan Cooper holds back his wages so that he may not run away. He has paid him nothing for three months. I tell him to be patient. But he is angry, he will not listen to reason. If the Tuan continues to use him ill there will be a misfortune."

"You were right to tell me."

The fool! Did he know so little of the Malays as to think he could safely injure them? It would serve him damned well right if he got a kris in his back. A kris. Mr Warburton's heart seemed on a sudden to miss a beat. He had only to let things take their course and one fine day he would be rid of Cooper. He smiled faintly as the phrase, a masterly inactivity, crossed his mind. And now his heart beat a little quicker, for he saw the man he hated lying on his face in a pathway of the jungle with a knife in his back. A fit end for the cad and the bully.

Mr Warburton sighed. It was his duty to warn him, and of course he must do it. He wrote a brief and formal note to Cooper asking him to come to the Fort at once.

In ten minutes Cooper stood before him. They had not spoken to one another since the day when Mr Warburton had nearly struck him. He did not now ask him to sit down.

"Did you wish to see me?" asked Cooper.

He was untidy and none too clean. His face and hands were covered with little red blotches where mosquitoes had bitten him and he had scratched himself till the blood came. His long, thin face bore a sullen look.

"I understand that you are again having trouble with your servants. Abas, my head-boy's nephew, complains that you have held back his wages for three months. I consider it a most arbitrary proceeding. The lad wishes to leave you, and I certainly do not blame him. I must insist on your paying what is due to him."

"I don't choose that he should leave me. I am holding back his wages as a pledge of his good behaviour."

"You do not know the Malay character. The Malays are very sensitive to injury and ridicule. They are passionate and revengeful. It is my duty to warn you that if you drive this boy beyond a certain point you run a great risk."

Cooper gave a contemptuous chuckle.

"What do you think he'll do?"

"I think he'll kill you."

"Why should you mind?"

"Oh, I wouldn't," replied Mr Warburton, with a faint laugh. "I should bear it with the utmost fortitude. But I feel the official obligation to give you a proper warning."

"Do you think I'm afraid of a damned nigger?"

"It's a matter of entire indifference to me."

"Well, let me tell you this, I know how to take care of myself; that boy Abas is a dirty, thieving rascal, and if he tries any monkey tricks on me, by God, I'll wring his bloody neck."

"That was all I wished to say to you," said Mr Warburton. "Good evening."

Mr Warburton gave him a little nod of dismissal. Cooper flushed, did not for a moment know what to say or do, turned on his heel, and stumbled out of the room. Mr Warburton watched him go with an icy smile on his lips. He had done his duty. But what would he have thought had he known that when Cooper got back to his bungalow, so silent and cheerless, he threw himself down on his bed and in his bitter loneliness on a sudden lost all control of himself? Painful sobs tore his chest and heavy tears rolled down his thin cheeks.

After this Mr Warburton seldom saw Cooper, and never spoke to him. He read his *Times* every morning, did his work at the office, took his exercise, dressed for dinner, dined, and sat by the river smoking his cheroot. If by chance he ran across Cooper he cut him dead. Each, though never for a moment unconscious of the propinquity, acted as though the other did not exist. Time did nothing to assuage their animosity. They watched one another's actions and each knew what the other did. Though Mr Warburton had been a keen shot in his youth, with age he had acquired a distaste for killing the wild things of the jungle, but on Sundays and holidays Cooper went out with his gun: if he got something it was a triumph over Mr Warburton; if not, Mr Warburton shrugged his shoulders and chuckled. These counter-jumpers trying to be sportsmen! Christmas was a bad time for both of them: they ate their dinners alone, each in his own quarters, and they got deliberately drunk. They were the only white men within two hundred miles and they lived within shouting distance of each other. At the beginning of the year Cooper went down with fever, and when Mr Warburton caught sight of him again he was surprised to see how thin he had grown. He looked ill and worn. The solitude, so much more unnatural because it was due to no necessity, was getting on his nerves. It was getting on Mr Warburton's too, and often he could not sleep at night. He lay awake brooding. Cooper was drinking heavily and surely the breaking point was near; but in his dealings with the natives he took care to do nothing that might expose him to his chief's rebuke. They fought a grim and silent battle with one another. It was a test of endurance. The months passed, and neither gave sign of weakening. They were like men dwelling in regions of eternal night, and their souls were oppressed with the knowledge that never would the day dawn for them. It looked as though their lives would continue for ever in this dull and hideous monotony of hatred.

And when at last the inevitable happened it came upon Mr Warburton with all the shock of the unexpected. Cooper accused the boy Abas of stealing some of his clothes, and when the boy denied the theft took him by the scruff of the neck and kicked him down the steps of the bungalow. The boy demanded his wages and Cooper flung at his head every word of abuse he knew. If he saw him in the compound in an hour he would hand him over to the police. Next morning the boy waylaid him outside the Fort when he was walking over to his office, and again demanded his wages. Cooper struck him in the face with his clenched fist. The boy fell to the ground and got up with blood streaming from his nose.

Cooper walked on and set about his work. But he could not attend to it. The blow had calmed his irritation, and he knew that he had gone too far. He was worried. He felt ill, miserable, and discouraged. In the adjoining office sat Mr Warburton, and his impulse was to go and tell him what he had done; he made a movement in his chair, but he knew with what icy scorn he would listen to the story. He could see his patronizing smile. For a moment he had an uneasy fear of what Abas might do. Warburton had warned him all right. He sighed. What a fool he had been! But he shrugged his shoulders impatiently. He did not care; a fat lot he had to live for. It was all Warburton's fault; if he hadn't put his back up nothing like this would have happened. Warburton had made life a hell for him from the start. The snob. But they were all like that: it was because he was a Colonial. It was a damned shame that he had never got his commission in the war; he was as good as anyone else. They were a lot of dirty snobs. He was damned if he was going to knuckle under now. Of course Warburton would hear of what had happened; the old devil knew everything. He wasn't afraid. He wasn't afraid of any Malay in Borneo, and Warburton could go to blazes.

He was right in thinking that Mr Warburton would know what had happened. His head-boy told him when he went in to tiffin.

"Where is your nephew now?"

"I do not know, Tuan. He has gone."

Mr Warburton remained silent. After luncheon as a rule he slept a little, but today he found himself very wide awake. His eyes involuntarily sought the bungalow where Cooper was now resting.

The idiot! Hesitation for a little was in Mr Warburton's mind. Did the man know in what peril he was? He supposed he ought to send for him. But each time he had tried to reason with Cooper, Cooper had insulted him. Anger, furious anger welled up suddenly in Mr Warburton's heart, so that the veins on his temples stood out and he clenched his fists. The cad had had his warning. Now let him take what was coming to him. It was no business of his, and if anything happened it was not his fault. But perhaps they would wish in Kuala Solor that they had taken his advice and transferred Cooper to another station.

He was strangely restless that night. After dinner he walked up and down the veranda. When the boy went away to his own quarters, Mr Warburton asked him whether anything had been seen of Abas.

"No, Tuan, I think maybe he has gone to the village of his mother's brother."

Mr Warburton gave him a sharp glance, but the boy was looking down, and their eyes did not meet. Mr Warburton went down to the river and sat in his arbour. But peace was denied him. The river flowed ominously silent. It was like a great serpent gliding with sluggish movement towards the sea. And the trees of the jungle over the water were heavy with a breathless menace. No bird sang. No breeze ruffled the leaves of the cassias. All around him it seemed as though something waited.

He walked across the garden to the road. He had Cooper's bungalow in full view from there. There was a light in his sitting-room, and across the road floated the sound of ragtime. Cooper was playing his gramophone. Mr Warburton shuddered; he had never got over his instinctive dislike of that instrument. But for that he would have gone over and spoken to Cooper. He turned and went back to his own house. He read late into the night, and at last he slept. But he did not sleep very long, he had terrible dreams, and he seemed to be awakened by a cry. Of course that was a dream too, for no cry – from the bungalow for instance – could be heard in his room. He lay awake till dawn. Then he heard hurried steps and the sound of voices, his head-boy burst suddenly into the room without his fez, and Mr Warburton's heart stood still.

"Tuan, Tuan."

Mr Warburton jumped out of bed.

"I'll come at once."

He put on his slippers, and in his sarong and pyjama jacket walked across his compound and into Cooper's. Cooper was lying in bed, with his mouth open, and a kris sticking in his heart. He had been killed in his sleep. Mr Warburton started, but not because he had not expected to see just such a sight, he started because he felt in himself a sudden glow of exultation. A great burden had been lifted from his shoulders.

Cooper was quite cold. Mr Warburton took the kris out of the wound, it had been thrust in with such force that he had to use an effort to get it out, and looked at it. He recognized it. It was a kris that a dealer had offered him some weeks before, and which he knew Cooper had bought.

"Where is Abas?" he asked sternly.

"Abas is at the village of his mother's brother."

The sergeant of the native police was standing at the foot of the bed.

"Take two men and go to the village and arrest him."

Mr Warburton did what was immediately necessary. With set face he gave orders. His words were short and peremptory. Then he went back to the Fort. He shaved and had his bath, dressed, and went into the dining-room. By the side of his plate *The Times* in its wrapper lay waiting for him. He helped himself to some fruit. The head-boy poured out his tea while the second handed him a dish of eggs. Mr Warburton ate with a good appetite. The head-boy waited.

"What is it?" asked Mr Warburton.

"Tuan, Abas, my nephew, was in the house of his mother's brother all night. It can be proved. His uncle will swear that he did not leave the kampong."

Mr Warburton turned upon him with a frown.

"Tuan Cooper was killed by Abas. You know it as well as I know it. Justice must be done."

"Tuan, you would not hang him?"

Mr Warburton hesitated an instant, and though his voice remained set and stern a change came into his eyes. It was a flicker which the Malay was quick to notice and across his own eyes flashed an answering look of understanding.

"The provocation was very great. Abas will be sentenced to a term of imprisonment." There was a pause while Mr Warburton helped himself to marmalade. "When he has served a part of his sentence in prison I will take him into this house as a boy. You can train him in his duties. I have no doubt that in the house of Tuan Cooper he got into bad habits."

"Shall Abas give himself up, Tuan?"

"It would be wise of him."

The boy withdrew. Mr Warburton took his *Times* and neatly slit the wrapper. He loved to unfold the heavy, rustling pages. The morning, so fresh and cool, was delicious and for a moment his eyes wandered out over the garden with a friendly glance. A great weight had been lifted from his mind. He turned to the columns in which were announced the births, deaths, and marriages. That was what he always looked at first. A name he knew caught his attention. Lady Ormskirk had had a son at last. By George, how pleased the old dowager must be! He would write her a note of congratulation by the next mail.

Abas would make a very good house-boy.

That fool Cooper!

RED

THE SKIPPER THRUST his hand into one of his trouser pockets and with difficulty, for they were not at the sides but in front and he was a portly man, pulled out a large silver watch. He looked at it and then looked again at the declining sun. The Kanaka at the wheel gave him a glance, but did not speak. The skipper's eyes rested on the island they were approaching. A white line of foam marked the reef. He knew there was an opening large enough to get his ship through, and when they came a little nearer he counted on seeing it. They had nearly an hour of daylight still before them. In the lagoon the water was deep and they could anchor comfortably. The chief of the village which he could already see among the coconut trees was a friend of the mate's, and it would be pleasant to go ashore for the night. The mate came forward at that minute and the skipper turned to him.

"We'll take a bottle of booze along with us and get some girls in to dance," he said.

"I don't see the opening," said the mate.

He was a Kanaka, a handsome, swarthy fellow, with somewhat the look of a later Roman emperor, inclined to stoutness; but his face was fine and clean-cut.

"I'm dead sure there's one right here," said the captain, looking through his glasses. "I can't understand why I can't pick it up. Send one of the boys up the mast to have a look."

The mate called one of the crew and gave him the order. The captain watched the Kanaka climb and waited for him to speak. But the Kanaka shouted down that he could see nothing but the unbroken line of foam. The captain spoke Samoan like a native, and he cursed him freely.

"Shall he stay up there?" asked the mate.

"What the hell good does that do?" answered the captain. "The blame fool can't see worth a cent. You bet your sweet life I'd find the opening if I was up there."

He looked at the slender mast with anger. It was all very well for a native who had been used to climbing up coconut trees all his life. He was fat and heavy.

"Come down," he shouted. "You're no more use than a dead dog. We'll just have to go along the reef till we find the opening."

It was a seventy-ton schooner with paraffin auxiliary, and it ran, when there was no head wind, between four and five knots an hour. It was a bedraggled object; it had been painted white a very long time ago, but it was now dirty, dingy, and mottled. It smelt strongly of paraffin, and of the copra which was its usual cargo. They were within a hundred feet of the reef now and the captain told the steersman to run along it till they came to the opening. But when they had gone a couple of miles he realized that they had missed it. He went about and slowly worked back again. The white foam of the reef continued without interruption and now the sun was setting. With a curse at the stupidity of the crew the skipper resigned himself to waiting till next morning.

"Put her about," he said. "I can't anchor here."

They went out to sea a little and presently it was quite dark. They anchored. When the sail was furled the ship began to roll a good deal.

They said in Apia that one day she would roll right over; and the owner, a German-American who managed one of the largest stores, said that no money was big enough to induce him to go out in her. The cook, a Chinese in white trousers, very dirty and ragged, and a thin white tunic, came to say that supper was ready, and when the skipper went into the cabin he found the engineer already seated at table. The engineer was a long, lean man with a scraggy neck. He was dressed in blue overalls and a sleeveless jersey which showed his thin arms tattooed from elbow to wrist.

"Hell, having to spend the night outside," said the skipper.

The engineer did not answer, and they ate their supper in silence. The cabin was lit by a dim oil-lamp. When they had eaten the canned apricots with which the meal finished the Chink brought them a cup of tea. The skipper lit a cigar and went on the upper deck. The island now was only a darker mass against the night. The stars were very bright. The only sound was the ceaseless breaking of the surf. The skipper sank into a deck-chair and smoked idly. Presently three or four members of the crew came up and sat down. One of them had a banjo and another a concertina. They began to play, and one of them sang. The native song sounded strange on these instruments. Then to the singing a couple began to dance. It was a barbaric dance, savage and primeval, rapid, with quick movements of the hands and feet and contortions of the body; it was sensual, sexual even, but sexual without passion. It was very animal, direct, weird without mystery, natural in short, and one might almost say childlike. At last they grew tired. They stretched themselves on the deck and slept, and all was silent. The skipper lifted himself heavily out of his chair and clambered down the companion. He went into his cabin and got out of his clothes. He climbed into his bunk and lay there. He panted a little in the heat of the night.

But next morning, when the dawn crept over the tranquil sea, the opening in the reef which had eluded them the night before was seen a little to the east of where they lay. The schooner entered the lagoon. There was not a ripple on the surface of the water. Deep down among the coral rocks you saw little coloured fish swim. When he had anchored his ship the skipper ate his breakfast and went on deck. The sun shone from an unclouded sky, but in the early morning the air was grateful and cool. It was Sunday, and there was a feeling of quietness, a silence as though nature were at rest, which gave him a peculiar sense of comfort. He sat, looking at the wooded coast, and felt lazy and well at ease. Presently a slow smile moved his lips and he threw the stump of his cigar into the water.

"I guess I'll go ashore," he said. "Get the boat out."

He climbed stiffly down the ladder and was rowed to a little cove. The coconut trees came down to the water's edge, not in rows, but spaced out with an ordered formality. They were like a ballet of spinsters, elderly but flippant, standing in affected attitudes with the simpering graces of a bygone age. He sauntered idly through them, along a path that could be just seen winding its tortuous way, and it led him presently to a broad creek. There was a bridge across it, but a bridge constructed of single trunks of coconut trees, a dozen of them, placed end to end and supported where they met by a forked branch driven into the bed of the creek. You walked on a smooth, round surface, narrow and slippery, and there was no support for the hand. To cross such a bridge required sure feet and a stout heart. The skipper hesitated. But he saw on the other side, nestling among the trees, a white man's house; he made up his mind and, rather gingerly, began to walk. He watched his feet carefully, and where one trunk joined on to the next and there was a difference of level, he tottered a little. It was with a gasp of relief that he reached the last tree and finally set his feet on the firm ground of the other side. He had been so intent on the difficult crossing that he never noticed anyone was watching him, and it was with surprise that he heard himself spoken to.

"It takes a bit of nerve to cross these bridges when you're not used to them."

He looked up and saw a man standing in front of him. He had evidently come out of the house which he had seen.

"I saw you hesitate," the man continued, with a smile on his lips, "and I was watching to see you fall in."

"Not on your life," said the captain, who had not recovered his confidence.

"I've fallen in myself before now. I remember, one evening I came back from shooting, and I fell in, gun and all. Now I get a boy to carry my gun for me."

He was a man no longer young, with a small beard, now somewhat grey, and a thin face. He was dressed in a singlet, without arms, and a pair of duck trousers. He wore neither shoes nor socks. He spoke English with a slight accent.

"Are you Neilson?" asked the skipper.

"I am."

"I've heard about you. I thought you lived somewheres round here."

The skipper followed his host into the little bungalow and sat down heavily in the chair which the other motioned him to take. While Neilson went out to fetch whisky and glasses he took a look round the room. It filled him with amazement. He had never seen so many books. The shelves reached from floor to ceiling on all four walls, and they were closely packed. There was a grand piano littered with music, and a large table on which books and magazines lay in disorder. The room made him feel embarrassed. He remembered that Neilson was a queer fellow. No one knew very much about him, although he had been in the islands for so many years, but those who knew him agreed that he was queer. He was a Swede.

"You've got one big heap of books here," he said, when Neilson returned.

"They do no harm," answered Neilson with a smile.

"Have you read them all?" asked the skipper.

"Most of them."

"I'm a bit of a reader myself. I have the *Saturday Evening Post* sent me regler."

Neilson poured his visitor a good stiff glass of whisky and gave him a cigar. The skipper volunteered a little information.

"I got in last night, but I couldn't find the opening, so I had to anchor outside. I never been this run before, but my people had some stuff they wanted to bring over here. Gray, d'you know him?"

"Yes, he's got a store a little way along."

"Well, there was a lot of canned stuff he wanted over, an' he's got some copra. They thought I might just as well come over as lie idle at Apia. I run between Apia and Pago-Pago mostly, but they've got smallpox there just now, and there's nothing stirring."

He took a drink of his whisky and lit a cigar. He was a taciturn man, but there was something in Neilson that made him nervous,

632

and his nervousness made him talk. The Swede was looking at him with large dark eyes in which there was an expression of faint amusement.

"This is a tidy little place you've got here."

"I've done my best with it."

"You must do pretty well with your trees. They look fine. With copra at the price it is now. I had a bit of a plantation myself once, in Upolu it was, but I had to sell it."

He looked round the room again, where all those books gave him a feeling of something incomprehensible and hostile.

"I guess you must find it a bit lonesome here though," he said.

"I've got used to it. I've been here for twenty-five years."

Now the captain could think of nothing more to say, and he smoked in silence. Neilson had apparently no wish to break it. He looked at his guest with a meditative eye. He was a tall man, more than six feet high, and very stout. His face was red and blotchy, with a network of little purple veins on the cheeks, and his features were sunk into its fatness. His eyes were bloodshot. His neck was buried in rolls of fat. But for a fringe of long curly hair, nearly white, at the back of his head, he was quite bald; and that immense, shiny surface of forehead, which might have given him a false look of intelligence, on the contrary gave him one of peculiar imbecility. He wore a blue flannel shirt, open at the neck and showing his fat chest covered with a mat of reddish hair, and a very old pair of blue serge trousers. He sat in his chair in a heavy ungainly attitude, his great belly thrust forward and his fat legs uncrossed. All elasticity had gone from his limbs. Neilson wondered idly what sort of man he had been in his youth. It was almost impossible to imagine that this creature of vast bulk had ever been a boy who ran about. The skipper finished his whisky, and Neilson pushed the bottle towards him.

"Help yourself."

The skipper leaned forward and with his great hand seized it.

"And how come you in these parts anyways?" he said.

"Oh, I came out to the islands for my health. My lungs were bad and they said I hadn't a year to live. You see they were wrong."

"I meant, how come you to settle down right here?"

"I am a sentimentalist."

"Oh!"

Neilson knew that the skipper had not an idea what he meant, and he looked at him with an ironical twinkle in his dark eyes. Perhaps just because the skipper was so gross and dull a man the whim seized him to talk further.

"You were too busy keeping your balance to notice, when you crossed the bridge, but this spot is generally considered rather pretty."

"It's a cute little house you've got here."

"Ah, that wasn't here when I first came. There was a native hut, with its beehive roof and its pillars, overshadowed by a great tree with red flowers; and the croton bushes, their leaves yellow and red and golden, made a pied fence around it. And then all about were the coconut trees, as fanciful as women, and as vain. They stood at the water's edge and spent all day looking at their reflections. I was a young man then – good heavens, it's a quarter of a century ago – and I wanted to enjoy all the loveliness of the world in the short time allotted to me before I passed into the darkness. I thought it was the most beautiful spot I had ever seen. The first time I saw it I had a catch at my heart, and I was afraid I was going to cry. I wasn't more than twenty-five, and though I put the best face I could on it, I didn't want to die. And somehow it seemed to me that the very beauty of this place made it easier for me to accept my fate. I felt when I came here that all my past life had fallen away, Stockholm and its University, and then Bonn: it all seemed the life of somebody else, as though now at last I had achieved the reality which our doctors of philosophy – I am one myself, you know – had discussed so much. 'A year,' I cried to myself. 'I have a year. I will spend it here and then I am content to die.'

"We are foolish and sentimental and melodramatic at twenty-five, but if we weren't perhaps we should be less wise at fifty.

"Now drink, my friend. Don't let the nonsense I talk interfere with you."

He waved his thin hand towards the bottle, and the skipper finished what remained in his glass.

"You ain't drinking nothin'," he said, reaching for the whisky.

"I am of sober habit," smiled the Swede. "I intoxicate myself in ways which I fancy are more subtle. But perhaps that is only vanity. Anyhow, the effects are more lasting and the results less deleterious."

"They say there's a deal of cocaine taken in the States now," said the captain.

Neilson chuckled.

"But I do not see a white man often," he continued, "and for once I don't think a drop of whisky can do me any harm."

He poured himself out a little, added some soda, and took a sip.

"And presently I found out why the spot had such an unearthly loveliness. Here love had tarried for a moment like a migrant bird that happens on a ship in mid-ocean and for a little while folds its tired wings. The fragrance of a beautiful passion hovered over it like the fragrance of hawthorn in May in the meadows of my home. It seems to me that the places where men have loved or suffered keep about them always some faint aroma of something that has not wholly died. It is as though they had acquired a spiritual significance which mysteriously affects those who pass. I wish I could make myself clear." He smiled a little. "Though I cannot imagine that if I did you would understand."

He paused.

"I think this place was beautiful because here for a period the ecstasy of love had invested it with beauty." And now he shrugged his shoulders. "But perhaps it is only that my aesthetic sense is gratified by the happy conjunction of young love and a suitable setting."

Even a man less thick-witted than the skipper might have been forgiven if he were bewildered by Neilson's words. For he seemed faintly to laugh at what he said. It was as though he spoke from emotion which his intellect found ridiculous. He had said himself that he was a sentimentalist, and when sentimentality is joined with scepticism there is often the devil to pay.

He was silent for an instant and looked at the captain with eyes in which there was a sudden perplexity.

"You know, I can't help thinking that I've seen you before somewhere or other," he said.

"I couldn't say as I remember you," returned the skipper.

"I have a curious feeling as though your face were familiar to me. It's been puzzling me for some time. But I can't situate my recollection in any place or at any time."

The skipper massively shrugged his heavy shoulders.

"It's thirty years since I first come to the islands. A man can't figure on remembering all the folk he meets in a while like that."

The Swede shook his head.

"You know how one sometimes has the feeling that a place one has never been to before is strangely familiar. That's how I seem to see you." He gave a whimsical smile. "Perhaps I knew you in some past existence. Perhaps, perhaps you were the master of a galley in ancient Rome and I was a slave at the oar. Thirty years have you been here?"

"Every bit of thirty years."

"I wonder if you knew a man called Red?"

"Red?"

"That is the only name I've ever known him by. I never knew him personally. I never even set eyes on him. And yet I seem to see him more clearly than many men, my brothers, for instance, with whom I passed my daily life for many years. He lives in my imagination with the distinctness of a Paolo Malatesta or a Romeo. But I daresay you have never read Dante or Shakespeare?"

"I can't say as I have," said the captain.

Neilson, smoking a cigar, leaned back in his chair and looked vacantly at the ring of smoke which floated in the still air. A smile played on his lips, but his eyes were grave. Then he looked at the captain. There was in his gross obesity something extraordinarily repellent. He had the plethoric self-satisfaction of the very fat. It was an outrage. It set Neilson's nerves on edge. But the contrast between the man before him and the man he had in mind was pleasant.

"It appears that Red was the most comely thing you ever saw. I've talked to quite a number of people who knew him in those days, white men, and they all agree that the first time you saw him his beauty just took your breath away. They called him Red on account of his flaming hair. It had a natural wave and he wore it long. It must have been of that wonderful colour that the pre-Raphaelites raved over. I don't think he was vain of it, he was much too ingenuous for that, but no one could have blamed him if he had been. He was tall, six feet and an inch or two – in the native house that used to stand here was the mark of his height cut with a knife on the central trunk that supported the roof – and he was made like a Greek god, broad in the shoulders and thin in the flanks; he was like Apollo, with just that soft roundness which Praxiteles gave him, and that suave, feminine grace which has in it something troubling and mysterious. His skin was dazzling white, milky, like satin; his skin was like a woman's."

"I had kind of a white skin myself when I was a kiddie," said the skipper, with a twinkle in his bloodshot eyes.

But Neilson paid no attention to him. He was telling his story now and interruption made him impatient.

"And his face was just as beautiful as his body. He had large blue eyes, very dark, so that some say they were black, and unlike most red-haired people he had dark eyebrows and long dark lashes. His features were perfectly regular and his mouth was like a scarlet wound. He was twenty."

On these words the Swede stopped with a certain sense of the dramatic. He took a sip of whisky.

"He was unique. There never was anyone more beautiful. There was no more reason for him than for a wonderful blossom to flower on a wild plant. He was a happy accident of nature.

"One day he landed at that cove into which you must have put this morning. He was an American sailor, and he had deserted from a man-of-war in Apia. He had induced some good-humoured native to give him a passage on a cutter that happened to be sailing from Apia to Safoto, and he had been put ashore here in a dug-out. I do not know why he deserted. Perhaps life on a man-of-war with its restrictions irked him, perhaps he was in trouble, and perhaps it was the South Seas and these romantic islands that got into his bones. Every now and then they take a man strangely, and he finds himself like a fly in a spider's web. It may be that there was a softness of fibre in him, and these green hills with their soft airs, this blue sea, took the northern strength from him as Delilah took the Nazarite's. Anyhow, he wanted to hide himself, and he thought he would be safe in this secluded nook till his ship had sailed from Samoa.

"There was a native hut at the cove and as he stood there, wondering where exactly he should turn his steps, a young girl came out and invited him to enter. He knew scarcely two words of the native tongue and she as little English. But he understood well enough what her smiles meant, and her pretty gestures, and he followed her. He sat down on a mat and she gave him slices of pineapple to eat. I can speak of Red only from hearsay, but I saw the girl three years after he first met her, and she was scarcely nineteen then. You cannot imagine how exquisite she was. She had the passionate grace of the hibiscus and the rich colour. She was rather tall, slim, with the delicate features of her race, and large eyes like pools of still water under the palm trees; her hair, black and curling, fell down her back, and she wore a wreath of scented flowers. Her hands were lovely. They were so small, so exquisitely formed, they gave your heart-strings a wrench. And in those days she laughed easily. Her smile was so delightful that it made your knees shake. Her skin was like a field of ripe corn on a summer day. Good heavens, how can I describe her? She was too beautiful to be real.

"And these two young things, she was sixteen and he was twenty, fell in love with one another at first sight. That is the real love, not the love that comes from sympathy, common interests, or intellectual community, but love pure and simple. That is the love that Adam felt for Eve when he awoke and found her in the garden gazing at him with dewy eyes. That is the love that draws the beasts to one another, and the Gods. That is the love that makes the world a miracle. That is the love which gives life its pregnant meaning. You have never heard of the wise, cynical French duke who said that with two lovers there is always one who loves and one who lets himself be loved; it is bitter truth to which most of us have to resign ourselves; but now and then there are two who love and two who let themselves be loved. Then one might fancy that the sun stands still as it stood when Joshua prayed to the God of Israel.

"And even now after all these years, when I think of these two, so young, so fair, so simple, and of their love, I feel a pang. It tears my heart just as my heart is torn when on certain nights I watch the full moon shining on the lagoon from an unclouded sky. There is always pain in the contemplation of perfect beauty.

"They were children. She was good and sweet and kind. I know nothing of him, and I like to think that then at all events he was ingenuous and frank. I like to think that his soul was as comely as his body. But I daresay he had no more soul than the creatures of the woods and forests who made pipes from reeds and bathed in the mountain streams when the world was young, and you might catch sight of little fawns galloping through the glade on the back of a bearded centaur. A soul is a troublesome possession and when man developed it he lost the Garden of Eden.

"Well, when Red came to the island it had recently been visited by one of those epidemics which the white man brought to the South Seas, and one third of the inhabitants had died. It seems that the girl had lost all her near kin and she lived now in the house of distant cousins. The household consisted of two ancient crones, bowed and wrinkled, two younger women, and a man and a boy. For a few days he stayed there. But perhaps he felt himself too near the shore, with the possibility that he might fall in with white men who would reveal his hiding-place; perhaps the lovers could not bear that the company of others should rob them for an instant of the delight of being together. One morning they set out, the pair of them, with a few things that belonged to the girl, and walked along a grassy path under the coconuts, till they came to the creek you see. They had to cross the bridge you crossed, and the girl laughed gleefully because he was afraid. She held his hand till they came to the end of the first tree, and then his courage failed him and he had to go back. He was obliged to take off all his clothes before he could risk it, and she carried them over for him on her head. They settled down in the empty hut that stood there. Whether she had any rights over it (land tenure is a complicated business in the islands), or whether the owner had died during the epidemic, I do not know, but anyhow no one questioned them, and they took possession. Their furniture consisted of a couple of grass mats on which they slept, a fragment of looking-glass, and a bowl or two. In this pleasant land that is enough to start housekeeping on.

"They say that happy people have no history, and certainly a happy love has none. They did nothing all day long and yet the days seemed all too short. The girl had a native name, but Red called her Sally. He picked up the easy language very quickly, and he used to lie on the mat for hours while she chattered gaily to him. He was a silent fellow, and perhaps his mind was lethargic. He smoked incessantly the cigarettes which she made him out of the native tobacco and pandanus leaf, and he watched her while with deft fingers she made grass mats. Often natives would come in and tell long stories of the old days when the island was disturbed by tribal wars. Sometimes he would go fishing on the reef, and bring home a basket full of coloured fish. Sometimes at night he would go out with a lantern to catch lobster. There were plantains round the hut and Sally would roast them for their frugal meal. She knew how to make delicious messes from coconuts, and the breadfruit tree by the side of the creek gave them its fruit. On feast-days they killed a little pig and cooked it on hot stones. They bathed together in the creek; and in the evening they went down to the lagoon and paddled about in a dug-out, with its great outrigger. The sea was deep blue, wine-coloured at sun-down, like the sea of Homeric Greece; but in the lagoon the colour had an infinite variety, aquamarine and amethyst and emerald; and the setting sun turned it for a short moment to liquid gold. Then there was the colour of the coral, brown, white, pink, red, purple; and the shapes it took were marvellous. It was like a magic garden, and the hurrying fish were like butterflies. It strangely lacked reality. Among the coral were pools with a floor of white sand and here, where the water was dazzling clear, it was very good to bathe. Then, cool and happy, they wandered back in the gloaming over the soft grass road to the creek, walking hand in hand, and now the mynah birds filled the coconut trees with their clamour. And then the night, with that great sky shining with gold, that seemed to stretch more widely than the skies of Europe, and the soft airs that blew gently through the open hut, the long night again was all too short. She was sixteen and he was barely twenty. The dawn crept in among the wooden pillars of the hut and looked at those lovely children sleeping in one another's arms. The sun hid behind the great tattered leaves of the plantains so that it might not disturb them, and then, with playful malice, shot a golden ray, like the outstretched paw of a Persian cat, on their faces. They opened their sleepy eyes and they smiled to welcome another day. The weeks lengthened into months, and a year passed. They seemed to love one another as – I hesitate to say passionately, for passion has in it always a shade of sadness, a touch of bitterness or anguish, but as wholeheartedly, as simply and naturally as on that first day on which, meeting, they had recognized that a god was in them.

"If you had asked them I have no doubt that they would have thought it impossible to suppose their love could ever cease. Do we not know that the essential element of love is a belief in its own eternity? And yet perhaps in Red there was already a very little seed, unknown to himself and unsuspected by the girl, which would in time have grown to weariness. For one day one of the natives from the cove told them that some way down the coast at the anchorage was a British whaling-ship.

" 'Gee,' he said, 'I wonder if I could make a trade of some nuts and plantains for a pound or two of tobacco.'

"The pandanus cigarettes that Sally made him with untiring hands were strong and pleasant enough to smoke, but they left him unsatisfied; and he yearned on a sudden for real tobacco, hard, rank, and pungent. He had not smoked a pipe for many months. His mouth watered at the thought of it. One would have thought some premonition of harm would have made Sally seek to dissuade him, but love possessed her so completely that it never occurred to her any power on earth could take him from her. They went up into the hills together and gathered a great basket of wild oranges, green, but sweet and juicy; and they picked plantains from around the hut, and coconuts from their trees, and breadfruit and mangoes; and they carried them down to the cove. They loaded the unstable canoe with them, and Red and the native boy who had brought them the news of the ship paddled along outside the reef.

"It was the last time she ever saw him.

"Next day the boy came back alone. He was all in tears. This is the story he told. When after their long paddle they reached the ship and Red hailed it, a white man looked over the side and told them to come on board. They took the fruit they had brought with them and Red piled it up on the deck. The white man and he began to talk, and they seemed to come to some agreement. One of them went below and brought up tobacco. Red took some at once and lit a pipe. The boy imitated the zest with which he blew a great cloud of smoke from his mouth. Then they said something to him and he went into the cabin. Through the open door the boy, watching curiously, saw a bottle brought out and glasses. Red drank and smoked. They seemed to ask him something, for he shook his head and laughed. The man, the first man who had spoken to them, laughed too, and he filled Red's glass once more. They went on talking and drinking, and presently, growing tired of watching a sight that meant nothing to him, the boy curled himself up on the deck and slept. He was awakened by a kick; and jumping to his feet, he saw that the ship was slowly sailing out of the lagoon. He caught sight of Red seated at the table, with his head resting heavily on his arms, fast asleep. He made a movement towards him, intending to wake him, but a rough hand seized his arm, and a man, with a scowl and words which he did not understand, pointed to the side. He shouted to Red, but in a moment he was seized and flung overboard. Helpless, he swam round to his canoe, which was drifting a little way off, and pushed it on to the reef. He climbed in and, sobbing all the way, paddled back to shore.

"What had happened was obvious enough. The whaler, by desertion or sickness, was short of hands, and the captain when Red came aboard had asked him to sign on; on his refusal he had made him drunk and kidnapped him.

"Sally was beside herself with grief. For three days she screamed and cried. The natives did what they could to comfort her, but she would not be comforted. She would not eat. And then, exhausted, she sank into a sullen apathy. She spent long days at the cove, watching the lagoon, in the vain hope that Red somehow or other would manage to escape. She sat on the white sand, hour after hour, with the tears running down her cheeks, and at night dragged herself wearily back across the creek to the little hut where she had been happy. The people with whom she had lived before Red came to the island wished her to return to them, but she would not; she was convinced that Red would come back, and she wanted him to find her where he had left her. Four months later she was delivered of a still-born child, and the old woman who had come to help her through her confinement remained with her in the hut. All joy was taken from her life. If her anguish with time became less intolerable it was replaced by a settled melancholy. You would not have thought that among these people, whose emotions, though so violent, are very transient, a woman could be found capable of so enduring a passion. She never lost the profound conviction that sooner or later Red would come back. She watched for him, and every time someone crossed this slender little bridge of coconut trees she looked. It might at last be he."

Neilson stopped talking and gave a faint sigh.

"And what happened to her in the end?" asked the skipper.

Neilson smiled bitterly.

"Oh, three years afterwards she took up with another white man."

The skipper gave a fat, cynical chuckle.

"That's generally what happens to them," he said.

The Swede shot him a look of hatred. He did not know why that gross, obese man excited in him so violent a repulsion. But his thoughts wandered and he found his mind filled with memories of the past. He went back five-and-twenty years. It was when he first came to the island, weary of Apia, with its heavy drinking, its gambling and coarse sensuality, a sick man, trying to resign himself to the loss of the career which had fired his imagination with ambitious thought. He set behind him resolutely all his hopes of making a great name for himself and strove to content himself with the few poor months of careful life which was all that he could count on. He was boarding with a half-caste trader who had a store a couple of miles along the coast at the edge of a native village; and one day, wandering aimlessly along the grassy paths of the coconut groves, he had come upon the hut in which Sally lived. The beauty of the spot had filled him with a rapture so great that it was almost painful, and then he had seen Sally. She was the loveliest creature he had ever seen, and the sadness in those dark, magnificent eyes of hers affected him strangely. The Kanakas were a handsome race, and beauty was not rare among them, but it was the beauty of shapely animals. It was empty. But those tragic eyes were dark with mystery, and you felt in them the bitter complexity of the groping, human soul. The trader told him the story and it moved him.

"Do you think he'll ever come back?" asked Neilson.

"No fear. Why, it'll be a couple of years before the ship is paid off, and by then he'll have forgotten all about her. I bet he was pretty mad when he woke up and found he'd been shanghaied, and I shouldn't wonder but he wanted to fight somebody. But he'd got to grin and bear it, and I guess in a month he was thinking it the best thing that had ever happened to him that he got away from the island."

But Neilson could not get the story out of his head. Perhaps because he was sick and weakly, the radiant health of Red appealed to his imagination. Himself an ugly man, insignificant of appearance, he prized very highly comeliness in others. He had never been passionately in love, and certainly he had never been passionately loved. The mutual attraction of those two young things gave him a singular delight. It had the ineffable beauty of the Absolute. He went again to the little hut by the creek. He had a gift for languages and an energetic mind, accustomed to work, and he had already given much time to the study of the local tongue. Old habit was strong in him and he was gathering together material for a paper on the Samoan speech. The old crone who shared the hut with Sally invited him to come in and sit down. She gave him *kava* to drink and cigarettes to smoke. She was glad to have someone to chat with and while she talked he looked at Sally. She reminded him of the Psyche in the museum at Naples. Her features had the same clear purity of line, and though she had borne a child she had still a virginal aspect.

It was not till he had seen her two or three times that he induced her to speak. Then it was only to ask him if he had seen in Apia a man called Red. Two years had passed since his disappearance, but it was plain that she still thought of him incessantly.

It did not take Neilson long to discover that he was in love with her. It was only by an effort of will now that he prevented himself from going every day to the creek, and when he was not with Sally his thoughts were. At first, looking upon himself as a dying man, he asked only to look at her, and occasionally hear her speak, and his love gave him a wonderful happiness. He exulted in its purity. He wanted nothing from her but the opportunity to weave around her graceful person a web of beautiful fancies. But the open air, the equable temperature, the rest, the simple fare, began to have an unexpected effect on his health. His temperature did not soar at night to such alarming heights, he coughed less and began to put on weight; six months passed without his having a haemorrhage; and on a sudden he saw the possibility that he might live. He had studied his disease carefully, and the hope dawned upon him that with great care he might arrest its course. It exhilarated him to look forward once more to the future. He made plans. It was evident that any active life was out of the question, but he could live on the islands, and the small income he had, insufficient elsewhere, would be ample to keep him. He could grow coconuts; that would give him an occupation; and he would send for his books and a piano; but his quick mind saw that in all this he was merely trying to conceal from himself the desire which obsessed him.

He wanted Sally. He loved not only her beauty, but that dim soul which he divined behind her suffering eyes. He would intoxicate her with his passion. In the end he would make her forget. And in an ecstasy of surrender he fancied himself giving her too the happiness which he had thought never to know again, but had now so miraculously achieved.

He asked her to live with him. She refused. He had expected that and did not let it depress him, for he was sure that sooner or later she would yield. His love was irresistible. He told the old woman of his wishes, and found somewhat to his surprise that she and the neighbours, long aware of them, were strongly urging Sally to accept his offer. After all, every native was glad to keep house for a white man, and Neilson according to the standards of the island was a rich one. The trader with whom he boarded went to her and told her not to be a fool; such an opportunity would not come again, and after so long she could not still believe that Red would ever return. The girl's resistance only increased Neilson's desire, and what had been a very pure love now became an agonizing passion. He was determined that nothing should stand in his way. He gave Sally no peace. At last, worn out by his persistence and the persuasions, by turns pleading and angry, of everyone around her, she consented. But the day after, when exultant he went to see her he found that in the night she had burnt down the hut in which she and Red had lived together. The old crone ran towards him full of angry abuse of Sally, but he waved her aside; it did not matter; they would build a bungalow on the place where the hut had stood. A European house would really be more convenient if he wanted to bring out a piano and a vast number of books.

And so the little wooden house was built in which he had now lived for many years, and Sally became his wife. But after the first few weeks of rapture, during which he was satisfied with what she gave him, he had known little happiness. She had yielded to him, through weariness, but she had only yielded what she set no store on. The soul which he had dimly glimpsed escaped him. He knew that she cared nothing for him. She still loved Red, and all the time she was waiting for his return. At a sign from him, Neilson knew that, notwithstanding his love, his tenderness, his sympathy, his generosity, she would leave him without a moment's hesitation. She would never give a thought to his distress. Anguish seized him and he battered at that impenetrable self of hers which sullenly resisted him. His love became bitter. He tried to melt her heart with kindness, but it remained as hard as before; he feigned indifference, but she did not notice it. Sometimes he lost his temper and abused her, and then she wept silently. Sometimes he thought she was nothing but a fraud, and that soul simply an invention of his own, and that he could not get into the sanctuary of her heart because there was no sanctuary there. His love became a prison from which he longed to escape, but he had not the strength merely to open the door – that was all it needed – and walk out into the open air. It was torture and at last he became numb and hopeless. In the end the fire burnt itself out and, when he saw her eyes rest for an instant on the slender bridge, it was no longer rage that filled his heart but impatience. For many years now they had lived together bound by the ties of habit and convenience, and it was with a smile that he looked back on his old passion. She was an old woman, for the women on the islands age quickly, and if he had no love for her any more he had tolerance. She left him alone. He was contented with his piano and his books.

His thoughts led him to a desire for words.

"When I look back now and reflect on that brief passionate love of Red and Sally, I think that perhaps they should thank the ruthless fate that separated them when their love seemed still to be at its height. They suffered, but they suffered in beauty. They were spared the real tragedy of love."

"I don't know exactly as I get you," said the skipper.

"The tragedy of love is not death or separation. How long do you think it would have been before one or other of them ceased to care? Oh, it is dreadfully bitter to look at a woman whom you have loved with all your heart and soul, so that you felt you could not bear to let her out of your sight, and realize that you would not mind if you never saw her again. The tragedy of love is indifference."

But while he was speaking a very extraordinary thing happened. Though he had been addressing the skipper he had not been talking to him, he had been putting his thoughts into words for himself, and with his eyes fixed on the man in front of him he had not seen him.

But now an image presented itself to them, an image not of the man he saw, but of another man. It was as though he were looking into one of those distorting mirrors that make you extraordinarily squat or outrageously elongate, but here exactly the opposite took place, and in the obese, ugly old man he caught the shadowy glimpse of a stripling. He gave him now a quick, searching scrutiny. Why had a haphazard stroll brought him just to this place? A sudden tremor of his heart made him slightly breathless. An absurd suspicion seized him. What had occurred to him was impossible, and yet it might be a fact.

"What is your name?" he asked abruptly.

The skipper's face puckered and he gave a cunning chuckle. He looked then malicious and horribly vulgar.

"It's such a damned long time since I heard it that I almost forget it myself. But for thirty years now in the islands they've always called me Red."

His huge form shook as he gave a low, almost silent laugh. It was obscene. Neilson shuddered. Red was hugely amused, and from his bloodshot eyes tears ran down his cheeks.

Neilson gave a gasp, for at that moment a woman came in. She was a native, a woman of somewhat commanding presence, stout without being corpulent, dark, for the natives grow darker with age, with very grey hair. She wore a black Mother Hubbard, and its thinness showed her heavy breasts. The moment had come.

She made an observation to Neilson about some household matter and he answered. He wondered if his voice sounded as unnatural to her as it did to himself. She gave the man who was sitting in the chair by the window an indifferent glance, and went out of the room. The moment had come and gone.

Neilson for a moment could not speak. He was strangely shaken. Then he said:

"I'd be very glad if you'd stay and have a bit of dinner with me. Pot luck."

"I don't think I will," said Red. "I must go after this fellow Gray. I'll give him his stuff and then I'll get away. I want to be back in Apia tomorrow."

"I'll send a boy along with you to show you the way."

"That'll be fine."

Red heaved himself out of his chair, while the Swede called one of the boys who worked on the plantation. He told him where the skipper wanted to go, and the boy stepped along the bridge. Red prepared to follow him.

"Don't fall in," said Neilson.

"Not on your life."

Neilson watched him make his way across and when he had disappeared among the coconuts he looked still. Then he sank heavily in his chair. Was that the man who had prevented him from being happy? Was that the man whom Sally had loved all these years and for whom she had waited so desperately? It was grotesque. A sudden fury seized him so that he had an instinct to spring up and smash everything around him. He had been cheated. They had seen each other at last and had not known it. He began to laugh, mirthlessly, and his laughter grew till it became hysterical. The Gods had played him a cruel trick. And he was old now.

At last Sally came in to tell him dinner was ready. He sat down in front of her and tried to eat. He wondered what she would say if he told her now that the fat old man sitting in the chair was the lover whom she remembered still with the passionate abandonment of her youth. Years ago, when he hated her because she made him so unhappy, he would have been glad to tell her. He wanted to hurt her then as she hurt him, because his hatred was only love. But now he did not care. He shrugged his shoulders listlessly.

"What did that man want?" she asked presently.

He did not answer at once. She was too old, a fat old native woman. He wondered why he had ever loved her so madly. He had laid at her feet all the treasures of his soul, and she had cared nothing for them. Waste, what waste! And now, when he looked at her, he felt only contempt. His patience was at last exhausted. He answered her question.

"He's the captain of a schooner. He's come from Apia."

"Yes."

"He brought me news from home. My eldest brother is very ill and I must go back."

"Will you be gone long?"

He shrugged his shoulders.

MISS KING

IT WAS NOT till the beginning of September that Ashenden, a writer by profession, who had been abroad at the outbreak of the war, managed to get back to England. He chanced soon after his arrival to go to a party and was there introduced to a middle-aged colonel whose name he did not catch. He had some talk with him. As he was about to leave, this officer came up to him and asked:

"I say, I wonder if you'd mind coming to see me. I'd rather like to have a chat with you."

"Certainly," said Ashenden. "Whenever you like."

"What about tomorrow at eleven?"

"All right."

"I'll just write down my address. Have you a card on you?"

Ashenden gave him one and on this the colonel scribbled in pencil the name of a street and the number of a house. When Ashenden walked along next morning to keep his appointment he found himself in a street of rather vulgar red-brick houses in a part of London that had once been fashionable, but was now fallen in the esteem of the house-hunter who wanted a good address. On the house at which Ashenden had been asked to call there was a board up to announce that it was for sale, the shutters were closed, and there was no sign that anyone lived in it. He rang the bell and the door was opened by a non-commissioned officer so promptly that he was startled. He was not asked his business, but led immediately into a long room at the back, once evidently a dining-room, the florid decoration of which looked oddly out of keeping with the office furniture, shabby and sparse, that was in it. It gave Ashenden the impression of a room in which the brokers had taken possession. The colonel, who was known in the Intelligence Department, as Ashenden later discovered, by the letter R. rose when he came in and shook hands with him. He was a man somewhat above the middle height, lean, with a yellow, deeply-lined face, thin grey hair, and a toothbrush moustache. The thing immediately noticeable about him was the closeness with which his blue eyes were set. He only just escaped a squint. They were hard and cruel eyes, and very wary; and they gave him a cunning, shifty look. Here was a man that you could neither like nor trust at first sight. His manner was pleasant and cordial.

He asked Ashenden a good many questions and then, without further to-do, suggested that he had particular qualifications for the secret service. Ashenden was acquainted with several European languages and his profession was excellent cover; on the pretext that he was writing a book he could without attracting attention visit any neutral country. It was while they were discussing this point that R. said:

"You know, you ought to get material that would be very useful to you in your work."

"I shouldn't mind that," said Ashenden.

"I'll tell you an incident that occurred only the other day and I can vouch for its truth. I thought at the time it would make a damned good story. One of the French ministers went down to Nice to recover from a cold and he had some very important documents with him that he kept in a dispatch-case. They were very important indeed. Well, a day or two after he arrived he picked up a yellow-haired lady at some restaurant or other where there was dancing, and he got very friendly with her. To cut a long story short, he took her back to his hotel – of course it was a very imprudent thing to do – and when he came to himself in the morning the lady and the dispatch-case had disappeared. They had one or two drinks up in his room and his theory is that when his back was turned the woman slipped a drug into his glass."

R. finished and looked at Ashenden with a gleam in his close-set eyes.

"Dramatic, isn't it?" he asked.

"Do you mean to say that happened the other day?"

"The week before last."

"Impossible," cried Ashenden. "Why, we've been putting that incident on the stage for sixty years, we've written it in a thousand novels. Do you mean to say that life has only just caught up with us?"

R. was a trifle disconcerted.

"Well, if necessary, I could give you names and dates, and believe me, the Allies have been put to no end of trouble by the loss of the documents that the dispatch-case contained."

"Well, sir, if you can't do better than that in the secret service," sighed Ashenden, "I'm afraid that as a source of inspiration to the writer of fiction it's a wash-out. We really *can't* write that story much longer."

It did not take them long to settle things and when Ashenden rose to go he had already made careful note of his instructions. He was to start for Geneva next day. The last words that R. said to him, with a casualness that made them impressive, were:

"There's just one thing I think you ought to know before you take on this job. And don't forget it. If you do well you'll get no thanks and if you get into trouble you'll get no help. Does that suit you?"

"Perfectly."

"Then I'll wish you good afternoon."

Ashenden was on his way back to Geneva. The night was stormy and the wind blew cold from the mountains, but the stodgy little steamer plodded sturdily through the choppy waters of the lake. A scudding rain, just turning into sleet, swept the deck in angry gusts, like a nagging woman who cannot leave a subject alone. Ashenden had been to France in order to write and dispatch a report. A day or two before, about five in the afternoon, an Indian agent of his had come to see him in his rooms; it was only by a lucky chance that he was in, for he had no appointment with him, and the agent's instructions were to come to the hotel only in a case of urgent importance. He told Ashenden that a Bengali in the German service had recently come from Berlin with a black cane trunk in which were a number of documents interesting to the British Government. At that time the Central Powers were doing their best to foment such an agitation in India as would make it necessary for Great Britain to keep her troops in the country and perhaps send others from France. It had been found possible to get the Bengali arrested in Berne on a charge that would keep him out of harm's way for a while, but the black cane trunk could not be found. Ashenden's agent was a very brave and very clever fellow and he mixed freely with such of his countrymen as were disaffected to the interests of Great Britain. He had just discovered that the Bengali before going to Berne had, for greater safety, left the trunk in the cloak-room at Zürich station, and now that he was in gaol, awaiting trial, was unable to get the *bulletin* by which it might be obtained into the hands of any of his confederates. It was a matter of great urgency for the German Intelligence Department to secure the contents of the trunk without delay, and since it was impossible for them to get hold of it by the ordinary official means, they had decided to break into the station that very night and steal it. It was a bold and ingenious scheme and Ashenden felt a pleasant exhilaration (for a great deal of his work was uncommonly dull) when he heard of it. He recognized the dashing and unscrupulous touch of the head of the German secret service at Berne. But the burglary was arranged for two o'clock on the following morning and there was not a moment to lose. He could trust neither the telegraph nor the telephone to communicate with the British officer at Berne, and since the Indian agent could not go (he was taking his life in his hands by coming to see Ashenden and if he were noticed leaving his room it might easily be that he would be found one day floating in the lake with a knife-thrust in his back), there was nothing for it but to go himself.

There was a train to Berne that he could just catch and he put on his hat and coat as he ran downstairs. He jumped into a cab. Four hours later he rang the bell of the headquarters of the Intelligence Department. His name was known there but to one person, and it was for him that Ashenden asked. A tall tired-looking man, whom he had not met before, came out and without a word led him into an office. Ashenden told him his errand. The tall man looked at his watch.

"It's too late for us to do anything ourselves. We couldn't possibly get to Zürich in time."

He reflected.

"We'll put the Swiss authorities on the job. They can telephone, and when your friends attempt their little burglary, I have no doubt they'll find the station well guarded. Anyhow, you had better get back to Geneva."

He shook hands with Ashenden and showed him out. Ashenden was well aware that he would never know what happened then. Being no more than a tiny rivet in a vast and complicated machine, he never had the advantage of seeing a completed action. He was concerned with the beginning or the end of it, perhaps, or with some incident in the middle, but what his own doings led to he had seldom a chance of discovering. It was as unsatisfactory as those modern novels that give you a number of unrelated episodes and expect you by piecing them together to construct in your mind a connected narrative.

Notwithstanding his fur coat and his muffler, Ashenden was chilled to the bone. It was warm in the saloon and there were good lights to read by, but he thought it better not to sit there in case some habitual traveller, recognizing him, wondered why he made these constant journeys between Geneva in Switzerland and Thonon in France; and so, making the best of what shelter could be found, he passed the tedious time in the darkness of the deck. He looked in the direction of Geneva, but could see no lights, and the sleet, turning into snow, prevented him from recognizing the landmarks. Lake Leman, on fine days so trim and pretty, artificial like a piece of water in a French garden, in this tempestuous weather was as secret and as menacing as the sea. He made up his mind that, on getting back to his hotel, he would have a fire lit in his sitting-room, a hot bath, and dinner comfortably by the fireside in pyjamas and a dressing-gown. The prospect of spending an evening by himself with his pipe and a book was so agreeable that it made the misery of that journey across the lake positively worth while. Two sailors tramped past him heavily, their heads bent down to save themselves from the sleet that blew in their faces, and one of them shouted to him: *Nous arrivons*; they went to the side and withdrew a bar to allow passage for the gangway, and looking again Ashenden through the howling darkness saw mistily the lights of the quay. A welcome sight. In two or three minutes the steamer was made fast and Ashenden, muffled to the eyes, joined himself to the little knot of passengers that waited to step ashore. Though he made the journey so often – it was his duty to cross the lake into France once a week to deliver his reports and to receive instructions – he had always a faint sense of trepidation when he stood among the crowd at the gangway and waited to land. There was nothing on his passport to show that he had been in France; the steamer went round the lake touching French soil at two places, but going from Switzerland to Switzerland, so that his journey might have been to Vevey or to Lausanne; but he could never be sure that the secret police had not taken note of him, and if he had been followed and seen to land in France, the fact that there was no stamp on his passport would be difficult to explain. Of course he had his story ready, but he well knew that it was not a very convincing one, and though it might be impossible for the Swiss authorities to prove that he was anything but a casual traveller, he might nevertheless spend two or three days in gaol, which would be uncomfortable, and then be firmly conducted to the frontier, which would be mortifying. The Swiss knew well that their country was the scene of all manner of intrigues; agents of the secret service, spies, revolutionaries, and agitators infested the hotels of the principal towns and, jealous of their neutrality, they were determined to prevent conduct that might embroil them with any of the belligerent powers.

There were as usual two police officers on the quay to watch the passengers disembark and Ashenden, walking past them with as unconcerned an air as he could assume, was relieved when he had got safely by. The darkness swallowed him up and he stepped out briskly for his hotel. The wild weather with a scornful gesture had swept all the neatness from the trim promenade. The shops were closed and Ashenden passed only an occasional pedestrian who sidled along, scrunched up, as though he fled from the blind wrath of the unknown. You had a feeling in that black and bitter night that civilization, ashamed of its artificiality, cowered before the fury of elemental things. It was hail now that blew in Ashenden's face, and the pavement was wet and slippery so that he had to walk with caution. The hotel faced the lake. When he reached it and a page-boy opened the door for him, he entered the hall with a flurry of wind that sent the papers on the porter's desk flying into the air. Ashenden was dazzled by the light. He stopped to ask the porter if there were letters for him. There was nothing, and he was about to get into the lift when the porter told him that two gentlemen were waiting in his room to see him. Ashenden had no friends in Geneva.

"Oh?" he answered, not a little surprised. "Who are they?"

He had taken care to get on friendly terms with the porter and his tips for trifling services had been generous. The porter gave a discreet smile.

"There is no harm in telling you. I think they are members of the police."

"What do they want?" asked Ashenden.

"They did not say. They asked me where you were, and I told them you had gone for a walk. They said they would wait till you come back."

"How long have they been there?"

"An hour."

Ashenden's heart sank, but he took care not to let his face betray his concern.

"I'll go up and see them," he said. The liftman stood aside to let him step into the lift, but Ashenden shook his head. "I'm so cold," he said, "I'll walk up."

He wished to give himself a moment to think, but as he ascended the three flights slowly his feet were like lead. There could be small doubt why two police officers were so bent upon seeing him. He felt on a sudden dreadfully tired. He did not feel he could cope with a multitude of questions. And if he were arrested as a secret agent he must spend at least the night in a cell. He longed more than ever for a hot bath and a pleasant dinner by his fireside. He had half a mind to turn tail and walk out of the hotel, leaving everything behind him; he had his passport in his pocket and he knew by heart the hours at which trains started for the frontier: before the Swiss authorities had made up their minds what to do he would be in safety. But he continued to trudge upstairs. He did not like the notion of abandoning his job so easily; he had been sent to Geneva, knowing the risks, to do work of a certain kind, and it seemed to him that he had better go through with it. Of course it would not be very nice to spend two years in a Swiss prison, but the chance of this was, like assassination to kings, one of the inconveniences of his profession. He reached the landing of the third floor and walked to his room. Ashenden had in him, it seems, a strain of flippancy (on account of which, indeed, the critics had often reproached him) and as he stood for a moment outside the door his predicament appeared to him on a sudden rather droll. His spirits went up and he determined to brazen the thing out. It was with a genuine smile on his lips that he turned the handle and entering the room faced his visitors.

"Good evening, gentlemen," said he.

The room was brightly lit, for all the lights were on, and a fire burned in the hearth. The air was grey with smoke, since the strangers, finding it long to wait for him, had been smoking strong and inexpensive cigars. They sat in their greatcoats and bowler-hats as though they had only just that moment come in; but the ashes in the little tray on the table would alone have suggested that they had been long enough there to make themselves familiar with their surroundings. They were two powerful men, with black moustaches, on the stout side, heavily built, and they reminded Ashenden of Fafner and Fasolt, the giants in *The Rhinegold*; their clumsy boots, the massive way they sat in their chairs, and the ponderous alertness of their expression made it obvious that they were members of the detective force. Ashenden gave his room an enveloping glance. He was a neat creature and saw at once that his things, though not in disorder, were not as he had left them. He guessed that an examination had been made of his effects. That did not disturb him, for he kept in his room no document that would compromise him; his code he had learned by heart and destroyed before leaving England, and such communications as reached him from Germany were handed to him by third parties and transmitted without delay to the proper places. There was nothing he need fear in a search, but the impression that it had been made confirmed his suspicion that he had been denounced to the authorities as a secret agent.

"What can I do for you, gentlemen?" he asked affably. "It's warm in here, wouldn't you like to take off your coats – and hats?"

It faintly irritated him that they should sit there with their hats on.

"We're only staying a minute," said one of them. "We were passing and as the *concierge* said you would be in at once, we thought we would wait."

He did not remove his hat. Ashenden unwrapped his scarf and disembarrassed himself of his heavy coat.

"Won't you have a cigar?" he asked, offering the box to the two detectives in turn.

"I don't mind if I do," said the first, Fafner, taking one, upon which the second, Fasolt, helped himself without a word, even of thanks.

The name on the box appeared to have a singular effect on their manners, for both now took off their hats.

"You must have had a very disagreeable walk in this bad weather," said Fafner, as he bit half an inch off the end of his cigar and spat it in the fire-place.

Now it was Ashenden's principle (a good one in life as well as in the Intelligence Department) always to tell as much of the truth as he conveniently could; so he answered as follows:

"What do you take me for? I wouldn't go out in such weather if I could help it. I had to go to Vevey today to see an invalid friend and I came back by boat. It was bitter on the lake."

"We come from the police," said Fafner casually.

Ashenden thought they must consider him a perfect idiot if they imagined he had not guessed that, but it was not a piece of information to which it was discreet to reply with a pleasantry.

"Oh, really," he said.

"Have you your passport on you?"

"Yes. In these war-times I think a foreigner is wise always to keep his passport on him."

"Very wise."

Ashenden handed the man the nice new passport, which gave no information about his movements other than that he had come from London three months before and had since then crossed no frontier. The detective looked at it carefully and passed it on to his colleague.

"It appears to be all in order," he said.

Ashenden, standing in front of the fire to warm himself, a cigarette between his lips, made no reply. He watched the detectives warily, but with an expression, he flattered himself, of amiable unconcern. Fasolt handed back the passport to Fafner, who tapped it reflectively with a thick forefinger.

"The chief of police told us to come here," he said, and Ashenden was conscious that both of them now looked at him with attention, "to make a few inquiries of you."

Ashenden knew that when you have nothing apposite to say it is better to hold your tongue; and when a man has made a remark that calls to his mind for an answer, he is apt to find silence a trifle disconcerting. Ashenden waited for the detective to proceed. He was not quite sure, but it seemed to him that he hesitated.

"It appears that there have been a good many complaints lately of the noise that people make when they come out of the Casino late at night. We wish to know if you personally have been troubled by the disturbance. It is evident that as your rooms look on the lake and the revellers pass your windows, if the noise is serious, you have heard it."

For an instant Ashenden was dumbfounded. What balderdash was this the detective was talking to him (boom, boom, he heard the big drum as the giant lumbered on the scene), and why on earth should the chief of police send to him to find out if his beauty sleep had been disturbed by vociferous gamblers? It looked very like a trap. But nothing is so foolish as to ascribe profundity to what on the surface is merely inept; it is a pitfall into which many an ingenuous reviewer has fallen headlong. Ashenden had a confident belief in the stupidity of the human animal, which in the course of his life had stood him in good stead. It flashed across him that if the detective asked him such a question it was because he had no shadow of proof that he was engaged in any illegal practice. It was clear that he had been denounced, but no evidence had been offered, and the search of his rooms had been fruitless. But what a silly excuse was this to make for a visit and what a poverty of invention it showed! Ashenden immediately thought of three reasons the detectives might have given for seeking an interview with him and he wished that he were on terms sufficiently familiar with them to make the suggestions. This was really an insult to the intelligence. These men were even stupider than he thought; but Ashenden had always a soft corner in his heart for the stupid and now he looked upon them with a feeling of unexpected kindliness. He would have liked to pat them gently. But he answered the question with gravity.

"To tell you the truth, I am a very sound sleeper (the result doubtless of a pure heart and an easy conscience), and I have never heard a thing."

Ashenden looked at them for the faint smile that he thought his remark deserved, but their countenances remained stolid. Ashenden, as well as an agent of the British Government, was a humorist, and he stifled the beginnings of a sigh. He assumed a slightly imposing air and adopted a more serious tone.

"But even if I had been awakened by noisy people I should not dream of complaining. At a time when there is so much trouble, misery, and unhappiness in the world, I cannot but think it very wrong to disturb the amusement of persons who are lucky enough to be able to amuse themselves."

"*En effet,*" said the detective. "But the fact remains that people have been disturbed and the chief of police thought the matter should be inquired into."

His colleague, who had hitherto preserved a silence that was positively sphinx-like, now broke it.

"I noticed by your passport that you are an author, *monsieur,*" he said.

Ashenden in reaction from his previous perturbation was feeling exceedingly debonair and he answered with good-humour:

"It is true. It is a profession full of tribulation, but it has now and then its compensations."

"*La gloire,*" said Fafner politely.

"Or shall we say notoriety?" hazarded Ashenden.

"And what are you doing in Geneva?"

The question was put so pleasantly that Ashenden felt it behoved him to be on his guard. A police officer amiable is more dangerous to the wise than a police officer aggressive.

"I am writing a play," said Ashenden.

He waved his hand to the papers on his table. Four eyes followed his gesture. A casual glance told him that the detectives had looked and taken note of his manuscripts.

"And why should you write a play here rather than in your own country?"

Ashenden smiled upon them with even more affability than before, since this was a question for which he had long been prepared, and it was a relief to give the answer. He was curious to see how it would go down.

"*Mais, monsieur,* there is the war. My country is in turmoil, it would be impossible to sit there quietly and write a play."

"Is it a comedy or a tragedy?"

"Oh, a comedy, and a light one at that," replied Ashenden. "The artist needs peace and quietness. How do you expect him to preserve that detachment of spirit that is demanded by creative work unless he can have perfect tranquillity? Switzerland has the good fortune to be neutral, and it seemed to me that in Geneva I should find the very surroundings I wanted."

Fafner nodded slightly to Fasolt, but whether to indicate that he thought Ashenden an imbecile or whether in sympathy with his desire for a safe retreat from a turbulent world, Ashenden had no means of knowing. Anyhow the detective evidently came to the conclusion that he could learn nothing more from talking to Ashenden, for his remarks grew now desultory and in a few minutes he rose to go.

When Ashenden, having warmly shaken their hands, closed the door behind the pair he heaved a great sigh of relief. He turned on the water for his bath, as hot as he thought he could possibly bear it, and as he undressed reflected comfortably over his escape.

The day before, an incident had occurred, that had left him on his guard. There was in his service a Swiss, known in the Intelligence Department as Bernard, who had recently come from Germany, and Ashenden, desiring to see him, had instructed him to go to a certain café at a certain time. Since he had not seen him before, so that there might be no mistake he had informed him through an intermediary what question he himself would ask and what reply he was to give. He chose the luncheon hour for the meeting, since then the café was unlikely to be crowded, and it chanced that on entering he saw but one man of about the age he knew Bernard to be. He was by himself, and going up to him Ashenden casually put to him the pre-arranged question. Then Ashenden ordered himself a Dubonnet. The spy was a stocky little fellow, shabbily dressed, with a bullet-shaped head, close-cropped, fair, with shifty blue eyes and a sallow skin. He did not inspire confidence, and but that Ashenden knew by experience how hard it was to find men willing to go into Germany he would have been surprised that his predecessor had engaged him. He was a German-Swiss and spoke French with a strong accent. He immediately asked for his wages and these Ashenden passed over to him in an envelope. They were in Swiss francs. He gave a general account of his stay in Germany and answered Ashenden's careful questions. He was by calling a waiter and had found a job in a restaurant near one of the Rhine bridges, which gave him good opportunity to get the information that was required of him. His reasons for coming to Switzerland for a few days were plausible and there could apparently be no difficulty in his crossing the frontier on his return. Ashenden expressed his satisfaction with his behaviour, gave him his orders and was prepared to finish the interview.

"Very good," said Bernard. "But before I go back to Germany I want two thousand francs."

"Do you?"

"Yes, and I want them now, before you leave this café. It's a sum I have to pay, and I've got to have it."

"I'm afraid I can't give it to you."

A scowl made the man's face even more unpleasant to look at than it was before.

"You've got to."

"What makes you think that?"

The spy leaned forward and, not raising his voice, but speaking so that only Ashenden could hear, burst out angrily:

"Do you think I'm going on risking my life for that beggarly sum you give me? Not ten days ago a man was caught at Mainz and shot. Was that one of your men?"

"We haven't got anyone at Mainz," said Ashenden, carelessly, and for all he knew it was true. He had been puzzled not to receive his usual communications from that place and Bernard's information might afford the explanation. "You knew exactly what you were to get when you took on the job, and if you weren't satisfied you needn't have taken it. I have no authority to give you a penny more."

"Do you see what I've got here?" said Bernard.

He took a small revolver out of his pocket and fingered it significantly.

"What are you going to do with it? Pawn it?"

With an angry shrug of the shoulders he put it back in his pocket. Ashenden reflected that had he known anything of the technique of the theatre Bernard would have been aware that it was useless to make a gesture that had no ulterior meaning.

"You refuse to give me the money?"

"Certainly."

The spy's manner, which at first had been obsequious, was now somewhat truculent, but he kept his head and never for a moment raised his voice. Ashenden could see that Bernard, however big a ruffian, was a reliable agent, and he made up his mind to suggest to R. that his salary should be raised. The scene diverted him. A little way off two fat citizens of Geneva, with black beards, were playing dominoes, and on the other side a young man with spectacles was with great rapidity writing sheet after sheet of an immensely long letter. A Swiss family (who knows, perhaps Robinson by name), consisting of a father and mother and four children, were sitting round a table making the best of two small cups of coffee. The *caissière* behind the counter, an imposing brunette with a large bust encased in black silk, was reading the local paper. The surroundings made the melodramatic scene in which Ashenden was engaged perfectly grotesque. His own play seemed to him much more real.

Bernard smiled. His smile was not engaging.

"Do you know that I have only to go to the police and tell them about you to have you arrested? Do you know what a Swiss prison is like?"

"No, I've often wondered lately. Do you?"

"Yes, and you wouldn't much like it."

One of the things that had bothered Ashenden was the possibility that he would be arrested before he finished his play. He disliked the notion of leaving it half done for an indefinite period. He did not know whether he would be treated as a political prisoner or as a common criminal and he had a mind to ask Bernard whether in the latter case (the only one Bernard was likely to know anything about) he would be allowed writing materials. He was afraid Bernard would think the inquiry an attempt to laugh at him. But he was feeling comparatively at ease and was able to answer Bernard's threat without heat.

"You could of course get me sentenced to two years' imprisonment."

"At least."

"No, that is the maximum, I understand, and I think it is quite enough. I won't conceal from you that I should find it extremely disagreeable. But not nearly so disagreeable as you would."

"What could you do?"

"Oh, we'd get you somehow. And after all, the war won't last for ever. You are a waiter, you want your freedom of action. I promise you that if I get into any trouble, you will never be admitted into any of the Allied countries for the rest of your life. I can't help thinking it would cramp your style."

Bernard did not reply, but looked down sulkily at the marble-topped table. Ashenden thought this was the moment to pay for the drinks and go.

"Think it over, Bernard," he said. "If you want to go back to your job, you have your instructions, and your usual wages shall be paid through the usual channels."

The spy shrugged his shoulders, and Ashenden, though not knowing in the least what was the result of their conversation, felt that it behoved him to walk out with dignity. He did so.

And now as he carefully put one foot into the bath, wondering if he could bear it, he asked himself what Bernard had in the end decided on. The water was just not scalding and he gradually let himself down into it. On the whole it seemed to him that the spy had thought it would be as well to go straight, and the source of his denunciation must be looked for elsewhere. Perhaps in the hotel itself. Ashenden lay back, and as his body grew used to the heat of the water gave a sigh of satisfaction.

"Really," he reflected, "there are moments in life when all this to-do that has led from the primeval slime to myself seems almost worth while."

Ashenden could not but think he was lucky to have wriggled out of the fix he had found himself in that afternoon. Had he been arrested and in due course sentenced, R., shrugging his shoulders, would merely have called him a damned fool and set about looking for someone to take his place. Already Ashenden knew his chief well enough to be aware that when he had told him that if he got into trouble he need look for no help he meant exactly what he said.

Ashenden, lying comfortable in his bath, was glad to think that in all probability he would be able to finish his play in peace. The police had drawn a blank and though they might watch him from now on with some care it was unlikely that they would take a further step until he had at least roughed out his third act. It behoved him to be prudent (only a fortnight ago his colleague at Lausanne had been sentenced to a term of imprisonment), but it would be foolish to be alarmed: his predecessor in Geneva, seeing himself, with an exaggerated sense of his own importance, shadowed from morning till night, had been so affected by the nervous strain that it had been found necessary to withdraw him. Twice a week Ashenden had to go to the market to receive instructions that were brought to him by an old peasant woman from French Savoy who sold butter and eggs. She came in with the other market-women and the search at the frontier was perfunctory. It was barely dawn when they crossed and the officials were only too glad to have done quickly with these chattering noisy women and get back to their warm fires and their cigars. Indeed this old lady looked so bland and innocent, with her corpulence, her fat red face, and her smiling good-natured mouth, it would have been a very astute detective who could imagine that if he took the trouble to put his hand deep down between those voluminous breasts of hers, he would find a little piece of paper that would land in the dock an honest old woman (who kept her son out of the trenches by taking this risk) and an English writer approaching middle age. Ashenden went to the market about nine when the housewives of Geneva for the most part had done their provisioning, stopped in front of the basket by the side of which, rain or wind, hot or cold, sat that indomitable creature and bought half a pound of butter. She slipped the note into his hand when he was given change for ten francs and he sauntered away. His only moment of risk was when he walked back to his hotel with the paper in his pocket, and after this scare he made up his mind to shorten as much as possible the period during which it could be found on him.

Ashenden sighed, for the water was no longer quite so hot; he could not reach the tap with his hand nor could he turn it with his toes (as every properly regulated tap should turn) and if he got up enough to add more hot water he might just as well get out altogether. On the other hand he could not pull out the plug with his foot in order to empty the bath and so force himself to get out, nor could he find in himself the will-power to step out of it like a man. He had often heard people tell him that he possessed character and he reflected that people judge hastily in the affairs of life because they judge on insufficient evidence: they had never seen him in a hot, but diminishingly hot, bath. His mind, however, wandered back to his play, and telling himself jokes and repartees that he knew by bitter experience would never look so neat on paper nor sound so well on the stage as they did then, he abstracted his mind from the fact that his bath was growing almost tepid, when he heard a knock at the door. Since he did not want anyone to enter, he had the presence of mind not to say come in, but the knocking was repeated.

"Who is it?" he cried irascibly.

"A letter."

"Come in then. Wait a minute."

Ashenden heard his bedroom-door open and getting out of the bath flung a towel round him and went in. A page-boy was waiting with a note. It needed only a verbal answer. It was from a lady staying in the hotel asking him to play bridge after dinner and was signed in the continental fashion Baronne de Higgins. Ashenden, longing for a cosy meal in his own room, in slippers and with a book leaned up against a reading-lamp, was about to refuse when it occurred to him that in the circumstances it might be discreet to show himself in the dining-room that night. It was absurd to suppose that in that hotel the news would not have spread that he had been visited by the police and it would be as well to prove to his fellow-guests that he was not disconcerted. It had passed through his mind that it might be someone in the hotel who had denounced him and indeed the name of the sprightly baroness had not failed to suggest itself to him. If it was she who had given him away there would be a certain humour in playing bridge with her. He gave the boy a message that he would be pleased to come and proceeded slowly to don his evening clothes.

The Baroness von Higgins was an Austrian, who on settling in Geneva during the first winter of the war had found it convenient to make her name look as French as possible. She spoke English and French perfectly. Her surname, so far from Teutonic, she owed to her grandfather, a Yorkshire stable-boy, who had been taken over to Austria by a Prince Blankenstein early in the nineteenth century. He had had a charming and romantic career; a very good-looking man, he attracted the attention of one of the arch-duchesses and then made such good use of his opportunities that he ended his life as a baron and minister plenipotentiary to an Italian court. The baroness, his only descendant, after an unhappy marriage, the particulars of which she was fond of relating to her acquaintance, had resumed her maiden name. She mentioned not infrequently the fact that her grandfather had been an ambassador, but never that he had been a stable-boy and Ashenden had learned this interesting detail from Vienna; for as he grew friendly with her he had thought it necessary to get a few particulars about her past, and he knew among other things that her private income did not permit her to live on the somewhat lavish scale on which she was living in Geneva. Since she had so many advantages for espionage, it was fairly safe to suppose that an alert secret service had enlisted her services and Ashenden took it for granted that she was engaged somehow on the same kind of work as himself. It increased if anything the cordiality of his relations with her.

When he went into the dining-room it was already full. He sat down at his table and feeling jaunty after his adventure ordered himself (at the expense of the British Government) a bottle of champagne. The baroness gave him a flashing, brilliant smile. She was a woman of more than forty, but in a hard and glittering manner extremely beautiful. She was a high-coloured blonde with golden hair of a metallic lustre, lovely no doubt but not attractive, and Ashenden had from the first reflected that it was not the sort of hair you would like to find in your soup. She had fine features, blue eyes, a straight nose, and a pink and white skin, but her skin was stretched over her bones a trifle tightly; she was generously *décolletée* and her white and ample bosom had the quality of marble. There was nothing in her appearance to suggest the yielding tenderness that the susceptible find so alluring. She was magnificently gowned, but scantily bejewelled, so that Ashenden, who knew something of these matters, concluded that the superior authority had given her *carte blanche* at a dress-maker's but had not thought it prudent or necessary to provide her with rings or pearls. She was notwithstanding so showy that but for R.'s story of the minister, Ashenden would have thought the sight of her alone must have aroused in anyone on whom she desired to exercise her wiles the sense of prudence.

While he waited for his dinner to be served, Ashenden cast his eyes over the company. Most of the persons gathered were old friends by sight. At that time Geneva was a hot-bed of intrigue and its home was the hotel at which Ashenden was staying. There were French-men there, Italians and Russians, Turks, Rumanians, Greeks, and Egyptians. Some had fled their country, some doubtless represented it. There was a Bulgarian, an agent of Ashenden, whom for greater safety he had never even spoken to in Geneva; he was dining that night with two fellow-countrymen and in a day or so, if he was not killed in the interval, might have a very interesting communication to make. Then there was a little German prostitute, with china-blue eyes and a doll-like face, who made frequent journeys along the lake and up to Berne, and in the exercise of her profession got little titbits of information over which doubtless they pondered with deliberation in Berlin. She was of course of a different class from the baroness and hunted much easier game. But Ashenden was surprised to catch sight of Count von Holzminden and wondered what on earth he was doing there. This was the German agent in Vevey and he came over to Geneva only on occasion. Once Ashenden had seen him in the old quarter of the city, with its silent houses and deserted streets, talking at a corner to a man whose appearance very much suggested the spy and he would have given a great deal to hear what they said to one another. It had amused him to come across the Count, for in London before the war he had known him fairly well. He was of great family and indeed related to the Hohenzollerns. He was fond of England; he danced well, rode well, and shot well; people said he was more English than the English. He was a tall, thin fellow, in well-cut clothes, with a close-cropped Prussian head, and that peculiar bend of the body – as though he were just about to bow to a royalty – that you feel, rather than see, in those who have spent their lives about a court. He had charming manners and was much interested in the Fine Arts. But now Ashenden and he pretended they had never seen one another before. Each of course knew on what work the other was engaged and Ashenden had had a mind to chaff him about it – it seemed absurd when he had dined with a man off and on for years and played cards with him, to act as though he did not know him from Adam – but refrained in case the German looked upon his behaviour as further proof of the British frivolity in face of war. Ashenden was perplexed: Holzminden had never set foot in that hotel before and it was unlikely that he had done so now without good reason.

Ashenden asked himself whether this event had anything to do with the unusual presence in the dining-room of Prince Ali. At that juncture it was imprudent to ascribe any occurrence, however accidental it looked, to the hazard of coincidence. Prince Ali was an Egyptian, a near relation of the Khedive, who had fled his country when the Khedive was deposed. He was a bitter enemy of the English and was known to be actively engaged in stirring up trouble in Egypt. The week before, the Khedive in great secrecy had passed three days at the hotel and the pair of them had held constant meetings in the prince's apartments. He was a little fat man with a heavy black moustache. He was living with his two daughters and a certain pasha, Mustapha by name, who was his secretary and managed his affairs. The four of them were now dining together; they drank a great deal of champagne, but sat in a stolid silence. The two princesses were emancipated young women who spent their nights dancing in restaurants with the bloods of Geneva. They were short and stout, with fine black eyes and heavy sallow faces; and they were dressed with a rich loudness that suggested the Fish-market at Cairo rather than the Rue de la Paix. His Highness usually ate upstairs but the princesses dined every evening in the public dining-room: they were chaperoned vaguely by a little old Englishwoman, a Miss King, who had been their governess; but she sat at a table by herself and they appeared to pay no attention to her. Once Ashenden, going along a corridor, had come upon the elder of the two fat princesses berating the governess in French with a violence that took his breath away. She was shouting at the top of her voice and suddenly smacked the old woman's face. When she caught sight of Ashenden she gave him a furious look and flinging into her room slammed the door. He walked on as though he had noticed nothing.

On his arrival Ashenden had tried to scrape acquaintance with Miss King, but she had received his advances not merely with frigidity but with churlishness. He had begun by taking off his hat when he met her, and she had given him a stiff bow, then he had addressed her and she had answered with such brevity that it was evident that she wished to have nothing much to do with him. But it was not his business to be discouraged, so with what assurance he could muster he took the first opportunity to enter into conversation with her. She drew herself up and said in French, but with an English accent:

"I don't wish to make acquaintance with strangers."

She turned her back on him and, next time he saw her, cut him dead.

She was a tiny woman, just a few little bones in a bag of wrinkled skin, and her face was deeply furrowed. It was obvious that she wore a wig, it was of a mousy brown, very elaborate and not always set quite straight, and she was heavily made up, with great patches of scarlet on her withered cheeks and brilliantly red lips. She dressed fantastically in gay clothes that looked as though they had been bought higgledy-piggledy from an old-clothes shop and in the day-time she wore enormous, extravagantly girlish hats. She tripped along in very small smart shoes with very high heels. Her appearance was so grotesque that it created consternation rather than amusement. People turned in the street and stared at her with open mouths.

Ashenden was told that Miss King had not been to England since she was first engaged as governess of the prince's mother and he could not but be amazed to think of all she must have seen during those long years in the harems of Cairo. It was impossible to guess how old she was. How many of those short Eastern lives must have run their course under her eyes and what dark secrets must she have known! Ashenden wondered where she came from; an exile from her own country for so long, she must possess in it neither family nor friends: he knew that her sentiments were anti-English and if she had answered him so rudely he surmised that she had been told to be on her guard against him. She never spoke anything but French. Ashenden wondered what it was she thought of as she sat there, at luncheon and dinner by herself. He wondered if ever she read. After meals she went straight upstairs and was never seen in the public sitting-rooms. He wondered what she thought of those two emancipated princesses who wore garish frocks and danced with strange men in second-rate cafés. But when Miss King passed him on her way out of the dining-room it seemed to Ashenden that her mask of a face scowled. She appeared actively to dislike him. Her gaze met his and the pair of them looked at one another for a moment: he imagined that she tried to put into her stare an unspoken insult. It would have been pleasantly absurd in that painted, withered visage if it had not been for some reason rather oddly pathetic.

But now the Baroness de Higgins, having finished her dinner, gathered up her handkerchief and her bag, and with waiters bowing on either side sailed down the spacious room. She stopped at Ashenden's table. She looked magnificent.

"I'm so glad you can play bridge tonight," she said in perfect English, with no more than a trace of German accent. "Will you come to my sitting-room when you are ready and have your coffee?"

"What a lovely dress," said Ashenden.

"It is frightful. I have nothing to wear, I don't know what I shall do now that I cannot go to Paris. Those horrible Prussians," and her r's grew guttural as she raised her voice, "why did they want to drag my poor country into this terrible war?"

She gave a sigh, and a flashing smile, and sailed on. Ashenden was among the last to finish and when he left the dining-room it was almost empty. As he walked past Count Holzminden, Ashenden feeling very gay hazarded the shadow of a wink. The German agent could not be quite sure of it and if he suspected it might rack his brains to discover what mystery it portended. Ashenden walked up to the second floor and knocked at the baroness's door.

"*Entrez, entrez,*" she said and flung it open.

She shook both his hands with cordiality and drew him into the room. He saw that the two persons who were to make the four had already arrived. They were Prince Ali and his secretary. Ashenden was astounded.

"Allow me to introduce Mr Ashenden to Your Highness," said the baroness, speaking in her fluent French.

Ashenden bowed and took the proffered hand. The prince gave him a quick look, but did not speak. Madame de Higgins went on:

"I do not know if you have met the Pasha."

"I am delighted to make your acquaintance, Mr Ashenden," said the prince's secretary, warmly shaking his hand. "Our beautiful baroness has talked to us of your bridge and His Highness is devoted to the game. *N'est-ce pas, Altesse?*"

"*Oui, oui,*" said the prince.

Mustapha Pasha was a huge fat fellow, of forty-five perhaps, with large mobile eyes and a big black moustache. He wore a dinner jacket with a large diamond in his shirt-front and the *tarboosh* of his country. He was exceedingly voluble, and the words tumbled out of his mouth tumultuously, like marbles out of a bag. He took pains to be extremely civil to Ashenden. The prince sat in silence, looking at Ashenden quietly from under his heavy eyelids. He seemed shy.

"I have not seen you at the club, *Monsieur,*" said the pasha. "Do you not like baccarat?"

"I play but seldom."

"The baroness, who has read everything, tells me that you are a remarkable writer. Unfortunately I do not read English."

The baroness paid Ashenden some very fulsome compliments to which he listened with a proper and grateful politeness, and then, having provided her guests with coffee and liqueurs, she produced the cards. Ashenden could not but wonder why he had been asked to play. He had (he flattered himself) few illusions about himself, and so far as bridge was concerned none. He knew that he was a good player of the second class, but he had played often enough with the best players in the world to know that he was not in the same street with them. The game played now was contract, with which he was not very familiar, and the stakes were high; but the game was obviously but a pretext and Ashenden had no notion what other game was being played under the rose. It might be that knowing he was a British agent the prince and his secretary had desired to see him in order to find out what sort of person he was. Ashenden had felt for a day or two that something was in the air and this meeting confirmed his suspicions, but he had not the faintest notion of what nature this something was. His spies had told him of late nothing that signified. He was now persuaded that he owed that visit of the Swiss police to the kindly intervention of the baroness and it looked as though the bridge-party had been arranged when it was discovered that the detectives had been able to do nothing. The notion was mysterious, but diverting, and as Ashenden played one rubber after another, joining in the incessant conversation, he watched what was said by himself no less closely than what was said by the others. The war was spoken of a good deal and the baroness and the pasha expressed very anti-German sentiments. The baroness's heart was in England whence her family (the stable-boy from Yorkshire) had sprung, and the pasha looked upon Paris as his spiritual home. When the pasha talked of Montmartre and its life by night the prince was roused from his silence.

"*C'est une bien belle ville, Paris,*" he said.

"The Prince has a beautiful apartment there," said his secretary, "with beautiful pictures and life-sized statues."

Ashenden explained that he had the greatest sympathy for the national aspirations of Egypt and that he looked upon Vienna as the most pleasing capital in Europe. He was as friendly to them as they were to him. But if they were under the impression that they would get any information out of him that they had not already seen in the Swiss papers he had a notion that they were mistaken. At one moment he had a suspicion that he was being sounded upon the possibility of selling himself. It was done so discreetly that he could not be quite sure, but he had a feeling that a suggestion floated in the air that a clever writer could do his country a good turn and make a vast amount of money for himself if he cared to enter into an arrangement that would bring to a troubled world the peace that every humane man must so sincerely desire. It was plain that nothing very much would be said that first evening, but Ashenden as evasively as he could, more by general amiability than by words, tried to indicate that he was willing to hear more of the subject. While he talked with the pasha and the beautiful Austrian he was conscious that the watchful eyes of Prince Ali were upon him, and had an uneasy suspicion that they read too much of his thoughts. He felt rather than knew that the prince was an able and astute man. It was possible that after he left them the prince would tell the other two that they were wasting their time and there was nothing to be done with Ashenden.

Soon after midnight, a rubber having been finished, the prince rose from the table.

"It is getting late," he said, "and Mr Ashenden has doubtless much to do tomorrow. We must not keep him up."

Ashenden looked upon this as a signal to take himself off. He left the three together to discuss the situation and retired not a little mystified. He could only trust that they were no less puzzled than he. When he got to his room he suddenly realized that he was dog-tired. He could hardly keep his eyes open while he undressed, and the moment he flung himself into bed he fell asleep.

He would have sworn that he had not been asleep five minutes when he was dragged back to wakefulness by a knocking at the door. He listened for a moment.

"Who is it?"

"It's the maid. Open. I have something to say to you."

Cursing, Ashenden turned on his light, ran a hand through his thinning and rumpled hair (for like Julius Caesar he disliked exposing an unbecoming baldness) and unlocked and opened the door. Outside it stood a tousled Swiss maid. She wore no apron and looked as though she had thrown on her clothes in a hurry.

"The old English lady, the governess of the Egyptian princesses, is dying and she wants to see you."

"Me?" said Ashenden. "It's impossible. I don't know her. She was all right this evening."

He was confused and spoke his thoughts as they came to him.

"She asks for you. The doctor says, will you come. She cannot last much longer."

"It must be a mistake. She can't want me."

"She said your name and the number of your room. She says quick, quick."

Ashenden shrugged his shoulders. He went back into his room to put on slippers and a dressing-gown, and as an afterthought dropped a small revolver into his pocket. Ashenden believed much more in his acuteness than in a firearm, which is apt to go off at the wrong time and make a noise, but there are moments when it gives you confidence to feel your fingers round its butt, and this sudden summons seemed to him exceedingly mysterious. It was ridiculous to suppose that those two cordial stout Egyptian gentlemen were laying some sort of trap for him, but in the work upon which Ashenden was engaged the dullness of routine was apt now and again to slip quite shamelessly into the melodrama of the 'sixties. Just as passion will make use brazenly of the hackneyed phrase, so will chance show itself insensitive to the triteness of the literary convention.

Miss King's room was two floors higher than Ashenden's, and as he accompanied the chamber-maid along the corridor and up the stairs he asked her what was the matter with the old governess. She was flurried and stupid.

"I think she has had a stroke. I don't know. The night-porter woke me and said Monsieur Bridet wanted me to get up at once."

Monsieur Bridet was the assistant-manager.

"What is the time?" asked Ashenden.

"It must be three o'clock."

They arrived at Miss King's door and the maid knocked. It was opened by Monsieur Bridet. He had evidently been roused from his sleep; he wore slippers on his bare feet, grey trousers and a frock-coat over his pyjamas. He looked absurd. His hair as a rule plastered neatly on his head stood on end. He was extremely apologetic.

"A thousand excuses for disturbing you, Monsieur Ashenden, but she kept asking for you and the doctor said you should be sent for."

"It doesn't matter at all."

Ashenden walked in. It was a small back room and all the lights were on. The windows were closed and the curtains drawn. It was intensely hot. The doctor, a bearded, grizzled Swiss, was standing at the bedside. Monsieur Bridet, notwithstanding his costume and his evident harassment, found in himself the presence of mind to remain the attentive manager, and with ceremony effected the proper introduction.

"This is Mr Ashenden, for whom Miss King has been asking. Dr Arbos of the Faculty of Medicine of Geneva."

Without a word the doctor pointed to the bed. On it lay Miss King. It gave Ashenden a shock to look at her. She wore a large white cotton nightcap (on entering Ashenden had noticed the brown wig on a stand on the dressing-table) tied under the chin, and a white, voluminous nightdress that came high up in the neck. Nightcap and nightdress belonged to a past age and reminded you of Cruikshank's illustrations to the novels of Charles Dickens. Her face was greasy still with the cream she had used before going to bed to remove her make-up, but she had removed it summarily and there were streaks of black on her eyebrows and of red on her cheeks. She looked very small, lying in the bed, no larger than a child, and immensely old.

"She must be well over eighty," thought Ashenden.

She did not look human, but like a doll, the caricature of an old, old witch that an ironic toymaker had amused himself with modelling. She lay perfectly still on her back, the tiny little body hardly marked under the flatness of the blanket, her face even smaller than usual because she had removed her teeth; and you would have thought she was dead but for the black eyes, strangely large in the shrunken mask, that stared unblinkingly. Ashenden thought their expression changed when she saw him.

"Well, Miss King, I'm sorry to see you like this," he said with forced cheerfulness.

"She cannot speak," said the doctor. "She had another little stroke when the maid went to fetch you. I have just given her an injection.

She may partly recover the use of her tongue in a little while. She has something to say to you."

"I will gladly wait," said Ashenden.

He fancied that in those dark eyes he saw a look of relief. For a moment or two the four of them stood round the bed and stared at the dying woman.

"Well, if there is nothing I can do, I may just as well go back to bed," said Monsieur Bridet then.

"*Allez, mon ami*," said the doctor. "You can do nothing."

Monsieur Bridet turned to Ashenden.

"May I have a word with you?" he asked.

"Certainly."

The doctor noticed a sudden fear in Miss King's eyes.

"Do not be alarmed," he said kindly. "Monsieur Ashenden is not going. He will stay as long as you wish."

The assistant-manager took Ashenden to the door and partly closed it so that those within should not hear his undertones.

"I can count on your discretion, Monsieur Ashenden, can I not? It is a very disagreeable thing to have anyone die in a hotel. The other guests do not like it and we must do all we can to prevent their knowing. I shall have the body removed the first possible moment and I shall be extremely obliged if you will not say that there has been a death."

"You can have every confidence in me," said Ashenden.

"It is very unfortunate that the manager should be away for the night. I am afraid he will be exceedingly displeased. Of course if it had been possible I would have sent for an ambulance and had her taken to the hospital, but the doctor said she might die before we got her downstairs and absolutely refused to let me. It is not my fault if she dies in the hotel."

"Death so often chooses its moments without consideration," murmured Ashenden.

"After all she is an old woman, she should have died years ago. What did this Egyptian prince want to have a governess of that age for? He ought to have sent her back to her own country. These Orientals, they are always giving trouble."

"Where is the prince now?" asked Ashenden. "She has been in his service for many years. Ought you not to wake him?"

"He is not in the hotel. He went out with his secretary. He may be playing baccarat. I do not know. Anyhow I cannot send all over Geneva to find him."

"And the princesses?"

"They have not come in. They seldom return to the hotel till dawn. They are mad about dancing. I do not know where they are; in any case they would not thank me for dragging them away from their diversions because their governess has had a stroke. I know what they are. The night-porter will tell them when they arrive and then they can please themselves. She does not want them. When the night-porter fetched me and I went into her room I asked where His Highness was and she cried with all her strength: no, no."

"She could talk then?"

"Yes, after a fashion, but the thing that surprised me was that she spoke in English. She always insisted on talking French. You know, she hated the English."

"What did she want with me?"

"That I cannot tell you. She said she had something that she must say to you at once. It is funny, she knew the number of your room. At first when she asked for you I would not let them send. I cannot have my clients disturbed in the middle of the night because a crazy old woman asks for them. You have the right to your sleep, I imagine. But when the doctor came he insisted. She gave us no peace and when I said she must wait till morning she cried."

Ashenden looked at the assistant-manager. He seemed to find nothing at all touching in the scene he related.

"The doctor asked who you were and when I told him he said that perhaps she wished to see you because you were a compatriot."

"Perhaps," said Ashenden dryly.

"Well, I shall try to get a little sleep. I shall give the night-porter orders to wake me when everything is over. Fortunately the nights are long now and if everything goes well we may be able to get the body away before it is light."

Ashenden went back into the room and immediately the dark eyes of the dying woman fixed upon him. He felt that it was incumbent upon him to say something, but as he spoke he reflected on the foolish way in which one speaks to the sick.

"I'm afraid you're feeling very ill, Miss King."

It seemed to him that a flash of anger crossed her eyes and Ashenden could not but imagine that she was exasperated by his futile words.

"You do not mind waiting?" asked the doctor.

"Of course not."

It appeared that the night-porter had been roused by the ringing of the telephone from Miss King's room, but on listening could get no one to speak. The bell continued to ring, so he went upstairs and knocked at the door. He entered with his pass-key and found Miss King lying on the floor. The telephone had fallen too. It looked as though, feeling ill, she had taken off the receiver to call for help and then collapsed. The night-porter hurried to fetch the assistant-manager and together they had lifted her back into bed. Then the maid was wakened and the doctor sent for. It gave Ashenden a queer feeling to listen to the doctor giving him these facts in Miss King's hearing. He spoke as though she could not understand his French. He spoke as though she were already dead.

Then the doctor said:

"Well, there is really nothing more that I can do. It is useless for me to stay. I can be rung up if there is any change."

Ashenden, knowing that Miss King might remain in that condition for hours, shrugged his shoulders.

"Very well."

The doctor patted her raddled cheek as though she were a child.

"You must try to sleep. I will come back in the morning."

He packed up the dispatch-case in which he had his medical appliances, washed his hands, and shuffled himself into a heavy coat. Ashenden accompanied him to the door and as he shook hands the doctor gave his prognosis in a pout of his bearded mouth. Ashenden, coming back, looked at the maid. She sat on the edge of a chair, uneasily, as though in the presence of death she feared to presume. Her broad, ugly face was bloated with fatigue.

"There's no use in your staying up," Ashenden said to her. "Why don't you go to bed?"

"*Monsieur* wouldn't like to remain here alone. Somebody must stay with him."

"But good heavens, why? You have your day's work to do tomorrow."

"In any case I have to get up at five."

"Then try to get a little sleep now. You can give me a look in when you get up. *Allez*."

She rose heavily to her feet.

"As the gentleman wishes. But I will stay very willingly."

Ashenden smiled and shook his head.

"*Bonsoir, ma pauvre mademoiselle*," said the maid.

She went out and Ashenden was left alone. He sat by the bedside and again his eyes met Miss King's. It was embarrassing to encounter that unshrinking stare.

"Don't worry yourself, Miss King. You've had a slight stroke. I'm sure your speech will come back to you in a minute."

He felt certain then that he saw in those dark eyes a desperate effort to speak. He could not be mistaken. The mind was shaken by desire, but the paralysed body was incapable of obedience. For her disappointment expressed itself quite plainly, tears came to her eyes and ran down her cheeks. Ashenden took out his handkerchief and dried them.

"Don't distress yourself, Miss King. Have a little patience and I'm sure you'll be able to say anything you want."

He did not know if it was his fancy that he read in her eyes now the despairing thought that she had not the time to wait. Perhaps it was only that he ascribed to her the notions that came to himself. On the dressing-table were the governess's poor little toilet things, silver-backed embossed brushes and a silver mirror, in a corner stood a shabby black trunk, and on the top of the wardrobe a large hat-box in shiny leather. It all looked poor and mean in that trim hotel room, with its suite in highly varnished rosewood. The glare was intolerable.

"Wouldn't you be more comfortable if I turned out some of the lights?" asked Ashenden.

He put out all the lamps but the one by the bedside and then sat down again. He had a longing to smoke. Once more his eyes were held by those other eyes in which was all that remained alive of that old, old woman. He felt certain that she had something that she wanted urgently to say to him. But what was it? What was it? Perhaps she had asked him only because feeling death near, she had had a sudden yearning, she the exile of so many years, to die with someone of her own people, so long forgotten, by her side. That was what the doctor thought. But why should she have sent for him? There were other English people in the hotel. There was an old pair, a retired Indian Civilian and his wife, to whom it seemed more natural that she should turn. No one could be more of a stranger to her than Ashenden.

"Have you got something to say to me, Miss King?"

He tried to read an answer in her eyes. They continued to stare at him meaningly, but what the meaning was he had no notion.

"Don't be afraid I shall go, I will stay as long as you want me."

Nothing, nothing. The black eyes, and as he looked at them they seemed to glow mysteriously as though there were fire behind them, the eyes continued to hold him with that insistent stare. Then Ashenden asked himself if she had sent for him because she knew that he was a British agent. Was it possible that at that last moment she had had some unexpected revulsion of feeling from everything that had signified to her for so many years? Perhaps at the moment of death a love for her country, a love that had been dead for half a century, awakened again in her – ("I'm silly to fancy these idiotic things," thought Ashenden, "it's cheap and tawdry fiction") – and she had been seized with a desire to do something for what was after all her own. No one was quite himself just then and patriotism (in peacetime an attitude best left to politicians, publicists, and fools, but in the dark days of war an emotion that can wring the heart-strings), patriotism made one do odd things. It was curious that she had been unwilling to see the prince and his daughters. Did she on a sudden hate them? Did she feel herself a traitor on their account and now at the last hour wish to make amends? ("It's all very improbable, she's just a silly old maid who ought to have died years ago.") But you couldn't ignore the improbable. Ashenden, his common sense protesting, became strangely convinced that she had some secret that she wished to impart to him. She had sent for him knowing who he was because he could make use of it. She was dying and feared nothing. But was it really important? Ashenden leaned forward trying more eagerly to read what her eyes had to say. Perhaps it was only some trivial thing that was important only in her addled old brain. Ashenden was sick of the people who saw spies in every inoffensive passer-by and plots in the most innocent combination of circumstances. It was a hundred to one that if Miss King recovered her speech she would tell him something that could be of no use to anybody.

But how much must that old woman know! With her sharp eyes and sharp ears she must have had the chance to discover matters that were closely hidden from persons that seemed less insignificant. Ashenden thought again how he had the impression that something of real consequence was being prepared round about him. It was curious that Holzminden should have come to the hotel that day; and why had Prince Ali and the pasha, those wild gamblers, wasted an evening in playing contract-bridge with him? It might be that some new plan was in question, it might be that the very greatest affairs were afoot, and perhaps what the old woman had to say might make all the difference in the world. It might mean defeat or victory. It might mean anything. And there she lay powerless to speak. For a long time Ashenden stared at her in silence.

"Has it got anything to do with the war, Miss King?" he said on a sudden, loudly.

Something passed through her eyes and a tremor shot across her little old face. It was a distinct movement. Something strange and horrible was happening and Ashenden held his breath. The tiny frail body was suddenly convulsed and that old woman, as though by a final desperate effort of will, raised herself up in the bed. Ashenden sprang forward to support her.

"England," she said, just that one word, in a harsh cracked voice, and fell back in his arms.

When he laid her down on the pillow, he saw that she was dead.

THE HAIRLESS MEXICAN

"DO YOU LIKE macaroni?" said R.

"What do you mean by macaroni?" answered Ashenden. "It is like asking me if I like poetry. I like Keats and Wordsworth and Verlaine and Goethe. When you say macaroni, do you mean *spaghetti, tagliatelli, vermicelli, fettuccini, tufali, farfalli,* or just macaroni?"

"Macaroni," replied R., a man of few words.

"I like all simple things, boiled eggs, oysters and caviare, *truite au bleu,* grilled salmon, roast lamb (the saddle by preference), cold grouse, treacle tart, and rice pudding. But of all simple things the only one I can eat day in and day out, not only without disgust but with the eagerness of an appetite unimpaired by excess, is macaroni."

"I am glad of that because I want you to go down to Italy."

Ashenden had come from Geneva to meet R. at Lyons and having got there before him had spent the afternoon wandering about the dull, busy and prosaic streets of that thriving city. They were sitting now in a restaurant on the *place* to which Ashenden had taken R. on his arrival because it was reputed to give you the best food in that part of France. But since in so crowded a resort (for the Lyonese like a good dinner) you never knew what inquisitive ears were pricked up to catch any useful piece of information that might fall from your lips, they had contented themselves with talking of indifferent things. They had reached the end of an admirable repast.

"Have another glass of brandy?" said R.

"No, thank you," answered Ashenden, who was of an abstemious turn.

"One should do what one can to mitigate the rigours of war," remarked R. as he took the bottle and poured out a glass for himself and another for Ashenden.

Ashenden, thinking it would be affectation to protest, let the gesture pass, but felt bound to remonstrate with his chief on the unseemly manner in which he held the bottle.

"In my youth I was always taught that you should take a woman by the waist and a bottle by the neck," he murmured.

"I am glad you told me. I shall continue to hold a bottle by the waist and give women a wide berth."

Ashenden did not know what to reply to this and so remained silent. He sipped his brandy and R. called for his bill. It was true that he was an important person, with power to make or mar quite a large number of his fellows, and his opinions were listened to by those who held in their hands the fate of empires; but he could never face the business of tipping a waiter without an embarrassment that was obvious in his demeanour. He was tortured by the fear of making a fool of himself by giving too much or of exciting the waiter's icy scorn by giving too little. When the bill came he passed some hundred-franc notes over to Ashenden and said:

"Pay him, will you? I can never understand French figures."

The groom brought them their hats and coats.

"Would you like to go back to the hotel?" asked Ashenden.

"We might as well."

It was early in the year, but the weather had suddenly turned warm, and they walked with their coats over their arms. Ashenden knowing that R. liked a sitting-room had engaged one for him, and to this, when they reached the hotel, they went. The hotel was old-fashioned and the sitting-room was vast. It was furnished with a heavy mahogany suite upholstered in green velvet and the chairs were set primly round a large table. On the walls, covered with a dingy paper, were large steel engravings of the battles of Napoleon, and from the ceiling hung an enormous chandelier once used for gas, but now fitted with electric bulbs. It flooded the cheerless room with a cold, hard light.

"This is very nice," said R., as they went in.

"Not exactly cosy," suggested Ashenden.

"No, but it looks as though it were the best room in the place. It all looks very *good* to me."

He drew one of the green velvet chairs away from the table and, sitting down, lit a cigar. He loosened his belt and unbuttoned his tunic.

"I always thought I liked a cheroot better than anything," he said, "but since the war I've taken quite a fancy to Havanas. Oh well, I suppose it can't last for ever." The corners of his mouth flickered with the beginning of a smile. "It's an ill wind that blows nobody any good."

Ashenden took two chairs, one to sit on and one for his feet, and when R. saw him he said: "That's not a bad idea," and swinging another chair out from the table with a sigh of relief put his boots on it.

"What room is that next door?" he asked.

"That's your bedroom."

"And on the other side?"

"A banqueting hall."

R. got up and strolled slowly about the room and when he passed the windows, as though in idle curiosity, peeped through the heavy rep curtains that covered them, and then returning to his chair once more comfortably put his feet up.

"It's just as well not to take any more risk than one need," he said.

He looked at Ashenden reflectively. There was a slight smile on his thin lips, but the pale eyes, too closely set together, remained cold and steely. R.'s stare would have been embarrassing if Ashenden had not been used to it. He knew that R. was considering how he would broach the subject that he had in mind. The silence must have lasted for two or three minues.

"I'm expecting a fellow to come and see me tonight," he said at last. "His train gets in about ten." He gave his wrist-watch a glance. "He's known as the Hairless Mexican."

"Why?"

"Because he's hairless and because he's a Mexican."

"The explanation seems perfectly satisfactory," said Ashenden.

"He'll tell you all about himself. He talks nineteen to the dozen. He was on his uppers when I came across him. It appears that he was mixed up in some revolution in Mexico and had to get out with nothing but the clothes he stood up in. They were rather the worse for wear when I found him. If you want to please him you call him General. He claims to have been a general in Huerta's army, at least I think it was Huerta; anyhow he says that if things had gone right he would be Minister of War now and no end of a big bug. I've found him very useful. Not a bad chap. The only thing I really have against him is that he will use scent."

"And where do I come in?" asked Ashenden.

"He's going down to Italy. I've got rather a ticklish job for him to do and I want you to stand by. I'm not keen on trusting him with a lot of money. He's a gambler and he's a bit too fond of the girls. I suppose you came from Geneva on your Ashenden passport?"

"Yes."

"I've got another for you, a diplomatic one, by the way, in the name of Somerville with visas for France and Italy. I think you and he had better travel together. He's an amusing cove when he gets going, and I think you ought to know one another."

"What is the job?"

"I haven't yet quite made up my mind how much it's desirable for you to know about it."

Ashenden did not reply. They eyed one another in a detached manner, as though they were strangers who sat together in a railway carriage and each wondered who and what the other was.

"In your place I'd leave the General to do most of the talking. I wouldn't tell him more about yourself than you find absolutely necessary. He won't ask you any questions, I can promise you that, I think he's by way of being a gentleman after his own fashion."

"By the way, what is his real name?"

"I always call him Manuel. I don't know that he likes it very much, his name is Manuel Carmona."

"I gather by what you have not said that he's an unmitigated scoundrel."

R. smiled with his pale blue eyes.

"I don't know that I'd go quite as far as that. He hasn't had the advantages of a public-school education. His ideas of playing the game are not quite the same as yours or mine. I don't know that I'd leave a gold cigarette-case about when he was in the neighbourhood, but if he lost money to you at poker and had pinched your cigarette-case he would immediately pawn it to pay you. If he had half a chance he'd seduce your wife, but if you were up against it he'd share his last crust with you. The tears will run down his face when he hears Gounod's *Ave Maria* on the gramophone, but if you insult his dignity he'll shoot you like a dog. It appears that in Mexico it's an insult to get between a man and his drink and he told me himself that once when a Dutchman who didn't know passed between him and the bar he whipped out his revolver and shot him dead."

"Did nothing happen to him?"

"No, it appears that he belongs to one of the best families. The matter was hushed up and it was announced in the papers that the Dutchman had committed suicide. He did practically. I don't believe the Hairless Mexican has a great respect for human life."

Ashenden, who had been looking intently at R., started a little and he watched more carefully than ever his chief's tired, lined, and yellow face. He knew that he did not make this remark for nothing.

"Of course a lot of nonsense is talked about the value of human life. You might just as well say that the counters you use at poker have an intrinsic value. Their value is what you like to make it; for a general giving battle, men are merely counters and he's a fool if he allows himself for sentimental reasons to look upon them as human beings."

"But, you see, they're counters that feel and think and if they believe they're being squandered they are quite capable of refusing to be used any more."

"Anyhow, that's neither here nor there. We've had information that a man called Constantine Andreadi is on his way from Constantinople with certain documents that we want to get hold of. He's a Greek. He's an agent of Enver Pasha and Enver has great confidence in him. He's given him verbal messages that are too secret and too important to be put on paper. He's sailing from the Piraeus, on a boat called the *Ithaca*, and will land at Brindisi on his way to Rome. He's to deliver his dispatches at the German Embassy and impart what he has to say personally to the ambassador."

"I see."

At this time Italy was still neutral; the Central Powers were straining every nerve to keep her so; the Allies were doing what they could to induce her to declare war on their side.

"We don't want to get into trouble with the Italian authorities, it might be fatal, but we've got to prevent Andreadi from getting to Rome."

"At any cost?" asked Ashenden.

"Money's no object," answered R., his lips twisting into a sardonic smile.

"What do you propose to do?"

"I don't think you need bother your head about that."

"I have a fertile imagination," said Ashenden.

"I want you to go down to Naples with the Hairless Mexican. He's very keen on getting back to Cuba. It appears that his friends are organizing a show and he wants to be as near at hand as possible so that he can hop over to Mexico when things are ripe. He needs cash.

685

I've brought money down with me, in American dollars, and I shall give it to you tonight. You'd better carry it on your person."

"Is it much?"

"It's a good deal, but I thought it would be easier for you if it wasn't bulky, so I've got it in thousand-dollar notes. You will give the Hairless Mexican the notes in return for the documents that Andreadi is bringing."

A question sprang to Ashenden's lips, but he did not ask it. He asked another instead.

"Does this fellow understand what he has to do?"

"Perfectly."

There was a knock at the door. It opened and the Hairless Mexican stood before them.

"I have arrived. Good evening, Colonel. I am enchanted to see you."

R. got up.

"Had a nice journey, Manuel? This is Mr Somerville, who's going to Naples with you, General Carmona."

"Pleased to meet you, sir."

He shook Ashenden's hand with such force that he winced.

"Your hands are like iron, General," he murmured.

The Mexican gave them a glance.

"I had them manicured this morning. I do not think they were very well done. I like my nails much more highly polished."

They were cut to a point, stained bright red, and to Ashenden's mind shone like mirrors. Though it was not cold the General wore a fur coat with an astrakhan collar and with his every movement a wave of perfume was wafted to your nose.

"Take off your coat, General, and have a cigar," said R.

The Hairless Mexican was a tall man, and though thinnish gave you the impression of being very powerful; he was smartly dressed in a blue serge suit, with a silk handkerchief neatly tucked in the breast pocket of his coat, and he wore a gold bracelet on his wrist. His features were good, but a little larger than life-size, and his eyes were brown and lustrous. He was quite hairless. His yellow skin had the smoothness of a woman's and he had no eyebrows nor eyelashes; he wore a pale brown wig, rather long, and the locks were arranged in artistic disorder. This and the unwrinkled sallow face, combined with his dandified dress, gave him an appearance that was at first glance a trifle horrifying. He was repulsive and ridiculous, but you could not take your eyes from him. There was a sinister fascination in his strangeness.

He sat down and hitched up his trousers so that they should not bag at the knee.

"Well, Manuel, have you been breaking any hearts today?" said R. with his sardonic joviality.

The General turned to Ashenden.

"Our good friend, the Colonel, envies me my successes with the fair sex. I tell him he can have just as many as I if he will only listen to me. Confidence, that is all you need. If you never fear a rebuff you will never have one."

"Nonsense, Manuel, one has to have your way with the girls. There's something about you that they can't resist."

The Hairless Mexican laughed with a self-satisfaction that he did not try to disguise. He spoke English very well, with a Spanish accent, but with an American intonation.

"But since you ask me, Colonel, I don't mind telling you that I got into conversation on the train with a little woman who was coming to Lyons to see her mother-in-law. She was not very young and she was thinner than I like a woman to be, but she was possible, and she helped me to pass an agreeable hour."

"Well, let's get to business," said R.

"I am at your service, Colonel." He gave Ashenden a glance. "Is Mr Somerville a military man?"

"No," said R., "he's an author."

"It takes all sorts to make a world, as you say. I am happy to make you acquaintance, Mr Somerville. I can tell you many stories that will interest you; I am sure that we shall get on well together. You have a sympathetic air. I am very sensitive to that. To tell you the truth I am nothing but a bundle of nerves and if I am with a person who is antipathetic to me I go all to pieces."

"I hope we shall have a pleasant journey," said Ashenden.

"When does our friend arrive at Brindisi?" asked the Mexican, turning to R.

"He sails from the Piraeus in the *Ithaca* on the fourteenth. It's probably some old tub, but you'd better get down to Brindisi in good time."

"I agree with you."

R. got up and with his hands in his pockets sat on the edge of the table. In his rather shabby uniform, his tunic unbuttoned, he looked a slovenly creature beside the neat and well-dressed Mexican.

"Mr Somerville knows practically nothing of the errand on which you are going and I do not desire to tell him anything. I think you had much better keep your own counsel. He is instructed to give you the funds you need for your work, but your actions are your own affair. If you need his advice of course you can ask for it."

"I seldom ask other people's advice and never take it."

"And should you make a mess of things I trust you to keep Mr Somerville out of it. He must on no account be compromised."

"I am a man of honour, Colonel," answered the Hairless Mexican with dignity, "and I would sooner let myself be cut in a thousand pieces than betray my friends."

"That is what I have already told Mr Somerville. On the other hand, if everything pans out OK Mr Somerville is instructed to give you the sum we agreed on in return for the papers I spoke to you about. In what manner you get them is no business of his."

"That goes without saying. There is only one thing I wish to make quite plain; Mr Somerville understands of course that I have not accepted the mission with which you have entrusted me on account of the money?"

"Quite," replied R. gravely, looking him straight in the eyes.

"I am with the Allies body and soul, I cannot forgive the Germans for outraging the neutrality of Belgium, and if I accept the money that you have offered me it is because I am first and foremost a patriot. I can trust Mr Somerville implicitly, I suppose?"

R. nodded. The Mexican turned to Ashenden.

"An expedition is being arranged to free my unhappy country from the tyrants that exploit and ruin it and every penny that I receive will go on guns and cartridges. For myself I have no need of money; I am a soldier and I can live on a crust and a few olives. There are only three occupations that befit a gentleman, war, cards, and women; it costs nothing to sling a rifle over your shoulder and take to the mountains – and that is real warfare, not this manoeuvring of battalions and firing of great guns – women love me for myself, and I generally win at cards."

Ashenden found the flamboyance of this strange creature, with his scented handkerchief and his gold bracelet, very much to his taste. This was far from being just the man in the street (whose tyranny we rail at but in the end submit to) and to the amateur of the baroque in human nature he was a rarity to be considered with delight. He was a purple patch on two legs. Notwithstanding his wig and his hairless big face, he had undoubtedly an air; he was absurd, but he did not give you the impression that he was a man to be trifled with. His self-complacency was magnificent.

"Where is your kit, Manuel?" asked R.

It was possible that a frown for an instant darkened the Mexican's brow at the abrupt question that seemed a little contemptuously to brush to one side his eloquent statement, but he gave no other sign of displeasure. Ashenden suspected that he thought the Colonel a barbarian insensitive to the finer emotions.

"I left it at the station."

"Mr Somerville has a diplomatic passport so that he can get it through with his own things at the frontier without examination if you like."

"I have very little, a few suits and some linen, but perhaps it would be as well if Mr Somerville would take charge of it. I bought half a dozen suits of silk pyjamas before I left Paris."

"And what about you?" asked R., turning to Ashenden.

"I've only got one bag. It's in my room."

"You'd better have it taken to the station while there's someone about. Your train goes at one ten."

"Oh?"

This was the first Ashenden had heard that they were to start that night.

"I think you'd better get down to Naples as soon as possible."

"Very well."

R. got up.

"I'm going to bed. I don't know what you fellows want to do."

"I shall take a walk about Lyons," said the Hairless Mexican. "I am interested in life. Lend me a hundred francs, Colonel, will you? I have no change on me."

R. took out his pocket-book and gave the General the note he asked for. Then to Ashenden:

"What are you going to do? Wait here?"

"No," said Ashenden, "I shall go to the station and read."

"You'd both of you better have a whisky and soda before you go, hadn't you? What about it, Manuel?"

"It is very kind of you, but I never drink anything but champagne and brandy."

"Mixed?" asked R. dryly.

"Not necessarily," returned the other with gravity.

R. ordered brandy and soda and when it came, whereas he and Ashenden helped themselves to both, the Hairless Mexican poured himself out three parts of a tumbler of neat brandy and swallowed it into two noisy gulps. He rose to his feet and put on his coat with the astrakhan collar, seized in one hand his bold black hat and, with the gesture of a romantic actor giving up the girl he loves to one more worthy of her, held out the other to R.

"Well, Colonel, I will bid you good night and pleasant dreams. I do not expect that we shall meet again so soon."

"Don't make a hash of things, Manuel, and if you do, keep your mouth shut."

"They tell me that in one of your colleges where the sons of gentlemen are trained to become naval officers it is written in letters of gold: There is no such word as impossible in the British Navy. I do not know the meaning of the word failure."

"It has a good many synonyms," retorted R.

"I will meet you at the station, Mr Somerville," said the Hairless Mexican, and with a flourish left them.

R. looked at Ashenden with that little smile of his that always made his face look so dangerously shrewd.

"Well, what d'you think of him?"

"You've got me beat," said Ashenden. "Is he a mountebank? He seems as vain as a peacock. And with that frightful appearance can he really be the lady's man he pretends? What makes you think you can trust him?"

R. gave a low chuckle and he washed his thin, old hands with imaginary soap.

"I thought you'd like him. He's quite a character, isn't he? I think we can trust him." R.'s eyes suddenly grew opaque. "I don't believe it would pay him to double-cross us." He paused for a moment. "Anyhow we've got to risk it. I'll give you the tickets and the money and then you can take yourself off; I'm all in and I want to go to bed."

Ten minutes later Ashenden set out for the station with his bag on a porter's shoulder.

Having nearly two hours to wait he made himself comfortable in the waiting-room. The light was good and he read a novel. When the time drew near for the arrival of the train from Paris that was to take them direct to Rome, and the Hairless Mexican did not appear, Ashenden, beginning to grow a trifle anxious, went out on the platform to look for him. Ashenden suffered from that distressing malady known as train fever: an hour before his train was due he began to have apprehensions lest he should miss it; he was impatient with the porters who would never bring his luggage down from his room in time and he could not understand why the hotel bus cut it so fine; a block in the street would drive him to frenzy and the languid movements of the station porters infuriate him. The whole world seemed in a horrid plot to delay him; people got in his way as he passed through the barriers; others, a long string of them, were at the ticket-office getting tickets for other trains than his and they counted their change with exasperating care; his luggage took an interminable time to register; and then if he was travelling with friends they would go to buy newspapers, or would take a walk along the platform, and he was certain they would be left behind, they would stop to talk to a casual stranger or suddenly be seized with a desire to telephone and disappear at a run. In fact the universe conspired to make him miss every train he wanted to take and he was not happy unless he was settled in his corner, his things on the rack above him, with a good half-hour to spare. Sometimes by arriving at the station too soon he had caught an earlier train than the one he had meant to, but that was nerve-racking and caused him all the anguish of very nearly missing it.

The Rome express was signalled and there was no sign of the Hairless Mexican; it came in and he was not to be seen. Ashenden became more and more harassed. He walked quickly up and down the platform, looked in all the waiting-rooms, went to the *consigne* where the luggage was left; he could not find him. There were no sleeping-cars, but a number of people got out and he took two seats in a first-class carriage. He stood by the door, looking up and down the platform and up at the clock; it was useless to go if his travelling companion did not turn up, and Ashenden made up his mind to take his things out of the carriage as the porter cried *en voiture*; but, by George! he would give the brute hell when he found him. There were three minutes more, then two minutes, then one; at that late hour there were few persons about and all who were travelling had taken their seats. Then he saw the Hairless Mexican, followed by two porters with his luggage and accompanied by a man in a bowler-hat, walk leisurely on to the platform. He caught sight of Ashenden and waved to him.

"Ah, my dear fellow, there you are, I wondered what had become of you."

"Good God, man, hurry up or we shall miss the train."

"I never miss a train. Have you got good seats? The *chef de gare* has gone for the night; this is his assistant."

The man in the bowler-hat took it off when Ashenden nodded to him.

"But this is an ordinary carriage. I am afraid I could not travel in that." He turned to the stationmaster's assistant with an affable smile. "You must do better for me than that, *mon cher*."

"*Certainement, mon général*, I will put you into a *salon-lit*. Of course."

The assistant stationmaster led them along the train and opened the door of an empty compartment where there were two beds. The Mexican eyed it with satisfaction and watched the porters arrange the luggage.

"That will do very well. I am much obliged to you." He held out his hand to the man in the bowler-hat. "I shall not forget you and next time I see the Minister I will tell him with what civility you have treated me."

"You are too good, General. I shall be very grateful."

A whistle was blown and the train started.

"This is better than an ordinary first-class carriage, I think, Mr Somerville," said the Mexican. "A good traveller should learn how to make the best of things."

But Ashenden was still extremely cross.

"I don't know why the devil you wanted to cut it so fine. We should have looked a pair of damned fools if we'd missed the train."

"My dear fellow, there was never the smallest chance of that. When I arrived I told the stationmaster that I was General Carmona, Commander-in-Chief of the Mexican Army, and that I had to stop off in Lyons for a few hours to hold a conference with the British Field-Marshal. I asked him to hold the train for me if I was delayed and suggested that my government might see its way to conferring an order on him. I have been to Lyons before, I like the girls here; they have not the *chic* of the Parisians, but they have something, there is no denying that they have something. Will you have a mouthful of brandy before you go to sleep?"

"No, thank you," said Ashenden morosely.

"I always drink a glass before going to bed, it settles the nerves."

He looked in his suit-case and without difficulty found a bottle. He put it to his lips and had a long drink, wiped his mouth with the back of his hand and lit a cigarette. Then he took off his boots and lay down. Ashenden dimmed the light.

"I have never yet made up my mind," said the Hairless Mexican reflectively, "whether it is pleasanter to go to sleep with the kisses of a beautiful woman on your mouth or with a cigarette between your lips. Have you ever been to Mexico? I will tell you about Mexico tomorrow. Good night."

Soon Ashenden heard from his steady breathing that he was asleep and in a little while himself dozed off. Presently he woke. The Mexican, deep in slumber, lay motionless; he had taken off his fur coat and was using it as a blanket; he still wore his wig. Suddenly there was a jolt and the train with a noisy grinding of brakes stopped; in the twinkling of an eye, before Ashenden could realize that anything had happened, the Mexican was on his feet with his hand to his hip.

"What is it?" he cried.

"Nothing. Probably only a signal against us."

The Mexican sat down heavily on his bed. Ashenden turned on the light.

"You wake quickly for such a sound sleeper," he said.

"You have to in my profession."

Ashenden would have liked to ask him whether this was murder, conspiracy, or commanding armies, but was not sure that it would be discreet. The General opened his bag and took out the bottle.

"Will you have a nip?" he asked. "There is nothing like it when you wake suddenly in the night."

When Ashenden refused he put the bottle once more to his lips and poured a considerable quantity of liquor down his throat. He sighed and lit a cigarette. Although Ashenden had seen him now drink nearly a bottle of brandy, and it was probable that he had had a good deal more when he was going about the town, he was certainly quite sober. Neither in his manner nor in his speech was there any indication that he had drunk during the evening anything but lemonade.

The train started and Ashenden again fell asleep. When he awoke it was morning and turning round lazily he saw that the Mexican was awake too. He was smoking a cigarette. The floor by his side was strewn with burnt-out butts and the air was thick and grey. He had begged Ashenden not to insist on opening a window, for he said the night air was dangerous.

"I did not get up, because I was afraid of waking you. Will you do your toilet first or shall I?"

"I'm in no hurry," said Ashenden.

"I am an old campaigner, it will not take me long. Do you wash your teeth every day?"

"Yes," said Ashenden.

"So do I. It is a habit I learned in New York. I always think that a fine set of teeth are an adornment to a man."

There was a wash-basin in the compartment and the General scrubbed his teeth, with gurglings and garglings, energetically. Then he got a bottle of eau-de-Cologne from his bag, poured some of it on a towel and rubbed it over his face and hands. He took a comb and carefully arranged his wig; either it had not moved in the night or else he had set it straight before Ashenden awoke. He got another bottle out of his bag, with a spray attached to it, and squeezing a bulb covered his shirt and coat with a fine cloud of scent, did the same to his handkerchief, and then with a beaming face, like a man who has done his duty by the world and is well pleased, turned to Ashenden and said:

"Now I am ready to brave the day. I will leave my things for you, you need not be afraid of the eau-de-Cologne, it is the best you can get in Paris."

"Thank you very much," said Ashenden. "All I want is soap and water."

"Water? I never use water except when I have a bath. Nothing can be worse for the skin."

When they approached the frontier, Ashenden, remembering the General's instructive gesture when he was suddenly awakened in the night, said to him:

"If you've got a revolver on you I think you'd better give it to me. With my diplomatic passport they're not likely to search me, but they might take it into their heads to go through you and we don't want to have any bothers."

"It is hardly a weapon, it is only a toy," returned the Mexican, taking out of his hip-pocket a fully loaded revolver of formidable dimensions. "I do not like parting with it even for an hour, it gives me the feeling that I am not fully dressed. But you are quite right, we do not want to take any risks; I will give you my knife as well. I would always rather use a knife than a revolver; I think it is a more elegant weapon."

"I daresay it is only a matter of habit," answered Ashenden. "Perhaps you are more at home with a knife."

"Anyone can pull a trigger, but it needs a man to use a knife."

To Ashenden it looked as though it were in a single movement that he tore open his waistcoat and from his belt snatched and opened a long knife of murderous aspect. He handed it to Ashenden with a pleased smile on his large, ugly, and naked face.

"There's a pretty piece of work for you, Mr Somerville. I've never seen a better bit of steel in my life, it takes an edge like a razor and it's strong; you can cut a cigarette-paper with it and you can hew down an oak. There is nothing to get out of order and when it is closed it might be the knife a schoolboy uses to cut notches in his desk."

He shut it with a click and Ashenden put it along with the revolver in his pocket.

"Have you anything else?"

"My hands," replied the Mexican with arrogance, "but those I daresay the Custom officials will not make trouble about."

Ashenden remembered the iron grip he had given him when they shook hands and slightly shuddered. They were large and long and smooth; there was not a hair on them or on the wrists, and with the pointed, rosy, manicured nails there was really something sinister about them.

Ashenden and General Carmona went through the formalities at the frontier independently and when they returned to their carriage Ashenden handed back to his companion the revolver and the knife. He sighed.

"Now I feel more comfortable. What do you say to a game of cards?"

"I should like it," said Ashenden.

The Hairless Mexican opened his bag again and from a corner extracted a greasy pack of French cards. He asked Ashenden whether he played *écarté* and when Ashenden told him that he did not suggested piquet. This was a game that Ashenden was not unfamiliar with, so they settled the stakes and began. Since both were in favour of quick action, they played the game of four hands, doubling the first and last. Ashenden had good enough cards, but the General seemed notwithstanding always to have better. Ashenden kept his eyes open and he was not careless of the possibility that his antagonist might correct the inequalities of chance, but he saw nothing to suggest that everything was not above board. He lost game after game. He was capoted and rubiconed. The score against him mounted up and up till he had lost something like a thousand francs, which at that time was a tidy sum. The General smoked innumerable cigarettes. He made them himself with a twist of the finger, a lick of his tongue and incredible celerity. At last he flung himself against the back of his seat.

"By the way, my friend, does the British Government pay your card losses when you are on a mission?" he asked.

"It certainly doesn't."

"Well, I think you have lost enough. If it went down on your expense account I would have proposed playing till we reached Rome, but you are sympathetic to me. If it is your own money I do not want to win any more of it."

He picked up the cards and put them aside. Ashenden somewhat ruefully took out a number of notes and handed them to the Mexican. He counted them and with his usual neatness put them carefully folded into his pocket-book. Then, leaning forward, he patted Ashenden almost affectionately on the knee.

"I like you, you are modest and unassuming, you have not the arrogance of your countrymen, and I am sure that you will take my advice in the spirit in which it is meant. Do not play piquet with people you don't know."

Ashenden was somewhat mortified and perhaps his face showed it, for the Mexican seized his hand.

"My dear fellow, I have not hurt your feelings? I would not do that for the world. You do not play piquet worse than most piquet players. It is not that. If we were going to be together longer I would teach you how to win at cards. One plays cards to win money and there is no sense in losing."

"I thought it was only in love and war that all things were fair," said Ashenden, with a chuckle.

"Ah, I am glad to see you smile. That is the way to take a loss. I see that you have good humour and good sense. You will go far in life. When I get back to Mexico and am in possession of my estates again you must come and stay with me. I will treat you like a king. You shall ride my best horses, we will go to bullfights together, and if there are girls you fancy you have only to say the word and you shall have them."

He began telling Ashenden of the vast territories, the *haciendas* and the mines in Mexico, of which he had been dispossessed. He told him of the feudal state in which he lived. It did not matter whether what he said was true or not, for those sonorous phrases of his were fruity with the rich-distilled perfumes of romance. He described a spacious life that seemed to belong to another age and his eloquent gestures brought before the mind's eyes tawny distances and vast green plantation, great herds of cattle and in the moonlit night the song of the blind singers that melted in the air and the twanging of guitars.

"Everything I lost, everything. In Paris I was driven to earn a pittance by giving Spanish lessons or showing Americans – *Americanos del Norte*, I mean – the night life of the city. I who have flung away a thousand *duros* on a dinner have been forced to beg my bread like a blind Indian. I who have taken pleasure in clasping a diamond bracelet round the wrist of a beautiful woman have been forced to accept a suit of clothes from a hag old enough to be my mother. Patience. Man is born to trouble as the sparks fly upward, but misfortune cannot last for ever. The time is ripe and soon we shall strike our blow."

He took up the greasy pack of cards and set them out in a number of little piles.

"Let us see what the cards say. They never lie. Ah, if I had only had greater faith in them I should have avoided the only action of my life that has weighed heavily on me. My conscience is at ease. I did what any man would do under the circumstances, but I regret that necessity forced upon me an action that I would willingly have avoided."

He looked through the cards, set some of them on one side on a system Ashenden did not understand, shuffled the remainder and once more put them in little piles.

"The cards warned me, I will never deny that, their warning was clear and definite. Love and a dark woman, danger, betrayal and death. It was as plain as the nose on your face. Any fool would have known what it meant and I have been using the cards all my life. There is hardly an action that I make without consulting them. There are no excuses. I was besotted. Ah, you of the northern races do not know what love means, you do not know how it can prevent you from sleeping, how it can take your appetite for food away so that you dwindle as if from a fever, you do not understand what a frenzy it is so that you are like a madman and you will stick at nothing to satisfy your desire. A man like me is capable of every folly and every crime when he is in love, *si, Señor,* and of heroism. He can scale mountains higher than Everest and swim seas broader than the Atlantic. He is god, he is devil. Women have been my ruin."

Once more the Hairless Mexican glanced at the cards, took some out of the little piles and left others in. He shuffled them again.

"I have been loved by multitudes of women. I do not say it in vanity. I offer no explanation. It is mere matter of fact. Go to Mexico City and ask them what they know of Manuel Carmona and of his triumphs. Ask them how many women have resisted Manuel Carmona."

Ashenden, frowning a little, watched him reflectively. He wondered whether R., that shrewd fellow who chose his instruments with such a sure instinct, had not this time made a mistake, and he was uneasy. Did the Hairless Mexican really believe that he was irresistible or was he merely a blatant liar? In the course of his manipulations he had thrown out all the cards in the pack but four, and these now lay in front of him face downwards and side by side. He touched them one by one but did not turn them up.

"There is fate," he said, "and no power on earth can change it. I hesitate. This is a moment that ever fills me with apprehension and I have to steel myself to turn over the cards that may tell me that disaster awaits me. I am a brave man, but sometimes I have reached this stage and not had the courage to look at the four vital cards."

Indeed now he eyed the backs of them with an anxiety he did not try to hide.

"What was I saying to you?"

"You were telling me that women found your fascinations irresistible," replied Ashenden dryly.

"Once all the same I found a woman who resisted me. I saw her first in a house, a *casa de mujeres* in Mexico City, she was going down the stairs as I went up; she was not very beautiful, I had had a hundred more beautiful, but she had something that took my fancy and I told the old woman who kept the house to send her to me. You will know her when you go to Mexico City; they call her La Marqueza. She said that the girl was not an inmate, but came there only from time to time and had left. I told her to have her there next evening and not to let her go till I came. But I was delayed and when I arrived La Marqueza told me that the girl had said she was not used to being kept waiting and had gone. I am a good-natured fellow and I do not mind if women are capricious and teasing, that is part of their charm, so with a laugh I sent her a note of a hundred *duros* and promised that on the following day I would be punctual. But when I went, on the minute, La Marqueza handed me back my hundred *duros* and told me the girl did not fancy me. I laughed at her impertinence. I took off the diamond ring I was wearing and told the old woman to give her that and see whether it would induce her to change her mind. In the morning La Marqueza brought me in return for my ring – a red carnation. I did not know whether to be amused or angry. I am not used to being thwarted in my passions, I never hesitate to spend money (what is it for but to squander on pretty women?), and I told La Marqueza to go to the girl and say that I would give her a thousand *duros* to dine with me that night. Presently she came back with the answer that the girl would come on the condition that I allowed her to go home immediately after dinner. I accepted with a shrug of the shoulders. I did not think she was serious. I thought that she was saying that only to make herself more desired. She came to dinner at my house. Did I say she was not beautiful? She was the most beautiful, the most exquisite creature I had ever met. I was intoxicated. She had charm and she had wit. She had all the *gracia* of the Andalusian. In one word she was adorable. I asked her why she had treated me so casually and she laughed in my face. I laid myself out to be agreeable. I exercised all my skill. I surpassed myself. But when we finished dinner she rose from her seat and bade me good night. I asked her where she was going. She said I had promised to let her go and she trusted me as a man of honour to keep my word. I expostulated, I reasoned, I raved, I stormed. She held me to my word. All I could induce her to do was to consent to dine with me the following night on the same terms.

"You will think I was a fool, I was the happiest man alive; for seven days I paid her a thousand silver *duros* to dine with me. Every evening I waited for her with my heart in my mouth, as nervous as a *novillero* at his first bullfight, and every evening she played with me, laughed at me, coquetted with me and drove me frantic. I was madly in love with her. I have never loved anyone so much before or since. I could think of nothing else. I was distracted. I neglected everything. I am a patriot and I love my country. A small band of us had got together and made up our minds that we could no longer put up with the misrule from which we were suffering. All the lucrative posts were given to other people, we were being made to pay taxes as though we were tradesmen, and we were exposed to abominable affronts. We had money and men. Our plans were made and we were ready to strike. I had an infinity of things to do, meetings to go to, ammunition to get, orders to give, I was so besotted over this woman that I could attend to nothing.

"You would have thought that I should be angry with her for making such a fool of me, me who had never known what it was not to gratify my smallest whim; I did not believe that she refused me to inflame my desires, I believed that she told the plain truth when she said that she would not give herself to me until she loved me. She said it was for me to make her love me. I thought her an angel. I was ready to wait. My passion was so consuming that sooner or later, I felt, it must communicate itself to her; it was like a fire on the prairie that devours everything around it; and at last − at last she said she loved me. My emotion was so terrific that I thought I should fall down and die. Oh, what rapture! Oh, what madness! I would have given her everything I possessed in the world, I would have torn down the stars from heaven to deck her hair; I wanted to do something to prove to her the extravagance of my love, I wanted to do the impossible, the incredible, I wanted to give her myself, my soul, my honour, all, all I had and all I was; and that night when she lay in my arms I told her of our plot and who we were that were concerned in it. I felt her body stiffen with attention, I was conscious of a flicker of her eyelids, there was something, I hardly knew what, the hand that stroked my face was dry and cold; a sudden suspicion seized me and all at once I remembered what the cards had told me: love and a dark woman, danger, betrayal, and death. Three times they'd said it and I wouldn't heed. I made no sign that I had noticed anything. She nestled up against my heart and told me that she was frightened to hear such things and asked me if So-and-so was concerned. I answered her. I wanted to make sure. One after the other, with infinite cunning, between her kisses she cajoled me into giving every detail of the plot, and now I was certain, as certain as I am that you sit before me, that she was a spy. She was a spy of the President's and she had been set to allure me with her devilish charm and now she had wormed out of me all our secrets. The lives of all of us were in her hands and I knew that if she left that room in twenty-four hours we should be dead men. And I loved her, I loved her; oh, words cannot tell you the agony of desire that burned my heart; love like that is no pleasure; it is pain, pain, but the exquisite pain that transcends all pleasure. It is that heavenly anguish that the saints speak of when they are seized with a divine ecstasy. I knew that she must not leave the room alive and I feared that if I delayed my courage would fail me.

"'I think I shall sleep,' she said.

"'Sleep, my dove,' I answered.

"'*Alma de mi corazon*,' she called me. 'Soul of my heart.' They were the last words she spoke. Those heavy lids of hers, dark like a grape and faintly humid, those heavy lids of hers closed over her eyes and in a little while I knew by the regular movement of her breast against mine that she slept. You see, I loved her, I could not bear that she should suffer; she was a spy, yes, but my heart bade me spare her the terror of knowing what must happen. It is strange, I felt no anger because she had betrayed me, I should have hated her because of her vileness; I could not, I only felt that my soul was enveloped in night. Poor thing, poor thing. I could have cried in pity for her. I drew my arm very gently from around her, my left arm that was, my right was free, and raised myself on my hand. But she was so beautiful, I turned my face away when I drew the knife with all my strength across her lovely throat. Without awaking she passed from sleep to death."

He stopped and stared frowning at the four cards that still lay, their backs upward, waiting to be turned up.

"It was in the cards. Why did I not take their warning? I will not look at them. Damn them. Take them away."

With a violent gesture he swept the whole pack on to the floor.

"Though I am a free-thinker I had masses said for her soul." He shrugged his shoulders. "The Colonel said you were a writer. What do you write?"

"Stories," replied Ashenden.

"Detective stories?"

"No."

"Why not? They are the only ones I read. If I were a writer I should write detective stories."

"They are very difficult. You need an incredible amount of invention. I devised a murder story once, but the murder was so ingenious that I could never find a way of bringing it home to the murderer, and, after all, one of the conventions of the detective story is that the mystery should in the end be solved and the criminal brought to justice."

"If your murder is as ingenious as you think the only means you have of proving the murderer's guilt is by the discovery of his motives. When once you have found a motive the chances are that you will hit upon evidence that till then had escaped you. If there is no motive the most damning evidence will be inconclusive. Imagine for instance that you went up to a man in a lonely street on a moonless night and stabbed him to the heart. Who would ever think of you? But if he was your wife's lover, or your brother, or had cheated or insulted you, then a scrap of paper, a bit of string or a chance remark would be enough to hang you. What were your movements at the time he was killed? Are there not a dozen people who saw you before and after? But if he was a total stranger you would never for a moment be suspected. It was inevitable that Jack the Ripper should escape unless he was caught in the act."

Ashenden had more than one reason to change the conversation. They were parting at Rome and he thought it necessary to come to an understanding with his companion about their respective movements. The Mexican was going to Brindisi and Ashenden to Naples. He meant to lodge at the Hotel de Belfast, which was a large second-rate hotel near the harbour frequented by commercial travellers and the thriftier kind of tripper. It would be as well to let the General have the number of his room so that he could come up if necessary without inquiring of the porter, and at the next stopping-place Ashenden got an envelope from the station-buffet and made him address it in his own writing to himself at the post-office in Brindisi. All Ashenden had to do then was to scribble a number on a sheet of paper and post it.

The Hairless Mexican shrugged his shoulders.

"To my mind all these precautions are rather childish. There is absolutely no risk. But whatever happens you may be quite sure that I will not compromise you."

"This is not the sort of job which I'm very familiar with," said Ashenden. "I'm content to follow the Colonel's instructions and know no more about it than it's essential I should."

"Quite so. Should the exigencies of the situation force me to take a drastic step and I get into trouble I shall of course be treated as a political prisoner. Sooner or later Italy is bound to come into the war on the side of the Allies and I shall be released. I have considered everything. But I beg you very seriously to have no more anxiety about the outcome of our mission than if you were going for a picnic on the Thames."

But when at last they separated and Ashenden found himself alone in a carriage on the way to Naples he heaved a great sigh of relief. He was glad to be rid of that chattering, hideous, and fantastic creature. He was gone to meet Constantine Andreadi at Brindisi and if half of what he had told Ashenden was true, Ashenden could not but congratulate himself that he did not stand in the Greek spy's shoes. He wondered what sort of man he was. There was a grimness in the notion of his coming across the blue Ionian, with his confidential papers and his dangerous secrets, all unconscious of the noose into which he was putting his head. Well, that was war, and only fools thought it could be waged with kid gloves on.

Ashenden arrived in Naples and, having taken a room at the hotel, wrote its number on a sheet of paper in block letters and posted it to the Hairless Mexican. He went to the British Consulate, where R. had arranged to send any instructions he might have for him, and found that they knew about him and everything was in order. Then he put aside these matters and made up his mind to amuse himself. Here in the South the spring was well advanced and in the busy streets the sun was hot. Ashenden knew Naples pretty well. The Pizza di San Ferdinando, with its bustle, the Piazza del Plebiscito, with its handsome church, stirred in his heart pleasant recollections. The Strada di Chiara was as noisy as ever. He stood at corners and looked up the narrow alleys that climbed the hill precipitously, those alleys of high houses with the washing set out to dry on lines across the streets like pennants flying to mark a feast-day: and he sauntered along the shore, looking at the burnished sea with Capri faintly outlined against the bay, till he came to Posilippo, where there was an old, rambling, and bedraggled *palazzo* in which in his youth he had spent many a romantic hour. He observed the curious little pain with which the memories of the past wrung his heart-strings. Then he took a fly drawn by a small and scraggy pony and rattled back over the stones to the Galleria, where he sat in the cool and drank an *americano* and looked at the people who loitered there, talking, for ever talking with vivacious gestures, and, exercising his fancy, sought from their appearance to divine their reality.

For three days Ashenden led the idle life that fitted so well the fantastical, untidy, and genial city. He did nothing from morning till night but wander at random, looking, not with the eye of the tourist who seeks for what ought to be seen, nor with the eye of the writer who looks for his own (seeing in a sunset a melodious phrase or in a face the inkling of a character), but with that of the tramp to whom whatever happens is absolute. He went to the museum to look at the statue of Agrippina the Younger, which he had particular reasons for remembering with affection, and took the opportunity to see once more the Titian and the Brueghel in the picture gallery. But he always came back to the church of Santa Chiara. Its grace, its gaiety, the airy persiflage with which it seemed to treat religion and at the back of this its sensual emotion; its extravagance, its elegance of line; to Ashenden it seemed to express, as it were in one absurd and grandiloquent metaphor, the sunny, dusty, lovely city and its bustling inhabitants. It said that life was charming and sad; it's a pity one hadn't any money but money wasn't everything, and anyway why bother when we are here today and gone tomorrow, and it was all very exciting and amusing, and after all we must make the best of things: *Facciamo una piccola combinazione.*

But on the fourth morning, when Ashenden, having just stepped out of his bath, was trying to dry himself on a towel that absorbed no moisture, his door was quickly opened and a man slipped into his room.

"What d'you want?" cried Ashenden.

"It's all right. Don't you know me?"

"Good Lord, it's the Mexican. What have you done to yourself?"

He had changed his wig and wore now a black one, close-cropped, that fitted on his head like a cap. It entirely altered the look of him and though this was still odd enough, it was quite different from that which he had borne before. He wore a shabby grey suit.

"I can only stop a minute. He's getting shaved."

Ashenden felt his cheeks suddenly redden.

"You found him then?"

"That wasn't difficult. He was the only Greek passenger on the ship. I went on board when she got in and asked for a friend who had sailed from the Piraeus. I said I had come to meet a Mr George Diogenidis. I pretended to be much puzzled at his not coming, and I got into conversation with Andreadi. He's travelling under a false name. He calls himself Lombardos. I followed him when he landed and do you know the first thing he did? He went into a barber's and had his beard shaved. What do you think of that?"

"Nothing. Anyone might have his beard shaved."

"That is not what I think. He wanted to change his appearance. Oh, he's cunning. I admire the Germans, they leave nothing to chance, he's got his whole story pat, but I'll tell you that in a minute."

"By the way, you've changed your appearance too."

"Ah, yes, this is a wig I'm wearing; it makes a difference, doesn't it?"

"I should never have known you."

"One has to take precautions. We are bosom friends. We had to spend the day in Brindisi and he cannot speak Italian. He was glad to have me help him and we travelled up together. I have brought him to this hotel. He says he is going to Rome tomorrow, but I shall not let him out of my sight; I do not want him to give me the slip. He says that he wants to see Naples and I have offered to show him everything there is to see."

"Why isn't he going to Rome today?"

"That is part of the story. He pretends he is a Greek business man who has made money during the war. He says he was the owner of two coasting steamers and has just sold them. Now he means to go to Paris and have his fling. He says he has wanted to go to Paris all his life and at last has the chance. He is close. I tried to get him to talk. I told him I was a Spaniard and had been to Brindisi to arrange communications with Turkey about war material. He listened to me and I saw he was interested, but he told me nothing and of course I did not think it wise to press him. He has the papers on his person."

"How do you know?"

"He is not anxious about his grip, but he feels every now and then round his middle. They're either in a belt or in the lining of his vest."

"Why the devil did you bring him to this hotel?"

"I thought it would be more convenient. We may want to search his luggage."

"Are you staying here too?"

"No, I am not such a fool as that. I told him I was going to Rome by the night train and would not take a room. But I must go, I promised to meet him outside the barber's in fifteen minutes."

"All right."

"Where shall I find you tonight if I want you?"

Ashenden for an instant eyed the Hairless Mexican, then with a slight frown looked away.

"I shall spend the evening in my room."

"Very well. Will you just see that there's nobody in the passage?"

Ashenden opened the door and looked out. He saw no one. The hotel in point of fact at that season was nearly empty. There were few foreigners in Naples and trade was bad.

"It's all right," said Ashenden.

The Hairless Mexican walked boldly out. Ashenden closed the door behind him. He shaved and slowly dressed. The sun was shining as brightly as usual on the square and the people who passed, the shabby little carriages with their scrawny horses, had the same air as before, but they did not any longer fill Ashenden with gaiety. He was not comfortable. He went out and called as was his habit at the Consulate to ask if there was a telegram for him. Nothing. Then he went to Cook's and looked out the trains to Rome: there was one soon after midnight and another at five in the morning. He wished he could catch the first. He did not know what were the Mexican's plans; if he really wanted to get to Cuba he would do well to make his way to Spain, and, glancing at the notices in the office, Ashenden saw that next day there was a ship sailing from Naples to Barcelona.

Ashenden was bored with Naples. The glare in the streets tired his eyes, the dust was intolerable, the noise was deafening. He went to the Galleria and had a drink. In the afternoon he went to a cinema. Then, going back to his hotel, he told the clerk that since he was starting so early in the morning he preferred to pay his bill at once, and he took his luggage to the station, leaving in his room only a dispatch-case in which were the printed part of his code and a book or two. He dined. Then returning to the hotel he sat down to wait for the Hairless Mexican. He could not conceal from himself the fact that he was exceedingly nervous. He began to read, but the book was tiresome, and he tried another; his attention wandered and he glanced at his watch. It was desperately early; he took up his book again, making up his mind that he would not look at his watch till he had read thirty pages, but though he ran his eyes conscientiously down one page after another he could not tell more than vaguely what it was he read. He looked at the time again. Good God, it was only half past ten. He wondered where the Hairless Mexican was, and what he was doing; he was afraid he would make a mess of things. It was a horrible business. Then it struck him that he had better shut the window and draw the curtains. He smoked innumerable cigarettes. He looked at his watch and it was a quarter past eleven. A thought struck him and his heart began to beat against his chest; out of curiosity he counted his pulse and was surprised to find that it was normal. Though it was a warm night and the room was stuffy his hands and feet were icy. What a nuisance it was, he reflected irritably, to have an imagination that conjured up pictures of things that you didn't in the least want to see! From his standpoint as a writer he had often considered murder, and his mind went to that fearful description of one in *Crime and Punishment*. He did not want to think of this topic, but it forced itself upon him; his book dropped to his knees and staring at the wall in front of him (it had a brown wall-paper with a pattern of dingy roses) he asked himself how, if one had to, one would commit a murder in Naples. Of course there was the Villa, the great leafy garden facing the bay in which stood the aquarium; that was deserted at night and very dark; things happened there that did not bear the light of day and prudent persons after dusk avoided its sinister paths. Beyond Posilippo the road was very solitary and there were byways that led up the hill in which by night you would never meet a soul, but how would you induce a man who had any nerves to go there? You might suggest a row in the bay, but the boatman who hired the boat would see you; it was doubtful indeed if he would let you go on the water alone; there were disreputable hotels down by the harbour where no questions were asked of persons who arrived late at night without luggage; but here again the waiter who showed you your room had the chance of a good look at you and you had on entering to sign an elaborate questionnaire.

Ashenden looked once more at the time. He was very tired. He sat now not even trying to read, his mind a blank.

Then the door opened softly and he sprang to his feet. His flesh crept. The Hairless Mexican stood before him.

"Did I startle you?" he asked smiling. "I thought you would prefer me not to knock."

"Did anyone see you come in?"

"I was let in by the night-watchman; he was asleep when I rang and didn't even look at me. I'm sorry I'm so late, but I had to change."

The Hairless Mexican wore now the clothes he had travelled down in and his fair wig. It was extraordinary how different he looked. He was bigger and more flamboyant; the very shape of his face was altered. His eyes were shining and he seemed in excellent spirits. He gave Ashenden a glance.

"How white you are, my friend! Surely you're not nervous?"

"Have you got the documents?"

"No. He hadn't got them on him. This is all he had."

He put down on the table a bulky pocket-book and a passport.

"I don't want them," said Ashenden quickly. "Take them."

With a shrug of the shoulders the Hairless Mexican put the things back in his pocket.

"What was in his belt? You said he kept feeling round his middle."

"Only money. I've looked through the pocket-book. It contains nothing but private letters and photographs of women. He must have locked the documents in his grip before coming out with me this evening."

"Damn," said Ashenden.

"I've got the key of his room. We'd better go and look through his luggage."

Ashenden felt a sensation of sickness in the pit of his stomach. He hesitated. The Mexican smiled not unkindly.

"There's no risk, *amigo*," he said, as though he were reassuring a small boy, "but if you don't feel happy, I'll go alone."

"No, I'll come with you," said Ashenden.

"There's no one awake in the hotel and Mr Andreadi won't disturb us. Take off your shoes if you like."

Ashenden did not answer. He frowned because he noticed that his hands were slightly trembling. He unlaced his shoes and slipped them off. The Mexican did the same.

"You'd better go first," he said. "Turn to the left and go straight along the corridor. It's number thirty-eight."

Ashenden opened the door and stepped out. The passage was dimly lit. It exasperated him to feel so nervous when he could not but be aware that his companion was perfectly at ease. When they reached the door the Hairless Mexican inserted the key, turned the lock, and went in. He switched on the light. Ashenden followed him and closed the door. He noticed that the shutters were shut.

"Now we're all right. We can take our time."

He took a bunch of keys out of his pocket, tried one or two and at last hit upon the right one. The suitcase was filled with clothes.

"Cheap clothes," said the Mexican contemptuously as he took them out. "My own principle is that it's always cheaper in the end to buy the best. After all one is a gentleman or one isn't a gentleman."

"Are you obliged to talk?" asked Ashenden.

"A spice of danger affects people in different ways. It only excites me, but it puts you in a bad temper, *amigo*."

"You see, I'm scared and you're not," replied Ashenden with candour.

"It's merely a matter of nerves."

Meanwhile he felt the clothes, rapidly but with care, as he took them out. There were no papers of any sort in the suitcase. Then he took out his knife and slit the lining. It was a cheap piece and the lining was gummed to the material of which the suitcase was made. There was no possibility of anything being concealed in it.

"They're not here. They must be hidden in the room."

"Are you sure he didn't deposit them in some office? At one of the consulates, for example?"

"He was never out of my sight for a moment except when he was getting shaved."

The Hairless Mexican opened the drawers and the cupboard. There was no carpet on the floor. He looked under the bed, in it, and under the mattress. His dark eyes shot up and down the room, looking for a hiding-place, and Ashenden felt that nothing escaped him.

"Perhaps he left them in charge of the clerk downstairs?"

"I should have known it. And he wouldn't dare. They're not here. I can't understand it."

He looked about the room irresolutely. He frowned in the attempt to guess at a solution of the mystery.

"Let's get out of here," said Ashenden.

"In a minute."

The Mexican went down on his knees, quickly and neatly folded the clothes, and packed them up again. He locked the bag and stood up. Then, putting out the light, he slowly opened the door and looked out. He beckoned to Ashenden and slipped into the passage. When Ashenden had followed him he stopped and locked the door, put the key in his pocket, and walked with Ashenden to his room. When they were inside it and the bolt drawn Ashenden wiped his clammy hands and his forehead.

"Thank God, we're out of that!"

"There wasn't really the smallest danger. But what are we to do now? The Colonel will be angry that the papers haven't been found."

"I'm taking the five o'clock train to Rome. I shall wire for instructions there."

"Very well, I will come with you."

"I should have thought it would suit you better to get out of the country more quickly. There's a boat tomorrow that goes to Barcelona. Why don't you take that and if necessary I can come to see you there?"

The Hairless Mexican gave a little smile.

"I see that you are anxious to be rid of me. Well, I won't thwart a wish that your inexperience in these matters excuses. I will go to Barcelona. I have a visa for Spain."

Ashenden looked at his watch. It was a little after two. He had nearly three hours to wait. His companion comfortably rolled himself a cigarette.

"What do you say to a little supper?" he asked. "I'm as hungry as a wolf."

The thought of food sickened Ashenden, but he was terribly thirsty. He did not want to go out with the Hairless Mexican, but neither did he want to stay in that hotel by himself.

"Where could one go at this hour?"

"Come along with me. I'll find you a place."

Ashenden put on his hat and took his dispatch-case in his hand. They went downstairs. In the hall the porter was sleeping soundly on a mattress on the floor. As they passed the desk, walking softly in order not to wake him, Ashenden noticed in the pigeon-hole belonging to his room a letter. He took it out and saw that it was addressed to him. They tiptoed out of the hotel and shut the door behind them. They then walked quickly away. Stopping after a hundred yards or so under a lamp-post Ashenden took the letter out of his pocket and read it; it came from the Consulate and said: *The enclosed telegram arrived tonight and in case it is urgent I am sending it round to your hotel by messenger.* It had apparently been left some time before midnight while Ashenden was sitting in his room. He opened the telegram and saw that it was in code.

"Well, it'll have to wait," he said, putting it back in his pocket.

The Hairless Mexican walked as though he knew his way through the deserted streets and Ashenden walked by his side. At last they came to a tavern in a blind alley, noisome and evil, and this the Mexican entered.

"It's not the Ritz," he said, "but at this hour of the night it's only in a place like this that we stand a chance of getting something to eat."

Ashenden found himself in a long sordid room at one end of which a wizened young man sat at a piano; there were tables standing out from the wall on each side and against them benches. A number of persons, men and women, were sitting about. They were drinking beer and wine. The women were old, painted, and hideous; and their harsh gaiety was at once noisy and lifeless. When Ashenden and the Hairless Mexican came in they all stared and when they sat down at one of the tables Ashenden looked away in order not to meet the leering eyes, just ready to break into a smile, that sought his insinuatingly. The wizened pianist strummed a tune and several couples got up and began to dance. Since there were not enough men to go round some of the women danced together. The General ordered two plates of spaghetti and a bottle of Capri wine. When the wine was brought he drank a glassful greedily and then waiting for the *pasta* eyed the women who were sitting at the other tables.

"Do you dance?" he asked Ashenden. "I'm going to ask one of these girls to have a turn with me."

He got up and Ashenden watched him go up to one who had at least flashing eyes and white teeth to recommend her; she rose and he put his arm round her. He danced well. Ashenden saw him begin talking; the woman laughed and presently the look of indifference with which she had accepted his offer changed to one of interest.

Soon they were chatting gaily. The dance came to an end and putting her back at her table he returned to Ashenden and drank another glass of wine.

"What do you think of my girl?" he asked. "Not bad, is she? It does one good to dance. Why don't you ask one of them? This is a nice place, is it not? You can always trust me to find anything like this. I have an instinct."

The pianist started again. The woman looked at the Hairless Mexican and when with his thumb he pointed to the floor she jumped up with alacrity. He buttoned up his coat, arched his back, and standing up by the side of the table waited for her to come to him. He swung her off, talking smiling, and already he was on familiar terms with everyone in the room. In fluent Italian, with his Spanish accent, he exchanged badinage with one and the other. They laughed at his sallies. Then the waiter brought two heaped platefuls of macaroni and when the Mexican saw them he stopped dancing without ceremony and, allowing his partner to get back to her table as she chose, hurried to his meal.

"I'm ravenous," he said. "And yet I ate a good dinner. Where did you dine? You're going to eat some macaroni, aren't you?"

"I have no appetite," said Ashenden.

But he began to eat and to his surprise found that he was hungry. The Hairless Mexican ate with huge mouthfuls, enjoying himself vastly; his eyes shone and he was loquacious. The woman he had danced with had in that short time told him all about herself and he repeated now to Ashenden what she had said. He stuffed huge pieces of bread into his mouth. He ordered another bottle of wine.

"Wine?" he cried scornfully. "Wine is not a drink, only champagne; it does not even quench your thirst. Well, *amigo*, are you feeling better?"

"I'm bound to say I am," smiled Ashenden.

"Practice, that is all you want, practice."

He stretched out his hand to pat Ashenden on the arm.

"What's that?" cried Ashenden with a start. "What's that stain on your cuff?"

The Hairless Mexican gave his sleeve a glance.

"That? Nothing. It's only blood. I had a little accident and cut myself."

713

Ashenden was silent. His eyes sought the clock that hung over the door.

"Are you anxious about your train? Let me have one more dance and then I'll accompany you to the station."

The Mexican got up and with his sublime self-assurance seized in his arms the woman who sat nearest to him and danced away with her. Ashenden watched him moodily. He was a monstrous, terrible figure, with that blond wig and his hairless face, but he moved with a matchless grace; his feet were small and seemed to hold the ground like the pads of a cat or a tiger; his rhythm was wonderful and you could not but see that the bedizened creature he danced with was intoxicated by his gestures. There was music in his toes and in the long arms that held her so firmly, and there was music in those long legs that seemed to move strangely from the hips. Sinister and grotesque though he was, there was in him now a feline elegance, even something of beauty, and you felt a secret, shameful fascination. To Ashenden he suggested one of those sculptures of the pre-Aztec hewers of stone, in which there is barbarism and vitality, something terrible and cruel, and yet withal a brooding and significant loveliness. All the same he would gladly have left him to finish the night by himself in that sordid dance-hall, but he knew that he must have a business conversation with him. He did not look forward to it without misgiving. He had been instructed to give Manuel Carmona certain sums in return for certain documents. Well, the documents were not forth-coming, and as for the rest – Ashenden knew nothing about that; it was no business of his. The Hairless Mexican waved gaily as he passed him.

"I will come the moment the music stops. Pay the bill and then I shall be ready."

Ashenden wished he could have seen into his mind. He could not even make a guess at its workings. Then the Mexican, with his scented handkerchief wiping the sweat from his brow, came back.

"Have you had a good time, General?" Ashenden asked him.

"I always have a good time. Poor white trash, but what do I care? I like to feel the body of a woman in my arms and see her eyes grow languid and her lips part as her desire for me melts the marrow in her bones like butter in the sun. Poor white trash, but women."

They sallied forth. The Mexican proposed that they should walk and in that quarter, at that hour, there would have been little chance of finding a cab; but the sky was starry. It was a summer night and the air was still. The silence walked beside them like the ghost of a dead man. When they neared the station the houses seemed on a sudden to take on a greyer, more rigid line, and you felt that the dawn was at hand. A little shiver trembled through the night. It was a moment of apprehension and the soul for an instant was anxious; it was as though, inherited down the years in their countless millions, it felt a witless fear that perhaps another day would not break. But they entered the station and the night once more enwrapped them. One or two porters lolled about like stage-hands after the curtain has rung down and the scene is struck. Two soldiers in dim uniforms stood motionless.

The waiting-room was empty, but Ashenden and the Hairless Mexican went to sit in the most retired part of it.

"I still have an hour before my train goes. I'll just see what this cable's about."

He took it out of his pocket and from the dispatch-case got his code. He was not then using a very elaborate one. It was in two parts, one contained in a slim book, and the other, given him on a sheet of paper and destroyed by him before he left allied territory, committed to memory. Ashenden put on his spectacles and set to work. The Hairless Mexican sat in a corner of the seat, rolling himself cigarettes and smoking; he sat there placidly, taking no notice of what Ashenden did, and enjoyed his well-earned repose. Ashenden deciphered the groups of numbers one by one and as he got it out jotted down each word on a piece of paper. His method was to abstract his mind from the sense till he had finished, since he had discovered that if you took notice of the words as they came along you often jumped to a conclusion and sometimes were led into error. So he translated quite mechanically, without paying attention to the words as he wrote them one after the other. When at last he had done he read the complete message. It ran as follows:

> *Constantine Andreadi has been detained by illness at Piraeus. He will be unable to sail. Return Geneva and await instructions.*

At first Ashenden could not understand. He read it again. He shook from head to foot. Then, for once robbed of his self-possession, he blurted out, in a hoarse, agitated, and furious whisper:

"You bloody fool, you've killed the wrong man."

GIULIA LAZZARI

ASHENDEN WAS IN the habit of asserting that he was never bored. It was one of his notions that only such persons were as had no resources in themselves and it was but the stupid that depended on the outside world for their amusement. Ashenden had no illusions about himself and such success in current letters as had come to him had left his head unturned. He distinguished acutely between fame and the notoriety that rewards the author of a successful novel or a popular play; and he was indifferent to this except in so far as it was attended with tangible benefits. He was perfectly ready to take advantage of his familiar name to get a better state-room in a ship than he had paid for, and if a Customs-house officer passed his luggage unopened because he had read his short stories Ashenden was pleased to admit that the pursuit of literature had its compensations. He sighed when eager young students of the drama sought to discuss its technique with him, and when gushing ladies tremulously whispered in his ear their admiration of his books he often wished he was dead. But he thought himself intelligent and so it was absurd that he should be bored. It was a fact that he could talk with interest to persons commonly thought so excruciatingly dull that their fellows fled from them as though they owed them money. It may be that here he was but indulging the professional instinct that was seldom dormant in him; they, his raw material, did not bore him any more than fossils bore the geologist. And now he had everything that a reasonable man could want for his entertainment. He had pleasant rooms in a good hotel and Geneva is one of the most agreeable cities in Europe to live in. He hired a boat and rowed on the lake or hired a horse and trotted sedately, for in that neat and orderly canton it is difficult to find a stretch of turf where you can have a good gallop, along the macadamized roads in the environs of the town. He wandered on foot about its old streets, trying among those grey stone houses, so quiet and dignified, to recapture the spirit of a past age. He read again with delight Rousseau's *Confessions*, and for the second or third time tried in vain to get on with *La Nouvelle Héloïse*. He wrote. He knew few people, for it was his business to keep in the background, but he had picked up a chatting acquaintance with several persons living in his hotel and he was not lonely. His life was sufficiently filled, it was varied, and when he had nothing else to do he could enjoy his own reflections; it was absurd to think that under these circumstances he could possibly be bored, and yet, like a little lonely cloud in the sky, he did see in the offing the possibility of boredom. There is a story that Louis XIV, having summoned a courtier to attend him on a ceremonial occasion, found himself ready to go as the courtier appeared; he turned to him and with icy majesty said, *J'ai failli attendre*, of which the only translation I can give, but a poor one, is, I have but just escaped waiting: so Ashenden might have admitted that he now but just escaped being bored.

It might be, he mused, as he rode along the lake on a dappled horse with a great rump and a short neck, like one of those prancing steeds that you see in old pictures, but his horse never pranced and he needed a firm jab with the spur to break even into a smart trot – it might be, he mused, that the great chiefs of the secret service in their London offices, their hands on the throttle of this great machine, led a life full of excitement; they moved their pieces here and there, they saw the pattern woven by the multitudinous threads (Ashenden was lavish with his metaphors), they made a picture out of the various pieces of the jigsaw puzzle; but it must be confessed that for the small fry like himself to be a member of the secret service was not as adventurous an affair as the public thought. Ashenden's official existence was as orderly and monotonous as a city clerk's. He saw his spies at stated intervals and paid them their wages; when he could get hold of a new one he engaged him, gave him his instructions and sent him off to Germany; he waited for the information that came through and despatched it; he went into France once a week to confer with his colleague over the frontier and to receive his orders from London; he visited the market-place on market-day to get any message the old butter-woman had brought him from the other side of the lake; he kept his eyes and ears open; and he wrote long reports which he was convinced no one read, till having inadvertently slipped a jest into one of them he received a sharp reproof for his levity. The work he was doing was evidently necessary, but it could not be called anything but monotonous. At one moment for something better to do he had considered the possibility of a flirtation with the Baroness von Higgins. He was confident now that she was an agent in the service of the Austrian Government and he looked forward to a certain entertainment in the duel he foresaw. It would be amusing to set his wits against hers. He was quite aware that she would lay snares for him and to avoid them would give him something to keep his mind from rusting. He found her not unwilling to play the game. She wrote him gushing little notes when he sent her flowers. She went for a row with him on the lake and letting her long white hand drag through the water talked of Love and hinted at a Broken Heart. They dined together and went to see a performance, in French and in prose, of *Romeo and Juliet*. Ashenden had not made up his mind how far he was prepared to go when he received a sharp note from R. to ask him what he was playing at: information "had come to hand" that he (Ashenden) was much in the society of a woman calling herself the Baroness de Higgins, who was known to be an agent of the Central Powers and it was most undesirable that he should be on any terms with her but those of frigid courtesy. Ashenden shrugged his shoulders. R. did not think him as clever as he thought himself. But he was interested to discover, what he had not known before, that there was someone in Geneva part of whose duties at all events was to keep an eye on him. There was evidently someone who had orders to see that he did not neglect his work or get into mischief. Ashenden was not a little amused. What a shrewd, unscrupulous old thing was R.! He took no risks; he trusted nobody; he made use of his instruments, but, high or low, had no opinion of them. Ashenden looked about to see whether he could spot the person who had told R. what he was doing. He wondered if it was one of the waiters in the hotel. He knew that R. had a great belief in waiters; they had the chance of seeing so much and could so easily get into places where information was lying about to be picked up. He even wondered whether R. had got his news from the Baroness herself; it would not be so strange if after all she was employed by the secret service of one of the Allied nations. Ashenden continued to be polite to the Baroness, but ceased to be attentive.

He turned his horse and trotted gently back to Geneva. An ostler from the riding-stables was waiting at the hotel door and slipping out of the saddle. Ashenden went into the hotel. At the desk the porter handed him a telegram. It was to the following effect:

> Aunt Maggie not at all well. Staying at Hôtel Lotti, Paris. If possible please go and see her. Raymond.

Raymond was one of R.'s facetious *noms de guerre*, and since Ashenden was not so fortunate as to possess an Aunt Maggie he concluded that this was an order to go to Paris. It had always seemed to Ashenden that R. had spent much of his spare time in reading detective fiction and especially when he was in a good humour he found a fantastic pleasure in aping the style of the shilling shocker. If R. was in good humour it meant that he was about to bring off a coup, for when he had brought one off he was filled with depression and then vented his spleen on his subordinates.

Ashenden, leaving his telegram with deliberate carelessness on the desk, asked at what time the express left for Paris. He glanced at the clock to see whether he had time to get to the Consulate before it closed and secure his visa. When he went upstairs to fetch his passport the porter, just as the lift doors were closed, called him.

"*Monsieur* has forgotten his telegram," he said.

"How stupid of me," said Ashenden.

Now Ashenden knew that if an Austrian baroness by any chance wondered why he had so suddenly gone to Paris she would discover that it was owing to the indisposition of a female relative. In those troublous times of war it was just as well that everything should be clear and above board. He was known at the French Consulate and so lost little time there. He had told the porter to get him a ticket and on his return to the hotel bathed and changed. He was not a little excited at the prospect of this unexpected jaunt. He liked the journey. He slept well in a sleeping-car and was not disturbed if a sudden jolt wakened him; it was pleasant to lie a while smoking a cigarette and to feel oneself in one's little cabin so enchantingly alone; the rhythmical sound as the wheels rattled over the points was an agreeable background to the pattern of one's reflections, and to speed through the open country and the night made one feel like a star speeding through space. And at the end of the journey was the unknown.

When Ashenden arrived in Paris it was chilly and a light rain was falling; he felt unshaved and he wanted a bath and clean linen; but he was in excellent spirits. He telephoned from the station to R. and asked how Aunt Maggie was.

"I'm glad to see that your affection for her was great enough to allow you to waste no time in getting here," answered R., with the ghost of a chuckle in his voice. "She's very low, but I'm sure it'll do her good to see you."

Ashenden reflected that this was the mistake the amateur humorist, as opposed to the professional, so often made; when he made a joke he harped on it. The relations of the joker to his joke should be as quick and desultory as those of a bee to its flower. He should make his joke and pass on. There is of course no harm if, like the bee approaching the flower, he buzzes a little; for it is just as well to announce to a thick-headed world that a joke is intended. But Ashenden, unlike most professional humorists, had a kindly tolerance for other people's humour and now he answered R. on his own lines.

"When would she like to see me, do you think?" he asked. "Give her my love, won't you?"

Now R. quite distinctly chuckled. Ashenden sighed.

"She'll want to titivate a little before you come, I expect. You know what she is, she likes to make the best of herself. Shall we say half past ten, and then when you've had a talk to her we might go out and lunch together somewhere."

"All right," said Ashenden. "I'll come to the Lotti at ten-thirty."

When Ashenden, clean and refreshed, reached the hotel, an orderly whom he recognized met him in the hall and took him up to R.'s apartment. He opened the door and showed Ashenden in. R. was standing with his back to a bright log fire dictating to his secretary.

"Sit down," said R. and went on with his dictation.

It was a nicely furnished sitting-room and a bunch of roses in a bowl gave the impression of a woman's hand. On a large table was a litter of papers. R. looked older than when last Ashenden had seen him. His thin yellow face was more lined and his hair was greyer. The work was telling on him. He did not spare himself. He was up at seven every morning and he worked late into the night. His uniform was spick and span, but he wore it shabbily.

"That'll do," he said. "Take all this stuff away and get on with the typing. I'll sign before I go out to lunch." Then he turned to the orderly. "I don't want to be disturbed."

The secretary, a second-lieutenant in the thirties, obviously a civilian with a temporary commission, gathered up a mass of papers and left the room. As the orderly was following, R. said:

"Wait outside. If I want you I'll call."

"Very good, sir."

When they were alone R. turned to Ashenden with what for him was cordiality.

"Have a nice journey up?"

"Yes, sir."

"What do you think of this?" he asked, looking round the room. "Not bad, is it? I never see why one shouldn't do what one can to mitigate the hardships of war."

While he was idly chatting R. gazed at Ashenden with a singular fixity. The stare of those pale eyes of his, too closely set together, gave you the impression that he looked at your naked brain and had a very poor opinion of what he saw there. R. in rare moments of expansion made no secret of the fact that he looked upon his fellow-men as fools or knaves. That was one of the obstacles he had to contend with in his calling. On the whole he preferred them knaves; you knew then what you were up against and could take steps accordingly. He was a professional soldier and had spent his career in India and the Colonies. At the outbreak of the war he was stationed in Jamaica and someone in the War Office who had had dealings with him, remembering him, brought him over and put him in the Intelligence Department. His astuteness was so great that he very soon occupied an important post. He had an immense energy and a gift for organization, no scruples, but resource, courage and determination. He had perhaps but one weakness. Throughout his life he had never come in contact with persons, especially women, of any social consequence; the only women he had ever known were the wives of his brother officers, the wives of government officials and of business men; and when, coming to London at the beginning of the war, his work brought him into contact with brilliant, beautiful, and distinguished women he was unduly dazzled. They made him feel shy, but he cultivated their society; he became quite a lady's man, and to Ashenden, who knew more about him than R. suspected, that bowl of roses told a story.

Ashenden knew that R. had not sent for him to talk about the weather and the crops, and wondered when he was coming to the point. He did not wonder long.

"You've been doing pretty well in Geneva," he said.

"I'm glad you think that, sir," replied Ashenden.

Suddenly R. looked very cold and stern. He had done with idle talk.

"I've got a job for you," he said.

Ashenden made no reply, but he felt a happy little flutter somewhere about the pit of his stomach.

"Have you ever heard of Chandra Lal?"

"No, sir."

A frown of impatience for an instant darkened the Colonel's brow. He expected his subordinates to know everything he wished them to know.

"Where have you been living all these years?"

"At 36 Chesterfield Street, Mayfair," returned Ashenden.

The shadow of a smile crossed R.'s yellow face. The somewhat impertinent reply was after his own sardonic heart. He went over to the big table and opened a dispatch-case that lay upon it. He took out a photograph and handed it to Ashenden.

"That's him."

To Ashenden, unused to Oriental faces, it looked like any of a hundred Indians that he had seen. It might have been the photograph of one or other of the rajahs who come periodically to England and are portrayed in the illustrated papers. It showed a fat-faced, swarthy man, with full lips and a fleshy nose; his hair was black, thick, and straight, and his very large eyes even in the photograph were liquid and cow-like. He looked ill-at-ease in European clothes.

"Here he is in native dress," said R., giving Ashenden another photograph.

This was full-length, whereas the first had shown only the head and shoulders, and it had evidently been taken some years earlier. He was thinner and his great, serious eyes seemed to devour his face. It was done by a native photographer in Calcutta and the surroundings were naïvely grotesque. Chandra Lal stood against a background on which had been painted a pensive palm tree and a view of the sea. One hand rested on a heavily carved table on which was a rubber-plant in a flower-pot. But in his turban and long, pale tunic he was not without dignity.

"What d'you think of him?" asked R.

"I should have said he was a man not without personality. There is a certain force there."

"Here's his dossier. Read it, will you?"

R. gave Ashenden a couple of typewritten pages and Ashenden sat down. R. put on his spectacles and began to read the letters that awaited his signature. Ashenden skimmed the report and then read it a second time more attentively. It appeared that Chandra Lal was a dangerous agitator. He was a lawyer by profession, but had taken up politics and was bitterly hostile to the British rule in India. He was a partisan of armed force and had been on more than one occasion responsible for riots in which life had been lost. He was once arrested, tried, and sentenced to two years' imprisonment; but he was at liberty at the beginning of the war and seizing his opportunity began to foment active rebellion. He was at the heart of plots to embarrass the British in India and so prevent them from transferring troops to the seat of war and with the help of immense sums given to him by German agents he was able to cause a great deal of trouble. He was concerned in two or three bomb outrages which, though beyond killing a few innocent bystanders they did little harm, yet shook the nerves of the public and so damaged its morale. He evaded all attempts to arrest him, his activity was formidable, he was here and there; but the police could never lay hands on him, and they only learned that he had been in some city when, having done his work, he had left it. At last a high reward was offered for his arrest on a charge of murder, but he escaped the country, got to America, from there went to Sweden and eventually reached Berlin. Here he busied himself with schemes to create disaffection among the native troops that had been brought to Europe. All this was narrated dryly, without comment or explanation, but from the very frigidity of the narrative you got a sense of mystery and adventure, of hairbreadth escapes and dangers dangerously encountered. The report ended as follows: C. has a wife in India and two children. He is not known to have anything to do with women. He neither drinks nor smokes. He is said to be honest. Considerable sums of money have passed through his hands and there has never been any question as to his not having made a proper (!) use of them. He has undoubted courage and is a hard worker. He is said to pride himself on keeping his word.

Ashenden returned the document to R.

"Well?"

"A fanatic." Ashenden thought there was about the man something rather romantic and attractive, but he knew that R. did not want any nonsense of that sort from him. "He looks like a very dangerous fellow."

"He is the most dangerous conspirator in or out of India. He's done more harm than all the rest of them put together. You know that there's a gang of these Indians in Berlin; well, he's the brains of it. If he could be got out of the way I could afford to ignore the others; he's the only one who has any guts. I've been trying to catch him for a year, I thought there wasn't a hope; but now at last I've got a chance and, by God, I'm going to take it."

"And what'll you do then?"

R. chuckled grimly.

"Shoot him and shoot him damn quick."

Ashenden did not answer. R. walked once or twice across the small room and then, again with his back to the fire, faced Ashenden. His thin mouth was twisted by a sarcastic smile.

"Did you notice at the end of that report I gave you it said he wasn't known to have anything to do with women? Well, that *was* true, but it isn't any longer. The damned fool has fallen in love."

R. stepped over to his dispatch-case and took out a bundle tied up with pale blue ribbon.

"Look, here are his love-letters. You're a novelist, it might amuse you to read them. In fact you should read them, it will help you to deal with the situation. Take them away with you."

R. flung the neat little bundle back into the dispatch-case.

"One wonders how an able man like that can allow himself to get besotted over a woman. It was the last thing I ever expected of him."

Ashenden's eyes travelled to the bowl of beautiful roses that stood on the table, but he said nothing. R., who missed little, saw the glance and his look suddenly darkened. Ashenden knew that he felt like asking him what the devil he was staring at. At that moment R. had no friendly feelings towards his subordinate, but he made no remark. He went back to the subject in hand.

"Anyhow that's neither here nor there. Chandra has fallen madly in love with a woman called Giulia Lazzari. He's crazy about her."

"Do you know how he picked her up?"

"Of course I do. She's a dancer, and she does Spanish dances, but she happens to be an Italian. For stage purposes she calls herself La Malagueña. You know the kind of thing. Popular Spanish music and a mantilla, a fan and a high comb. She's been dancing all over Europe for the last ten years."

"Is she any good?"

"No, rotten. She's been in the provinces in England and she's had a few engagements in London. She never got more than ten pounds a week. Chandra met her in Berlin in a Tingel-tangel, you know what that is, a cheap sort of music-hall. I take it that on the Continent she looked upon her dancing chiefly as a means to enhance her value as a prostitute."

"How did she get to Berlin during the war?"

"She's been married to a Spaniard at one time; I think she still is though they don't live together, and she travelled on a Spanish passport. It appears Chandra made a dead set for her." R. took up the Indian's photograph again and looked at it thoughtfully. "You wouldn't have thought there was anything very attractive in that greasy little nigger. God, how they run to fat! The fact remains that she fell very nearly as much in love with him as he did with her. I've got her letters too, only copies of course, he's got the originals and I daresay he keeps them tied up in pink ribbon. She's mad about him. I'm not a literary man, but I think I know when a thing rings true; anyhow you'll be reading them, and you can tell me what you think. And then people say there's no such thing as love at first sight."

R. smiled with faint irony. He was certainly in a good humour this morning.

"But how did you get hold of all these letters?"

"How did I get hold of them? How do you imagine? Owing to her Italian nationality Giulia Lazzari was eventually expelled from Germany. She was put over the Dutch frontier. Having an engagement to dance in England she was granted a visa and" – R. looked up a date among the papers – "and on the twenty-fourth of October last sailed from Rotterdam to Harwich. Since then she has danced in London, Birmingham, Portsmouth, and other places. She was arrested a fortnight ago at Hull."

"What for?"

"Espionage. She was transferred to London and I went to see her myself at Holloway."

Ashenden and R. looked at one another for a moment without speaking and it may be that each was trying his hardest to read the other's thoughts. Ashenden was wondering where the truth in all this lay and R. wondered how much of it he could advantageously tell him.

"How did you get on to her?"

"I thought it odd that the Germans should allow her to dance quite quietly in Berlin for weeks and then for no particular reason decide to put her out of the country. It would be a good introduction for espionage. And a dancer who was not too careful of her virtue might make opportunities of learning things that it would be worth somebody's while in Berlin to pay a good price for. I thought it might be as well to let her come to England and see what she was up to. I kept track of her. I discovered that she was sending letters to an address in Holland two or three times a week and two or three times a week was receiving answers from Holland. Hers were written in a queer mixture of French, German, and English; she speaks English a little and French quite well, but the answers were written entirely in English; it was good English, but not an Englishman's English, flowery and rather grandiloquent; I wondered who was writing them. They seemed to be just ordinary love-letters, but they were by way of being rather hot stuff. It was plain enough that they were coming from Germany and the writer was neither English, French, nor German. Why did he write in English? The only foreigners who know English better than any continental language are Orientals, and not Turks or Egyptians either; they know French. A Jap would write English and so would an Indian. I came to the conclusion that Giulia's lover was one of that gang of Indians that were making trouble for us in Berlin. I had no idea it was Chandra Lal till I found the photograph."

"How did you get that?"

"She carried it about with her. It was a pretty bit of work, that. She kept it locked up in her trunk, with a lot of theatrical photographs of comic singers and clowns and acrobats; it might easily have passed for the picture of some music-hall artiste in his stage dress. In fact, later, when she was arrested and asked who the photograph represented she said she didn't know, it was an Indian conjuror who had given it her and she had no idea what his name was. Anyhow I put a very smart lad on the job and he thought it queer that it should be the only photograph in the lot that came from Calcutta. He noticed that there was a number on the back, and he took it, the number, I mean; of course the photograph was replaced in the box."

"By the way, just as a matter of interest how did your very smart lad get at the photograph at all?"

R.'s eyes twinkled.

"That's none of your business. But I don't mind telling you that he was a good-looking boy. Anyhow it's of no consequence. When we got the number of the photograph we cabled to Calcutta and in a little while I received the grateful news that the object of Giulia's affections was no less a person than the incorruptible Chandra Lal. Then I thought it my duty to have Giulia watched a little more carefully. She seemed to have a sneaking fondness for naval officers. I couldn't exactly blame her for that; they are attractive, but it is unwise for ladies of easy virtue and doubtful nationality to cultivate their society in war-time. Presently I got a very pretty little body of evidence against her."

"How was she getting her stuff through?"

"She wasn't getting it through. She wasn't trying to. The Germans had turned her out quite genuinely; she wasn't working for them, she was working for Chandra. After her engagement was through in England she was planning to go to Holland again and meet him. She wasn't very clever at the work; she was nervous, but it looked easy; no one seemed to bother about her, it grew rather exciting; she was getting all sorts of interesting information without any risk. In one of her letters she said: 'I have so much to tell you, *mon petit chou* darling, and what you will be *extrêmement intéressé* to know,' and she underlined the French words."

R. paused and rubbed his hands together. His tired face bore a look of devilish enjoyment of his own cunning.

"It was espionage made easy. Of course I didn't care a damn about her, it was him I was after. Well, as soon as I'd got the goods on her I arrested her. I had enough evidence to convict a regiment of spies."

R. put his hands in his pockets and his pale lips twisted to a smile that was almost a grimace.

"Holloway's not a very cheerful place, you know."

"I imagine no prison is," remarked Ashenden.

"I left her to stew in her own juice for a week before I went to see her. She was in a very pretty state of nerves by then. The wardress told me she'd been in violent hysterics most of the time. I must say she looked like the devil."

"Is she handsome?"

"You'll see for yourself. She's not my type. I daresay she's better when she's made up and that kind of thing. I talked to her like a Dutch uncle. I put the fear of God into her. I told her she'd get ten years. I think I scared her, I know I tried to. Of course she denied everything, but the proofs were there, I assured her she hadn't got a chance. I spent three hours with her. She went all to pieces and at last she confessed everything. Then I told her that I'd let her go scot-free if she'd get Chandra to come to France. She absolutely refused, she said she'd rather die; she was very hysterical and tiresome, but I let her rave. I told her to think it over and said I'd see her in a day or two and we'd have another talk about it. In point of fact I left her for a week. She'd evidently had time to reflect, because when I came again she asked me quite calmly what it was exactly that I proposed. She'd been in a gaol a fortnight then and I expect she'd had about enough of it. I put it to her as plainly as I could and she accepted."

"I don't think I quite understand," said Ashenden.

"Don't you? I should have thought it was clear to the meanest intelligence. If she can get Chandra to cross the Swiss frontier and come into France she's to go free, either to Spain or to South America, with her passage paid."

"And how the devil is she to get Chandra to do that?"

"He's madly in love with her. He's longing to see her. His letters are almost crazy. She's written to him to say that she can't get a visa to Holland (I told you she was to join him there when her tour was over), but she can get one for Switzerland. That's a neutral country and he's safe there. He jumped at the chance. They've arranged to meet at Lausanne."

"Yes."

"When he reaches Lausanne he'll get a letter from her to say that the French authorities won't let her cross the frontier and that she's going to Thonon, which is just on the other side of the lake from Lausanne, in France, and she's going to ask him to come there."

"What makes you think he will?"

R. paused for an instant. He looked at Ashenden with a pleasant expression.

"She must make him if she doesn't want to go to penal servitude for ten years."

"I see."

"She's arriving from England this evening in custody and I should like you to take her down to Thonon by the night train."

"Me?" said Ashenden.

"Yes, I thought it the sort of job you could manage very well. Presumably you know more about human nature than most people. It'll be a pleasant change for you to spend a week or two at Thonon. I believe it's a pretty little place, fashionable too – in peace-time. You might take the baths there."

"And what do you expect me to do when I get the lady down to Thonon?"

"I leave you a free hand. I've made a few notes that may be useful to you. I'll read them to you, shall I?"

Ashenden listened attentively. R.'s plan was simple and explicit. Ashenden could not but feel unwilling admiration for the brain that had so neatly devised it.

Presently R. suggested that they should have luncheon and he asked Ashenden to take him to some place where they could see smart people. It amused Ashenden to see R., so sharp, sure of himself and alert in his office, seized as he walked into the restaurant with shyness. He talked a little too loud in order to show that he was at his ease and made himself somewhat unnecessarily at home. You saw in his manner the shabby and commonplace life he had led till the hazards of war raised him to a position of consequence. He was glad to be in that fashionable restaurant cheek by jowl with persons who bore great or distinguished names, but he felt like a schoolboy in his first top-hat, and he quailed before the steely eye of the *maitre d'hôtel*. His quick glance darted here and there and his sallow face beamed with a self-satisfaction of which he was slightly ashamed. Ashenden drew his attention to an ugly woman in black, with a lovely figure, wearing a long row of pearls.

"That is Madame de Brides. She is the mistress of the Grand Duke Theodore. She's probably one of the most influential women in Europe, she's certainly one of the cleverest."

R.'s clever eyes rested on her and he flushed a little.

"By George, this is life," he said.

Ashenden watched him curiously. Luxury is dangerous to people who have never known it and to whom its temptations are held out too suddenly. R., that shrewd, cynical man, was captivated by the vulgar glamour and the shoddy brilliance of the scene before him. Just as the advantage of culture is that it enables you to talk nonsense with distinction, so the habit of luxury allows you to regard its frills and furbelows with a proper contumely.

But when they had eaten their luncheon and were drinking their coffee Ashenden, seeing that R. was mellowed by the good meal and his surroundings, went back to the subject that was in his thoughts.

"That Indian fellow must be a rather remarkable chap," he said.

"He's got brains, of course."

"One can't help being impressed by a man who had the courage to take on almost single-handed the whole British power in India."

"I wouldn't get sentimental about him if I were you. He's nothing but a dangerous criminal."

"I don't suppose he'd use bombs if he could command a few batteries and half a dozen battalions. He uses what weapons he can. You can hardly blame him for that. After all, he's aiming at nothing for himself, is he? He's aiming at freedom for his country. On the face of it it looks as though he were justified in his actions."

But R. had no notion of what Ashenden was talking about.

"That's very far-fetched and morbid," he said. "We can't go into all that. Our job is to get him and when we've got him to shoot him."

"Of course. He's declared war and he must take his chance. I shall carry out your instructions, that's what I'm here for, but I see no harm in realizing that there's something to be admired and respected in him."

R. was once more the cool and astute judge of his fellows.

"I've not yet made up my mind whether the best men for this kind of job are those who do it with passion or those who keep their heads. Some of them are filled with hatred for the people we're up against and when we down them it gives them a sort of satisfaction like satisfying a personal grudge. Of course they're very keen on their work. You're different, aren't you? You look at it like a game of chess and you don't seem to have any feeling one way or the other. I can't quite make it out. Of course for some sort of jobs it's just what one wants."

Ashenden did not answer. He called for the bill and walked back with R. to the hotel.

The train started at eight. When he had disposed of his bag Ashenden walked along the platform. He found the carriage in which Giulia Lazzari was, but she sat in a corner looking away from the light, so that he could not see her face. She was in the charge of two detectives who had taken her over from English police at Boulogne. One of them worked with Ashenden on the French side of the Lake Geneva and as Ashenden came up he nodded to him.

"I've asked the lady if she will dine in the restaurant-car, but she prefers to have dinner in the carriage, so I've ordered a basket. Is that quite correct?"

"Quite," said Ashenden.

"My companion and I will go into the diner in turn so that she will not remain alone."

"That is very considerate of you. I will come along when we've started and have a chat with her."

"She's not disposed to be very talkative," said the detective.

"One could hardly expect it," replied Ashenden.

He walked on to get his ticket for the second service and then returned to his own carriage. Giulia Lazzari was just finishing her meal when he went back to her. From a glance at the basket he judged that she had not eaten with too poor an appetite. The detective who was guarding her opened the door when Ashenden appeared and at Ashenden's suggestion left them alone.

Giulia Lazzari gave him a sullen look.

"I hope you've had what you wanted for dinner," he said as he sat down in front of her.

She bowed slightly, but did not speak. He took out his case.

"Will you have a cigarette?"

She gave him a glance, seemed to hesitate, and then, still without a word, took one. He struck a match and, lighting it, looked at her. He was surprised. For some reason he had expected her to be fair, perhaps from some notion that an Oriental would be more likely to fall for a blonde; but she was almost swarthy. Her hair was hidden by a close-fitting hat, but her eyes were coal-black. She was far from young, she might have been thirty-five, and her skin was lined and sallow. She had at the moment no make-up on and she looked haggard. There was nothing beautiful about her but her magnificent eyes. She was big, and Ashenden thought she must be too big to dance gracefully; it might be that in Spanish costume she was a bold and flaunting figure, but there in the train, shabbily dressed, there was nothing to explain the Indian's infatuation. She gave Ashenden a long, appraising stare. She wondered evidently what sort of man he was. She blew a cloud of smoke through her nostrils and gave it a glance, then looked back at Ashenden. He could see that her sullenness was only a mask, she was nervous and frightened. She spoke in French with an Italian accent.

"Who are you?"

"My name would mean nothing to you, *madame*. I am going to Thonon. I have taken a room for you at the Hôtel de la Place. It is the only one open now. I think you will find it quite comfortable."

"Ah, it is you the Colonel spoke to me of. You are my gaoler."

"Only as a matter of form. I shall not intrude upon you."

"All the same you are my gaoler."

"I hope not for very long. I have in my pocket your passport with all the formalities completed to permit you to go to Spain."

She threw herself back into the corner of the carriage. White with those great black eyes, in the poor light, her face was suddenly a mask of despair.

"It's infamous. Oh, I think I could die happy if I could only kill that old Colonel. He has no heart. I'm so unhappy."

"I am afraid you have got yourself into a very unfortunate situation. Did you not know that espionage was a dangerous game?"

"I never sold any of the secrets. I did no harm."

"Surely only because you had no opportunity. I understand that you signed a full confession."

Ashenden spoke to her as amiably as he could, a little as though he were talking to a sick person, and there was no harshness in his voice.

"Oh, yes, I made a fool of myself. I wrote the letter the Colonel said I was to write. Why isn't that enough? What is to happen to me if he does not answer? I cannot force him to come if he does not want to."

"He has answered," said Ashenden. "I have the answer with me."

She gave a gasp and her voice broke.

"Oh, show it to me, I beseech you to let me see it."

"I have no objection to doing that. But you must return it to me."

He took Chandra's letter from his pocket and gave it to her. She snatched it from his hand. She devoured it with her eyes, there were eight pages of it, and as she read the tears streamed down her cheeks. Between her sobs she gave little exclamations of love, calling the writer by pet names French and Italian. This was the letter that Chandra had written in reply to hers telling him, on R.'s instructions, that she would meet him in Switzerland. He was mad with joy at the prospect. He told her in passionate phrases how long the time had seemed to him since they were parted, and how he had yearned for her, and now that he was to see her again so soon he did not know how he was going to bear his impatience. She finished it and let it drop to the floor.

"You can see he loves me, can't you? There's no doubt about that. I know something about it, believe me."

"Do you really love him?" asked Ashenden.

"He's the only man who's ever been kind to me. It's not very gay, the life one leads in these music-halls, all over Europe, never resting, and men – they are not much, the men who haunt those places. At first I thought he was just like the rest of them."

Ashenden picked up the letter and replaced it in his pocket-book.

"A telegram was sent in your name to the address in Holland to say that you would be at the Hotel Gibbons at Lausanne on the 14th."

"That is tomorrow."

"Yes."

She threw up her head and her eyes flashed.

"Oh, it is an infamous thing that you are forcing me to do. It is shameful."

"You are not obliged to do it," said Ashenden.

"And if I don't?"

"I'm afraid you must take the consequences."

"I can't go to prison," she cried out suddenly, "I can't, I can't; I have such a short time before me; he said ten years. Is it possible I could be sentenced to ten years?"

"If the Colonel told you so it is very possible."

"Oh, I know him. That cruel face. He would have no mercy. And what should I be in ten years? Oh, no no."

At that moment the train stopped at a station and the detective waiting in the corridor tapped on the window. Ashenden opened the door and the man gave him a picture-postcard. It was a dull little view of Pontarlier, the frontier station between France and Switzerland, and showed a dusty *place* with a statue in the middle and a few plane-trees. Ashenden handed her a pencil.

"Will you write this postcard to your lover. It will be posted at Pontarlier. Address it to the hotel at Lausanne."

She gave him a glance, but without answering took it and wrote as he directed.

"Now on the other side write: 'Delayed at frontier but everything all right. Wait at Lausanne.' Then add whatever you like, *tendresses*, if you like."

He took the postcard from her, read it to see that she had done as he directed and then reached for his hat.

"Well, I shall leave you now, I hope you will have a sleep. I will fetch you in the morning when we arrive at Thonon."

The second detective had now returned from his dinner and as Ashenden came out of the carriage the two men went in. Giulia Lazzari huddled back into her corner. Ashenden gave the postcard to an agent who was waiting to take it to Pontarlier and then made his way along the crowded train to his sleeping-car.

It was bright and sunny, though cold, next morning when they reached their destination. Ashenden, having given his bags to a porter, walked along the platform to where Giulia Lazzari and the two detectives were standing. Ashenden nodded to them.

"Well, good morning. You need not trouble to wait."

They touched their hats, gave a word of farewell to the woman, and walked away.

"Where are they going?" she asked.

"Off. You will not be bothered with them any more."

"Am I in your custody then?"

"You're in nobody's custody. I'm going to permit myself to take you to your hotel and then I shall leave you. You must try to get a good rest."

Ashenden's porter took her hand-luggage and she gave him the ticket for her trunk. They walked out of the station. A cab was waiting for them and Ashenden begged her to get in. It was a longish drive to the hotel and now and then Ashenden felt that she gave him a sidelong glance. She was perplexed. He sat without a word. When they reached the hotel the proprietor – it was a small hotel, prettily situated at the corner of a little promenade and it had a charming view – showed them the room that had been prepared for Madame Lazzari. Ashenden turned to him.

"That'll do very nicely, I think. I shall come down in a minute."

The proprietor bowed and withdrew.

"I shall do my best to see that you are comfortable, *madame*," said Ashenden. "You are here absolutely your own mistress and you may order pretty well anything you like. To the proprietor you are just a guest of the hotel like any other. You are absolutely free."

"Free to go out?" she asked quickly.

"Of course."

"With a policeman on either side of me, I suppose."

"Not at all. You are as free in the hotel as though you were in your own house and you are free to go out and come in when you choose. I should like an assurance from you that you will not write letters without my knowledge or attempt to leave Thonon without my permission."

She gave Ashenden a long stare. She could not make it out at all. She looked as though she thought it a dream.

"I am in a position that forces me to give you any assurance you ask. I give you my word of honour that I will not write a letter without showing it to you or attempt to leave this place."

"Thank you. Now I will leave you. I will do myself the pleasure of coming to see you tomorrow morning."

Ashenden nodded and went out. He stopped for five minutes at the police-station to see that everything was in order and then took the cab up the hill to a little secluded house on the outskirts of the town at which on his periodic visits to this place he stayed. It was pleasant to have a bath and a shave and get into slippers. He felt lazy and spent the rest of the morning reading a novel.

Soon after dark, for even at Thonon, though it was in France, it was thought desirable to attract attention to Ashenden as little as possible, an agent from the police-station came to see him. His name was Félix. He was a little dark Frenchman with sharp eyes and an unshaven chin, dressed in a shabby grey suit and rather down at heel, so that he looked like a lawyer's clerk out of work. Ashenden offered him a glass of wine and they sat down by the fire.

"Well, your lady lost no time," he said. "Within a quarter of an hour of her arrival she was out of the hotel with a bundle of clothes and trinkets that she sold in a shop near the market. When the afternoon boat came in she went down to the quay and bought a ticket to Évian."

Évian, it should be explained, was the next place along the lake in France and from there, crossing over, the boat went to Switzerland.

"Of course she hadn't a passport, so permission to embark was denied her."

"How did she explain that she had no passport?"

"She said she'd forgotten it. She said she had an appointment to see friends in Évian and tried to persuade the official in charge to let her go. She attempted to slip a hundred francs into his hand."

"She must be a stupider woman than I thought," said Ashenden.

But when next day he went about eleven in the morning to see her he made no reference to her attempt to escape. She had had time to arrange herself, and now, her hair elaborately done, her lips and cheeks painted, she looked less haggard than when he had first seen her.

"I've brought you some books," said Ashenden. "I'm afraid the time hangs heavy on your hands."

"What does that matter to you?"

"I have no wish that you should suffer anything that can be avoided. Anyhow, I will leave them and you can read them or not as you choose."

"If you only knew how I hated you."

"It would doubtless make me very uncomfortable. But I really don't know why you should. I am only doing what I have been ordered to."

"What do you want of me now? I do not suppose you have come only to ask after my health."

Ashenden smiled.

"I want you to write a letter to your lover telling him that owing to some irregularity in your passport the Swiss authorities would not let you cross the frontier, so you have come here where it is very nice and quiet, so quiet that one can hardly realize there is a war, and you propose that Chandra should join you."

"Do you think he is a fool? He will refuse."

"Then you must do your best to persuade him."

She looked at Ashenden a long time before she answered. He suspected that she was debating within herself whether by writing the letter and so seeming docile she could not gain time.

"Well, dictate and I will write what you say."

"I should prefer you to put it in your own words."

"Give me half an hour and the letter shall be ready."

"I will wait here," said Ashenden.

"Why?"

"Because I prefer to."

Her eyes flashed angrily, but controlling herself she said nothing. On the chest of drawers were writing materials. She sat down at the dressing-table and began to write. When she handed Ashenden the letter he saw that even through her rouge she was very pale. It was the letter of a person not much used to expressing herself by means of pen and ink, but it was well enough, and when towards the end, starting to say how much she loved the man, she had been carried away and wrote with all her heart, it had really a certain passion.

"Now add: 'The man who is bringing this is Swiss, you can trust him absolutely. I didn't want the censor to see it.'"

She hesitated an instant, but then wrote as he directed.

"How do you spell absolutely?"

"As you like. Now address an envelope and I will relieve you of my unwelcome presence."

He gave the letter to the agent who was waiting to take it across the lake. Ashenden brought her the reply the same evening. She snatched it from his hands and for a moment pressed it to her heart. When she read it she uttered a little cry of relief.

"He won't come."

The letter, in the Indian's flowery, stilted English, expressed his bitter disappointment. He told her how intensely he had looked forward to seeing her and implored her to do everything in the world to smooth the difficulties that prevented her from crossing the frontier. He said that it was impossible for him to come, impossible, there was a price on his head, and it would be madness for him to think of risking it. He attempted to be jocular, she did not want her little fat lover to be shot, did she?

"He won't come," she repeated, "he won't come."

"You must write and tell him that there is no risk. You must say that if there were you would not dream of asking him. You must say that if he loves you he will not hesitate."

"I won't. I won't."

"Don't be a fool. You can't help yourself."

She burst into a sudden flood of tears. She flung herself on the floor and seizing Ashenden's knees implored him to have mercy on her.

"I will do anything in the world for you if you will let me go."

"Don't be absurd," said Ashenden. "Do you think I want to become your lover? Come, come, you must be serious. You know the alternative."

She raised herself to her feet and changing on a sudden to fury flung at Ashenden one foul name after another.

"I like you much better like that," he said. "Now will you write or shall I send for the police?"

"He will not come. It is useless."

"It is very much to your interest to make him come."

"What do you mean by that? Do you mean that if I do everything in my power and fail, that . . . "

She looked at Ashenden with wild eyes.

"Yes, it means either you or him."

She staggered. She put her hand to her heart. Then without a word she reached for pen and paper. But the letter was not to Ashenden's liking and he made her write it again. When she had finished she flung herself on the bed and burst once more into passionate weeping. Her grief was real, but there was something theatrical in the expression of it that prevented it from being peculiarly moving to Ashenden. He felt his relation to her as impersonal as a doctor's in the presence of a pain that he cannot alleviate. He saw now why R. had given him this peculiar task; it needed a cool head and an emotion well under control.

He did not see her next day. The answer to the letter was not delivered to him till after dinner, when it was brought to Ashenden's little house by Félix.

"Well, what news have you?"

"Our friend is getting desperate," smiled the Frenchman. "This afternoon she walked up to the station just as a train was about to start for Lyons. She was looking up and down uncertainly so I went to her and asked if there was anything I could do. I introduced myself as an agent of the Sûreté. If looks could kill I should not be standing here now."

"Sit down, *mon ami*," said Ashenden.

"*Merci*. She walked away, she evidently thought it was no use to try to get on the train, but I have something more interesting to tell you. She has offered a boatman on the lake a thousand francs to take her across to Lausanne."

"What did he say to her?"

"He said he couldn't risk it."

"Yes?"

The little agent gave his shoulders a slight shrug and smiled.

"She's asked him to meet her on the road that leads to Évian at ten o'clock tonight so that they can talk of it again, and she's given him to understand that she will not repulse too fiercely the advances of a lover. I have told him to do what he likes so long as he comes and tells me everything that is of importance."

"Are you sure you can trust him?" asked Ashenden.

"Oh, quite. He knows nothing, of course, but that she is under surveillance. You need have no fear about him. He is a good boy. I have known him all his life."

Ashenden read Chandra's letter. It was eager and passionate. It throbbed strangely with the painful yearning of his heart. Love? Yes, if Ashenden knew anything of it there was the real thing. He told her how he spent the long hours walking by the lakeside and looking towards the coast of France. How near they were and yet so desperate parted! He repeated again and again that he could not come, and begged her not to ask him, he would do everything in the world for her, but that he dared not do, and yet if she insisted how could he resist her? He besought her to have mercy on him. And then he broke into a long wail at the thought that he must go away without seeing her, he asked her if there were not some means by which she could slip over, he swore that if he could ever hold her in his arms again he would never let her go. Even the forced and elaborate language in which it was written could not dim the hot fire that burned the pages; it was the letter of a madman.

"When will you hear the result of her interview with the boatman?" asked Ashenden.

"I have arranged to meet him at the landing-stage between eleven and twelve."

Ashenden looked at his watch.

"I will come with you."

They walked down the hill and reaching the quay for shelter from the cold wind stood in the lee of the custom-house. At last they saw a man approaching and Félix stepped out of the shadow that hid them.

"Antoine."

"*Monsieur Félix?* I have a letter for you; I promised to take it to Lausanne by the first boat tomorrow."

Ashenden gave the man a brief glance, but did not ask what had passed between him and Giulia Lazzari. He took the letter and by the light of Félix's electric torch read it. It was in faulty German:

> On no account come. Pay no attention to my letters.
> Danger. I love you. Sweetheart. Don't come.

He put it in his pocket, gave the boatman fifty francs, and went home to bed. But the next day when he went to see Giulia Lazzari he found her door locked. He knocked for some time, there was no answer. He called her.

"Madame Lazzari, you must open the door. I want to speak to you."

"I am in bed. I am ill and can see no one."

"I am sorry, but you must open the door. If you are ill I will send for a doctor."

"No, go away. I will see no one."

"If you do not open the door I shall send for a locksmith and have it broken open."

There was a silence and then he heard the key turned in the lock. He went in. She was in a dressing-gown and her hair was dishevelled. She had evidently just got out of bed.

"I am at the end of my strength. I can do nothing more. You have only to look at me to see that I am ill. I have been sick all night."

"I shall not keep you long. Would you like to see a doctor?"

"What good can a doctor do me?"

He took out of his pocket the letter she had given the boatman and handed it to her.

"What is the meaning of this?" he asked.

She gave a gasp at the sight of it and her sallow face went green.

"You gave me your word that you would neither attempt to escape nor write a letter without my knowledge."

"Did you think I would keep my word?" she cried, her voice ringing with scorn.

"No. To tell you the truth it was not entirely for your convenience that you were placed in a comfortable hotel rather than in the local gaol, but I think I should tell you that though you have your freedom to go in and out as you like you have no more chance of getting away from Thonon than if you were chained by the leg in a prison cell. It is silly to waste your time writing letters that will never be delivered."

"*Cochon.*"

She flung the opprobrious word at him with all the violence that was in her.

"But you must sit down and write a letter that *will* be delivered."

"Never. I will do nothing more. I will not write another word."

"You came here on the understanding that you would do certain things."

"I will not do them. It is finished."

"You had better reflect a little."

"Reflect! I have reflected. You can do what you like; I don't care."

"Very well, I will give you five minutes to change your mind."

Ashenden took out his watch and looked at it. He sat down on the edge of the unmade bed.

"Oh, it has got on my nerves, this hotel. Why did you not put me in the prison? Why, why? Everywhere I went I felt that spies were on my heels. It is infamous what you are making me do. Infamous! What is my crime? I ask you, what have I done? Am I not a woman? It is infamous what you are asking me to do. Infamous."

She spoke in a high shrill voice. She went on and on. At last the five minutes were up. Ashenden had not said a word. He rose.

"Yes, go, go," she shrieked at him.

She flung foul names at him.

"I shall come back," said Ashenden.

He took the key out of the door as he went out of the room and locked it behind him. Going downstairs he hurriedly scribbled a note, called the boots and dispatched him with it to the police-station. Then he went up again. Giulia Lazzari had thrown herself on her bed and turned her face to the wall. Her body was shaken with hysterical sobs. She gave no sign that she heard him come in. Ashenden sat down on the chair in front of the dressing-table and looked idly at the odds and ends that littered it. The toilet things were cheap and tawdry and none too clean. There were little shabby pots of rouge and cold-cream and little bottles of black for the eyebrows and eyelashes. The hairpins were horrid and greasy. The room was untidy and the air was heavy with the smell of cheap scent. Ashenden thought of the hundreds of rooms she must have occupied in third-rate hotels in the course of her life wandering from provincial town to provincial town in one country after another. He wondered what had been her origins. She was a coarse and vulgar woman, but what had she been when young? She was not the type he would have expected to adopt that career, for she seemed to have no advantages that could help her, and he asked himself whether she came of a family of entertainers (there are all over the world families in which for generations the members have become dancers or acrobats or comic singers) or whether she had fallen into the life accidentally through some lover in the business who had for a time made her his partner. And what men must she have known in all these years, the comrades of the shows she was in, the agents and managers who looked upon it as a perquisite of their position that they should enjoy her favours, the merchants or well-to-do trades-men, the young sparks of the various towns she played in, who were attracted for the moment by the glamour of the dancer or the blatant sensuality of the woman! To her they were the paying customers and she accepted them indifferently as the recognized and admitted supplement to her miserable salary, but to them perhaps she was romance. In her bought arms they caught sight for a moment of the brilliant world of the capitals, and ever so distantly and however shoddily of the adventure and the glamour of a more spacious life.

There was a sudden knock at the door and Ashenden immediately cried out:

"*Entrez.*"

Giulia Lazzari sprang up in bed to a sitting posture.

"Who is it?"

She gave a gasp as she saw the two detectives who had brought her from Boulogne and handed her over to Ashenden at Thonon.

"You! What do you want?"

"*Allons, levez-vous,*" said one of them, and his voice had a sharp abruptness that suggested that he would put up with no nonsense.

"I'm afraid you must get up, Madame Lazzari," said Ashenden. "I am delivering you once more to the care of these gentlemen."

"How can I get up! I'm ill, I tell you. I cannot stand. Do you want to kill me?"

743

"If you won't dress yourself, we shall have to dress you, and I'm afraid we shouldn't do it very cleverly. Come, come, it's no good making a scene."

"Where are you going to take me?"

"They're going to take you back to England."

One of the detectives took hold of her arm.

"Don't touch me, don't come near me," she screamed furiously.

"Let her be," said Ashenden. "I'm sure she'll see the necessity of making as little trouble as possible."

"I'll dress myself."

Ashenden watched her as she took off her dressing-gown and slipped a dress over her head. She forced her feet into shoes obviously too small for her. She arranged her hair. Every now and then she gave the detectives a hurried, sullen glance. Ashenden wondered if she would have the nerve to go through with it. R. would call him a damned fool, but he almost wished she would. She went up to the dressing-table and Ashenden stood up in order to let her sit down. She greased her face quickly and then rubbed off the grease with a dirty towel, she powdered herself and made up her eyes. But her hand shook. The three men watched her in silence. She rubbed the rouge on her cheeks and painted her mouth. Then she crammed a hat down on her head. Ashenden made a gesture to the first detective and he took a pair of handcuffs out of his pocket and advanced towards her.

At the sight of them she started back violently and flung her arms wide.

"*Non, non, non. Je ne veux pas.* No, not them. No. No."

"Come, *ma fille*, don't be silly," said the detective roughly.

As though for protection (very much to his surprise) she flung her arms round Ashenden.

"Don't let them take me, have mercy on me, I can't, I can't."

Ashenden extricated himself as best he could.

"I can do nothing more for you."

The detective seized her wrists and was about to affix the handcuffs when with a great cry she threw herself down on the floor.

"I will do what you wish. I will do everything."

On a sign from Ashenden the detectives left the room. He waited for a little till she had regained a certain calm. She was lying on the

744

floor sobbing passionately. He raised her to her feet and made her sit down.

"What do you want me to do?" she gasped.

"I want you to write another letter to Chandra."

"My head is in a whirl. I could not put two phrases together. You must give me time."

But Ashenden felt that it was better to get her to write a letter while she was under the effect of her terror. He did not want to give her time to collect herself.

"I will dictate the letter to you. All you have to do is to write exactly what I tell you."

She gave a deep sigh, but took the pen and the paper and sat down before them at the dressing-table.

"If I do this and . . . and you succeed, how do I know that I shall be allowed to go free?"

"The Colonel promised that you should. You must take my word for it that I shall carry out his instructions."

"I *should* look a fool if I betrayed my friend and then went to prison for ten years."

"I'll tell you your best guarantee of our good faith. Except by reason of Chandra you are not of the smallest importance to us. Why should we put ourselves to the bother and expense of keeping you in prison when you can do us no harm?"

She reflected for an instant. She was composed now. It was as though, having exhausted her emotion, she had become on a sudden a sensible and practical woman.

"Tell me what you want me to write."

Ashenden hesitated. He thought he could put the letter more or less in the way she would naturally have put it, but he had to give it consideration. It must be neither fluent nor literary. He knew that in moments of emotion people are inclined to be melodramatic and stilted. In a book or on the stage this always rings false and the author has to make his people speak more simply and with less emphasis than in fact they do. It was a serious moment, but Ashenden felt that there were in it elements of the comic.

"I didn't know I loved a coward," he started. "If you loved me you couldn't hesitate when I ask you to come . . . Underline *couldn't* twice." He went on. "When I promise you there is no danger. If you don't love me, you are right not to come. Don't come. Go back to Berlin where you are in safety. I am sick of it. I am alone here. I have made myself ill by waiting for you and every day I have said he is coming. If you loved me you would not hesitate so much. It is quite clear to me that you do not love me. I am sick and tired of you. I have no money. The hotel is impossible. There is nothing for me to stay for. I can get an engagement in Paris. I have a friend there who has made me serious propositions. I have wasted long enough over you and look what I have got from it. It is finished. Good-bye. You will never find a woman who will love you as I have loved you. I cannot afford to refuse the proposition of my friend, so I have telegraphed to him and as soon as I shall receive his answer I go to Paris. I do not blame you because you do not love me, that is not your fault, but you must see that I should be a stupid to go on wasting my life. One is not young for ever. Good-bye. Giulia."

When Ashenden read over the letter he was not altogether satisfied. But it was the best he could do. It had an air of verisimilitude which the words lacked because, knowing little English, she had written phonetically, the spelling was atrocious and the handwriting like a child's; she had crossed out words and written them over again. Some of the phrases she had put in French. Once or twice tears had fallen on the pages and blurred the ink.

"I leave you now," said Ashenden. "It may be that when next you see me I shall be able to tell you that you are free to go where you choose. Where do you want to go?"

"Spain."

"Very well, I will have everything prepared."

She shrugged her shoulders. He left her.

There was nothing now for Ashenden to do but wait. He sent a messenger to Lausanne in the afternoon, and next morning went down to the quay to meet the boat. There was a waiting-room next to the ticket-office and here he told the detectives to hold themselves in readiness. When a boat arrived the passengers advanced along the pier in line and their passports were examined before they were allowed to go ashore. If Chandra came and showed his passport, and it was very likely that he was travelling with a false one, issued probably by a neutral nation, he was to be asked to wait and Ashenden was to identify him. Then he would be arrested. It was with some excitement that Ashenden watched the boat come in and the little group of people gathered at the gangway. He scanned them closely but saw no one who looked in the least like an Indian. Chandra had not come. Ashenden did not know what to do. He had played his last card. There were not more than half a dozen passengers for Thonon, and when they had been examined and gone their way he strolled along the pier.

"Well, it's no go," he said to Félix, who had been examining the passports. "The gentleman I expected hasn't turned up."

"I have a letter for you."

He handed Ashenden an envelope addressed to Madame Lazzari on which he immediately recognized the spidery handwriting of Chandra Lal. At that moment the steamer from Geneva which was going to Lausanne and the end of the lake hove in sight. It arrived at Thonon every morning twenty minutes after the steamer going in the opposite direction had left. Ashenden had an inspiration.

"Where is the man who brought it?"

"He's in the ticket-office."

"Give him the letter and tell him to return to the person who gave it to him. He is to say that he took it to the lady and she sent it back. If the person asks him to take another letter he is to say that it is not much good as she is packing her trunk and leaving Thonon."

He saw the letter handed over and the instructions given and then walked back to his little house in the country.

The next boat on which Chandra could possibly come arrived about five and having at that hour an important engagement with an agent working in Germany he warned Félix that he might be a few minutes late. But if Chandra came he could easily be detained; there was no great hurry since the train in which he was to be taken to Paris did not start till shortly after eight. When Ashenden had finished his business he strolled leisurely down to the lake. It was light still and from the top of the hill he saw the steamer pulling out. It was an anxious moment and instinctively he quickened his steps. Suddenly he saw someone running towards him and recognized the man who had taken the letter.

"Quick, quick," he cried. "He's there."

Ashenden's heart gave a great thud against his chest.

"At last."

He began to run too and as they ran the man, panting, told him how he had taken back the unopened letter. When he put it in the Indian's hand he turned frightfully pale ("I should never have thought an Indian could turn that colour," he said), and turned it over and over in his hand as though he could not understand what his own letter was doing there. Tears sprang to his eyes and rolled down his cheeks. ("It was grotesque, he's fat, you know.") He said something in a language the man did not understand and then in French asked him when the boat went to Thonon. When he got on board he looked about, but did not see him, then he caught sight of him, huddled up in an ulster with his hat drawn down over his eyes, standing alone in the bows. During the crossing he kept his eyes fixed on Thonon.

"Where is he now?" asked Ashenden.

"I got off first and Monsieur Félix told me to come for you."

"I suppose they're holding him in the waiting-room."

Ashenden was out of breath when they reached the pier. He burst into the waiting-room. A group of men, talking at the top of their voices and gesticulating wildly, were clustered round a man lying on the ground.

"What's happened?" he cried.

"Look," said Monsieur Félix.

Chandra Lal lay there, his eyes wide open and a thin line of foam on his lips, dead. His body was horribly contorted.

"He's killed himself. We've sent for the doctor. He was too quick for us."

A sudden thrill of horror passed through Ashenden.

When the Indian landed Félix recognized from the description that he was the man they wanted. There were only four passengers. He was the last. Félix took an exaggerated time to examine the passports of the first three, and then took the Indian's. It was a Spanish one and it was all in order. Félix asked the regulation questions and noted them on the official sheet. Then he looked at him pleasantly and said:

"Just come into the waiting-room for a moment. There are one or two formalities to fulfil."

"Is my passport not in order?" the Indian asked.

"Perfectly."

Chandra hesitated, but then followed the official to the door of the waiting-room. Félix opened it and stood aside.

"*Entrez.*"

Chandra went in and the two detectives stood up. He must have suspected at once that they were police-officers and realized that he had fallen into a trap.

"Sit down," said Félix. "I have one or two questions to put to you."

"It is hot in here," he said, and in point of fact they had a little stove there that kept the place like an oven. "I will take off my coat if you permit."

"Certainly," said Félix graciously.

He took off his coat, apparently with some effort, and he turned to put it on a chair, and then before they realized what had happened they were startled to see him stagger and fall heavily to the ground. While taking off his coat Chandra had managed to swallow the contents of a bottle that was still clasped in his hand. Ashenden put his nose to it. There was a very distinct odour of almonds.

For a little while they looked at the man who lay on the floor. Félix was apologetic.

"Will they be very angry?" he asked nervously.

"I don't see that it was your fault," said Ashenden. "Anyhow, he can do no more harm. For my part I am just as glad he killed himself. The notion of his being executed did not make me very comfortable."

In a few minutes the doctor arrived and pronounced life extinct.

"Prussic acid," he said to Ashenden.

Ashenden nodded.

"I will go and see Madame Lazzari," he said. "If she wants to stay a day or two longer I shall let her. But if she wants to go tonight of course she can. Will you give the agents at the station instructions to let her pass?"

"I shall be at the station myself," said Félix.

Ashenden once more climbed the hill. It was night now, a cold, bright night with an unclouded sky and the sight of the new moon, a white shining thread, made him turn three times the money in his pocket. When he entered the hotel he was seized on a sudden with distaste for its cold banality. It smelt of cabbage and boiled mutton.

On the walls of the hall were coloured posters of railway companies advertising Grenoble, Carcassonne, and the bathing places of Normandy. He went upstairs and after a brief knock opened the door of Giulia Lazzari's room. She was sitting in front of her dressing-table, looking at herself in the glass, just idly, despairingly, apparently doing nothing, and it was in this that she saw Ashenden as he came in. Her face changed suddenly as she caught sight of his and she sprang up so vehemently that the chair fell over.

"What is it? Why are you so white?" she cried.

She turned round and stared at him and her features were gradually twisted to a look of horror.

"*Il est pris*," she gasped.

"*Il est mort*," said Ashenden.

"Dead! He took the poison. He had the time for that. He's escaped you after all."

"What do you mean? How did you know about the poison?"

"He always carried it with him. He said that the English should never take him alive."

Ashenden reflected for an instant. She had kept that secret well. He supposed the possibility of such a thing should have occurred to him. How was he to anticipate these melodramatic devices?

"Well, now you are free. You can go wherever you like and no obstacle shall be put in your way. Here are your ticket and your passport and here is the money that was in your possession when you were arrested. Do you wish to see Chandra?"

She started.

"No, no."

"There is no need. I thought you might care to."

She did not weep. Ashenden supposed that she had exhausted all her emotion. She seemed apathetic.

"A telegram will be sent tonight to the Spanish frontier to instruct the authorities to put no difficulties in your way. If you will take my advice you will get out of France as soon as you can."

She said nothing, and since Ashenden had no more to say he made ready to go.

"I am sorry that I have had to show myself so hard to you. I am glad to think that now the worst of your troubles are over and I hope that time will assuage the grief that I know you must feel for the death of your friend."

Ashenden gave her a little bow and turned to the door. But she stopped him.

"One little moment," she said. "There is one thing I should like to ask. I think you have some heart."

"Whatever I can do for you, you may be sure I will."

"What are they going to do with his things?"

"I don't know. Why?"

Then she said something that confounded Ashenden. It was the last thing he expected.

"He had a wrist-watch that I gave him last Christmas. It cost twelve pounds. Can I have it back?"

THE TRAITOR

WHEN ASHENDEN, GIVEN charge of a number of spies working from Switzerland, was first sent there, R., wishing him to see the sort of report that he would be required to obtain, handed him the communications, a sheaf of typewritten documents, of a man known in the secret service as Gustav.

"He's the best fellow we've got," said R. "His information is always very full and circumstantial. I want you to give his reports your very best attention. Of course Gustav is a clever little chap, but there's no reason why we shouldn't get just as good reports from the other agents. It's merely a question of explaining exactly what we want."

Gustav, who lived at Basle, represented a Swiss firm with branches at Frankfurt, Mannheim and Cologne, and by virtue of his business was able to go in and out of Germany without risk. He travelled up and down the Rhine, and gathered material about the movement of troops, the manufacture of munitions, the state of mind of the country (a point on which R. laid stress), and other matters upon which the Allies desired information. His frequent letters to his wife hid an ingenious code and the moment she received them in Basle she sent them to Ashenden in Geneva, who extracted from them the important facts and communicated these in the proper quarter. Every two months Gustav came home and prepared one of the reports that served as models to the other spies in this particular section of the secret service.

His employers were pleased with Gustav and Gustav had reason to be pleased with his employers. His services were so useful that he was not only paid more highly than the others, but for particular scoops had received from time to time a handsome bonus.

This went on for more than a year. Then something aroused R.'s quick suspicions; he was a man of an amazing alertness, not so much of mind, as of instinct, and he had suddenly a feeling that some hanky-panky was going on. He said nothing definite to Ashenden (whatever R. surmised he was disposed to keep to himself), but told him to go to Basle, Gustav being then in Germany, and have a talk with Gustav's wife. He left it to Ashenden to decide the tenor of the conversation.

Having arrived at Basle, and leaving his bag at the station, for he did not yet know whether he would have to stay or not, he took a tram to the corner of the street in which Gustav lived and, with a quick look to see that he was not followed, walked along to the house he sought. It was a block of flats that gave you the impression of decent poverty and Ashenden conjectured that they were inhabited by clerks and small tradespeople. Just inside the door was a cobbler's shop and Ashenden stopped.

"Does Herr Grabow live here?" he asked in his none too fluent German.

"Yes, I saw him go up a few minutes ago. You'll find him in."

Ashenden was startled, for he had but the day before received through Gustav's wife a letter addressed from Mannheim in which Gustav by means of his code gave the numbers of certain regiments that had just crossed the Rhine. Ashenden thought it unwise to ask the cobbler the question that rose to his lips, so thanked him and went up to the third floor, on which he knew already that Gustav lived. He rang the bell and heard it tinkle within. In a moment the door was opened by a dapper little man with a close shaven round head and spectacles. He wore carpet slippers.

"Herr Grabow?" asked Ashenden.

"At your service," said Gustav.

"May I come in?"

Gustav was standing with his back to the light and Ashenden could not see the look on his face. He felt a momentary hesitation and gave the name under which he received Gustav's letters from Germany.

"Come in, come in. I am very glad to see you."

Gustav led the way into the stuffy little room, heavy with carved oak furniture, and on the large table covered with a table-cloth of green velveteen was a typewriter. Gustav was apparently engaged in composing one of his invaluable reports. A woman was sitting at the open window darning socks, but at a word from Gustav rose, gathered up her things and left. Ashenden had disturbed a pretty picture of connubial bliss.

"Sit down, please. How very fortunate that I was in Basle! I have long wanted to make your acquaintance. I have only just this minute returned from Germany." He pointed to the sheets of paper by the typewriter. "I think you will be pleased with the news I bring. I have some very valuable information." He chuckled. "One is never sorry to earn a bonus."

He was very cordial, but to Ashenden his cordiality rang false. Gustav kept his eyes, smiling behind the glasses, fixed watchfully on Ashenden, and it was possible that they held a trace of nervousness.

"You must have travelled quickly to get here only a few hours after your letter, sent here and then sent on by your wife, reached me in Geneva."

"That is very probable. One of the things I had to tell you is that the Germans suspect that information is getting through by means of commercial letters and so they have decided to hold up all mail at the frontier for eight-and-forty hours."

"I see," said Ashenden amiably. "And was it on that account that you took the precaution of dating your letter forty-eight hours after you sent it?"

"Did I do that? That was very stupid of me. I must have mistaken the day of the month."

Ashenden looked at Gustav with a smile that was very thin. Gustav, a business man, knew too well how important in his particular job was the exactness of a date. The circuitous routes by which it was necessary to get information from Germany made it difficult to transmit news quickly and it was essential to know precisely on what days certain events had taken place.

"Let me look at your passport a minute," said Ashenden.

"What do you want with my passport?"

"I want to see when you went into Germany and when you came out."

"But you do not imagine that my comings and goings are marked on my passport? I have methods of crossing the frontiers."

Ashenden knew a good deal of this matter. He knew that both the Germans and the Swiss guarded the frontier with severity.

"Oh? Why should you not cross in the ordinary way? You were engaged because your connexion with a Swiss firm supplying necessary goods to Germany made it easy for you to travel backwards and forwards without suspicion. I can understand that you might get past the German sentries with the connivance of the Germans, but what about the Swiss?"

Gustav assumed a look of indignation.

"I do not understand you. Do you mean to suggest that I am in the service of the Germans? I give you my word of honour . . . I will not allow my integrity to be impugned."

"You would not be the only one to take money from both sides and provide information of value to neither."

"Do you pretend that my information is of no value? Why then have you given me more bonuses than any other agent has received? The Colonel has repeatedly expressed the highest satisfaction with my services."

It was Ashenden's turn now to be cordial.

"Come, come, my dear fellow, do not try to ride the high horse. You do not wish to show me your passport and I will not insist. You are not under the impression that we leave the statements of our agents without corroboration or that we are so foolish as not to keep track of their movements? Even the best of jokes cannot bear an indefinite repetition. I am in peace-time a humorist by profession and I tell you that from bitter experience." Now Ashenden thought the moment had arrived to attempt his bluff; he knew something of the excellent but difficult game of poker. "We have information that you have not been to Germany now, nor since you were engaged by us, but have sat here quietly in Basle, and all your reports are merely due to your fertile imagination."

Gustav looked at Ashenden and saw a face expressive of nothing but tolerance and good-humour. A smile slowly broke on his lips and he gave his shoulder a little shrug.

"Did you think I was such a fool as to risk my life for fifty pounds a month? I love my wife."

Ashenden laughed outright.

"I congratulate you. It is not everyone who can flatter himself that he has made a fool of our secret service for a year."

"I had the chance of earning money without any difficulty. My firm stopped sending me into Germany at the beginning of the war, but I learned what I could from the other travellers. I kept my ears open in restaurants and beer-cellars, and I read the German papers. I got a lot of amusement out of sending you reports and letters."

"I don't wonder," said Ashenden.

"What are you going to do?"

"Nothing. What can we do? You are not under the impression that we shall continue to pay you a salary?"

"No, I cannot expect that."

"By the way, if it is not indiscreet, may I ask if you have been playing the same game with the Germans?"

"Oh, no," Gustav cried vehemently. "How can you think it? My sympathies are absolutely pro-Ally. My heart is entirely with you."

"Well, why not?" asked Ashenden. "The Germans have all the money in the world and there is no reason why you should not get some of it. We could give you information from time to time that the Germans would be prepared to pay for."

Gustav drummed his fingers on the table. He took up a sheet of the now useless report.

"The Germans are dangerous people to meddle with."

"You are a very intelligent man. And after all, even if your salary is stopped, you can always earn a bonus by bringing us news that can be useful to us. But it will have to be substantiated; in future we pay only by results."

"I will think of it."

For a moment or two Ashenden left Gustav to his reflections. He lit a cigarette and watched the smoke he had inhaled fade into the air. He thought too.

"Is there anything particular you want to know?" asked Gustav suddenly.

Ashenden smiled.

"It would be worth a couple of thousand Swiss francs to you if you could tell me what the Germans are doing with a spy of theirs in Lucerne. He is an Englishman and his name is Grantley Caypor."

"I have heard the name," said Gustav. He paused a moment. "How long are you staying here?"

"As long as necessary. I will take a room at the hotel and let you know the number. If you have anything to say to me you can be sure of finding me in my room at nine every morning and at seven every night."

"I should not risk coming to the hotel. But I can write."

"Very well."

Ashenden rose to go and Gustav accompanied him to the door.

"We part without ill-feeling then?" he asked.

"Of course. Your reports will remain in our archives as models of what a report should be."

Ashenden spent two or three days visiting Basle. It did not much amuse him. He passed a good deal of time in the book-shops turning over the pages of books that would have been worth reading if life were a thousand years long. Once he saw Gustav in the street. On the fourth morning a letter was brought up with his coffee. The envelope was that of a commercial firm unknown to him and inside it was a typewritten sheet. There was no address and no signature. Ashenden wondered if Gustav was aware that a typewriter could betray its owner as certainly as a handwriting. Having twice carefully read the letter, he held the paper up to the light to see the watermark (he had no reason for doing this except that the sleuths of detective novels always did it), then struck a match and watched it burn. He scrunched up the charred fragments in his hand.

He got up, for he had taken advantage of his situation to breakfast in bed, packed his bag and took the next train to Berne. From there he was able to send a code telegram to R. His instructions were given to him verbally two days later, in the bedroom of his hotel at an hour when no one was likely to be seen walking along a corridor, and within twenty-four hours, though by a circuitous route, he arrived at Lucerne.

Having taken a room at the hotel at which he had been instructed to stay, Ashenden went out; it was a lovely day, early in August, and the sun shone in an unclouded sky. He had not been to Lucerne since he was a boy and but vaguely remembered a covered bridge, a great stone lion and a church in which he had sat, bored yet impressed, while they played an organ; and now, wandering along a shady quay (and the lake looked just as tawdry and unreal as it looked on the picture-postcards) he tried not so much to find his way about a half-forgotten scene as to re-form in his mind some recollection of the shy and eager lad, so impatient for life (which he saw not in the present of his adolescence but only in the future of his manhood) who so long ago had wandered there. But it seemed to him that the most vivid of his memories was not of himself, but of the crowd; he seemed to remember sun and heat and people; the train was crowded and so was the hotel, the lake steamers were packed and on the quays and in the streets you threaded your way among the throng of holiday-makers. They were fat and old and ugly and odd, and they stank. Now, in war-time, Lucerne was as deserted as it must have been before the world at large discovered that Switzerland was the playground of Europe. Most of the hotels were closed, the streets were empty, the rowing boats for hire rocked idly at the water's edge and there was none to take them, and in the avenues by the lake the only persons to be seen were serious Swiss taking their neutrality, like a dachshund, for a walk with them. Ashenden felt exhilarated by the solitude and, sitting down on a bench that faced the water, surrendered himself deliberately to the sensation. It was true that the lake was absurd, the water was too blue, the mountains too snowy, and its beauty, hitting you in the face, exasperated rather than thrilled; but all the same there was something pleasing in the prospect, an artless candour, like one of Mendelssohn's *Songs Without Words*, that made Ashenden smile with complacency. Lucerne reminded him of wax flowers under glass cases and cuckoo clocks and fancy-work in Berlin wool. So long at all events as the fine weather lasted he was prepared to enjoy himself. He did not see why he should not at least try to combine pleasure to himself with profit to his country. He was travelling with a brand-new passport in his pocket, under a borrowed name, and this gave him an agreeable sense of owning a new personality. He was often slightly tired of himself and it diverted him for a while to be merely a creature of R.'s facile invention. The experience he had just enjoyed appealed to his acute sense of the absurd. R., it is true, had not seen the fun of it: what humour R. possessed was of a sardonic turn and he had no facility for taking in good part a joke at his own expense. To do that you must be able to look at yourself from the outside and be at the same time spectator and actor in the pleasant comedy of life. R. was a soldier and regarded introspection as unhealthy, un-English, and unpatriotic.

Ashenden got up and strolled slowly to his hotel. It was a small German hotel, of the second class, spotlessly clean, and his bedroom had a nice view; it was furnished with brightly varnished pitch-pine, and though on a cold wet day it would have been wretched, in that warm and sunny weather it was gay and pleasing. There were tables in the hall and he sat down at one of these and ordered a bottle of beer. The landlady was curious to know why in that dead season he had come to stay and he was glad to satisfy her curiosity. He told her that he had recently recovered from an attack of typhoid and had come to Lucerne to get back his strength. He was employed in the Censorship Department and was taking the opportunity to brush up his rusty German. He asked her if she could recommend to him a German teacher. The landlady was a blonde and blowzy Swiss, good-humoured and talkative, so that Ashenden felt pretty sure that she would repeat in the proper quarter the information he gave her. It was his turn now to ask a few questions. She was voluble on the subject of the war on account of which the hotel, usually in that month so full that rooms had to be found for visitors in neighbouring houses, was nearly empty. A few people came in from outside to eat their meals *en pension* but she had only two lots of resident guests. One was an old Irish couple who lived in Vevey and passed their summers in Lucerne and the other was an Englishman and his wife. She was a German and they were obliged on that account to live in a neutral country. Ashenden took care to show little curiosity about them – he recognized in the description Grantley Caypor – but of her own accord she told him that they spent most of the day walking about the mountains. Herr Caypor was a botanist and much interested in the flora of the country. His lady was a very nice woman and she felt her position keenly. Ah, well, the war could not last for ever. The landlady bustled away and Ashenden went upstairs.

Dinner was at seven, and, wishing to be in the dining-room before anyone else so that he could take stock of his fellow-guests as they entered, he went down as soon as he heard the bell. It was a very plain, stiff, white-washed room, with chairs of the same shiny pitch-pine as in his bedroom, and on the walls were oleographs of Swiss lakes. On each little table was a bunch of flowers. It was all neat and clean and presaged a bad dinner. Ashenden would have liked to make up for it by ordering a bottle of the best Rhine wine to be found in the hotel, but did not venture to draw attention to himself by extravagance (he saw on two or three tables half-empty bottles of table hock, which made him surmise that his fellow-guests drank thriftily), and so contented himself with ordering a pint of lager. Presently one or two persons came in, single men with some occupation in Lucerne and obviously Swiss, and sat down each at his own little table and untied the napkins that at the end of luncheon they had neatly tied up. They propped newspapers against their water-jugs and read while they somewhat noisily ate their soup. Then entered a very old tall bent man, with white hair and a drooping white moustache, accompanied by a little old white-haired lady in black. These were certainly the Irish colonel and his wife of whom the landlady had spoken. They took their seats and the colonel poured out a thimbleful of wine for his wife and a thimbleful for himself. They waited in silence for their dinner to be served to them by the buxom, hearty maid.

At last the persons arrived for whom Ashenden had been waiting. He was doing his best to read a German book and it was only by an exercise of self-control that he allowed himself only for one instant to raise his eyes as they came in. His glance showed him a man of about forty-five with short dark hair, somewhat grizzled, of middle height, but corpulent, with a broad red clean-shaven face. He wore a shirt open at the neck, with a wide collar, and a grey suit. He walked ahead of his wife, and of her Ashenden only caught the impression of a German woman self-effaced and dusty. Grantley Caypor sat down and began in a loud voice explaining to the waitress that they had taken an immense walk. They had been up some mountain the name of which meant nothing to Ashenden, but which excited in the maid expressions of astonishment and enthusiasm. Then Caypor, still in fluent German but with a marked English accent, said that they were so late they had not even gone up to wash, but had just rinsed their hands outside. He had a resonant voice and a jovial manner.

"Serve me quick, we're starving with hunger, and bring beer, bring three bottles. *Lieber Gott*, what a thirst I have!"

He seemed to be a man of exuberant vitality. He brought into that dull, overclean dining-room the breath of life, and everyone in it appeared on a sudden more alert. He began to talk to his wife, in English, and everything he said could be heard by all; but presently she interrupted him with a remark made in an undertone. Caypor stopped and Ashenden felt that his eyes were turned in his direction. Mrs Caypor had noticed the arrival of a stranger and had drawn her husband's attention to it. Ashenden turned the page of the book he was pretending to read, but he felt that Caypor's gaze was fixed intently upon him. When he addressed his wife again it was in so low a tone that Ashenden could not even tell what language he used, but when the maid brought them their soup Caypor, his voice still low, asked her a question. It was plain that he was inquiring who Ashenden was. Ashenden could catch of the maid's reply but the one word *länder*.

One or two people finished their dinner and went out picking their teeth. The old Irish colonel and his old wife rose from their table and he stood aside to let her pass. They had eaten their meal without exchanging a word. She walked slowly to the door; but the colonel stopped to say a word to a Swiss who might have been a local attorney, and when she reached it she stood there, bowed and with a sheep-like look, patiently waiting for her husband to come and open it for her. Ashenden realized that she had never opened a door for herself. She did not know how to. In a minute the colonel with his old, old gait came to the door and opened it; she passed out and he followed. The little incident offered a key to their whole lives, and from it Ashenden began to reconstruct their histories, circumstances, and characters; but he pulled himself up; he could not allow himself the luxury of creation. He finished his dinner.

When he went into the hall he saw tied to the leg of a table a bull-terrier and in passing mechanically put down his hand to fondle the dog's drooping, soft ears. The landlady was standing at the foot of the stairs.

"Whose is this lovely beast?" asked Ashenden.

"He belongs to Herr Caypor. Fritzi, he is called. Herr Caypor says he has a longer pedigree than the King of England."

Fritzi rubbed himself against Ashenden's leg and with his nose sought the palm of his hand. Ashenden went upstairs to fetch his hat, and when he came down saw Caypor standing at the entrance of the hotel talking with the landlady. From the sudden silence and their constrained manner he guessed that Caypor had been making inquiries about him. When he passed between them, into the street, out of the corner of his eye he saw Caypor give a suspicious stare. That frank, jovial red face bore then a look of shifty cunning.

Ashenden strolled along till he found a tavern where he could have his coffee in the open and to compensate himself for the bottle of beer that his sense of duty had urged him to drink at dinner ordered the best brandy the house provided. He was pleased at last to have come face to face with the man of whom he had heard so much and in a day or two hoped to become acquainted with him. It is never very difficult to get to know anyone who has a dog. But he was in no hurry; he would let things take their course; with the object he had in view he could not afford to be hasty.

Ashenden reviewed the circumstances. Grantley Caypor was an Englishman, born according to his passport in Birmingham, and he was forty-two years of age. His wife, to whom he had been married for eleven years, was of German birth and parentage. That was public knowledge. Information about his antecedents was contained in a private document. He had started life, according to this, in a lawyer's office in Birmingham and then had drifted into journalism. He had been connected with an English paper in Cairo and with another in Shanghai. There he got into trouble for attempting to get money on false pretences and was sentenced to a short term of imprisonment. All trace of him was lost for two years after his release, when he reappeared in a shipping-office in Marseilles. From there, still in the shipping business, he went to Hamburg, where he married, and to London. In London he set up for himself in the export business, but after some time failed and was made a bankrupt. He returned to journalism. At the outbreak of war he was once more in the shipping business, and in August 1914 was living quietly with his German wife at Southampton. In the beginning of the following year he told his employers that owing to the nationality of his wife the position was intolerable; they had no fault to find with him and, recognizing that he was in an awkward fix, granted his request that he should be transferred to Genoa. Here he remained till Italy entered the war, but then gave notice and with his papers in perfect order crossed the border and took up his residence in Switzerland.

All this indicated a man of doubtful honesty and unsettled disposition, with no background and of no financial standing; but the facts were of no importance to anyone till it was discovered that Caypor, certainly from the beginning of the war and perhaps sooner, was in the service of the German Intelligence Department. He had a salary of forty pounds a month. But though dangerous and wily no steps would have been taken to deal with him if he had contented himself with transmitting such news as he was able to get in Switzerland. He could do no great harm there and it might even be possible to make use of him to convey information that it was desirable to let the enemy have. He had no notion that anything was known of him. His letters, and he received a good many, were closely censored; there were few codes that the people who dealt with such matters could not in the end decipher and it might be that sooner or later through him it would be possible to lay hands on the organization that still flourished in England. But then he did something that drew R.'s attention to him. Had he known it none could have blamed him for shaking in his shoes: R. was not a very nice man to get on the wrong side of. Caypor scraped acquaintance in Zürich with a young Spaniard, Gomez by name, who had lately entered the British secret service, by his nationality inspired him with confidence, and managed to worm out of him the fact that he was engaged in espionage. Probably the Spaniard, with a very human desire to seem important, had done no more than talk mysteriously; but on Caypor's information he was watched when he went to Germany and one day caught just as he was posting a letter in a code that was eventually deciphered. He was tried, convicted, and shot. It was bad enough to lose a useful and disinterested agent, but it entailed besides the changing of a safe and simple code. R. was not pleased. But R. was not the man to let any desire of revenge stand in the way of his main object, and it occurred to him that if Caypor was merely betraying his country for money it might be possible to get him to take more money to betray his employers. The fact that he had succeeded in delivering into their hands an agent of the Allies must seem to them an earnest of his good faith. He might be very useful. But R. had no notion what kind of man Caypor was, he had lived his shabby, furtive life obscurely, and the only photograph that existed of him was one taken for a passport. Ashenden's instructions were to get acquainted with Caypor and see whether there was any chance that he would work honestly for the British: if he thought there was, he was entitled to sound him and if his suggestions were met with favour to make certain propositions. It was a task that needed tact and a knowledge of men. If on the other hand Ashenden came to the conclusion that Caypor could not be bought, he was to watch and report his movements. The information he had obtained from Gustav was vague, but important; there was only one point in it that was interesting, and this was that the head of the German Intelligence Department in Berne was growing restive at Caypor's lack of activity. Caypor was asking for a higher salary and Major von P. had told him that he must earn it. It might be that he was urging him to go to England. If he could be induced to cross the frontier Ashenden's work was done.

"How the devil do you expect *me* to persuade him to put his head in a noose?" asked Ashenden.

"It won't be a noose, it'll be a firing squad," said R.

"Caypor's clever."

"Well, be cleverer, damn your eyes."

Ashenden made up his mind that he would take no steps to make Caypor's acquaintance, but allow the first advances to be made by him. If he was being pressed for results it must surely occur to him that it would be worth while to get into conversation with an Englishman who was employed in the Censorship Department. Ashenden was prepared with a supply of information that it could not in the least benefit the Central Powers to possess. With a false name and a false passport he had little to fear that Caypor would guess that he was a British agent.

Ashenden did not have to wait long. Next day he was sitting in the doorway of the hotel, drinking a cup of coffee and already half asleep after a substantial *Mittagessen*, when the Caypors came out of the dining-room. Mrs Caypor went upstairs and Caypor released his dog. The dog bounded along and in a friendly fashion leaped up against Ashenden.

"Come here, Fritzi," cried Caypor, and then to Ashenden: "I'm so sorry. But he's quite gentle."

"Oh, that's all right. He won't hurt me."

Caypor stopped at the doorway.

"He's a bull-terrier. You don't often see them on the Continent." He seemed while he spoke to be taking Ashenden's measure; he called to the maid: "A coffee, please, *Fräulein*. You've just arrived, haven't you?"

"Yes, I came yesterday."

"Really? I didn't see you in the dining-room last night. Are you making a stay?"

"I don't know. I've been ill and I've come here to recuperate."

The maid came with the coffee and seeing Caypor talking to Ashenden put the tray on the table at which he was sitting. Caypor gave a laugh of faint embarrassment.

"I don't want to force myself upon you. I don't know why the maid put my coffee on your table."

"Please sit down," said Ashenden.

"It's very good of you. I've lived so long on the Continent that I'm always forgetting that my countrymen are apt to look upon it as confounded cheek if you talk to them. Are you English, by the way, or American?"

"English," said Ashenden.

Ashenden was by nature a very shy person, and he had in vain tried to cure himself of a failing that at his age was unseemly, but on occasion he knew how to make effective use of it. He explained now in a hesitating and awkward manner the facts that he had the day before told the landlady and that he was convinced she had already passed on to Caypor.

"You couldn't have come to a better place than Lucerne. It's an oasis of peace in this war-weary world. When you're here you might almost forget that there is such a thing as a war going on. That is why I've come here. I'm a journalist by profession."

"I couldn't help wondering if you wrote," said Ashenden, with an eagerly timid smile.

It was clear that he had not learnt that "oasis of peace in a war-weary world" at the shipping-office.

"You see, I married a German lady," said Caypor gravely.

"Oh, really?"

"I don't think anyone could be more patriotic than I am. I'm English through and through and I don't mind telling you that in my opinion the British Empire is the greatest instrument for good that the world has ever seen, but having a German wife I naturally see a good deal of the reverse of the medal. You don't have to tell me that the Germans have faults, but frankly I'm not prepared to admit that they're devils incarnate. At the beginning of the war my poor wife had a very rough time in England and I for one couldn't have blamed her if she'd felt rather bitter about it. Everyone thought she was a spy. It'll make you laugh when you know her. She's the typical German *Hausfrau* who cares for nothing but her house and her husband and our only child Fritzi." Caypor fondled his dog and gave a little laugh. "Yes, Fritzi, you are our child, aren't you? Naturally it made my position very awkward. I was connected with some very important papers, and my editors weren't quite comfortable about it. Well, to cut a long story short I thought the most dignified course was to resign and come to a neutral country till the storm blew over. My wife and I never discuss the war, though I'm bound to tell you that it's more on my account than hers, she's much more tolerant than I am and she's more willing to look upon this terrible business from my point of view than I am from hers."

"That is strange," said Ashenden. "As a rule women are so much more rabid than men."

"My wife is a very remarkable person. I should like to introduce you to her. By the way, I don't know if you know my name. Grantley Caypor."

"My name is Somerville," said Ashenden.

He told him then of the work he had been doing in the Censorship Department, and he fancied that into Caypor's eyes came a certain intentness. Presently he told him that he was looking for someone to give him conversation lessons in German so that he might rub up his rusty knowledge of the language; and as he spoke a notion flashed across his mind: he gave Caypor a look and saw that the same notion had come to him. It had occurred to them at the same instant that it would be a very good plan for Ashenden's teacher to be Mrs Caypor.

"I asked our landlady if she could find me someone and she said she thought she could. I must ask her again. It ought not to be very hard to find a man who is prepared to come and talk German to me for an hour a day."

"I wouldn't take anyone on the landlady's recommendation," said Caypor. "After all you want someone with a good North-German accent and she only talks Swiss. I'll ask my wife if she knows anyone. My wife's a very highly educated woman and you could trust her recommendation."

"That's very kind of you."

Ashenden observed Grantley Caypor at his ease. He noticed how the small, grey-green eyes, which last night he had not been able to see, contradicted the red good-humoured frankness of the face. They were quick and shifty, but when the mind behind them was seized by an unexpected notion they were suddenly still. It gave one a peculiar feeling of the working of the brain. They were not eyes that inspired confidence; Caypor did that with his jolly, good-natured smile, the openness of his broad, weatherbeaten face, his comfortable obesity and the cheeriness of his loud deep voice. He was doing his best now to be agreeable. While Ashenden talked to him, a little shyly still but gaining confidence from that breezy, cordial manner, capable of putting anyone at his ease, it intrigued him to remember that the man was a common spy. It gave a tang to his conversation to reflect that he had been ready to sell his country for no more than forty pounds a month. Ashenden had known Gomez, the young Spaniard whom Caypor had betrayed. He was a high-spirited youth, with a love of adventure, and he had undertaken his dangerous mission not for the money he earned by it, but from a passion for romance. It amused him to outwit the clumsy German and it appealed to his sense of the absurd to play a part in a shilling shocker. It was not very nice to think of him now six feet underground in a prison yard. He was young and he had a certain grace of gesture. Ashenden wondered whether Caypor had felt a qualm when he delivered him up to destruction.

"I suppose you know a little German?" asked Caypor, interested in the stranger.

"Oh, yes, I was a student in Germany, and I used to talk it fluently, but that is long ago and I have forgotten. I can still read it very comfortably."

"Oh, yes, I noticed you were reading a German book last night."

Fool! It was only a little since he had told Ashenden that he had not seen him at dinner. He wondered whether Caypor had observed the slip. How difficult it was never to make one! Ashenden must be on his guard; the thing that made him most nervous was the thought that he might not answer readily enough to his assumed name of Somerville. Of course there was always the chance that Caypor had made the slip on purpose to see by Ashenden's face whether he noticed anything. Caypor got up.

"There is my wife. We go for a walk up one of the mountains every afternoon. I can tell you some charming walks. The flowers even now are lovely."

"I'm afraid I must wait till I'm a bit stronger," said Ashenden, with a little sigh.

He had naturally a pale face and never looked as robust as he was. Mrs Caypor came downstairs and her husband joined her. They walked down the road, Fritzi bounding round them, and Ashenden saw that Caypor immediately began to speak with volubility. He was evidently telling his wife the results of his interview with Ashenden. Ashenden looked at the sun shining so gaily on the lake; the shadow of a breeze fluttered the green leaves of the trees; everything invited to a stroll: he got up, went to his room and throwing himself on his bed had a very pleasant sleep.

He went into dinner that evening as the Caypors were finishing, for he had wandered melancholy about Lucerne in the hope of finding a cocktail that would enable him to face the potato salad that he foresaw, and on their way out of the dining-room Caypor stopped and asked him if he would drink coffee with them. When

Ashenden joined them in the hall Caypor got up and introduced him to his wife. She bowed stiffly and no answering smile came to her face to respond to Ashenden's civil greeting. It was not hard to see that her attitude was definitely hostile. It put Ashenden at his ease. She was a plainish woman, nearing forty, with a muddy skin and vague features; her drab hair was arranged in a plait round her head like that of Napoleon's Queen of Prussia; and she was squarely built, plump rather than fat, and solid. But she did not look stupid; she looked on the contrary, a woman of character, and Ashenden, who had lived enough in Germany to recognize the type, was ready to believe that though capable of doing the housework, cooking the dinner, and climbing a mountain, she might be also prodigiously well-informed. She wore a white blouse that showed a sunburned neck, a black skirt and heavy walking boots. Caypor, addressing her in English, told her in his jovial way, as though she did not know it already, what Ashenden had told him about himself. She listened grimly.

"I think you told me you understood German," said Caypor, his big red face wreathed in polite smiles but his little eyes darting about restlessly.

"Yes, I was for some time a student in Heidelberg."

"Really?" said Mrs Caypor in English, an expression of faint interest for a moment chasing away the sullenness from her face. "I know Heidelberg very well. I was at school there for one year."

Her English was correct, but throaty, and the mouthing emphasis she gave her words was disagreeable. Ashenden was diffuse in praise of the old university town and the beauty of the neighbourhood. She heard him, from the standpoint of her Teutonic superiority, with toleration rather than with enthusiasm.

"It is well known that the valley of the Neckar is one of the beauty places of the whole world," she said.

"I have not told you, my dear," said Caypor then, "that Mr Somerville is looking for someone to give him conversation lessons while he is here. I told him that perhaps you could suggest a teacher."

"No, I know no one whom I could conscientiously recommend," she answered. "The Swiss accent is hateful beyond words. It could do Mr Somerville only harm to converse with a Swiss."

"If I were in your place, Mr Somerville, I would try and persuade my wife to give you lessons. She is, if I may say so, a very cultivated and highly educated woman."

"*Ach*, Grantley, I have not the time. I have my own work to do."

Ashenden saw that he was being given his opportunity. The trap was prepared and all he had to do was to fall in. He turned to Mrs Caypor with a manner that he tried to make shy, deprecating and modest.

"Of course it would be too wonderful if you would give me lessons. I should look upon it as a real privilege. Naturally I wouldn't want to interfere with your work. I am just here to get well, with nothing in the world to do, and I would suit my time entirely to your convenience."

He felt a flash of satisfaction pass from one to the other and in Mrs Caypor's blue eyes he fancied that he saw a dark glow.

"Of course it would be a purely business arrangement," said Caypor. "There's no reason that my good wife shouldn't earn a little pin-money. Would you think ten francs an hour too much?"

"No," said Ashenden, "I should think myself lucky to get a first-rate teacher for that."

"What do you say, my dear? Surely you can spare an hour, and you would be doing this gentleman a kindness. He would learn that all Germans are not the devilish fiends that they think them in England."

On Mrs Caypor's brow was an uneasy frown and Ashenden could not but think with apprehension of that hour's conversation a day that he was going to exchange with her. Heaven only knew how he would have to rack his brain for subjects of discourse with that heavy and morose woman. Now she made a visible effort.

"I shall be very pleased to give Mr Somerville conversation lessons."

"I congratulate you, Mr Somerville," said Caypor noisily. "You're in for a treat. When will you start, tomorrow at eleven?"

"That would suit me very well if it suits Mrs Caypor."

"Yes, that is as good an hour as another," she answered.

Ashenden left them to discuss the happy outcome of their diplomacy. But when, punctually at eleven next morning, he heard a knock at his door (for it had been arranged that Mrs Caypor should give him his lesson in his room) it was not without trepidation that he opened it. It behoved him to be frank, a trifle indiscreet, but obviously wary of a German woman, sufficiently intelligent, and impulsive. Mrs Caypor's face was dark and sulky. She plainly hated having anything to do with him. But they sat down and she began, somewhat peremptorily, to ask him questions about his knowledge of German literature. She corrected his mistakes with exactness and when he put before her some difficulty in German construction explained it with clearness and precision. It was obvious that though she hated giving him a lesson she meant to give it conscientiously. She seemed to have not only an aptitude for teaching, but a love of it, and as the hour went on she began to speak with greater earnestness. It was already only by an effort that she remembered that he was a brutal Englishman. Ashenden, noticing the unconscious struggle within her, found himself not a little entertained; and it was with truth that, when later in the day Caypor asked him how the lesson had gone, he answered that it was highly satisfactory; Mrs Caypor was an excellent teacher and a most interesting person.

"I told you so. She's the most remarkable woman I know."

And Ashenden had a feeling that when in his hearty, laughing way Caypor said this he was for the first time entirely sincere.

In a day or two Ashenden guessed that Mrs Caypor was giving him lessons only in order to enable Caypor to arrive at a closer intimacy with him, for she confined herself strictly to matters of literature, music, and painting; and when Ashenden, by way of experiment, brought the conversation round to the war, she cut him short.

"I think that is a topic that we had better avoid, Herr Somerville," she said.

She continued to give her lessons with the greatest thoroughness, and he had his money's worth, but every day she came with the same sullen face and it was only in the interest of teaching that she lost for a moment her instinctive dislike of him. Ashenden exercised in turn, but in vain, all his wiles. He was ingratiating, ingenuous, humble, grateful, flattering, simple, and timid. She remained coldly hostile. She was a fanatic. Her patriotism was aggressive, but disinterested, and obsessed with the notion of the superiority of all things German; she loathed England with a virulent hatred because in that country she saw the chief obstacle to their diffusion. Her ideal was a German world in which the rest of the nations under a hegemony greater than that of Rome should enjoy the benefits of German science and German art and German culture. There was in the conception a magnificent impudence that appealed to Ashenden's sense of humour. She was no fool. She had read much, in several languages, and she could talk of the books she had read with good sense. She had a knowledge of modern painting and modern music that not a little impressed Ashenden. It was amusing once to hear her before lunch-eon play one of those silvery little pieces of Debussy; she played it disdainfully because it was French and so light, but with an angry appreciation of its grace and gaiety. When Ashenden congratulated her she shrugged her shoulders.

"The decadent music of a decadent nation," she said. Then with powerful hands she struck the first resounding chords of a sonata by Beethoven; but she stopped. "I cannot play, I am out of practice, and you English, what do you know of music? You have not produced a composer since Purcell!"

"What do you think of that statement?" Ashenden, smiling, asked Caypor, who was standing near.

"I confess its truth. The little I know of music my wife taught me. I wish you could hear her play when she is in practice." He put his fat hand, with its square, stumpy fingers, on her shoulder. "She can wring your heartstrings with pure beauty."

"*Dummer Kerl*," she said, in a soft voice, "Stupid fellow," and Ashenden saw her mouth for a moment quiver, but she quickly recovered. "You English, you cannot paint, you cannot model, you cannot write music."

"Some of us can at times write pleasing verses," said Ashenden, with good-humour, for it was not his business to be put out, and he did not know why, two lines occurring to him he said them:

> *"Whither, O splendid ship, thy white sails crowding,*
> *Leaning across the bosom of the urgent West?"*

"Yes," said Mrs Caypor, with a strange gesture, "you can write poetry. I wonder why."

And to Ashenden's surprise she went on, in her guttural English, to recite the next two lines of the poem he had quoted.

"Come Grantley, *Mittagessen* is ready, let us go into the dining-room."

They left Ashenden reflective.

Ashenden admired goodness, but was not outraged by wickedness. People sometimes thought him heartless because he was more often interested in others than attached to them, and even in the few to whom he was attached his eyes saw with equal clearness the merits and the defects. When he liked people it was not because he was blind to their faults, he did not mind their faults but accepted them with a tolerant shrug of the shoulders, or because he ascribed to them excellencies that they did not possess; and since he judged his friends with candour they never disappointed him and so he seldom lost one. He asked from none more than he could give. He was able to pursue his study of the Caypors without prejudice and without passion. Mrs Caypor seemed to him more of a piece and therefore the easier of the two to understand; she obviously detested him; though it was necessary for her to be civil to him her antipathy was strong enough to wring from her now and then an expression of rudeness; and had she been safely able to do so she would have killed him without a qualm. But in the pressure of Caypor's chubby hand on his wife's shoulder and in the fugitive trembling of her lips Ashenden had divined that this unprepossessing woman and that mean fat man were joined together by a deep and sincere love. It was touching. Ashenden assembled the observations that he had been making for the past few days and little things that he had noticed but to which he had attached no significance returned to him. It seemed to him that Mrs Caypor loved her husband because she was of a stronger character than he and because she felt his dependence on her; she loved him for his admiration of her, and you might guess that till she met him this dumpy, plain woman with her dullness, good sense, and want of humour could not have much enjoyed the admiration of men; she enjoyed his heartiness and his noisy jokes, and his high spirits stirred her sluggish blood; he was a great big bouncing boy and he would never be anything else and she felt like a mother towards him; she had made him what he was, and he was her man and she was his woman, and she loved him, notwithstanding his weakness (for with her clear head she must always have been conscious of that), she loved him, *ach, was*, as Isolde loved Tristan. But then there was the espionage. Even Ashenden with all his tolerance for human frailty could not but feel that to betray your country for money is not a very pretty proceeding. Of course she knew of it, indeed it was probably through her that Caypor had first been approached; he would never have undertaken such work if she had not urged him to it. She loved him and she was an honest and an upright woman. By what devious means had she persuaded herself to force her husband to adopt so base and dishonourable a calling? Ashenden lost himself in a labyrinth of conjecture as he tried to piece together the actions of her mind.

Grantley Caypor was another story. There was little to admire in him, but at that moment Ashenden was not looking for an object of admiration; but there was much that was singular and much that was unexpected in that gross and vulgar fellow. Ashenden watched with entertainment the suave manner in which the spy tried to inveigle him in his toils. It was a couple of days after his first lesson that Caypor after dinner, his wife having gone upstairs, threw himself heavily into a chair by Ashenden's side. His faithful Fritzi came up to him and put his long muzzle with its black nose on his knee.

"He has no brain," said Caypor, "but a heart of gold. Look at those little pink eyes. Did you ever see anything so stupid? And what an ugly face, but what incredible charm!"

"Have you had him long?" asked Ashenden.

"I got him in 1914 just before the outbreak of war. By the way, what do you think of the news today? Of course my wife and I never discuss the war. You can't think what a relief to me it is to find a fellow-countryman to whom I can open my heart."

He handed Ashenden a cheap Swiss cigar and Ashenden, making a rueful sacrifice to duty, accepted it.

"Of course they haven't got a chance, the Germans," said Caypor, "not a dog's chance. I knew they were beaten the moment we came in."

His manner was earnest, sincere, and confidential. Ashenden made a commonplace rejoinder.

"It's the greatest grief of my life that owing to my wife's nationality I was unable to do any war work. I tried to enlist the day war broke out, but they wouldn't have me on account of my age, but I don't mind telling you, if the war goes on much longer, wife or no wife, I'm going to do something. With my knowledge of languages

I ought to be of some service in the Censorship Department. That's where you were, wasn't it?"

That was the mark at which he had been aiming and in answer now to his well-directed questions Ashenden gave him the information that he had already prepared. Caypor drew his chair a little nearer and dropped his voice.

"I'm sure you wouldn't tell me anything that anyone shouldn't know, but after all these Swiss are absolutely pro-German and we don't want to give anyone the chance of overhearing."

Then he went on another tack. He told Ashenden a number of things that were of a certain secrecy.

"I wouldn't tell this to anybody else, you know, but I have one or two friends who are in pretty influential positions, and they know they can trust me."

Thus encouraged, Ashenden was a little more deliberately indiscreet and when they parted both had reason to be satisfied. Ashenden guessed that Caypor's typewriter would be kept busy next morning and that extremely energetic Major in Berne would shortly receive a most interesting report.

One evening, going upstairs after dinner, Ashenden passed an open bathroom. He caught sight of the Caypors.

"Come in," cried Caypor in his cordial way. "We're washing our Fritzi."

The bull-terrier was constantly getting himself very dirty, and it was Caypor's pride to see him clean and white. Ashenden went in. Mrs Caypor with her sleeves turned up and a large white apron was standing at one end of the bath, while Caypor, in a pair of trousers and a singlet, his fat, freckled arms bare, was soaping the wretched hound.

"We have to do it at night," he said, "because the Fitzgeralds use this bath and they'd have a fit if they knew we washed the dog in it. We wait till they go to bed. Come along, Fritzi, show the gentleman how beautifully you behave when you have your face scrubbed."

The poor brute, woebegone but faintly wagging his tail to show that however foul was this operation performed on him he bore no malice to the god who did it, was standing in the middle of the bath in six inches of water. He was soaped all over and Caypor, talking the while, shampooed him with his great fat hands.

"Oh, what a beautiful dog he's going to be when he's as white as the driven snow. His master will be as proud as Punch to walk out with him and all the little lady-dogs will say: Good gracious, who's that beautiful aristocratic-looking bull-terrier walking as though he owned the whole of Switzerland? Now stand still while you have your ears washed. You couldn't bear to go out into the street with dirty ears, could you? like a nasty little Swiss schoolboy. *Noblesse oblige*. Now the black nose. Oh, and all the soap in going into his little pink eyes and they'll smart."

Mrs Caypor listened to this nonsense with a good-humoured sluggish smile on her broad, plain face, and presently gravely took a towel.

"Now he's going to have a ducking. Upsie-daisy."

Caypor seized the dog by the fore-legs and ducked him once and ducked him twice. There was a struggle, a flurry and a splashing. Caypor lifted him out of the bath.

"Now go to mother and she'll dry you."

Mrs Caypor sat down and taking the dog between her strong legs rubbed him till the sweat poured off her forehead. And Fritzi, a little shaken and breathless, but happy it was all over, stood, with his sweet stupid face, white and shining.

"Blood will tell," cried Caypor exultantly. "He knows the names of no less than sixty-four of his ancestors, and they were all nobly born."

Ashenden was faintly troubled. He shivered a little as he walked upstairs.

Then, one Sunday, Caypor told him that he and his wife were going on an excursion and would eat their luncheon at some little mountain restaurant; and he suggested that Ashenden, each paying his share, should come with them. After three weeks at Lucerne Ashenden thought that his strength would permit him to venture the exertion. They started early, Mrs Caypor businesslike in her walking boots and Tyrolese hat and alpenstock, and Caypor in stockings and plus-fours looking very British. The situation amused Ashenden and he was prepared to enjoy his day; but he meant to keep his eyes open; it was not inconceivable that the Caypors had discovered what he was and it would not do to go too near a precipice; Mrs Caypor would not hesitate to give him a push and Caypor for all his jolliness was an ugly customer. But on the face of it there was nothing to mar Ashenden's pleasure in the golden morning. The air was fragrant. Caypor was full of conversation. He told funny stories. He was gay and jovial. The sweat rolled off his great red face and he laughed at himself because he was so fat. To Ashenden's astonishment he showed a peculiar knowledge of the mountain flowers. Once he went out of the way to pick one he saw a little distance from the path and brought it back to his wife. He looked at it tenderly.

"Isn't it lovely?" he cried, and his shifty grey-green eyes for a moment were as candid as a child's. "It's like a poem by Walter Savage Landor."

"Botany is my husband's favourite science," said Mrs Caypor. "I laugh at him sometimes. He is devoted to flowers. Often when we have hardly had enough money to pay the butcher he has spent everything in his pocket to bring me a bunch of roses."

"*Qui fleurit sa maison fleurit son cœur,*" said Grantley Caypor.

Ashenden had once or twice seen Caypor, coming in from a walk, offer Mrs Fitzgerald a nosegay of mountain flowers with an elephantine courtesy that was not entirely displeasing; and what he had just learned added a certain significance to the pretty little action. His passion for flowers was genuine and when he gave them to the old Irish lady he gave her something he valued. It showed a real kindness of heart. Ashenden had always thought botany a tedious science, but Caypor, talking exuberantly as they walked along, was able to impart to it life and interest. He must have given it a good deal of study.

"I've never written a book," he said. "There are too many books already and any desire to write I have is satisfied by the more immediately profitable and quite ephemeral composition of an article for a daily paper. But if I stay here much longer I have half a mind to write a book about the wild flowers of Switzerland. Oh, I wish you'd been here a little earlier. They were marvellous. But one wants to be a poet for that, and I'm only a poor newspaper-man."

It was curious to observe how he was able to combine real emotion with false fact.

When they reached the inn, with its view of the mountains and the lake, it was good to see the sensual pleasure with which he poured down his throat a bottle of ice-cold beer. You could not but feel sympathy for a man who took so much delight in simple things. They lunched deliciously off scrambled eggs and mountain trout. Even Mrs Caypor was moved to an unwonted gentleness by her surroundings; the inn was in an agreeably rural spot, it looked like a picture of a Swiss chalet in a book of early nineteenth-century travels; and she treated Ashenden with something less than her usual hostility. When they arrived she had burst into loud German exclamations on the beauty of the scene, and now, softened perhaps too by food and drink, her eyes, dwelling on the grandeur before her, filled with tears. She stretched out her hand.

"It is dreadful and I am ashamed, notwithstanding this horrible and unjust war I can feel in my heart at the moment nothing but happiness and gratitude."

Caypor took her hand and pressed it and, an unusual thing with him, addressing her in German, called her little pet-names. It was absurd, but touching. Ashenden, leaving them to their emotions, strolled through the garden and sat down on a bench that had been prepared for the comfort of the tourist. The view was of course spectacular, but it captured you; it was like a piece of music that was obvious and meretricious, but for the moment shattered your self-control.

And as Ashenden lingered idly in that spot he pondered over the mystery of Grantley Caypor's treachery. If he liked strange people he had found in him one who was strange beyond belief. It would be foolish to deny that he had amiable traits. His joviality was not assumed, he was without pretence a hearty fellow, and he had real good nature. He was always ready to do a kindness. Ashenden had often watched him with the old Irish colonel and his wife who were the only other residents of the hotel; he would listen good-humouredly to the old man's tedious stories of the Egyptian war, and he was charming with her. Now that Ashenden had arrived at terms of some familiarity with Caypor he found that he regarded him less with repulsion than with curiosity. He did not think that he had become a spy merely for the money; he was a man of modest tastes and what he had earned in a shipping-office must have sufficed to so good a manager as Mrs Caypor; and after war was declared there was no lack of remunerative work for men over the military age. It might be that he was one of those men who prefer devious ways to straight for some intricate pleasure they get in fooling their fellows; and that he had turned spy, not from hatred of the country that had imprisoned him, not even from love of his wife, but from a desire to score off the big-wigs who never even knew of his existence. It might be that it was vanity that impelled him, a feeling that his talents had not received the recognition they merited, or just a puckish, impish desire to do mischief. He was a crook. It is true that only two cases of dishonesty had been brought home to him, but if he had been caught twice it might be surmised that he had often been dishonest without being caught. What did Mrs Caypor think of this? They were so united that she must be aware of it. Did it make her ashamed, for her own uprightness surely none could doubt, or did she accept it as an inevitable kink in the man she loved? Did she do all she could to prevent it or did she close her eyes to something she could not help?

How much easier life would be if people were all black or all white and how much simpler it would be to act in regard to them! Was Caypor a good man who loved evil or a bad man who loved good? And how could such unreconcilable elements exist side by side and in harmony within the same heart? For one thing was clear, Caypor was disturbed by no gnawing of conscience; he did his mean and despicable work with gusto. He was a traitor who enjoyed his treachery. Though Ashenden had been studying human nature more or less consciously all his life, it seemed to him that he knew as little about it now in middle age as he had done when he was a child. Of course R. would have said to him: Why the devil do you waste your time with such nonsense? The man's a dangerous spy and your business is to lay him by the heels.

That was true enough. Ashenden had decided that it would be useless to attempt to make any arrangement with Caypor. Though doubtless he would have no feeling about betraying his employers he could certainly not be trusted. His wife's influence was too strong. Besides, notwithstanding what he had from time to time told Ashenden, he was in his heart convinced that the Central Powers must win the war, and he meant to be on the winning side. Well, then Caypor must be laid by the heels, but how he was to effect that Ashenden had no notion. Suddenly he heard a voice.

"There you are. We've been wondering where you had hidden yourself."

He looked around and saw the Caypors strolling towards him. They were walking hand in hand.

"So this is what has kept you so quiet," said Caypor as his eyes fell on the view. "What a spot!"

Mrs Caypor clasped her hands.

"*Ach Gott, wie schön!*" she cried. "*Wie schön.* When I look at that blue lake and those snowy mountains I feel inclined, like Goethe's Faust, to cry to the passing moment: Tarry."

"This is better than being in England with the excursions and alarums of war, isn't it?" said Caypor.

"Much," said Ashenden.

"By the way, did you have any difficulty in getting out?"

"No, not the smallest."

"I'm told they make rather a nuisance of themselves at the frontier nowadays."

"I came through without the smallest difficulty. I don't fancy they bother much about the English. I thought the examination of passports was quite perfunctory."

A fleeting glance passed between Caypor and his wife. Ashenden wondered what it meant. It would be strange if Caypor's thoughts were occupied with the chances of a journey to England at the very moment when he was himself reflecting on its possibility. In a little while Mrs Caypor suggested that they had better be starting back and they wandered together in the shade of trees down the mountain paths.

Ashenden was watchful. He could do nothing (and his inactivity irked him) but wait with his eyes open to seize the opportunity that might present itself. A couple of days later an incident occurred that made him certain something was in the wind. In the course of his morning lesson Mrs Caypor remarked:

"My husband has gone to Geneva today. He had some business to do there."

"Oh," said Ashenden, "will he be gone long?"

"No, only two days."

It is not everyone who can tell a lie and Ashenden had the feeling, he hardly knew why, that Mrs Caypor was telling one then. Her

manner perhaps was not quite as indifferent as you would have
expected when she was mentioning a fact that could be of no interest
to Ashenden. It flashed across his mind that Caypor had been
summoned to Berne to see the redoubtable head of the German
secret service. When he had the chance he said casually to the
waitress:

"A little less work for you to do, *Fräulein*. I hear that Herr Caypor
has gone to Berne."

"Yes. But he'll be back tomorrow."

That proved nothing, but it was something to go upon.
Ashenden knew in Lucerne a Swiss who was willing on emergency
to do odd jobs, and looking him up, asked him to take a letter
to Berne. It might be possible to pick up Caypor and trace his
movements. Next day Caypor appeared once more with his wife
at the dinner-table, but merely nodded to Ashenden and afterwards
both went straight upstairs. They looked troubled. Caypor, as a
rule so animated, walked with bowed shoulders and looked neither
to the right nor to the left. Next morning Ashenden received a
reply to his letter: Caypor had seen Major von P. It was possible to
guess what the Major had said to him. Ashenden well knew how
rough he could be; he was a hard man and brutal, clever and
unscrupulous, and he was not accustomed to mince his words.
They were tired of paying Caypor a salary to sit still in Lucerne
and do nothing; the time was come for him to go to England.
Guesswork? Of course it was guesswork, but in that trade it mostly
was; you had to deduce the animal from its jaw-bone. Ashenden
knew from Gustav that the Germans wanted to send someone
to England. He drew a long breath; if Caypor went he would have
to get busy.

When Mrs Caypor came in to give him his lesson she was dull and
listless. She looked tired and her mouth was set obstinately. It
occurred to Ashenden that the Caypors had spent most of the night
talking. He wished he knew what they had said. Did she urge him to
go or did she try to dissuade him? Ashenden watched them again at
luncheon. Something was the matter, for they hardly spoke to one
another and as a rule they found plenty to talk about. They left the
room early, but when Ashenden went out he saw Caypor sitting in
the hall by himself.

"Hullo," he cried jovially, but surely the effort was patent, "how are you getting on? I've been to Geneva."

"So I heard," said Ashenden.

"Come and have your coffee with me. My poor wife's got a headache. I told her she'd better go and lie down." In his shifty green eyes was an expression that Ashenden could not read. "The fact is, she's rather worried, poor dear; I'm thinking of going to England."

Ashenden's heart gave a sudden leap against his ribs, but his face remained impassive:

"Oh, are you going for long? We shall miss you."

"To tell you the truth, I'm fed up with doing nothing. The war looks as though it were going on for years and I can't sit here indefinitely. Besides, I can't afford it, I've got to earn my living. I may have a German wife, but I am an Englishman, hang it all, and I want to do my bit. I could never face my friends again if I just stayed here in ease and comfort till the end of the war and never attempted to do a thing to help the country. My wife takes her German point of view and I don't mind telling you that she's a bit upset. You know what women are."

Now Ashenden knew what it was that he saw in Caypor's eyes. Fear. It gave him a nasty turn. Caypor didn't want to go to England, he wanted to stay safely in Switzerland; Ashenden knew now what the major had said to him when he went to see him in Berne. He had got to go or lose his salary. What was it that his wife had said when he told her what had happened? He had wanted her to press him to stay, but, it was plain, she hadn't done that; perhaps he had not dared tell her how frightened he was; to her he had always been gay, bold, adventurous, and devil-may-care; and now, the prisoner of his own lies, he had not found it in him to confess himself the mean and sneaking coward he was.

"Are you going to take your wife with you?" asked Ashenden.

"No, she'll stay here."

It had been arranged very neatly. Mrs Caypor would receive his letters and forward the information they contained to Berne.

"I've been out of England so long that I don't quite know how to set about getting war-work. What would you do in my place?"

"I don't know; what sort of work are you thinking of?"

"Well, you know, I imagine I could do the same thing as you did. I wonder if there's anyone in the Censorship Department that you could give me a letter of introduction to."

It was only by a miracle that Ashenden saved himself from showing by a smothered cry or by a broken gesture how startled he was; but not by Caypor's request, but what had just dawned upon him. What an idiot he had been! He had been disturbed by the thought that he was wasting his time at Lucerne, he was doing nothing, and though in fact, as it turned out, Caypor was going to England it was due to no cleverness of his. He could take to himself no credit for the result. And now he saw that he had been put in Lucerne, told how to describe himself and given the proper information, so that what actually had occurred should occur. It would be a wonderful thing for the German secret service to get an agent into the Censorship Department; and by a happy accident there was Grantly Caypor, the very man for the job, on friendly terms with someone who had worked there. What a bit of luck! Major von P. was a man of culture and, rubbing his hands, he must surely have murmured: *stultum facit fortuna quem vult perdere.* It was a trap of that devilish R. and the grim major at Berne had fallen into it. Ashenden had done his work just by sitting still and doing nothing. He almost laughed as he thought what a fool R. had made of him.

"I was on very good terms with the chief of my department, I could give you a note to him if you liked."

"That would be just the thing."

"But of course I must give the facts. I must say I've met you here and only known you a fortnight."

"Of course. But you'll say what else you can for me, won't you?"

"Oh, certainly."

"I don't know yet if I can get a visa. I'm told they're rather fussy."

"I don't see why. I shall be very sick if they refuse me one when I want to go back."

"I'll go and see how my wife is getting on," said Caypor suddenly, getting up. "When will you let me have that letter?"

"Whenever you like. Are you going at once?"

"As soon as possible."

Caypor left him. Ashenden waited in the hall for a quarter of an hour so that there should appear in him no sign of hurry. Then he went upstairs and prepared various communications. In one he informed R. that Caypor was going to England; in another he made arrangements through Berne that wherever Caypor applied for a visa it should be granted to him without question; and these he dispatched forthwith. When he went down to dinner he handed Caypor a cordial letter of introduction.

Next day but one Caypor left Lucerne.

Ashenden waited. He continued to have his hour's lesson with Mrs Caypor and under her conscientious tuition began now to speak German with ease. They talked of Goethe and Winckelmann, of art and life and travel. Fritzi sat quietly by her chair.

"He misses his master," she said, pulling his ears. "He only really cares for him, he suffers me only as belonging to him."

After his lesson Ashenden went every morning to Cook's to ask for his letters. It was here that all communications were addressed to him. He could not move till he received instructions, but R. could be trusted not to leave him idle long; and meanwhile there was nothing for him to do but have patience. Presently he received a letter from the consul in Geneva to say that Caypor had there applied for his visa and had set out for France. Having read this Ashenden went on for a little stroll by the lake and on his way back happened to see Mrs Caypor coming out of Cook's office. He guessed that she was having her letters addressed there too. He went up to her.

"Have you had news of Herr Caypor?" he asked her.

"No," she said. "I suppose I could hardly expect to yet."

He walked along by her side. She was disappointed, but not yet anxious; she knew how irregular at that time was the post. But next day during the lesson he could not but see that she was impatient to have done with it. The post was delivered at noon and at five minutes to she looked at her watch and him. Though Ashenden knew very well that no letter would ever come for her he had not the heart to keep her on tenter-hooks.

"Don't you think that's enough for the day? I'm sure you want to go down to Cook's," he said.

"Thank you. That is very amiable of you."

When a little later he went there himself he found her standing in the middle of the office. Her face was distraught. She addressed him wildly.

"My husband promised to write from Paris. I am sure there is a letter for me, but these stupid people say there's nothing. They're so careless, it's a scandal."

Ashenden did not know what to say. While the clerk was looking through the bundle to see if there was anything for him she came up to the desk again.

"When does the next post come in from France?" she asked.

"Sometimes there are letters about five."

"I'll come then."

She turned and walked rapidly away. Fritzi followed her with his tail between his legs. There was no doubt of it, already the fear had seized her that something was wrong. Next morning she looked dreadful; she could not have closed her eyes all night; and in the middle of the lesson she started up from her chair.

"You must excuse me, Herr Somerville. I cannot give you a lesson today. I am not feeling well."

Before Ashenden could say anything she had flung nervously from the room, and in the evening he got a note from her to say that she regretted that she must discontinue giving him conversation lessons. She gave no reason. Then Ashenden saw no more of her; she ceased coming in to meals; except to go morning and afternoon to Cook's she spent apparently the whole day in her room. Ashenden thought of her sitting there hour after hour with that hideous fear gnawing at her heart. Who could help feeling sorry for her? The time hung heavy on his hands too. He read a good deal and wrote a little, he hired a canoe and went for long leisurely paddles on the lake; and at last one morning the clerk at Cook's handed him a letter. It was from R. It had all the appearance of a business communication, but between the lines he read a good deal.

Dear Sir, [it began] The goods, with accompanying letter, dispatched by you from Lucerne have been duly delivered. We are obliged to you for executing our instructions with such promptness.

It went on in this strain. R. was exultant. Ashenden guessed that Caypor had been arrested and by now had paid the penalty of his crime. He shuddered. He remembered a dreadful scene. Dawn. A cold grey dawn, with a drizzling rain falling. A man, blindfolded, standing against a wall, an officer very pale giving an order, a volley, and then a young soldier, one of the firing-party, turning round and holding on to his gun for support, vomiting. The officer turning paler still, and he, Ashenden, feeling dreadfully faint. How terrified Caypor must have been! It was awful when the tears ran down their faces. Ashenden shook himself. He went to the ticket-office and obedient to his orders bought himself a ticket for Geneva.

As he was waiting for his change Mrs Caypor came in. He was shocked at the sight of her. She was blowzy and dishevelled and there were heavy rings round her eyes. She was deathly pale. She staggered up to the desk and asked for a letter. The clerk shook his head.

"I'm sorry, madam, there's nothing yet."

"But look, look. Are you sure? Please look again."

The misery in her voice was heartrending. The clerk with a shrug of the shoulders took out the letters from a pigeon-hole and sorted them once more.

"No, there's nothing, madam."

She gave a hoarse cry of despair and her face was distorted with anguish.

"Oh, God, oh, God," she moaned.

She turned away, the tears streaming from her weary eyes, and for a moment she stood there like a blind man groping and not knowing which way to go. Then a fearful thing happened. Fritzi, the bull-terrier, sat down on his haunches and threw back his head and a gave a long, long melancholy howl. Mrs Caypor looked at him with terror; her eyes seemed really to start from her head. The doubt, the gnawing doubt that had tortured her during those dreadful days of suspense, was a doubt no longer. She knew. She staggered blindly into the street.

HIS EXCELLENCY

WHEN ASHENDEN WAS sent to X and looked about him he could not but see that his situation was equivocal. X was the capital of an important belligerent state; but a state divided against itself; there was a large party antagonistic to the war and revolution was possible if not imminent. Ashenden was instructed to see what under the circumstances could best be done; he was to suggest a policy and, if it was approved by the exalted personages who had sent him, to carry it out. A vast amount of money was put at his disposal. The Ambassadors of Great Britain and the United States had been directed to afford him such facilities as were at their command, but Ashenden had been told privately to keep himself to himself; he was not to make difficulties for the official representatives of the two powers by divulging to them facts that might be inconvenient for them to know; and since it might be necessary for him to give support under cover to a party that was at daggers drawn with that in office and with which the relations of the United States and Great Britain were extremely cordial it was just as well that Ashenden should keep his own counsel. The exalted personages did not wish the ambassadors to suffer the affront of discovering that an obscure agent had been sent to work at cross-purposes with them. On the other hand it was thought just as well to have a representative in the opposite camp, who in the event of a sudden upheaval would be at hand with adequate funds and in the confidence of the new leaders of the country.

But ambassadors are sticklers for their dignity and they have a keen nose to scent any encroachment on their authority. When Ashenden on his arrival at X paid an official call on Sir Herbert Witherspoon, the British ambassador, he was received with a politeness to which no exception could be taken, but with a frigidity that would have sent a little shiver down the spine of a polar bear. Sir Herbert was a diplomat *de carrière* and he cultivated the manner of his profession to a degree that filled the observer with admiration. He did not ask Ashenden anything about his mission because he knew that Ashenden would reply evasively, but he allowed him to see that it was a perfectly foolish one. He talked with acidulous tolerance of the exalted personages who had sent Ashenden to X. He told Ashenden that he had instructions to meet any demands for help that he made and stated that if Ashenden at any time desired to see him he had only to say so.

"I have received the somewhat singular request to dispatch telegrams for you in a private code which I understand has been given to you and to hand over to you telegrams in code as they arrive."

"I hope they will be few and far between, sir," answered Ashenden. "I know nothing so tedious as coding and decoding."

Sir Herbert paused for an instant. Perhaps that was not quite the answer he expected. He rose.

"If you will come into the Chancellery I will introduce you to the Counsellor and to the Secretary to whom you can take your telegrams."

Ashenden followed him out of the room, and after handing him over to the Counsellor the ambassador gave him a limp hand to shake.

"I hope I shall have the pleasure of seeing you again one of these days," he said, and with a curt nod left him.

Ashenden bore his reception with composure. It was his business to remain in obscurity and he did not wish any official attentions to attract notice to him. But when on the afternoon of the same day he made his call at the American Embassy he discovered why Sir Herbert Witherspoon had shown him so much coldness. The American ambassador was Mr Wilbur Schäfer; he came from Kansas City and had been given his post when few suspected that a war was on the point of breaking out, as a reward for political services. He was a big stout man, no longer young, for his hair was white, but well-preserved and exceedingly robust. He had a square, red face, clean-shaven, with a little snub nose and a determined chin. His face was very mobile and he twisted it continually into odd and amusing grimaces. It looked as though it were made out of the red india-rubber from which they make hot-water bottles. He greeted Ashenden with cordiality. He was a hearty fellow.

"I suppose you've seen Sir Herbert. I reckon you've got his dander up. What do they mean in Washington and London by telling us to dispatch your code telegrams without knowing what they're all about? You know, they've got no right to do that."

"Oh, Your Excellency, I think it was only done to save time and trouble," said Ashenden.

"Well, what is this mission anyway?"

This of course was a question that Ashenden was not prepared to answer, but not thinking it politic to say so, he determined to give a reply from which the ambassador could learn little. He had already made up his mind from the look of him that Mr Schäfer, though doubtless possessed of the gifts that enable a man to swing a presidential election this way or that, had not, at least nakedly for all men to see, the acuteness that his position perhaps demanded. He gave you the impression of a bluff, good-humoured creature who liked good cheer. Ashenden would have been wary when playing poker with him, but where the matter in hand was concerned felt himself fairly safe. He began to talk in a loose, vague way of the world at large and before he had gone far managed to ask the ambassador his opinion of the general situation. It was as the sound of the trumpet to the war-horse: Mr Schäfer made him a speech that lasted without a break for twenty-five minutes, and when at last he stopped in exhaustion, Ashenden with warm thanks for his friendly reception was able to take his leave.

Making up his mind to give both the ambassadors a wide berth, he set about his work and presently devised a plan of campaign. But by chance he was able to do Sir Herbert Witherspoon a good turn and so was thrown again into contact with him. It has been suggested that Mr Schäfer was more of a politician than a diplomat and it was his position rather than his personality that gave weight to his opinions. He looked upon the eminence to which he had risen as an opportunity to enjoy the good things of life and his enthusiasm led him to lengths that his constitution could ill support. His ignorance of foreign affairs would in any case have made his judgement of doubtful value, but his state at meetings of the Allied ambassadors so often approached the comatose that he seemed hardly capable of forming a judgement at all. He was known to have succumbed to the fascination of a Swedish lady of undoubted beauty, but of antecedents that from the point of view of a secret service agent were suspect. Her relations with Germany were such as to make her sympathy with the Allies dubious. Mr Schäfer saw her every day and was certainly much under her influence. Now it was noticed that there was from time to time a leakage of very secret information and the question arose whether Mr Schäfer did not in these daily interviews inadvertently say things that were promptly passed on to the headquarters of the enemy. No one could have doubted Mr Schäfer's honesty and patriotism, but it was permissible to be uncertain of his discretion. It was an awkward matter to deal with, but the concern was as great in Washington as in London and Paris, and Ashenden was instructed to deal with it. He had of course not been sent to X without help to do with work he was expected to do and among his assistants was an astute, powerful, and determined man, a Galician Pole, named Herbartus. After consultation with him it happened by one of those fortunate coincidences that occasionally come about in the secret service that a maid in the service of the Swedish lady fell ill and in her place the countess (for such she was) was very luckily able to engage an extremely respectable person from the neighbourhood of Cracow. The fact that before the war she had been secretary to an eminent scientist made her doubtless no less competent a housemaid.

The result of this was that Ashenden received every two or three days a neat report upon the goings-on at this charming lady's apartment, and though he learned nothing that could confirm the vague suspicions that had arisen, he learned something else of no little importance. From conversations held at the cosy little *tête-à-tête* dinners that the countess gave the ambassador it appeared that His Excellency was harbouring a bitter grievance against his English colleague. He complained that the relations between himself and Sir Herbert were deliberately maintained on a purely official level. In his blunt way he said he was sick of the frills that damned Britisher put on. He was a he-man and a hundred-per-cent American and he had no more use for protocol and etiquette than for a snowball in hell. Why didn't they get together, like a couple of regular fellows, and have a good old crack? Blood was thicker than water, he'd say, and they'd do more towards winning the war by sitting down in their shirt-sleeves and talking things out over a bottle of rye than by all their diplomacy and white spats. Now it was obviously very undesirable that there should not exist between the two ambassadors a perfect cordiality, so Ashenden thought it well to ask Sir Herbert whether he might see him.

He was ushered into Sir Herbert's library.

"Well, Mr Ashenden, what can I do for you? I hope you're quite satisfied with everything. I understand that you've been keeping the telegraph lines busy."

Ashenden, as he sat down, gave the ambassador a glance. He was beautifully dressed in a perfectly cut tail-coat that fitted his slim figure like a glove, in his black silk tie was a handsome pearl, there was a perfect line in his grey trousers, with their quiet and distinguished stripe, and his neat, pointed shoes looked as though he had never worn them before. You could hardly imagine him sitting in his shirt-sleeves over a whisky highball. He was a tall, thin man, with exactly the figure to show off modern clothes, and he sat in his chair, rather upright, as though he were sitting for an official portrait. In his cold and uninteresting way he was really a very handsome fellow. His neat grey hair was parted on one side, his pale face was clean-shaven, he had a delicate, straight nose and grey eyes under grey eyebrows, his mouth in youth might have been sensual and well-shaped, but now it was set to an expression of sarcastic determination and the lips were pallid. It was the kind of face that suggested centuries of good breeding, but you could not believe it capable of expressing emotion. You would never expect to see it break into the hearty distortion of laughter, but at the most be for a moment frigidly kindled by an ironic smile.

Ashenden was uncommonly nervous.

"I'm afraid you'll think I'm meddling in what doesn't concern me, sir. I'm quite prepared to be told to mind my own business."

"We'll see. Pray go on."

Ashenden told his story and the ambassador listened attentively. He did not turn his cold, grey eyes from Ashenden's face, and Ashenden knew that his embarrassment was obvious.

"How did you find out all this?"

"I have means of getting hold of little bits of information that are sometimes useful," said Ashenden.

"I see."

Sir Herbert maintained his steady gaze, but Ashenden was surprised to see on a sudden in the steely eyes a little smile. The bleak, supercilious face became for an instant quite attractive.

"There is another little bit of information that perhaps you'd be good enough to give me. What does one do to be a regular fellow?"

"I am afraid one can do nothing, Your Excellency," replied Ashenden gravely. "I think it is a gift of God."

The light vanished from Sir Herbert's eyes, but his manner was slightly more urbane than when Ashenden was brought into the room. He rose and held out his hand.

"You did quite right to come and tell me this, Mr Ashenden. I have been very remiss. It is inexcusable on my part to offend that inoffensive old gentleman. But I will do my best to repair my error. I will call at the American Embassy this afternoon."

"But not in too great state, sir, if I may venture a suggestion."

The ambassador's eyes twinkled. Ashenden began to think him almost human.

"I can do nothing but in state, Mr Ashenden. That is one of the misfortunes of my temperament." Then as Ashenden was leaving he added: "Oh, by the way, I wonder if you'd care to come to dinner with me tomorrow night. Black tie. At eight-fifteen."

He did not wait for Ashenden's assent, but took it for granted, and with a nod of dismissal sat down once more at his great writing-table.

Ashenden looked forward with misgiving to the dinner to which Sir Herbert Witherspoon had invited him. The black tie suggested a small party, perhaps only Lady Anne, the ambassador's wife, whom Ashenden did not know, or one or two young secretaries. It did not presage a hilarious evening. It was possible that they might play bridge after dinner, but Ashenden knew that professional diplomats do not play bridge with skill: it may be supposed that they find it difficult to bend their great minds to the triviality of a parlour game. On the other hand he was interested to see a little more of the ambassador in circumstances of less formality. For it was evident that Sir Herbert Witherspoon was not an ordinary person. He was in appearance and manner a perfect specimen of his class and it is always entertaining to come upon good examples of a well-known type. He was exactly what you expected an ambassador to be. If any of his characteristics had been ever so slightly exaggerated he would have been a caricature. He escaped being ridiculous only by a hair's breadth and you watched him with a kind of breathlessness as you might watch a tight-rope dancer doing perilous feats at a dizzy height. He was certainly a man of character. His rise in the diplomatic service had been rapid and though doubtless it helped him to be connected by marriage with powerful families his rise had been due chiefly to his merit. He knew how to be determined when determination was necessary and conciliatory when conciliation was opportune. His manners were perfect; he could speak half a dozen languages with ease and accuracy; he had a clear and logical brain. He was never afraid to think out his thoughts to the end, but was wise enough to suit his actions to the exigencies of the situation. He had reached his post at X at the early age of fifty-three and had borne himself in the exceedingly difficult conditions created by the war and contending parties within the state with tact, confidence, and once at least with courage. For on one occasion, a riot having arisen, a band of revolutionaries forced their way into the British Embassy and Sir Herbert from the head of his stairs had harangued them and, not-withstanding revolvers flourished at him, had persuaded them to go to their homes. He would end his career in Paris. That was evident. He was a man whom you could not but admire but whom it was not easy to like. He was a diplomat of the school of those Victorian ambassadors to whom could confidently be entrusted great affairs and whose self-reliance, sometimes it must be admitted tinctured with arrogance, was justified by its results.

When Ashenden drove up to the doors of the Embassy they were flung open and he was received by a stout and dignified English butler and three footmen. He was ushered up that magnificent flight of stairs on which had taken place the dramatic incident just related and shown into an immense room, dimly lit with shaded lamps, in which at the first glance he caught sight of large pieces of stately furniture and over the chimney-piece an immense portrait in coron-ation robes of King George IV. But there was a bright fire blazing on the hearth and from a deep sofa by the side of it his host, as his name was announced, slowly rose. Sir Herbert looked very elegant as he came towards him. He wore his dinner jacket, the most difficult costume for a man to look well in, with notable distinction.

"My wife has gone to a concert, but she'll come in later. She wants to make your acquaintance. I haven't asked anybody else. I thought I would give myself the pleasure of enjoying your company *en tête-à-tête*."

Ashenden murmured a civil rejoinder, but his heart sank. He wondered how he was going to pass at least a couple of hours alone with this man who made him, he was bound to confess, feel extremely shy.

The door was opened again and the butler and a footman entered bearing very heavy silver salvers.

"I always have a glass of sherry before my dinner," said the ambassador, "but in case you have acquired the barbarous custom of drinking cocktails I can offer you what I believe is called a dry Martini."

Shy though he might be, Ashenden was not going to give in to this sort of thing with complete tameness.

"I move with the times," he replied. "To drink a glass of sherry when you can get a dry Martini is like taking a stage-coach when you can travel by the Orient Express."

A little desultory conversation after this fashion was interrupted by the throwing open of two great doors and the announcement that His Excellency's dinner was served. They went into the dining-room. This was a vast apartment in which sixty people might have comfortably dined, but there was now only a small round table in it so that Sir Herbert and Ashenden sat intimately. There was an immense mahogany sideboard on which were massive pieces of gold plate, and above it, facing Ashenden, was a fine picture by Canaletto. Over the chimney-piece was a three-quarter-length portrait of Queen Victoria as a girl with a little gold crown on her small, prim head. Dinner was served by the corpulent butler and the three very tall English footmen. Ashenden had the impression that the ambassador enjoyed in his well-bred way the sensation of ignoring the pomp in which he lived. They might have been dining in one of the great country houses of England; it was a ceremony they performed, sumptuous without ostentation, and it was saved from a trifling absurdity only because it was in a tradition; but the experience gained for Ashenden a kind of savour from the thought that dwelt with him that on the other side of the wall was a restless, turbulent population that might at any moment break into bloody revolution, while not two hundred miles away men in the trenches were sheltering in their dug-outs from the bitter cold and the pitiless bombardment.

Ashenden need not have feared that the conversation would proceed with difficulty and the notion he had had that Sir Herbert had asked him in order to question him about his secret mission was quickly dispelled. The ambassador behaved to him as though he were a travelling Englishman who had presented a letter of introduction and to whom he desired to show civility. You would hardly have thought that a war was raging, for he made to it only such references as showed that he was not deliberately avoiding a distressing subject. He spoke of art and literature, proving himself to be a diligent reader of catholic taste, and when Ashenden talked to him, from personal acquaintance, of the writers whom Sir Herbert knew only through their works, he listened with the friendly condescension which the great ones of the earth affect towards the artist. (Sometimes, however, they paint a picture or write a book, and then the artist gets a little of his own back.) He mentioned in passing a character in one of Ashenden's novels, but did not make any other reference to the fact that his guest was a writer. Ashenden admired his urbanity. He disliked people to talk to him of his books, in which indeed, once written, he took small interest, and it made him self-conscious to be praised or blamed to his face. Sir Herbert Witherspoon flattered his self-esteem by showing that he had read him, but spared his delicacy by withholding his opinion of what he had read. He spoke too of the various countries in which during his career he had been stationed and of various persons, in London and elsewhere, that he and Ashenden knew in common. He talked well, not without a pleasant irony that might very well have passed for humour, and intelligently. Ashenden did not find his dinner dull, but neither did he find it exhilarating. He would have been more interested if the ambassador had not so invariably said the right, wise, and sensible thing upon every topic that was introduced. Ashenden was finding it something of an effort to keep up with this distinction of mind and he would have liked the conversation to get into its shirt-sleeves, so to speak, and put its feet on the table. But of this there was no chance and Ashenden once or twice caught himself wondering how soon after dinner he could decently take his leave. At eleven he had an appointment with Herbartus at the Hotel de Paris.

The dinner came to an end and coffee was brought in. Sir Herbert knew good food and good wine and Ashenden was obliged to admit that he had fared excellently. Liqueurs were served with the coffee, and Ashenden took a glass of brandy.

"I have some very old Benedictine," said the ambassador. "Won't you try it?"

"To tell you the honest truth I think brandy is the only liqueur worth drinking."

"I'm not sure that I don't agree with you. But in that case I must give you something better than that."

He gave an order to the butler, who presently brought in a cobwebbed bottle and two enormous glasses.

"I don't really want to boast," said the ambassador as he watched the butler pour the golden liquid into Ashenden's glass, "but I venture to think that if you like brandy you'll like this. I got it when I was counsellor for a short time in Paris."

"I've had a good deal to do lately with one of your successors there."

"Byring?"

"Yes."

"What do you think of the brandy?"

"I think it's marvellous."

"And of Byring?"

The question came so oddly on the top of the other that it sounded faintly comic.

"Oh, I think he's a damned fool."

Sir Herbert leaned back in his chair, holding the huge glass with both hands in order to bring out the aroma, and looked slowly round the stately and spacious room. The table had been cleared of superfluous things. There was a bowl of roses between Ashenden and his host. The servants switched off the electric light as they finally left the room and it was lit now only by the candles that were on the table and by the fire. Notwithstanding its size it had an air of sober comfort. The ambassador's eyes rested on the really distinguished portrait of Queen Victoria that hung over the chimney-piece.

"I wonder," he said at last.

"He'll have to leave the diplomatic service."

"I'm afraid so."

Ashenden gave him a quick glance of inquiry. He was the last man from whom he would have expected sympathy for Byring.

"Yes, in the circumstances," he proceeded, "I suppose it's inevitable that he should leave the service. I'm sorry. He's an able fellow and he'll be missed. I think he had a career before him."

"Yes, that is what I've heard. I'm told that at the FO they thought very highly of him."

"He has many of the gifts that are useful in this rather dreary trade," said the ambassador, with a slight smile, in his cold and judicial manner. "He's handsome, he's a gentleman, he has nice manners, he speaks excellent French, and he has a good head on his shoulders. He'd have done well."

"It seems a pity that he should waste such golden opportunities."

"I understand he's going into the wine business at the end of the war. Oddly enough he's going to represent the very firm from whom I got this brandy."

Sir Herbert raised the glass to his nose and inhaled the fragrance. Then he looked at Ashenden. He had a way of looking at people, when he was thinking of something else perhaps, that suggested that he thought them somewhat peculiar but rather disgusting insects.

"Have you ever seen the woman?" he asked.

"I dined with her and Byring at Larue's."

"How very interesting. What is she like?"

"Charming."

Ashenden tried to describe her to his host, but meanwhile with another part of his mind he recollected the impression she had made on him at the restaurant when Byring had introduced him to her. He had been not a little interested to meet a woman of whom for some years he had heard so much. She called herself Rose Auburn, but what her real name was few knew. She had gone to Paris originally as one of a troupe of dancers, called the Glad Girls, who performed at the Moulin Rouge, but her astonishing beauty had soon caused her to be noticed and a wealthy French manufacturer fell in love with her. He gave her a house and loaded her with jewels, but could not long meet the demands she made upon him, and she passed in rapid succession from lover to lover. She became in a short time the best-known courtesan in France. Her expenditure was prodigal and she ruined her admirers with cynical unconcern. The richest men found themselves unable to cope with her extravagance. Ashenden, before the war, had seen her once at Monte Carlo lose a hundred and eighty thousand francs at a sitting and that then was an important sum. She sat at the big table, surrounded by curious onlookers, throwing down packets of thousand-franc notes with a self-possession that would have been admirable if it had been her own money that she was losing.

When Ashenden met her she had been leading this riotous life, dancing and gambling all night, racing most afternoons a week, for twelve or thirteen years and she was no longer very young; but there was hardly a line on that lovely brow, scarcely a crow's-foot round those liquid eyes, to betray the fact. The most astonishing thing about her was that notwithstanding this feverish and unending round of senseless debauchery she had preserved an air of virginity. Of course she cultivated the type. She had an exquisitely graceful and slender figure, and her innumerable frocks were always made with a perfect simplicity. Her brown hair was very plainly done. With her oval face, charming little nose, and large blue eyes she had all the air of one or other of Anthony Trollope's charming heroines. It was the keepsake style raised to such rareness that it made you catch your breath. She had a lovely skin, very white and red, and if she painted it was not from necessity but from wantonness. She irradiated a sort of dewy innocence that was as attractive as it was unexpected.

Ashenden had heard of course that Byring for a year or more had been her lover. Her notoriety was such that a hard light of publicity was shed on everyone with whom she had any affair, but in this instance the gossips had more to say than usual because Byring had no money to speak of and Rose Auburn had never been known to grant her favours for anything that did not in some way represent hard cash. Was it possible that she loved him? It seemed incredible and yet what other explanation was there? Byring was a young man with whom any woman might have fallen in love. He was somewhere in the thirties, very tall and good-looking with a singular charm of manner and of an appearance so debonair that people turned round in the street to look at him; but unlike most handsome men he seemed entirely unaware of the impression he created. When it became known that Byring was the *amant de cœur* (a prettier phrase than our English fancy man) of this famous harlot he became an object of admiration to many women and of envy to many men; but when a rumour spread abroad that he was going to marry her consternation seized his friends and ribald laughter everyone else. It became known that Byring's chief had asked him if it was true and he had admitted it. Pressure was put upon him to relinquish a plan that could only end in disaster. It was pointed out to him that the wife of a diplomat has social obligations that Rose Auburn could not fulfil.

Byring replied that he was prepared to resign his post whenever by so doing he would not cause inconvenience. He brushed aside every expostulation and every argument; he was determined to marry.

When first Ashenden met Byring he did not very much take to him. He found him slightly aloof. But as the hazards of his work brought him from time to time into contact with him he discerned that the distant manner was due merely to shyness and as he came to know him better he was charmed by the uncommon sweetness of his disposition. Their relations, however, remained purely official so that it was a trifle unexpected when Byring one day asked him to dinner to meet Miss Auburn, and he could not but wonder whether it was because already people were beginning to turn the cold shoulder on him. When he went he discovered that the invitation was due to the lady's curiosity. But the surprise he got on learning that she had found time to read (with admiration, it appeared) two or three of his novels was not the only surprise he got that evening. Leading on the whole a quiet and studious life he had never had occasion to penetrate into the world of the higher prostitution and the great courtesans of the period were known to him only by name. It was somewhat astonishing to Ashenden to discover that Rose Auburn differed so little in air and manner from the smart women of Mayfair with whom through his books he had become more or less intimately acquainted. She was perhaps a little more anxious to please (indeed one of her agreeable traits was the interest she took in whomever she was talking to), but she was certainly no more made-up and her conversation was as intelligent. It lacked only the coarseness that society has lately affected. Perhaps she felt instinctively that those lovely lips should never disfigure themselves with foul words; perhaps only she was at heart still a trifle suburban. It was evident that she and Byring were madly in love with one another. It was really moving to see their mutual passion. When Ashenden took his leave of them, as he shook hands with her (and she held his hand a moment and with her blue, starry eyes looked into his) she said to him:

"You will come and see us when we're settled in London, won't you? You know we're going to be married."

"I heartily congratulate you," said Ashenden.

"And him?" she smiled, and her smile was like an angel's; it had the freshness of dawn and the tender rapture of a southern spring.

"Have you never looked at yourself in the glass?"

Sir Herbert Witherspoon watched him intently while Ashenden (he thought not without a trace of humour) was describing the dinner-party. No flicker of a smile brightened his cold eyes.

"Do you think it'll be a success?" he asked now.

"No."

"Why not?"

The question took Ashenden aback.

"A man not only marries his wife, he marries her friends. Do you realize the sort of people Byring will have to mix with, painted women of tarnished reputation and men who've gone down in the social scale, parasites and adventurers? Of course they'll have money, her pearls must be worth a hundred thousand pounds, and they'll be able to cut a dash in the smart Bohemia of London. Do you know the gold fringe of society? When a woman of bad character marries she earns the admiration of her set, she has worked the trick, she's caught a man and become respectable, but he, the man, only earns its ridicule. Even her own friends, the old hags with their gigolos and the abject men who earn a shabby living by introducing the unwary to tradesmen on a ten per cent commission, even they despise him. He is the mug. Believe me, to conduct yourself gracefully in such a position you need either great dignity of character or an unparalleled effrontery. Besides, do you think there's a chance of its lasting? Can a woman who's led that wild career settle down to domestic life? In a little while she'll grow bored and restless. And how long does love last? Don't you think Byring's reflections will be bitter when, caring for her no longer, he compares what he is with what he might have been?"

Witherspoon helped himself to another drop of his old brandy. Then he looked up at Ashenden with a curious expression.

"I'm not sure if a man isn't wiser to do what he wants very much to do and let the consequences take care of themselves."

"It must be very pleasant to be an ambassador," said Ashenden.

Sir Herbert smiled thinly.

"Byring rather reminds me of a fellow I knew when I was a very junior clerk at the FO. I won't tell you his name because he's by way of being very well-known now and highly respected. He's made a great success of his career. There is always something a little absurd in success."

Ashenden slightly raised his eyebrows at this statement, somewhat unexpected in the mouth of Sir Herbert Witherspoon, but did not say anything.

"He was one of my fellow-clerks. He was a brilliant creature, I don't think anyone ever denied that, and everyone prophesied from the beginning that he would go far. I venture to say that he had pretty well all the qualifications necessary for a diplomatic career. He was of a family of soldiers and sailors, nothing very grand, but eminently respectable, and he knew how to behave in the great world without bumptiousness or timidity. He was well-read. He took an interest in painting. I daresay he made himself a trifle ridiculous; he wanted to be in the movement, he was very anxious to be modern, and at a time when little was known of Gauguin and Cézanne he raved over their pictures. There was perhaps a certain snobbishness in his attitude, a desire to shock and astonish the conventional, but at heart his admiration of the arts was genuine and sincere. He adored Paris and whenever he had the chance ran over and put up at a little hotel in the Latin Quarter, where he could rub shoulders with painters and writers. As is the habit with gentry of that sort they patronized him a little because he was nothing but a diplomat and laughed at him a little because he was evidently a gentleman. But they liked him because he was always ready to listen to their speeches, and when he praised their works they were even willing to admit that, although a philistine, he had a certain instinct for the Right Stuff."

Ashenden noted the sarcasm and smiled at the fling at his own profession. He wondered what this long description was leading to. The ambassador seemed to linger over it partly because he liked it, but also because for some reason he hesitated to come to the point.

"But my friend was modest. He enjoyed himself enormously and he listened open-mouthed when these young painters and unknown scribblers tore to pieces established reputations and talked with enthusiasm of persons of whom the sober but cultured secretaries in Downing Street had never even heard. At the back of his mind he knew that they were rather a common, second-rate lot, and when he went back to his work in London it was with no regret, but with the feeling that he had been witnessing an odd and diverting play; now the curtain had fallen he was quite ready to go home. I haven't told you that he was ambitious. He knew that his friends expected him to do considerable things and he had no notion of disappointing them. He was perfectly conscious of his abilities. He meant to succeed. Unfortunately he was not rich, he had only a few hundreds a year, but his father and mother were dead and he had neither brother nor sister. He was aware that this freedom from close ties was an asset. His opportunity to make connexions that would be of use to him was unrestricted. Do you think he sounds a very disagreeable young man?"

"No," said Ashenden in answer to the sudden question. "Most clever young men are aware of their cleverness, and there is generally a certain cynicism in their calculations with regard to the future. Surely young men should be ambitious."

"Well, on one of these little trips to Paris my friend became acquainted with a talented young Irish painter called O'Malley. He's an RA now and paints highly-paid portraits of Lord Chancellors and Cabinet Ministers. I wonder if you remember one he did of my wife, which was exhibited a couple of years ago."

"No, I don't. But I know his name."

"My wife was delighted with it. His art always seems to me very refined and agreeable. He's able to put on canvas the distinction of his sisters in a very remarkable way. When he paints a woman of breeding, you know that it is a woman of breeding and not a trollop."

"It is a charming gift," said Ashenden. "Can he also paint a slut and make her look like one?"

"He could. Now doubtless he would scarcely wish to. He was living then in a small and dirty studio in the rue du Cherche Midi with a little Frenchwoman of the character you describe and he painted several portraits of her which were extremely like."

It seemed to Ashenden that Sir Herbert was going into somewhat excessive detail, and he asked himself whether the friend of whom he was telling a story that till now seemed to lead no-whither was in point of fact himself. He began to give it more of his attention.

"My friend liked O'Malley. He was good company, the type of the agreeable rattle, and he had a truly Irish gift of the gab. He talked incessantly and in my friend's opinion brilliantly. He found it very amusing to go and sit in the studio while O'Malley was painting and listen to him chattering away about the technique of his art. O'Malley was always saying that he would paint a portrait of him and his vanity was tickled. O'Malley thought him far from plain and said it would do him good to exhibit the portrait of someone who at least looked like a gentleman."

"By the way, when was all this?" asked Ashenden.

"Oh, thirty years ago ... They used to talk of their future and when O'Malley said the portrait he was going to paint of my friend would look very well in the National Portrait Gallery, my friend had small doubt in the back of his mind, whatever he modestly said, that it would eventually find its way there. One evening when my friend – shall we call him Brown? – was sitting in the studio and O'Malley, desperately taking advantage of the last light of day, was trying to get finished for the Salon that portrait of his mistress which is now in the Tate Gallery, O'Malley asked him if he would like to come and dine with them. He was expecting a friend of hers, she was called Yvonne by the way, and he would be glad if Brown would make a fourth. This friend of Yvonne's was an acrobat and O'Malley was anxious to get her to pose for him in the nude. Yvonne said she had a marvellous figure. She had seen O'Malley's work and was willing enough to sit and dinner was to be devoted to settling the matter. She was not performing then, but was about to open at the Gaietés Montparnasses and with her days free was not disinclined to oblige a friend and earn a little money. The notion amused Brown, who had never met an acrobat, and he accepted. Yvonne suggested that he might find her to his taste and if he did she could promise him that he would not find her very difficult to persuade. With his grand air and English clothes she would take him for a *milord anglais*. My friend laughed. He did not take the suggestion very seriously. '*On ne sait jamais*,' he said. Yvonne looked at him with mischievous eyes. He sat on. It was Easter time and cold, but the studio was comfortably warm, and though it was small and everything was higgledy-piggledy and the dust lay heavy on the rim of the window, it was most friendly and cosy. Brown had a tiny flat in Waverton Street, in London, with very good mezzotints on the walls and several pieces of early Chinese pottery here and there, and he wondered to himself why his tasteful sitting-room had none of the comforts of home nor the romance that he found in that disorderly studio.

"Presently there was a ring at the door and Yvonne ushered in her friend. Her name, it appeared, was Alix, and she shook hands with Brown, uttering a stereotyped phrase, with the mincing politeness of a fat woman in a *bureau de tabac*. She wore a long cloak in imitation mink and an enormous scarlet hat. She looked incredibly vulgar. She was not even pretty. She had a broad flat face, a wide mouth and an upturned nose. She had a great deal of hair, golden, but obviously dyed, and large china-blue eyes. She was heavily made-up."

Ashenden began to have no doubt that Witherspoon was narrating an experience of his own, for otherwise he could never have remembered after thirty years what hat the young woman wore and what coat, and he was amused at the ambassador's simplicity in thinking that so thin a subterfuge could disguise the truth. Ashenden could not but guess how the story would end and it tickled him to think that this cold, distinguished, and exquisite person should ever have had anything like an adventure.

"She began to talk away to Yvonne, and my friend noticed that she had one feature that oddly enough he found very attractive: she had a deep and husky voice as though she were just recovering from a bad cold and, he didn't know why, it seemed to him exceedingly pleasant to listen to. He asked O'Malley if that was her natural voice and O'Malley said she had had it as long as ever he had known her. He called it a whisky voice. He told her what Brown said about it and she gave him a smile of her wide mouth and said it wasn't due to drink, it was due to standing so much on her head. That was one of the inconveniences of her profession. Then the four of them went to a beastly little restaurant off the boulevard St Michel where for two francs fifty including wine my friend ate a dinner that seemed to him more delicious than any he had ever eaten at the Savoy or Claridge's. Alix was a very chatty young person and Brown listened with amusement, with amazement even, while in her rich, throaty voice she talked of the varied incidents of the day. She had a great command of slang, and, though he could not understand half of it, he was immensely tickled with its picturesque vulgarity. It was pungent of the heated asphalt, the zinc bars of cheap taverns, and racy of the crowded squares in the poorer districts of Paris. There was an energy in those apt and vivid metaphors that went like champagne to his anaemic head. She was a guttersnipe, yes, that's what she was, but she had a vitality that warmed you like a blazing fire. He was conscious that Yvonne had told her that he was an unattached Englishman, with plenty of money; he saw the appraising glance she gave him and then, pretending that he had noticed nothing, he caught the phrase, *il n'est pas mal*. It faintly amused him: he had a notion himself that he was not so bad. There were places, indeed, where they went farther than that. She did not pay much attention to him, in point of fact they were talking of things of which he was ignorant and he could do little more than show an intelligent interest, but now and again she gave him a long look, passing her tongue quickly round her lips, that suggested to him that he only had to ask for her to give. He shrugged a mental shoulder. She looked healthy and young, she had an agreeable vivacity, but beyond her husky voice there was nothing particularly attractive in her. But the notion of having a little affair in Paris did not displease him, it was life, and the thought that she was a music-hall artiste was mildly diverting: in middle age it would doubtless amuse him to remember that he had enjoyed the favours of an acrobat. Was it la Rochefoucauld or Oscar Wilde who said that you should commit errors in youth in order to have something to regret in old age? At the end of dinner (and they sat over their coffee and brandy till late), they went out into the street and Yvonne proposed that he should take Alix home. He said he would be delighted. Alix said it was not far and they walked. She told him that she had a little apartment, of course mostly she was on tour, but she liked to have a place of her own, a woman, you know, had to be in her furniture, without that she received no consideration; and presently they reached a shabby house in a bedraggled street. She rang the bell for the *concierge* to open the door. She did not press him to enter. He did not know if she looked upon it as a matter of course. He was seized with timidity. He racked his brains, but could not think of a single thing to say. Silence fell upon them. It was absurd. With a little click the door opened; she looked at him expectantly; she was puzzled; a wave of shyness swept over him. Then she held out her hand, thanked him for bringing her to the door, and bade him good night. His heart beat nervously. If she had asked him to come in he would have gone. He wanted some sign that she would like him to. He shook her hand, said good night, raised his hat and walked away. He felt a perfect fool. He could not sleep; he tossed from side to side of his bed, thinking what a noodle she must take him for, and he could hardly wait for the day that would permit him to take steps to efface the contemptible impression he must have made on her. His pride was lacerated. Wanting to lose no time he went round to her house at eleven to ask her to lunch with him, but she was out; he sent round some flowers and later in the day called again. She had been in, but was gone out once more. He went to see O'Malley on the chance of finding her, but she was not there, and O'Malley facetiously asked him how he had fared. To save his face he told him that he had come to the conclusion that she did not mean very much to him and so like a perfect gentleman he had left her. But he had an uneasy feeling that O'Malley saw through his story. He sent her a *pneumatique* asking her to dine with him next day. She did not answer. He could not understand it, he asked the porter of his hotel a dozen times if there was nothing for him, and at last, almost in desperation, just before dinner went to her house. The *concierge* told him she was in and he went up. He was very nervous, inclined to be angry because she had treated his invitation so cavalierly, but at the same time anxious to appear at his ease. He climbed the four flights of stairs, dark and smelly, and rang at the door to which he had been directed. There was a pause, he heard sounds within and rang again Presently she opened. He had an absolute certitude that she did not in the least know who he was. He was taken aback, it was a blow to his vanity; but he assumed a cheerful smile.

"'I came to find out if you were going to dine with me tonight. I sent you a *pneumatique*.'

"Then she recognized him. But she stood at the door and did not ask him in.

"'Oh, no, I can't dine with you tonight. I have a terrible megrim and I am going to bed. I couldn't answer your *pneumatique*, I mislaid it, and I'd forgotten your name. Thank you for the flowers. It was nice of you to send them.'

"'Then won't you come and dine with me tomorrow night?'

"'*Justement*, I have an engagement tomorrow night. I'm sorry.'

"There was nothing more to say. He had not the nerve to ask her anything else and so bade her good night and went. He had the impression that she was not vexed with him, but that she had entirely forgotten him. It was humiliating. When he went back to London without having seen her again, it was with a curious sense of dissatisfaction. He was not in the least in love with her, he was annoyed with her, but he could not get her quite out of his mind. He was honest enough to realize that he was suffering from nothing more than wounded vanity.

"During that dinner at the little restaurant off the Boul' Mich' she had mentioned that her troupe was going to London in the spring, and in one of his letters to O'Malley he slipped in casually a phrase to the effect that if his young friend Alix happened to be coming to town he (O'Malley) might let him know and he would look her up. He would like to hear from her own ingenuous lips what she thought of the nude O'Malley had painted of her. When the painter some time afterwards wrote and told him that she was appearing a week later at the Metropolitan in the Edgware Road, he felt a sudden rush of blood to his head. He went to see her play. If he had not taken the precaution to go earlier in the day and look at the programme he would have missed her, for her turn was the first on the list. There were two men, a stout one and a thin one, with large black moustaches, and Alix. They were dressed in ill-fitting pink tights with green satin trunks. The men did various exercises on twin trapezes while Alix tripped about the stage, giving them handkerchiefs to wipe their hands on, and occasionally turned a somersault. When the fat man raised the thin one on his shoulders she climbed up and stood on the shoulders of the second, kissing her hand to the audience. They did tricks with safety bicycles. There is often grace, and even beauty, in the performance of clever acrobats, but this one was so crude, so vulgar that my friend felt positively embarrassed. There is something shameful in seeing grown men publicly make fools of themselves. Poor Alix, with a fixed and artificial smile on her lips, in her pink tights and green satin trunks, was so grotesque that he wondered how he could have let himself feel a moment's annoyance because when he went to her apartment she had not recognized him. It was with a shrug of the shoulders, condescendingly, that he went round to the stage door afterwards and gave the doorkeeper a shilling to take her his card. In a few minutes she came out. She seemed delighted to see him.

"'Oh, how good it is to see the face of someone you know in this sad city,' she said. 'Ah, now you can give me that dinner you asked me to in Paris. I'm dying of hunger. I never eat before the show. Imagine that they should have given us such a bad place on the programme. It's an insult. But we shall see the agent tomorrow. If they think they can put upon us like that they are mistaken. *Ah, non, non et non!* And what an audience! No enthusiasm, no applause, nothing.'

"My friend was staggered. Was it possible that she took her performance seriously? He almost burst out laughing. But she still spoke with that throaty voice that had such a queer effect on his nerves. She was dressed all in red and wore the same red hat in which he had first seen her. She looked so flashy that he did not fancy the notion of asking her to a place where he might be seen, and so suggested Soho. There were hansoms still in those days, and the hansom was more conducive to love-making, I imagine, than is the taxi of the present time. My friend put his arm round Alix's waist and kissed her. It left her calm, but on the other hand did not wildly excite him. While they ate a late dinner he made himself very gallant and she played up to him agreeably; but when they got up to go and he proposed that she should come round to his rooms in Waverton Street she told him that a friend had come over from Paris with her and that she had to meet him at eleven: she had only been able to dine with Brown because her companion had a business engagement. Brown was exasperated, but did not want to show it, and when, as they walked down Wardour Street (for she said she wanted to go to the Café Monico), pausing in front of a pawnbroker's to look at the jewellery in the window, she went into ecstasies over a bracelet of sapphires and diamonds that Brown thought incredibly vulgar, he asked her if she would like it.

"'But it's marked fifteen pounds,' she said.

"He went in and bought it for her. She was delighted. She made him leave her just before they came to Piccadilly Circus.

"'Now listen, *mon petit*,' she said, 'I cannot see you in London because of my friend, he is jealous as a wolf, that is why I think it is more prudent for you to go now, but I am playing at Boulogne next week, why do you not come over? I shall be alone there. My friend has to go back to Holland, where he lives.'

" 'All right,' said Brown, 'I'll come.'

"When he went to Boulogne – he had two days' leave – it was with the one idea of salving the wound to his pride. It was odd that he should care. I daresay to you it seems inexplicable. He could not bear the notion that Alix looked upon him as a fool, and he felt that when once he had removed that impression from her he would never bother about her again. He thought of O'Malley too, and of Yvonne. She must have told them, and it galled him to think that people whom in his heart he despised should laugh at him behind his back. Do you think he was very contemptible?"

"Good gracious, no," said Ashenden. "All sensible people know that vanity is the most devastating, the most universal, and the most ineradicable of the passions that afflict the soul of man, and it is only vanity that makes him deny its power. It is more consuming than love. With advancing years, mercifully, you can snap your fingers at the terror and the servitude of love, but age cannot free you from the thraldom of vanity. Time can assuage the pangs of love, but only death can still the anguish of wounded vanity. Love is simple and seeks no subterfuge, but vanity cozens you with a hundred disguises. It is part and parcel of every virtue: it is the mainspring of courage and the strength of ambition; it gives constancy to the lover and endurance to the stoic; it adds fuel to the fire of the artist's desire for fame and is at once the support and the compensation of the honest man's integrity; it leers even cynically in the humility of the saint. You cannot escape it, and should you take pains to guard against it, it will make use of those very pains to trip you up. You are defenceless against its onslaught because you know not on what unprotected side it will attack you. Sincerity cannot protect you from its snare nor humour from its mockery."

Ashenden stopped, not because he had said all he had to say, but because he was out of breath. He noticed also that the ambassador, desiring to talk rather than to listen, heard him with a politeness that was strained. But he had made this speech not so much for his host's edification as for his own entertainment.

"It is vanity finally that makes man support his abominable lot."

For a minute Sir Herbert was silent. He looked straight in front of him as though his thoughts lingered distressfully on some far horizon of memory.

"When my friend came back from Boulogne he knew that he was madly in love with Alix and he had arranged to meet her again in a fortnight's time when she would be performing at Dunkirk. He thought of nothing else in the interval, and the night before he was to start, he only had thirty-six hours this time, he could not sleep, so devouring was the passion that consumed him. Then he went over for a night to Paris to see her, and once when she was disengaged for a week he persuaded her to come to London. He knew that she did not love him. He was just a man among a hundred others and she made no secret of the fact that he was not her only lover. He suffered agonies of jealousy but knew that it would only excite her ridicule or her anger if he showed it. She had not even a fancy for him. She liked him because he was a gentleman and well dressed. She was quite willing to be his mistress so long as the claims he made on her were not irksome. But that was all. His means were not large enough to enable him to make her any serious offers, but even if they had been, liking her freedom, she would have refused."

"But what about the Dutchman?" asked Ashenden.

"The Dutchman? He was a pure invention. She made him up on the spur of the moment because for one reason or another she did not just then want to be bothered with Brown. What should one lie more or less matter to her? Don't think he didn't struggle against his passion. He knew it was madness; he knew that a permanent connexion between them could only lead to disaster for him. He had no illusions about her; she was common, coarse, and vulgar. She could talk of none of the things that interested him, nor did she try, she took it for granted that he was concerned with her affairs and told him interminable stories of her quarrels with fellow-performers, her disputes with managers, and her wrangles with hotel-keepers. What she said bored him to death, but the sound of her throaty voice made his heart beat so that sometimes he thought he would suffocate."

Ashenden sat uneasily in his chair. It was a Sheraton chair very good to look at, but hard and straight; and he wished that Sir Herbert had had the notion of going back to the other room where there was a comfortable sofa. It was quite plain now that the story he was telling was about himself, and Ashenden felt a certain indelicacy in the man's stripping his soul before him so nakedly. He did not desire this confidence to be forced upon him. Sir Herbert Witherspoon meant nothing to him. By the light of the shaded candles Ashenden saw that he was deathly pale and there was a wildness in his eyes that in that cold and composed man was strangely disconcerting. He poured himself out a glass of water; his throat was dry so that he could hardly speak. But he went on pitilessly.

"At last my friend managed to pull himself together. He was disgusted by the sordidness of his intrigue; there was no beauty in it, nothing but shame; and it was leading to nothing. His passion was as vulgar as the woman for whom he felt it. Now it happened that Alix was going to spend six months in the North of Africa with her troupe and for that time at least it would be impossible for him to see her. He made up his mind that he must seize the opportunity and make a definite break. He knew bitterly that it would mean nothing to her. In three weeks she would have forgotten him.

"And then there was something else. He had come to know very well some people, a man and his wife, whose social and political connexions were extremely important. They had an only daughter and, I don't know why, she fell in love with him. She was everything that Alix was not, pretty in the real English way, with blue eyes and pink and white cheeks, tall and fair; she might have stepped out of one of du Maurier's pictures in *Punch*. She was clever and well-read, and since she had lived all her life in political circles she could talk intelligently of the sort of things that interested him. He had reason to believe that if he asked her to marry him she would accept. I have told you that he was ambitious. He knew that he had great abilities and he wanted the chance to use them. She was related to some of the greatest families in England and he would have been a fool not to realize that a marriage of this kind must make his path infinitely easier. The opportunity was golden. And what a relief to think that he could put behind him definitely that ugly little episode, and what a happiness, instead of that wall of cheerful indifference and matter-of-fact good nature against which in his passion for Alix he had vainly battered his head, what a happiness to feel that to someone else he really meant something! How could he help being flattered and touched when he saw her face light up as he came into the room? He wasn't in love with her, but he thought her charming, and he wanted to forget Alix and the vulgar life into which she had led him. At last he made up his mind. He asked her to marry him and was accepted. Her family was delighted. The marriage was to take place in the autumn, since her father had to go on some political errand to South America and was taking his wife and daughter with him. They were to be gone the whole summer. My friend Brown was transferring from the FO to the diplomatic service and had been promised a post at Lisbon. He was to go there immediately.

"He saw his fiancée off. Then it happened that owing to some hitch the man whom Brown was going to replace was kept at Lisbon three months longer and so for that period my friend found himself at a loose end. And just when he was making up his mind what to do with himself he received a letter from Alix. She was coming back to France and had a tour booked; she gave him a long list of the places she was going to, and in her casual, friendly way said that they would have fun if he could manage to run over for a day or two. An insane, a criminal notion seized him. If she had shown any eagerness for him to come he might have resisted, it was her airy, matter-of-fact indifference that took him. On a sudden he longed for her. He did not care if she was gross and vulgar, he had got her in his bones, and it was his last chance. In a little while he was going to be married. It was now or never. He went down to Marseilles and met her as she stepped off the boat that had brought her from Tunis. His heart leaped at the pleasure she showed on seeing him. He knew he loved her madly. He told her that he was going to be married in three months and asked her to spend the last of his freedom with him. She refused to abandon her tour. How could she leave her companions in the lurch? He offered to compensate them, but she would not hear of it; they could not find someone to take her place at a moment's notice, nor could they afford to throw over a good engagement that might lead to others in the future; they were honest people, and they kept their word, they had their duty to their managers and their duty to their public. He was exasperated; it seemed absurd that his whole happiness should be sacrificed to that wretched tour. And at the end of the three months? What was to happen to her then? Oh, no, he was asking something that wasn't reasonable. He told her that he adored her. He did not know till then how insanely he loved her. Well, then, she said, why did he not come with her and make the tour with them? She would be glad of his company; they could have a good time together and at the end of three months he could go and marry his heiress and neither of them would be any the worse. For a moment he hesitated, but now that he saw her again he could not bear the thought of being parted from her so soon. He accepted. And then she said:

"'But listen, my little one, you mustn't be silly, you know. The managers won't be too pleased with me if I make a lot of *chichi*, I have to think of my future, and they won't be so anxious to have me back if I refuse to please old customers of the house. It won't be very often, but it must be understood that you are not to make me scenes if now and then I give myself to someone whose fancy I take. It will mean nothing, that is business, you will be my *amant de cœur*.'

"He felt a strange, excruciating pain in his heart, and I think he went so pale that she thought he was going to faint. She looked at him curiously.

"'Those are the terms,' she said. 'You can either take them or leave them.'

"He accepted."

Sir Herbert Witherspoon leaned forward in his chair and he was so white that Ashenden thought too that he was going to faint. His skin was drawn over his skull so that his face looked like a death's head, but the veins on his forehead stood out like knotted cords. He had lost all reticence. And Ashenden once more wished that he would stop, it made him shy and nervous to see the man's naked soul: no one has the right to show himself to another in that destitute state. He was inclined to cry:

"Stop, stop. You mustn't tell me any more. You'll be so ashamed."

But the man had lost all shame.

"For three months they travelled together from one dull provincial town to another, sharing a filthy little bedroom in frowzy hotels; Alix would not let him take her to good hotels, she said she had not the clothes for them and she was more comfortable in the sort of hotel she was used to; she did not want her companions in the business to say that she was putting on side. He sat interminable hours in shabby cafés. He was treated as a brother by members of the troupe, they called him by his Christian name and chaffed him coarsely and slapped him on the back. He ran errands for them when they were busy with their work. He saw the good-humoured contempt in the eyes of managers and was obliged to put up with the familiarity of stagehands. They travelled third-class from place to place and he helped to carry the luggage. He with whom reading was a passion never opened a book because Alix was bored by reading and thought that anyone who did was just giving himself airs. Every night he went to the music-hall and watched her go through that grotesque and ignoble performance. He had to fall in with her pathetic fancy that it was artistic. He had to congratulate her when it had gone well and condole with her when some feat of agility had gone amiss. When she had finished he went to a café and waited for her while she changed, and sometimes she would come in rather hurriedly and say:

"'Don't wait for me tonight, *mon chou*, I'm busy.'

"And then he would undergo agonies of jealousy. He would suffer as he never knew a man could suffer. She would come back to the hotel at three or four in the morning. She wondered why he was not asleep. Sleep! How could he sleep with that misery gnawing at his heart? He had promised he would not interfere with her. He did not keep his promise. He made her terrific scenes. Sometimes he beat her. Then she would lose her patience and tell him she was sick of him, she would pack her things to go, and then he would go grovelling to her, promising anything, any submission, vowing to swallow any humiliation, if she would not leave him. It was horrible and degrading. He was miserable. Miserable? No, he was happier than he'd ever been in his life. It was the gutter that he wallowed in, but he wallowed in it with delight. Oh, he was so bored with the life he'd led hitherto, and this one seemed to him amazing and romantic. This was reality. And that frowzy, ugly woman with the whisky voice, she had such a splendid vitality, such a zest for life that she seemed to raise his own to some more vivid level. It really did seem to him to burn with a pure, gem-like flame. Do people still read Pater?"

"I don't know," said Ashenden. "I don't."

"There was only three months of it. Oh, how short the time seemed and how quickly the weeks sped by! Sometimes he had wild dreams of abandoning everything and throwing in his lot with the acrobats. They had come to have quite a liking for him and they said he could easily train himself to take a part in the turn. He knew they said it more in jest than in earnest, but the notion vaguely tickled him. But these were only dreams and he knew that nothing would come of them. He never really chaffered with the thought that when the three months came to an end he would not return to his own life with its obligations. With his mind, that cold, logical mind of his, he knew it would be absurd to sacrifice everything for a woman like Alix; he was ambitious, he wanted power; and besides, he could not break the heart of that poor child who loved and trusted him. She wrote to him once a week. She was longing to get back, the time seemed endless to her and he, he had a secret wish that something would happen to delay her arrival. If he could only have a little more time! Perhaps if he had six months he would have got over his infatuation. Already sometimes he hated Alix.

"The last day came. They seemed to have little to say to one another. They were both sad; but he knew that Alix only regretted the breaking of an agreeable habit, in twenty-four hours she would be as gay and full of spirits with her stray companion as though he had never crossed her path; he could only think that next day he was going to Paris to meet his fiancée and her family. They spent their last night in one another's arms weeping. If she'd asked him then not to leave her it may be that he would have stayed; but she didn't, it never occurred to her, she accepted his going as a settled thing, and she wept not because she loved him, she wept because he was unhappy.

"In the morning she was sleeping so soundly that he had not the heart to wake her to say good-bye. He slipped out very quietly, with his bag in his hand, and took the train to Paris."

Ashenden turned away his head, for he saw two tears form themselves in Witherspoon's eyes and roll down his cheeks. He did not even try to hide them. Ashenden lit another cigar.

"In Paris they cried out when they saw him. They said he looked like a ghost. He told them he'd been ill and hadn't said anything about it in order not to worry them. They were very kind. A month later he was married. He did very well for himself. He was given opportunities to distinguish himself and he distinguished himself. His rise was spectacular. He had the well-ordered and distinguished establishment that he had wanted. He had the power for which he had craved. He was loaded with honours. Oh, he made a success of life and there were hundreds who envied him. It was all ashes. He was bored, bored to distraction, bored by that distinguished, beautiful lady he had married, bored by the people his life forced him to live with; it was a comedy he was playing and sometimes it seemed intolerable to live for ever and ever behind a mask, sometimes he felt he couldn't bear it. But he bore it. Sometimes he longed for Alix so fiercely that he felt it would be better to shoot himself than to suffer such anguish. He never saw her again. Never. He heard from O'Malley that she had married and left her troupe. She must be a fat old woman now and it doesn't matter any more. But he had wasted his life. And he never even made that poor creature whom he married happy. How could he go on hiding from her year after year that he had nothing to give her but pity? Once in his agony he told her about Alix and she tortured him ever after with her jealousy. He knew that he should never have married her; in six months she would have got over her grief if he had told her he could not bear to, and in the end would have happily married somebody else. So far as she was concerned his sacrifice was vain. He was terribly conscious that he had only one life and it seemed so sad to think that he had wasted it. He could never surmount his immeasurable regret. He laughed when people spoke of him as a strong man: he was as weak and unstable as water. And that's why I tell you that Byring is right. Even though it only lasts five years, even though he ruins his career, even though this marriage of his ends in disaster, it will have been worth while. He will have been satisfied. He will have fulfilled himself."

At that moment the door opened and a lady came in. The ambassador glanced at her and for an instant a look of cold hatred crossed his face, but it was only for an instant; then, rising from the table, he composed his ravaged features to an expression of courteous suavity. He gave the incomer a haggard smile.

"Here is my wife. This is Mr Ashenden."

"I couldn't imagine where you were. Why didn't you go and sit in your study? I'm sure Mr Ashenden's been dreadfully uncomfortable."

She was a tall, thin woman of fifty, rather drawn and faded, but she looked as though she had once been pretty. It was obvious that she was very well-bred. She vaguely reminded you of an exotic plant, reared in a hot-house, that had begun to lose its bloom. She was dressed in black.

"What was the concert like?" asked Sir Herbert.

"Oh, not bad at all. They gave a Brahms Concerto and the Fire-music from the *Walküre*, and some Hungarian dances of Dvořák. I thought them rather showy." She turned to Ashenden. "I hope you haven't been bored all alone with my husband. What have you been talking about? Art and Literature?"

"No, its raw material," said Ashenden.

He took his leave.

SANATORIUM

FOR THE FIRST six weeks that Ashenden was at the sanatorium he stayed in bed. He saw nobody but the doctor who visited him morning and evening, the nurses who looked after him, and the maid who brought him his meals. He had contracted tuberculosis of the lungs, and since at the time there were reasons that made it difficult for him to go to Switzerland the specialist he saw in London had sent him up to a sanatorium in the north of Scotland. At last the day came that he had been patiently looking forward to when the doctor told him he could get up; and in the afternoon his nurse, having helped him to dress, took him down to the veranda, placed cushions behind him, wrapped him up in rugs, and left him to enjoy the sun that was streaming down from a cloudless sky. It was mid-winter. The sanatorium stood on the top of a hill and from it you had a spacious view of the snow-clad country. There were people lying all along the veranda in deckchairs, some chatting with their neighbours and some reading. Every now and then one would have a fit of coughing and you noticed that at the end of it he looked anxiously at his handkerchief. Before the nurse left Ashenden she turned with a kind of professional briskness to the man who was lying in the next chair.

"I want to introduce Mr Ashenden to you," she said. And then to Ashenden: "This is Mr McLeod. He and Mr Campbell have been here longer than anyone else."

On the other side of Ashenden was lying a pretty girl, with red hair and bright blue eyes; she had on no make-up, but her lips were very red and the colour on her cheeks was high. It emphasized the astonishing whiteness of her skin. It was lovely even when you realized that its delicate texture was due to illness. She wore a fur coat and was wrapped up in rugs, so that you could see nothing of her body, but her face was extremely thin, so thin that it made her nose, which wasn't really large, look a trifle prominent. She gave Ashenden a friendly look, but did not speak, and Ashenden, feeling rather shy among all those strange people, waited to be spoken to.

"First time they've let you get up, is it?" said McLeod.

"Yes."

"Where's your room?"

Ashenden told him.

"Small. I know every room in the place. I've been here for seventeen years. I've got the best room here and so I damned well ought to have. Campbell's been trying to get me out of it, he wants it himself, but I'm not going to budge; I've got a right to it, I came here six months before he did."

McLeod, lying there, gave you the impression that he was immensely tall; his skin was stretched tight over his bones, his cheeks and temples hollow, so that you could see the formation of his skull under it; and in that emaciated face, with its great bony nose, the eyes were preternaturally large.

"Seventeen years is a long time," said Ashenden, because he could think of nothing else to say.

"Time passes very quickly. I like it here. At first, after a year or two, I went away in the summer, but I don't any more. It's my home now. I've got a brother and two sisters; but they're married and now they've got families; they don't want me. When you've been here a few years and you go back to ordinary life, you feel a bit out of it, you know. Your pals have gone their own ways and you've got

817

nothing in common with them any more. It all seems an awful rush. Much ado about nothing, that's what it is. It's noisy and stuffy. No, one's better off here. I shan't stir again till they carry me out feet first in my coffin."

The specialist had told Ashenden that if he took care of himself for a reasonable time he would get well, and he looked at McLeod with curiosity.

"What do you do with yourself all day long?" he asked.

"Do? Having TB is a whole-time job, my boy. There's my temperature to take and then I weigh myself. I don't hurry over my dressing. I have breakfast, I read the papers and go for a walk. Then I have my rest. I lunch and play bridge. I have another rest and then I dine. I play a bit more bridge and I go to bed. They've got quite a decent library here, we get all the new books, but I don't really have much time for reading. I talk to people. You meet all sorts here, you know. They come and they go. Sometimes they go because they think they're cured, but a lot of them come back, and sometimes they go because they die. I've seen a lot of people out and before I go I expect to see a lot more."

The girl sitting on Ashenden's other side suddenly spoke.

"I should tell you that few persons can get a heartier laugh out of a hearse than Mr McLeod," she said.

McLeod chuckled.

"I don't know about that, but it wouldn't be human nature if I didn't say to myself: Well, I'm just as glad it's him and not me they're taking for a ride."

It occurred to him that Ashenden didn't know the pretty girl, so he introduced him.

"By the way, I don't think you've met Mr Ashenden – Miss Bishop. She's English, but not a bad girl."

"How long have *you* been here?" asked Ashenden.

"Only two years. This is my last winter. Dr Lennox says I shall be all right in a few months and there's no reason why I shouldn't go home."

"Silly, I call it," said McLeod. "Stay where you're well off, that's what I say."

At that moment a man, leaning on a stick, came walking slowly along the veranda.

"Oh, look, there's Major Templeton," said Miss Bishop, a smile lighting up her blue eyes; and then, as he came up: "I'm glad to see you up again."

"Oh, it was nothing. Only a bit of a cold. I'm quite all right now."

The words were hardly out of his mouth when he began to cough. He leaned heavily on his stick. But when the attack was over he smiled gaily.

"Can't get rid of this damned cough," he said. "Smoking too much. Dr Lennox says I ought to give it up, but it's no good – I can't."

He was a tall fellow, good-looking in a slightly theatrical way, with a dusky, sallow face, fine very dark eyes, and a neat black moustache. He was wearing a fur coat with an astrakhan collar. His appearance was smart and perhaps a trifle showy. Miss Bishop made Ashenden known to him. Major Templeton said a few civil words in an easy, cordial way, and then asked the girl to go for a stroll with him; he had been ordered to walk to a certain place in the wood behind the sanatorium and back again. McLeod watched them as they sauntered off.

"I wonder if there's anything between those two," he said. "They do say Templeton was a devil with the girls before he got ill."

"He doesn't look up to much in that line just now," said Ashenden.

"You never can tell. I've seen a lot of rum things here in my day. I could tell you no end of stories if I wanted to."

"You evidently do, so why don't you?"

McLeod grinned.

"Well, I'll tell you one. Three or four years ago there was a woman here who was pretty hot stuff. Her husband used to come and see her every other week-end, he was crazy about her, used to fly up from London; but Dr Lennox was pretty sure she was carrying on with somebody here, but he couldn't find out who. So one night when we'd all gone to bed he had a thin coat of paint put down just outside her room and next day he had everyone's slippers examined. Neat, wasn't it? The fellow whose slippers had paint on them got the push. Dr Lennox has to be particular, you know. He doesn't want the place to get a bad name."

"How long has Templeton been here?"

"Three or four months. He's been in bed most of the time. He's for it all right. Ivy Bishop'll be a damned fool if she gets stuck on him. She's got a good chance of getting well. I've seen so many of them, you know, I can tell. When I look at a fellow I make up my mind at once whether he'll get well or whether he won't, and if he won't I can make a pretty shrewd guess how long he'll last. I'm very seldom mistaken. I give Templeton about two years myself."

McLeod gave Ashenden a speculative look, and Ashenden, knowing what he was thinking, though he tried to be amused, could not help feeling somewhat concerned. There was a twinkle in McLeod's eyes. He plainly knew what was passing through Ashenden's mind.

"You'll get all right. I wouldn't have mentioned it if I hadn't been pretty sure of that. I don't want Dr Lennox to hoof me out for putting the fear of God into his bloody patients."

Then Ashenden's nurse came to take him back to bed. Even though he had only sat out for an hour, he was tired, and was glad to find himself once more between the sheets. Dr Lennox came in to see him in the course of the evening. He looked at his temperature chart.

"That's not so bad," he said.

Dr Lennox was small, brisk, and genial. He was a good enough doctor, an excellent business man, and an enthusiastic fisherman. When the fishing season began he was inclined to leave the care of his patients to his assistants; the patients grumbled a little, but were glad enough to eat the young salmon he brought back to vary their meals. He was fond of talking, and now, standing at the end of Ashenden's bed, he asked him, in his broad Scots, whether he had got into conversation with any of the patients that afternoon. Ashenden told him the nurse had introduced him to McLeod. Dr Lennox laughed.

"The oldest living inhabitant. He knows more about the sanatorium and its inmates than I do. How he gets his information I haven't an idea, but there's not a thing about the private lives of anyone under this roof that he doesn't know. There's not an old maid in the place with a keener nose for a bit of scandal. Did he tell you about Campbell?"

"He mentioned him."

"He hates Campbell, and Campbell hates him. Funny, when you come to think of it, those two men, they've been here for seventeen years and they've got about one sound lung between them. They loathe the sight of one another. I've had to refuse to listen to the complaints about one another that they come to me with. Campbell's room is just below McLeod's and Campbell plays the fiddle. It drives McLeod wild. He says he's been listening to the same tunes for fifteen years, but Campbell says McLeod doesn't know one tune from another. McLeod wants me to stop Campbell playing, but I can't do that, he's got a perfect right to play so long as he doesn't play in the silence hours. I've offered to change McLeod's room, but he won't do that. He says Campbell only plays to drive him out of the room because it's the best in the house, and he's damned if he's going to have it. It's queer, isn't it, that two middle-aged men should think it worth while to make life hell for one another? Neither can leave the other alone. They have their meals at the same table, they play bridge together; and not a day passes without a row. Sometimes I've threatened to turn them both out if they don't behave like sensible fellows. That keeps them quiet for a bit. They don't want to go. They've been here so long, they've got no one any more who gives a damn for them, and they can't cope with the world outside. Campbell went away for a couple of months' holiday some years ago. He came back after a week; he said he couldn't stand the racket, and the sight of so many people in the streets scared him."

It was a strange world into which Ashenden found himself thrown when, his health gradually improving, he was able to mix with his fellow-patients. One morning Dr Lennox told him he could thenceforward lunch in the dining-room. This was a large, low room, with great window space; the windows were always wide open and on fine days the sun streamed in. There seemed to be a great many people and it took him some time to sort them out. They were of all kinds, young, middle-aged, and old. There were some, like McLeod and Campbell, who had been at the sanatorium for years and expected to die there. Others had only been there for a few months. There was one middle-aged spinster called Miss Atkin who had been coming every winter for a long time and in the summer went to stay with friends and relations. She had nothing much the matter with her any more, and might just as well have stayed away altogether, but she liked the life. Her long residence had given her a sort of position, she was honorary librarian and hand in glove with the matron. She was always ready to gossip with you, but you were soon warned that everything you said was passed on. It was useful to Dr Lennox to know that his patients were getting on well together and were happy, that they did nothing imprudent and followed his instructions. Little escaped Miss Atkin's sharp eyes, and from her it went to the matron and so to Dr Lennox. Because she had been coming for so many years, she sat at the same table as McLeod and Campbell, together with an old general who had been put there on account of his rank. The table was in no way different from any other, and it was not more advantageously placed, but because the oldest residents sat there it was looked upon as the most desirable place to sit, and several elderly women were bitterly resentful because Miss Atkin, who went away for four or five months every summer, should be given a place there while they who spent the whole year in the sanatorium sat at other tables. There was an old Indian Civilian who had been at the sanatorium longer than anyone but McLeod and Campbell; he was a man who in his day had ruled a province, and he was waiting irascibly for either McLeod or Campbell to die so that he might take his place at the first table. Ashenden made the acquaintance of Campbell. He was a long, big-boned fellow with a bald head, so thin that you wondered how his limbs held together; and when he sat crumpled in an armchair he gave you the uncanny impression of a manikin in a puppet-show. He was brusque, touchy, and bad-tempered. The first thing he asked Ashenden was:

"Are you fond of music?"

"Yes."

"No one here cares a damn for it. I play the violin. But if you like it, come to my room one day and I'll play to you."

"Don't you go," said McLeod, who heard him. "It's torture."

"How can you be so rude?" cried Miss Atkin. "Mr Campbell plays very nicely."

"There's no one in this beastly place that knows one note from another," said Campbell.

With a derisive chuckle McLeod walked off. Miss Atkin tried to smooth things down.

"You mustn't mind what McLeod said."

"Oh, I don't. I'll get back on him all right."

He played the same tune over and over again all that afternoon. McLeod banged on the floor, but Campbell went on. He sent a message by a maid to say that he had a headache and would Mr Campbell mind not playing; Campbell replied that he had a perfect right to play and if Mr McLeod didn't like it he could lump it. When next they met high words passed.

Ashenden was put at a table with the pretty Miss Bishop, with Templeton, and with a London man, an accountant, called Henry Chester. He was a stocky, broad-shouldered, wiry little fellow, and the last person you would ever have thought would be attacked by TB. It had come upon him as a sudden and unexpected blow. He was a perfectly ordinary man, somewhere between thirty and forty, married, with two children. He lived in a decent suburb. He went up to the City every morning and read the morning paper; he came down from the City every evening and read the evening paper. He had no interests except his business and his family. He liked his work; he made enough money to live in comfort, he put by a reasonable sum every year, he played golf on Saturday afternoon and on Sunday, he went every August for a three weeks' holiday to the same place on the east coast; his children would grow up and marry, then he would turn his business over to his son and retire with his wife to a little house in the country where he could potter about till death claimed him at a ripe old age. He asked nothing more from life than that, and it was a life that thousands upon thousands of his fellow-men lived with satisfaction. He was the average citizen. Then this thing happened. He had caught cold playing golf, it had gone to his chest, and he had had a cough that he couldn't shake off. He had always been strong and healthy, and had no opinion of doctors; but at last at his wife's persuasion he had consented to see one. It was a shock to him, a fearful shock, to learn that there was tubercle in both his lungs and that his only chance of life was to go immediately to a sanatorium. The specialist he saw then told him that he might be able to go back to work in a couple of years, but two years had passed and Dr Lennox advised him not to think of it for at least a year more. He showed him the bacilli in his sputum, and in an X-ray photograph the actively-diseased patches in his lungs. He lost heart. It seemed to him a cruel and unjust trick that fate had played upon him. He could have understood it if he had led a wild life, if he had drunk too much, played around with women, or kept late hours. He would have deserved it then. But he had done none of these things. It was monstrously unfair. Having no resources in himself, no interest in books, he had nothing to do but think of his health. It became an obsession. He watched his symptoms anxiously. They had to deprive him of a thermometer because he took his temperature a dozen times a day. He got it into his head that the doctors were taking his case too indifferently, and in order to force their attention used every method he could devise to make the thermometer register a temperature that would alarm; and when his tricks were foiled he grew sulky and querulous. But he was by nature a jovial, friendly creature, and when he forgot himself he talked and laughed gaily; then on a sudden he remembered that he was a sick man and you would see in his eyes the fear of death.

At the end of every month his wife came up to spend a day or two in a lodging house near by. Dr Lennox did not much like the visits that relatives paid the patients, it excited and unsettled them. It was moving to see the eagerness with which Henry Chester looked forward to his wife's arrival; but it was strange to notice that once she had come he seemed less pleased than one would have expected. Mrs Chester was a pleasant, cheerful little woman, not pretty, but neat, as commonplace as her husband, and you only had to look at her to know that she was a good wife and mother, a careful house-keeper, a nice, quiet body who did her duty and interfered with nobody. She had been quite happy in the dull, domestic life they had led for so many years, her only dissipation a visit to the pictures, her great thrill the sales in the big London shops; and it had never occurred to her that it was monotonous. It completely satisfied her. Ashenden liked her. He listened with interest while she prattled about her children and her house in the suburbs, her neighbours and her trivial occupations. On one occasion he met her in the road. Chester for some reason connected with his treatment had stayed in and she was alone. Ashenden suggested that they should walk together. They talked for a little of indifferent things. Then she suddenly asked him how he thought her husband was.

"I think he seems to be getting on all right."

"I'm so terribly worried."

"You must remember it's a slow, long business. One has to have patience."

They walked on a little and then he saw she was crying.

"You mustn't be unhappy about him," said Ashenden gently.

"Oh, you don't know what I have to put up with when I come here. I know I ought not to speak about it, but I must. I can trust you, can't I?"

"Of course."

"I love him. I'm devoted to him. I'd do anything in the world I could for him. We've never quarrelled, we've never even differed about a single thing. He's beginning to hate me and it breaks my heart."

"Oh, I can't believe that. Why, when you're not here he talks of you all the time. He couldn't talk more nicely. He's devoted to you."

"Yes, that's when I'm not here. It's when I'm here, when he sees me well and strong, that it comes over him. You see, he resents it so terribly that he's ill and I'm well. He's afraid he's going to die and he hates me because I'm going to live. I have to be on my guard all the time; almost everything I say, if I speak of the children, if I speak of the future, exasperates him, and he says bitter, wounding things. When I speak of something I've had to do to the house or a servant I've had to change it irritates him beyond endurance. He complains that I treat him as if he didn't count any more. We used to be so united, and now I feel there's a great wall of antagonism between us. I know I shouldn't blame him, I know it's only his illness, he's a dear good man really, and kindness itself, normally he's the easiest man in the world to get on with; and now I simply dread coming here and I go with relief. He'd be terribly sorry if I had TB but I know that in his heart of hearts it would be a relief. He could forgive me, he could forgive fate, if he thought I was going to die too. Sometimes he tortures me by talking about what I shall do when he's dead, and when I get hysterical and cry out to him to stop, he says I needn't grudge him a little pleasure when he'll be dead so soon and I can go on living for years and years and have a good time. Oh, it's so frightful to think that this love we've had for one another all these years should die in this sordid, miserable way."

Mrs Chester sat down on a stone by the roadside and gave way to passionate weeping. Ashenden looked at her with pity, but could find nothing to say that might comfort her. What she had told him did not come quite as a surprise.

"Give me a cigarette," she said at last. "I mustn't let my eyes get all red and swollen, or Henry'll know I've been crying and he'll think I've had bad news about him. Is death so horrible? Do we all fear death like that?"

"I don't know," said Ashenden.

"When my mother was dying she didn't seem to mind a bit. She knew it was coming and she even made little jokes about it. But she was an old woman."

Mrs Chester pulled herself together and they set off again. They walked for a while in silence.

"You won't think any the worse of Henry for what I've told you?" she said at last.

"Of course not."

"He's been a good husband and a good father. I've never known a better man in my life. Until this illness I don't think an unkind or ungenerous thought ever passed through his head."

The conversation left Ashenden pensive. People often said he had a low opinion of human nature. It was because he did not always judge his fellows by the usual standards. He accepted, with a smile, a tear, or a shrug of the shoulders, much that filled others with dismay. It was true that you would never have expected that good-natured, commonplace little chap to harbour such bitter and unworthy thoughts; but who has ever been able to tell to what depths man may fall or to what heights rise? The fault lay in the poverty of his ideals. Henry Chester was born and bred to lead an average life, exposed to the normal vicissitudes of existence, and when an unforeseeable accident befell him he had no means of coping with it. He was like a brick made to take its place with a million others in a huge factory, but by chance with a flaw in it so that it is inadequate to its purpose. And the brick too, if it had a mind, might cry: What have I done that I cannot fulfil my modest end, but must be taken away from all these other bricks that support me and thrown on the dust-heap? It was no fault of Henry Chester's that he was incapable of the conceptions that might have enabled him to bear his calamity with resignation. It is not everyone who can find solace in art or thought. It is the tragedy of our day that these humble souls have lost their faith in God, in whom lay hope, and their belief in a resurrection that might bring them the happiness that has been denied them on earth; and have found nothing to put in their place.

There are people who say that suffering ennobles. It is not true. As a general rule it makes man petty, querulous, and selfish; but here in this sanatorium there was not much suffering. In certain stages of tuberculosis the slight fever that accompanies it excites rather than depresses, so that the patient feels alert and, upborne by hope, faces the future blithely; but for all that the idea of death haunts the subconscious. It is a sardonic theme song that runs through a sprightly operetta. Now and again the gay, melodious arias, the dance measures, deviate strangely into tragic strains that throb menacingly down the nerves; the petty interests of every day, the small jealousies and trivial concerns are as nothing; pity and terror make the heart on a sudden stand still and the awfulness of death broods as the silence that precedes a tropical storm broods over the tropical jungle. After Ashenden had been for some time at the sanatorium there came a boy of twenty. He was in the navy, a sub-lieutenant in a submarine, and he had what they used to call in novels galloping consumption. He was a tall, good-looking youth, with curly brown hair, blue eyes, and a very sweet smile. Ashenden saw him two or three times lying on the terrace in the sun and passed the time of day with him. He was a cheerful lad. He talked of musical shows and film stars; and he read the paper for the football results and the boxing news. Then he was put to bed and Ashenden saw him no more. His relations were sent for and in two months he was dead. He died uncomplaining. He understood what was happening to him as little as an animal. For a day or two there was the same malaise in the sanatorium as there is in a prison when a man has been hanged; and then, as though by universal consent, in obedience to an instinct of self-preservation, the boy was put out of mind: life, with its three meals a day, its golf on the miniature course, its regulated exercise, its prescribed rests, its quarrels and jealousies, its scandal-mongering and petty vexations, went on as before. Campbell, to the exasperation of McLeod, continued to play the prize-song and "Annie Laurie" on his fiddle. McLeod continued to boast of his bridge and gossip about other people's health and morals. Miss Atkin continued to backbite.

Henry Chester continued to complain that the doctors gave him insufficient attention and railed against fate because, after the model life he had led, it had played him such a dirty trick. Ashenden continued to read, and with amused tolerance to watch the vagaries of his fellow-creatures.

He became intimate with Major Templeton. Templeton was perhaps a little more than forty years of age. He had been in the Grenadier Guards, but had resigned his commission after the war. A man of ample means, he had since then devoted himself entirely to pleasure. He raced in the racing season, shot in the shooting season, and hunted in the hunting season. When this was over he went to Monte Carlo. He told Ashenden of the large sums he had made and lost at baccarat. He was very fond of women and if his stories could be believed they were very fond of him. He loved good food and and good drink. He knew by their first names the head waiters of every restaurant in London where you ate well. He belonged to half a dozen clubs. He had led for years a useless, selfish, worthless life, the sort of life which maybe it will be impossible for anyone to live in the future, but he had lived it without misgiving and had enjoyed it. Ashenden asked him once what he would do if he had his time over again and he answered that he would do exactly what he had done. He was an amusing talker, gay and pleasantly ironic, and he dealt with the surface of things, which was all he knew, with a light, easy, and assured touch. He always had a pleasant word for the dowdy spinsters in the sanatorium and a joking one for the peppery old gentlemen, for he combined good manners with a natural kindliness. He knew his way about the superficial world of the people who have more money than they know what to do with as well as he knew his way about Mayfair. He was the kind of man who would always have been willing to take a bet, to help a friend, and to give a tenner to a rogue. If he had never done much good in the world he had never done much harm. He amounted to nothing. But he was a more agreeable companion than many of more sterling character and of more admirable qualities. He was very ill now. He was dying and he knew it. He took it with the same easy, laughing nonchalance as he had taken all the rest. He'd had a thundering good time, he regretted nothing, it was rotten tough luck getting TB but to hell with it, no one can live for ever, and when you came to think of it, he might have been killed in the war or broken his bloody neck in a point-to-point. His principle all through life had been, when you've made a bad bet, pay up and forget about it. He'd had a good run for his money and he was ready to call it a day. It had been a damned good party while it lasted, but every party's got to come to an end, and next day it doesn't matter much if you went home with the milk or if you left while the fun was in full swing.

Of all those people in the sanatorium he was probably from the moral standpoint the least worthy, but he was the only one who genuinely accepted the inevitable with unconcern. He snapped his fingers in the face of death, and you could choose whether to call his levity unbecoming or his insouciance gallant.

The last thing that ever occurred to him when he came to the sanatorium was that he might fall more deeply in love there than he had ever done before. His amours had been numerous, but they had been light; he had been content with the politely mercenary love of chorus girls and with ephemeral unions with women of easy virtue whom he met at house parties. He had always taken care to avoid any attachment that might endanger his freedom. His only aim in life had been to get as much fun out of it as possible, and where sex was concerned he found every advantage and no inconvenience in ceaseless variety. But he liked women. Even when they were quite old he could not talk to them without a caress in his eyes and a tenderness in his voice. He was prepared to do anything to please them. They were conscious of his interest in them and were agreeably flattered, and they felt, quite mistakenly, that they could trust him never to let them down. He once said a thing that Ashenden thought showed insight:

"You know, any man can get any woman he wants if he tries hard enough, there's nothing in that, but once he's got her, only a man who thinks the world of women can get rid of her without humiliating her."

It was simply from habit that he began to make love to Ivy Bishop. She was the prettiest and the youngest girl in the sanatorium. She was in point of fact not so young as Ashenden had first thought her, she was twenty-nine, but for the last eight years she had been wandering from one sanatorium to another, in Switzerland,

England, and Scotland, and the sheltered invalid life had preserved her youthful appearance so that you might easily have taken her for twenty. All she knew of the world she had learnt in these establishments, so that she combined rather curiously extreme innocence with extreme sophistication. She had seen a number of love affairs run their course. A good many men, of various nationalities, had made love to her; she accepted their attentions with self-possession and humour, but she had at her disposal plenty of firmness when they showed an inclination to go too far. She had a force of character unexpected in anyone who looked so flower-like, and when it came to a show-down knew how to express her meaning in plain, cool, and decisive words. She was quite ready to have a flirtation with George Templeton. It was a game she understood, and though always charming to him, it was with a bantering lightness that showed quite clearly that she had summed him up and had no mind to take the affair more seriously than he did. Like Ashenden, Templeton went to bed every evening at six and dined in his room, so that he saw Ivy only by day. They went for little walks together, but otherwise were seldom alone. At lunch the conversation between the four of them, Ivy, Templeton, Henry Chester, and Ashenden, was general, but it was obvious that it was for neither of the two men that Templeton took so much trouble to be entertaining. It seemed to Ashenden that he was ceasing to flirt with Ivy to pass the time, and that his feeling for her was growing deeper and more sincere; but he could not tell whether she was conscious of it nor whether it meant anything to her. Whenever Templeton hazarded a remark that was more intimate than the occasion warranted she countered it with an ironic one that made them all laugh. But Templeton's laugh was rueful. He was no longer content to have her take him as a play-boy. The more Ashenden knew Ivy Bishop the more he liked her. There was something pathetic in her sick beauty, with that lovely transparent skin, the thin face in which the eyes were so large and so wonderfully blue; and there was something pathetic in her plight, for like so many others in the sanatorium she seemed to be alone in the world. Her mother led a busy social life, her sisters were married; they took but a perfunctory interest in the young woman from whom they had been separated now for eight years. They corresponded, they came to see her occasionally, but there was no longer very much between them. She accepted the situation without bitterness. She was friendly with everyone and prepared always to listen with sympathy to the complaints and the distress of all and sundry. She went out of her way to be nice to Henry Chester and did what she could to cheer him.

"Well, Mr Chester," she said to him one day at lunch, "it's the end of the month, your wife will be coming tomorrow. That's something to look forward to."

"No, she's not coming this month," he said quietly, looking down at his plate.

"Oh, I am sorry. Why not? The children are all right, aren't they?"

"Dr Lennox thinks it's better for me that she shouldn't come."

There was a silence. Ivy looked at him with troubled eyes.

"That's tough luck, old man," said Templeton in his hearty way. "Why didn't you tell Lennox to go to hell?"

"He must know best," said Chester.

Ivy gave him another look and began to talk of something else.

Looking back, Ashenden realized that she had at once suspected the truth. For next day he happened to walk with Chester.

"I'm awfully sorry your wife isn't coming," he said. "You'll miss her visit dreadfully."

"Dreadfully."

He gave Ashenden a sidelong glance. Ashenden felt that he had something he wanted to say, but could not bring himself to say it. He gave his shoulders an angry shrug.

"It's my fault if she's not coming. I asked Lennox to write and tell her not to. I couldn't stick it any more. I spend the whole month looking forward to her coming and then when she's here I hate her. You see, I resent so awfully having this filthy disease. She's strong and well and full of beans. It maddens me when I see the pain in her eyes. What does it matter to her really? Who cares if you're ill? They pretend to care, but they're jolly glad it's you and not them. I'm a swine, aren't I?"

Ashenden remembered how Mrs Chester had sat on a stone by the side of the road and wept.

"Aren't you afraid you'll make her very unhappy, not letting her come?"

"She must put up with that. I've got enough with my own unhappiness without bothering with hers."

Ashenden did not know what to say and they walked on in silence. Suddenly Chester broke out irritably.

"It's all very well for you to be disinterested and unselfish, you're going to live. I've going to die, and God damn it, I don't want to die. Why should I? It's not fair."

Time passed. In a place like the sanatorium where there was little to occupy the mind it was inevitable that soon everyone should know that George Templeton was in love with Ivy Bishop. But it was not so easy to tell what her feelings were. It was plain that she liked his company, but she did not seek it, and indeed it looked as though she took pains not to be alone with him. One or two of the middle-aged ladies tried to trap her into some compromising admission, but ingenuous as she was, she was easily a match for them. She ignored their hints and met their straight questions with incredulous laughter. She succeeded in exasperating them.

"She can't be so stupid as not to see that he's mad about her."

"She has no right to play with him like that."

"I believe she's just as much in love with him as he is with her."

"Dr Lennox ought to tell her mother."

No one was more incensed than McLeod.

"Too ridiculous. After all, nothing can come of it. He's riddled with TB and she's not much better."

Campbell on the other hand was sardonic and gross.

"I'm all for their having a good time while they can. I bet there's a bit of hanky-panky going on if one only knew, and I don't blame 'em."

"You cad," said McLeod.

"Oh, come off it. Templeton isn't the sort of chap to play bumble-puppy bridge with a girl like that unless he's getting something out of it, and she knows a thing or two, I bet."

Ashenden, who saw most of them, knew them better than any of the others. Templeton at last had taken him into his confidence. He was rather amused at himself.

"Rum thing at my time of life, falling in love with a decent girl. Last thing I'd ever expected of myself. And it's no good denying it, I'm in it up to the neck; if I were a well man I'd ask her to marry me tomorrow. I never knew a girl could be as nice as that. I've always thought girls, decent girls, I mean, damned bores. But she isn't a bore, she's as clever as she can stick. And pretty too. My God, what a skin! And that hair: but it isn't any of that that's bowled me over like a row of ninepins. D'you know what's got me? Damned ridiculous when you come to think of it. An old rip like me. Virtue. Makes me laugh like a hyena. Last thing I've ever wanted in a woman, but there it is, no getting away from it, she's good, and it makes me feel like a worm. Surprises you, I suppose?"

"Not a bit," said Ashenden. "You're not the first rake who's fallen to innocence. It's merely the sentimentality of middle age."

"Dirty dog," laughed Templeton.

"What does she say to it?"

"Good God, you don't suppose I've told her. I've never said a word to her that I wouldn't have said before anyone else. I may be dead in six months, and besides, what have I got to offer a girl like that?"

Ashenden by now was pretty sure that she was just as much in love with Templeton as he was with her. He had seen the flush that coloured her cheeks when Templeton came into the dining-room and he had noticed the soft glance she gave him now and then when he was not looking at her. There was a peculiar sweetness in her smile when she listened to him telling some of his old experiences. Ashenden had the impression that she basked comfortably in his love as the patients on the terrace, facing the snow, basked in the hot sunshine; but it might very well be that she was content to leave it at that, and it was certainly no business of his to tell Templeton what perhaps she had no wish that he should know.

Then an incident occurred to disturb the monotony of life. Though McLeod and Campbell were always at odds they played bridge together because, till Templeton came, they were the best players in the sanatorium. They bickered incessantly, their post-mortems were endless, but after so many years each knew the other's game perfectly and they took a keen delight in scoring off one another. As a rule Templeton refused to play with them; though a fine player he preferred to play with Ivy Bishop, and McLeod and Campbell were agreed on this, that she ruined the game. She was the kind of player who, having made a mistake that lost the rubber, would laugh and say: Well, it only made the difference of a trick. But one afternoon, since Ivy was staying in her room with a headache, Templeton consented to play with Campbell and McLeod. Ashenden was the fourth. Though it was the end of March there had been heavy snow for several days, and they played, in a veranda open on three sides to the wintry air, in fur coats and caps, with mittens on their hands. The stakes were too small for a gambler like Templeton to take the game seriously and his bidding was overbold, but he played so much better than the other three that he generally managed to make his contract or at least to come near it. But there was much doubling and redoubling. The cards ran high, so that an inordinate number of small slams were bid; it was a tempestuous game, and McLeod and Campbell lashed one another with their tongues. Half past five arrived and the last rubber was started, for at six the bell rang to send everyone to rest. It was a hard-fought rubber, with sets on both sides, for McLeod and Campbell were opponents and each was determined that the other should not win. At ten minutes to six it was game all and the last hand was dealt. Templeton was McLeod's partner and Ashenden Campbell's. The bidding started with two clubs from McLeod; Ashenden said nothing; Templeton showed that he had substantial help, and finally McLeod called a grand slam. Campbell doubled and McLeod redoubled. Hearing this, the players at other tables who had broken off gathered round and the hands were played in deadly silence to a little crowd of onlookers. McLeod's face was white with excitement and there were beads of sweat on his brow. His hands trembled. Campbell was very grim. McLeod had to take two finesses and they both came off. He finished with a squeeze and got the last of the thirteen tricks. There was a burst of applause from the onlookers. McLeod, arrogant in victory, sprang to his feet. He shook his clenched fist at Campbell.

"Play that off on your blasted fiddle," he shouted. "Grand slam doubled and redoubled. I've wanted to get it all my life and now I've got it. By God, By God."

He gasped. He staggered forward and fell across the table. A stream of blood poured from his mouth. The doctor was sent for. Attendants came. He was dead.

He was buried two days later, early in the morning so that the patients should not be disturbed by the sight of a funeral. A relation in black came from Glasgow to attend it. No one had liked him. No one regretted him. At the end of a week so far as one could tell, he was forgotten. The Indian Civilian took his place at the principal table and Campbell moved into the room he had so long wanted.

"Now we shall have peace," said Dr Lennox to Ashenden. "When you think that I've had to put up with the quarrels and complaints of those two men for years and years . . . Believe me, one has to have patience to run a sanatorium. And to think that after all the trouble he's given me he had to end up like that and scare all those people out of their wits."

"It was a bit of a shock, you know," said Ashenden.

"He was a worthless fellow and yet some of the women have been quite upset about it. Poor little Miss Bishop cried her eyes out."

"I suspect that she was the only one who cried for him and not for herself."

But presently it appeared that there was one person who had not forgotten him. Campbell went about like a lost dog. He wouldn't play bridge. He wouldn't talk. There was no doubt about it, he was moping for McLeod. For several days he remained in his room, having his meals brought to him, and then went to Dr Lennox and said he didn't like it as well as his old one and wanted to be moved back. Dr Lennox lost his temper, which he rarely did, and told him he had been pestering him to give him that room for years and now he could stay there or get out of the sanatorium. He returned to it and sat gloomily brooding.

"Why don't you play your violin?" the matron asked him at length. "I haven't heard you play for a fortnight."

"I haven't."

"Why not?"

"It's no fun any more. I used to get a kick out of playing because I knew it maddened McLeod. But now nobody cares if I play or not. I shall never play again."

Nor did he for all the rest of the time that Ashenden was at the sanatorium. It was strange, now that McLeod was dead, life had lost its savour for him. With no one to quarrel with, no one to infuriate, he had lost his incentive and it was plain that it would not be long before he followed his enemy to the grave.

But on Templeton McLeod's death had another effect, and one which was soon to have unexpected consequences. He talked to Ashenden about it in his cool, detached way.

"Grand, passing out like that in his moment of triumph. I can't make out why everyone got in such a state about it. He'd been here for years, hadn't he?"

"Eighteen, I believe."

"I wonder if it's worth it. I wonder if it's not better to have one's fling and take the consequences."

"I suppose it depends on how much you value life."

"But is this life?"

Ashenden had no answer. In a few months he could count on being well, but you only had to look at Templeton to know that he was not going to recover. The death-look was on his face.

"D'you know what I've done?" asked Templeton. "I've asked Ivy to marry me."

Ashenden was startled.

"What did she say?"

"Bless her little heart, she said it was the most ridiculous idea she'd ever heard in her life and I was crazy to think of such a thing."

"You must admit she was right."

"Quite. But she's going to marry me."

"It's madness."

"I daresay it is; but anyhow, we're going to see Lennox and ask him what he thinks about it."

The winter had broken at last; there was still snow on the hills, but in the valleys it was melted and on the lower slopes the birch trees were in bud all ready to burst into delicate leaf. The enchantment of spring was in the air. The sun was hot. Everyone felt alert and some felt happy. The old stagers who came only for the winter were making their plans to go south. Templeton and Ivy went to see Dr Lennox together. They told him what they had in mind. He examined them; they were X-rayed and various tests were taken. Dr Lennox fixed a day when he would tell them the results and in the light of this discuss their proposal. Ashenden saw them just before they went to keep the appointment. They were anxious, but did their best to make a joke of it. Dr Lennox showed them the results of his examinations and explained to them in plain language what their condition was.

"All that's very fine and large," said Templeton then, "but what we want to know is whether we can get married."

"It would be highly imprudent."

"We know that, but does it matter?"

"And criminal if you had a child."

"We weren't thinking of having one," said Ivy.

"Well, then I'll tell you in very few words how the matter stands. Then you must decide for yourselves."

Templeton gave Ivy a little smile and took her hand. The doctor went on.

"I don't think Miss Bishop will ever be strong enough to lead a normal life, but if she continues to live as she has been doing for the last eight years . . . "

"In sanatoriums?"

"Yes. There's no reason why she shouldn't live very comfortably, if not to a ripe old age, as long as any sensible person wants to live. The disease is quiescent. If she marries, if she attempts to live an ordinary life, the foci of infection may very well light up again, and what the results of that may be no one can foretell. So far as you are concerned, Templeton, I can put it even more shortly. You've seen the X-ray photos yourself. Your lungs are riddled with tubercle. If you marry you'll be dead in six months."

"And if I don't how long can I live?"

The doctor hesitated.

"Don't be afraid. You can tell me the truth."

"Two or three years."

"Thank you, that's all we wanted to know."

They went as they had come, hand in hand; Ivy was crying softly. No one knew what they said to one another; but when they came into luncheon they were radiant. They told Ashenden and Chester that they were going to be married as soon as they could get a licence. Then Ivy turned to Chester.

"I should so much like your wife to come up for my wedding. D'you think she would?"

"You're not going to be married here?"

837

"Yes. Our respective relations will only disapprove, so we're not going to tell them until it's all over. We shall ask Dr Lennox to give me away."

She looked mildly at Chester, waiting for him to speak, for he had not answered her. The other two men watched him. His voice shook a little when he spoke.

"It's very kind of you to want her. I'll write and ask her."

When the news spread among the patients, though everyone congratulated them, most of them privately told one another that it was very injudicious; but when they learnt, as soon or later everything that happened in the sanatorium was learnt, that Dr Lennox had told Templeton that if he married he would be dead in six months, they were awed to silence. Even the dullest were moved at the thought of these two persons who loved one another so much that they were prepared to sacrifice their lives. A spirit of kindliness and good will descended on the sanatorium: people who hadn't been speaking spoke to one another again; others forgot for a brief space their own anxieties. Everyone seemed to share in the happiness of the happy pair. And it was not only the spring that filled those sick hearts with new hope, the great love that had taken possession of the man and the girl seemed to spread its effulgence on all that came near them. Ivy was quietly blissful; the excitement became her and she looked younger and prettier. Templeton seemed to walk on air. He laughed and joked as if he hadn't a care in the world. You would have said that he looked forward to long years of uninterrupted felicity. But one day he confided in Ashenden.

"This isn't a bad place, you know," he said. "Ivy's promised me that when I hand in my checks she'll come back here. She knows the people and she won't be so lonely."

"Doctors are often mistaken," said Ashenden. "If you live reasonably I don't see why you shouldn't go on for a long time yet."

"I'm only asking for three months. If I can have that it'll be worth it."

Mrs Chester came up two days before the wedding. She had not seen her husband for several months and they were shy with one another. It was easy to guess that when they were alone they felt awkward and constrained. Yet Chester did his best to shake off the

ABOUT THE INTRODUCER

NICHOLAS SHAKESPEARE spent his first eight years in Paris, Singapore and Phnom Penh. In 1990, he was awarded the Somerset Maugham Prize for his first novel, *The Vision of Elena Silves*. Among his other books are *The High Flyer*, *The Dancer Upstairs*, *Snowleg* and the authorized biography of Bruce Chatwin.

depression that was now habitual and at all events at mealtimes showed himself the jolly, hearty little fellow that he must have been before he fell ill. On the eve of the wedding day they all dined together, Templeton and Ashenden both sitting up for dinner; they drank champagne and stayed up till ten joking, laughing, and enjoying themselves. The wedding took place next morning in the kirk. Ashenden was best man. Everyone in the sanatorium who could stand on his feet attended it. The newly married couple were setting out by car immediately after lunch. Patients, doctors, and nurses assembled to see them off. Someone had tied an old shoe on the back of the car, and as Templeton and his wife came out of the door of the sanatorium rice was flung over them. A cheer was raised as they drove away, as they drove away to love and death. The crowd separated slowly. Chester and his wife went silently side by side. After they had gone a little way he shyly took her hand. Her heart seemed to miss a beat. With a sidelong glance she saw that his eyes were wet with tears.

"Forgive me, dear," he said. "I've been very unkind to you."

"I knew you didn't mean it," she faltered.

"Yes, I did. I wanted you to suffer because I was suffering. But not any more. All this about Templeton and Ivy Bishop – I don't know how to put it, it's made me see everything differently. I don't mind dying any more. I don't think death's very important, not so important as love. And I want you to live and be happy. I don't grudge you anything any more and I don't resent anything. I'm glad now it's me that must die and not you. I wish for you everything that's good in the world. I love you."

This book is set in BEMBO which was cut
by the punch-cutter Francesco Griffo
for the Venetian printer-publisher
Aldus Manutius in early 1495
and first used in a pamphlet
by a young scholar
named Pietro
Bembo.